Trisha Telep was the romance and fantasy book buyer at Murder One, the UK's premier crime and romance bookstore. She has recently re-launched this classic bookshop online at www.murderone. co.uk. Originally from Vancouver, Canada, she completed the Master of Publishing program at Simon Fraser University before moving to London. She lives in Hackney with her boyfriend, filmmaker Christopher Joseph.

THE MAMMOTH BOOK OF

VAMPIRE ROMANCE 2

EDITED BY TRISHA TELEP

ROBINSON

RUNNING PRESS
PHILADELPHIA · LONDON

Constable & Robinson Ltd
3 The Lanchesters
162 Fulham Palace Road
London W6 9ER
www.constablerobinson.com

First published in the UK by Robinson,
an imprint of Constable & Robinson, 2009

A copy of the British Library Cataloguing in Publication
Data is available from the British Library

UK ISBN 978-1-84901-043-6

1 3 5 7 9 10 8 6 4 2

First published in the United States in 2009 by Running Press Book Publishers

US Library of Congress number: 2008944141
US ISBN 978-0-7624-3796-2

Running Press Book Publishers
2300 Chestnut Street
Philadelphia, PA 19103-4371

Visit us on the web!

www.runningpress.com

Printed and bound in the EU

Contents

Acknowledgments   vii
Introduction   ix

Paris After Dark   1
Jordan Summers

Coven of Mercy   36
Deborah Cooke

Le Cirque de la Nuit   64
Karen MacInerney

Perdition   84
Caitlin Kittredge

Deliver Us From Evil   108
Dina James

Blood and Thyme   135
Camille Bacon-Smith

Into the Mist For Ever   155
Rosemary Laurey

Blood Feud   179
Patti O'Shea

Love Bites   200
Angie Fox

Flotsam   231
Caitlín R. Kiernan

The Murder King's Woman   236
Jamie Leigh Hansen

Butterfly Kiss   256
Carole Nelson Douglas

Crimson Kisses   282
Diane Whiteside

Vampsploitation   305
Jaye Wells

Trust Me   333
Stacia Kane

The Scotsman and the Vamp   359
Jennifer Ashley

I Need More You   381
Justine Musk

Point of No Return   394
Jennifer St Giles

With Friends Like These   425
Dawn Cook

Blood Gothic   441
Nancy Holder

Eternity Embraced   447
Larissa Ione

The Ghost of Leadville   472
Jeanne C. Stein

The Vampire, the Witch and the Yenko   487
Tiffany Trent

Circle Unbroken   506
Ann Aguirre

Skein of Sunlight   537
Devon Monk

Author Biographies   557

Acknowledgments

"Paris After Dark" © by Jordan Summers. First publication, original to this anthology. Printed by permission of the author.

"Coven of Mercy" © by Deborah Cooke. First publication, original to this anthology. Printed by permission of the author.

"Le Cirque de la Nuit" © by Karen MacInerney. First publication, original to this anthology. Printed by permission of the author.

"Perdition" © by Caitlin Kittredge. First publication, original to this anthology. Printed by permission of the author.

"Deliver Us From Evil" © by Dina James. First publication, original to this anthology. Printed by permission of the author.

"Blood and Thyme" © by Camille Bacon-Smith. First publication, original to this anthology. Printed by permission of the author.

"Into the Mist For Ever" © by Rosemary Laurey. First publication, original to this anthology. Printed by permission of the author.

"Blood Feud" © by Patti O'Shea. First publication, original to this anthology. Printed by permission of the author.

"Love Bites" © by Angie Fox. First publication, original to this anthology. Printed by permission of the author.

"Flotsam" © by Caitlín R. Kiernan. First published in *Not One of Us* #40, October 2008.

"The Murder King's Woman" © by Jamie Leigh Hansen. First publication, original to this anthology. Printed by permission of the author.

Introduction

Urban fantasy is the ultimate milieu for a little vamp action. Vampires can get romantic in some pretty freaky ways. So, although this is *The Mammoth Book of Vampire Romance 2*, don't go expecting too much gentle foreplay and whispers of sweet nothings. These can be dark, brooding, vicious creatures who like it . . . a little rough. And sometimes they come bearing romance with just the slightest hint of menace. But you'll also find the lighter side of vamps in here, too. Just be warned: the vampire really does push the boundaries of "romance" – often to its bloodiest limits. You just might have to rework your definition of love once you sink your teeth into many of these tales.

From the get-go, this collection was moving at lightning speed into the dark and dirty waters of urban fantasy. My new co-pilot, YA urban fantasy writer Karen Mahoney (check out her short story in the new YA vamp anthology, *The Eternal Kiss*) who had started work at Murder One with me, was a definite influence. She has the infectious enthusiasm of a kid in a candy store (or Wonder Woman with a new invisible plane). When I told her that I was compiling *Love Bites* she immediately put me in contact with urban fantasy writers she knew through Live Journal, Facebook and Twitter. She told me of urban fantasy writers who were going to be in London soon and were keen to come to Murder One for a signing (this is how I met Caitlin Kittredge [think of a goth Sandy in *Grease* with pink streaks in her hair], Stacia Kane and Jordan Summers (who had a great deal of fun laughing at my prudishness over her friend Cheyenne McCray's formerly ultra-hot Succubus story in *The Mammoth Book of Paranormal Romance*). And Devon Monk, Justine Musk and Jaye Wells should basically be in touch with the police after I stalked them mercilessly à la Facebook, with Karen's gleeful encouragement. I hope you enjoy this dark new collection of vampires and the fantastic writers who write them.

Paris After Dark

Jordan Summers

One

Rachel Chang pinched the cigarette between her lips and reached into her pocket for her lighter. Five years of being nicotine free was about to go up in smoke, if she could just get this damn thing to light. She flicked the Zippo and inhaled, then proceeded to choke. Eyes watering, Rachel flicked the cigarette onto the cobblestone as a high-pitched scream pierced the night.

One hand moved to where her weapon should be, while the other automatically reached for the St Michael medal around her neck. For a moment Rachel saw her partner lying in a puddle of blood. She closed her eyes and took a deep breath as the panic attack eased. This wasn't New York. The vision wasn't real. And this wasn't her problem. Let someone else clean up the mess for a change.

A second scream followed the first, then ended abruptly. Rachel remained immobile, while her conscience called her every foul name in the book. Unfortunately, the voice in her head wasn't loud enough to drown out the struggle she could hear taking place on the dimly lit road off Boulevard Raspail.

"You have no authority here. You don't even speak French. Let the Parisian police handle it," she muttered under her breath as she came upon a man grappling with a woman. The woman's arms were flailing as she beat at the man's broad shoulders with her clenched fists.

The dark-haired man wasn't striking her back, but he was holding her tight to deflect her blows. It looked like a typical domestic dispute. Only a fool got in the middle of those. Rachel had been foolish once and it had cost her dearly. *Never again.* She shoved her hands in her pockets and kept walking.

Rachel saw a sign for the Cimetière du Montparnasse affixed to a high, grey brick wall. She glanced at the sky. "Trying to tell me something, partner?" Of course Paul Veretti didn't answer. No one did. Like the residents of the fancy French cemetery, he was dead. All that was left of him was her memories and the St Michael medal around her neck.

The patron saint must have been on a coffee break the day her partner caught a bullet in the chest – a bullet that was meant for her. It was Rachel's idea to answer the domestic battery call on the drive home. It wasn't even part of their job. She should've been the one to stay in the house and try to calm the battered wife, not Paul. But he'd insisted she escort the husband outside and wait for a patrol car to pick him up. Rachel had barely made it to the porch, when the shot rang out. There was a shocked cry and a loud thump. She knew without looking what had happened. She felt like that bullet had been chasing her ever since.

Rachel glanced at the cemetery once more, then asked herself what Paul would do. The answer was obvious. She cursed, then tromped back to the mouth of the street. This was a bad idea. Her gun and NYPD badge currently resided an ocean away inside her captain's desk. She'd have to count on the man fleeing when she confronted him. Rachel ran the odds of that happening in her head and let out a string of expletives.

The woman had stopped struggling and now hung loosely in the man's arms. Had he struck her after Rachel left? She hated bullies. Hated people who thought their size gave them free rein to do as they pleased. The man stood in the shadows with his back to her, but Rachel could tell he outweighed her and the woman by a good fifty pounds. *This was such a bad idea.*

"Hey buddy," she shouted.

The dark-haired man didn't acknowledge her, but Rachel saw his broad shoulders tense.

"Yeah, I'm talking to you. *Parlez-vous . . . anglais*? Let the woman go," she said in frustration, wishing she'd paid attention to the French CDs she'd checked out of the library.

He slowly turned. Rachel caught a glimpse of shimmering green eyes, the colour so unnatural it couldn't possibly be found outside the animal kingdom. Had to be contact lenses. But it wasn't his eyes that held her in place. It was his teeth – his long, very bloody teeth.

Rachel watched the blood drip down his chin onto his dark suit before he stepped back into the shadows. What in the hell had he been doing? When she'd walked by earlier it had looked like the woman was the aggressor. She'd been wrong . . . *again*. How many people had to die for her to get it right?

She automatically catalogued the scene, so she could give her statement to the police later. He released the woman. She slumped to the ground like discarded rags. The man grinned, his attention now riveted on the new arrival.

Rachel knew that the fact she was a petite Chinese-American woman made her look like an easy target, but her size was deceptive. "Before you do anything stupid," she said, knowing it was already too late for that, "I think you should know I've called the police. I'm placing you under citizen's arrest." She pointed to the sidewalk. "Get down on the ground."

If the dark-haired man understood her, he didn't let on. He kept approaching at a steady pace. The light should've revealed his face, but the shadows seemed to follow him, obscuring his pale features. It didn't matter. Rachel was sure she could identify him from his eyes alone, although they didn't seem as bright as they'd been moments ago. Must've been a trick of the light.

"Stay back," she said. "This is your last warning." Rachel held her hands up like her Krav Maga instructor taught her to do. It looked like a defensive posture. It wasn't.

The man smiled, giving her an up close and personal look at his mouth. He had abnormally long incisors that had been filed into jagged points. He used his blood-covered tongue to caress them as he closed the distance between them.

Give an asshole prosthetic fangs and he thinks he's a fucking vampire.

Rachel took a step back, a chill snaking down her spine. She didn't dare look over her shoulder; he'd be on her before she could make it twenty yards. She needed to draw someone's attention. The man must've read her mind because in a blink he went from ten feet away to in her face. Rachel didn't have time to scream as he slammed her into the wall surrounding the cemetery. She landed with a sickening thud. The air rushed out of her lungs with a loud whoosh as pain shot through her body.

She blinked to clear her vision. The shadows still obscured his features. Rachel brushed at the darkness as he approached. He growled. She gagged as his coppery breath fanned out over her face. The guttural sound grew louder. It was the only warning she received.

Instinct made Rachel throw her hand up a second before his teeth clamped onto her forearm. Her leather jacket ripped as he tore through the thick material like it was made of butterfly wings. His sharp incisors punctured her skin. The excruciating pain snapped her out of her initial shock.

Rachel drove her palm into her attacker's nose and heard something crunch, then saw blood splatter across his face. She wasn't sure who was more surprised. Her hand came away covered in crimson. She swung again, but her slick palm only grazed his cheek.

Fury filled his glowing green eyes. The grip he had on her with his teeth tightened and he shook his head, shredding muscle. The human pit bull was going to break her arm, if she didn't get him to release her.

Rachel hit his nose again, spilling more blood. He grabbed her arm, while his other hand latched on to her throat and began to squeeze. Blood roared in her ears as he tried to kill her. It was one thing to contemplate taking her own life, it was quite another to have him take it from her. Rachel thrust her hips forwards and kneed his groin hard. He grunted and released her arm, but the hand around her throat remained.

She tried to break the grip on her neck, using every technique she'd been taught at the police academy, but nothing worked. Rachel hit him until her palm hurt, then hit him some more. His nose was now bent at an odd angle and made a strange whistling snort every time he inhaled. She reached for his fingers and began prying them off one at a time as he tightened his hold. The chain on her neck sliced her skin, then Rachel felt the links snap.

"No," she gritted out.

He didn't respond to her plea. Instead, his head whipped around. He stared into the darkness, his gaze searching the shadows. Beyond the dark side street, the lights of Paris twinkled. One second he was strangling her and trying to rip her arm off, the next, he ran ... taking her broken St Michael medal with him.

Rachel dropped to her knees, clutching her injured arm and coughing as she gulped air into her lungs. It took a second to remember the woman lying on the ground. She didn't appear to be breathing. Rachel crawled to her and felt for a pulse. There wasn't one.

"Damn it."

She dragged herself to Boulevard Raspail and saw her attacker duck into a nearby building. He hadn't gone far. Rachel had no doubt if he got away he'd be back on the streets in a few days to do the same thing to another woman.

She forced herself to her feet and stumbled down the sidewalk. Rachel gave a quick glance at the oncoming traffic and rushed across the road. Horns blared as the Parisian drivers narrowly missed her. No one braked. She pushed on until she reached a small park that butted up against the building she'd seen the man enter.

Rachel stepped over the low fence, keeping to the shadows. She couldn't afford to let him catch her off guard. He'd done it once and it had nearly killed her. A tall wrought-iron fence ran alongside the green gothic-looking building that resembled an ornate shed. Rachel continued across the garden until she reached the end of the grass.

The wrought iron ended at a small gate, which squeaked in the cool evening breeze. A short nose of an entrance poked out of the front of the building. The door was covered in metal mesh. Or at least it had been. The mesh had been ripped away. She glanced down and saw a lock on the ground. It had been smashed. She hadn't seen a weapon on him – with those teeth he didn't need one. Yet he'd obviously been carrying something, unless he'd suddenly become a character out of a James Bond film.

Rachel knew she should call the police. It was the sensible thing to do, but by the time she found a phone, and someone who could understand her broken French, the killer would be long gone, along with Paul's necklace. She couldn't allow that to happen, even if all she managed to do was find his hiding place. Despite what the department shrinks thought, she didn't have a death wish . . . *most days*.

She pushed the gate open. The metal screeched, announcing her arrival. He'd have to be deaf not to have heard her. Rachel cringed, but kept going until she could squeeze through. The light over the sign above the building had been smashed. Broken bits of bulb crunched under her shoes. The main door was open a crack, just enough for her to see the darkness beyond. Rachel turned back and grabbed the mangled lock. It wasn't a perfect weapon, but at least it would aid her punches. Maybe she could manage to knock out his expensive dental work this time.

Rachel walked back to the door and inched it open. She tilted her head and listened. She could hear the soft fall of footsteps growing fainter by the second. He was getting away. She took a breath and stepped through the opening. The door slid shut behind her, extinguishing what little light had been cast.

She pulled out her lighter and flicked it on. There was a closed door on the left. It was flanked by a tiny archway that opened into a crude office, which lay empty except for a lone chair. Rachel raised the lighter and spotted a ramp, leading off to her right. There didn't appear to be anywhere else he could've gone.

She shored up her courage and followed. Rachel stepped lightly, praying the sound wouldn't carry. The ramp ended abruptly at a set of winding stairs. She couldn't see the bottom.

What in the hell was this place?

Her arm ached and her neck began to sting, reminding her once more why she was here. Rachel flipped the lighter closed and began a slow, steady descent. Every twenty or so stairs she'd stop and listen. She couldn't hear footsteps any longer, only the steady drip of water pinging off rock. The air had gone from fresh to stale.

Rachel was just about to call it quits and turn around, when the stairs ended abruptly. Did she dare use her lighter again? What if he was waiting in the shadows? Did she really have a choice? Rachel's heart began to pound as she flicked on the lighter.

She was standing at the mouth of a tunnel. It appeared to be the only way she could go unless she wanted to climb the hundred or so stairs she'd just come down. If Rachel hadn't been claustrophobic before, she would be now. The narrow tunnel had a low ceiling like the entrance of a tomb. She couldn't stretch her arms out without hitting rock walls.

Rachel began walking. It was impossible to be quiet with loose gravel beneath her feet, so she left the lighter on. She stopped every few yards to listen. It was hard to hear anything over the pounding of her heart. The sound of water dripping grew louder. The tunnel eventually opened up into a larger chamber. Rachel read the sign above the door. It was written in French: ARRÊTE! ICI C'EST L'EMPIRE DES MORTS.

It was easy enough to translate: STOP! THIS IS THE EMPIRE OF THE DEAD.

"Terrific," she murmured, half-expecting someone to cue horror music.

Rachel stepped through the archway into a nightmare. Walls of human remains rose from the floor nearly touching the ceiling. Faces of people who'd lived long ago stared at her from empty eye sockets, their bones neatly arranged in macabre designs around their skulls.

Suddenly the room was too warm. Rachel pulled at her coat as her heart slammed into her ribs. The freak had lured her into the catacombs. There were miles of tunnels down here, according to the brochures she'd picked up in the airport. No one would hear her scream this far below the surface. They wouldn't even find her body, if he didn't want it to be found. So much for discovering his hiding place and reporting it to the police. She had to get out of here.

Rachel took a step back – right into a hard male body. She couldn't think. Couldn't breathe. For a moment, fear kept her paralysed, then panic set in. A large pale hand covered her mouth before Rachel could draw breath and scream. Her lighter burned her fingers and she dropped it, plunging them into darkness.

She elbowed the man and tried to smash his nose with her head, but only succeeded in hitting his chest. Rachel braced, expecting a fist to the face. The man made no attempt to strike her. Why should he? He had her right where he wanted her.

A warm breath brushed her neck. His jagged teeth flashed in her mind. He was going to bite her just like he'd bitten the woman and there wasn't a damn thing she could do to stop him.

"No." The plea came out garbled behind his hand, but Rachel knew he understood. "Don't." She jerked her head and only succeeded in hurting herself.

"Stop fighting," he hissed, tightening his grip.

Her breath rushed past his long fingers as she bit him.

"Ow, stop that!" He pressed his face closer.

Rachel tensed and began to tremble as she waited to feel the slice of those fake fangs on her flesh. The pain never came. Heat from the body holding her began to sink into her bones. A moment later firm lips brushed her ear lobe and she quivered. What was he playing at?

Nuzzling her hair, he inhaled. "American. Figures," he said with distaste in a low French accent. "You must have a death wish, *mademoiselle.*"

Two

"You're trespassing," Gabriel Dumont said, ignoring the smell of wild flowers coming from the woman's hair. He resisted the urge to bury his nose in her dark tresses once more. Instead, Gabriel released her. She scurried away. He reached into his pocket and pulled out a flashlight. Not that he needed it to see, but he had no doubt she did. "The catacombs are closed. You want to tell me what you're doing down here?"

Her soft Asian eyes narrowed as she carefully took in his appearance. The woman wasn't as young as he'd initially thought. Mid to late thirties if he had to guess. The press of her warm lithe body had thrown him off. He was glad to be wrong. Time seasoned a woman. Though it had little meaning to creatures such as himself. Gabriel kept still, trying to look harmless, though he was anything but.

She opened her mouth to reply, but stopped. He could tell by her expression that she was trying to come up with a plausible story for her presence. Smart and beautiful. "Do you work here?" she asked, attempting to commandeer the conversation. This was a woman used to being in charge.

Gabriel's lips quirked. "Why else would I be here?" It wasn't like she knew this was the entrance to the Otherworld. Was she simply a tourist trying to sneak in to the catacombs after dark? There were plenty who tried and succeeded. Not all got out to tell of their adventures.

"I was attacked by a man. He came down here." She ran a trembling hand through her hair.

He arched a brow. "And you followed him?" Gabriel corrected his earlier assessment of her. The woman was clearly insane.

"He took something of mine," she said softly. "I want it back." She glanced around the cavern, her gaze hopping from skull to skull. "Did you happen to see anyone else down here?"

"No." He shook his head. "Only you." Gabriel watched her scan the area. She didn't miss much. He rarely met humans who paid close attention to their surroundings. That's what made them such easy prey. "What did he take, miss? Miss . . . ?"

"Rachel Chang. And you are?" she asked, avoiding his question.

She was good at changing conversational direction. He'd give her that. "My name is Gabriel Dumont."

"Can I see your eyes, Mr Dumont?" she asked, taking another step back.

Gabriel blinked at her question, then slowly raised the flashlight beam to his face.

"They're blue," Rachel said, then visibly relaxed.

He frowned. "I know. Is that a problem?"

Rachel waved the question away. "I need to notify the police. There's been a murder."

"I thought you said you were attacked and robbed," he said, feeling suddenly uneasy.

"I was. The man who attacked me killed a woman."

Gabriel ran a hand over his face. So much for spending a quiet evening at home. "Let's start at the beginning, shall we?"

She groaned in frustration. "We don't have time. We have to get back to the scene."

"At least tell me what he took."

"My St Michael's medal."

That hadn't been the answer Gabriel expected. Diamonds, yes. Gold maybe. But not a worthless medal. "They are easy to obtain. Allow me to get you another."

"Thanks, but it wouldn't be the same." Rachel forced herself to concentrate on getting out of the catacombs. She was sure Gabriel hadn't been the man who'd attacked her, but the place was making her uneasy. She rolled her shoulders, but the sensation of being watched didn't go away. The killer was nearby. Maybe he was waiting for an opportunity to attack Gabriel. She wasn't going to be responsible for another death tonight.

"Let's get out of here," she said.

"Right this way, madam." He motioned for her to go ahead of him.

"After you," she said.

Rachel was huffing from climbing the stairs by the time they reached street level. Gabriel wasn't even out of breath. She stared at him, getting a better look now that they were under a street light. Gabriel's raven-coloured hair framed a boxer's face. His features were several fights past handsome, but strangely intriguing. Lines bracketed his blue eyes, but she couldn't gauge his age. Rachel craned her neck. He was taller than her assailant, well over six feet. And she couldn't help but notice how nicely his broad shoulders filled out his jacket.

She tore her gaze away, when he caught her looking. "It's this way." Rachel led him to the side street where she'd last seen the body, but the woman had vanished.

She searched the bushes. The woman had been lying in the middle of the sidewalk where the man dropped her. Maybe she'd been further along the street than Rachel had realized.

"Where is she?" Gabriel asked.

"She should be right here. I don't understand." Rachel scanned the shadows.

He looked up and down the street. "Sure she was dead?"

Rachel glowered at him. "Positive. I checked her pulse."

"Maybe someone reported the incident and they've already picked her up," he suggested.

"I'm not sure how the Parisian police work, but back in New York we don't clean up a crime scene this fast," she said. "Where's the tape? Where are the homicide detectives? Someone should still be here canvassing the neighbourhood for witnesses."

Gabriel stiffened. "Are you police?"

"Homicide detective," she said absently, ignoring his broken English.

He inhaled again. "Have you been drinking, detective?"

Rachel tensed. "I had a few flutes of champagne with dinner, but I know what I saw."

"Is this perhaps an elaborate ruse to get out of a trespassing charge?" Gabriel asked.

Her almond-shaped eyes narrowed to glittering slits. "Listen, if you don't believe me that's fine. Just point me in the direction of the nearest police station so I can report the incident."

"OK." Gabriel reached for her arm to turn her towards the station. She winced. He instantly released her. "Are you injured?"

"I'll live," she said. "The guy bit me after he bit the woman. He'd reshaped his teeth. Fancied himself a friggin' vampire." Rachel snorted. "More like a drugged-out psycho." She shook out her arm and winced.

Gabriel maintained a placid expression, when inside his thoughts were in turmoil. If what she was saying was true, then it was possible Rachel had been bitten by a *vampyre*. "May I see?" he asked.

She shrugged and unbuttoned her coat. The second she slipped it off, the scent of blood filled the air. Gabriel swallowed hard, his nostrils flaring to draw the delicious fragrance in. "That looks bad. You're going to need stitches," he said, fighting the urge to lick her arm from wrist to elbow.

Rachel glanced down. "It'll wait."

"You really should get that seen to." He looked away as his mouth began to water. It certainly looked like a vamp bite, although it was in an odd location. Most vamps preferred to feed from softer tissue.

"Police station first. Hospital second."

"As you wish, detective." Gabriel was nearly mad with the desire to feed by the time they reached the station. Without a body to back her claims, Rachel was just another tipsy tourist who'd been mugged. The police would take a report, check out the scene, then it would be filed away.

Rachel came out of the station two hours later, cursing under her breath and scowling. When Gabriel stepped out of the shadows, she startled, clutching her chest.

"Stop sneaking up on me." She glared at him.

"I wasn't sneaking," he said. "How did it go?"

"Just peachy. Can't you tell? They're going to contact my captain in New York. That should be an interesting conversation." She muttered something unintelligible about stupid men under her breath, then looked around in confusion. "What are you still doing here?"

He held up his hands in defence. "Nothing nefarious I assure you. I believe I said you needed to go to the hospital to get that wound cleaned and stitched. I'm here to take you." He gave her a gallant bow. The move seemed natural, like he'd performed it hundreds of times.

Despite his easy charm, there was something off about Gabriel. It wasn't how he spoke or behaved. He'd been nothing but courteous. It wasn't how he moved. For a big man, he was incredibly light on his feet. Rachel couldn't pin down what was bothering her and wouldn't let it go until she could. She scrubbed a hand over her face. Maybe she was shaken up more than she realized.

She eyed Gabriel cautiously, debating whether to accept his offer. Eventually, she gave in. Rachel had no idea where the nearest hospital was in Paris. She could be standing next to it and wouldn't know it given the architecture in this town. "Lead the way."

He grinned. The act transformed his face from weary boxer into something altogether unexpected, taking her breath away. Rachel's heart jumped and her knees turned to jelly. At least she knew she wasn't dead.

Three

Gabriel waited for the doctor to finish patching Rachel up. It didn't take long once he found the physician he was looking for. It helped to have a *vampyre*, one of the *sanguis* – *the blood* – on the inside. Vamp bites weren't fatal unless a blood exchange had occurred, but the bad ones were painful and did take a long time to heal.

The doctor drew a vial of Rachel's blood. Gabriel watched him walk into the other room and drink it. His palate was quicker than any lab test. Since *sanguis*' blood didn't show up in a victim for twenty-four to forty-eight hours, he could only confirm the presence of *sanguis*' saliva and check for contaminants, along with diseases.

"You're all set," the doctor said, returning to the room minutes later. He met Gabriel's gaze and nodded, confirming his suspicions. She'd been bitten by a member of the *sanguis*, which lent credibility to her story.

Rachel was given a shot to stave off infection and carefully stitched. With any luck, she'd be on the mend in a few weeks.

Gabriel's phone vibrated as Rachel was being discharged. He flipped it open.

The text contained two words: "*Corps trouvé*". Body found.

He cursed under his breath and closed the phone as Rachel approached. "Ready?"

She nodded and wobbled on her feet.

Gabriel grabbed her hand to steady her and awareness flared between them. The warmth of her skin scalded his fingertips and sent shock waves through his body. He slowly released her and cleared his throat. "We'd better get you back to your hotel."

Her soft brown eyes peered up at him and Gabriel felt his chest constrict. He could get trapped in that gaze if he wasn't careful. The urge to touch her again made Gabriel's hands itch, but *sanguis* and human relationships were never a good idea. No matter how careful one was in the beginning, the human inevitably paid the price.

"You've done more than enough," she said sounding sincere. "I can find my own way home."

"Nonsense. Let me at least call you a taxi. I don't want your last impression of Parisian men to be that of a deranged dentally challenged biter."

Rachel laughed, then tilted her chin, sending her long brown hair into her face. Gabriel reached out and brushed the downy soft strands over her shoulder. "Why are you so concerned about my impression of the men here?"

Gabriel hesitated. Anything he said would be far too revealing.

Rachel's lips canted. "Don't worry, you've more than made up for the mad biter."

He smiled, more pleased than he should be about her admission. He hiked a thumb over his shoulder. "I'd better call you that taxi. Where are you staying?"

"Hotel Luxembourg Parc." Her voice faded with exhaustion.

"Take a seat. I'll let you know when it arrives." Gabriel ducked out the front of the hospital.

Rachel watched him go. She wasn't quite sure what to make of Gabriel Dumont. On the one hand, he'd gone well out of his way to help her. It would never have happened had they been in New York. She could've been bleeding on the sidewalk and no one would've stopped. Maybe the French were different, but they hadn't seemed like it at the police station.

If Gabriel had an ulterior motive for helping her, Rachel couldn't see what it could be. She didn't have money, the only thing stolen was her necklace, and they hadn't been able to find the body. Despite all that, she couldn't stop the gnawing at her gut that told her she was missing something vital.

Gabriel popped his head in the door and smiled. The unease she'd felt seconds ago melted under that grin, morphing into something far more dangerous. Rachel didn't have time for romantic liaisons. She needed to find the psycho who'd attacked her and get Paul's necklace back. She felt naked without its protection, without its comfort.

*   *   *

The taxi drove off with Rachel slumped in the back seat. Gabriel reached into his pocket for his phone and called his partner. "I'll be there in ten minutes."

"Hurry up or there won't be anything left to do," he said.

Gabriel found his partner, Claude Russo, off Rue Balard leaning over the body of a blonde-haired woman. Her throat had been ripped out like the other victims they'd found over the past few months, leaving only tendon and bone behind. She wore a long black skirt and a purple shirt with a multi-coloured scarf thrown over her shoulders. Her grey eyes were open, frozen with fright.

He glanced around and saw a sign for Parc Andre. The location was nowhere near Boulevard Raspail where Rachel had been attacked, so it was doubtful there was a connection.

"What took you so long?" Claude asked, laying out a tarp next to the body. A jug nearby contained a mixture of bleach and water.

"It's been a hell of a night," Gabriel said.

"Do tell." Claude rolled the body onto the tarp. He reached for the jug and began to spray the area where the body had been lying.

"I ran into this crazy American woman down in the catacombs."

Claude shook his head. "When will they learn it's not smart to sneak in there after dark?"

"That's just it, she wasn't down there stealing bones or exploring. She claimed to have witnessed a murder over by Cimetière du Montparnasse. She was chasing her attacker, when I found her."

"Drinking makes you see things that aren't there," Claude said.

"I'd have thought so, too if it wasn't for the fact she'd been bitten by one of the *sanguis*."

Claude's shoulders stiffened. "Then I suppose it's exceedingly lucky for her that she didn't catch him."

"Yes, it is." Fear trickled down Gabriel's spine at the thought of Rachel fighting a *sanguis*. She was lucky she'd survived the initial attack. And even more fortunate he'd come upon her before round two.

"Come help me roll her." Claude indicated to the body.

Gabriel walked over and grabbed the edge of the tarp and slowly covered the woman, then rolled her up tight. "What do you think?" he asked.

"I think you had it pegged right. The woman is obviously crazy. Who's to say she was even bitten by one of us. Could've been a dog." His laugh came out as a congested snort.

Gabriel looked at him. "No, it was definitely a *sanguis* bite. I didn't believe her at first, but the hospital confirmed it."

Claude frowned. "So you found the body?"

He paused. "That's the weird part. There wasn't one. I mean I saw blood. Smelled it everywhere, but the bulk of it was coming from Rachel."

Claude arched a brow. "Her name is Rachel. Just how well did you get to know this woman?"

Gabriel tensed at the underlying implication in Claude's tone. "Not well."

"But you'd like to, eh, *ami*?" he asked.

"She needed help, so I helped her." Gabriel looked away. He wasn't sure how he felt about Rachel. She brought out a protective side of him Gabriel thought he'd lost long ago.

"How does she taste? Good?" Claude asked.

Gabriel shifted impatiently on his feet. "I wouldn't know."

"You didn't bite her?" he asked, sounding surprised. "It's always important to know how she tastes before you make her a regular donor."

Gabriel glared. "She's not going to be a donor. Rachel's already been through enough between the bite and her necklace being stolen. Damn fool is determined to get it back. It obviously has sentimental meaning."

"Is that so?" Claude murmured. "It doesn't really matter what she wants. It's not like she'll be able to find the guy when even the Trackers haven't succeeded. And they've been hunting him far longer."

"Did I mention she's a New York City homicide detective?"

Claude's head whipped around. "No, you left that part out."

"I've seen her type. She's not going to let this go." Gabriel slipped a plastic tie around one end of the tarp. "I have to try to find the necklace for her. The sooner she leaves Paris, the better. We don't need a credible witness running around screaming about *vampyres*."

"She actually used the 'v' word?" His disgust over the use of the derogatory term was evident.

Gabriel lifted the woman's feet as Claude tied the other end of the tarp. "Yes, but she thinks he's a fake, assumes he's had cosmetic dentistry. Thank God for goths and movies."

"*Oui.*" Claude snorted, then wheezed.

"Are you all right?" Gabriel asked.

"I accidentally inhaled some of the bleach fumes when I was mixing tonight's batch of cleaners." They lifted the body into Claude's van. "Hopefully the Trackers will catch the killer soon."

"It would certainly make our job easier," Gabriel said. "Let's hurry. I want to drop by Luxembourg Parc to make sure Rachel's OK before reporting the incident to the Sang High Council."

Claude's attention sharpened. "Sounds like you're developing a bit of a soft spot for this mortal."

Gabriel avoided his partner's knowing gaze. "*Sanguis* don't have soft spots, remember? They're ripped out at rebirth."

Claude's green eyes narrowed. "Whatever you say, my friend."

Rachel could see the woman clearly. She wore a blue sweatsuit and a black cap. Her long red ponytail bobbed as she set off at a brisk pace on her jog. The sun had faded, leaving streaks of purple and grey behind. Her pale skin looked nearly translucent despite the blood pumping beneath and it gave off a faint musky aroma. Rachel could see the veins networking through her neck. They were a blue relief against the alabaster. She was so hungry, so very thirsty. Rachel licked her cracked lips, but nothing but the woman's blood could quench her burning need. She had to catch her, stop her, taste her.

Suddenly Rachel was moving. Slowly at first, then gaining speed. The distance between her and the woman closed rapidly. The bushes beside her blurred as she raced to catch her. One hand reached out for the woman's red ponytail, while the other sealed her mouth. There was a flash of teeth, then a muffled scream as she sank fangs into the woman's throat. Desire – thick, rich, and tantalizing – flooded Rachel. She wanted more, needed more. Her body craved completion.

Gaze riveted, Rachel watched blood drip down the woman's throat and her mouth began to water. The woman slumped. Rachel could hear the sound of the redhead's heart thump erratically in her chest. One thump, then three in quick succession. Then there were no more. The silence was broken by a loud menacing growl.

Rachel jerked awake and looked around. The TV was on low and her suitcase was poking out of the closet where she'd left it. Her stomach rumbled and she fell back onto the bed.

The dream had been so real. She could almost taste the blood in her mouth. Another wave of desire scorched her. Her stomach growled again. Rachel swallowed hard and tossed the covers off, then sprinted to the bathroom. She barely made it to the toilet before she threw up.

When nothing else would come up, Rachel gripped the sink and pulled herself to her feet. How could she feel anything but revulsion at the thought of drinking someone's blood? It had to be her subconscious working overtime. She was simply reliving the trauma of last night . . . even though this woman wasn't wearing a long black skirt and a purple shirt like the first victim.

Rachel turned on the tap and splashed water on her face. It did little to remove the haze her mind was shrouded in. She needed a shower then maybe she'd be able to face the day. Rachel carefully unwound the dressing on her arm. The bite stank and oozed thick green pus. If the doctor hadn't said that would happen, she would be worried that it was infected. She dropped the dirty bandages into the trash and turned on the shower.

It didn't take long to strip out of her clothes. Rachel stepped under the spray and immediately jumped back as the water peppered her body. She could feel every drop pierce her flesh. She looked down half expecting to see blood. There wasn't any, but her skin was abnormally red where the water had touched.

"You're just bruised from the fight," Rachel told herself as she made her way back under the spray. It didn't get any better. If anything, the sensation was worse.

She stayed in the shower just long enough to wash her hair and rinse off. She'd never been hypersensitive before. Hell, maybe it was the water pressure in Paris, Rachel thought as she turned off the tap.

She wrapped a towel around her hair and body, then ran a hand over the fogged mirror. At first glance, she didn't see herself. Rachel swiped her hand again, then caught a glimpse of her face. It was faint, but she could at least make out her features. Parisian steam was obviously tougher than New York bathroom steam. She looked up at the ceiling. They really should put fans in these places.

Rachel put on her make-up the best she could, then got dressed and bound her wound. She wanted to revisit the side street where she'd been attacked. Maybe the killer had dropped something she could use to locate him. She had a far better chance of finding proof in the daylight than she did at night. He wouldn't be the first perp stupid enough to leave a cell phone or a business card behind.

She glanced at the clock to see if there was enough time to grab breakfast first. It was six. She'd gone to bed at four in the morning. Rachel had never felt this rested after so little sleep. She turned the volume up on the television and flipped it to the English-language channel. The evening news had just begun. She looked back at the clock. It couldn't be. Rachel walked over to the phone and called the front desk.

"Hello, could you please tell me what time it is?" she asked.

"But of course, madam. It is six o' clock," the woman said politely.

"In the evening?"

"*Oui*, madam."

"Thank you." Rachel's legs were trembling as she slowly hung up the phone. She ran a hand through her hair. "Pull yourself together," she muttered.

Rachel walked over to the window and threw back the curtain. So much for finding proof in the daylight. She stared at the Jardin du Luxembourg across the street. The park's gates were closed for the night. She was about to shut the drapes when she noticed movement near the sidewalk.

The shadows surrounding the park shifted and a man appeared. Rachel watched in horror as he grinned, flashing glaring white fangs. He held up his hand and let something drop. Light from the street light caught the silver chain dangling from his fingertips. It swayed gently back and forth like a pendulum. Rachel could see it clearly. It was her St Michael medal – Paul's St Michael medal. The bastard was taunting her with it, daring her to come and get it. How did he find her?

"Son of a bitch!" she growled, grabbing her coat as she headed out the door.

Rachel reached the front of the hotel within a minute and glanced up and down the street. There was no one around. She picked a direction and ran up the road. He had to be here somewhere. He wouldn't go to all this trouble, and then hide.

She scanned the cafes, but didn't spot him. He couldn't have gone far. Rachel had left the hotel room the second she'd seen him. At most, he'd be a block ahead of her. She was looking down a side street, trying to decide whether to head in another direction, when she collided with a hard, unyielding male chest. Strong arms enveloped her. Rachel took a deep breath to scream and caught a familiar scent. She looked up and all thoughts of fleeing disappeared as she fell into Gabriel Dumont's blue eyes.

Four

Gabriel continued to hold her, enjoying the feel of soft womanly curves in his hands. He longed to pull her closer, taste her full lips, answer the need he could see burning in her eyes. Rachel recovered before he could act on those impulses.

She grabbed the front of his shirt and yanked. "Did you see him?"

"See who?" He looked around, but didn't immediately spot anyone. Gabriel inhaled, catching the familiar fragrance of her floral shampoo. He forced his senses to move on. There were *sanguis* about, but none nearby.

"The killer. He was here." She craned her neck to scan the street.

Something fluttered dangerously in Gabriel's chest. "What do you mean he was here?" The calm in his voice belied the building rage scorching his veins.

Rachel released him. "I just saw him outside my hotel. He had my necklace. Held it up so I could see it. The son-of-a bitch all but dared me to come and get it."

Her skin tone had faded to milk, emphasizing the dark circles under her eyes.

"Are you feeling all right?"

"Don't change the subject," Rachel snapped. "I can tell by your expression that you don't believe me."

There was no deception that Gabriel could sense in her speech. Rachel believed every word coming out of her mouth. She'd obviously seen something that shook her up, but could it really be her attacker?

"How did he find me?" she asked quietly. If it wasn't for the fine tension thrumming through her body, he would've believed the calm she projected.

"No idea," Gabriel said. "Are you sure it was him?"

"Positive." A muscle in Rachel's jaw began to tic. "You're the only one who knows where I'm staying."

Gabriel flinched, his temper pricked by her insinuation. "Are you accusing me of something?"

Rachel stepped closer. Waves of heat emanated from her tiny body as she peered up at him. "No one else knew where I was staying."

"The police knew, but I take it you've already ruled them out." They stood nose to nose. "So you think I moved the body, took you to the police, and then the hospital so that I could turn around and tell your attacker where to find you? Are you even listening to yourself?"

"I know how it sounds, but that scenario is far more likely than my attacker tailing us all night," Rachel said. "He's not an idiot. He isn't going to sit outside a police station and wait for me to come out. And the police aren't likely to assist a killer by giving him my address."

Gabriel kept his temper in check. "I can assure you that I've told no one where you're staying," he lied easily. He'd had to list her whereabouts in the report he'd given the high council. All random *sanguis* attacks had to be reported. It was Sang law. The thought that his actions had somehow endangered her made him ill.

Rachel touched her head and swayed.

Gabriel moved quickly, catching her arm. "When was the last time you ate?"

She shrugged, ignoring the revulsion she felt at the thought of ingesting anything solid. What was wrong with her? Blood made her hungry and the idea of food made her sick. Rachel's lack of an answer was all the encouragement Gabriel needed.

"You're coming with me. We have to get some food in you before you pass out on the street." He led her down the sidewalk towards Rue de Seine.

Cafes, galleries, patisseries and used bookstores lined the quaint French street that bordered St Germain-des-Prés and the Latin Quarter. Gabriel found a cafe he liked, then quickly deposited her in a seat.

"That wasn't necessary," Rachel said, shaking her head to ease the dizziness. Her arm ached and her body trembled. If she'd been throwing up this whole time, Rachel would've thought she'd caught the flu. She rubbed her arm. Maybe she was experiencing side effects from the tetanus shot she'd been given. It had happened before. Or it could be the bite.

Gabriel gave her an entirely too male condescending look. "Obviously it was necessary, if you haven't even bothered to eat today."

"Give me a break," she said. "I just got up."

His long lashes shuttered his eyes. "What?"

"Up until – " she glanced at her watch "– an hour ago, I thought it was morning. I slept all day. Getting mugged takes it out of me, I guess."

His frown deepened.

"I'm sure it's nothing," she assured him. "Probably just coming down with something. They did all the important tests at the hospital. The guy didn't have HIV, according to the doctor. Never thought to have them check for rabies."

Gabriel's lips twitched. "It's doubtful he had rabies."

Rachel smiled, happy that she'd been able to relieve the worry she'd seen on his face moments ago. "I'm sure once I eat I'll be all right."

Gabriel sat forwards. "You're sure it was him?"

Her grin faded. "I've been a cop for fifteen years. My job has made me good at remembering details. It was him."

His expression turned pensive once more.

Rachel squeezed his hand. It was cool to the touch, but warmed quickly. "I'm sorry I accused you of selling me out."

Gabriel shook his head and dark hair fell over one eye. She brushed it back, her fingers lingering longer than necessary. He was watching her carefully, but he didn't try to pull away. The tension between them rose, but this time it had nothing to do with discussing her attacker. It had been easy to ignore the simmering attraction between them the first time, given the circumstances, but now there was no denying it.

He cleared his throat. "You better order. I need to get you back to the hotel so you can rest. You've been through a lot."

"Yeah." Rachel glanced away. She couldn't believe how bold she'd been. She never made moves on men, especially men she didn't know. Rachel wondered what she would've done had Gabriel responded in kind. From the look on his face, she could tell he'd been tempted, but he hadn't acted. Instead, Gabriel had remained chivalrous to his core.

A lot of predators sought victims by gaining their trust. Even as the thought fluttered through her cop brain, Rachel knew that wasn't the case here. Gabriel had been just as shocked by her attacker's audacity as she'd been. She'd seen it in his eyes before he'd carefully schooled his expression. Now he was brooding. Or at least he had been until she'd touched him.

Rachel had felt his muscles lock under her fingertips, but for some reason she couldn't stop herself. She'd wanted to feel his hair since he'd taken her to the hospital. It had looked so soft, so tempting. She forced her traitorous gaze away from his rough-hewn face.

"Aren't you going to eat?" she asked, staring at the menu like she could understand French.

"Later," he said. "The French don't dine this early, only tourists do." Gabriel grinned at her, then caught the waiter's attention.

"I'll have beef stew. You do have beef stew, right?" she asked.

"*Oui, madame,*" the waiter said.

"And bring us a bottle of house red," Gabriel added.

"I don't think I can drink anything." Rachel looked at Gabriel. "I'm not even sure I'm going to be able to eat."

He touched her forehead. "You're a little warm. How are you feeling?"

"Flu-ish."

"For how long?" he asked. Gone was the flirting.

Rachel sighed. "Since yesterday. Could be the shot, but it's probably the bite working its way through my system. It's not unheard of for people who suffer from a human bite to get sick afterwards. I've been through it before. I'll live."

The waiter returned with the stew and their wine. He placed the steaming bowl in front of Rachel. "Smells delicious," she said, looking at the beads of fat floating on top of the broth. Her stomach threatened to rebel as she lifted the spoon.

"I think you need to tell me exactly what happened last night," Gabriel said after the waiter retreated into the kitchen. "Start from the beginning and don't leave anything out, including the significance of the necklace."

"That's personal." Rachel put the spoon down. She couldn't share the pain she'd been through with a stranger. Could she?

"You have my word of honour I will not tell anyone," Gabriel said.

There was no denying he meant what he said. Rachel could see the sincerity in his eyes. If she were prone to fantasy, she'd say she could see his very soul. It glowed like a soft beacon inside of him, warming her.

Once Rachel decided to open the floodgates, the words flowed out. She told Gabriel everything, starting with the domestic battery she and Paul had investigated. She explained what had occurred the days after he'd been shot. How Paul had lingered in a coma and had eventually been taken off life support. His family had given her the St Michael's medal he'd been wearing the day of the shooting. The bullet had grazed the edge of the medal leaving a permanent gash behind. She'd put the necklace on at the funeral and hadn't removed it since.

Rachel described the man who'd attacked her. Talked about his teeth, the blood, and green glowing eyes. She gave a blow-by-blow account of how she'd struck him and broken his nose, then how something had spooked him.

When she was done, Rachel felt as if she'd been put through an industrial tumble dryer. She hadn't talked about Paul and the shooting since it had happened. She still couldn't believe she'd told Gabriel everything, but there was no denying the relief coursing through her. An invisible weight had been lifted. And it was all thanks to the man sitting across from her. "Thank you for listening," she said.

"Anytime." Gabriel reached for her hand, but drew back before he touched her. "How are you feeling now that you've had some food?"

She shrugged. "The same."

Gabriel forced a grin as dread filled him. He'd listened to Rachel pour her heart out. She'd been carrying so much pain, so much guilt. It wasn't fair. She didn't deserve to have this forced upon her. No one did. If he'd had doubts about the symptoms before, they were gone now. Rachel had caused a blood exchange with the vamp that had attacked her when she'd broken his nose.

She was infected. No longer human, Rachel was now a revenant that would soon be crawling back to the grave.

Like most viruses, the *sanguis* virus would take a few days to fully incubate. Once it did, if Rachel didn't receive more blood from her sire, she'd die.

Anger engulfed him as he glanced at the vibrant, brave woman seated across from him. How dare a *stray* take the life of one so noble? It wouldn't mean anything to her in the end, but Gabriel vowed to himself to avenge her. In the meantime, he'd make Rachel as comfortable as possible.

"What he has taken from you is unforgivable, but you must move on. Enjoy your time. There is no getting your –" he paused "– life back."

"St Michael's medal back," Rachel said at the same time.

For a moment their words hung in the air, a jumble of sentences not meant to be strewn together. Then her brows slowly drew down over her brown eyes.

"What did you just say?" she asked. "Better yet, what do you mean?"

Gabriel didn't know what to say. He was shocked as much by her statement as she'd been by his. How could she still be worrying about such a trivial item when her life as she knew it was over?

"He bit you," he said slowly.

"Uh-huh, and I told you I've been bitten before," Rachel said as if she were speaking to a child.

Gabriel took a sip of wine. "You don't understand."

"You said he didn't have rabies." Rachel glanced at her bandaged arm.

Most women in Rachel's position would be in hysterics by now. "No, not rabies. Something far worse." Gabriel stared at her, taking in the arch of her brow, the soft curve of her neck, the gentle rise of her breasts. So beautiful and full of life. He wanted to reach out and pull her into his arms. Hold her tight and never let her go. He had to say something. Explain what had happened, but . . .

How do you tell someone you are beginning to care about that they'll be dead by the weekend?

Five

"I don't feel so good." Rachel clutched her stomach and hunched over.

He rose to his feet. "We need to get you back to the hotel."

She swayed. "Not until you explain what's happening to me."

Gabriel sighed. "I will, but this is not the place. What I need to tell you requires privacy."

"Fine, but you're not leaving until you do," she said, daring him to argue.

Sadness clouded his eyes. "You're not going to like what I have to say."

Rachel stood as Gabriel threw money down on the table. "I've got news for you. There's nothing you can say that will be worse than the day I learned my partner had been removed from life support."

Gabriel's expression was grave when he finally answered. "Remember you said that after we talk."

Rachel's feet were dragging and they still had a block to go before they reached the luxurious Luxembourg Parc boutique hotel. She felt worse now that she'd eaten, and the dread of the upcoming conversation wasn't helping matters. What could Gabriel possibly say that was worse than Paul's death? And what had he meant by the attack costing her life? She glanced his way. He remained focused on the sidewalk, lost in thought.

Her head spun and Rachel reached out to steady herself. Her hand missed and she began to fall. Strong arms swept her up before she hit.

"This is embarrassing." Rachel fidgeted and looked around to see if anyone was watching. "Put me down."

His blue gaze arrested her, stopping her struggles. "You are in no condition to argue."

As much as she'd hate to admit it, Gabriel was right. Besides, Rachel enjoyed being in his arms. He carried her as if she weighed nothing, cradling her close to his chest. Each step he took lulled her, until she eventually nodded off.

The dark-haired woman left the party, bidding her friends goodbye. She walked down the busy boulevard, then turned left onto a quiet street. The crowds faded in the distance as her long strides took her further away from safety.

Her ebony skin shimmered in the darkness. It flowed like the black fabric of her cocktail dress. The tap, tap, tap of her heels sounded obscenely loud in the stillness of the night. Rachel watched the pulse jump under the skin at her neck. It throbbed in time to her steps. A coppery fragrance reached her, so enticing that Rachel had to find out where it was coming from. The woman turned, startled by someone behind her. Then she smiled.

"Oh, it's just you," she said.

Rachel's mouth was sand dry as she licked her lips. So thirsty. So hungry. So hot. She shifted, trying to get comfortable, but it was impossible.

Fangs flashed and the woman's smile faded. She didn't get a chance to scream as the sharp teeth tore at her slender throat. Blood bubbles escaped from her mouth as unnatural desires were fed.

Rachel cried out and bolted upright. Gabriel was seated in a nearby chair. He rose instantly and came forwards.

"What happened?" he asked.

She blinked. "I saw him. I saw . . . she's dead."

He frowned. "Who's dead?"

"The woman." Her body arched as she threw the covers off. "How did I get here?" A moan escaped before Rachel could stop it.

"You fell asleep in my arms. I fished the key out of your pocket and put you to bed."

Rachel rubbed her hands down her thighs. "I ache. What's happening to me?"

A pained expression passed over Gabriel's face. "What I'm about to say is going to sound crazy."

Rachel writhed on the bed. She couldn't seem to ease the need burning through her body. If she didn't get relief soon, she wouldn't hear a word that Gabriel had to say. She bit her lip and blood welled.

Gabriel's gaze locked on her mouth. He hadn't moved, but the heat coming off him was approaching nuclear. His eyes devoured her. Everywhere his gaze touched ignited an answering flame inside of her.

She mewed. "What are you doing to me?"

"I could ask you the same thing," he said. His nostrils flared and his muscles tensed, revealing the outline of his straining arousal.

Rachel's breath caught as a new kind of hunger struck. "We'll talk later." She reached for him, and he came to her without a fight.

The second their lips fused Rachel was lost. Her mind took a back seat to her need. She blindly stripped Gabriel's shirt off, feeling the hard planes of muscle that had been hiding beneath. She couldn't get enough of him. Rachel followed the dark trail of hair down his stomach, her greedy fingers seeking his hard length. Gabriel gasped when she closed around him, but stopped her from exploring further.

"Not yet," he said through gritted teeth. "I want this to last."

He reached for the front of her blouse and ripped, sending buttons and material flying. Rachel threaded her fingers through his hair as she pulled him into another embrace. Tongues, lips and teeth collided as they devoured one another in a frenzy of melding flesh.

Gabriel's hands seemed to be everywhere at once, stroking and teasing her until Rachel was convinced she'd expire from sheer delight. Somehow he managed to finish undressing them both then went to work pleasuring her from head to toe. Gabriel had a very talented mouth that he put to good use. It didn't take long for Rachel to reach her first peak.

Her body continued to quiver as he slipped inside of her and began to move. Sweat glistened on his forehead. Her hands danced along his spine, feeling the muscles bunch beneath her fingertips. Rachel couldn't tell where she left off and he began. He reached between their bodies and stroked until she soared ever higher. Rachel was still crying out in passion, when she felt a slight sting below her ear. Gabriel nuzzled her neck, gently lapping the spot, while he rolled his hips, driving deep to tumble her over the edge. He gave one last thrust, then followed her into oblivion.

It took several minutes before either of them could move. Gabriel slowly withdrew from her and gently kissed her lips. "Thank you," he said.

"For what?"

"For sharing something so precious with me." His thumb gently brushed her neck.

"It was just sex," Rachel said, knowing it was so much more.

Gabriel met her gaze and shook his head. "No, it wasn't."

Rachel's heart fluttered at his admission. It would be so easy to love this man. She shied away from the idea. She still hadn't heard what he had to say. She might not feel the same afterwards. Even Rachel realized it was already too late. The vulnerability and need she'd seen in Gabriel's blue eyes had allowed her to unlock the pain she'd been harbouring. Whether he realized it or not, they needed each other.

"We better get this over with," she said reluctantly.

Gabriel rolled off her, taking his warmth with him. "I was hoping we could ... "

She smiled. "Maybe later."

His lips thinned. "I doubt you'll be in the mood after I explain what really happened the night you were attacked. In fact, I'll be amazed if you don't toss me out of the room."

"Not much shocks me these days," Rachel said, growing weary.

"This is going to sound utterly mad, but it's the absolute truth." He waited until he had her attention. "The man who attacked you wasn't a man at all."

"He was a woman?" she asked in confusion.

Gabriel shook his head. "No, he was a *sanguis*, a blood. You're more familiar with the term *vampyre*."

Rachel slowly sat up, pulling the covers close as fear engulfed her. He was insane. She'd been so blinded by the promise of passion that she'd ignored what her gut had been telling her all along. "Could you repeat that please?"

His chin dropped. "You heard me. I know how it sounds, but I can prove it."

Rachel judged the distance to the door, then asked, "How?"

"Just know that I would never hurt you." Gabriel's voice cracked. "Ever."

Rachel rose from the bed and grabbed her robe. "You are freaking me out."

Gabriel gave her a sad smile. "Not as much as I'm about to," he said, revealing the tips of his fangs.

Rachel nearly tripped over her feet trying to get away. "Oh my God! What are you?"

"I'm a *sanguis*. We call it *sang* here in France. It means blood."

Her hands trembled as she tied her robe. "Are you telling me you're like the creep who attacked me?" Horrified, Rachel reached for the spot on her neck where she'd felt the prick.

"No!" Gabriel's jaw tensed. "I am nothing like the animal that attacked you. I clean up his messes."

"You know who did this and you didn't tell me." Fear was instantly replaced with anger. "How can you live with yourself?"

"What kind of man do you think I am?" he asked. "Wait –" he held up his hands "– don't answer that."

Rachel stared at him, waiting for him to sprout horns. "You must really think I'm a fool."

Gabriel looked tired when he finally met her gaze. "You are many things, Rachel Chang, but a fool is not one of them. I don't know who attacked you. If I did, justice would've been swift. I assure you. I've been trying to keep you safe."

"How? By lying to me?"

"Would you have believed me had I said something sooner?" he asked.

Hell, Rachel wasn't sure she believed him now. Trouble was she'd been a cop long enough to know when someone was lying and, as much as she didn't like what he had to say, Rachel knew Gabriel wasn't.

"What did the asshole that bit me really do to me?" She sank into the chair by the window.

Gabriel sat up on the bed. The duvet fell to his waist, revealing a sculpted abdomen. Rachel drank the sight in, then forced her gaze away. The desire she felt now was tempered by anger.

"A normal *sang* or *vampyre* bite doesn't do anything to the mortal other than leave them a little weak. Unfortunately when the vamp bit your arm, you struck him, shattering his nose. This caused a blood exchange."

"What does that mean exactly?" she asked.

He took a deep breath. "There's no easy way to say this."

"I don't know if you noticed, but I'm not a patient person, Gabriel. Just tell me."

"You've been infected. You're dying, Rachel." Gabriel's voice held no emotion when he delivered the news.

Rachel had spent the last several months dodging the bullet that had been meant for her and now it had finally found her. Of course it wasn't a real bullet this time, but the infection had the same effect. It was just a little slower acting. Instead of fearing the future, she was strangely relieved. "How long do I have?"

"A day. Maybe three max."

The news sucker-punched her in the gut. Rachel had hoped it would be longer than that, but she recovered quickly. Her mind raced to comprehend all she'd been told. "You were obviously infected, how come you're still alive?"

"Because my sire stayed around to make sure I was fed," he said quietly.

Rachel looked at him. "Since mine's a psycho that's not going to happen."

Gabriel slowly shook his head. "No."

"That doesn't leave us much time," she said.

His brow furrowed. "Time for what?"

"To catch this bastard and get my necklace back."

Gabriel stood, gloriously at ease with his nakedness. "Didn't you hear what I said?"

"Every word." Rachel closed the distance between them. Gabriel flinched when she touched his cheek. "If what you say is true, I don't have much time left. I plan to make every second count, starting with bringing the bastard down. Help or stay out of my way. It's your choice."

"You know I won't let you go after him alone. It would be a slaughter."

"I didn't go down easy the first time."

Gabriel kissed her. "No, you did not. You are a remarkable woman."

Rachel blushed. "Bet you say that to all the girls."

He stared at her. "I've never said that to anyone until now." Gabriel sighed. "Where should we start?"

"That's easy," Rachel said, grateful for the change in subject. "The catacombs. I chased him there once. There's a good possibility he'll show again. Besides, we have an advantage."

Gabriel cocked his head. "What's that?"

"Me." Rachel shrugged. "He's obviously after me."

He nodded. "You've seen his face. He knows you can identify him. That makes you a threat."

She grinned. "Perfect, so let's give him what he wants."

Gabriel turned away. "It's too dangerous."

Rachel snorted. "I'm dying. There's nothing else he can do to me."

"That's where you're wrong," Gabriel said. "There are a lot of things worse than death."

Six

The plan wasn't foolproof, but it was the best they could do under the circumstances. The bodies of the two women Rachel had seen in her dreams had been discovered, one by Gabriel's team and the other by the Parisian police. The fact that the police had been brought in troubled the Sang High Council. A termination order was given to the Trackers of Paris. There would be no trial.

Somehow the killer was keeping tabs on Rachel. She and Gabriel were counting on the fact that he'd follow her, if she left herself open for attack. The best place to do that was in the catacombs.

Hiding until it closed for the evening hadn't been difficult, although it did require crawling on mountains of bones. Rachel lay on a pile swallowed by shadows and concentrated on not moving. Mentally she kept apologizing to the dead for the inconvenience. When the last employee did his rounds, she slowly made her way off her bed of bones. Human remains from the eighteenth century crunched beneath her booted feet. Somewhere nearby Gabriel was waiting, careful not to give his presence away.

Despite everything she'd been told over the last two days, Rachel felt at peace for the first time in a year. She turned on her flashlight and made her way down the path towards the sound of water dripping. There was no guarantee the killer would show tonight or any other night for that matter. They were counting on his arrogance to bring him.

Rachel reached the stone chalice, which held water that steadily dripped from the ceiling. She and Gabriel had picked the spot earlier because the area was wider here than along the rest of the trail. There were no benches, so Rachel had to stand. She leaned against a wide column that looked to be holding up the cave-like roof. Rachel extinguished the flashlight allowing the darkness to envelop her. Nothing left to do but wait.

The drip, drip, drip of the water onto the stone lulled her mind. Rachel replayed much of her life and realized that, with the exception of Paul's death, she had few regrets. She'd come to Paris to contemplate ending her life, only to discover a reason to live. Too bad it was too late.

Drip, drip, drip, *silence*.

She waited for the next drip, but it never came. Rachel slowly straightened, her ears straining to hear. Something nearby had stopped the water. The hair on Rachel's neck rose, leaving gooseflesh in its wake. "I know you're here," she said.

"Come for your necklace?" a male voice said, far too close for comfort.

"Yes, and to get justice for the women you killed."

He laughed, the sound rusty from disuse. "We both know that's not going to happen."

A cool chain touched the skin on the back of her hand. Paul's necklace. Rachel snatched for it, but missed.

"So close," he said smugly. "Now, what am I going to do with you?"

The floodlights came on suddenly. Rachel blinked, temporarily blinded.

"Claude? What are you doing here?" Gabriel asked.

Rachel's vision cleared and she saw the dark-haired man from the side street standing four feet from her. His green gaze was locked on Gabriel.

"You know this man?" she asked.

Gabriel didn't take his gaze off the other man when he answered. "This is my partner – my friend. We work together."

Rachel's stomach pitched. "This is the man who attacked me. He killed those women."

"Claude, what is she talking about?" Gabriel's disbelief was clear.

"The woman is obviously mad. You said so yourself. Why else would she be down here so close to the Otherworld entrance?"

Gabriel's blue eyes burned holes in his partner. "I heard what you said. Every word. Looking back, I should've known. You knew she'd been drinking the night of the attack before I even said anything. The only way you could've known that was if you were there."

He tugged at his cuff, straightening it. "That is a shame, *mon ami*. It would've been easier had you stayed out of it." Claude launched himself at Gabriel, knocking him into the wall of bones, then proceeded to pound on him with his fists.

Rachel hadn't even seen him move. It would be a very short fight if she didn't do something quick. "Claude," she shouted, then grabbed a thigh bone and hit him on the side of the head as he turned, giving Gabriel time to scramble to his feet.

The men circled, taking swipes at each other with their bare hands. Given the power behind their blows and the sharpness of their teeth, they didn't need weapons. Rachel watched in fascinated horror as each man tore chunks of flesh from the other. Gabriel was bleeding badly now and didn't look nearly as focused as he'd been earlier. Claude dodged right and struck Gabriel across the head with his fist. Gabriel went down – hard.

"Let's end this so we can have some alone time." Claude smiled viciously at Rachel as he pulled a long antique dagger out of his sleeve.

Gabriel moaned and tried to stand.

She'd already seen what Claude did to women and had no intention of joining his little *club*. Rachel looked around quickly and snatched up two damaged bones. The joints had been snapped off, leaving jagged points behind.

He grabbed Gabriel by the hair and bared his neck. Claude raised the dagger, preparing to slash his throat. Rachel didn't think. She roared in anger and rushed forwards, bones held like stakes in front of her.

Claude blinked in surprise. He quickly dropped Gabriel to face the oncoming threat. Rachel ploughed into him. It was like smashing into marble. She drove the bones into his shoulders. They went in a few inches then splintered in her hands.

Rachel stumbled back. Pain blossomed. Burned. She looked down at the dagger sticking out of her abdomen. So much blood. She shivered. Cold. Rachel fell, still clutching the weapon in her gut.

Claude's fangs extended. His green eyes began to glow. He stalked towards her. "You should've waited your turn. But if you insist on going first." He hauled Rachel to her feet and slammed her against the pillar. "Don't move."

She was too numb to feel anything.

"What, no begging or pleading for your life? How about the life of your lover?" He glanced at Gabriel.

Rachel glared. "Just get on with it."

The bones made sucking noises as Claude pulled them out of his body and dropped them on the ground in disgust. He growled, then wrenched her neck back and opened his mouth. His warm fetid breath bathed her throat. "Painful, but pointless. Do you not know how to kill a *vampyre*?"

Rachel braced herself.

Claude's body jerked once. He released her and looked down. Rachel followed his gaze to see the sharp edges of a bone protruding from the middle of his chest.

"I do," Gabriel hissed, driving the bone deeper.

There was no drama to Claude's death. He didn't burst into flames, shrivel up and age, or flail about. He simply fell to his knees, grimaced and died.

Rachel's legs gave out and she slid to the ground. "We got him," she said, then coughed. Blood smeared her delicate lips.

"Yes, we did." Gabriel rifled through Claude's pockets until he found what he was looking for. He dropped the St Michael medal into Rachel's hand. "I believe this is yours." He choked on the words. "I told you I'd get it back for you."

She smiled and touched his cheek, leaving a streak of blood behind. "Thank you."

"Listen," Gabriel said. "We don't have much time."

Rachel laughed and winced. "We knew that going in."

"No." He shook his head. "You don't understand. You have a choice to make. Normally this is done by the *sanguis* who sired you. But since he's dead, I can offer."

Rachel's lids drooped shut. Gabriel shook her hard. "Wake up and listen." He sounded desperate, even to his own ears. Her eyes fluttered open, but they didn't focus. "I can change you into what I am, but it has to be done with your permission."

"What are you saying?"

"Do you want to live?" Gabriel asked. "Yes or no."

Ever since Paul's death Rachel had been asking herself that question. Up until now the answer had always been the same – no. But that was before she'd met Gabriel. He reminded her that she was indeed alive. She glanced at the St Michael's medal in her hand. It used to bring her pain and comfort in equal measure. Now as she stroked the necklace with her thumb all she had was fond memories. She met Gabriel's eyes.

He trembled under her regard. She could tell what it was costing him to wait. He'd live with whatever she decided, but hope burned eternal in his gaze.

"Do it," she said, then braced herself.

Just like when they'd made love, Rachel felt a slight sting as his teeth broke the skin on her neck. Gabriel held her close, comforting her as he drank. The drips from the water faded and the world began to dim. Rachel felt her heart stutter. Before it stopped, Gabriel pulled the dagger out of her and sliced open his wrist, then pressed the bleeding wound to her mouth.

"Drink for our future." Gabriel forced her to swallow, when every instinct inside her revolted.

Two Days Later ...

Rachel woke up in her bed at the Hotel Luxembourg. She reached down and winced as her hand touched her tender abdomen. She lifted her shirt and saw a clean white bandage. Rachel glanced around. Nothing looked different, but the bandage meant it definitely hadn't been a dream.

She heard the shower running in the bathroom. A moment later the door opened with a billow of steam and Gabriel stepped out with a white fluffy towel wrapped around his trim waist.

"You're finally awake," he said, not bothering to hide his relief. "How are you feeling?"

Rachel sat up. "Fine, I think. How did we get here?"

He grinned and her heart skittered. "I carried you."

"You do realize the hotel is never going to let me stay here again, right?"

"This is Paris. The city of love." His expression grew solemn. "What are you going to do now that you've recovered?"

He watched her carefully. The vulnerability she'd seen in the catacombs was back in full force. Rachel made a show of thinking about it. She had nothing to go back to in New York other than a small apartment, an empty refrigerator and months of psychological evaluations.

"I thought maybe I'd stick around. My French is rusty and I need to learn the ropes of this whole *vampyre* thing," she said.

Hope blossomed in his blue eyes. "I'd be more than happy to teach you, if you like."

"What would I do for work?" she asked. "You can't live on love alone, not even in Paris."

Gabriel's smile was back, wider than before. "I happen to know of a job opening now that my partner has retired."

"Is that so?" Rachel had a hard time keeping a straight face.

"Of course, I'll have to interview you." His heated gaze raked her and she felt an answering pull deep inside.

Rachel arched a brow. "What does a *vampyric* interview entail?"

Gabriel dropped his towel, revealing his growing desire. "It starts with a very thorough physical."

Rachel grinned, admiring the view. "Did I ever tell you I received the Presidential patch for fitness when I was in school?"

Gabriel's lips quirked. "Prove it."

Coven of Mercy

Deborah Cooke

I hate the month of March. It's an indecisive month, hovering on the cusp between winter and spring. Indecision drives me wild.

I like clear-cut strategies, battles that are victories or failures. Nothing in between.

March hovers, indecisive whether it should herald warm and sunny spring, or more winter – cold and overcast, the skies thick with falling snow. It ends up in that mucky zone, somewhere in between. Freezing rain and relentless grey, dampness and dull days, are followed by teasing intervals of sunshine. It's unreliable, untrustworthy, despicable.

Give me black or white. Give me winter or spring. Give me February or April. You can keep March.

My mother died in March; maybe that's part of it. Diagnosed early in the month, gone by the end of it, hers was a chaotic and whirlwind departure, a roller-coaster ride of triumphs and setbacks. That journey to death – the one no one wanted to take, the one that changed everything forever – is echoed for me every year in the weather.

March makes me restless and impatient, sharp and irritable.

That year was no different.

My hospital was a research hospital. That gave me the option of working in the labs, researching instead of practising. There are no mucky grey zones in the labs – a new drug is effective or it isn't – and that polarity always worked for me.

I had a bit of a reputation on the wards, where I would be called in as a specialist on the tough cases. 'Icicle' Taylor cut to the chase, took risks, won more than she lost. Each case, for me, was an array of statistics, a flotilla of blood test results, and I chose the armaments with which I would engage based upon experience and the sum of results to date. I never wanted to know the patient – that was just extraneous detail. I never wanted to familiarize myself with the territory in dispute.

I just wanted to win.

But that March, one patient wasn't having any of that. Mrs Curtis was in her forties and had a wry smile. She refused to let me slide in and out of her life without making a connection. She continued to insist that I call her by her first name, for example, even though I never did. She always wanted a conversation when I slipped in to check her charts or progress. She introduced me to her family and friends. There are many points of contact in an aggressive routine of chemotherapy and radiation, and Mrs Curtis put every one to work in her effort to charm me.

In a way, she waged her own campaign against my clinical detachment while I fought the disease that had invaded her body.

She had one advantage she never realized and it was the one that made the difference – she looked like my mother. She was taller and more buxom, but that glint in her eye, that ability to see right through my carefully composed lines to what I really meant, was my mother back from the grave. It caught at my heart, ripped a hole in my composure, and exposed a small vulnerability.

So, I was even more determined than usual to ensure that Mrs Curtis was a triumph. My mother, you see, had lost her battle right before my eyes. Mrs Curtis was my chance to prove that I wasn't some helpless twelve-year-old forced to stand aside and watch while her life disintegrated before her eyes.

Mrs Curtis was a territory I intended to win back from the enemy, one cell at a time.

And that's why I was back at the hospital close to midnight that night, on the way home from a date that I hadn't wanted to keep. It had been a double date, set up by a friend despairing of my "perverse affection" for solitude, and it had been a disaster. They all were. He'd been nice enough, but not nearly as fascinating as the mutating opponent I met in the lab every single day. And he didn't understand what it was to be passionate about anything – other than football and sex. I'd tapped my fingers on the table and smiled thinly throughout the meal.

We were probably all relieved when the cheque came.

I'd immediately gone back to the hospital to look over the most recent bout of test results, just to make sure I hadn't missed anything. I knew I hadn't, I never do, but it gave me the excuse to look in on Mrs Curtis again.

She was probably awake. We shared a kind of insomnia, a restlessness in the middle of the night that only conversation cured. She had a private room, so I knew I wouldn't be troubling anyone else.

I needed to talk to her about doing another biopsy anyway. The last had been painful, deeper than anticipated. I'd feared that the subsequent radiation would finish her before the cancer did. But Mrs Curtis had rallied, as she always did.

So, unfortunately, had my determined foe – the cancer.

The ward was quiet. I've always preferred the hospital at night. During the day, it can be fraught with emotional energy, people demanding answers and desperate to do something to help. I'd never done well with that kind of anxiety.

I was always better with test results, percentages, calculations, cold hard maths. Winter, if you will – relentless but consistent, instead of the capricious and fleeting charm of spring.

In the quiet darkness, the hospital was more pure in its function. Monitors beeped and intravenous tubes dripped. The machines ran the show, which worked for me. Patients slept. Visitors had left. Gurneys were moved as the dead journeyed quietly down to the morgue. The nurses focused on the checking of patients and keeping records.

I savoured the dimness of the lights and the emptiness of the lobby as I crossed the threshold that night. I was looking forward to seeing Mrs Curtis too, even with the discussion ahead of us. The elevator came immediately and, in the comparative silence, I heard the whirr of its mechanism as I stood alone in it.

I nodded to the night nurse, Miriam, one of the most watchful and competent of the nursing team. I hesitated outside Mrs Curtis's room, my steps frozen at the sound of voices.

She had a guest.

How could that be?

I looked at my watch. It was almost midnight. Outrage rose within me that anyone would disturb a patient as she healed, but then Mrs Curtis laughed.

It was a different laugh than the one I usually heard in her presence. Low. Breathy. Sexy.

"I can't dance now!" she protested in a tone of voice that indicated she'd like to be persuaded otherwise.

"Of course you can," a man insisted. His voice was low and rich, a murmur that made me shiver.

"The IV . . . "

"We'll ignore it."

"But there's no music," Mrs Curtis argued, her tone light. Flirtatious.

Did Mrs Curtis have a lover? She'd never mentioned it, but then I made a point of not asking after personal details. I knew nothing about her life and, until this moment, that had suited me just fine. I peeked around the edge of the door, curious.

There was a man on the far side of Mrs Curtis's bed, standing with his back to the window. He had dark hair and dark eyes, and seemed to be younger than Mrs Curtis. He was handsome, handsome enough to make me yearn for something I hadn't had in a long time. He was wearing a black leather jacket, black jeans and a black T-shirt. A silver earring gleamed from his left ear lobe. No pretty boy – he was older, knowing, a little bit world-weary.

Sexy.

Familiar.

Although I knew I'd never seen him before.

Mrs Curtis had braced herself on one elbow, her hair a tangle of silver and russet on the back of her neck. Her skin was pale and she was thinner than I'd realized. The back of her hospital gown was open, and I was shocked at how clearly the individual vertebrae were delineated. The IV in her right hand looked enormous in comparison to her delicate hands.

"Isn't there?" he asked, his smile broadening. He had a sensual mouth, a full and mobile one, and his smile looked positively decadent. I couldn't identify his accent, but it was European. Exotic.

And then I heard the waltz. It seemed as if an orchestra had struck up in the ward, although that made no sense. The music lilted through the room, barely audible to me in the doorway, but achingly beautiful.

Mrs Curtis was laughing at the man, who watched her as if she was the most beautiful woman in the world. A lump rose in my throat at his kindness.

Or maybe the state of his infatuation.

"How did you do that?" she demanded.

"Does it matter? Or should we simply dance?" He offered his hand to her, palm up, and I was struck by how tiny her right hand looked when she placed it in his. How wrong that IV needle looked in the back of her hand, with its three strips of tape.

I had never seen Mrs Curtis healthy.

I had never before heard her laugh.

"OK," she agreed, conspiratorial. "Let's dance."

He gathered her in his arms, bodily lifting her from the bed. My mouth went dry at the tenderness in his expression. She was all bones and pale skin, a rag doll, a wisp of the woman she must have been.

She slid her hands up to his shoulders, rapturous in his embrace. He smiled down at her, loving, possessive, gentle.

She laid her head on his shoulder and sighed. I saw her eyes close. I saw the glimmer of a tear on her cheek. She looked so fragile and faded, like a rose left in a vase too long. I thought he was going to kiss her and I knew I should look away.

But his gaze suddenly locked on mine.

That one glance stopped my heart cold. I was caught.

But there was no surprise in his expression: he'd known all along that I was there. That realization shook me, rooted me, made it impossible for me to move.

He knew me as well as I knew him.

Impossible.

He had smouldering dark eyes, eyes filled with a thousand shadows, eyes that seemed to see straight through to my heart. His hair was long, tied back; his features could have been sculpted out of marble. But his dark eyes, his eyes saw so much.

More than I allowed anyone to see. I wanted to avert my gaze, to hide. I saw the glimmer of a smile, as if he were amused by me.

Then he bent his head and sank his teeth into Mrs Curtis' neck. Mrs Curtis gasped and arched her neck, as if in pleasure, then laid her cheek upon his shoulder in surrender.

I knew that my eyes had to be deceiving me. There were no vampires in real life.

But the blood was flowing, easing from the corner of the stranger's mouth to slide down Mrs Curtis' fair skin. The rivulet was red against her pale flesh, and he drank steadily. The music soared and swirled as I gaped at them, then I saw her fingers go slack on his shoulder.

That made me move.

"Stop it!" I almost flew across the room, intending to pull him bodily away.

He stole one last massive gulp, then straightened. By the time I crossed the room, he'd laid Mrs Curtis back in her bed with that remarkable tenderness. He was a good foot taller than me, broad and imposing, but I shoved past him in my haste.

He stepped gracefully aside, as if he'd meant to move all along. I bent over Mrs Curtis, checking her monitors and her IV, placing my fingers under her chin.

Her pulse was weak, irregular, but still there.

The music, the lilting music that seemed to have drifted from another world, faded to nothing. I doubted I had even heard it in the first place.

"It's too late," the stranger said quietly. At close proximity, I was even more aware of his potent voice. It was more than low – it was languid. Melted chocolate on fruit.

Dark chocolate.

Tropical fruit.

I could feel the heat of him beside me, feel his scrutiny, almost hear his pulse. He was flesh and blood, like me, not an illusion.

Not a fable.

Before I could decide that my eyes had deceived me, I saw the proof: there were two perfectly round punctures in Mrs Curtis' throat.

He *was* a vampire.

I sputtered, far from my usual coherence. "How could you do this? Who are you?"

His smile broadened, but there was a tinge of sadness in his eyes. I had the sense that he knew more than I did, but I was too angry to care. "My name is Micah," he said softly.

Mrs Curtis' pulse faltered beneath my fingers and I forgot his alluring gaze. I reached past him and slapped the alarm button for Miriam. "We need an infusion, Miriam, stat," I said, not waiting for her query.

She knew where I was and would call up the blood type.

The stranger, meanwhile, had stepped around the end of the bed. He leaned over Mrs Curtis and, before I could stop him, touched her throat gently with his fingertips. The gesture was reverent, that of a lover saying farewell.

When he lifted his hand, those two round holes were gone.

As if they'd never been there.

I blinked and stared, but the flesh was perfect.

I had seen them, though. I had seen what he had done.

Mrs Curtis sighed and her head fell to one side. The pulse monitor began to sound an alarm.

Everything happened quickly then: Miriam arrived with the blood and we worked together, two other nurses following instructions. Mrs Curtis' vitals rapidly went from bad to worse. Her pulse rate slowed and became erratic. Her breathing became more laboured, rattling in her throat, her skin became paler. Nothing we did made a difference. Miriam was the perfect partner, both of us knowing exactly what had to be done when.

But it was too late.

My hands were on her scarred chest when Mrs Curtis' heart stopped right beneath my palms. I would have kept trying, but Miriam touched my shoulder.

"There's no point, Dr Taylor," she said quietly, and even knowing she was right, it was hard to lift my hands away.

This battle had been more important to me, although they all were critical. I blinked back unexpected tears as Miriam pulled the sheet over Mrs Curtis' face. The two other nurses left quietly and I took a shaking breath. I turned away from the sight of Mrs Curtis' still figure.

I'd lost.

The night was inky black beyond the windows, a perfect echo of my mood.

No. I hadn't lost. I'd been cheated.

By Micah.

I spun, finding Miriam halfway to the door. "That man, Miriam, did you see him? Where did he go?"

Miriam gave me a quizzical look. "What man, Dr Taylor?"

"Mrs Curtis' visitor; you couldn't have missed him. You must have passed him on your way in here with the blood."

She frowned. "I didn't see anyone but staff tonight."

"Maybe he works here." I shrugged. "He was with Mrs Curtis when I arrived, talking to her. He was tall and dark, about thirty-five, leather jacket and long dark hair . . . " I faltered to silence as I realized Miriam had no idea who I was talking about.

"I think I'd remember a man like that," Miriam said with a smile. "Are you sure, Dr Taylor?"

I glanced back at Mrs Curtis again. I knew what I had seen. Why hadn't Miriam seen him? I remembered the way he had made the marks of his feasting disappear, and bit my tongue.

No one would believe that I'd seen a vampire.

And I wasn't going to ask Miriam about bats in the ward.

Miriam crossed the floor, her shoe soles squeaking on the linoleum. She touched my elbow briefly and I started in surprise. No one ever touched me, especially not at work. "Time to go, Dr Taylor." She gestured to the door and I knew she was right. Lingering wouldn't change anything.

"I'll call her family," Miriam said kindly when we were in the hall. "Does she have a partner?"

"A sister. I have the number. I'll tell her how hard you tried." Miriam studied me, then smiled. "Go home, Dr Taylor, go home and get some sleep."

I was confused by her compassion. "I'm fine. I'll go down to the lab . . . "

She exhaled sharply and looked stern. "I understand that you did rounds at seven this morning, and now it's almost midnight."

There was frost hanging from every word of my response. "I always work long hours." And they were no one's business but mine.

"But you don't always see people who aren't there, Dr Taylor, do you?"

I could have argued that the stranger *had* been there, that I knew what I had seen, but I saw that Miriam wouldn't be persuaded. I nodded an acknowledgment, thanked her and returned to the elevator.

But I didn't go home.

I went to the cafeteria and nursed a coffee from the vending machine, reviewing everything I had done, seeking the error in my judgment. I always do this kind of examination, always try to improve my strategy.

I'd done nothing wrong.

I just hadn't allowed for vampires in my statistical analysis.

Vampires. Maybe there was something to Miriam's concern. Maybe I had been pushing myself too hard. I was tired, there was no disputing that.

But how can anyone sleep when the battle is so relentless? Cancer never sleeps and it takes advantage of every weakness. It would win, maybe even while I was sleeping, and I couldn't let that happen. There already weren't enough hours in the day.

It was getting light when I ditched the cold coffee, then left the hospital. If nothing else, I'd shower and change my clothes at home before returning for morning rounds. I tried to swallow the lump in my throat to keep from looking back to Mrs Curtis' room. I ignored the cars of my co-workers pulling into their parking spaces.

I was halfway across the lot when I saw the stranger leaning against the front fender of my car.

Waiting.

For me.

He had that amused smile again, which was more than enough to set me off.

I was across the parking lot in record time, fury and exhaustion making me more volatile than usual. "You killed her!"

The stranger didn't move away from my anger. He leaned one hip against my car, his arms folded across his chest. He was dark and large and could have been carved from stone.

No, he could have been sculpted from stone. He was beautiful, his dark eyes thickly lashed, his mouth sensuously curved. I felt an awareness of him and our proximity, an awareness I resented.

He was a predator, a murderer, a vampire. He might as well have been on the enemy side.

Micah. It was a name that suited him. Just a little bit different. Unexpected. Old and strong.

I glared at him. "You did, didn't you?"

He inclined his head slightly. "Yes." He moved slowly, elegantly, every gesture thoughtful. He closed his eyes briefly, his features touched with a sadness I didn't understand.

"How could you do that?"

"I have to feed."

"Isn't there someone else you could kill? A criminal or a wild animal? Someone who deserves to die?"

"Everyone will die, deserving or not."

"But she was going to live. I was winning . . . "

"Maybe she's at peace now."

"No. She's dead now."

He was amused again. "Not in heaven?"

I was as impatient with this idea as ever. My father and I had argued this up, down and sideways and I knew my position well. "There is no heaven and there is no hell. There is life and there is death and everything else is just romance."

"*Just* romance?"

"There's no point in self-delusion. Get away from my car."

"You need to understand . . . "

"I understand everything, thanks. You *fed*, and she died because of it. That's evil."

He didn't move. He frowned and averted his gaze, and I thought that maybe I had touched his conscience. But to my surprise, he spoke with regret and changed the subject. "Once I had a child," he began softly, but his own history didn't interest me.

"No. I don't care. No matter what you've lost, you have no right to decide whether another person lives or dies."

He met my gaze steadily and parted his lips, letting me see the sharp points of his fangs. "I have every right."

"No. No. Vampires don't exist," I said. I jammed my key into the lock of the door on the driver's side. He still didn't move.

"Then who killed the woman?" he asked mildly. "You?"

"No! I was the one who would have saved her. You stole that victory away."

"Victory?"

I heard my own fears in that single word. "Sure, it was back, but it hadn't won yet. I had a treatment plan prepared. We would have gone after it, hard." I held his gaze, knowing my own was filled with accusation and anger. "I would have *won*. I would have saved her. But you stole her first." I took a deep breath and glared at him. He watched me steadily, those full lips curving in that damned amusement. "You cheated me and you cheated Mrs Curtis."

"Are you sure?"

"Yes!"

But I wasn't and he knew it. You can never be sure. Remission might be permanent or might not be. I'd been sure that Mrs Curtis' previous round of treatment would finish the cancer, but the blood tests don't lie.

He was watching me. "Don't you want to know the rest of the story?"

There was something seductive about his voice, something that I feared I would find compelling. There was something more seductive about the notion that he knew more than I did, and that he would share. Why did I recognize him? How could it be possible?

How could I not remember?

I felt charmed by him and didn't trust the jumbled feelings I felt in his presence. I was aroused. I was furious. I wanted to know how he kissed. I wanted him to disappear for ever. "No," I said with a heat that was rare for me.

His eyes twinkled, their darkness lit as the night sky had been lit with stars. "What if I don't want to go?"

I shoved him and he moved from the fender of my car. There was nothing virtual about him. He felt muscled, as if he worked out, solid and real, and I tingled in an unwelcome way.

"You can't stop the coven of mercy, Rosemary," Micah whispered, his words making me catch my breath.

"How do you know my name?" He'd known which car was mine, too.

"I know a lot of things." He arched a dark brow. "I've watched you for a long time. Not everyone prefers solitude."

His words startled me, in more ways than one, but he didn't have a shard of doubt. He was too smug, too sure.

Maybe a little bit too much like me.

I needed to get some sleep.

"There is no coven of mercy and there was no mercy in what you did. Get away from my car."

"Is her death what's really bothering you?" he asked, his words low. "Or is it that you lost a chance to win? Is this about the person or the score?"

I slapped him then, hard, right across the face. His head jerked to one side and the red mark of my hand showed on his cheek.

I was afraid then, afraid for a moment that I'd pushed him too hard.

What he did next astonished me.

He looked at me steadily for a long moment in which my heart thundered in terror, then he pivoted with the grace of a giant cat. He strode silently across the parking lot, towards the surrounding scrub of trees.

The hospital was new, built slightly outside of town, surrounded by undeveloped land. There were scrubby trees and a little creek, a tangle of undergrowth and a nature trail. There was still snow there, caught in the bit of brush, and the tree branches were dark and bare.

The sky was turning pink in the east by then, and my hands clenched as I watched his dark figure move away. His boots crunched on the snow, as real as I was. I was so angry that I was tempted to go after him, argue some more, shake him.

Kiss him.

A car door slammed near me and I jumped, surprised to find Dr Bradley stepping out of his Subaru so close at hand. He ran the labs and was my boss. "Are you all right, Dr Taylor?"

"Good morning, Dr Bradley." I forced a smile.

He didn't smile, just came to my side, his expression concerned. "Have you been here all night? Again?" He was paternal, a good twenty years older than me.

I made a gesture of futility, not knowing how much I wanted to share and too tired to work it out. "I was just going home for a shower."

"And arguing with yourself about it."

"What?"

"You were shadow-boxing when I pulled in."

"No, there was a guy here . . . " I recognized immediately that Dr Bradley hadn't seen the stranger.

Just like Miriam.

I stopped talking before I condemned myself.

Dr Bradley cleared his throat. "I know you've been working really hard lately, Dr Taylor, but indulge me, will you?"

I was wary. "What do you mean?"

"You look exhausted and have for a while. I'm wondering about your iron and iron stores. You're probably not eating well any more often than you're sleeping well. And I'm probably being cautious, but your expertise is valuable to the team."

He smiled, softening the impact of his words, but I got the drift. No one was glad to have me around, but they liked my abilities. Someone like Dr Bradley would never understand why a lack of human connection didn't bother me.

Even if, this time, it did. A bit.

"Meaning?" I asked in my most professional tone.

"That prevention is the best medicine. Indulge me and get a routine suite of blood work done. We both know that it'll be easier to improve your iron counts sooner rather than later."

"There's nothing wrong with me. I just didn't sleep last night."

"When did you last have a physical?"

I shrugged. I wasn't the only one who never got around to it.

He smiled, the way he always did when he wanted something extra from his staff. For once, it worked like a charm on me. "Just humor me." He winked and turned away, giving me a last wave. "I'll leave the requisitions on your desk this morning. Promise?"

"Sure, Dr Bradley." It wasn't as if I was afraid of needles and test results. And I had felt as if I was running on empty lately. I knew I just needed more sleep, but it wouldn't hurt to have my haemoglobin checked.

I got in my car, went home and had a shower.

Then I drank the better part of a pot of good coffee and came back to work. Cancer doesn't need to rest, after all. The battle rages, even when we leave the field. Maybe it moves faster when we aren't looking.

Coven of mercy. What had the stranger meant?

His name was Micah.

Micah.

Two days after Mrs Curtis' death, her last batch of test results came back from the lab. There was also a reminder from Dr Bradley that I hadn't given my blood samples yet. I crumpled the message and tossed it out. I'd just been too busy for details.

I wasn't going to look at Mrs Curtis' results, as I was still unable to accept what I'd seen. But on some level, I needed to prove to myself that I'd been right, that Micah had been wrong, just in case I ever saw him again and could tell him so. I needed data to argue my point of view.

I knew this was ridiculous – that I needed to muster my resources to argue with a vampire – but couldn't put it out of my thoughts. I argued with myself until close to midnight.

Then I gave it up. I got a coffee from the vending machine, sat down at my desk and clicked through on the file. I stared at the numbers for so long that my coffee got cold.

I checked them four times. I assumed initially that they had to be wrong, but they were completely consistent. The cancer had efficiently progressed while we'd thought we were killing every last cell.

Against all expectation, it had turned even more virulent and metastasized. It had used the highways and byways of her lymphatic system to colonize every corner of her territory. Despite the treatment regimen. Mrs Curtis had been so much more ill than she had appeared to be. The counts were staggering and impressive.

Cancer had already won. I had maybe slowed its progress, but I hadn't come close to stopping it.

I remembered how Mrs Curtis had cheerfully suffered through her more recent bout of treatment, enduring more no matter how violent her reactions were. I had been so sure that short-term pain would lead to long-term gain. I had never underestimated the disease so much.

I felt a bit sick that she'd gone through that for nothing.

Just like my mother.

Yes, my mother's treatment had been just as futile. I'd found copies of the correspondence with her doctors in the house after my father's death, when Rick and I were cleaning things out, still refusing to speak to each other. I had reviewed them with the eyes of a trained oncologist, seeing then the inevitability of her counts. She was diagnosed too late for the treatment protocols available at the time to turn the tide.

I had known at twelve that she would die, even without that training, and I had been right. Later, I saw that there was mercy in the speed of the disease's progression. Three weeks of knowing, two weeks of suffering, then the battle had been won.

It wasn't always that kind.

I stared at Mrs Curtis' charts.

Coven of mercy. I recalled Micah's words and had to consider them. If Mrs Curtis hadn't died two days before, would these two days of treatment have been merciful? No, of course not. Chemotherapy and radiation are seldom easy, and we would have had to hit her harder this time. I had to face the truth.

With counts like this, she would have been gone in a week or two anyway, barring a miracle.

I felt a presence at my side and knew who it was. It was the warmth, the watchfulness, the scent of leather that gave Micah away.

"You knew," I said, without looking.

"I knew," he agreed.

I spun in my chair to face him, surprised at his size and intensity. He was all male – brooding thoughtful male – and he filled the bit of spare space in my crowded small office. "How?"

He frowned and folded his arms across his chest, scanning the floor as he sought the words. I liked that he didn't dismiss my question, that he didn't rush into explanations.

I felt a strange sense of union with him and was struck by the fact that it was easier to talk to him than any other person I'd known.

"We can smell it."

"Cancer?"

"Death." His gaze collided with mine, his eyes filled with enigmatic shadows. "You have to understand that it's our biological need to feed on blood. Some of us choose to use that need for compassionate ends. Some of us choose to feed strategically."

"Why?"

His smile was fleeting and his eyes gleamed as he watched me. "Some of us have an inexplicable fondness for humanity." He shrugged. "Or maybe we just remember the pain of being mortal."

"You're immortal, then?"

He nodded.

"But every day, you have to kill somebody?"

He shook his head. "The hunger comes with some regularity, but not daily. Exertion affects the appetite, as does quality and quantity consumed."

It made sense to me, in biological terms. I could understand him as a different species better than as a fable. I looked at my computer screen again, fighting the sense that I could fall into his eyes and lose myself for ever.

I looked up. "'We'? You said 'we'. How many of you are there?"

"The coven has twelve members right now . . . "

"Shouldn't there be thirteen?" I joked but he didn't smile.

"Yes," he agreed, then continued with his original point. "We are committed to mercy, to using our power to improve the lives of individual humans."

"To killing."

"Sometimes it is kinder to die. Sometimes suffering achieves nothing but pain."

That was a sentiment too close to my own recent thoughts. My tone was more sarcastic than he deserved. "So, you're all stalking cancer wards and palliative care units?"

He didn't respond to my tone, which only made me feel rude.

"We all have our tendencies and our passions. Beatrice is sensitive to victims of abuse, perhaps because of her own history. She knows some scars cannot be healed. Adrian hears the anguish of broken children, and Lucinda shares her kiss with the old and infirm. Ignatius can be found in war zones, Petronella in areas struck by famine, Augustine near outbreaks of plague."

"And you?"

That sad knowing smile curved his lips. "I have my own quest." His words were soft and he seemed to have turned inwards, away from me. I felt the loss of his attention and the weight of his grief and had to say something.

To my surprise, I didn't want him to leave. "Tell me about your child," I invited. His gaze locked with mine, a familiar sorrow lighting its shadows, then he swallowed. "You said you had a child. Tell me."

Micah shook his head and stood, facing the window and the night. I was struck that he seemed overcome with emotion. I had thought that he would be a monster, a cold and calculating predator, but his anguish was raw.

And I was astonished by my own wave of compassion for him. I stood, but couldn't bring myself to go to him, to touch him.

"Boy or girl?" I asked quietly, not expecting him to answer. He sighed – a shudder that rolled right through him – and glanced over his shoulder at me.

That gaze, so filled with torment, caught at my heart. I couldn't look away.

"Elsebietta," he murmured, reverence and love resonant in every syllable. He swallowed. "Her mother died in labour and they said she would be a sad child." He fell silent for a moment, and his voice was thick when he continued. "But she was as radiant as sunlight." He raised a hand, closing it on nothing. "She was my joy. The centre of my world."

I had to ask. "Did you kill her?"

The quick shake of his head was no lie. "It was before, before the coven." He swallowed. "I had to watch her die, and then there was no point in living any more."

"But you're alive now."

"The coven came to me and I found their proposition appealing."

"Why?"

"Elsebietta had consumption. There was no real treatment and no cure. She wasted to nothing before my eyes." He inhaled sharply, then eyed me. I couldn't avert my gaze. I knew that consumption was an historic diagnosis that contemporary researchers believed meant cancer. "My daughter needed my help and I had nothing to give her."

I swallowed then, knowing that sense of helplessness all too well. We had been to the same place, Micah and I.

"Only her hair held its colour." He smiled, lost in recollection. "It was so beautiful, like spun gold."

I knew then that his wife and daughter had been blonde, like me. My hair has always been wavy and unruly, so I keep it tightly controlled, captured beneath dozens of pins and clips. I saw the yearning in Micah's eyes, though, and I wanted to console him, this haunted man who mourned his only child.

It was such a small thing to give. Even if I was clumsy with such gestures.

I unpinned my hair and shook it out. It fell just past my shoulders, and seemed to writhe with pleasure to be free for once. I shoved the pins in the pocket of my lab coat and looked up to find his dark gaze fixed upon me.

Filled with admiration.

In an instant Micah was beside me, although I never saw him move. He lifted a hand and gently captured one tendril between finger and thumb. That secretive smile touched his lips again.

"So soft," he whispered, then bent his head and kissed that lock of my hair. When he glanced up, those dark eyes were near mine, that mouth so close that I could almost feel it on my own lips. I caught my breath, felt my eyes widen, and saw that sparkle light his eyes. There was a moment in which we stared at each other, a moment in which time stood still, a moment in which there was nowhere else I wanted to be.

Then he kissed me.

I could have stepped back. I could have ensured that he never touched me. But one kiss, one kiss was nothing. A taste. A tease. A temptation.

And it had been so long since I'd kissed anyone.

I let him kiss me, and he seemed to understand that I wouldn't give much, not without being persuaded to do so. The first touch of his lips was as light as the brush of a butterfly's wings. Ethereal. Almost illusory. I made some small involuntary sound – one of disappointment – and he bent close again, his kiss soft upon my mouth.

Persuasive.

Tender.

I thought of Micah helpless to save his child. I thought of the wife he had lost. I recalled my own mourning of my mother. I remembered how our small family had dissolved and scattered in her absence, and guessed that he had experienced a similar loss. The same sense of having no direction. Of being lost. Adrift.

Alone.

The isolation must have been worse for Micah. I had had my father, barricaded as he had been in his own grief. And my brother, Rick, now on the other side of the world and estranged. We had had the comfort of each other's physical presence, at least.

But Micah . . . Micah had been all alone.

I kissed him back. There was solace in the common ground of sorrow, purpose in consoling another. Our kiss was sweet and gentle, but then it changed. Then it became more sensual, more rooted in desire than in consolation, more demanding.

More exciting.

I opened my mouth and gripped his shoulders, leaning against him as he caught me close. He knew when to entreat and when to wait, how to drive me crazy as if we'd been lovers for years. I wanted more. I wanted it immediately, and I knew he tasted that in my kiss.

It was unlike any kiss I'd ever had, making all others look like pale shadows of this perfection. It was the kiss I had always wanted and

I realized, as he let his tongue tempt mine, that I had been looking for just this kiss.

Then I felt the brush of Micah's sharp tooth against my lower lip. There could be no stronger reminder of the predator he was.

And I heard music.

I broke the kiss and backed away from him in fear.

He let me go, watching as intently as I'd come to expect. "Now you look alive," he murmured with satisfaction.

I pivoted to check my reflection, and was shocked at my own appearance. My hair was loose and wild as it had never been, my eyes sparkling, my lips swollen. I looked like a woman who had been thoroughly kissed, and as different from my usual prim self as could be.

I would have blamed Micah for that, but when I turned back, he was gone.

As surely as if he had never been. My hands were shaking as I scooped up the scattered pins from my hair, and I pulled my hair up so tightly that it made me wince.

I could still taste that kiss, though.

I knew I would relive it in my dreams.

We aren't supposed to become involved.

We learned that in med school. Oncologists should be professional and detached, in order to make the best logical decision for treatment. We are the rudders, the realists, the rational ones. It's the only way to balance the emotions we encounter, the ones that cancer rouses.

It's the only way to fight the battle over the long term. I may have been called Icicle Taylor, but I haven't been the only one with my moat filled and my portcullis dropped. I have waded through buckets of emotional reactions every day since graduation, but always kept my eyes fixed on the prize.

Maybe it's not an accident that I chose to stay in research, to be a specialist called in for tough cases, but never the primary contact.

But, two years before this particular March, a little boy named Jason had reached in and grabbed my heart.

He had been all of five years old when he came to the ward with leukaemia, the adored elder child of a devoted couple. They were a picture-perfect husband and wife, trim and attractive, affluent and kind, professionals. They were affectionate with each other and with their adorable son and daughter. They were the kind of people who get what they want, and what they wanted was their son healthy again.

They would do whatever it took.

Jason was solemn, with a tangle of dark hair and eyes that seemed too big for his face. He had beautiful dark lashes and a surprising ability to understand what was really going on. His leukaemia was aggressive and I was testing a new drug. Their oncologist, pushed by Jason's parents to do more, called me in.

I was not used to being noticed in these situations. I'd explain the drug or the protocol, the risks and advantages, the unknowns, then step back and let the patient's oncologist handle the rest. I witnessed but didn't really participate.

Jason was the first to challenge that. We were at the end of our meeting, the oncologist summing up the strategy for Jason's parents, when this boy reached out and grabbed my hand. I jumped. I had thought they had all forgotten my presence.

"Will it hurt, Dr Taylor?" he demanded, his eyes wide.

I was so surprised that I couldn't lie to him. "Yes," I said. "But if you can do this, you will get better."

His mother caught her breath sharply. His father watched in horror. The oncologist closed his eyes. The tension in the room was palpable.

But Jason studied me, his gaze searching mine. I stared back at him steadily. I knew we would win and I let him see my conviction. His lips set and he nodded then, as committed to the course as I was.

And he was a trooper. Never complained. I went to his second marrow transplant as an observer, unable to stay away. The first hadn't been easy and the second was likely to be worse. Jason had seized my finger in pre-op, insisting that I hold his hand.

The whole team was shocked when Icicle Taylor agreed.

I was more shocked when Jason ran to give me a hug on the day of his final discharge. No one had spontaneously hugged me since my mother's death. I didn't think to hug him back. I was surprised and touched, and although I had rationalized it since, I still relived that moment of triumph.

It was a battle we had won.

But a week after Mrs Curtis died, Jason came back.

Capricious, deceitful March.

I'd been working even more hours, cross-checking everything, determined not to let anyone down the way I'd almost let Mrs Curtis down. Dr Bradley was a genial nag about my apparent inability to give the lab some blood. I'd never logged so many hours and I was exhausted, but I felt on the cusp of a breakthrough.

Until I saw Jason's parents in the ward. My heart stopped cold with the knowledge of why they were there. I have never wanted to be wrong as badly as I did then. Headaches, lassitude, infections that wouldn't go away, night sweats. His parents knew the truth as well as we did.

Jason had always reminded me of somebody I couldn't quite remember. I was so shocked at the sight of him this time that I realized who he resembled.

He looked like Micah. He had the intensity of focus and thoughtfulness that characterized Micah. That solemnity, that intensity, that watchfulness. Never mind the dark eyes and dark hair, the beautiful features.

It made no sense. I had met Jason *before* Micah.

No. That wasn't true. I remembered suddenly that I *had* seen Micah before. He'd been at my mother's funeral, a stranger on the perimeter of the gathering of mourners, watching.

Watching me.

My father had told me to pay attention and had been impatient with my insistence about the stranger. He had said that there was no one there.

I had never told anyone about the dreams I'd had later, dreams of that same man who didn't exist. I had shoved the recollection of those dreams aside, like so much else that made no sense that year.

Once recalled, I couldn't forget them. Micah had been watching me.

Why me?

I had a dreadful feeling about Jason's prognosis. We ordered the tests and tried to make cheerful noises, but the oncologist on the case and I avoided each other's gaze.

I was there the night the tests came back from the lab, a little ping from my computer indicating that the file I was watching had been updated. I didn't get coffee, just sat and read.

The results were terrible.

Inescapable.

I shut the door of my office and wept. Optimism isn't nearly a good enough weapon. I know the statistics and the survival rates as well as my own name. I looked again at Jason's blood work, even though I knew.

I was caught. We couldn't deny him treatment. I couldn't be fatalistic. I couldn't send Jason home to be happy for as many months – or weeks – as he had left. But I didn't want to put that darling boy with his trusting eyes through a treatment ordeal that wouldn't matter at the end.

I didn't want him to suffer more than he would anyway.

I wanted mercy for him.

I knew that Jason's parents would spare no expense and no trouble in their quest to see him cured. They had proven to be great allies in his past treatment regimen.

But this time they would fight, and they would lose.

And so I cried. I sat alone in my office and I wept for the futility of it all. I wept for Jason and his parents and the fact that he would never grow up to be the heartbreaker I wanted him to be. I wept for Mrs Curtis, believing at the end that she was dancing with a handsome man. I wept for my mother, and my father who had never been able to talk about his own pain, and my brother who had run as far away from the past as was physically possible. I wept for Micah and his lost wife and his beautiful daughter.

It was late when I had shed all my tears – two decades worth of them – and the night was still and dark. I wiped my face and blew my nose and decided I needed some sleep. I was straightening my desk when I grimaced at another email from Dr Bradley. The message from the day before was still unopened as I'd assumed it to be a nag about iron supplements. This one was marked urgent.

Some people don't like to be ignored.

I had done the blood work, for goodness sake.

I rolled my eyes and flicked open the file, guessing that he'd been right in his diagnosis. Low iron is a common problem among women, and I knew I wasn't that special in biological terms. I certainly didn't practice good self-care.

But it was a referral to the head oncologist on our team.

I clicked through to my own blood tests and sat back, stunned. My haemoglobin was down, but my white blood counts high. Worst of all, Dr Bradley had requested a cancer antigen test, because of my family history, and its high result told me all I needed to know.

My old adversary had moved the field of battle into my own cells.

Cancer is sneaky. It takes advantage of your mistakes. I've learned that, but I had left one flank undefended. My mother, after all, had died of ovarian cancer. Her death was what got me into this line of work. I wanted the power to do something other than stand by and watch for the inevitable. I've made a lot of saves in my time, and spearheaded a lot of research. I've done good work.

Maybe that's why it came after me. Maybe I was too worthy an opponent. Maybe that's why it took advantage of my genetic weakness.

It had certainly taken advantage of my slip-up. How long had it been since I'd had a physical examination? A suite of blood work done? A Pap smear? I just never had the time. Or maybe, I'd thought I was invincible, since I was fighting for the good guys.

It didn't really matter. I knew too much about treatment, about pain and suffering, and I knew the statistics. I knew that the oncologist would review my family history and immediately order an ultrasound of my lower abdomen, and I knew what he would find. I understood suddenly why I couldn't shed that round belly I'd developed, and it wasn't the food in the cafeteria.

I had a tumour and, with these counts, I would bet that it had already metastasized. It made too much sense. I knew that by the time there are symptoms of ovarian cancer, it's all over.

Even more damning, I had known my mother would die, with unshakeable certainty, when she was diagnosed and I had the same conviction that this cancer would take me, too.

Maybe I had always known that. Maybe that was why I hated March so much. Maybe it was a kind of foresight.

I didn't cry for myself. I'd cried all my tears for Jason and for Mrs Curtis. I was too angry that the fight would go on without me, that the battle would rage without my contribution. It wasn't fair. I was surprised by how much I wanted a different answer than the one I routinely gave.

I looked out the window at the night, seething.

Micah was leaning against the fender of my car again, and he looked as if his gaze was fixed upon my window. I understood then why I was the only one who could see him. Just as Mrs Curtis had seen him.

He was waiting for me.

And I knew why.

"You knew," I said when I was still twenty feet away from him.

Micah inclined his head in agreement, that same graceful gesture, but there was no amused curve to his lips this time. He was as watchful as ever, though.

Still.

I couldn't simply stand, not with this chaotic need to do something swirling inside me. I was excited, agitated, uncertain. Could I battle my old enemy in a different way?

"I need to walk." I headed for the scrap of wilderness around the parking lot.

Micah followed. I walked quickly, striding through the brush, ignoring the patches of snow underfoot and the brambles snatching at my clothes. It felt good to push my body, a denial of the disease that lurked inside my cells.

When I finally halted and spun, there was nothing but Micah, his glittering eyes and the stars overhead. I was aware of the warm strength of him, aware of the lump in my throat.

I saw no need for pretence. "Tell me about the coven."

"We offer relief to those who suffer, especially those who suffer needlessly. It's a choice on our part."

"When treatment is futile."

"When there is no chance of healing."

"Like Elsebietta."

He nodded once and looked away, still tormented by that loss. "It was hell."

I knew exactly what he meant and so I did what I never do – I reached out and touched him. I offered solace.

He eyed my hand, then reached down and captured it in his. My heart skipped at the heat in his eyes and I sounded breathless. "So, you joined the coven."

"I saw the chance to diminish suffering." He grimaced and bent his head, staring at the glint of the creek. "I follow the edicts of the coven of mercy, but I've been looking for something different than the others. Something more."

"Like what?"

He looked at me so quickly that I couldn't look away, his eyes gleaming. "I don't want to be alone," he whispered.

I swallowed, guessing his implication. "You said the coven is short one member."

He nodded once. "I asked for the right to fill that place. I have been waiting for a dance partner for a long time."

"How long?" I knew the answer, but I had to hear it.

"Twenty years, this very month."

"I thought I saw you at the funeral," I guessed. "But no one else did."

"No, you could only glimpse me then. It was too soon." He smiled. "But you dreamed me. I managed that."

He was right. "Why me?"

"Because I saw the same passion in you that burns in me."

I caught my breath and looked away, dizzy at the implication. I heard the music begin, sounding as if it carried from a distant orchestra, and panicked. "But Mrs Curtis died."

"Because I didn't stop."

I eyed him, seeing that he looked paler than he had, seeing a gauntness to his cheeks. "You're hungry."

He nodded, licked his lips and looked away. "I've been waiting for you, Rosemary."

"For a long time?"

He smiled. "Always."

"And I would be able to do what you do, to give mercy?"

"Yes."

"But I would be your partner?"

"Maybe. Maybe not. We can only try when we have similar powers and objectives." His smile was fleeting, barely curving his lips. "I'm inviting you on an adventure."

It was an invitation that I was destined to accept. Another chance, an opportunity to make a difference . . . with Micah.

There was only one element in my past, only one detail that I wanted to resolve. "Will you show mercy to Jason?"

He shook his head and my heart sank. "I think he should be yours."

In a way, my decision had been made when I saw my own test results. I offered my other hand to him, palm up. My words were thick, my voice not sounding like my own. "I've never learned to waltz."

"I'll teach you," he pledged. He pulled me into his arms and that music became louder. It was evocative of another time and place, romantic and sweet and ethereal. As seductive as he was.

"How do you do that?" I asked.

"It's easy," he whispered and I believed him. I felt his hand on my back, his chest against mine, then he pulled me close. His breath fanned against my ear, my neck, and I gasped at the tiny prick of his teeth.

Then my blood was leaving me, its heat flowing from the wound on my neck. I felt him drink, felt him take the life force into his body. With every beat of my heart, Micah felt stronger and larger, firmer and warmer. And with every beat, I felt less substantial, weaker.

I was becoming a ghost. The cares of the world fell away from me and I saw the course of my life with perfect clarity. I saw that every step had been on the same journey, bringing me to this place at this moment with this man. I relived that forgotten glimpse of Micah at my mother's funeral, reviewed those dreams, and tasted the force of destiny in my life.

I saw the pattern in my dating, my dissatisfaction with all those dark-eyed, dark-haired men, none of whom could hold a candle to Micah. I saw my own impatience with any relationship that was not a perfect communion, and knew what I had been seeking.

This.

Him.

I saw how the past shapes the future, but gained a sense of how the future could shape the past. My life had brought me inexorably to this destination, to this junction, to this destiny.

Who could tell where the adventure would lead from here?

I wanted to know.

And just when it seemed that I would cease to exist for ever, just when it seemed that I was no more substantial than the wind, Micah lifted his head. He bit his own hand, then fitted my mouth to the wound. The blood was salty, not truly to my taste, but he coaxed me to drink of it.

Once I had started, I couldn't stop. Micah's blood flooded through me like a draught of starlight. It set me tingling with a physiological change that I knew I would have to analyse later. For the moment, though, there was only the sense that I was changing, becoming something closer to ice and moonlight than before.

I was trading the sun for the moon, in more ways than one. I felt stronger and more vital, purposeful and focused. When Micah made me stop drinking, I believed I truly was invincible.

Finally.

I smiled at him, seeing him fully for the first time. He was larger and darker than I'd imagined, the secrets in his eyes more profound. His skin was finer, his presence stronger, his hair more luxurious. My desire for him had multiplied tenfold.

My gaze was sharper, my ability to perceive detail almost dizzying. All of my senses were heightened and my body was stronger. I flexed my hand, awed by the change. There was so much to learn.

And I had all of eternity.

Then I lifted my arms, astounded to find myself rising above the earth by will alone. I looked down upon the collapsed body of Dr Rosemary Taylor, that mortal shell I needed no longer. She lay on the bank of the creek as if she were sleeping, no more a part of me than the shoes I'd kicked into my closet.

Micah offered his hand and we moved like the wind through the air, the speed leaving me dizzy and disconnected from space and time. I knew where we would go and trusted him to take me there.

Jason awakened to find me by his bedside. He smiled, this thoughtful gem of a boy, trust filling his eyes. I heard the music again, that ghostly waltz, and my throat tightened at its import.

"Would you like to dance, Jason?"

He looked between me and Micah, with uncertainty. "Will it hurt, Dr Taylor?"

"Never again," I vowed and he searched my gaze as he had once before.

And then he smiled.

"OK." Jason opened his arms to me.

I smiled and leaned closer, gathering the precious burden of him into my arms as Micah watched. I smelled the death in Jason and my heart swelled that I could give him this gift.

This mercy.

"Listen to the music," I murmured.

"Pretty," he said and closed his eyes, his dark lashes thick upon his cheek. He'd never awaken again and I was fiercely glad of that. I bent my head to his sweet neck, tore the flesh and drank until he was gone.

Until he was at peace for ever.

Micah brushed my fingertips across the two puncture marks, showing me how to remove the proof of our presence. His hand was warm over mine, protective. As I stared at Jason, finally so tranquil, I was fiercely glad of the choice I'd made. I had become something new, and was determined to use my power as Micah did.

For mercy.

So, I smiled when Micah took my hand in his and I squeezed his fingers in mine. His eyes glowed with promise.

I went willingly. There was so much to learn, and all the time to do it. I had been waiting for this opportunity and I knew that I – we – would make the most of it.

For ever.

Le Cirque de la Nuit

Karen MacInerney

Bella sensed him before she saw him.

There was something different in the air that night – beyond the sweet scent of kettle corn, of bodies packed together in the darkness, the hush of anticipation and desire beyond the footlights.

Bella waited backstage, muscles warm and limber, make-up applied, the red sequins of her costume glittering in the reflected light. Beside her stood Boris – a necessary evil, stinking of garlic. His teeth a line of broken fence posts. Handsome from a distance though, which was all that mattered. He was proud in the sparkling Lycra bodysuit that clung to his muscular frame.

The ringmaster had announced their act in his rolling, mellifluous voice . . . and as the first brash strains of *Carmen* filled the tent, Bella and Boris stepped out of the shadows and into the spotlight's caress.

Bella felt the intake of breath at their arrival, the barely contained desire of the husbands in the audience – locked in next to their doughy wives – as she climbed the ladder to the platform, Boris' garlicky presence a few rungs behind. A moment later, it began. She leaped from the platform, trapeze clenched in her calloused hands, and transformed into an airborne bird, beautiful, powerful, the object of every eye in the audience. Together with Boris, Bella began her seductive dance fifty feet above a sea of upturned faces, each one wishing he or she could fly with her.

That night though – even in the throes of the intricate dance she performed six times a week, floating and leaping to the rasping pulse of a modernized Bizet – a new electricity sparked in the tent. There was, as always, an intimate connection with the audience. Bella arched her back, stretched a graceful arm, made her taut body a question mark, an unattainable invitation suspended from a slender wooden bar, death the merest slip away. Death and beauty – the twin charms of the trapeze artist, the source of Bella's nightly seduction, a heady brew that caught men's breaths in their throats and launched a million fantasies. Tonight though, there was a new urgency in the audience, an erotic throb that went beyond the throaty siren song smouldering in the hazy air. It followed her as she danced, an invisible lover's caress, so that by the time she alighted on the platform for the last time, Boris' chalky hand gripping hers, Bella's body was aflame under the tight red costume.

She bowed deeply, extending one graceful arm as if to embrace the sea of earthbound souls below, rising higher on the swell of applause, the hidden gaze that followed every move of her glittering, lithe body. She felt that gaze as she climbed down the ladder, felt the eyes lingering on the curve of her waist, the swell of her small breasts, the long, lean line of her legs. She felt it follow her all the way to the edge of the ring, where she stepped out of the spotlight and back into darkness.

"Did you feel something different?" she asked Boris, slightly breathless, as they left the stage behind them and the last strain of *Carmen* died, leaving the dusty ring to the clowns.

Boris shrugged, his blond hair streaked with sweat. "They liked us. They always do."

Bella glanced over her shoulder, thinking of that gaze, like a lover's touch. Was she imagining things?

"I'm going to skip the workout tonight," Boris said then, stretching.

Bella's mouth tightened. "That's the third time this week," she said. Uneasiness dimmed the spell's hold on her. Though she loved the intimacy of having the trapeze to herself, Boris had skipped too many late-night practices recently. If he became soft, or careless . . .

"I'll catch you tomorrow," he said.

"Let's hope so," Bella said, but he was already gone, striding away through a sea of silk costumes and painted faces.

Bella glanced back towards the ring again, listening to the familiar antics of Rocky – the strongman was lifting the anvil now, she knew – and then stepped aside as Franco bustled past. The clown paused when he saw her.

"Why the sour face?" he asked. "He eat too much garlic again?"

Bella laughed. "Always."

"You could run away to another circus," he said.

"It's easier to go with a partner. Besides, I'd miss you. "

"I tell him to use the mouthwash," Franco said, his dark eyes intelligent and full of humour above the white greasepaint and painted red mouth. "He does not deserve such a beautiful partner."

"Thank you, Franco." Bella's ruby-painted lips formed a Cupid's bow smile. "You're my knight in shining armour."

He bent over in a mock courtly bow, his baggy clown pants gaping, his huge red shoes gleaming. "I am at your service, *mademoiselle*."

Bella bent over to kiss his white-painted cheek. He staggered back in feigned ecstasy, almost bumping into one of the jugglers. "I shall never wash again."

"You're up next," she reminded him. "Better hurry!"

He hurried towards the stage door. Still thinking about the erotic charge that had filled the tent during her performance, Bella drifted back to her trailer.

The big top was empty when she returned two hours later, wearing a simple black leotard, her oval face scrubbed of rouge and eye shadow. Although the roustabouts had already swept up the stray popcorn, the sweet familiar scent still filled the tent. The intensity that had permeated the place was gone though, erased by the empty bleachers and the blaze of white light overhead.

Bella stretched for a minute or two, feeling the blood run through her cooled muscles, then climbed the ladder to the platform. The safety net was not in place tonight; so instead of unhooking the trapeze, she reached for the long, purple silks that the circus' soloist, Irina, used during her performance. Rather than return to the ground, Bella stepped off the platform and slowly lowered herself down the silk, savouring the feeling of the fabric pressed against her body as she moved through the routine she had been developing on her own for a year. It was a sensuous dance, suspended only by two sheer lengths of fabric, hung high above the mats below.

Bella had been practising for thirty minutes when she sensed a change. The throaty siren song of *Carmen* had long faded, but the tent was filled with the same dark, erotic presence she had felt earlier.

Goosebumps rose on her slender arms and legs, and, as Bella wrapped each foot in a length of fabric and slowly pushed her body until her legs were stretched into a full split, she searched for its source. There, in the corner by the north entrance, a man sat.

He tilted his head as Bella watched; the lights gleamed on his hair, which was chestnut brown. Even from this distance she could make out wide shoulders in a dark suit jacket. It was the man she had sensed earlier. Suddenly, the rote of practice became something else altogether.

Again, Bella felt the caress of his gaze on her body as she hung suspended in the air. Her familiar movements transformed into an intimate dance, the watched and the watcher, each slow move studied, devoured by the presence in the corner of the tent.

Finally, her entire body burning with desire, Bella unrolled herself and slid down the silks to the mats. She looked up to where her silent watcher sat.

He was gone.

Bella woke late the next morning, after a night of erotic dreams, which slipped through her fingers when she tried to grasp them. She exited her trailer to the sharp cold of a Canadian winter, and the familiar smell of animals, canvas and stale popcorn. A few flakes of snow fluttered down as she passed the shuttered midway on the way to the cookhouse.

The tent was blissfully warm and, despite the fact that it was less than an hour till noon, smelled deliciously of sizzling bacon. Boris was there, arm slung around Jade, the petite contortionist who had joined Circus Renaldi a few months ago. One hand was curled around her narrow waist possessively; the other was busy cutting a sausage in half with a fork.

Bella passed them by with a brief nod. A few minutes later, with a bowl of bran flakes and half a grapefruit (she allowed herself bacon and eggs only once a week), she retreated to a table at the far end of the tent. The cookhouse was sparsely inhabited, and Bella could hear the intimate tones of Jade and Boris from several yards away. Had Boris slept at all last night? Should Bella talk to the ringmaster about his skipped practices? So far, he hadn't missed a catch, but if he continued to avoid rehearsals, that would likely change. What Bella really longed to do was her solo act with the silks. But while the supple Russian gymnast Irina was firmly ensconced as the ringmaster's favourite, Bella knew she would have to eschew the silks for a trapeze – at least for a while.

Bella was spooning up the last of her cereal when someone slipped through the tent door, letting a blast of cold air sweep through inside. The circus would be moving further south in a few days, and Bella welcomed the thought of warmer weather. But she would miss the erotic thrill of last night's audience. Would her mysterious admirer return again tonight? Bella toyed with her spoon, reliving the strange intimacy of last night's performance, wondering how it was that one single person out of hundreds could charge the atmosphere so completely. She was thinking about that glimpse of chestnut hair, wondering what his face looked like, when Franco slid into the chair across from her.

Bella smiled. "Hi, Franco."

"Good morning, Bella. Your boyfriend is busy again this morning," he said, eyeing Boris and Jade.

"I know," she said, biting her lip.

"Too much schnapps last night," Franco said, shaking his head. Without the greasepaint, the pitted scars of adolescent acne gave his skin the appearance of a moonscape. Bella had often wondered if the thick layers of camouflaging paint had influenced his decision to become a clown. For a few hours a night, he was allowed to leave his ravaged face behind. He smiled sadly. "He is not good for you."

"As long as he can hold his own on the rigging, he can do what he wants," Bella said, resignation in her voice. Distant as it was, their partnership had survived at least two of Boris' flings; initially passionate, each one had burned out quickly, both times ending in his paramour's flight to another circus. If she could ride out this one, things would likely even out again, and Bella could wait for the ringmaster to lose interest in Irina. By then she would be ready.

Franco leaned towards her, his voice just above a whisper. "Replace him," he said.

Bella blinked, her blue eyes wide. "How?"

"Quietly," he said. "There is another circus in town. Le Cirque de la Nuit. Perhaps there is an aerialist there who is not happy with his lot."

Bella felt a frisson of excitement. She had heard rumours about the Cirque for years, but had never met anyone who worked for it. The tickets were reputed to sell for hundreds of dollars, even thousands, apiece. The Cirque's engagements were strictly limited. Bella doubted anyone in such a prestigious circus would be willing to trade down to Renaldi. But if there was an opening for an aerialist . . .

"Where are they playing?" she asked, urgency in her voice. She had a matinee show that afternoon, but she might have time to visit, see if she could get an audition. The routine she'd been working on, with the silks – Bella might be able to leave Boris behind permanently. She might even be able to find a spot for Franco . . .

Franco pushed a paper across the checkered tablecloth to her. "I found out where they play. If you go now –"

Bella glanced down at the address scrawled on the paper, then tucked it into the pocket of her jeans. "Thanks, Franco."

As the clown slipped back out the tent entrance, she gathered her bowl and spoon and stood up.

"Are we rehearsing this morning, Bella?" It was Boris. He had disentangled himself from his pretty contortionist and was now standing behind Bella. "I'm sorry I missed you last night."

Normally, Bella would have cared more – about both his abdication and his attempt at restitution – but her thoughts were full of the legendary Cirque. "I've got a few things to do this morning," she said. "I'll see you at show time. Three o'clock."

His face was a mask of contrition. "We haven't been working together as much lately."

"We'll practise together tomorrow. Go have fun with Jade," she said, glancing at the pretty girl, who was observing their exchange with interest. Boris looked tired, Bella thought. Perhaps another bout with the contortionist wasn't the best idea after all. "Or take a nap," she suggested.

"Thank you," Boris said, with another gap-toothed smile. Bella glanced at her watch; she had two and a half hours if she was going to make it back in time for make-up. Buttoning her coat against the cold, she hurried out of the tent and into the knife-sharp wind.

Her breath caught at the sight of the deep blue tent, its sides spangled with silver moons and stars, surrounded by a small array of trailers. A silver banner flew from the big top's apex, fluttering in the cold winter wind.

The taxi slowed to a halt at the deserted entrance, and Bella checked her hair and make-up in a compact before snapping it shut and tucking it back into her bag. "Will you stay here for a few minutes?" she asked, smiling winningly at the driver, a pale young man with circles under his eyes.

"How long?"

"Twenty at most," she said. Bella hadn't come prepared for an audition; all she wanted was a chance to talk to the ringmaster.

The driver nodded brusquely, and Bella exited the warmth of the cab into the biting wind. She stepped over the chain that stretched across the entryway and searched for someone to direct her to the ringmaster.

The problem was, there was nobody around to talk to. Despite the huge blue tent and the jumble of trailers, the place was desolate.

Thinking the cold weather might have driven everyone indoors, she hurried to the back of the lot where the trailers stood, then mounted the stairs to the nearest one and hammered on the door. The windows were dark, and nothing stirred in response. Bella knocked again, then moved to the next trailer. Again nothing. After the fifth trailer, she stood for a moment, thinking – and then decided to find the cookhouse. She sniffed the air, searching for the smell of a kitchen, but the only scents were asphalt and canvas. No animals, no popcorn, no bacon frying.

And no people.

Confounded, Bella returned to the main tent, admiring the spangled moons and stars sprinkled on the deep blue canvas. The entrance was laced tight and locked, the tent's base lashed to the ground; short of cutting through the lacing or canvas, there was no way to get in.

The young woman stood outside the main tent, shivering and confused. Where was everyone?

Her dreams, so buoyant that morning, seemed to shrink to nothing in the cold winter wind. The thought of returning to Circus Renaldi, to a matinee performance in a half-filled tent with the garlic-scented Boris, was more repellent than ever. Casting her eyes around the area one last time, she crossed the pitted pavement to the waiting taxi.

"Nobody home?" the driver asked. She climbed into the back seat.

"Nobody at all," she said with a sigh, and watched out the window until the spangled blue tent disappeared from sight.

*   *   *

Boris had obviously not taken advantage of the opportunity to sleep that afternoon. When Bella found him backstage, his eyes were more bloodshot than ever, and the reek of garlic mingled with the sour smell of alcohol. Jade was nowhere to be seen – in make-up, probably, Bella thought – but the solo aerialist Irina, lithe and graceful in white sequins and spandex, pranced by, earning the smouldering gaze of the ringmaster. His lust had lasted eighteen months so far. Bella was hoping it would die soon, but it showed no signs. She glanced over at Boris, noticing the sweat stains on his red leotard, and sighed.

As Bella chalked her hands, wondering if the mystery man would be at the performance tonight, Franco hurried over to her. "Did you talk to the ringmaster?" he whispered, glancing over his hunched shoulder to make sure they were alone. His face was painted white, with the traditional clown smile obscuring the worried set of his mouth.

"There was no one there," she said.

He blinked in surprise. "No one?"

"Nobody – no roustabouts, no performers – not even a cookhouse. The tents and trailers were there, but it was deserted."

"It couldn't have been."

"It was," Bella said.

"Try again tomorrow," he said. "Maybe they all went into town."

"Can you find out when the performances are?" Bella asked. Chances were good they coincided with Renaldi's, but there might be one she could slip away for.

"I will see what I can find out," he said.

Before he could say more, the ringmaster strutted up, his belly thrust out in front of him. "Your act is next, Franco," he said.

"I'm ready," he said.

The ringmaster looked at Bella, his eyes running up and down her body, checking her costume and make-up. "Where is your partner?" he barked.

"Over there," Bella said, pointing to where Boris slouched against one of the tent posts.

"You haven't been practising together lately," he said, turning to study Boris.

"You should talk to Boris about that," Bella said. "I think he's been . . . distracted."

As Bella spoke, Jade sauntered by, resplendent in a green sequined bodysuit that hugged her slim body. Boris stood at attention as Jade sent him a sidelong look from her heavily made-up eyes.

"I see," said the ringmaster in a chilly tone of voice. "I will speak to him after the act." He strode away. A few minutes later, Boris and Bella strode into the spotlight together to perform before stands only half-filled – and devoid of the chestnut-haired man who had watched her perform last night.

"You talked to him about me, didn't you?" Boris demanded as he and Bella waited behind the scenes that night, preparing for their second performance of the day. Outside, the icy wind blew, the temperature even lower with the sun below the horizon. But inside, the heaters roared, making it almost too warm despite Bella's brief leotard. The tent was packed tonight; there was an almost tangible sense of excitement from the audience. Though it would mean nothing – the circus would be packing up in a few days – Bella was hoping that last night's spectator would be among the faces ranged around the stage.

"Talked to who?" Bella asked Boris. Her partner's face was bright red, to match the veins in his eyes.

"The ringmaster. He told me I've been slacking off."

Bella shrugged a narrow shoulder. "I haven't said anything. But you have been missing a lot of rehearsals lately."

"You want to replace me, don't you?" His face was red with anger. "I hear what you say about me – that I smell bad, that you don't like me."

Bella stepped back. "Boris," she said in a low voice. "We have to go on in a minute. This is not the time."

"I'm right, aren't I?" he asked, a crafty glint in his eye.

"Boris! Bella!" One of the jugglers was waving at them frantically. Bella could hear the ringmaster's voice rolling, echoing through the tent, preparing the audience for their act.

"Let's go," she hissed, grabbing Boris' chalky hand and pulling him towards the entrance. As the ringmaster gave the two aerialists their cue and they stepped into the glaring spotlights, Boris plastered a smile onto his face; but Bella could feel the anger radiating off of him.

She could feel something else, too. As she strutted to the rope ladder, her eyes scanned the crowd, searching for that gleaming brown hair. She couldn't locate him, but she knew he was there.

As she had last night, she performed with Boris, but every move of her body, every leap, every arch of her slender back, was an act of seduction, directed at a man she had never really seen. Her focus during the last leap was split between the hidden presence in the audience and the demands of the physical task. Her body sang with pleasure as she flew through the air.

They were on the last minute of the song, the routine perfectly synchronized with the sultry music, when it happened. Bella propelled herself through the air, clinging to the trapeze with her knees and, at the very apex of the swing, released her grip and sailed into the air, just as she had a thousand times before.

Only Boris wasn't there.

The crowd caught its breath in a collective sigh as Bella tumbled. The net flexed beneath her, the spell broken – by Boris. Fuming, Bella slid off the net onto the mats and quickly climbed the rigging again, but with only thirty seconds left in the act, there was little she could do to recover.

"Bella and Boris!" the ringmaster announced as they took their last bow. Bella smiled, but her face felt wooden. The applause died quickly, and they turned and strutted out of the public eye.

"How could you miss that?" she asked once they were safely backstage.

"I'm sorry," he said. "I got the timing wrong."

"You drank too much last night, you haven't slept, and you haven't practised," she said, seething. Falling to the net was better than plummeting to the mats, but it was still dangerous – and embarrassing.

"I'm sorry," he repeated, looking belligerent. "You've missed a time or two before."

"Not for two years," she shot back. "And nobody fell."

"Whatever," he said, and turned and stalked away.

Bella took a few deep breaths, trying to control her anger. Irina gave her a slow, cruel smile. News of her fall had spread quickly. Bella usually stayed to the end of the night, to talk with Franco. Tonight though, she wrapped her coat around her and left the tent, heading back to her tiny trailer.

The cold wind needled Bella as she hurried across the packed snow towards her trailer. Quickly, she climbed the two metal steps to her door and fumbled with the key. Wedged into the crack beneath the door was an envelope. She reached down and grabbed it, then hurried inside and slammed the door behind her, happy for the warmth of the crowded space and the absence of other performers.

Bella shrugged off her coat and lowered herself onto her bed, examining the envelope. It was thick, creamy linen, and her name – Ms Bella Volynski – was written on the front in a firm, old-fashioned script. She tore it open with a fingernail, and swallowed hard at the letterhead.

Le Cirque de la Nuit.

She devoured the note, heart hammering against her ribcage.

> *Dear Ms Volynski*
>
> *Your recent performance on the aerial silks has come to our attention. We are pleased to extend an invitation to audition for the position of aerialist for le Cirque de la Nuit.*

Silks? But her act was on the trapeze. Unless . . .

Goosebumps rose on her arms as she remembered her solitary practice of last night.

> *This is an unusual invitation, as an opening is very rare. If you are interested, please arrive, prepared to audition, between eleven pm and one am tonight or tomorrow. We eagerly anticipate your visit.*
>
> *Cordially,*
> *M. Rideau*
> *Ringmaster*
> *Cirque de la Nuit*

Bella read it three times. *Eagerly anticipate your visit.* Had they somehow known she'd visited today? Had M. Rideau – the ringmaster – been the silent observer in the big top? And why such strange hours for an audition?

She checked the clock on the bedside table. Not quite ten. Another hour until eleven. She'd arrive at midnight, she decided. So she looked interested . . . but not desperate.

Bella turned to her mirror and reached for her make-up case.

It was a different driver this time. She decided not to ask him to wait; she had taken her cell phone, and would call another cab when she was done.

The blue tent glowed under the spotlight, the silver moons shimmering in the white lights. Despite the late hour, the place was anything but deserted. Although the audience had long since driven home, a few figures hurried from the main tent to the midway, and lights glowed in many of the trailers. Bella paid the taxi driver and slammed the door behind her, taking a deep breath of the icy air before hurrying forwards, her coat pulled tight around her, the audition invitation jammed into her pocket.

She paused near the big tent, wondering where to go. A man in a long overcoat was striding by. She called out to him as he passed her.

"Excuse me, sir."

He turned quickly, staring at her in a strange way – almost hungrily – and took a step towards her. Bella lifted her chin. "I'm supposed to see the ringmaster for an audition," she said. "Can you tell me where to find him?"

The look on the man's face went from hunger to something different – curiosity? "He's in the big top," he said. Then he smiled. Even in the darkness, his teeth seemed very white. "Good luck."

"Thank you," she said, and hurried on, bracing herself against the wind and the nervousness that coiled in her stomach.

The entrance to the big top was unlaced tonight. Bella pushed the flap aside and ducked inside.

It was as if she had stepped into a tropical night. The air was warm and lush, and overhead, a swath of stars twinkled, shining through the rigging suspended from the top of the tent. Three rows of plush seats ringed the centre stage, above which dangled a flashing crescent moon. Two red silks hung from the centre of the tent, puddling on the black mat and billowing slightly in the breeze from the doorway.

"Hello?" she called out, starting tentatively down the walkway towards the stage.

When no one answered, she climbed to the centre platform and walked across the mats to the hanging silks, caressing them with one hand. To perform here, under that magical, twinkling starlight . . .

"You came."

Bella whirled around, still holding one of the silks. She knew before she saw him that it was the man with the chestnut hair.

He stood at least six feet tall, his brown hair tumbling over a face that took her breath away. Her trained eye took in the rest of him at a sweep; broad shoulders tapering to a narrow waist, well muscled under his tailored black suit. Overall, he gave the impression of barely restrained power. His dark eyes seemed to consume her. Again, she felt the erotic charge that had filled the tent at Circus Renaldi just last night.

"Are you Mr Rideau?" she asked, head held high.

He nodded. "I am pleased that you responded to my invitation, Bella." His voice was deep and smooth, with a faint accent. "The name suits you."

Bella felt the blood rush to her cheeks. "Thank you," she said, hearing the throatiness in her own voice. She hadn't taken her eyes from his face. Those intense eyes, the half-smile.

"I have prepared the stage for you," he said quietly, gesturing to the silks she still held in her hand. "Do you need time to warm up?"

"Yes, please," she said.

"I will watch, if you do not mind," he said.

"Of course." Conscious of his eyes on her, she shrugged off her heavy coat, letting it slide down her shoulders with as much grace as she could muster. Rideau moved to the edge of the stage, extending a hand to take it from her. She surrendered it to him, revealing the blue velvet leotard, sprinkled with sequins, that she had borrowed from wardrobe.

"Lovely," he breathed.

Aware of his eyes on her, she performed an abbreviated set of stretches, her mind awash in the thrill of anticipation – and many questions. Why had the lot been empty earlier that day? Why was this audition at night? Would she accept the job if it was offered?

When her muscles had warmed up, she glanced back at Rideau, at the dark hair tumbling over his brow, the desire in his eyes, and felt an answering frisson in her body. Then she stood tall and approached the silks, grasping the fabric in her hands.

And just as it had the previous night, the dance began.

She climbed the silks slowly, sensuously, and moved through the routine she had been perfecting for months, feeling his eyes on every glissade, every drop, every caress of the silk against the bare skin of her thighs. Despite the two performances, her body was singing with strength and grace, singing its siren song to the man who sat, still and quiet, in the front row. She could almost feel his touch against her skin as she wrapped the silky fabric around her.

She emerged from the silks, which she'd held like a veil before her, her body humming with desire, when she realized something had changed. Rideau was no longer sitting in the front row. He had mounted the stage, and now stood beneath her, looking up. The world suddenly contracted. There was Bella, and the two red silks she clutched in her hands, and the magnetic presence of him on the mats beneath. She swung around one more time, one foot hooked in the silk, describing a slow circle around the centre of the stage and the man beneath her. Then, still gripping the fabric, she lowered herself slowly, gracefully, until she was standing mere inches away from Rideau's tall, silent form. Her breath came in short gasps.

He stared at her, then reached with one hand, pupils dilated, to touch her flushed cheek. "So beautiful," he whispered. Then, in one fluid movement, he pulled her towards him, lowering his mouth to hers. She could sense his hunger; it fed her own raw desire. Slowly, slowly, he traced a trail down her neck with fervent kisses. Something sharp grazed her skin. Startled, she pulled away.

"You are irresistible," he said, his voice husky. "I am sorry."

"No," Bella said, reaching for him. "It's fine. Really."

He smiled then, and she drew in her breath at the sight of his teeth, sharp and pointed, against the red of his full lips. "You're . . . "

He studied her. "Yes," he said.

Bella took an involuntary step back. Everything pointed to one thing – he had confirmed it himself – but how could it be? It wasn't possible. "When I was here earlier . . . and everything was closed. No one was out . . . "

"We were asleep. That is why we are le Cirque de la Nuit." He reached out, ran a long finger down her jaw. "So beautiful, so exotic . . . so very, very talented . . . "

She drew in her breath. "You liked the routine?"

"It set my blood on fire," he said, his voice again hoarse.

"But . . . " Bella started, then trailed off.

"You are asking if everyone who works with the Cirque is subject to my condition," he finished.

Bella nodded, feeling caught between twin urges: the impulse to flee, and the desire to succumb.

"I think you know the answer to that," he said.

She was silent.

"The position is yours, if you desire it," he said, still looking at her with that dark, smouldering gaze.

"What's it like?" she asked, her voice a whisper. It was too much, too sudden. But to be with Rideau, and to perform before him every night, under that spangled tent . . .

"I can show you," he said and, before she could respond, he pulled her to him, his mouth hot against the fragile skin of her neck. She gasped as his teeth punctured her, but after a flash of pain, there was a warm, flooding ecstasy.

With a palpable effort, he withdrew, breathing hard; Bella watched through half-lidded eyes as he took something from his pocket and bared his own neck. He made a quick slicing movement. A moment later, red droplets appeared against his pale skin, like a string of dark pearls.

"Drink," he commanded.

She hesitated.

"It won't make you like me. It will only give you a taste. Drink," he repeated, reaching for her head, guiding her mouth to his neck.

The taste was salty, coppery, repellent. At first she gagged. Then she took a breath, inhaling Rideau's clean musk scent, and something stirred in her. The blood was flowing more freely now, and as she pressed her lips to his neck, warmth suffused her, a warmth that pulled her closer to the tall vampire, until their bodies were pressed against one another. Bella drank hungrily now, intoxicated with his blood, and resisted when he pulled her head away.

"Enough," he said, his voice rough, pressing one hand to the gash on his neck.

She pulled back then, the spell broken, and held one hand to her mouth. When she lowered it, it was stained with blood.

"Can you feel it now?" he asked.

"Yes," she said, looking up from her bloodstained hand, the horror at what she'd done fading. Every detail in the tent seemed a little sharper, a little more luminous. The stars overhead glowed like trapped fireflies. Even the howl of the wind past the canvas seemed to contain a hidden melody. "Is it like this all the time for you?"

"Always," he said. "Only more intense." He reached to touch her skin again; the contact felt like an electric charge. "Come with me. Perform for me every night, never dying, never fading. A perfect, ageless rose. For ever Bella."

"Yes," she said, her voice a moan. "Yes. I want it."

He drew closer, the scent of him intoxicating. Her eyes were drawn to the cut on his neck, already healing.

"Are you certain?" he whispered.

She hesitated then. "Will I ever see the sun again?"

He shook his head. "The moon will be your sun, Bella."

Her eyes moved from the gash on his throat to his teeth. She remembered the feel of them on her neck, and the hungry look of the man – the vampire. "I would have to kill people," she said slowly.

"There is always a cost," he said. "But it is a gentle kill – a release. A dark blessing."

The desire to succumb was overwhelming ... but to never see the sun again? To consent to becoming a killer. "Can I change my mind?"

He laughed, then lowered his mouth to her neck again. The same dark ecstasy flowed through her as he suckled from her, an act somehow more intimate even than sex. She never wanted it to end. Finally though, he pulled away, his breath coming in rough gasps, his pupils dilated with desire.

"Don't stop," she said.

He smiled then, her blood stained his white teeth. "Take one more day, my Bella." He pulled his collar away, proffered his neck to her again. "This will help you regain your strength." Hungrily, she latched on to him, feeling no disgust this time. She sucked hard until he reached down and detached her with a firm hand. "Tomorrow," he said.

She reached for him again, but he held her away, his hands on her shoulders. "I would have you come willingly," he said. "Take one last look at the sun, Bella. Enjoy one last day among your companions. And then, when the sun has sunk beyond the horizon, when you are truly ready ... come to me."

He leaned down then and kissed her. Bella's entire body seemed to dissolve at his touch. She did not resist as he led her to the chair where he had laid her coat. He bundled her in it. "Go home now," he said. "Tomorrow night, we will be together."

She left the tent in a daze, his hand on her arm. He bent to kiss her forehead and then slipped away, leaving her alone in the icy wind, save for the handful of dark forms moving soundlessly between the tents.

*   *   *

The next day was a kaleidoscope of colour and form. With Rideau's blood in her system, everything was somehow magnified. Bella's appetite had faded. She had to force down her bran flakes and orange juice, and they churned in her stomach.

Boris was attentive and rested at their practice, anxious to make amends, but Bella no longer cared. This was her last day with Circus Renaldi. After tonight, she would leave this existence behind. The last swing, the last time she'd hear *Carmen* echoing from the tent walls, the last time she would have to endure Boris' pungent smell as his calloused hands gripped hers. The puncture wounds throbbed under the hidden bandage on her neck – but it was a pleasant throb, a throb of pleasure, not of pain.

Franco approached her backstage as she wiped the chalk off of her hands with a damp rag. "You look different today, Bella," he said. "Are you all right?"

She pulled him over towards the side of the tent, away from the other performers. "I'm going to the Cirque," she whispered. "I auditioned last night, and they offered me a job."

"Bella, that's amazing!" he said in a low voice. "Do they have room for me?"

She took a breath, about to tell him the price of admission. That after tonight, she would never see the sun again. That she might soon be forced to take a life in order for her own to continue. That she had no idea what the circus consisted of – or even what she would be paid. For a second, the spell of the vampire's blood wavered, and she felt a deep unease.

"I'll see what I can do," she said.

He sensed her hesitation; the hurt flashed in his eyes.

"It's complicated," she said, not sure what else to say. She thought of the feel of the silk against her body, the heat of Rideau's gaze. It might be crazy to run away to the circus, but she couldn't think of anything she wanted more. Besides, she'd already done it once, hadn't she?

"I understand," he said, although it was obvious he didn't understand at all. She watched him retreat, shoulders slumped in his red-and-white silk costume, and felt her heart contract a little.

Then she shrugged it off and went back to her trailer to take off her costume for the last time.

*   *   *

The taxi arrived an hour before the night-time performance was to begin at Circus Renaldi. The driver helped as she loaded her trunks. She ignored the burning gazes of her former co-workers, but knew the news would be all over the lot within minutes. Bella felt a stab of guilt – she would be leaving Boris without a partner. And as for Franco – she'd tucked a note under the door of his trailer, and would try to get back to see him before she left town. She knew it would hurt him, but she did not want his soul on her head. As for her own . . .

Her excitement grew as they crossed town. The vampire blood in her veins had dwindled as the day progressed, but the street lights still had an unusual shimmering quality, seeming to dance beyond the clouded windows of the cab.

It wasn't long before the blue tent of the Cirque de la Nuit came into sight, glowing blue and silver under the spotlights, the parking lot lined with cars.

"Please wait here for a moment," she said when the driver let her out at the front gate. "I need to see where to take my things."

There were people in the lot, but their numbers were few, the women clad in expensive furs, the men in dark overcoats, their polished shoes gleaming. Among them were the Cirque's staff members – hunters in a swarm of prey, Bella realized.

She walked up to the nearest vampire, a tall man, cheeks tinged with pink – from the cold, or from blood? – and touched his arm.

He whirled around with a speed that startled her.

"I'm looking for Mr Rideau," she said. "I'm a new performer."

The vampire raked his eyes over her, a cold, appraising glance. "Go back to where the trailers are," he said. "Someone will tell you where to go."

"Thank you," Bella said, and hurried off past the big top to the knot of silver trailers in the back of the lot. Anticipation thrummed through her; she could not wait to see Rideau again. Could not wait to taste his blood, to feel that intense bond yet again . . .

But there was no one there.

Frustrated, she turned to go back to the front gate, to ask again. Then she heard a noise, a scuffle, and what sounded like a moan.

It was coming from one of the trailers.

She hurried over to it, mouth open to enquire about Rideau, and stopped suddenly.

A man and woman stood, locked in what appeared to be a passionate embrace. Only they weren't kissing. His mouth was attached to her neck.

The man's back was to Bella. All she could see was the woman, her fur-clad arms draped over the man's broad back. Her face was pale in the silvery moonlight, her head lolling at an unnatural angle. A brief moan escaped her glossy lips. She was beautiful, Bella saw, with high cheekbones and a small, straight nose. Then her mouth fell open, her eyelids fluttered, and her body went limp.

The man bent over her a moment longer, holding her tight. Then he raised his head and let her go. As Bella stared, the beautiful woman crumpled to the cold, hard ground. The man who had held her so tightly now stepped away from her as if in disgust, pushing her away with the tip of his shoe.

Bella stood frozen for a moment, then started to turn. She scuttled backwards, pressing her body against the side of the trailer, fighting to still her ragged breathing. A moment later, the man walked past her, straightening his lapels. She caught a glimpse of his face in profile.

It was Rideau.

She waited until he had passed, striding towards the big top, and then slid around the trailer. The woman was dead, her large eyes staring sightlessly at the moon, her fur coat lying open, her neck smeared with blood.

Blindly, Bella turned and ran, her only thought to get back to the cab, to get away from the Cirque de la Nuit as fast as possible. She passed the trailers, passed the blue and silver glowing tent, passed the women in furs and greatcoats. She had almost reached the front gate when a hand grasped her arm, pulling her back.

"Bella."

He was there, filling her field of vision, his eyes dark with lust.

"No," she said, struggling to go. "I can't."

He bent down and kissed her then. She could taste the woman's blood on her lips and, despite the horror of what she'd just seen, found herself hungering for more. Then he was drawing her away from the crowd, into a dark corner, away from the waiting taxi, peeling back the scarf from her throat, lowering his lips to her neck . . .

She was lost again, drowning in the pull of him, the feel of his mouth on hers. When he tore his own skin again, she locked her mouth to the gash, and drank until she could drink no more.

The silks clung to her like a lover – like the eyes of Matthieu, who stood, as always, just beside the curtain, watching her every move, devouring her with his dark eyes. The eyes of the audience followed her too. She had found her target already. He was in the third row back, muscled shoulders, pale blue irises, a shock of blond hair like corn. She dropped to the mats, preened for the audience. A standing ovation again. She locked eyes with the blond young man for just long enough before strutting off the stage.

She found him right where she expected to, lingering by the side of the tent, hoping to catch even a glimpse of the woman who had seduced him as she hung between the silks. Bella smiled, beckoned him to follow her. She let her hips sway as she led him deep into the forest of trailers behind the big top. She could hear his breathing, feel his desire. When she could stand it no more, she turned, arms open in submission, and waited for him to come to her.

He was in her arms in a second, smelling of soap and sweat and young, virile male. She savoured the feel of him for a moment, the urgency of his mouth against hers, then traced her tongue along his neck, feeling for the throb of his pulse, quickened by her presence. Then, slowly, slowly, she let her teeth penetrate the skin of his neck, let his blood fill her mouth, let the ecstasy wash over her. He gasped slightly, but did not pull away as she sucked, locking him tight in her arms, the most intimate embrace, until finally he was drained.

She stepped back, and his body dropped to the ground – empty, of no use to her, or to anyone. A soft laugh sounded behind her. It was Matthieu. He was waiting for her.

"Bella," he said, opening his arms. She went to him then, kissed him, the blood mingling on their lips. And together, arms entwined, they walked into the night.

Perdition

Caitlin Kittredge

From the personal files of Mr James Priestly, being a record of the events that occurred at Perdition, Arizona, on or about May 18 1888.

I beg you not to call me mad. I know that what I have set down here may seem like fancy, or the whiskey ravings of a drunk.

I was that in the spring of 1888. I admit it freely. But what I saw in that town, that mean dusty town hunched against the desert like a starving coyote waiting for a beast to die – that is the honest, clear and sober truth, best as I can recollect it these many years gone.

I was twenty-one years old that spring, going no particular direction but West and having been ejected from every respectable town along my route, I came to find myself in Perdition. A more aptly named township there never was, for it was the definition of Hell – no water, barely any whiskey, suspicious eyes and full up with the worst scum that Arizona Territory had to offer.

One of them myself, with three bodies to my credit through Kansas and Texas, I hunkered in and resolved to move on as quickly as I could gamble my way to a fresh horse.

The saloon didn't have a name, or if it did, the sign was long weathered away by the ever-moving dust of the desert, which stripped paint and skin with equal fastness, crept into every crevice and compounded my misery by finding its way to the bottom of my glass. The man I sat down to gamble with had nearly white eyes – I thought at first that he was blind and this would be a neat and profitable game indeed. But he looked at me, and he did not blink when he shoved the dog-eared deck in my direction.

"Cut the cards."

I did as he bid, and his hand came out fast, like a rattlesnake, and took them back. It was all bones, that hand, but it didn't shake. The man was just a bag of skin, but he didn't appear ill or malformed in any way as he dealt and threw his ante onto the table. I had the coins in my hand to return when the door of the nameless place swung open and a woman appeared.

She wore breeches, like a man, with a man's jacket over a woman's shirt. Her hair was falling out of its pins and streaked over with dust, but I judged it to be darker underneath. She wasn't pretty, too old for that, with too many sun lines wrought into her face, but she was striking. That's a word my mother used often – striking – and I'd always taken it, as a boy, to mean something more than merely pretty.

The woman arrested me with her square, open face, sure enough, but the Winchester rifle in her hands caught my eye a deal more.

My poker partner stopped moving, and breathing, as she stalked through the place and came to my shoulder. She said to the man, "You look like my John."

And then she shot him.

Arizona Territory, 1888

Kate Elder's horse died twenty miles from Perdition. The animal had been foaming and stumbling for at least ten more, so Kate didn't fault it much. Water was scarce, and if she hadn't filled her canteen when she left Prescott, she'd be in the same boat as the flea-bitten roan.

There should be water. Even in the desert, there's water if you know where to look. John had taught her that. He was an adaptable creature, John was, and he knew the desert as well as he knew the swamps and backwoods at home.

Known. John had *known* the desert. Kate didn't catch herself clinging to the dead, never had. Even calling him "John" inside her head instead of his nickname was a way of blocking him out, putting him in the past where he belonged.

She couldn't see the town when she picked up her pack and started walking. The Winchester seven-shot thumped against the back of her thigh, counting off steps and feet and miles. Perdition hunched at the base of a mesa, she knew that. Always in the shadow of the rocks, as the sun set behind it.

The sky was red, and she hadn't gone but six or seven miles at most. Kate tucked her jacket around her and kept walking. There would be no predators in this desert at night. Not when they could smell what spread its foulness and filth out from the little smear of dust road and shanty-house that made up Perdition.

John had called these places Death's acre, the spaces around the night creatures that no man, wildcat or coyote ever wanted to encounter. He did have a colourful way of putting things, John. He liked words, he liked names. Liked to hear himself talk.

"Why do they call you 'Big-Nose Kate'?" he asked the first time they spoke.

"The same reason they call you 'Doc', I suppose," she'd answered. "To differ you from all the other sawbones knocking around out there."

"I'm a dentist, truly," he said, and he smiled. Kate would learn later this wasn't a common occurrence, unless he'd had a few glasses of whiskey. "Got any molars troubling you? Bicuspids overstepping their bounds?"

"Don't mind him," said Doc's big, slow-spoken friend Wyatt. "He's drunk."

"So tell me, Kate with the prominent proboscis," Doc said. "How many other Kates are there?"

She'd blushed, which wasn't something she made a habit of. Blushing just gave men the wrong idea in a town like Griffin, tucked away in rough-and-tumble cattle-droving Texas. "Truthfully, Mr Holliday, there's just me."

Kate blew down the seams of her gloves, warming her hands. You wouldn't think a desert would get a chill at night. You wouldn't think a woman who should be well past roaming around in one would be out in it, either, but here she was, nearly forty years old and trudging through the brush towards what would probably be the last bad idea she'd ever get a chance to indulge herself with.

If only John hadn't called her here. If only he'd been strong in the end.

But John wasn't anything. John was dead.

And Kate Elder had eleven more miles to walk.

Fort Griffin, Texas
1877

Kate sees him first, across a room full of drovers who smell like dust and cowhide. He is dressed in dove grey and dealing faro with a concentration most men bring only to fighting or fornicating.

She is not in Exeley's Beer Hall to meet a man. She is in this mean, dirt-floored little place to seek employment. Exeley doesn't hire sporting women, but he does hire honest workers. At least, that's what the word at the train station was. Kate isn't proud. Not any more. She'll sweep and clean glasses, boil wash and do mending. She'll empty spittoons and carry the leaden trays of beer and whiskey bottles to and from the gambling tables.

She's stronger than most women her size, and she's got a good head. She can handle the drunken cowboys pressing in around her as if they were part of the herds they drive up to Kansas on the Chisholm Trail, handle them just fine.

Kate threads her way towards the barkeeper, the bald-pated Exeley.

She doesn't make it. A drover loops his arm like a lasso around her waist, pulls her against him so she can smell his sweat now, too. "And how much are you?" Cheap mash breathes into her face, chokes her nose and mouth.

Kate puts her hands on his barrel chest and shoves. "I'm not."

The drover's rheumy grin widens. "You're free? Must be my lucky day."

Kate feels like she's drowning in his stink and his heat. She can't get free. She can't lift up her leg and deliver a knee to where it'd hurt. She can barely breathe as his trail-hardened arm clamps down on her ribcage, his other hand pawing at her only decent dress.

Through the cacophony of hoots and shouts, a voice comes, flat and hard as a thunderclap.

"Why don't you leave the lady alone?"

Her head snaps, nearly catching the drover on the chin. He's staring. All of his friends are staring. Kate would know the face anyway, from the tintypes they sold in Dodge City and the penny novels hawked at every stop between Dodge and Fort Griffin. The down-turned moustache, the eyes that could fell you like a fist, the tall wide forehead and the nose crooked from breaking and resetting and breaking again.

Wyatt Earp has just saved her skin.

The drover lets go of her like her flesh is hot iron. "Sorry."

"Sorry, what?" Earp's eyebrows draw together like a storm front. The drover's eyes flick between Kate and the Marshal as his fear claws its way through his drunken stupor.

"Sorry, ma'am, for any offence I may have caused you."

"That's better." Earp waves him to the door. "Go on, get out."

Wyatt sits her in an empty seat at the faro table, asks her if she wants a drink. Kate asks for whiskey.

The faro dealer smiles. "A woman after my own heart." In all the places where Earp is broad and imposing as the landscape beyond the doors of Exeley's, the faro dealer is slight and quicksilver. Kate looks back at Earp, watches the crowd part as he walks through it.

"He's married, you know." The faro dealer collects his cards and his money and shuffles for a new hand. He doesn't watch his fingers. He's watching her.

Kate feels red sneaking up her neck. "I'm sure I don't know what you mean."

"I only tell you because his wife's a mean one. They're man and woman in every way but legal, and that just makes her meaner. And you're too pretty to get a laudanum bottle in the head."

Laughter bubbles out of her throat, that this man should not only presume so much but be telling tales about the great Marshal Earp in the same breath. The faro dealer taps the deck into shape. "See, I was right. Much too pretty."

When he's dealt the hand, he tips his hat to her. "I'm John Henry Holliday, but most folks call me Doc."

"And are you a lawman too, Doc?" she asks. Wyatt sets down a glass of whiskey. The glass still has the lip prints of the previous owner on the rim.

"This son of a bitch? He's a degenerate card player if there ever was one. If you'll excuse my language, ma'am."

Doc smiles, and Kate knows it's an old joke between the men. Even if the smile is stiff, and if Doc's eyes are more slate than silver when Wyatt laughs at his expense.

"I'm just a faro dealer, ma'am," he tells her. "At least until the sun goes down."

Perdition, Arizona
1888

Sunset came and went while Kate walked, and the moon was hung high overhead when she reached the outskirts of Perdition.

A small cemetery set outside the town limits was the first hint of civilization. The graves were wooden crosses or nothing at all, just humped dirt where the ground kept its secrets. A white shiny spot in the dirt turned out to be a leg bone, dug up and gnawed by a coyote.

Kate had the Winchester off her back, in her hands, the metal of the lever and the stock warming against her skin. There were sounds in the darkness, at last, and that could only mean she was getting close. Some of them could turn into rats, or wolves. Bugs, bats. Night creatures. Carrion-eaters.

The owl's call nearly made her scream, and Kate pulled up hard. She was too nervous, too tight. She'd end up shooting herself, or a citizen that still drew breath.

It swooped over the cemetery, dived, and picked up a fat wriggling rat. Its blunt-feathered wings made no sound as it climbed into the night, taking a perch in a cottonwood tree a little ways off.

Kate lowered the rifle. John always said owls watched for lost souls, to capture them and take them on to the netherworld. Said that in Greek mythos, owls were the keepers of the dead, neither harm nor help. They just watched. John was full of such facts, and during a long stage ride or a slow night at the tables, he told her because she listened.

He hadn't needed to teach her anatomy, though, when she'd found out about his side profession. Her father was a doctor and he made sure his Mary Katharine knew something about the ways a man could bend and break and be sewn back together. Kate knew where to aim and where to shoot.

But Doc taught her the lore, the stories. Without them, you couldn't hope to understand, not really.

The owl ripped a fat cut from the rat's belly and swallowed it. Kate grimaced. "I hope it's one of yours," she murmured to the dark, and kept walking into town.

"You're not from Texas," Doc had said, after they'd spent hours at the faro table talking, when it had gone full dark outside and Kate had given up hope of a job. "You're from a long way off."

"I was born in Europe," she admitted. "Hungary. And you, Mr Holliday – you're not from Texas either."

"Valdosta, Georgia," he admitted, although he ran the words together – *Valdostageorgia*, with As long and wide as a muddy river. "It seems we have something in common, Miss Kate." He took a drink from his flask, winked at her. "We neither of us ended up where destiny said we'd be."

Dodge City, Kansas
1878

Kate knows that something is not right with Doc. She's never been a particularly suspicious woman and certainly not a jealous one – jealousy is for married women and haggard old spinsters, like the ones that glare at her in the street when she and Doc are out taking the air.

The air in Kansas is thick and wet in summer, full of dust and dancing motes in autumn. Neither one helps Doc's coughing.

He told Kate the night they met that he was sick, and not to expect him to live any time at all. Kate doesn't make a habit of expecting anything from anyone, especially not gamblers who move from town to town, trailing their lawman friends like the Romany caravans that rumbled through the streets of Kate's childhood city.

Because of this, she and Doc have spent over a year together. Expecting nothing, and enjoying most things. He talks to her. He doesn't treat her like she's stupid, or even like she's a woman at times. He tells her stories about hunting fox in the swamps outside Valdosta, about his dentistry practice. He told her about a man who had every one of his teeth pulled while drunk, and made it funny, so that Kate had to hide herself behind her fan. Laughter until you're red-faced is unladylike.

There's always money, whiskey and a feather bed at the end of the night, if they go to bed. Doc is a better lover than most before, and what he lacks in consideration he makes up for in ardency. Doc is dying and he grasps on to her like she's the air that his rotted lungs can't breathe in.

Kate knows, if she were a different Kate than Big-Nose Kate Elder, woman of no particular skill but possessed of a sharp tongue, were he a different Doc than Doc Holliday, the fastest gunfighter since Bill Hickok, that she'd be in love with him.

But there's something not right about Doc, and it's eating Kate away as surely as the tuberculosis is eating at her lover.

That's why she follows him this time, when he slips out of bed, into a shirt and pants and his favourite overcoat. She waits, breathing slow and even in the dark, while he straps on his twin nickel-plated pistols and tucks a rifle up under his arm.

Doc has been leaving her at night for months, in Texas and in Kansas, and at first Kate, the other Kate, was furious and heartbroken. But she's never smelled another woman on him, not even the smoke and soot of a gambling house. Never seen anything except tired crescents under his eyes in the morning light.

She's left on her stockings, and it's a simple trick to pull on a shirtwaist and skirt, shove her feet into boots, and be after him once the door of their rooming house swings shut.

They'd retired early, Doc tired and pale and not in the mood to engage in couple's familiarity. Kate remembers the taut feeling of his shoulders as she slipped his jacket off.

"Somebody tried to kill Wyatt tonight," he says before she can ask.

"Knowing Wyatt, this somebody probably had a reason," she replies.

"I almost shot a man in the chest, Kate." Doc slumps on their bed, and she mounts it behind him, wrapping her arms around his torso, pressing her face into the ashy gold hair that smells of pomade. It's like putting your face into hay, clean and sweet.

"But you didn't, love," she tells him.

"But I was ready to," he says, so quiet it's difficult to hear over the street noise below their window.

Doc is a few dozen feet ahead of her, walking with purpose through the empty streets. The rifle is under his coat – not even the trusted friend of Marshal Earp can shirk the ordinance against firearms inside the limits of Dodge.

He turns into the shanty town where the Chinamen have their laundries and seamstressing concerns and opium parlours. Kate doesn't understand opium. Opium makes you stupid, and slow. Kate has learned from Doc the value of being sharp and fast.

Doc passes under someone's forgotten laundry line, his pale face and hair in shadow for a moment before the moon finds them again. And then he stops, and he turns in a slow circle.

Kate yanks herself into the alcove of a laundry, bags and bundles of clean clothes breathing out scratchy fibres and the scent of lye. He's almost seen her, and she can't articulate why, but she knows that Doc seeing her now would ruin something, kick out some foundation their time together is resting on.

Behind Doc, the shadows move.

Kate watches them unfold, grow arms and legs and teeth. The teeth shine under the moonlight, silver and brighter than the polish on Doc's pistols.

She's screaming before she can bite her tongue. "John, look out!"

In one motion, Doc raises his rifle, pumps the lever, aims and fires. The shadow drops back and falls to the ground. The shadow is hissing.

Kate moves from her hiding place but Doc stops her. "Stay put!" He draws the pistol from the left side of his belt and points it at the black mass on the ground. The mass that is wearing a man's clothing and a man's face, and has teeth like a hungry cougar. Bleeding clotted black blood from a chest wound, but still grinning and hissing.

Doc is a true shot – he doesn't miss eight times out of ten. He hasn't missed now. The thing's heart is shot out. And yet it still bleeds. It still moves. It looks her in the eye.

The pistol speaks, and the thing goes still, collapsing like the laundry sacks piled up under the tents all around them.

Kate doesn't think she can speak, but she manages. "Is he dead?"

"It." Doc's chest is moving like a bellows, short and shallow. "It, not 'he'. And no … " Doc doubles over, choking, and the spell holding Kate's feet breaks. She goes to him, rubs the centre of his back like she's done a hundred times before, waits for the fit to pass.

He stops coughing after a time. Spits the blood at the thing. Its eyes are still open and Kate can't look any more. There's something still in there. "It's looking at me."

Doc grips her shoulders. "I need something from our room. Can you wait here until I get back?"

Kate can't answer, can just nod limply. The expression on Doc's face is scaring her a thousand times more than any living shadow.

Doc is frightened.

"I can." She sits on an overturned water barrel to demonstrate her fastness.

"If it gets up again … " Doc presses the dead weight of the pistol into her hands. "Aim for the head, and don't you miss."

Then he's gone, a blacker spot on the black night, and Kate is alone with the thing, this shadow-thing that tried to kill her John Henry.

It is a very long time before Doc comes back, and Kate spends every minute in agony, imagining the worst. Her imagination is no match for the truth. But she hasn't learned the truth of Doc's nights. Not yet.

Perdition, Arizona
1888

She knew the truth, in the back of her mind. A rivulet of stories from her father, the doctor, caught up with the dime novels she'd read to pass the time on long rides or when Doc and Wyatt were out on men's affairs, combined into a flash flood with the instinct that lives in every breathing thing, far back, underneath civility and flesh.

Kate knew what the thing on the ground was. When Doc came back with his beaten-up black leather dentist's kit, she wasn't surprised. When he took out the wooden spike and the hammer, she didn't look away even though he told her to.

And when the body on the ground had turned to foul-smelling grey ashes, already starting to scatter on the light wind, she grabbed Doc and slapped him hard, then started to cry.

He held her and whispered in her ear. "You have to understand, Kate. It's not something I go telling every man, woman and child in creation."

As the ash blew away and was forgotten, so the companionship of Kate Elder and Doc Holliday began to change. She told him the stories from her father and her father's grandmother before that, related while she and her sister huddled around the coal fire in Budapest. The *vampir*, who had their heads cut off and their ashes mixed with holy water to keep their corpses from wandering home again.

Kate had passed the cemetery, and she could see the first sweep of shanties and tents that made up Perdition. There was no movement. Not even wind deigned to stir this forsaken patch of ground. The Winchester was growing sweaty in her grip and her shirtwaist was growing damp against her skin.

This wasn't a hunting vampire that John shot on the wing. This wasn't a red-eyed whore feeding on lonely cowboys. Kate didn't know what waited for her in Perdition.

She just knew that she had to come.

The telegram crackled under her touch as she reached down to check her bullet belt. Every loop a full round, every round tested and true. Just like John's.

She'd been in Aspen, Colorado when the news had come. It wasn't unexpected, sudden, a shot and a body falling. She'd been to see him already. She'd made her peace with John Henry Holliday.

Holliday dead. Gone to Perdition. Your svcs needed.

She'd shed her tears and broken her crockery and had her time with that ice-cold empty feeling that came from knowing what she had to do, here in Perdition.

Now it just remained to finish.

John told her stories in return, like he always had, only now they were about how he'd come across a woman in the swamp outside Valdosta one moonlit midnight. How she'd had a little freeman child with her. John was seventeen, but his father was a war veteran twice over and he taught his son to shoot first and think later.

The little girl survived. The woman ran into the swamp, wounded and needing to feed.

Next sundown, she came to the Holliday house with six of her kin. "They can't cross thresholds," John had said. "But she sure did put up a howl. Sent the fear of God straight through me."

He went to the free Negro town across the piney woods from the Hollidays' snug home in downtown Valdosta, and the little girl's grandmother told him how her people dealt with vampires.

The next night, Doc was ready.

Kate's chest clenched when she breathed in, ever so slightly. He'd taught her how to shoot straighter, how to make silver bullets to put them down, what trees to fashion stakes from to kill them.

John had taught her how to survive in a world where things that breathed were little better than cattle.

And he'd died. He'd up and died and left her behind, to pick up his mess and burn it clean and scatter the ashes to the four directions like the Navajo. Four corners, four ways to keep the ghosts of your dead from rising again.

Sound and movement spilled from a saloon at the far end of the street, and Kate wiped her hand down on the rough cotton pants she'd kept in her trunk for nearly five years.

Just in case she ever needed to ride as hard and fast as the devil himself again, to prevent something worse than the devil from rising and walking.

Her hand would be steady and her aim would be sure. She wouldn't shy away from doing the duty she'd tumbled into that night she'd followed Doc from the rooming house, going on ten years ago now.

Kate steadied her grip on the Winchester, and walked towards the saloon.

Tombstone, Arizona
1881

Tombstone is a young town, birthed from the rock and the sand of Arizona. It does not have a decent milliner's shop or a single fine dining establishment. The rooming house Doc finds for them on Fremont Street, Fly's, is barely better than the hovels Kate lived in on her quest down the Mississippi and across the plains to Kansas, but at least there are no bugs and the landlord keeps his remarks about an unmarried couple in a single room to himself. Tombstone has whores in abundance, springing up like flowers from the fertile soil of mining and railroad money.

Because Tombstone also has silver mines. They wind for miles under the earth, deep and dark and cramped. The perfect hiding place for a creature that cannot face the sun.

Kate has cleaned a nest before – the weight of the kerosene jug tugs on her arm as she and Doc venture into the mine. They are twelve miles from Tombstone, creeping down a vent tunnel in the Graveyard Mine. "A more apt name I've never heard," Doc mutters as they move through the dim and the dust. "The bastard who laid this claim had the devil's own humour."

His lantern doesn't pierce much more than ten feet ahead, and he needs his other hand free to put down anything that might be moving in this forgotten section of ground. So Kate carries the kerosene, the matches, the spikes and the mallet.

Silver will paralyse a vampire, but only fire or a piercing of the heart will kill it. It seems like they're mocking her, Kate thinks as they walk, by living so close to the very thing that can leave them helpless.

Kate has a Winchester strapped across her back, and a knife dipped in silver in the belt of her man's trousers. The mine is hot, and sweat works its way down her neck and over her ribs in a parody of Doc's touch.

"It's easy for them in a place like this," he says from ahead of her. "A man dies in a whore's bed, it's drink or vice that did him in. A whore dies in the street, it's what she had coming from on high. The marshal's more concerned with keeping the breathers from shooting each other over claims

and the rest of them are so blinded by silver they wouldn't notice if one walked into the smithy and asked to have its fangs filed."

"Even Wyatt?" Kate says. Wyatt knows that Doc is a gambler and that Kate is his woman. He doesn't know about the midnight assignations. He doesn't know what watches him from the dark places.

"Especially Wyatt," Doc says. His tone of late is flat and angry when Wyatt comes up. Kate knows that Wyatt has given up law and taken up speculating. He's become angrier and more inclined to cuff a drunkard than escort him out of Earp's preferred saloon. Wyatt and Doc's friendship is strained in this silver-veined, lawless place. The vampires don't provide a help.

They've spread among the whores like syphilis, and Kate has put a stake through the heart of no less than three soiled doves in their four months at Tombstone. The nest will be the end of it, killing the disease rather than a symptom, Kate hopes.

She's gotten stronger in the time she's been with Doc. Smarter, too. Vampires are like a creeping rash on the face of the night. They can be burned and destroyed, but they always come crawling back. And they come to Doc, like moths to a lantern. Fierce as his reputation is among the daylight denizens of the frontier, it's worse among the night creatures. All of them want a pound of flesh from the hide of Doc Holliday.

The lantern lights up pine boxes, crude coffins slapped together from knotty wood still oozing pitch. Tucked up against the earth, like mushrooms sprouting from a dead man's skin.

Doc sets the lantern down and, as he does, Kate catches sight of a pale hand in the dirt. "John Henry. There."

He bends and checks the girl's throat – one of the Chinese girls who smiles at Kate when she takes in their washing – and shakes his head. "She's dry."

Near the corpse are a litter of fine clothes and whiskey bottles, and a belt half full of bullets. "Damn it," Doc growls. "God damn it straight to hell."

Kate keeps one eye on the coffins, for any sign of stirring, one eye on Doc as he pokes through the detritus. "What's wrong, Doc?"

"All this doesn't come from thieving off corpses and skulking in shadows," he whispers. "They had it brought here." He stands, pushes back his coat and puts his hand on the butt of his left pistol, a reflexive motion. In that moment, in the low light, he becomes the legend and not the man *she knows.* "They have a familiar," *Doc says. His boot kicks aside a belt buckle, a brand-new hat, a cattle brand that reads D-8.*

"That's a rustler brand," *Kate says. She wishes later she hadn't.* "I heard Wyatt and Virgil talking. They use that brand to change US army cattle into that . . . D-8 for US."

Doc's face goes stony still. "Is that so," *he says, and picks up the brand, stares at it before tossing it into the recesses of the tunnel. Picks up the kerosene, and splashes it over the coffins.*

The vampires scream as they burn. Trapped-animal screams. Kate knows that Doc dreams about the men he's had to shoot, the living ones, but Kate dreams of the screaming.

At the mouth of the tunnel, Doc watches the smoke for a moment and then buttons his jacket. Kate finally gives voice to the black thought that arose when they found the dead girl. "You're going to have to kill him. The man helping the blood drinkers."

Doc drops his eyes to his dusty boots. "Yes."

Kate slides her hand into his. "He's giving those things aid and comfort. He got a woman killed. He doesn't deserve to live."

Doc surprises her by pressing a kiss against her dirty, sweaty forehead. "You're the angel on my shoulder, my Kate," *he whispers.* "And sometimes the devil, too."

Kate coaxes him away from the mine, and onto the horses. They don't speak while they ride back to Tombstone. In the rooming house, they make love while the sun sets, still wordless. After, when she's left watching cobwebs trail against the stained ceiling, Doc has his worst coughing fit in some months. Blood stains the sheets, and all Kate can do is watch as his body twitches.

After that he sleeps, light and restless to every sound. Kate doesn't attempt slumber. She'll just hear more screaming.

The familiar's name is Frank McLaury, and it takes Kate and Doc nearly a month of watching and waiting at the mine to find him.

McLaury and his brother Tom run with a gang of cattle rustlers, the Clantons, Billy Claiborne and a few others. He uses his brethren to bring women and whiskey and whatever the vampires desire back to the mine, claiming he works for a reclusive industrialist with peculiar tastes. The other cowboys are too drunk or too dumb to question him. They drink all night when they're not rustling cattle. During the day, the gang rarely leaves camp.

Doc is getting sicker, and he's getting angrier, and Kate knows that he can't keep up the constant strain of watching McLaury and killing the man's masters one by one much longer.

Kate goes to Virgil and begs him to intervene on the county's behalf. The gang robs stages, steals cattle . . . Kate knows the justice-minded Virgil will take action.

What action, she couldn't have imagined. Virgil gets his brothers deputy badges, and before any time at all has passed the Clantons and McLaurys are riding into Tombstone spoiling for a fight.

Doc walks with them down the alley behind Fremont Street. He orders Kate to stay inside and away from the windows, but she peers through the sheer curtains as the four men walk together in the October sun.

When Doc and McLaury meet, Doc doesn't say a word. He raises his shotgun and aims, but he doesn't fire. Letting McLaury say his last words.

McLaury sneers. "I know what you are, Holliday." He spits in the dirt. "I smell it on you, and you can call it consumption but we know different. I smell it on you strong as your whore's perfume."

Doc fires then, and McLaury goes back like a sack of skin and bones. He drops in the dirt. His living blood spills, red brown like the Georgia dirt of Doc's home soil.

Kate hits the floor as the Earps, the Clantons and the rest of the cowboys turn the alley into a shooting gallery. She can smell cordite and black powder, and hear screaming.

It's different than the vampires – it's human and it comes from a human's pain. A long while later, when she dares peer over the sill again, only Wyatt and Ike Clanton are left in the street. There are bodies, too. But not Doc's.

His footfalls when he finally comes to the room are heavy. There's blood on his collar and on his face, ranging like raindrops into his light gold hair. Doc collapses on the bed and puts his head into his hands. "That was awful," he mutters. "Just awful."

Kate goes to him and sits with him while the light changes to night. "It's done?" she asks finally.

"We kill the sire, burn the last of the sire's kin, and it's done," he affirms. "Tombstone is a habitable and civilized bastion of the living, once more."

Kate doesn't miss the blade-edge tone. Doc doesn't believe in civilization, any more than the average drover believes in vampires.

"What was he jabbering about? McLaury?" To move, Kate goes about

wetting a cloth in the basin, handing it to Doc. He daubs at the blood on his cheek and forehead. The cloth turns pink.

"Nothing."

"John Henry." *Kate sets the pitcher down with force.* "It was not nothing. I could see your face."

Doc lies back on the bed with his boots still on, after setting his hat carefully aside. He looks as thin and tired as Kate's ever seen him. Pale as a corpse. Cold as one of them when she goes to at least take off his gun belt and his tie before he has another coughing fit.

"Kate, a man in my line of work has some secrets that he keeps out of necessity, and some that he doesn't want to keep, but he does anyway, because they're just harmful, hateful things that do no one any good. You understand?"

Kate sighs. The pistols are heavy as she hangs them next to his hat and she lies next to Doc, curling her body so that it fits to the shape of his, like a gun in a holster. "So you won't tell me."

Doc puts one hand in her hair, his card-quick and gun-calloused fingers stroking her cheekbone. He kisses her forehead again. "Not today, my dear."

"But maybe some day?" *She reaches back and undoes the laces of her stays. She didn't bother putting on a dress when Doc walked out to meet the Earps. He'd need her, when he came back. If.*

Doc gives her a quick smile, really only half of one, and it's a lie but she pretends it's not. "Someday. Yes."

Perdition, Arizona
1888

She found him at the card table, and for a moment she couldn't breathe. He looked so familiar there, so much like Doc, that it took Kate a full half-turn of the clock hands before she could move any further than the rude clapboard contraption that passed for a door.

A pasty-faced Irish boy was playing cards with him, red hair sticking out from his hat every which way. Doc's eyes never blinked, never wavered from the boy's wrists where blue veins pulsed as he laid his cards on the table.

"Three jacks, partner. That makes three hands to me ... " He trailed off when he spotted Kate's shadow across his cards and coins.

Doc's gaze shifted more slowly. His eyes, when he met hers, were as blank as an open sky. Kate's bile rose and she tasted her meagre breakfast of dried venison and hardtack in the back of her throat.

"You look like my John," she whispered. The motion was so familiar, but it seemed to take a thousand seconds. Pump the Winchester, squeeze the trigger. Repeat the motion twice more, until the thing sitting at the card table went over backwards, crashing to the ground.

"But you're not," Kate said. Doc began to laugh. Clotted blood caught itself up in his teeth, turned his grin to a shark's grin.

"Going to kill me, Kate? Going to get the stake and the mallet and drive it in yourself, through the gristle and the bone? Going to listen to me scream while you do?"

There was silence in the saloon. Utter silence, the kind you only found in the eyes of storms. Death's acre, Kate thought. The place where nothing lives, not even sound.

"Ma'am?" The red-headed boy broke the silence. "Maybe you should put that rifle down?"

Doc clambered up, brushing at his coat where the rifle has shot holes. "You ruined my suit, Kate."

The boy squeaked in shock. "Mister . . . maybe you should sit down. You got shot up pretty bad . . . "

"Maybe, maybe. Maybe's a weak word, boy. You should be more direct, you want people to listen." Doc grinned again. Blood dribbled down his chin.

Kate lifted the Winchester, jerked it. "Outside. The next ones won't just be lead shot."

He inclined his head and, before the staring gamblers and cowboys, they moved into the street, a matched pair, step for step.

The moon had climbed high up, shedding cold pale light on the scene. Kate caught eyeshine from behind windows, down side alleys, watching her. Unblinking.

Behind her, the boy followed them into the street. "Ma'am, I don't rightly know what's happening here . . . "

"And you shouldn't, child." Kate didn't take her gaze off Doc. He stood in the middle of the hard-packed street. He wore a gun belt, but his ivory-handled pistols were gone. Doc didn't need the thing that made him Doc any more.

"I'm not leaving you alone with that . . . man," the kid piped up.

Kate dared to glance at him. "What's your name?"

"James Priestly, ma'am. Out of Chattanooga, Tennessee."

"Well, James Priestly from Tennessee, I suggest you go back into that gin mill and you drink yourself stupid and forget everything that you just saw. For your own peace of mind, forget."

Priestly's thin, freckled face crinkled into a frown that was too old for the boy wearing it. "I don't understand . . ."

"And you don't want to. Scoot."

The kid backed up to the saloon door, but didn't go inside. Kate turned her attentions back to Doc. He was still, that dead stillness one could only achieve by not being possessed of a heartbeat.

"Well?" Doc called.

"You know why I'm here," Kate shouted back.

He moved, and the space between them closed, fluid, like air slipping from lungs. Doc's skinny fingers knotted in Kate's dusty hair, and his dry cheek pressed against hers. He jerked her neck back, exposing her throat to the sky and the moon. "You can't do it, Kate. You wouldn't do it to me."

Kate looked into Doc's eyes, cloudy and cataract-covered as they were. "I have to," she whispered, and felt a twist like a boot in her gut.

Doc's lips, cold like the night air, passed down her neck. "You won't kill me, Kate."

Kate shuddered. She missed him. She'd missed him. Every night, and every morning. Every time she saw a tall slender man in dove grey in the street.

"I will," she told Doc. "Because I promised you I would."

Glenwood Springs, Colorado
1887

It is spring when the stage deposits Kate in Glenwood Springs. She and her carpetbag proceed down the street to the Hotel Glenwood, taking in the swelling green on the hillsides and the fragrant air. The desk man at the hotel points her to John's room.

She's prepared for the worst, but not for what she sees.

There are buds on the trees outside Doc's window, and a soft mist clinging to the mountains beyond, but inside the room smells of funerals and graveyards.

Doc is small against the pillows, and his hair has leached of colour along with the rest of him, hanging on his sweaty forehead, lank and grey.

He smiles at her, and presses a stained handkerchief against his lips. "Kate."

She's resolved to stay away, stay aloof, but she flies to him and lets him put his free arm about her. "You came," he says into her hair.

"Of course I did, you stupid man." He smells sick, of stale sweat and staler soap, but he's still John. She doesn't move away.

Doc coughs and she hears the rattle in his chest. "Nobody else did."

"You know people." She's trying to be kind, and she sits up and straightens his blanket, fetches a fresh handkerchief from the neat stack some maid or laundress has left on the dressing table. "They don't want to see a man dying of consumption. They haven't seen what we have, so plain death . . . it scares them off."

"Kate." Her back is to him as she refolds the handkerchiefs out of want of something to do. She can see him in the mirror, almost a ghost on glass. "Kate, I don't have consumption."

Her hands stop. For a movement of a watch, everything stops. "What are you babbling about, John Henry?"

His words are lost in coughing for a long moment, but he wrestles his body still and speaks. "I need you to listen to me, Kate. Without judgment and without anger. I don't deserve it, but I'll be damned if I have anyone else to ask. I don't."

When she approaches the bed again, he catches her hand. "All I have is you, Kate. I've lost every God-damned thing in the world besides."

Feeling the long shadow of ill omen on her, Kate sits beside him anyway and says, "All right, John. What is it that's got you in such a sentimental state?"

Doc tells her about the first vampire he killed, in that Georgia swamp. "She didn't die right away. She got her hooks into me right and proper, and she . . . she fed on me."

Kate tries to pull away but Doc is suddenly strong again. "It didn't make me one of them, Kate. I never drank dead blood. She didn't kill me that night, she just . . . changed me. I could see sharper and shoot straighter. Wasn't until I spent a few more years in wet air, breathing in graveyard dust at nights, that I realized I was getting sicker, too."

Doc's gaze goes to the window, to the mountains. It's started to rain softly, drops dribbling down the glass. "For the time I had left, I was a man possessed of the skill I needed to kill them. For the time I had left, and it wasn't any time at all."

Kate is shaking now, and it's not out of fear for her neck. "You couldn't tell me the truth? God damn you, John Holliday."

And there you have it, reader – the truth of what happened in Perdition, to Miss Kate Elder (née Mary Katharine Horony) and to Mr John Holliday, plain and accurate as I could make it.

Miss Elder never wept when I came up on her with fresh horses. She took the smaller of the two, thanked me in a most decorous manner, and advised me to forget what I had seen.

I could not accede to her wishes, of course, but in my truthful retelling have tried to be accurate and logical, without giving over to sensation. I swore that morning that I would put away the whiskey bottle and the demons it conjured, and I've largely managed. There are worse demons in this world.

I went back to Tennessee and then to the Great Lakes, and along the way I had tried my best to impart the truth, where the truth need be told:

There are things in the night that are not people, and there are people in the night who stand guard. I endeavour only to be one of them, and to watch over the daylight world as those who came before me did, ever vigilant and never resting.

That is the whole of it. That is the truth, and nothing more.

James Priestly
Chicago, Illinois
December 12 1913

Deliver Us From Evil

Dina James

How he hated rainy nights.

Water rejected the dead, and though he wasn't technically "dead", he was certainly soulless, and the deluge from the sky apparently made no distinction.

Beneath his long black coat his skin burned in protest as he trudged through the downpour. All right, it wasn't a "downpour" or a "shower" . . . this was a storm. The meteorologist should be eviscerated for that deception. The harsh wind didn't make the rain coming down in curtains and sheets any easier to navigate through.

A nightclub he knew that boasted a generous clientele boasted nothing tonight but an empty parking lot. The sign advertising "live nude girls" flickered valiantly in its struggle against the weather.

His hunger urged him on, in spite of the vacant parking lot. It was a driving, persistent need that he could never satisfy, no matter how often he fed.

Marcos crossed the street, and another, then turned the corner and walked on through the deserted city. He was about to resign himself to another hungry night when a light several blocks ahead of him caught his keen eyes.

He cursed the rain again. Water of any kind made it difficult to use his ethereal abilities, and flowing water made it even more so. Had it not been pouring, he could have simply thought about where he wanted to be and appeared there, safely veiled from the perception of any humans around. In this, however, he was forced to walk.

Like a human.

He rolled his eyes at the irony. He hadn't been human for well over 400 years.

As he neared the light, he curled his lip in disdain. Even if the harsh glow of hot pink neon hadn't stung his light-sensitive eyes, the tackiness of the sign alone would have blinded him: PSYCHIC OPEN.

Marcos almost turned away. Ravenous or not, he was not about to set foot in such a place. He crossed himself out of old habit, then laughed and shook his head. What was he trying to do, ward off evil?

He was the evil one. The soulless one.

The psychic one.

Just as he was about to go back the way he'd come, something on the small barred window caught his eye. It was the symbol on the glass of the shop, mostly hidden behind one of the bars that covered the window.

A human wouldn't have noticed it. Marcos stared at it, entranced, forgetting his insistent hunger momentarily as he tried to remember what it meant. He knew it meant *something* important, but he couldn't quite recall what it was. A vague feeling of comfort – of safety – stirred within him. It was almost similar to the momentary sensation of peace that echoed through him after he'd fed, before the hunger returned, merciless and unrelenting, demanding more.

He remembered the word for the feeling. *Relief.*

Why would he be relieved by that symbol? What did it mean?

He found himself reaching for the glass door to the small shop. It, too, was barred. It would be, in this part of town. Even as he opened the door, Marcos heard gunshots and sirens piercing the night. They were far away, but his sensitive ears heard a great deal, even with the falling rain deafening him as it splattered against the pavement of the empty city streets.

The additional weight of the bars didn't prevent him from jerking the door open effortlessly. Bells clanged loudly above his head and at his side as he entered. Marcos winced against the noise and glared at them in annoyance as the door shut behind him.

Ay, Madre de Dios.

Marcos was tempted to cross himself again out of sheer horror. His eyes widened as they took in the room.

Dark purple and red fabrics of every hue and texture seemed to drape every possible surface, from the walls and countertops to lamps and tables. Even the chairs, in which one presumably waited while the . . . "psychic" was busy with other clients, were adorned with bits of hemmed cloth over the arms and backs.

The room was also bedecked in stars, angels, various crystals and prisms, and drowning in the overwhelming scent of incense. The pungent odour of patchouli assaulted him, and Marcos wrinkled his nose. He crossed the room to the "burner" that held the offending, noxious sticks and glared down at it. A card on the table next to it read "Madam Marina – Psychic, Spiritualist and Astrologer", along with a telephone number, the address of the shop, and a list of her offered services in purple ink.

What was it with purple?

A tinkling sound caused him to turn, and he stifled his laughter with effort. The woman that had emerged through the curtain of large brass discs stopped in the doorway and eyed him coolly, appraising him. He returned the favour.

She looked as tacky as the room did, and may as well have been one of the chairs, dressed as she was in a flowing tunic of purple and equally loose trousers of red. Scarves adorned her neck and hair, reminding one of a pirate wench or a Renaissance Faire worker gone mad.

He doesn't look like a thug, Marina thought to herself as she looked over the man who had entered her shop. Clean, and well dressed and, though his dark hair was longer than usual, it wasn't like the gang types wore theirs. He didn't look like a punk. Besides, he was too old. Not that his age really made a difference, but the ones who made trouble for her weren't usually his age. He looked a little older than she was – maybe thirty or thirty-five. He was certainly good-looking. Gorgeous black eyes. Dark, handsome features, with a day's growth of beard roughening his upper lip and chin.

"Have you come in seeking answers, or just a moment out of the storm?" Marina asked.

Marcos stifled his laughter again. What kind of accent was she trying to fake? He'd rarely heard such an affectation – it sounded more like she was covering up an unwanted speech impediment than any kind of regional inflection. He supposed that she was aiming for something Old World. Romanian, or possibly Italian. Whatever her aim, she was missing her mark. Woefully.

"Neither," he replied, his own rich, cultured voice seeming out of place in this tacky, fake environment. He pointed to the symbol painted on the window that had drawn his attention. "I . . . that symbol . . . "

"Yes?"

"Why is it there?" Marcos asked, his own brow furrowing as he considered the symbol from the inside this time, unhindered by bars.

"What do you mean?" Marina asked, trying not to let her discomfort show. This guy was seriously starting to creep her out. "It is a guardian spirit – a protector. An avenging angel, if you will."

Angels. He remembered something now. Not an avenging angel. A vengeful angel. Wroth and powerful, cursing him to endure limitless hunger until he –

Until? Until what?

He couldn't remember.

Marcos turned to the woman again. By God, her clothes were garish. It was hard to look at her.

"Do you have a question you wish to address to your spirit guide?" she asked.

Marcos snorted rudely. "No. Nor is there any such thing. Spirits don't guide, and angels do not watch protectively over each of us."

"Well, that is what that 'symbol' you show so much interest in is meant to portray," Marina replied. "If you have no questions, perhaps you should leave now. The rain seems to have lessened a bit."

His eyes swept over her. Her nervousness had caused her blood to rise, colouring her cheeks, inciting his ravenousness further. Why was he hesitating?

A glint of silver hidden by the ridiculous folds of her top caught his eye. The pendant that flashed into view was the same symbol as that gracing the window.

Again, his hunger quieted at the sight of it.

"Unless of course you wish a reading. Your aura is very strong. Or perhaps tarot?" he heard her ask.

Marcos made a rude noise. Auras radiated from the soul, and he didn't have one for her to read. He'd exchanged his soul for immortality, as all his kind had.

He was a vampire, cursed to maintain his own existence by feeding on the blood of those he sought to outlive. And then some, he thought wryly.

"I have no need of your . . . services, *mujer*." Marcos laughed at himself for his choice of words. She was far from any kind of "lady".

"Then it is certainly time for you to be on your way," Marina said, annoyance serving to muster her courage. She stepped into him and took him by the forearm, attempting to twist it as she'd seen the bouncer do more than a few times at the club where she used to work.

Marcos looked down at her hands on his arm and raised an eyebrow. Did she think she could physically remove him? Harm him?

He almost laughed, but managed to keep it contained.

Marina let go of his arm – he wasn't about to budge if he didn't want to, it seemed. Strong for someone who didn't look like he had a lot of muscle. Deceptive. She scowled at him.

"I will ask you once more to please leave," she said, exasperated.

Marcos noticed her "accent" slipped slightly. Her cheeks were pink and her blue eyes flashed. She was upset with him.

For some reason, Marcos didn't want to be the cause of this woman's annoyance. He wanted to move her, certainly, and it shocked him to realize he wanted to goad her passion – albeit passion of a different sort.

Her tone made him study her carefully, his sensitive eyes seeing past the ridiculous layers of red and purple material to the woman wearing them. She wasn't as tall as he – no surprise there. Few reached his six-foot four-inch height. The hair that had escaped the scarf she'd wrapped around her head was dark brown, or possibly black, and it didn't go well with her soft blue eyes. A light mask of freckles dotted her nose and cheeks, but didn't take away from her fair complexion as her dark hair did.

He smiled inwardly for noticing such details. He'd long since ceased paying attention to humans. They were food – a biological necessity for continued survival – nothing more, so . . . what did she or her upset matter? Why hadn't he simply entered, taken her blood as well as her life, and been done with it? Why was he attempting to be a gentleman? He wasn't even human, and she appeared to be a poor excuse for one. Still, oaths meant something to his kind, even if they didn't mean a great deal to humans.

Marcos lowered his eyes, and bowed his head, then turned and left the shop without another word. The bells on the door announced his departure with a bang as he vanished into the night.

Marina raised her eyebrows, stunned. She went to the door and pushed it open slowly, poking her head out and looking down one side of the street and then the other to see where he'd gone. There was no sign of him.

Shaking her head, she went back into the shop and pulled the door shut. She locked it and pulled the chain on her lit sign, turning it off. There wasn't a need to be open any longer; not with this weather. Other than . . . Strange Weirdo Man, no one had even passed by her window since the rain had started earlier that afternoon.

Besides, she didn't have any more appointments – not that she'd had any today, anyway – and it *was* almost closing time. Sighing, Marina pulled the curtains across the storefront windows and door.

Her brow knitted in confusion and she knelt down. She pressed her fingertips to the carpet where he'd stood, surprised to find that it wasn't at all wet. There wasn't any water trailing from the doorway, either.

And, she realized as she stood, his hair hadn't been wet. He'd been completely dry, though she'd heard him come in from the rain, and watched him . . . *watched him disappear* back into it.

Marina shivered, then laughed at herself for being freaked out. It was cold in here, and rainy and spooky outside in the darkness. Suddenly the candles in the room seemed a lot more comforting.

Ah, Mar, you're letting all this psychic stuff get to you, she chastised herself. *You know none of it is real.*

Her stomach growled, reminding her of the hour. She reminded it that she had no money for takeout and, since she was sleeping in the shop on the futon in the "waiting area", no kitchen either. She'd been evicted from her apartment a month ago, and was just barely making the rent and utilities on this place.

At least she still had another month on her gym membership, which was most useful now for the showers. Oh, God, a shower. A hot bath. Such ordinary things now seemed like such luxury to her. She didn't know what she was going to do in another month when her membership ran out. She didn't have any way to pay for another year's membership. Hell, in her present situation, she couldn't even afford another *month's* membership.

Maybe she should think more about taking Benny up on his offer of a few shifts a week at the club. Ever since Heidi had left, he was stuck with only Lisa and Amber. People still asked if she was going to come back. Benny always shrugged and smiled, saying, "You never know."

Marina's stomach growled again, unsympathetic about money or memberships.

Returning to the back, she took off the scarf around her head and shook out her hair with a deep sigh. Her stomach growled even louder, insisting on being acknowledged. She glared down at her middle and gave it a light smack of rebuke as she changed her clothes; her uncomfortable feeling eased as she performed the mundane activity. She grabbed her pillow and blanket and headed out to the futon.

It was early – dark, but early – and she had nowhere to go, no money to spend, no television to watch, and no one to visit. Bed was about the only option left to her, since there was no dinner to get tonight. Her stomach's protests aside, it wasn't like she hadn't gone to bed without dinner a night or two before. A few missed meals wouldn't hurt her.

Maybe I should take Benny up on those shifts, she thought again as she went back out to the futon and lay down. At least then she would have had something to order dinner with. Chinese sounded wonderful.

But Marina was trying to regain a modicum of her pride. She didn't want Benny's kind of money. *Needed*, yes. Wanted, no.

There were a lot of things she didn't want. She didn't want to go back to waitressing in the evenings and making up fortunes during the day, or vice versa. She didn't want to go back to stripping at night. It was embarrassing to have a client come in for a fortune when just the night before you'd either served him a steak or he'd seen you practically naked.

I wonder what Weirdo would look like practically naked, she thought, surprising herself.

She rolled her eyes and shrugged it off. Why were all the crazy ones drop-dead gorgeous?

*   *   *

Marcos' thoughts ran along the same line, but not in so much detail.

He'd wanted her. Hungered for her. Had all but felt her heart beating beneath the pale skin of her throat as his mouth closed over it.

Had he been one second more in turning away and leaving her presence, he would have felt it somewhere other than only in his wishful thoughts.

Why then? Why hadn't he just done it? Why had he spoken to her like he was a man? He hadn't shown that much restraint . . . hadn't had that much control over his overwhelming hunger in . . . Marcos couldn't remember the last time he'd been the master of his need and not the other way around.

A stray cat ran across the sidewalk in front of him, dashing across the empty street and disappearing into the alley on the other side, trying to find a dry place out of the rain.

Buena suerte, gato, Marcos thought with a wry smile. The little black cat would need all the luck it could get in this storm. It was a good thing he didn't feed on animals the way some of his kind did, or there wouldn't be enough luck in the world to help that feline.

He smiled again at the superstition that came to mind. A black cat crossing one's path was thought to be an omen of ill luck in many cultures, but Marcos didn't think it would hurt him. His luck had run out generations ago.

Perhaps now, though, it was changing a bit.

The girl. The human. There was something about her he didn't understand, and some strange part of him wanted to. What did it mean?

Marcos looked down at the business card he'd pocketed. Fat raindrops set to work disintegrating the cheap paper almost immediately. He cleared them away with his thumb, contemplating her name. Her true name. The one he'd heard in her thoughts, not the false one touting the services of the fortune-teller.

Marcos snorted. Fortune.

Did fortune ever favour the damned?

*   *   *

Fortune favoured Marina.

Well, fortune and the tips she'd made at the club this last week. Benny had made her too good an offer, and people were still paying for *that* kind of entertainment.

She smiled at the thought – and the inadvertent pun – as she thanked her last reading of the day. Marina followed behind the young woman stepping into the dark to meet the friends awaiting her outside, intending to lock up.

A strong hand reached for the door and held it open for the departing woman. Blushing without knowing why, the woman stammered her thanks and appreciated the tall man out of the corner of her eye as she left.

Marcos offered her a silent nod before looking up at Marina, who stood in the doorway, stunned.

"Will *la señorita* permit me entry?" he asked hesitantly. Not that he needed an invitation. He didn't know why he felt the need to ask for one this time. He hadn't needed one before – she had a public premises and a welcome sign encouraging entry to any who wished it. Perhaps he was attempting to make up for his rudeness during their last encounter.

That had been three weeks ago, and he hadn't been able to get her out of his mind since. No, not her, his behaviour. He hadn't been able to get the way he'd acted out of his mind. Not her.

Marina just looked at him, confused, but nodded slowly. She had to be out of her mind to let him back in when he'd been such a jerk last time, but he looked so . . . hopeful. Like he was afraid she'd say "no", or tell him to get lost. She probably should, but he seemed apologetic. She could at least give him a chance to talk before kicking him to the sidewalk. She'd done as much for ex-boyfriends who hadn't deserved time to say three words to her. This guy was at least trying to be nice. Or so it seemed.

"*Gracias,*" he murmured as she stepped aside and let him in.

Marcos stepped inside, just far enough to have a look around. The room appeared just as tacky as it had the last time, for the most part, and still smelled of that rancid incense.

She lived here, he realized, catching a scent beneath the incense that no human would have been able to detect. The scent of life. Of home and belonging and independence.

His eyes went to the beaded pillows on the futon, and he moved silently, drawn to the weight of the fragrance. She slept there. He could all but see it in his mind.

"I was just about to lock up," she said in that atrocious phony accent of hers. "Something you need? It's not raining today."

Marina knew she was rambling, and hoped her accent didn't give away that she was scared out of her mind. He was back. What was he doing back here? She had convinced herself that he hadn't been real, that he wouldn't be back, and here he was, standing in front of her. She'd dreamed about him in some way every night since he'd come into her shop, and now that he was here, she didn't know what to do, or say. God, he was gorgeous.

"I ... I am uncertain ... " Marcos offered lamely. She already thought him a madman, and perhaps she was right. Thinking back on their first encounter, he had seemed quite out of his mind. But then, his hunger had been nearly overwhelming, and it was the fact that she remained unharmed in spite of his need that mystified him.

He gestured at the low table he'd stood next to the last time he'd been there. There was a large glass jar there now, filled with coloured stones. Wedged between them were several sticks of patchouli incense, burning slowly.

"You've moved things around. There was a different holder for your incense here last time."

Marina nodded slowly, making sure to study him more closely this time. He was wearing the same clothes as he had been the night he'd come in, but then, so was she. It wasn't raining, but he still had on his long black coat. She noted his hair as well – shiny black, curling gently at his shoulders near his collar. He was paler than she remembered, but his features gave away his Latin heritage. He was even more gorgeous in front of her than in her dreams.

"It is put away, in the back," she replied.

Marcos nodded and didn't say anything more. He merely looked at her, studying her, taking in every detail of her, though he knew them already, having played her image in his mind every day, every hour, since their first encounter.

Realizing what he was doing, he turned his attention to the objects in the room.

"Why did you do that?" he asked, not knowing where the words came from. Why was he asking? What did he care?

Because, he realized, he was enjoying speaking to someone for the first time in he-couldn't-remember-when. Actually *speaking* to someone – having a conversation with another being.

Someone ... human. Someone who reminded him of who he had been. What he had been. What he'd once had, and –

And what he had lost.

No, not lost. Traded. Sold. Bartered. Willingly given away, truth be told.

Marina considered him for a long moment. His tone, his words. He was being way more polite than he had been a few weeks ago. Still, he didn't look like a psycho, and she didn't get the "creep" vibe from him, and she knew creeps. She dealt with plenty of creeps. Even dated more than a few. This guy didn't seem at all creepy. Strange, sure, but not creepy.

"I often change the décor to reflect the seasons, and spring is a season of growth and change," she replied. "As I said, I was about to lock up, so if you wouldn't mind."

She gestured meaningfully towards the door.

"I thought . . . perhaps . . . you might assist me in . . . finding some answers to questions I have," Marcos found himself saying. "That is, if you are willing. I realize that our last encounter wasn't the most pleasant."

Marina smiled. At least he recognized he'd been kind of a jerk. Was he trying to apologize? She had time before her shift at the club for one last client. It might as well be Weirdo.

"I am willing. However, I do need to lock up," she replied. "You don't mind being locked in, do you? I promise, I won't make you stay the night."

Marcos laughed and shook his head. "I'm accustomed to staying up nights."

"Have a seat in the back, through there," Marina said, gesturing towards the metallic curtain separating the waiting area from the reading room. "I'll be with you in a moment."

He nodded and started towards the curtain as she went to the door, keys in hand. She pulled it shut and locked it, then turned off her sign and drew the curtains across the door and windows.

Then she realized what she'd just done. She'd just locked herself in with Weirdo. Maybe she should unlock the door . . . just in case.

The door moved as if in answer to that, and Marina heard a female voice curse before footsteps carried it away. No, it was a good idea to be closed. Besides, she had to get to her shift at the club soon, and didn't have time for another client after Weirdo tonight. The ad in the paper she'd spent her last dime on a few weeks ago seemed to be working. Business was slow, but at least it was business, which was more than a lot of the other shops on this block had these days.

She moved slowly towards the curtain that Weirdo had gone through. She glanced through the strings of metallic discs to see him studying the incense burner she'd had in the waiting area before, his long, graceful fingers caressing the carved wooden base reverently. It reminded him of something, but he couldn't quite remember what.

"You are musical," she said after a moment, mostly for lack of anything better to say.

"What makes you say that?" Marcos asked without looking at her.

"Your hands, the way you move and touch things," she replied with a shrug.

"It is not so," he said, his black eyes meeting hers intensely. "I have no talent for music of any kind, Madam Marina."

"You know my name," she said lightly. "Perhaps you would honour me with yours? I will need it in order to give you a satisfactory reading."

"You claim to be a psychic," he countered. "Don't you know it outright?"

Marina scowled at him. "'Psychic' does not equal 'mind-reader'. No one can read minds."

"Nor does 'gypsy' equal 'psychic'," Marcos said flatly. "Look at this place. Look at yourself. Even your name sounds like you chose it from a pizza menu."

"And here I thought you said you wished me to assist you in answering questions you have," Marina retorted, glaring at him. "I can see that you still need to figure out what questions those are. Now, if you are finished insulting me and my profession, I'll see you out. As you've said yourself, you have no need of my services."

"You were intending to service me?" Marcos replied, raising an eyebrow at her choice of words.

Marina realized what she'd said and how it could be interpreted and blushed. "My professional services," she clarified.

"Out of my shop. Come. The door is this way."

She moved away from the curtain and gestured behind her,

beckoning him to follow. When he didn't, she returned to the doorway and pushed aside the curtain. The discs tinkled merrily, in complete opposition to her mood.

He still stood there, smiling.

"You are coming, yes?" she asked. "Your legs work? Or must I call the police?"

Marcos snorted again. "And they will take, what? Forty minutes to answer your call about a man upsetting you? I could do much more than upset you in that time, if I so chose."

Marina narrowed her eyes at his thinly veiled threat. "Out, now."

She pointed firmly at the door.

"You're quite fetching when you're angry," he replied, studying her. "Your cheeks turn the most brilliant shade of pink. It's a nice thing to see."

"So you insult me just to see that?" she demanded, rolling her eyes. "I won't be your entertainment. Out."

"But you have been 'entertainment'," Marcos replied, not moving. He cocked his head and met her eyes meaningfully.

Marina crossed her arms over her chest. She didn't remember seeing him at the club, but that didn't mean he wasn't a regular. She'd only started working at Benny's place again last week, and had yet to even receive her first pay cheque. If he was a regular there, he was a new one.

"And you frequent places of 'entertainment'?" she asked acidly.

Marcos laughed and shook his head.

"Hardly," he replied. "But is that not what you do? Entertain people? Your card states what you do is 'for entertainment purposes only' . . . "

Marcos trailed off, letting his words hang meaningfully between them. He shrugged. Her anger would warm her blood beautifully. Perhaps he should make it a habit to anger all his prey. Fear always left a bitter aftertaste. Anger, on the other hand – now that was a sweet emotion. Hot and spicy, just the way he preferred his food.

"Even the title before your 'name'," he continued, enjoying the tension filling the room, "implies you oversee a brothel."

How he'd closed the distance between them without her noticing Marina couldn't fathom. One moment he was studying a lotus flower candleholder, and the next he was holding the metallic curtain back, his hand resting lazily against the door frame as he leaned into it and smiled down at her.

"Some can read minds," he murmured.

Why wasn't his closeness making her uncomfortable? Why couldn't she look anywhere but his eyes?

"No, they can't," she heard herself reply. "There isn't a soul who can."

Marcos chuckled softly and leaned in close, brushing aside the wisp of hair at her ear that had escaped the scarf tied around.

"Perhaps then that talent lies only with the soulless," he said, his voice barely more than a whisper. "For I can hear your thoughts as clearly as if they were my own, and you are not afraid, are you, Mary?"

Marina swallowed hard. She was afraid, but not . . . not frightened. Not of him. She'd had men want something she wasn't willing to give before. Getting scared didn't help the situation.

"How . . . How did you—"

"—know your real name?" he finished her question for her. "As I said, there are some who can read minds."

He didn't wait for her to reply as his mouth found the pulse at her throat.

She gasped as his fangs pierced the delicate flesh of her neck. Her eyes slid shut as her arms wound around his neck, clinging to him before they went lax again.

His arms went around her waist effortlessly. He supported the weight of humans nightly – sometimes more than once – and could easily carry her weight. Not that there was all that much to support. Beneath her voluminous layers, there was an average-sized woman. A little thinner than he liked – the women from his home country had more meat on their bones than these would-be skeletons in this one – but her thinness seemed to be due more to hunger than any desire to keep her weight down.

Hunger?

Marcos rarely, if ever, read the information conveyed in his prey's blood. Oh, there was a great deal of knowledge carried in the lifeblood of any creature – it would drive one mad if they allowed it to surface. If they attempted to fathom it all. It had been one of his first, early, and most difficult lessons when he'd initially become a lost soul.

Vampire.

Might as well call it what it was. *Vampiro*, his people – former people – called those like him. Every language had a word for what he was, and they all meant the same thing. Blood-drinker.

He was no fledgling now. He could allow himself to absorb the knowledge in her blood without risking madness, and so he did.

Much more personal than simply reading – or rather hearing – her thoughts, this allowed him to feel her emotions as she felt them. Experience her worries as she experienced them. Essentially it allowed him to *be her* for a moment – live her life – know who she was, who she felt herself to be.

To share her soul.

It was exquisite, yet painful. He'd been soulless for so long that even a brief encounter with the living force of another such as this was intoxicating.

Some, he knew, lived for this moment. Some of his kind did this with each and every kill.

Marcos found that perverted. You didn't get to know a cow before you ate it. Humans were food. There was no need to know their names, or their loves, their losses, their triumphs.

For some, it was the knowledge they took and carried with them that made their existence bearable. Marcos found that parasitical and vicarious. It was barely a step above common thievery. Rifling through the life of another and taking that which wasn't yours.

So then . . . why was he doing it now?

Her blood.

Dios, it reminded him of something he'd blissfully forgotten.

Hunger left a taint in the blood. Suffering and strife and worry and upset – they all left a mark, not only upon the body. They marked the soul as well.

Unwilling to take her life, Marcos lifted his mouth from her throat with a groan of effort. Looking down at her in his arms, Marcos felt something he hadn't in centuries.

Shame.

Sick with guilt, Marcos gestured at the futon in the opposite room.

It folded itself out neatly and he carried Marina's – *Mary's* – limp form to it and laid her down.

He touched the wound on her neck reverently. Already it had sealed itself so that she bled no more. He straightened and looked down at her, studying her for a long moment. His eyes were again drawn to the pendant that lay defiantly against her breast. The six-winged seraph seemed to glare up at him, offended.

Perhaps she was an angel herself, lying there so peacefully.

No. She had blood – human blood – so he knew she wasn't any kind of ethereal in human form. Besides, angels, when they deigned to take human form, were vain creatures. It was their nature to be beautiful, even in the most wretched of forms. They couldn't hide their beauty any more than he could claim to have a soul.

Though she was indeed beautiful, she was no angel. Nor demon. Simply a human. But . . . there was something.

He knew who she was . . . but *who was* she?

Whoever she was, she was not for him.

Marcos shook his head, took a step back and vanished.

* * *

Marina woke up with her head pounding. Holy crap, what a nightmare. She sat up and looked around, blinking furiously in the dark.

Dark didn't mean much. Her curtains kept the light low in here anyway. The candles had all been extinguished, and she was lying in bed. Huh.

She didn't remember going to bed. She didn't remember . . . much of anything at all. Seeing her last client out. Locking the door. Dreaming about Weirdo again.

Her stomach growled, impressing its existence upon her. Wow, was she thirsty. Like, mega-uber-thirsty. Like she hadn't had a drink in days.

She struggled to her feet. Why was it so hard to move? She hadn't worked out that hard at the gym, and hadn't done any unusual moves on the stage at the club last night. Oh, hell! The club! Her shift!

Every muscle in her body protested, and when she finally got to her feet, the room seemed to spin, and she sat down hard again.

Whoa. Oh, please don't let her be coming down with anything.

She couldn't afford to be sick now. Literally. She couldn't afford to take time off for any reason. Not if she was going to have a place to shower next month. Food would be nice, too.

Marina waited for a few minutes and, when the room stopped moving, slowly got to her feet.

They stayed under her, and she breathed a sigh of relief. She took another step. The room remained where it was. Gingerly she made it to the small bathroom in the back and snapped on the light.

Her eyes widened in horror at how pale her reflection in the mirror looked. She was white as a sheet. Except for . . .

She turned her head slightly. There, in the harsh light of the bathroom's bare bulb, glared a dark purple and yellow bruise along her neck. She touched it softly, then prodded it a little harder.

No pain.

Whatever she'd done, it hadn't hurt. Yet. Or maybe it had, and she just didn't remember. Still, something that left that kind of mark was something she'd remember. Enough guys had tried to strangle her –

Guys.

Guy.

Weirdo.

She remembered now. He'd come in . . . when? Last night? What day was it? How long had she been lying there?

What had he done to her?

Marina ripped off her clothes and searched everywhere she could see for a pinprick or other bruise. Had he drugged her? Robbed her?

She didn't want to think about what else he might have done to her, but she didn't feel like . . . he'd done anything else. Her clothes were all intact, and everything else seemed fine.

Restoring order to her attire, the dripping faucet reminded her that she was desperately thirsty, and she gulped handfuls of water straight from the tap. She dried her mouth on the sleeve of her shirt and made her way to the cash register.

She turned on the rarely used overhead light in the room – fluorescent and harsh, it illuminated the small space with an annoying buzzing accompaniment.

Everything seemed in order. Nothing was disturbed or missing. She pushed the "no sale" button on the register. Everything was there. The money she'd made over the last few weeks was all there.

Every penny. She closed the cash drawer and went into the other room.

There, too. Not one item out of place.

She wandered back into the main room and considered the futon. Then she went to the door and pulled aside the curtain. It was dark outside, and the lit bank sign across the street that flashed the day, time and temperature said it was 3.17 am. So much for making her shift at the club. It closed at 2 am.

Nine hours. She'd been asleep for nine hours? Her last client had left just after six o'clock. Had she really just pulled out the futon and slept in her clothes? What about Weirdo? What about the phone? It should have awakened her, if Benny tried to call her when she didn't show for her shift. It was too bad she'd pawned the answering machine, or he could have left her an angry message. Oh, well. She'd smooth things over tomorrow, somehow.

Marina looked down at the door as she restored the curtain. It was locked, from the inside. So, if Weirdo had done anything to her, he was a bloody magician to let himself out then lock the door behind him. She'd already found her keys, and she had the only one to the place.

No way Weirdo had a key. Besides, the door was locked from inside. Inside. Which meant, if Weirdo had been here, he should still be here. And he wasn't, unless he was hiding in the U-bend of the toilet.

There weren't a whole lot of places to hide in here.

Man, she was thirsty.

Marina went back to the bathroom and gulped more water. Shaking her head at her reflection in the small mirror, she went into the back room, changed her clothes and went to the futon. Hopefully she would look better in the morning. If she didn't, she'd have to borrow some of Lisa's make-up to hide her pallor.

Marcos scowled at the dark window of Marina's shop. He hated himself, but he'd become something of an unwilling stalker. He told himself he was hunting in the area – as usual – but he knew better.

Her shop window was never dark this early on a Friday night.

Hating himself even more, Marcos ducked into an alley, out of human sight, and thought about where he wanted to be.

Patchouli assaulted him. Would she never desist using that foul incense? She could at least choose another scent.

Still, it was comforting to him in a way. It was her. It was this place.

He looked to the futon. Yes, the scent of her was still heavy there. She still slept here. Nightly. Perhaps she'd merely gone to obtain a meal. But she was never gone this early on a Friday night. It was one of her busiest.

Perhaps she was contracted to read fortunes for a party. It was one of the things she advertised she was available for.

Marcos wandered into the back room, where she kept her things. There was a bookcase he ran his fingers over the top of and smiled. She'd polished it. He could still feel the oil along the grain. He could see her in his mind, rubbing the surface with a cloth and the orange oil he could still smell faintly. She'd done it perhaps a week ago. She liked things clean.

A hardcover book rested open to a page depicting a tarot card. Marcos reached for the cover and lifted it, wishing to see the title of what she was reading.

An envelope slipped from the pages and fluttered to the floor at his feet.

He curled his fingers in a beckoning gesture and the envelope came to his hand. His brow furrowed at the name scrawled on it.

"Angel".

Inside was a yellow scrap of square paper with a rough, unmistakably uneducated note scrawled on it: "*Ain't much, but good for your first week back. Pass these around and there'll be more* – Benny."

In the envelope were black cards emblazoned with stars and the logo of the "gentleman's club" two streets over.

"*Featuring the return of Angel! Two shows on Fridays!*" the cards proclaimed across the bottom in silver letters.

He remembered their brief conversation about "entertainment".

And it was Friday.

Surely not. Not her. She was his. *His* Angel. She should be here for him, not . . . not *there* . . . sharing any part of herself with . . . anyone else.

Marcos scowled. He didn't think about anything but his need and disappeared.

The envelope wafted to the floor, scattering the cards beneath it.

★   ★   ★

One more show to go, Marina thought, staring wearily into the mirror that stood in what Benny laughably called the "dressing room". She was just about to apply more mascara when she was jerked to her feet by strong hands.

Her eyes widened as she realized it wasn't Benny.

Oh, God, Weirdo. How had he found her, and how had he gotten in here?

She tried to speak, even scream, but no sound would come.

Even so, Marcos brought up a hand and stilled any sound she would have made with a thought. It would not do to have her screams summon anyone.

As though they would do so, in this place, even if they could be heard over that noise they call music, Marcos thought wryly.

Marcos looked helplessly at the woman before him.

He should simply take her memories of him and leave. Or kill her and be done with it. It would be for the best. *Madre de Dios*, he could not do it. Marcos brought a fist to his forehead with a groan.

He shook his head and waved a hand at the woman before him, releasing her from the suspension he'd put on her.

"What are you doing here?!" she demanded, taking a step back. She groped behind her for anything she might use as a weapon. "Get out!"

"Stop," Marcos ordered firmly, gesturing at her again. "I won't harm you. I will answer all of your questions, I swear, if you will answer one for me."

Marina couldn't move.

"O–OK," she stammered.

"I will release my hold on you if you assure me you will not run or otherwise be a problem," Marcos said, glaring at her pointedly.

His hold? He wasn't even touching her. But then . . . why couldn't she move?

"Sure," she replied, barely able to get the word out past the fear choking her throat. "No problem."

"Not here," he said, shaking his head. He reached out and touched her shoulder, and suddenly they were no longer in the noisy club, but in the back room of her shop.

Marcos lowered his hand and recalled his power.

"What the—" she began. "How did you—"

"As I said, I will answer all of your questions, after you answer mine," he reminded her. "Your pendant," he said, his eyes deliberately trailing to her cleavage. "It means something. I know it does. What?"

Was he serious? What was it about that thing that he was so fascinated with?

"It's been in the family for ever," she said hesitantly. "One of my great-great-great grandmothers or something had it. Look, if you want it, just take it. There's no need to hurt me. It's yours, OK?"

Marcos scowled at her. "I'm no thief," he replied in disdain.

"Then what do you want?" Marina asked, taking another step back. She snapped on the fluorescent light above them. "You . . . you kidnap me . . . somehow, break in here—"

"I haven't 'broken in'," Marcos interrupted. "But that makes no difference now. You've already given me 'what I want'. All that remains now is what I wish to do with it."

"The pendant?" Marina ventured, confused.

"Your answer," he replied, shaking his head. "Would you mind turning off that overhead light? I find it particularly disturbing," she heard him say.

"Um . . . OK," she found herself replying, but before she could move, the fluorescent light went out and every candle in the place illuminated.

"Much better," Marcos said, smiling again. He studied Marina carefully. Heard her thoughts, her rapid heartbeat, the pulse of the blood beneath her pale skin.

"Calm yourself, Mary. I said, I won't harm you. I do wish to be more comfortable, however, now that it is time for me to fulfil my end of our bargain."

He didn't look so frightening in the candlelight.

Their bargain?

"I said I would answer your questions if you answered mine," he reminded her.

"Who are you?" Marina blurted.

Marcos gestured to the futon behind her. "Do you wish to sit? A glass of water, perhaps? Tea?"

Marina crossed her arms over her chest. "No, I want you to answer me," she said, unyielding. "I've asked you who you are several times now and you keep dodging the question. Who *are* you? And why is my angel pendant so important to you?"

"My name is Marcos Aquino de los Santos," he replied quietly.

"And that pendant . . . the symbol you display on your window. Do you know what kind of angel it is?"

Marina shrugged. "It bears a sword. It's likely Michael or possibly Uriel."

Marcos shook his head. "Michael and Uriel are Archangels. Your angel has six wings. It is a seraph."

"Seraph?" Marina echoed.

"Surely you're aware of the difference in the choirs of the Host," he said, disbelieving.

Marina shrugged again. "Angels are angels."

"I doubt very much they would agree with you," Marcos replied wryly. He nodded to her pendant. "That particular depiction is not only a seraph, it is the device of the Destrati."

"And that means what to me?" Marina asked, rapidly losing her patience with his condescension.

"It is the symbol used by a vampire clan," Marcos said.

Marina just looked at him and took another slow step back away from him. "OK, well, that's nice to know. Now, why don't you leave and not come back," she said.

Marcos heard her disparaging thoughts and scowled at her again.

"I'm not crazy, or delusional," he said, unimpressed. "You're perfectly happy to assist people in contacting their supposed spirit guides and dead relatives, but you're unwilling to acknowledge the existence of other immortal creatures? Even those standing right before you?"

"So you think you're a vampire?" Marina asked with a contemptuous snort.

"Just because you can't fathom the fact that I am indeed centuries old doesn't make me the liar in the room."

"Hey! No one's calling you a liar," Marina protested. "So you carry the vampire fantasy a little far with your black coat and fangs and the idea that you're some really old Spanish guy. What, did one of your history books fall on your head or something while you were in school? Whatever happened, it's OK. You don't need me to believe you in order to leave."

"Nor do I claim to be that which I am not for my own gain," Marcos replied with a smirk. His eyes swept over her meaningfully. "I wouldn't say anything about carrying a fantasy too far, *madam*."

Marina opened her mouth to say something, then blushed and

shook her head, lowering her eyes in shame. He crossed to her and brought a finger under her chin, and raised it slowly.

"Look at me," he ordered.

She did so.

He flashed a wicked smile at her.

Marina gasped at the sight of his pointed incisors. He should seriously see a dentist about those.

"Truth does not require belief," he said quietly, laughing inwardly at himself for quoting an oft-used ethereal adage. It was one of the things he'd first learned, as a fledgling. From Clan Destrati. The clan who'd found and fostered him. Who'd helped him live again, instead of merely survive.

The Clan – *the family* – he'd all but forgotten until he found the angel. His *Angel*.

Dios. How could he have forgotten? How could he have not understood? His endless hunger would be sated by an angel. That was the curse laid on him ages ago by one of the Host he'd inadvertently fed upon. One that had been masquerading as human, performing a task or other such thing it had been set to on the mortal plane.

His all-consuming hunger had driven everything else from his mind, including the fact that such ravenousness was part of the blight set upon him by an angel. The Messenger did not find his inadvertent attack amusing, and decided to teach Marcos a lesson in being more selective in his hunting.

He continued. "Something about you was familiar. The pendant. The angel on the window. Your blood. Nothing made sense."

"You bit me!" Marina cried suddenly, her hand going to her neck as she remembered the bruise that had only recently faded enough not to need to be concealed with make-up. Bruises were bad for business, according to Benny.

"Yes," Marcos said, nonchalant and unrepentant. "But I did not kill you. I stopped feeding from you once the familiarity overwhelmed me, and now I know why."

He cut himself off, unable to go on. He dropped his hold and walked a few paces away.

"Why?" she prompted, taking a hesitant step towards him. "Go on. Why, Marcos?"

Marina was always good at remembering names. She had to be,

in her business. It's the only real talent she had – her memory for names, faces and personal information.

He looked up at her.

"'*And ye shall wander, alone and unfulfilled, awaiting a merciful angel that will deliver thee.*'"

"What?" Marina asked softly.

"I remember," Marcos said in quiet wonder. "I remember it all now. You're the answer. You've broken the curse, my merciful Angel."

"Curse?"

Marcos laughed softly. "I even forgot the answer to ending my torment. Even if I hadn't, I doubt I would have considered that the 'merciful angel' would be one such as you."

"What? A psychic? An erotic dancer?" Marina asked, scowling at him.

"A human," Marcos answered bluntly.

The device of Clan Destrati remained unchanged over the centuries – a six-winged seraph standing with a blazing sword. The pendant marked the wearer as under the protection of the clan. Marcos lifted the chain with a finger.

"Even one wearing the device of my clan," he continued. "How did you come by this?"

"There's an old story my grandma used to tell, about how one of our ancestors lived after being attacked by a vampire," Marina stammered, unsure. "Since there's no such thing, and it was an old story – every family has one – we just thought it was, you know, something she told us just to get us to behave or the reason we had to go to church or something. In it a priest came by and gave my ancestor help of some kind, and this pendant. Grandma said it would keep me safe when she gave it to me, and it might be silly, but so far, it's worked. I just wear it now because . . . you know . . . angels."

She shrugged.

Marcos nodded slowly. "Humans are prey to my kind, and though I should do so, I cannot renounce you," Marcos said softly, beside her again without her noticing him move. "No matter what symbol you wear . . . or what clothes you're wearing . . . or not wearing . . ."

His closeness was overpowering. Marina looked up at him. He was taller than she remembered, than he was in her dreams. He had no scent, except the smell of his long leather coat. His dark eyes were hard to look away from, and she found she didn't want to. His arm found her waist, and he bent his head to place a gentle kiss on her brow.

"Mmm," Marina murmured as she found herself leaning in to him, in spite of the fact that she'd sworn off men for a long time to come. She'd had enough of men to last her a while. "Why haven't I been able to forget you since the night you stormed in here?"

"Because I'm in your blood, quite literally," he replied. "It knows me. I acted upon the overwhelming hunger within me, and it realized, even if I didn't, what it was I held in my arms. Had I known . . . "

His lips brushed against hers lightly.

"How would you like to sleep elsewhere tonight?" Marcos asked gently. He brushed an errant lock of her hair back over her ear. "In a real bed?"

"Yours?" she asked wryly. "You're gorgeous, honey, I'll give you that, and seriously sexy, but I don't do dead guys. That's just wrong."

Marcos laughed and lowered his lips to her neck.

"I'm not dead," he whispered in her ear. "Do I feel dead to you?"

He pressed his lean body against hers. She felt his desire hard against her thigh as his hand moved from her waist to her behind.

She gasped as he caressed her bottom, so unlike the way some guys did when she'd been a waitress. Unlike the way they did at the club when they thought the bouncer wasn't looking.

Oh, God, please never let him stop doing what he is doing. Marina surprised herself with the thought. She couldn't remember the last time she'd wanted a man to touch her. She didn't like men fondling her. She didn't like their closeness or their hot, heavy breathing or the way they looked at her when they were turned on. The way they wanted her. Men were pigs.

"I'm not a pig, *Angel*."

Marina's eyes widened as he spoke her thought aloud. The way he said her name, with that sexy accent. "*Ahn-hel*."

Marcos laughed again at the incredulity in her mind. He nipped at her neck, teasing, and pulled back to smile at her.

"You have a great deal to learn about a great many things," he said indulgently. "The first of which is that, though I am a vampire, I am not one of the 'undead'. This body is soulless, to be sure, but it is still very much alive. I have never died. I traded my soul for immortality. I have spent the whole of a human lifetime drowning in desperate, unfulfilled hunger, and now that it is finally sated, I find another desire has taken its place."

He lowered his lips to hers again.

Marina whimpered at the feel of his kiss. It was unreal, unlike anything she'd ever experienced, and she had more experience than she cared to think about.

She slid her arms around his neck as the kiss deepened, grateful he was truly there doing what he'd done nightly in her dreams.

Oh, God. What if he'd never come back?

"I would have come back," Marcos assured her, hearing her thought. "If only because I was curious as to why I didn't take your blood that first night. Now how about that bed? A decent meal, a bath . . . "

"Hey now," Marina said, pulling back to glare at him. "I just took a shower at the gym this morning."

"And you reek of that foul incense, not to mention the sweat of lesser, though no less desirous men," Marcos replied. "A thorough shower wouldn't harm you. Those I'm going to take you to meet will insist upon it, besides. Their sensibilities are just as acute as mine are, and just as easily offended. Sometimes more so."

"Where are we going?" Marina asked through a nervous laugh.

"To meet my family," he replied quietly.

Clan Destrati. It had been so long. Would they remember him? Had they given him up for lost or slain? Clan wars still raged.

"Now?" she asked, pulling him back to her with an impish grin. "We were just getting acquainted and you're ready for me to meet the family?"

Marcos laughed in spite of himself and smiled back at her, baring his fangs unashamedly.

Those were seriously disturbing, but nonetheless impressive.

"So you're a vampire, huh? Have you come to suck my blood?" she teased, offering her neck playfully.

Marcos laughed again.

"Lead me not into temptation, señorita," he replied as he nipped at her throat. "I am perfectly capable of finding it on my own, especially with your intoxicating nearness. I've yet to eat this evening."

Marina whimpered. Her arms slid around his neck, her fingers curling into his dark hair.

Soft bites accompanied the kisses along her neck up to her mouth. Marcos looked into her eyes for a moment, wanting to see the breathless desire he knew would be there. Marinia was indeed finding it particularly difficult to breathe at the moment. Don't lead him into temptation, huh? She remembered the Lord's Prayer from Sunday school.

"Lead us not into temptation, but deliver us from evil."

He was one evil she found herself praying not to be delivered from.

Blood and Thyme

Camille Bacon-Smith

"Have you fed tonight?"

Martin Harris looked up from the computer screen with forks and spoons dancing in his head – Rachmaninoff played softly on his iPod, so it was a strange dance – and blinked a minute to backburner the flatware counts. It was dark in the tiny office tucked next to the pantry, with nothing but the glow of the laptop screen for light, but he could see well enough. The dim light from the kitchen picked up the silver in Frank's hair, carved shadows at the corners of his mouth as he waited patiently in the doorway, his sleeve already rolled past his wrist. A quick sip wouldn't hurt, but Martin had fed before the party. He didn't need it right now, and Frank was looking a little pale anyway – Helene had kept him busy tonight.

"No, I'm good."

"Do you need anything else before I go?"

Over Frank's shoulder, the dimmed kitchen overheads cast a pale glow on the gleaming stainless steel refrigerators, reminding Martin of his singular failure. "Can you cook?"

Frank laughed softly. "No better than the last time you asked. Unless you need something else, I'm going to send everybody home."

Martin thought a minute. Clean-up was done for the night. They could inventory plates in the morning. "No, that's fine. Let the staff know they did an excellent job. They should be pleased with their envelopes." Helene DeCourcy's tip had been outrageous even by Red Heart standards. Worth it though. The staff kept their mouths shut and his clients fed, and they showed up for the next gig every time he called. Sometimes, they were a little too loyal.

"You're sitting out the next one. And grab a roast beef sandwich before you go. It's bad for my reputation when my headwaiter faints in the hors d'oeuvres."

"Yeah, I know." Frank laughed, stripped off his jacket, a black tuxedo with a discreet red heart embroidered on the lapel. "But it was Helene and I need a new transmission." Frank never let the puncture marks show, but it would take a serious inspection to find where Helene DeCourcy had fed. Best customer, best headwaiter the company ever had, and Martin thought there was more than snacking going on there, maybe had been for thirty years. But he was no good to Martin if he showed up a quart low.

"One more thing. Second Street's off-limits tonight." Second Street had a couple of after-hours clubs where the restaurant crowd gathered for a drink when the customers had all gone home. But not his staff. Not tonight.

"Hunting?" Frank paused in the doorway, a silver brow raised speculatively.

Martin didn't deny it. Helene had used Red Heart Catering for over a hundred years, and he was still the only game in town for a party like they had tonight, where the guests fed on canapés and the well-turned wrist. But Helene had already warned him about the next one. The mayor was invited.

Martin needed a chef.

"Have you heard of Rita DeLeone?" He waited while Frank went through his own mental filing system.

"Didn't she run Prescot's catering side for a while? Last I heard, she'd left him for a little ten-table place of her own in a strip mall in Cherry Hill. Good food, by all accounts. Don't know what happened to it."

"Snow." Martin had done his homework. "The roof fell in. She's doing pick-up work this side of Broad."

Restaurant Row had a demanding clientele. Frank broke into a wide grin. "My God, we could finally get you out of the kitchen! For that I'd give up drinking entirely!" He left with a backwards wave of his hand. "Nobody will get in your way tonight."

Then Martin was alone with the hum of the refrigerators. He had to do this, for the good of the company. So he ran his fingers through his hair to bring the short blond spikes back to some sort of attention, left his tailored overcoat in the closet and slipped into the bomber jacket instead. Out there somewhere was the answer to all his problems. He just had to find her.

"Card?" Let-out, when the bars all tipped their customers onto the sidewalk to fend for themselves, had come and gone but Stan's place stayed open late for members only. At Stan's, that meant five bucks and a job in the business. Rita flashed her card and slipped in past the guard at the door. The club wasn't much wider than a railroad car but it went back for half a block under a narrow tin ceiling that hadn't dumped a ton of snow onto the kitchen in all its 150 years. The crowd was comfortable, winding down after a long night serving other people. Rita said a few "hellos" on her way to the bar and grabbed the last empty stool, caught some guy with spiky blond hair and a leather bomber jacket staring. He looked away quickly, fussed with the bottle of Sly Fox IPA in front of him, but she knew the look.

Her lucky night, except she doubted his interest involved her legs, her curves, or the long dark hair she let down in unruly waves after work. He probably just hadn't gotten the word yet. Her restaurant was still sitting under the rubble. She gave Doug behind the bar a half-hearted smile. "Yingling," she said, ordering a decent, reasonable local lager instead of her usual, and mentally put another five dollars in the piggy bank. Doug had already gone for the wine bottle, or she might have gotten away with it.

Behind her, something caught his eye. "Courtesy of the gentleman." He set a wine glass on the bar, filled it and left the bottle.

Bomber Jacket Guy angled in next to her, an elbow covered in old, worn leather propped on the dinged-up mahogany. She really was not in the mood. "Tell the gentleman I can buy my own drinks, thank you." But Doug was already pulling beers for a crew at the end of the bar and pointedly not listening.

"Looking for a job?" Bomber Jacket Guy was about thirty-five, she guessed, with blue eyes pale as ice. She'd already noticed the hair – a little too metro for her tastes, if she'd been looking. Which she wasn't.

She considered possible answers – *Not in that line of work. It'll cost you more than a bottle of wine* – but Bleu's chef was back on Monday and her restaurant, Sophie's, was in shambles. Rita was pretty desperate for a job, so she lifted the glass and said, "What've you got?" instead.

He leaned in, set his beer on the bar. "Martin Harris. And it's what I *don't* have that's the problem." He held out his hand, realized the bottle had dewed it up and grabbed a napkin from a stack next to the beer taps with a self-conscious smile on lips that really weren't bad. But that line? Awful.

He seemed to know it and was laughing at himself, so she had to laugh with him.

"Weak. I'd give it a six."

"True, though."

OK, she'd grant him the killer smile. Average height, average build. A little athletic, maybe, but he didn't look like he worked out, which was a plus. It might not cost him more than a bottle of wine after all.

The woman next to her slapped a ten on the bar and got up to leave. Martin Harris slid onto the abandoned stool like he'd been waiting for it all his life. Another Sly Fox appeared in front of him and Rita realized that she'd lost track of the conversation . . .

"High profile . . . Four hundred . . . Wednesday."

"I'm a chef. If you're looking for waiters, there're three of them down the bar."

"You're what I need. Really. My chef moved back to Paris. She taught me everything I know before she left but –"

"Right." Then she fed him the punchline just to see what he'd do. "Not everything *she* knew."

"She's my mother and even she said I was hopeless. I pay really well when I'm desperate." He slid a card across the bar – address printed on the right and a rounded red heart on the left. Red Heart Catering. They'd been around a long time. Very discreet, so she didn't know much about them, but very high end.

"You don't even know that I can cook!"

"Prescot's liked you well enough," he pointed out. And yeah, she could cook for a crowd. But then he said, "Sophie's, on Route 73. It needed a serious upgrade on the décor, but the veal medallions with sweetbreads were perfect."

If he thought the décor wasn't much then, he should see the place now. But he'd liked the food, which started a warm, blanket-by-the-fire feeling under her ribs that Rita knew meant trouble. She was not going to fall for a guy who was not her type just because he liked her sweetbreads. She drank the wine anyway, and it felt soft rolling down her throat. Hadn't expected the way his eyes warmed up when she tilted her head back. It threw her enough that she answered him with "Wednesday?" before she knew what she was saying, or offering.

Watching the play of muscles against the stretch of her throat as she swallowed, his mouth went dry. A good beer was fine, and he'd told Frank the truth, he didn't need to feed this soon. But his fingers itched for the nape of her neck and only force of will kept his points retracted. Her pulse filled his senses, throbbing on her skin and beating in his ears, and he matched her, heartbeat for heartbeat, without thinking. Oh, gods, the scent rising off her skin – warm living blood on the inside and the smells of a kitchen still clinging on the outside. Butternut squash and striped bass and truffles rising like the hope of heaven through the aloe and lilac of her soap. He'd pay anything she asked for just the occasional sip, but knew better than to make the proposition. He needed her too badly as his chef to risk a red-heart offer. Maybe after Helene's party for the mayor . . .

Her chin came down and she set the glass aside. The moment passed and he hadn't done anything to scare her away.

"Wednesday?" she said again, reminding him he had business to conduct here.

"At eight, with Helene DeCourcy, to finalize the menu." He poured her another glass of wine. She was pretty – especially her wide, dark eyes and, well, her throat – which complicated things. He'd already figured her for smart, which helped on the business end, and that also complicated things. But Helene had been adamant about the food.

"We've got the Great Stair Hall and balcony at the Art Museum. If you're free on Monday, around six, we can go over the plans. You can make any changes to the menu that seem appropriate, and we'll meet with Helene on Wednesday. She just needs some reassurance that I won't poison the mayor. When word gets around that we have a new chef, you'll have plenty to do. In the meantime, you'll want to revise menus, maybe make some changes in kitchen staff. I'll leave that all up to you."

Too much. He'd had her through the mayor's party, but she pulled back when he started talking about a longer calendar. By the time he'd reached "up to you" she had pushed her glass away and Martin clamped his mouth shut. He wished he'd done it a few minutes earlier, before she felt the need to remind him, "This is strictly short term. I'm just waiting for repairs to my roof. Best veal medallions with sweetbreads in New Jersey, remember?"

Martin had done a thorough job of the research. The owners of that strip mall had taken the insurance money and walked away, leaving the place without a roof and Sophie's without a home. "Just get me through dinner with the mayor." He nudged the card a little closer. "After that, we'll take it one party at a time."

She had the right address, had checked it out in daylight and remembered the three white candles in the window. Red Heart Catering stood at the corner of 20th and Delancey in a perfectly maintained Victorian brownstone mansion. Imposing. A little terrifying for a Jersey girl, but she needed the job. Rita took a deep breath, climbed the half-flight to the elegant red front door, and rang the bell below a brass plate with the company name and the little rounded heart on it.

Something was different. She looked more closely at the card and saw a perfectly formed bead, like a jewel or a drop of blood, falling from the heart. It had to be a flaw in the printing, but it glistened in the light from the gas lamps that bracketed the door. Heart's blood. The door opened and she took a startled step back, would have cracked her head on the pavement below if not for Martin Harris' hand under her elbow.

"Miss DeLeone. I'm glad you came." He was looking considerably more rumpled than he had on Saturday night, the spikes of his hair flattened on one side of his head and skewed oddly on the other. He saw her looking and rubbed self-consciously at the wrong side. "Not quite awake yet," he said. "Working nights." He turned to lead her into the house, and maybe it was just her imagination, but she thought he wouldn't look her in the eye when he said it.

"If I've interrupted something, I can come back." She half expected a girl to wander out dressed in a sheet. Or a boy. Whatever. She didn't want to be there when it happened, not if he was going to be her boss. Not if he was going to look that . . . rumpled.

But he waved his free hand, dismissing the offer. "No, I should have been up anyway. Don't want to start with a bad impression." The apology came with a wry twitch of his lips, as if a nap had used up all his currency for cool. She couldn't help but shake her head. She hadn't known him long enough to call him an idiot, but she was thinking it.

She'd expected elegance when she saw the address and the foyer didn't disappoint her – not the parquetry rosette under her feet or the pale blue silk on the walls. "This is my office," he said, and opened a side door onto a Victorian parlour with a very modern laptop on the correspondence desk. He closed the door again, led her to the centre pocket-doors, and nudged them open silently. "This is the ballroom."

She'd known that some of the Gilded-Age mansions in this part of town had them, but this perfectly preserved jewel of a ballroom still took her breath away—from the gleaming floors to the cream-coloured taffeta on the walls and the mirrors that reflected the light from the Austrian-crystal chandeliers hanging from a ceiling painted with woodland scenes of corseted ladies and frolicking nymphs. Draperies the same fabric as the wall-covering filled one end of the room. Martin Harris flipped a switch and the drapes parted to reveal a small stage behind them.

"Oh, my!"

"I know. Sometimes I don't believe it myself." He didn't turn off the lights, but led her across the polished-oak dance floor. "My great grandfather built the house in the 1870s. He lost most of the family fortune in the crash of 1893. My great-grandmother started as his cook then kept the house afloat cooking for other people. When it came to losing the house or making an honest woman of her, he married her. We've been in the business ever since."

It wasn't just a business to Martin Harris. She could hear the warmth in his voice, the pride and love for the house and the family that built it. Something clicked in Rita when he told his story. She felt a kinship with that long-ago grandmother who supported her family with her cooking. His mother too, he'd said. She'd been his chef until she left for Paris. Rita fought the feeling that she was a part of that line of women because she needed to be sensible about this job, needed to be wary. Waiters and under-cooks liked to tell stories, but nobody had stories about Red Heart Catering. They paid well and their clients liked privacy. That was it. Not even "Martin Harris is a really nice guy," or "Martin Harris is an asshole, but he pays well." Just the same zombified answer until she'd given up asking.

He had her – saw it in her eyes – and he started to relax, adding up the bill at Godshalls Poultry and Iovines and a half-dozen more of his suppliers. Metropolitan Bakery, too. Unless . . . did she want them to make the bread in-house? His mother had, but most places bought it in these days.

Then he was losing her again and he didn't know what to do. He didn't quite believe anyone with the stardust he'd just seen in Rita DeLeone's eyes could walk away from this house.

"Imagine what it was like in 1870," he tried, with a glance to fill the ballroom with long-ago dancers. "Ladies in their ruffled silk dresses, and gentlemen in their evening coats and dancing shoes. A little orchestra on the stage, playing Strauss."

He slid his left hand down her arm, lifted her wrist lightly while he settled his right hand at her back. "May I have this dance?" he whispered in her ear. The warmth of her filled his senses as he swept her into a waltz.

With each turn, more memories crowded the floor: the orchestra played Strauss under gas lights that glittered off the crystals of the chandeliers while the mirrors threw back the images of the dancers going round and round – his mother and father, Helene and her lover, scandalous even among their own kind, and a hundred more couples dancing until dawn. It made him dizzy, delirious with the heat and the music and the dance, whirling, whirling. The needle points of his teeth itched, but he suppressed every instinct to feed.

This was about the mayor's party. It had nothing to do with the soft curves in his arms or the moist heat rising from behind her ear with the promise of blood and thyme. He needed her desperately – in his kitchen. But golden memories fizzed like champagne in his blood, confusing now and then, need and desire. He looked into her eyes, saw the joy and the music shining back at him, and couldn't look away. His whole world shifted on its axis and settled in a new plane, fixed on the smell of her blood and the feel of her touch and the hunger in her eyes. He'd never be free of it, not until the day he died. And if he told her, and she walked away, he'd lose everything. He was lost. Knew it and couldn't do a thing about it.

He'd fixed on Rita DeLeone. Shit. Damn. Hell. I am so screwed, he thought. And he dropped her hand as if it burned.

Magical. The room or the dance, or his glance that kept shifting between the past glory of the house and the present with her in his arms, was magical. She didn't know what dazzled her more, the light from the crystal chandeliers or the hungry gleam in his eyes, but she could have fallen forever into that long-ago world he evoked with whispers in her ear. Unconsciously she arched her back, the better to look into his eyes, where the darkness at their centres had pushed back the blue, offering pools of mystery where ice had lain. She wanted those mysteries, every one of them, starting with his mouth and working down from there. Buttons. So many buttons.

Then he took a step back, wiped his hands self-consciously on his rumpled Dockers, and said, "Upstairs we have three smaller party rooms and a staging kitchen."

It was over. Whatever it was. Rita wanted to scream, wanted to run, but he kept on talking. "On the third floor we have a few guest bedrooms. I have the basement apartment, so I'm on-site most of the time if you need me." He was walking a pace ahead of her, taking them away from the magic, past a room with a couple of chairs next to the stage, to the very back of the house. "Guest bathrooms are on the other side of the stage, and this is the kitchen. Pantry here, staff bath, and your office."

The kitchen was adequate: clean, which mattered a lot; pantry well stocked. The refrigerators were new, the stove not as good as the one waiting in her garage, but it would do for somebody. Not Rita. She was out of here, just as soon as he finished his tour and she found a door.

The office was small, and he'd been using it between chefs. He riffled through a stack of menus and pulled one out with a triumphant "Aha!" before he handed it to her. "For Mrs DeCourcy's party. Starred items are her preferences. We want to make sure we cover them. The rest you can change if you like. Mom took her personal recipes with her, but we've got a good library of the basics.

"And now, if you don't mind, we have a late job in Baltimore and I have to get ready. If you need anything else, just make a list and give it to Frank. Frank McCaffey's our headwaiter and he should be here any minute. He'll take care of everything."

He was wandering away while he talked, then opened a door she hadn't seen before to a staircase leading down. His basement apartment, she figured. He was leaving her behind with the invoices and the menus.

"I can't take the job," she muttered. He couldn't hear her, was already gone, so she added, "Because you're making me crazy," under her breath, and tripped over a dignified man with silver hair and a tuxedo who had come in behind her.

"Sorry. I'm Frank McCaffey, by the way," he said, and took a step back. "I didn't know anyone was here."

"I'm Rita DeLeone," she answered tartly. "And I'm not staying."

"Is there anything I can say to change your mind?" Frank's eyes didn't pull her in like a vortex, but they crinkled in the corners with warm understanding that made her almost as nervous as his boss did. "He makes us all crazy sometimes, but is that any reason to let him poison the mayor?"

The mayor. The Great Stair Hall. She had to do it, just to prove to herself that she could still pull off an affair like that. "Just the one party," she told him and figured he'd get the message to his boss. "For the mayor, not for Mr Martin Harris. That's it."

"It's enough," he answered. She didn't believe he meant it, but she wasn't giving Mr Harris a choice. The menu would do for now. She could manage it and his next chef would want to change things to suit anyway. But it sure wasn't going to be her.

Helene welcomed them into her office, which was a sleek, modern contrast to the parts of the house the public got to see. Helene was a sleek contrast to the house as well, with silver hair cut short and angled to highlight her sharp, high cheekbones. She offered coffee waiting in a pot on the desk. Martin poured three cups. He didn't know how Rita DeLeone liked her coffee, or if she liked it at all, but she handed over the menu in its leather cover then took the cup, added a little cream, and smiled politely when Martin made the introduction.

Martin sat back and watched as Rita went quickly over the menu, answering Helene's questions and offering her own suggestions to balance simple but elegant options with the more challenging fare. When they were done, Helene handed back the leather folder and passed a measuring frown from Rita to Martin. "Does she know what she's getting into with Red Heart?"

That was the question he didn't want to hear. Because, no, he hadn't told her and didn't plan to, at least not until after the party. "I stole her from Prescot's." It answered the surface question Rita would understand – could she cook as well for 400 as she did for 40?

– but ignored the trouble he was in, because she wouldn't understand that at all.

"Very well." Helene didn't approve, but conceded the point for the moment. She rose to show them the door. Martin followed her and stumbled – damn, he hadn't expected to slip up like that.

"Are you all right?" Rita DeLeone's hand fell on his arm and it felt like fire burning right through his jacket.

Control. Control. He kept the needle points of his teeth retracted. "I'm fine."

Helene had known him since the day he was born, had known his mother when she'd built Red Heart. She didn't miss much, and she hadn't missed this. "Would you mind waiting in the hall for just a moment, Miss DeLeone?"

Rita left, reluctantly, and with a promise: "I'll be right outside this door if you need me." Then Helene pressed him back into his chair, which he didn't need because he was fine now, really.

"When was the last time you fed?" She held his face in her hands, watching for a lie.

He had to think about the answer. "Saturday." He stared at the three white candles on her mantel – sanctuary, hearth and home – counting up the days. He hadn't realized it had been so long. "I think it was Saturday."

"Why? Are you trying to kill yourself?"

"I'm not. I didn't realize—" Dani had stopped by and he'd turned her down, paid her anyway because it was her day and she depended on the money, but: "I just wasn't hungry. Nobody smells right any more."

Helene went very still. "You didn't." She sighed, because it could only mean one thing. "Oh God, child, you haven't fixed on the chef, have you? You haven't even told her what you are!"

"I don't know how it happened."

"I know, my dear, it happens that way sometimes." But he could tell from the sound of her voice that she didn't know, that she thought he was a fool. "You have to eat." Rasp of a pearl button on silk as she undid the cuff of her blouse, and her wrist was under his nose, not smelling like food and warmth and blood and home, but something sure and familiar nonetheless. He let his points come down this time. They ached because he hadn't fed in too long, and he'd been holding them back around Rita.

"I'll give Marcus a call; he'll come over tomorrow," she said, and stroked his hair while he fed. It wasn't quite the same from his own kind, wasn't human enough, but it would keep him alive until he figured out what to do.

He retracted the needle points into his teeth and wiped his mouth with the back of his hand. "I'll be fine." He shook his head and it didn't make him dizzy this time. "I can handle it."

"By not eating? Mind over matter won't help. Beef carpaccio in truffle oil won't help. Marcus and I won't help for long. If you don't have living human blood, you'll die."

"I won't let that happen."

"I think you will, my darling boy," she said, which was ridiculous. He was almost as old as his house. But she sighed again, and said, "Accept Marcus tomorrow. Promise me. It's not enough, but it will do for now. And I want a Red Heart party for next Saturday. Fifty guests, costumes for all, Gilded-Age theme. We'll take two rooms upstairs, card tables and refreshments in one, buffet supper in the other, and the bedrooms for privacy. Set up the ballroom for dancing. Hire the usual for music. A party like the old days. It will be a test of your new chef."

"There's not enough time." A party like that could take months to pull together. She'd given him three days. Rita was going to kill him.

"I know you'll manage. Red Heart never lets its clients down."

"She can't know," he said. Feeding was always a private matter, but a Red Heart party was supposed to be safe space. "I need her in the kitchen. If she walks, the business will die."

"More than the business will die, sweet boy. Give me my party. We'll see what we can do. Oh, and one other thing – send Frank over tomorrow? I'll discuss details of service with him and free you up for more pressing matters."

"Frank can't wear the red heart yet."

"Don't worry about Frank. I have other interests in him. Like my party."

And it was true that Helene had never fixed on Frank. She liked him, had preferred him at her parties from the moment he joined the company, but she had other favourites as well, and occasionally liked something new for variety. Unlike Helene, his mother had fixed on a human husband, and Martin had been the result of that.

Humans died, and his mother had mourned his father's loss through two world wars. He didn't want that in his life. Didn't want to watch Rita DeLeone grow old and die. Didn't want to mourn her into the next millennium. His mother might know what to do, but Martin wasn't ready to tell her how badly he'd screwed up until he solved the problem himself.

"Saturday," he agreed, and wiped his mouth again because he didn't want Rita to know. He couldn't believe that such a minor inconvenience could suddenly become this huge thing in his life. It was just blood. He only needed a sip, it was nothing. But he couldn't tell her. And he couldn't drink from anyone else.

"We'd better tell Rita. About the party."

Saturday. She could not believe Martin had agreed to do this, and she told Frank McCaffey so. "If he didn't own the property, and if he hadn't turned away his other clients with his cooking, we'd be having this party in the parking lot at Trader Joe's!"

Helene DeCourcy's house could easily handle a less ambitious party for fifty, but she didn't want a mill and swill with finger food. "Costumes!"

"It's almost Mardi Gras," Frank pointed out and kept on counting napkins – serviettes, he called them. She hadn't heard that term since cooking school.

"Parking lot. Trader Joe's," she answered back, satisfied that he really had to work to hide his smile. She had a prep cook on the buffet and two cooks working on the light refreshments for the card room. Martin had rejected her own suggestion for prep cook, but he'd had some kitchen staff already, so that turned out all right. She'd pulled in Doug to handle the drinks because he worked hard and didn't hit on the guests.

The waiters would arrive in about two hours. Frank had that well in hand. "The usuals," he assured her. "They know Helene, they know her parties. We'll be fine." Hard not to believe him when he called the client by her first name like he'd been doing it for a hundred years, so she took his word for it and went on to the next worry on her list, this one not as easy to let go of.

"Where's Martin?"

Frank checked his watch. "He should be up by now, probably in the shower. I'd give him another fifteen minutes before I started to worry." But the reminder cut a frown between his brows. It was after six. Helene's invitations said eleven thirty. The food was under control – a standing rib roast in one oven, a ham in the other for the card room, and the quail stuffed with fois gras was prepped and waiting in the fridge. But they needed to do a last walk-through upstairs, and Martin hadn't shown his face in the kitchen yet.

"So, what's his problem?" She pretended it was a casual question while she inspected the list on her clipboard. They were far enough from the prep area that they wouldn't be overheard. It turned out she liked working here. Liked Frank and the rest of the staff, and she liked Martin Harris. Hell, she felt like she'd drunk too much champagne whenever Martin Harris was in the room, which wasn't a good idea but wouldn't have been a disaster. She thought he felt the same way about her, and once she got her restaurant open again he wouldn't be her boss. Except that she started to notice things. Like, he was *never* up before six.

"Does he have a drinking problem? Drugs? I need to know if it's going to blow up all over Helene DeCourcy's party." All over Rita DeLeone too, but Frank didn't need to know that.

"I don't think Martin has ever taken anything stronger than an aspirin. For that matter, I don't think he's ever taken an aspirin. He isn't drinking either."

It was the truth. She figured that out about Frank already. He always told her the truth and generally relied on her not to get it anyway. Like now. She was clearly missing the subtext, and tried again. Set down her clipboard and leaned on the butler's table, a hand on each stack of napkins so that he couldn't pretend they weren't having this conversation.

"But he did?"

"Never to excess. The Harrises have always been excellent employers."

Time to back off and let Frank at the napkins. "So we can assume he will not dance naked on Mrs DeCourcy's card tables."

"We can so assume." Frank paused, thought a moment. "But Helene would pay extra if he did."

"She probably would."

"Would what?" Martin – shaved, showered, and in a dinner jacket with tails – wandered into the kitchen and threw an arm across Rita's shoulders. She would have slipped away but thought he might fall if she did.

"Pay extra to see you dance naked on her card tables."

"Ah." For a moment he stared off into the distance, as if considering it. "If we lose any more clients I may have to take her up on the offer. But you're here to save me from a fate worse than death, aren't you, Rita, Rita, Rita?"

"You are drunk, Mr Harris." She pushed him upright, balancing him against the butler's table, with a glare at Frank McCaffey. "We have to get him sober before the guests arrive."

But Frank was ignoring her, and her cooks had all stopped to watch. "Did you see Marcus Balfour today, Martin?" Frank took Martin's weight, looked into his eyes like he was trying to gauge a truth that Martin might not give him.

"Didn't want him. Sent him home."

"Have you fed at all?"

Martin smiled beatifically. "Does the carpaccio count?"

"No, Martin, it doesn't."

"That's what Helene said."

The back door opened then and three new arrivals pushed their way into the kitchen. Frank looked relieved, though they were at least an hour early and the owner was drunk. Or stoned. Or possibly starving himself to death on beef carpaccio, which didn't make sense at all.

"Dani," Frank said, and the woman with the blonde bun looked up, shot a questioning eyebrow just as Martin Harris fell to the floor, taking Rita with him.

"Jesus Christ!" Rita said, and Frank followed them to his knees, got an arm under Martin's head, and said to the room in general, "Does anybody know when he fed last?"

"He paid me last week, and again on Monday, but he didn't want to feed," Dani answered. "I thought . . . He acted like he'd fixed on somebody else. I thought he was just being nice, paying out my contract."

Frank looked really scared. Angry too. And that scared the hell out of Rita. "What? What's wrong with him?"

"He's an idiot." Frank caught his breath, started again. "He has a rare . . . chemical imbalance, you could call it. And right now it's killing him."

Rita stared at him, trying to process what he'd said, but it didn't make sense. Martin was *not* dying. She wouldn't allow it. "I don't have my cell on me. Somebody call nine-one-one!"

"He doesn't need a hospital." Nobody picked up the phone and Rita scrambled, tried to get to her office where she had two of them. Frank grabbed her arm. "Wait. I know what's wrong. We'll handle it."

"People die of an overdose all the time, Frank. You can't protect him from this—"

"It's nothing a hospital will help." They were all listening to him, even Doug, who was down on the floor with his sleeve rolled up and his arm out. But Frank gave him a nudge, said, "Get Helene. Tell her he won't feed."

Doug seemed to get more out of that than Rita did. He nodded, got up and ran.

"You have to be kidding me." Dani peered over his shoulder, glaring. "He fixed on *her*. And she won't even feed him?!"

"I've cooked for him all week. This isn't about my cooking."

"No, it isn't." Frank sank back on his heels, rubbed his head. "You can leave now and not see any of this."

"I'm not leaving him!" Couldn't. Wouldn't, even though she knew Frank planned to turn her world on its head.

"You'll wish you had."

"I know that." She figured they were going to give him more drugs, or an antagonist to the drugs he'd already taken, and she'd have to do something about it later. But right now they had to keep him alive. If Frank knew how to do that, she'd let him and say 'thank you'.

"Somebody give me a knife!" A blade came into view and he said, "Clean knife!" Took it when it came and pricked his finger, waited until a drop of blood formed.

"Martin," he said, softly, and smeared the welling blood on Martin's lip.

"What are you doing?"

Martin stirred, tried to escape the blood, but it was movement, more than they'd had a moment ago.

"Is he alive?" Helene DeCourcy had arrived, quite at home in a ruffled Gilded Age ball gown, and with a terrible, terrible expression on her face.

"So far." Frank stood up, deferred to her authority. "He needs to feed, but he won't do it."

"Get him off this floor and put him to bed. We'll have to make his excuses at the party."

The door to the basement apartment was still open and between them Frank and Doug got him down the stairs. Rita wanted to follow, but she had a kitchen to deal with first – and Helene DeCourcy. "We have to cancel," Rita said, "he needs a hospital."

"Trust me to know what he needs, my dear. For his reputation, no one must know what has happened here."

Helene followed Martin to the stairs, with Rita right behind her. "This is not the nineteenth century. We don't let people die to hide their problems."

Helene stopped. She turned on the stair and, for a moment, Rita saw something in her eyes that froze her like a stalked rabbit.

"He's a vampire, dear. It's not like he's snorting cocaine. And he nearly killed himself to keep you from finding out, so please do not lecture me on secrets and reputations."

"That's insane!" Really, really insane. If the situation wasn't so dire, Rita would have laughed. But Martin was unconscious and nobody else looked surprised.

"I know, dear. If these were different times . . . " Helene studied her for a full moment, waiting for something. Then her shoulders lifted. She grabbed Rita by the arm and tugged her down the stairs. "If these were different times, we'd lock you in a room together until you sorted it out between you."

Rita had a bad feeling about this, but it was getting her where she needed to be. So she let Helene lead her, through a tidy little kitchen and a living room with a big brown couch, all of it clean except for the dirt – not dust, but a scattering of soil like a flower pot had overturned – in a fine line across the bedroom doorway. Helene stepped over it and pulled Rita in after her.

The room, like the rest of the apartment, was masculine and clean except for a bit of soil across the hearth of the fireplace. On the mantelpiece sat three fat white candles, like the candles in the window and the ones at Helene DeCourcy's house. But it was the bed that held all of Rita's attention. They'd undressed him and covered him to the waist. His skin looked like marble, pale and blue veined, as still as death. Oh God, she thought. Oh God. She remembered the champagne fizz of excitement when he entered the room, and the dark pools of his eyes pushing back the blue with mysteries. Rita fell to her knees by the side of the bed, took his hand in hers, still soft, but cold, so cold. She almost didn't hear it when Helene said, "We are going to do this the old-fashioned way." Didn't care when Frank said, "We can't do that. Martin—"

"Martin will die if we don't. He is a foolish boy, but there we are. Do you want to tell his mother that you let him die?"

Frank said nothing, but he left and took Doug with him. Rita was glad they were gone. She didn't want anyone to see her cry. To hear her scream. Martin was dead, was dead, was dead.

The door closed, leaving her alone with Helene DeCourcy and Martin's body, but of the two, only Martin mattered. Until Helene crossed to the hearth and lit the three white candles. "Sanctuary, hearth and home," she said. "Sanctuary stands highest to light the way for the lost. We have two choices here. If what I said upstairs is true, do you still love him?"

Upstairs. She'd said that Martin was a vampire. Down here, she'd said they still had choices.

"Will I die?" That was one kind of movie. Helene said, "We all die, eventually. But Martin would never hurt you. He would die first. He *is* dying rather than upset you. He's a fool in that, but no, it will not kill you."

"Will I become like him?" Given his present state, that didn't sound much better, but Helene said, "No, I'm sorry. That isn't possible. It's genetic." Rita wasn't sorry, but she thought Helene might see it differently.

Helene waited, but Rita didn't have anything else to say except, "Choices?" like Martin was on the menu – pick one, pay for ever.

"He's fixed on you. Loves you. Because he hasn't fed yet, we can still stop it. I can wake him long enough for you to tell him 'no'. But then you have to go, and never see him again. It won't be comfortable, but he'll survive. If you choose to stay, he will need to feed from you, a tablespoon or so of blood every few days. Like insulin, if you like, only it has to be drawn living from your body."

When put that way, it sounded clinical. Simple. Not obscenely personal at all. "Why didn't he tell me?"

Tears simmered in Helene's eyes, but they didn't fall, and she managed to smile fondly in spite of them. "Because he is a foolish boy and he loves this house almost as much as he loves you. If he told you too soon, he risked losing you both. So he kept silent."

Rita wondered how far she'd go to put Sophie's back on its feet. The little restaurant meant a lot to her, but not this much. Not Martin's life.

"For ever."

"Until the day you die."

The thought terrified her. But Rita had learned all she needed to know about for ever watching Martin die. "Show me how," she said, and scarcely noticed when Helene undid the buttons on her jacket – the white one. Frank had told her the black jackets with the little red hearts on the pockets were for the special service staff, but she hadn't realized until now what that special service was. She supposed she'd be wearing a red-heart jacket after tonight.

Rita's jacket fell away, and then her shirt, her slacks, peeled down until she was naked in the warmth of the candles and reaching for Martin, sliding into the bed beside him as if in a dream, or a trance. She wondered if Helene had done something to her, but the thought didn't shake her resolve.

"Here," Helene said, and took a lancet from a small purse at her waist. Rita had watched as Frank pricked his finger, so she already knew that much of what she had to do. She reached out her finger for Helene to prick, winced at the cut, but she'd done worse in the kitchen. A bubble of blood formed at the tip of her finger.

"It's always better when both people are conscious," Helene remarked, "but this will have to do for now."

If Helene could make a joke, Rita figured, the worst was over. Her own sense of humour was still on hold. This close, she wanted him, wanted his eyes open and looking at her like they had when they danced together in his empty ballroom. She wanted his skin warm against hers, and she wondered about that; it almost stopped her, but just being close to her seemed to have warmed him. She remembered what Frank had done and touched his lip gently, let him sense the presence of her blood. His head followed her movement, reaching for it rather than escaping it. Frank couldn't save him, but she could. She felt powerful, and it gave her courage. She needed that when he opened his eyes and moaned her name.

"Your wrist will do for now. Let him hold your hand."

For a moment she'd forgotten that Helene DeCourcy was still there, and she blushed to her toes, knew Helene could see every fiery inch of her and blushed even more. But Martin was reaching for her, tugging at her arm, his lips soft on the inside of her wrist. A delicate lick and every muscle grew liquid and languorous. He found what he was looking for – her vein pulsed against his mouth.

She cried out at the little pain, the fierce need, as the needles of his teeth pierced her flesh. She felt it down in her belly, to the ends of her toes, the tidal pull starting in her wrist and emptying her, her soul drawn out like a sigh. She closed her eyes, trying to absorb the sensation, focus on the pleasure of that deep motion, the awareness of heart and veins and arteries pulsing down to one point of existence in her wrist. When she opened her eyes again, Helene was gone, and Martin was blinking at her.

"You're warm," Rita said, and Martin said, "You're here."

Epilogue

Martin was nervous. The food was packed, the trucks were waiting to head over to the Art Museum, but Frank had insisted that they make it official. So he was standing in his kitchen – Rita's now – in his dinner jacket, with his staff in an anxious circle. Rita looked nervous, but they'd made it through the worst.

"It's time," Frank said, and Martin took off Rita's white coat, handed it to Dani, who folded it over her arm. Then Frank brought out a new black jacket and handed it to Martin. There were a dozen more in the closet now, but he made a ceremony of the first.

"Two souls, one heart." Martin touched the small red heart embroidered on the pocket over her breast, let his fingers linger. Through the heart wove a thin gold ring. "For ever."

Martin was giving her that killer smile, and the dark of his eyes had swallowed the blue in a way Rita had come to recognize. Might as well break in the new jacket. She pushed back the sleeve, offered her wrist and he nipped, just a promise for later. They'd found much more interesting places for sipping, and Martin Harris was completely alive, everywhere. But right now the mayor was waiting for dinner.

Into the Mist For Ever

Rosemary Laurey

1

There were only two of them, dressed as Romans and armed. Hunting, like her no doubt. Everyone was hungering for fresh meat at this point in the winter. As the boar broke from the brush and raced across the open meadow, the taller of the two let his spear fly. With a loud squeal the boar turned, the spear embedded in its flank, and charged for the trees, in a direct line to where she was concealed.

Gwyltha let her own spear fly, with an accuracy that only a vampire possessed. It struck the animal between the eyes.

It stopped in its tracks and lay twitching on the winter grass. She flicked her horse's rump and sent horse and chariot flying out of the trees, towards the downed animal. The two Romans were already heading for it but it was her kill. She reached it before them. They raced towards her then stopped, one watching her, the other stepping towards the boar.

"My kill, I believe, centurions." She spoke in Latin, doubting they'd understand her own tongue.

"I hit it first," the taller one said.

"You did," she agreed, "but mine was the killing blow." Let them argue that, if they could. Or dared. She smiled. They no doubt thought her a lone, defenceless woman. This might be interesting.

Gwyltha waited as the taller one viewed the downed animal, exchanged glances with his companion then looked up at her with dark eyes that didn't hide his amazement.

*   *   *

Justin stared up at the woman. She was short, with the dark hair of the native Brigantes who inhabited this part of Northern Britain. But what she might lack in height, she more than made up for in presence. Hades! Seemed she was prepared to stare him down and fight over the kill. Understandable. Her people were no doubt half-starved at this point in the winter. But did she have no fear, facing two armed Romans as if they were barefoot peasants? Apparently not. "I hit it first."

"Indeed you did, centurion. You hit it and it veered in my direction. You made the kill easy for me. I thank you." She inclined her head

"You know without doubt you killed it, Briton?" his companion, Marcus asked.

"My spear did." She glanced towards the barely twitching animal.

"By Zeus!" Marcus muttered.

Justin's spear had pierced the creature's haunch. Hers was embedded between its eyes so deeply that the metal point was barely visible.

No question who'd made the kill.

"You dispute the evidence of your own eyes, centurion?" she asked, with a little twist of a smile. "Or perhaps you think I placed my spear after the animal fell." She raised a dark eyebrow and Justin found himself staring into the depths of her dark-blue eyes.

"What man would doubt that, madam? You split its brain in two."

She looked down at him again. Her manner suggested she was the wife of some local chieftain. "There have been occasions."

There had. Most recently a few weeks back when a man was killed over a disputed hunt.

"Not with us!" Marcus said, not concealing his annoyance.

"No, gentlemen. Seems I have the advantage of encountering noble Romans." She didn't have to say it in quite that tone. "Could I be less gracious?"

She leaped out of the chariot, giving them both a glimpse of a pair of very finely muscled legs, and stood over the boar.

Using one hand, she pulled out Justin's spear. Had his strike really been that light? After wiping the point on the grass, she handed it to him. "A good shot from that distance."

She'd been watching? Damn! These trees concealed too much at times, but now was not the time to consider the local arboretum. Not when Justin could watch her bend over the still warm animal.

As she reached for the knife at her belt, he tensed, putting his hand on the hilt of his sword. Marcus did the same. Both relaxed as she slit the animal's throat before deftly skinning the lower part of the creature, easing the hairy pelt off the hind leg before severing it.

It wasn't just her skill, or the body under her tunic, that fascinated Justin. By Zeus, she was strong – slicing the muscle in a few slashes, then cutting through the joint before she stood up and, reaching for a roll of coarse canvas from her chariot, cut off a length with her knife.

She rolled up the severed limb and handed it to Justin. "Would be churlish to take all of the animal that you helped me kill but I can spare no more. I hunt for a village. You Romans seldom starve no matter how harsh the winter."

Really? Wouldn't do to let her know that supplies were thin, transports being delayed by bad weather or, as the Legate suspected, ambushed en route from the south. Did she think they were hunting to fill idle hours? Fresh meat was a luxury everywhere this time of year.

But she'd given them a generous haunch. Justin stared as she wrapped the entire carcass and lifted it into the chariot, brushing off his rather tardy, and apparently unnecessary, offer of help.

"Enjoy your feast, centurions," she said as she took back the reins and manoeuvred the chariot backwards a little way.

"I'm not a centurion," Justin replied, "and neither is Marcus."

"Indeed. And not a centurion?"

She was arrogant, no doubt about it, but the temptation to snub her faded faster than it occurred. "I am Justinius Corvus, Regimental Surgeon."

"*Vale*, Justinius Corvus," she said, as she turned the chariot and headed back into the shelter of the trees.

"That was some woman," Marcus said. They turned back towards camp. "Did you see the body on her?"

Justin had. Very clearly. But somehow the thought that his assistant had noticed her strong, slim body rankled him. Considerably. "I wouldn't harbour designs on some chieftain's wife," Justin told him. "That way lies civil unrest and a swift transfer to some far flung outpost of the Empire."

"I thought we were already in one."

He had to laugh at the lad's wit but it was too close to truth to be truly funny.

On their return to camp, a message awaited Justin. As a ranking officer, he was summoned to dine with the Legate. With a warning to Marcus not to eat the entire leg of boar, Justin readied himself for a rather boring evening, enlivened only, he suspected, with stray thoughts of a dark-haired Brigante woman wielding a sharp knife with skill and confidence.

2

Once in the safety of the woods, Gwyltha took what blood she could from the carcass. Boar was not as sweet as human blood but would serve. In time of winter famine, she would never feed off any villager. Wiping her mouth, she returned to the village and handed over her kill to the baker. Once cooked, they'd portion it out among them. She'd paid for hospitality for another few days. She was welcome. No one in their right mind refused respect or hospitality to a Timeless One, but there was trouble brewing. She sensed it in the glances she wasn't intended to catch, the whispers shared between the elders and in the very air around her.

If there was trouble she would avoid it at all costs. She hoped everyone else would too. Any victory would be short lived once the Romans retaliated with more troops. She'd seen enough in the past couple of hundred years to learn there was no hope of defeating the Roman invaders. But could she rest neutral when the people she was supposed to protect went to war? She understood their frustration. Who rested content under an invader's heel? Even though the fort at Eboracum was so obviously under strength, the legion was well armed and well fed. There was no hope of defeating them. Unless there was a pact between the tribes . . .

What if?

Her mind spun.

This needed a mind older than hers. Once the village set to feasting on roasted boar, Gwyltha ran through woods and cross country to her mentor's home high on the moors.

Vorniax had transformed her, taught her the ways of the Timeless, and bade her never forget the old religion. "Even if the magic has left the land," he used to say, "we stay."

He'd always nagged at her to create her own offspring. Something she'd never done. Yet. Maybe she should have. An army of vampires would have a chance against the Roman spears and swords. But that would disturb the balance and, Vorniax always admonished, was unpardonable.

He reiterated this as they sat and talked. He answered her misgivings with more questions. As she ran back, her mind mulled over what she'd learned and not learned. She'd been right to suspect discontent. That he'd not denied, pointing out numerous incidents of insults and injustice and the many meetings between the leaders of the tribes. He'd also warned her of sickness in Eboracum and reminded her she was a healer.

Just like the Roman she'd met that afternoon and had difficulty forgetting. A soldier by his dress and bearing but he'd claimed to be a surgeon. A mender of bones and wounded soldiers.

She should stop thinking about him. She should not fixate on those dark eyes, the strong line of his jaw or the way the corners of his eyes crinkled as he squinted against the light. There was no point. He was the invader, to be watched with utmost wariness and caution.

When she returned to the village, only the sentries were awake. Unnoticed she slipped over the outer fence and found her resting place in her hut. A few hours' repose and she'd do as Vorniax suggested. She'd venture into the town and listen to gossip. Vampire hearing had its advantages.

The Legate dined well, given it was deep winter, but Justin rather mourned the roasted boar. He hoped Marcus and his companions were doing it justice.

He also hoped to keep his attention on the conversation. His mind kept wandering back to the Briton in the chariot and her impossible throwing skill and strength. A mere woman could never have slain that boar. Where had the spear come from? Someone concealed in the trees? If so, it was a damn good thing both he and Marcus were wearing breast and back plates. Proved what the Legate always said: it never paid to take risks in this barbaric country.

"Well, Corvus?"

Damn! "Sir?" Everyone was looking his way. What in Hades had he missed?

"The sickness in the town," Lucas Merinas said.

Justin gave him a grateful nod.

"It must be watched and contained if need be, sir. Have there been any deaths?" If there had, surely he'd have picked up talk.

"Only a couple, but too many might cause unrest, what with the trouble up north and reinforcements not arriving, to say nothing of delayed supplies. Best go down and give me your report. Can't have the natives getting restless. We need to maintain order."

Deaths meant nothing, order and discipline meant all. Of course. "I'll go down into the town in the morning, sir, and see what I can discover."

The child was sweating. Badly. Looking at the limp body and fever-clouded eyes, Justin shook his head. What could he do? He was a surgeon, not a Greek apothecary. Sword cuts and knife wounds he could stitch up, broken bones he knew how to set, but a disease that racked a little helpless body? He was lost. The child wasn't as old as his step-brother was the last time he'd examined him. But he was headed for the grave.

"Can you do anything, surgeon?" the frantic mother asked.

Relieve symptoms perhaps. "Bring some clean water and a linen cloth."

He told her to bathe the child and keep damp cloths on his head. It was unlikely to work. The little body was wasted and racked with fever.

Justin stood to leave and was about to suggest the family make an offering to their gods for the child's sake, when a voice called from the street.

He spun around in recognition then immediately gave his attention back to his patient.

How was this possible? It was her.

The mother admitted the female hunter from yesterday to the house. If it was any consolation, she appeared as stunned as he was.

"Surgeon," she said with a nod of acknowledgment, "I see you are before me."

Justin made himself not think of the breasts she revealed under her woollen tunic as she threw her cloak back.

"Healer." The mother was anxious. She was scared of offending one or both of them, no doubt. "The surgeon was asking who was sick in the town and I called him to see my son."

"As have I come," the woman replied. "Maybe two heads are better than one."

That Justin seriously doubted, in this case at least, but he returned to the bedside. He stood back to let her get close.

"You ordered the cool cloths?" she asked and he tried to suppress the satisfaction when she smiled at his assent. What did her approval or disapproval matter?

"It will ease his symptoms," Justin replied. "The fever is far advanced."

"Your son is very ill," she told the mother, "but I might be able to help."

She reached into her pack for a small, stoppered jar. Raising the boy's head, she forced him to swallow a small amount of its contents. Then she handed the jar to the mother. "Give him the contents of this throughout the day, a little at a time." She handed over another package. "Infuse half of this in boiling water. When it cools, give it to him tomorrow. Prepare the last half and give it to him on the third day. If his rash doesn't fade or his fever break, send word and I will return. Wash him daily and keep the cloths on his head as the surgeon ordered. They will help."

She barely gave Justin as much as a passing glance as the mother thanked her, and him. Justin followed her out into the street and the misting rain.

3

"You know how many cases there are, Surgeon Justin Corvus?" she asked as they stood in the street in the rain.

"You have the advantage over me, madam," he replied. "You never gave me your name."

"I am Gwyltha," she replied.

"Gwyltha," he said, inclining his head, "we meet again."

"Without spears this time." If she was surprised or impressed he pronounced her name correctly, she hid it. It hadn't been hard. It was close to his dead mother's name. Only she'd been from the civilized lands in the far south, a very different world from these barbaric northern wastes. Besides, no man would harbour for his mother the thoughts that sprung to mind standing close to Gwyltha. There was a strange and uncanny air about her. Arrogance, self-assurance, a burning sensuality. Whatever it was, he wanted her. Naked, preferably.

Short rations and damp weather were affecting his reason.

"You live in Eboracum?"

She shook her head. "No. I come when asked to see the sick. Two died yesterday. I fear we will lose more. Of course the death of a Briton is hardly a matter of importance to a Roman."

He looked her in the eye. "My mother was a Briton, of the Dumnonii. Her death was of importance."

Gwyltha wanted to bite her careless tongue. Perhaps it was because of his British blood that he fascinated her. Hardly! No one else had ever held her attention in this way. "My apologies, surgeon. And my condolences for your mother's death."

"It was years back. I was a child," he replied. He seemed to hesitate, as if about to say more, but then asked, "The potion you gave that boy? What is it?"

"A herbal concoction. Helps with fevers and cools the blood. I have more with me. You are here to attend the sick in the town? Don't you have your own sick and wounded?"

"My Legate told me to come and see how many are sick."

"Indeed? Maybe the town should send a deputation to thank him for his concern."

Justin Corvus smiled and she couldn't help smiling back. Gods of her fathers protect her! This man had an aura about him enough to make her forget her vows and heritage. "I doubt he would appreciate the sentiment in which the deputation might be sent," he replied.

The solemn line of his wide mouth, combined with the wicked twinkle in his dark eyes, almost undid her. "That would be a tragic misunderstanding," she replied. His deep peal of laughter almost completed her unravelling. Time to concentrate on the sick and dying. "I thank you at least for coming. There are several ailing. Not all will die but it seems to hit the young and the old hardest."

"Like so many diseases."

She nodded.

"What precisely was in the potion you gave the boy?" he asked, sounding hesitant. Afraid it was some deep held secret perhaps?

Why not tell him? "Fever bright and heartsease mixed with a soporific. It helps them rest and eases the fever. For the rash there's not much I can do. If they live it fades."

"Would you share what you do?"

She should refuse, tell him to go back to the camp and leave her in peace but his genuine interest swayed her. "Come with me. It's no secret. Watch me at the next stop and then you'll know what to do."

Watching her at each bedside was a pleasure, and gave him opportunities to touch her under the pretext of handing her a package or helping her on and off with her cloak. Was this insanity?

Maybe. But on her part, she did not appear to be repulsed by his company. Maybe she would welcome more? They could hunt together perhaps. Now that was a thought . . .

"If we split up," Gwyltha said, as they stood in the narrow street outside the last house they'd visited, "we can work in half the time."

This was definitely not what he'd had in mind but she handed him four small vials and a bundle of herbs. Perhaps sensing his hesitation – very real it was too; who knew if her potions killed or cured? – she smiled at him. He was ready to do her bidding in an instant. She led him around a couple of corners and indicated, across the street, a reasonably prosperous Roman-style house. "The father there is stricken with the sickness," she said. "They are Romanized enough to trust you more than they'd trust me perhaps. Tell them I sent you."

"And I have to trust that your potions are safe?"

Giving him the oddest, searching look, without a trace of a smile, she replied, "In this, you can trust me, surgeon Corvus. I am not one who kills."

Meaning she thought he was? Well, of course, he had killed before. "I will attend him," he said. "Meet me here?"

She indicated the next corner. "Down there. I have a house to visit. Two children are ailing."

After the initial surprise at finding him on their doorstep, Justin was admitted, greeted by the wife as if he were their saviour. He was taken to see the patient. One glance at the wasted body in the bed convinced him the woman was fated to be a widow, but he kept that to himself. He dosed the patient with Gwyltha's potion and instructed that he be bathed and given the infusion of the dried herbs. Would do no good, he was certain, but might ease the man's last hours.

Out on the street, Justin waited some minutes. He experienced an illogical pleasure as Gwyltha emerged from the low doorway and looked in his direction.

"How was Arius?" she asked, as they walked towards the next call.

"I doubt he'll last until morning. He could barely swallow the potion."

"But he swallowed it?" she asked. Justin nodded. "Then all we can do is hope. Secunda, his wife, will see that all care is taken. You told her that we would be back in three days?"

"I did."

"Then we'd best on to the next patient."

It was as if he were in a waking trance. He had to follow her, and was content to. He longed to be close to her, contrived more than once to brush her clothes or let his hand touch hers, or his arm to brush her cloak.

Whatever was happening to him was delightful – apart from the wild and insane need to take her into some narrow doorway and sate himself then and there.

Except he wouldn't. Demanding the conqueror's prerogative had never been his way. When he wanted a woman, he found one who was willing. What was different with Gwyltha? It had to be more than her eyes, blue as the sky in Rome, her smile that curved up the corners of her mouth, or the promise of her warm breasts beneath her tunic. He'd never met a woman who healed, walked the streets to tend the sick, was willing to share her knowledge (for whatever it might be worth) and could hit a bolting boar between the eyes at fifty paces.

Gwyltha smiled to herself as Justin fell in step beside her. She had him. Almost. He followed her as a newborn colt trailed its mother. With the very modicum of compulsion, he'd be hers. She had need of the blood in his veins. Two long runs last night used up the strength she'd taken from the boar.

After the last patient, she led him into a narrow street behind a temple, where they would be undisturbed. This entrance was little used except before festivals. For a moment he looked around, a flash of concern in his eyes, but she reached out and put her hand on his arm. "Justin Corvus, you have nothing to fear. I am Gwyltha, that is all." As she spoke, he looked into her eyes and she sent the full force of her vampire control into his mind.

He was hers, docile, on the edge of quiescence as she drew him close. Brushing his cloak and tunic from his neck, she stretched up to his height, and cradled his head in one hand. She tilted it to expose his neck and bit.

She took only what she needed. It was nowhere near enough. Never would be, she feared. Wild desire flowed from his veins and she wanted more, needed more, longed to sate herself in the richness of his human life and revel in the warmth from his blood.

She broke away, remembering to seal his wound with her saliva, and led him back towards the street.

Her mind was so caught up in the giddiness, she almost forgot to remove the compulsion.

He stood, a little dazed, looking around him as if wondering why he stood there in the mist and the failing light.

"Madam," he said, looking at her with the same amazement she'd seen when they met in the meadow.

"*Vale*, Justinius Corvus," she said, resisting the urge to pull him into her arms and kiss him right there in the public street. She turned and walked as fast as she dared. Whatever had happened between them stunned her and she needed solitude to consider the implications. Never in all her many years had she tasted blood as rich and heady as his. It wasn't because he was Roman. She'd had enough of them in her early days as a vampire, leaving more than one dead as she sated her youthful hungers. No, it was as if she'd shared his heartbeat, tasted his soul.

A decidedly anxiety-provoking thought. For which she had neither time nor patience.

4

Justin wandered back to camp in a daze. He'd partnered with a healer who seemed little better than a witch, had administered untested remedies to the sick and dying and was now consumed with a raging sexual desire for her that he almost couldn't control. Ridiculous! Impossible! He rubbed the side of his neck. It felt oddly stiff.

He returned to his hospital with all haste only to find Marcus and two wound dressers, bustling around a soldier with a spear point in his back.

"He and three others went hunting without armour," Marcus said, as Justin joined them. "Silly fools. They were attacked by an unknown assailant."

No point in arguing that point. The Legate would see to discipline. If the soldier survived.

The spear point was lodged deep in the man's ribs. Not as deep as Gwyltha's had been in the boar's skull though. At least this attack couldn't be pinned on her. She'd been with him almost all morning. Out of his sight at times, yes, but never long enough to run out and do this.

For some inexplicable reason, that knowledge flooded him with relief.

The next afternoon Justin left the camp, driven by a desire to get away from the Legate's reaction to the attack on the foot soldier – who had died despite all their efforts. At least he was spared the flogging that awaited his three companions.

Stupid fools going out into open country without armour. Justin had little sympathy for them, but did wonder what, if any, retaliation was planned. Not much was feasible with a legion at short strength. Whatever happened, he'd be told when he was told. Meanwhile, he wandered into Eboracum, his mind mulling over which wine shop to head for.

A slave, scrubbing the steps of a house, looked up as he passed. "Surgeon," she called out, "blessings on you and your house. Our master lives because of you!"

The greeting was unexpected enough to stop him in his tracks. Justin recognized the house from yesterday and remembered the man so close to death he'd almost not given him Gwyltha's potion. "Let me see your master," he told the slave.

It was impossible. But there was no mistaking it. As Justin left the house, the heartfelt thanks and blessings of the entire household following him down the street, he tried to make sense of what he'd just witnessed.

Did Gwyltha dispense magic potions, or did she just possess phenomenal knowledge of herb lore? Yesterday that man had been at death's door. Today he wasn't exactly hale, but he was sitting up and taking broth. All trace of fever gone.

Justin was tempted to stop at some of the other houses to see if the results were as astounding.

Or he *was* tempted, until he noticed a familiar dark head at a metalworker's stall, inspecting the craftsman's wares.

Tending to the sick and satisfying his curiosity about her cures was supplanted by his desire for a different kind of satisfaction.

He was surely moonstruck. Why this wild rush of desire and need? It was broad daylight, for Zeus' sake, and he was the regimental surgeon of the Ninth, not a randy apprentice losing his mind over the neighbourhood Venus.

He was drawn to Gwyltha like a moth to a lamp flame.

Why?

What a ridiculous question! He knew exactly why. He just didn't want to think about it right now. He wanted to ...

Her laugh broke into his thoughts. He couldn't see her face but imagined the light in her blue eyes as she smiled. He noticed the shrug of her shoulders as her laugh faded and heard what she said, clear enough to know it was the local language. She said a last word to the metalworker and turned to go. Justin stepped back out of her line of sight.

For some reason, he didn't want to appear to have been watching her.

He worked back through the crowd, as she turned down the street to walk away. He ran a few paces and called out to her.

She turned, looked right at him through the crowd and smiled. "*Ave*, Justinius Corvus."

"*Ave*, Gwyltha." He caught up with her. "Do you have another name? Title?"

"Gwyltha Briganteorum, if you like. But those who know me call me Gwyltha." Gwyltha of the Brigantes, that much he knew already. "You need me, *chirurge*?"

Why suddenly so formal? "Justin," he replied and yes, by all the gods, he needed her.

The light in her eyes suggested she could read his mind, hear his racing heartbeat and sense the wildness coursing through his veins. "The man yesterday, who lived in the white house by the potter's," he began.

"Arius Alba?" she asked. "You've seen him?"

"I have indeed. What is in the potion of yours? Yesterday I feared for his survival and today he is sitting up sipping broth."

"I'd hoped so," she said. "He is a good man and an honest merchant. To say nothing of being the father of a growing family."

"What is in that potion?" he repeated.

"Do not sound so accusatory, *chirurge*. Herbs, as I told you; nothing more, nothing less. Herbs best gathered at full moon but that is as far as healing magic goes. If you are still here in the spring, I will show you where they grow."

"I would be grateful. All knowledge helps save lives. It seems, lady, you possess great knowledge."

She also possessed enough vampire hearing to know blood coursed though his veins faster than was usual for a healthy mortal. The man was in dire need. Gwyltha looked up into his dark eyes and smiled. She couldn't help herself. Since tasting him yesterday, he'd occupied her thoughts, confused her thinking and clouded her reason. It should be so easy to dismiss him as one more Roman, but he was more, much more. "I will gladly share what knowledge I can, *chirurge*."

He looked as pleased as a child promised a treat. "Perhaps we can visit the patients together?"

Not now! "I have other business to attend to but tell me, surgeon Corvus, will you meet me this evening?"

"Where?"

Good question. Nights were cold for a mortal. "By the bridge is a wine shop, the Red Flagon. Next to it is a row of houses and shops. My home is the last one. Meet me there a little after sunset." She had stunned him. Hopefully, not too much. She reached out and took his hand. It was warm and strong and, she was sure, so was the rest of his body. "Until then, surgeon Corvus."

She walked away and whispered to herself, "Justinius."

5

What had happened to the discipline instilled in him through his years of army life? At least instinct was keeping him at attention, but that was about it. While the Legate harangued about the need for constant vigilance and his suspicions that the Brigantes were up to no good (a chronic conviction of the man), Justin kept his eyes forwards while his mind was still standing in the crowded street with Gwyltha. Then he was meeting Gwyltha in the middle of a damp meadow with a dead boar between them, then seeing Gwyltha beside a sick bed or, the best of all, imagining Gwyltha naked in his arms while he feasted his eyes, and the rest of him, on her beauty.

He was halfway to insane. Here they were, supposedly on the brink of an insurrection (assuming the Legate was right for once), and all he, Justin Corvus, wanted to do was consort with one particular Brigante. For the rest of his born days.

It was insanity. In a year the legion would move to a new posting. But a lot could happen in a year. It was utter stupidity and a total impossibility. He couldn't by law marry until he retired and somehow Gwyltha didn't strike him as the sort of woman to settle for living beyond the protection of law and convention. But she had made an assignation, and it wasn't to discuss herb lore or healing methods.

Gwyltha lit the fire in the brazier, saw there were supplies of wine – mortals did so like that – and some cakes and cheese, and waited. She'd been tempted to watch for his coming, perhaps from the roof of the wine shop, or one of the trees that edged the river, but trees this time of year offered little cover, even for a vampire.

She wondered how long he would take to get here. And even if he would. Romans were strange creatures. She'd learned to live with them better than many had, but she knew she would be here long after the Romans left. Mortals didn't have that to look forward to. There was restlessness among the tribes, not just the Brigantes, and it didn't take vampire sight to notice the numbers of horses that had been bred the past couple of seasons, to say nothing of the new chariots and the secret caches of knives and blades in the chieftains' houses.

They were brave, hopeful and foolish, and if they planned insurrection it had better be soon, before the garrison got reinforcements.

Mortals! She'd seen too much death and too many battles to think another would benefit anyone.

But . . .

Footsteps approached. Firm, confident steps and wide paces, such as the Romans marched.

Gwyltha stood and opened the door. He was coming, bearing a small torch.

Cautious man, the torch lighted his way but also made an extra weapon if anyone was foolish enough to attack a lone soldier.

If anyone were that foolhardy, they'd have her to reckon with.

He stopped, three or four paces from the open door, and looked at her. How could mere mortal eyes hold such promise, such heat and such desire? "Welcome," she said and stepped forwards.

She took his outstretched hand and as good as propelled him into the room, closing the door behind them.

"You came," she said.

"You asked me to," he replied.

"Yes." Was she lost? Found? Or just caught in the aura of his masculinity?

No matter. He was here, would soon be in her bed, and would sate her craving. "Take off your cloak, Justin, and let me pour you a drink. It's a cold night."

"But warm in here, lady."

He was back to formal address. Why? Was he unsure of her? He should be. Not that she'd harm him, but because she was not what he thought. No doubt she was unlike any other woman he'd ever known.

Still, why ponder any questions when she had her own Roman soldier at hand? "Wine, Justin?" she asked as he draped his cloak over the end of the bed. She handed him a goblet. Their fingers touched, his cool from the chill outside, hers cold as was her nature. But it was more than coolness in that brush of fingers: an awareness of what they had both come here for.

She poured herself a little wine – her body tolerated a modicum of alcohol – and raised her glass to his. "Your health, Justin."

"And yours, Gwlytha." He sipped, watching her over the rim of the goblet. "This is your house?"

She shook her head. "Borrowed. I did not think you would care to venture into the deep woods where I have my real home." Romans were still leery about the woods.

"You live out there?" Shock tinged his voice.

"I always have. A town is not where I am most at peace."

"But you're here now."

"Because you are." Three words. They held so much meaning, so much hope. Sitting beside him it was more than blood need she felt. A strange, almost mortal, longing gripped her.

"Will you eat, Justin? I have cheese and cakes."

"You offer me everything, Gwyltha."

She did but agreeing wholeheartedly might seem churlish since he was giving more than he dreamed. "You are my guest. What should I offer you but my hospitality?"

He tucked into the cheese with an appetite that suggested they were as short of food in the camp as they were in the villages.

"You do not join me, Gwyltha?" he asked after his third or fourth slice of cheese.

"I will feed later," she replied, resting her hand on his thigh.

Under the leather kilt, she felt strong male muscle. She'd picked well. A strong man, he could satisfy her need and be none the worse for the loss of a little more blood than last time.

"Lady," he said, setting the goblet down, "you did not ask me here for conversation and cheese."

Bless the woodland gods that Justin had no inkling what he was here for. Could not. Never would.

"How right." She stood and unpinned her house cloak, dropping it on the stool where she'd been sitting. She reached out her hand to him and smiled.

He needed no second invitation.

In only a few mortal heartbeats, they were in each other's arms, his mouth on hers. A wildness took them both. How could a mere mortal stir this passion? Share this racing pleasure? Her mouth opened to his and sensation possessed her.

They were touching, caressing, reaching for skin. She heard fabric rip. It seemed they were both driven by the same, wild need. He threw off his kilt and breastplate. She hauled off his tunic, while he ripped open her girdle and pulled off her gown. Without words they were on the thin mattress, rolling like crazed creatures as they kissed, stroked and scratched. He was caressing her and sending great waves of pleasure through her like a tempest of mutual need.

Before she had time to think – if she'd even wanted to – he was inside her, driving her to a climax, sweat pouring off him as he filled her.

He was groaning with the effort and she was crying out with passion. Shouting with her building need until she came to the brink. Sensation soared and burst in a thousand peaks of sheer joy. Only then did she remember her reason for enticing him here. As he slipped out of her, she rolled on her side and ran a line of kisses down his neck, feeling the strength and warmth beneath the skin, hearing the wild beating of his heart and the pumping of warm mortal life blood. She bit.

Sweet gods and goddesses! What was he? This was more than a taste of life. This was mortal existence on her tongue. She drank more, making herself stop long before she'd begun to slake the thirst and craving he stirred in her.

"By Zeus, Gwyltha," he muttered, obviously as worn as she was. "Your lips are like magic."

She couldn't enlighten him about the magic of Timelessness. But he was amazing. As he lay beside her, Justin opened his eyes and smiled. And dear heavens! He was aroused again. By her taking his blood? For most mortals it had the reverse effect but now . . .

"I will never get enough of you," he said, as he grasped her by the waist and lifted her on top of him. She'd heard that the Romans liked it that way. And why not? It gave her a perfect view of his manly chest and handsome face. He took every possible advantage of her breasts and body as they both came back to the peak together.

This time he was spent. She wondered, rather idly, if another bite would arouse him again, but didn't dare take any more. The man had to walk home after all.

Not something he appeared to relish. But after a while spent sated in each other's arms, he stirred.

"I must go, my love," he said, sounding quite worn out.

"I know," she replied, "duty calls."

His sigh suggested how much he honoured duty at this moment in time. "I must." He sat up and reached for his tunic.

It would have been rude to lie there and not help him. Besides it gave her one last chance to touch his gloriously warm, mortal flesh.

"I'll see you again," he said. "Tomorrow, if I can."

That would be such a mistake. She kissed him. "Farewell, my handsome surgeon."

Once he was out of sight, she dressed, quickly, as only a vampire could. She noticed the tear in her gown and shook her head. How had she been so unrestrained? No matter. With his blood inside her she had strength to last several days and could cover the ground she needed.

But all she wanted to do was sit and wait until he returned. Only that was impossible. Duty called her too.

6

For the next week, Justin was at his wit's end. Gwyltha had disappeared, leaving no word, no message. He'd asked around the town. The metalworker, where he'd met her the day before, professed ignorance of her. When he revisited patients, every single one sang her praise, as well they might, but knew her only as a wandering healer. Some barely knew her name. If that wasn't enough, the Legate had the entire legion on alert after agents had mentioned that the tribes were gathering. There were two more attacks on isolated soldiers foolish enough to venture too far from the camp. And, of course, the promised reinforcements and supplies were again delayed.

Justin was beginning to think he'd dreamed the entire encounter and that Gwyltha was a figment of his fevered imagination, when a lad appeared at the hospital with a wicker hamper.

"For you, sir," he said, when Marcus summoned Justin to the door. The lad had insisted he speak to Justin and no one else.

"What is it?" Justin asked, and knew the answer the minute he lifted the lid. There were six or seven large vials and several packages that he knew contained dried herbs. "From Gwyltha?"

The lad nodded. "She said I was to give them to you in person. Said you may have need of them."

He needed more than herbs and potions. He needed her! But it was unfair to take his very real frustration out on this boy.

"Where is Gwyltha now?"

The lad shrugged. "Who knows? The Timeless go where they please. She told me to prepare the herbs and potions for you. Took me a while. There are no fresh herbs this time of year."

Justin barely heard the end of the boy's speech. One word caught his ear. "What do you mean 'Timeless'?"

The question obviously bothered the boy, which piqued Justin's curiosity even more. "How is she 'Timeless'?"

The lad looked away as he emptied his basket. "That's what we call ones like her. Who come and go."

"She doesn't live in your village?" Now there was a hope!

"She lives where she goes. Best not to ask too closely where she is." He made her sound like a sneak thief or a vagrant. The lad finished unloading his basket, tied the lid shut and left, steadfastly resisting all Justin's attempts to learn anything more about Gwyltha.

By Hades, she couldn't just disappear like that. And if she really had, why send him enough supplies to cure the entire garrison and half the town?

He resolved to spend as much time as he could spare the next day asking through the town for more information.

Early next morning the Legate announced that the entire legion was confined to camp. Trying to ignore the gossip that announcement kindled, Justin spent his time taking care of his patients, dismissing a couple of malingerers and taking in three more stricken with the current sickness. At least those he could cure easily, thanks to Gwyltha.

It all rather defied reason. If she'd only seen him as a casual bed companion, why send him the very generous gift of remedy?

His pointless and useless musings were rudely interrupted by the arrival of one of the tribunes bearing orders from the Legate. Justin was to ready the camp hospital for action. Additional supplies were unlikely to be forthcoming and could he manage on what he had? Since he was obviously going to have to, Justin agreed, asking how many men he should take. He was told to take as many as necessary.

He then asked how many men under Justin's care would be fit to march in the morning. Since the tribune's voice was better suited to the parade ground than a friendly conversation, the news would be around the hospital and out of the door before he returned to his office.

Not that Justin had time to waste worrying about that. He and Marcus and two orderlies spent the rest of the day packing the hospital wagons.

That night Justin slept badly. It wasn't the prospect of battle that bothered him. It was dreams of Gwyltha that disturbed his rest.

"They are fools," Gwyltha said, standing at the sacred oak beside her mentor, Vorniax. "Even united with the other tribes, what chance do they have against Rome?"

"They are driven by a need to show the Romans they are not a contented subject people." At her exasperated frown, Vorniax went on: "We will outlive the Romans and many more invaders. Mortals won't. They need to make themselves heard."

That Gwyltha understood but still saw the fruitlessness of it. "They fight by different rules." They learned that in the south when the first Caesar came. "What chance do they have against a fortified camp? The town will surely suffer."

"They will lure them out, I think. These petty attacks and skirmishes are to stir their anger. An outpost or two burned to the ground and they will come. The tribes will be ready for them."

Being ready to fight was not the same as being fully prepared for battle but that she kept to herself. Was her judgment clouded by the lasting memory of one particular Roman surgeon whose name echoed in her mind just as the taste of his blood and the memory of his hands on her flesh refused to fade? "They want me to come as healer."

Vorniax nodded. "You will?"

How could she refuse her people, even if they were rash and foolish? If she were right there would be wounded aplenty.

The Legion waited three days, long enough that anticipation faded to boredom. Then, just as Justin began to contemplate unpacking needed items from the wagons, came the news another patrol had been attacked, followed only hours later by a runner bringing word that an outpost to the north had been sacked. Within minutes, the order to prepare to march was given and they left camp before dawn on a wet and dismal morning.

The march was hell, even to hardened soldiers. The few survivors would never forget it. It wasn't just the weather – they'd been trained to ignore cold, heat or damp. But the fog that came down a few hours beyond Eboracum didn't improve things, blocking sight and muffling sound so even the creak of armour and the thud of marching steps were quieted. In the gloom and mist it wasn't hard to imagine lurking natives behind every ghostly tree and rock.

Arriving at the sacked outpost revived spirits, or rather rekindled a desire to show the damned Brigantes who ruled here now.

Marcus seemed caught up in the general belligerence. Justin couldn't help wondering if Gwyltha was out there. Somewhere.

What would he do if he encountered her? What could he do? He was Roman and sworn to his Emperor.

They camped for the night near the destroyed outpost. It was a quiet night but the entire legion awoke to shock and horror. The posted sentries had all had their throats cut.

A declaration of war if ever there was one.

The fog had lifted slightly. Nothing could have dampened the desire for battle that rippled through the lines then. The order was given and, at double pace, they headed towards a cluster of villages to the north where intelligence claimed there was a gathering of neighbouring tribes.

After two days' march they found them. Or rather the tribes found the legion. Earlier, scouts had reported there was a massed gathering ahead. The legion halted, while more scouts were sent forward to assess the ground. Then the line was attacked from behind. Waiting by his wagons in the rear, Justin watched the Brigantes, and what had to be Picts, pour out of the mist and take out several ranks to the rear before the order was give to reassemble in formation.

Seeing the carnage before his eyes, Justin gave orders to Marcus and the others to pull the wagons back and set up a dressing station. The first wounded arrived before they'd had time to heat water to prepare their instruments.

Justin lost track of time, measured it only by injuries treated and the wounded brought in. The sounds of battle increased as the day wore on, then eased. Were the Brigantes withdrawing? Justin finished stitching up a particularly nasty knife wound and went outside to call for more hot water.

He'd gone no more than two paces when the arrow caught him in the throat.

7

Gwyltha was watching from a distance. Her vampire sight allowing her to see far more than any mortal ever could.

She, like Vorniax, understood far more than the tribes did. Their protest was useless, but she'd protect and help as best she could. There would be need of healing once the battle was over. If not long before.

The initial surprise attack went well. The tribes had the advantage, knowing the ground and not marching in formation. The ranged troops on the rise were only a small part of the united force.

Her eyes scanned the battlefield. At the rear she spied the supply wagons, and what had to be the hospital, complete with their surgeon. Sweet goddesses. Her body remembered and her deathless heart ached for him. Was this the price of immortality? To feel the pain of loss forever.

Any sort of enduring love was impossible, poised as they were on opposite sides of a battle that would only bring the tribes a fleeting victory – if that.

Her eyes glimpsed an image that burned into her brain.

Justin! Struck by an arrow and down on the ground!

Throwing caution to the winds, she ran, faster than mortal eyes could register. Through the battle and the fighting, she sped to the back of the line, to see Justin carried into the hospital tent.

His life was fading, his slowing heart was like a drum beating his own retreat from life.

"No!" The cry came out aloud. The cluster of Romans around him turned and stared. One, lying wounded on a pallet, reached for his sword.

She ignored every single one of them and strode over to where Justin poured out his lifeblood, a black-feathered arrow embedded in his throat.

Marcus at least recognized her. "Madam! You are the hunter!"

She nodded in acknowledgment. "Justin is dying." It wasn't a question.

Marcus nodded. "I've tried to take out the arrow but it made him bleed more. He's choking on his own blood and his lungs are collapsing."

"I will take him."

"Eh! No, madam! Impossible!"

But she had him in her arms. "One less for you to bury."

"He can't leave like that!" one of the assistants said.

"He's not deserting, you fools! He's dying. Let me have him." Not that she was about to give them any choice. "You have witnesses enough that he was struck. Get busy with the wounded you can heal."

No one stopped her. Didn't even try as she walked to the door of the makeshift hospital and ran. Knocking aside Roman and Brigante alike, she took the shortest path into the shelter of the deep woods.

He still lived, but only just. She had to find Vorniax and get his help. He had been telling her for at least a hundred years to build her own colony. Now was the time to begin. She ran on until she found him.

"A Roman?" he asked, his eyebrows raised.

"One who is worthy," she replied.

"Bring him in. I will tell you what to do."

She laid Justin down at the stone altar and raised her eyes to her mentor. "Is it too late?"

Vorniax bent over and frowned at Justin. "He lives but not for long. Is this truly what you want?"

"Yes."

"Then bite him and take the last of his life. You must take his life to return it."

She leaned over, turning his head away from her. Grimacing at the arrow still imbedded in his throat, she bit into his vein and drank.

It took what seemed an eternity itself until his heart pumped its last and he lay inert and cooling.

"Wait," Vorniax said, "we need to take care of that arrow. He won't want that in his neck for eternity." Using both hands he pulled and removed it in a swift tug. "A Pictish one," he said, looking at the arrow. "Now." He looked up at her. "If this Roman is truly worthy to become one of the Timeless, open your wrist and let him drink."

That took longer. She had to force the first blood down his throat. Was she too late? Vorniax muttered some ancient chant and Justin's lips moved. Just a soft brush against her skin but it was movement. His mouth fixed on her wrist, like a babe at the breast, and he drank, embracing immortality.

At Vorniax's signal she broke the connection. "Has he had enough?"

Her mentor nodded. "He has. Let him rest. Let the wound heal and then, my dear Gwyltha, you will have the task of explaining to this Roman what you have done to him."

It would not be easy but they had eternity ahead of them. That would surely be long enough to explain. Against all reason and expectation, Justin was now hers.

For ever.

Blood Feud

Patti O'Shea

The stench of death assaulted my senses as I stood on the sidewalk, looking up at the sooty, tan brick facade of the warehouse. White paint obliterated the name of the business that had once used it, but I could make out the words "Trading Company" anyway. Graffiti covered the lower portion of the warehouse, a riot of colour and symbols that meant nothing to me. Deserted roads, broken streetlights, and a full moon obscured by passing clouds made everything seem eerie.

Of course, it was just as likely that my unease was caused by what awaited me in the building – a demon and a dead vampire, the seventh member of my clan killed this month.

I glanced over my shoulder. For a moment, I thought about hopping in the Aston Martin DBS I'd left parked at the kerb and racing off. That wasn't an option because my clan lord had been adamant that I handle this. His insistence puzzled me. Given my past, I thought he'd want to keep me as far away from demons as possible.

While it continued to bother me, I had to trust my ruler. And I could come up with one strong reason for choosing me – I might be his sole option. Chances were no other enforcer was willing to work with a demon, and if the murderer wasn't caught tonight, there might be an all-out war by sundown tomorrow.

It had taken more than 300 years and cost countless lives before a truce had been negotiated between vampires and demons. Prejudice and hatred remained, but the peace had lasted nearly 800 years. Now, the entire thing might unravel before morning. It was my job to make sure that didn't happen.

Huffing out a breath, I extended my senses to scan the building. No sign of the demon I was supposed to meet, but they did have the ability to cloak themselves. Walking to the entrance, I opened the door and stepped inside. I gave my eyes a moment to adjust to the darkness. Slowly, things came into view – more graffiti covered the grey cinder-block walls, the dirt was deep enough on the floor to reach the toes of my black ankle boots, and piles of debris were scattered in random locations.

Since I would probably find my partner-to-be near the body, I scanned for it. With a bead on its location, I headed deeper into the warehouse. It was a large building, partitioned off into smaller spaces, but I took my time. And prepared myself for anything.

There'd been a pattern to the murders – three vampires killed on each of two separate nights at specific time intervals. There was every reason to believe that the demon who'd done it meant to take the lives of two more tonight. With no guarantee that this wasn't a set-up to make me today's second victim, I had to be cautious.

I was strong. Humans didn't worry me and neither did most vampires. But demons? They scared me. I might not hate them across the board like many of my clan members did, but I didn't blindly trust them either.

Yes, my clan lord had assured me that he'd spoken to the demon king himself, but it didn't mean there was no risk. Maybe the demon ruler was in on it, or maybe the killer was good enough to fool a vampire, either way I wasn't taking any chances.

As I neared the body, I slowed even further. Broken crates and pallets offered more places to hide and that had me on edge. Up ahead there was a metal door hanging ajar and I knew I'd reached my destination. I slipped through, not wanting to pull it open any wider, and saw a pair of legs sticking out from behind a mound of refuse. The demon stood about twenty feet away, arms crossed over his chest.

Six centuries had taught me to hide my reactions and doing so now was instinctive. I didn't break stride or gasp even though it felt as if all the oxygen had been sucked out of the universe. It didn't matter. He would have sensed the way my heart sped up, how my pulse tripped when I recognized him. But then I'd felt his pulse surge as well. Leisurely, he lifted his head and looked at me. As his light blue eyes connected with mine, my body had another kind of reaction.

Every woman should have a demon lover once in her life. Seere had been mine.

And this left me even more stunned. Had my clan lord known that the demon king was sending Seere? Instantly, I dismissed that. I never would have been allowed within a mile of this place if my ruler had been aware that the demon from my past would be here.

It didn't matter that it had been nearly 200 years since I'd last seen Seere, I remembered the way his hands had caressed me, the weight of him over me, the thrust of his body inside mine – and the screaming orgasms. Who could forget a male who made them come so hard they lost all control?

He'd grown out his dark brown hair until it was long enough to brush across his shoulders and had pulled the top part back, tying it off with what appeared to be a leather thong. I drank in the sight of him, spending a little extra time on the breadth of his chest, the width of his shoulders and the muscles of his thighs. My mouth went dry and I had to swallow hard.

Only Seere could pull off a black duster over faded, torn blue jeans, tennis shoes and a navy T-shirt. On anyone else, it would be ridiculous, but on him it looked perfect.

Stopping a few feet away, I tucked my hands in the front pockets of my black jeans. If I didn't, I was afraid I'd reach for him and I'd forfeited any right I had to touch him. Damn, though, he was as gorgeous as ever and I longed to run my fingers over his face, kiss those sexy lips.

"Isobel." There was no emotion in his voice and that didn't bode well. Demons felt things deeply.

"Prince Seere," I said, inclining my head slightly.

He raised his eyebrows. "I never told you that."

"Wikipedia. You have a listing there."

"You looked me up," he said and his lips curved. Interesting that he'd spent enough time in this world to know what I was talking about.

"Curiosity." But it had been more than that. I'd been hungry for any information about him that I could find. There wasn't much, but I'd devoured everything I'd come across. I changed the subject. "Do you know who's responsible for murdering members of my clan?"

Seere's smile disappeared. "No, but we want the killer found as badly as you do."

"Really? There's at least one demon who doesn't agree."

He growled and walked away from me before stalking back. Seere still moved with a sinuous grace and that made the ache I felt deepen. He scented my arousal, I knew it by the flare in his eyes and the way the pulse in his carotid artery picked up speed again. Before I could stop it, my fangs began to extend and I turned away to regain my self-command.

It took longer than I liked. Too many memories of too many nights spent sharing pleasure with Seere, and it didn't help that he'd allowed me to taste him. Without permission, demon blood was poisonous to vampires, but when we were given the privilege, their blood was ambrosia and no other was nearly as sweet.

When I had my teeth retracted, I wiped my palms on my thighs and shifted back to face Seere. The knowing expression on his face helped me tamp down the arousal even further.

"I'd forgotten how easily I can excite you."

"I'd forgotten how obnoxious you can be." I bared my fangs at him and this time it had nothing to do with sexual heat.

The bastard gave me a smug look, but then a demon prince wasn't going to be frightened of any vampire, not even an enforcer. "Redheads and their tempers," he said with mock sadness.

That comment pushed my anger level higher and it took all my will power to keep my talons from extending along with my teeth. With one last glare, I brushed past Seere and went to check out the body.

I recognized him, and although he was a member of my clan, I felt no remorse. Herb Cropper had been an arrogant little twit who'd never accomplished anything of import. Not that his ego let him believe that. If it wasn't illegal for one vampire to kill another, he would have been dead long ago. And if he had ever broken the canon, there would have been a dozen enforcers campaigning to be the one to eliminate him – including me.

★   ★   ★

Dispassionately, I examined him. There wasn't a mark on him, but he was twisted up into an unnatural position – the result of his body contorting and convulsing as it tried to fight the poison of demon blood. "Did you see the others who were killed?" I asked Seere when he came up beside me.

"I've been part of the search for the rogue since the beginning."

"Vampires are careful to avoid drinking from demons. How is he gaining our confidence to such a degree?"

"If I were to guess, I'd say the demon didn't convince his victims that it was OK to take his blood. It's more likely that he created a cloak to make himself appear human."

I didn't know they could do that, but instead of commenting on it, I said, "And they wouldn't know differently until it was too late."

"Yes." He paused, then added, "The demons don't want war, Iso. We survive for the same reason your people do – most humans don't believe we exist – but there's no way to hide a conflict and once they know we're here . . . "

"Fanatics will hunt us down and kill us."

Seere nodded. "And then there will be the others, the ones who want to become vampires or demons. It'll be hell on Earth," he said with a smirk.

This time I smiled with him. "At least the demons can disappear into their alternate world."

"For brief periods." Before I could question him about that, Seere said, "If the one committing the murders follows his usual routine, he'll seek out two more vampires tonight. Where would be the best place for him to find victims?"

I shrugged. The possibilities were nearly endless. There were vampires from my clan spread all over the world, but Los Angeles had a disproportionately high number because our ruler called this city home right now. If this were San Francisco, or some other place without a clan lord in residence, it would be easy to pinpoint a location or two. The sheer numbers here meant there were dozens of options.

"You must have some ideas," he pressed. "Where do you hang out?"

"It might be more productive to come up with somewhere that the victims routinely visited." And I wasn't about to tell him that aside from when I needed to feed or had an assignment, I spent most of my time on the clan lord's estate either training or learning from the elders. If Seere wanted to believe I was out every night, I wasn't about to dissuade him.

"That's why you're here – to add your knowledge of vampires to mine on demons."

Yeah, I knew that. The problem was that I hadn't been part of the investigation into the murders until tonight and the only one of the dead I'd had a passing acquaintance with was Herb. Since I did everything I could to avoid him, I wasn't sure I'd be able to come up with any of his hangouts.

"Give me a few minutes to think." After Seere nodded, I wandered from the body and found a crate that had enough wood left that it might support me. Gingerly, I lowered myself to seated and, once I was assured it would hold, I settled back.

The first thing I did was scrounge my brain for all the places I'd heard mentioned as favourite haunts. This wasn't easy. I wasn't quite an outcast among my people, but because I'd had a relationship with a demon, I remained suspect and countless conversations came to a halt when I neared.

It didn't help me concentrate when the demon in question sat beside me. The crate swayed and my muscles tensed, preparing themselves in case I needed to leap to my feet, but the dilapidated wood remained intact. As soon as I relaxed, my thigh pressed into Seere's and a flash fire roared through every cell in my body. Somehow, I managed to stop the full extension of my teeth and talons, but I was pretty sure my eyes had changed, that the irises had become bluish-white outlined with black.

Unable to prevent it, I looked at Seere and realized I wasn't the only one who felt something. The red glow in his eyes revealed his own arousal.

For an instant, I couldn't breathe. He still wanted me. Until this moment, I hadn't been sure of that. Demons were highly emotional and Seere hadn't seemed to react much to my presence, but he couldn't conceal his desire now. Of course, I wasn't hiding my ardour either. Hope was replaced by disappointment when he cooled the heat and stared at me stonily.

Shifting to give myself a few inches of space, I worked on banking my need and returned to my task. I came up with nine possible locations and began to narrow them down.

While Herb had earned the scorn of many members from our clan, it was the females who particularly disliked him. That allowed me to eliminate a few places. His snobbery had me crossing off some of the higher-end clubs from my list – not only wouldn't he fit in there, he wouldn't make an effort to try. That left me with three other possibilities.

One was a neighbourhood pub in a working-class part of the city, but it wasn't somewhere a vampire looking to feed would go. It was too small, too quiet, and for those same reasons, a demon on the hunt would likely rule it out as well.

"Any ideas yet?" Seere prompted.

"I'm trying to decide between a dance club called the Tiki-A-Go-Go and a goth club named House of the Damned."

"Which one would you go to?"

"Neither of them appeal to me, but I'm not Herb." I used my chin to indicate the dead vampire. "We're pretty much polar opposites."

"Then perhaps the question is which of them would you be least likely to go to?"

"House of the Damned," I said without hesitation.

"We'll start there."

Seere wasn't surprised by Isobel's sports car – 200 years ago it had been a fancy piece of horseflesh. When it came to transportation, the woman liked fast and flashy. The Aston Martin might not have the quickness of a Lamborghini or a Ferrari, but it had other things going for it and she looked good behind the wheel. Something she no doubt was aware of.

Music from Tchaikovsky's *Swan Lake* filled the car with lilting melodies, but didn't calm him. The first thing he'd done after getting in was to buckle up, but it took all his control not to clutch the door handle as she drove from the warehouse to the club. His edginess had more to do with Isobel than with her driving, but her hunger for speed unnerved him at the best of times and today was far from that.

Until his sexy little vampire walked in the warehouse tonight, he thought he'd gotten over her and he'd been happy in the delusion. Damn his father for insisting that Seere be the one to act as liaison on these murders. One glance was all it had taken to revive his old feelings for her.

He shifted slightly to get a better view of her face. His vision was as sharp at night as it was in daylight and he was able to see her clearly. Iso was even more beautiful than in his memories. Her dark red hair cascaded past her breasts – shorter than it had been – and her skin was porcelain smooth. Flawless.

Seere clenched his hands into fists to keep from touching her. Everything brought back memories. Her elfin chin reminded him of how she'd lift it when she was angry. Her emerald green eyes had often been smoky with arousal or blazing with passion before morphing to bluish-white. And her mouth . . . His body responded to the memory of her full lips open beneath his, and the way she'd used them to tease him.

Reaching out, he tilted one of the car's vents so the cool air was blowing directly onto him. If it was only lust, it would be easy, but what he felt for Isobel went far beyond that and into dangerous territory. Very dangerous territory.

She'd walked away from him once without a backwards glance and he'd have to be a complete masochist to invite her to trash his heart again. Seere just wasn't sure he'd be able to stop himself, not when he already struggled with his emotions. Why did she have this power over him? Why couldn't he leave the past behind the way she had when she'd left?

The car and the woman hummed with impatience when they were forced to stop for a traffic light. She'd always had a problem with waiting. Iso was quick to anger, quick to forgive, and quick to laugh. And her passionate nature had been one of the things he'd missed most.

She was dressed completely in black – a long-sleeved, V-neck shirt, black jeans and saucy ankle boots with four buckles across the front. Immediately, an image came into his mind of her wearing nothing except those boots. Seere fought to banish the idea before his body betrayed him. "You're dressed for a goth club," he said, hoping conversation would help him control his thoughts.

"Not quite, but I wanted to be able to blend into the night in case our meeting was a set-up."

"A demon doesn't have to see you in order to track you," he reminded Isobel. And now he was worrying about her. Great.

"I know."

Her half-smile made him wonder what had her amused, but Seere left it alone. "Can you run in those heels? Fight?"

"Yes, I've done it before."

He didn't ask about that either, but he wanted to. The idea of Isobel being at risk bothered him. Seere knew she was an enforcer for her clan – she'd held that position the last time he'd been with her – but he didn't like it any better now than he had back then. The fact that she regularly hunted down humans who targeted vampires, as well as rogues who violated the laws of her people, wasn't his concern. Not any more.

And he was lying to himself. Seere nearly growled in frustration. Fortunately he spotted the club and that allowed him to pull back from his roiling emotions. The front of the building was painted black and the only colour was a red neon sign above the door that proclaimed HOUSE OF THE DAMNED.

There was no valet parking, but that didn't bother Iso. She found a lot nearby and zipped the DBS into one of the spots. "Are you going to use some magic to change your clothes?" she asked as she turned off the engine.

"No." Seere opened the door and got out of the car. When they met at the rear, he added, "The demon we're after is powerful and I might need all my energy to defeat him."

She nodded. "You have me, too. Don't forget that." Isobel walked off, leaving him where he stood.

Seere caught up with her in a few strides. "I want you to stay out of this."

"Doesn't work that way, partner. We're in it together." She took a couple of steps, stopped, and grabbed his arm. "Can you cloak what you are? Not just from vampires, but from the demon we're after as well? If he senses you in the club, he'll guess that you're looking for him."

"He won't realize I'm there until it's too late," Seere said, and before he could stop himself, he pushed her hair off her face and behind her shoulder. He watched a flush spread over her cheeks, but he couldn't enjoy her reaction, not when such a simple touch left him burning, too. Iso had always had this effect on him and even their past history couldn't seem to cool his desire. He pulled back and was careful not to touch her again as they walked to the club's entrance.

Isobel tried to pay their cover charge, but he was faster than her. Seere wanted to be irritated by that – he was looking for excuses to keep her at arm's length – but he couldn't maintain the emotion, not after they got asked for ID. Who else could he share his amusement with except her?

Leaving the vestibule, they entered the bar proper. It was jammed with people, but he'd expected that on a Friday night. What did surprise him was the music – 80s techno-rock. This was what the goth set listened to?

Shaking that off, Seere looked around to get the lie of the land. The walls were painted a bright pink shade that made him think of bubble gum, the ceiling was black, and coloured strobes shot light around the shadowy interior of the club. A DJ was positioned on a dais overlooking the dance floor. Along the sides of the large room there were tables filled with patrons. His scan showed about twenty per cent of the crowd was vampires, but he didn't pick up any other demon.

If the murderer were here though, he'd be cloaked the same way Seere was. Vampires had senses nearly as acute as demons.

They'd chosen the right place, Seere felt certain of that. The dead vamps he'd seen had all been dressed similarly to the humans here, not in the kind of clothes they'd wear for somewhere called Tiki-A-Go-Go.

Of course, there were no guarantees that the vampires didn't hang out in more than one goth club or that the demon hadn't hunted in multiple locations, but he was betting against the second. His kind tended to be creatures of habit. As long as things had gone well in this club, the killer would keep coming back.

Iso went on her toes to holler near his ear. "Anything?"

"No," he shouted back then asked, "Is this the only goth club on your list of night spots?"

"Yeah, most prefer the higher-end places with a quieter atmosphere." She grinned up at him. "You know how the *old* folks feel about kids and their music today."

His lips quirked. Many of the vampires would have grown up listening to traditional folk songs, opera, or symphony and it was logical that this type of club wouldn't appeal to a large number of them.

"Let's make a circuit of the room." When she nodded, Seere took her hand. He had no other choice, not unless he was willing to risk them becoming separated. And he wasn't. No matter what, Isobel would remain safe tonight. He'd make sure of that.

Because of the crush, they had to move slowly, threading their way through the sea of people. Occasionally, another vampire would stare at them oddly, but they never acknowledged Isobel and she didn't give them a nod or smile either. It left him curious since there was no way any of them could know he was a demon. Maybe their reticence had to do with her being an enforcer. And it made Seere wonder if she was lonely. If her own people were leery of her, who did she have for friends?

When they finished their trek around the perimeter, Iso looked at him expectantly. Seere shook his head, then raised his eyebrows, asking her wordlessly if she'd picked up anything. With a grimace, she shook her head, too.

I must have chosen the wrong venue.

Seere started when he heard Isobel in his head. She hadn't been powerful enough to communicate like that 200 years ago. He studied her, wondering what else she could do now that she hadn't been able to do previously.

"Seere, I'm sorry. I chose the wrong —"

I heard you, he sent in reply, wincing as a human female elbowed him in the back as she walked by. *It's early yet. The demon might still show up. He has a timetable for his murders and if he pushes the second one to the last minute tonight, we could have another hour before he arrives.* Unable to stop himself, Seere asked, *When did you learn to use telepathy?*

Before she could answer, someone knocked into her hard enough to send her stumbling. Seere caught her, wrapping his arms around her to keep her steady. Hell. He was going under and he wasn't sure he gave a damn, not as long as he was holding her. His only hope was if she stepped back, away from him. But she didn't. Instead, she wrapped her arms around his waist and looked up at him.

I was about 400 years old when you knew me, still a fledgling. I came into more abilities when I grew older.

He nodded, but didn't comment. This was a difference between demons and vampires of which he'd been unaware. He'd had his full powers from the time he'd been twenty and it had never occurred to him that she wouldn't have all of hers as well. And Seere realized something else – by using this skill with him, she was indicating that she trusted him.

She had every reason to believe he felt nothing for her, he'd made sure of it, but she had enough faith in him to share something about herself that he didn't know. If he wanted to, he could use it against her, but he wouldn't. He couldn't.

More people pushed past, bumping into them. It was then that Seere realized they were directly in the path for the bar. He shifted Isobel out of the way, but he didn't let go of her.

Why don't we dance? she invited with a small smile. *It will put us nearly in the middle of the room, making it easier to scan the entire club. We'll blend in better. We've been attracting a few curious glances.*

Seere looked around and noticed she was right. They didn't belong here, not really. Iso was wearing black, the colour of choice, but she didn't have any tattoos or facial piercings. The only thing he had on that sort of made him fit in was his long, dark coat. If the killer walked in and noticed the humans casting odd looks in their direction, he might question their presence. And if he scanned closely enough, there was a good chance he'd detect Isobel's power, or depending on how strong he was, he might be able to penetrate the cloak Seere was using.

You know I can't dance worth a damn, but I guess it doesn't matter here.

All he had to do was gyrate, not like those intricate dances from way back when. He eased Isobel away and offered her his elbow before he realized how formal the gesture was. She didn't comment, simply looped her arm through his and let him lead her to the floor.

It wasn't long before he decided the old dances were easier. At least he knew there was a set of steps to follow even if he couldn't manage them with any finesse. Now? It was all free-form. Seere felt stiff, uncomfortable.

He watched Isobel, hoping he could imitate her. He quickly lost himself in the graceful way she moved. From there, it was too easy to recall how she'd undulated beneath him, and his temperature rose. Scan, Seere reminded himself, but he found nothing out of the ordinary in the club. And she was right in front of him – the woman he'd loved to distraction.

The DJ chose that moment to segue into a slow song and, with a smile, Isobel stepped into his arms. For an instant, he resisted, then he decided the hell with it and gathered her against his body.

Seere swayed, moving just enough to tease both of them. He'd missed this, he'd missed *her*. His Isobel.

She melted into him and he closed his eyes, not only to savour her breasts pressed into his chest, but to hide the red glow that likely was beginning to appear as his arousal deepened. He slipped a hand to her bottom and pulled her more firmly into him. Isobel didn't protest, simply held on tighter. Seere let her heat engulf his senses. At least he did until his brain circled back to all the questions that had never been answered between them.

Why? Why had she left him? She'd never told him she loved him, but he'd been certain she had. Would she walk away from him tonight after they took down the murderer? The same way she'd disappeared back then?

He couldn't stand the uncertainty, the not knowing. *Why, Iso? Why didn't you stay with me?*

I'd been lost in Seere, in the brush of his body against mine. His question dragged me back to earth with a bang. For an instant, I clutched him closer, then I leaned away far enough to look into his face. Passion burned in his eyes. As did hurt.

He wouldn't believe me, but I'd tell him the truth anyway – even if it did make me a traitor in the eyes of my clan.

I had no choice.

"There's always a choice." His hands flexed where they rested against me and I heard the impatience in his voice despite the volume of the music.

Swallowing hard, I gathered my courage. I wasn't violating canon, but sharing our business with outsiders was strongly discouraged. *No, there isn't. Not for a fledgling. Until we reach our five hundredth year, our sire can bend our will to his. Mine discovered my relationship with you and disapproved of it. We argued, and when it became clear that I wouldn't go along with him, he compelled me to obey.*

Seere didn't speak, simply stared at me. I met his gaze squarely. What I'd told him was the truth. I wanted – needed – him to believe me. It took a long time before the suspicion left his face.

Why didn't you seek me out when your status changed?

Two reasons. I'd disappeared from your life without a word, and it had been nearly a hundred years. I wasn't sure of my reception. He began to speak aloud, but I rested the pads of my fingers over his lips to stop him. *That's not all. The clan lord can compel anyone in his line to follow his will, fledgling or not. Seere, my sire* is *the clan lord.*

His eyes closed when what I'd revealed registered. He leaned down, resting his forehead to mine. Tears that I believed I'd cried out a couple of centuries ago gathered and I blinked to get rid of them. I thought I'd resigned myself to eternity without him, but that was before I'd seen him again, before I'd felt his arms around me once more. We had tonight and not a second longer. By morning, either the murderer would be caught and justice administered or Seere's people and mine would be at war.

Thoughts of the killer had me scanning the club for the first time in quite a while. But it was all clear. That made it easier to give in to temptation. I pressed my lips to Seere's in a slow, sweet kiss that held everything that I felt for him.

We gave up all pretence of dancing and simply stood in the centre of the dance floor, arms around each other, as we let passion take over. Or nearly so. I couldn't forget the mission, not entirely. When Seere raised his head, I could see the burden of responsibility weighed him down too.

"I want you, Iso."

"I feel the same. Maybe after we catch . . . " I let my words trail off.

The odds were good that if we did capture the demon who'd slain the vampires, our moment would be lost. Other enforcers would have to be summoned to help take the murderer to the clan's estate. I'd be expected to stay to watch the execution. By then it would be close to morning and any further contact with Seere would likely be prohibited. I shook my head.

"Come on," he said and, taking my hand, pulled me through the crowd to the back of the nightclub.

"Seere!" But as breathless as my voice had been, I doubted he heard me. *We can't make love here, not when the demon we're after could arrive at any moment.*

I know that. He didn't slow, just kept walking until we reached what appeared to be a storeroom at the rear of the club. He left the door ajar, tugged the collar of his jacket away from his neck, and bared his throat to me. With a smirk, he said, "Not as good as sex, but as close as we can chance."

"Are you certain?"

Instead of answering me directly, Seere spoke in a language I didn't understand. When he finished, he pressed me close.

The heels of my boots put me at the precise height and, wrapping my arms around his waist, I ran my tongue over the pulse point in his neck, tasting his skin. I wanted to sink into him, but couldn't allow myself the indulgence. Instead, I pressed a kiss against his throat and eased away to extend my fangs. Our eyes met and his hands settled at my hips, urging me tightly against the lower half of his body. Carefully, not wanting to hurt him, I bent my head and pierced his flesh.

Bliss flowed through me, but I sipped slowly. This wasn't about feeding, this was about love. And about faith in each other. Seere had to trust me not to take too much blood and I had to trust him to have truly granted me permission to drink from him. And it was about pleasure – for both of us.

The throb of his pulse was echoed between my thighs and he rocked against me. It was good, but it could be better. We could be naked with Seere deep inside me while I savoured him. There'd been times I'd orgasmed simply from tasting his blood, but I couldn't lose myself that deeply in the moment. Not now.

Long before I was ready, I eased from him. After retracting my teeth, I licked at the small punctures on his neck to heal them. Not that he needed it. Demons mended even faster than vampires, but I liked tending to him in this small way.

"You didn't take much," Seere said when I raised my head.

The huskiness in his voice made me shiver and I wished we were safely tucked away in bed, free to explore each other at our leisure. "You said if the demon was strong, you might need all your powers. I didn't want to risk weakening you."

"Yeah." He sounded resigned.

"We better get back to work," I said without enthusiasm as I stepped away from him.

He nodded and this time when he took my hand, I knew it was because he wanted the closeness. When we re-entered the bar, the press of the crowd and the volume of the music made me feel claustrophobic, but I took a deep breath and forced it aside. This was my job and Seere needed me to be his partner, not a love-struck idiot.

We'll make another circuit, he sent telepathically.

I smiled to let him know I'd heard and moved with him, staying slightly behind and allowing Seere to use his broad shoulders to cut a path for us through the crowd. Because of my position, I didn't see what made him stiffen and jerk to a stop. "What?" I asked sharply.

Without a word, Seere dropped my hand and took off running.

Muttering a curse, I chased after him, almost needing to fight my way through the humans who blocked my path. He'd seen our target, I was sure of it, and I was angry at being left in the dust. We were supposed to work together, damn it. I reached the vestibule and kept going, bursting out onto the sidewalk.

A sense of motion had me looking to my left, and calling on all my preternatural speed. I followed. Demons were just as fast as vampires. I didn't catch up to him, but I didn't fall farther behind either.

We raced on and on until my lungs ached and a stitch developed in my side, but I didn't slow. I couldn't. What if something happened to Seere because I wasn't there to help him?

I crossed intersections against the lights by going airborne and then running again. Humans would see nothing except a blur – the same as when I was on the ground – but it kept me in the hunt. But damn, I hated flying and the nausea it gave me.

By the time I reached the park, I'd lost track of how far I'd travelled or where I actually was in the Los Angeles area. I could tell by the graffiti sprayed on the benches that this wasn't a safe part of town. Since Seere and the other demon were already circling each other, eyes glowing red, it was a good thing there weren't going to be any credible witnesses in the vicinity.

Fangs and talons at the ready, I brushed my mind against Seere's to let him know I was there.

No teeth, damn it. Even telepathically he could growl. But he was right – I couldn't risk getting the demon's blood in my mouth. I pulled my fangs back in, reducing my weaponry by half.

Lightning crashed from the sky, narrowly missing Seere. I swallowed a gasp. The second bolt connected, but didn't seem to cause any harm. He raised his hands, formed a glowing ball of energy between them, and hurled it towards the killer. Our enemy shunted it aside as if it were nothing more than a beach ball.

I wasn't used to standing around, watching a fight, but I was out of my depth here. Far out of my depth. Vampires couldn't control the weather or harness fireballs. I was glad the demon wars had ended long before my birth.

They threw more lightning fireballs at each other. Then they added ropes of fire to the mix. What kind of shields did they possess? Neither of them seemed to feel any ill effects.

Apparently growing frustrated with his lack of success, the murderer hurled a burst of lightning at *me*. But I'd expected that and my own protective field took the hit. It wobbled, but didn't fall.

Seere threw himself at the demon with enough force that I heard the thud of bodies from where I stood. They went down, rolling on the grass, and when my lover ended up pinned beneath the other male, I launched myself at the enemy, my talons slashing at his exposed back.

My claws glanced off whatever shielding the killer had and, with a snarl, he turned on me, hitting me with enough force to send my body sailing backwards.

I landed hard. My head slammed into the ground and I had the wind knocked out of me. Lying there, I struggled to clear the black spots obscuring my vision and draw in air before the killer decided to jump me. Through the ringing in my ears, I heard Seere's growl and detected more sounds of battle.

Shaking my head to clear my eyesight, I got to my feet. I wasn't entirely steady, but I staggered towards the fight. Both males were fast, so fast that there were times even I couldn't detect what was happening.

The killer restrained Seere against a tree trunk so I ran at him again even though I hadn't penetrated his protection earlier. I didn't succeed now either and, when he hit me this time, I probably flew twice the distance I had before. I remained prone, struggling to recover.

"Trying to protect your vampire whore, cousin?"

"Trying to prevent a war, Berith," Seere replied, the final word punctuated with a grunt.

I heard sounds of impact, of flesh meeting flesh, but I couldn't prise my eyes open. Part of me longed to curl up and sleep, but that wasn't an option. I was a full-powered enforcer, damn it, and not some fledgling.

"You're weak," Berith said with a defiant sneer in his voice. "Your whole line is weak. There never should have been a truce. Vampires are an aberration and they need to be eradicated."

Coughing, I rolled to my hands and knees. I wasn't much help, I knew that, but I couldn't leave Seere to fight alone. My stomach heaved as I stood. There was another flurry of attacks, only half of which I saw clearly. Then Seere was on the ground again, his cousin poised above him.

Now, Iso! His protection is down.

With all my strength, I ran at the demon. When I reached him, I slashed the talons of my right hand across the side of his neck. There was enough force there to rip out a large chunk of flesh and drive him backwards, away from Seere. But Berith didn't fall. Blood spurted and I hurriedly closed my mouth.

Seere was on him then, his own claws extended. Before Berith could react, my lover sliced down, severing his head from his body.

I stood there, staring stupidly until Seere lurched over to me. "You're covered in blood," he said. "Keep your mouth closed until I clean you up." He lifted his hand and, without touching me, rubbed his fingers together. I felt the bloody moisture on my face, on my neck, arms and clothes disappear. "There."

"Are you OK?" I asked. He used magic to remove the blood from his own body as well.

"Healing already." I frowned, but Seere waved off my concern and framed my face between his hands. "He hurt you."

"I'm fine." I would be in about an hour or so. Right now, I felt as if I'd been tackled by the entire defensive line of the Oakland Raiders. I raised my arms so I could curl my hands around Seere's forearms. "I don't know why demons are worried about a war with my people. The way your cousin kicked my butt, you can handle us easily."

Seere shook his head. "From what I was told, the vampires came up with a way to even the playing field during the wars. I bet the enforcers who fought at that time could tell you how."

They probably could, but I didn't think they'd fill me in, not when they'd worry I'd spill the secret to Seere. It didn't matter, though – not this minute. Time was short, I knew it, and there was something I wanted to share. Needed to share. I held both his hands in mine and moved closer to lean in to him. "I loved you then, though I never said the words," I told him quietly. "I love you still and know that I'll love you in the centuries to come even though we're apart."

His hold tightened briefly before he relaxed his grip. "I love you too, Iso. Always have, always will."

I was blinking back tears when his lips found mine. Releasing his hands, I wrapped my arms around Seere and held him close. Our kiss was both passionate and sweet and I poured my heart into it, trying to make up for the empty years stretched out in front of me.

But with the demon dead and dawn still hours away, maybe we could steal some time. One night wasn't too much to ask, was it?

"Is Berith's body enough to calm your clan's need for vengeance?"

We jerked apart. The male who'd spoken was unknown to me, but he was a demon. With his dark hair and light blue eyes, he bore enough resemblance to Seere to be a relative. Considering the array of bodyguards I saw, I suspected it was his father – the demon king. My clan lord stood beside him, his own contingent of personal enforcers present as well.

"An execution would have been a safer course of action, but if we hoist his head and body on pikes in the courtyard, that should suffice," my sire said.

It was surreal. A vampire clan lord and a demon king conversing as if they were buddies. Neither one of them seemed the least bit shocked or surprised to find Seere and I locked in an embrace. As I recalled the anger I'd faced 200 years ago when my sire had discovered my relationship with a demon, it made it seem more bizarre.

"This whole thing was a set-up," Seere said, half in disbelief, half in realization.

"You think Berith wasn't a threat?" his father asked.

"Not that part; Berith was real. I'm talking about Isobel and I discovering we were assigned to work together. That's what the two of you arranged, isn't it? You were hoping we'd rekindle our past relationship."

The leaders shared a glance and it was my clan lord who answered. "It's difficult to end old hatreds when those who warred yet live."

"You didn't feel that way before when you ordered me to stay away from Seere," I told him.

"Times change. It's necessary for vampires and demons to become allies or the future might be grim indeed."

"Politics. With Seere a demon prince and me a daughter of your blood, if we bond, we're a symbol of unity for both sides."

My clan lord inclined his head and I scowled. I thought he'd saved me from an expedient marriage 600 years ago, but it appeared destiny – and my sire – had other plans. It angered me, but before I could work up enough ire to confront him, Seere took my hand and anchored me at his side.

"They might have manipulated us for their own ends," he said, cupping my cheek with his free hand, "but don't forget we get something we want out of this too. A future together."

That made my temper evaporate and I smiled slowly. "A win-win situation."

"Exactly."

Seere's father and my clan lord turned away, dismissing us, and began issuing orders to their troops. And as the demon and vampire guards worked together to collect the pieces of the murderer's body, Seere wrapped his arm around my shoulders and led me away. "Where are we going?" I asked.

"Somewhere private so we can start catching up on all the years we missed." His grin was erotically predatory. "I had this fantasy tonight about you and those boots you're wearing."

My blood heated and my fangs dropped down just the smallest amount. I remembered the pleasure I'd had in the past while playing out Seere's fantasies. Eternity had never looked better.

Love Bites

Angie Fox

Katarina Volholme D'Transylvania checked her teeth for lipstick and
then, as if to tempt fate, added another layer of Sinfully Scarlet gloss.
This was it. Her rebel moment. And it had only taken 873 years.

Her fingers shook as she stowed the gloss into the back pocket
of her black leather pants. They felt wickedly snug. Glorious. Her
mother would have had a heart attack. Well, if her mother's heart
still beat.

Katarina, or Kat as her family called her, belonged to one of the
oldest vampire families in Romania. She'd learned to sit straight,
mind her manners and never, ever drink from the help. She'd been
the perfect little princess. Until now.

Butterflies tickled her stomach. She parted the rich velvet stage
curtain, blinking at the overhead lights.

If she didn't do it now, she never would.

"You ready, sweetheart?" A handsome, grey-haired vamp clapped
her on the arm, treating her to a sly smile and a wink as he passed.

"More than you'll ever know." Once. Just once, she was going to
do something for herself. And if it ruined her reputation for the next
century? She'd worry about that tomorrow.

Adrenaline raced through her body as spotlights popped to life.

An exaggerated drum roll sounded as the grey-haired vamp
jogged out on stage. He threw his arms out, clearly eating it up.
"Welcome toooo Love Bites!" The audience went wild as the game-
show band started in on a lively round of theme music. The affable
vamp gave an exaggerated bow. Television cameras followed his
every move.

"Each week, one lucky lady gets to pick from not two, but three vampy studs to find her one true love. Will it last for the evening, or for all eternity? That's up for grabs on stage tonight. I'm your host, Frankie G. Winner, coming to you live from Kiev, the undead capital of the world, with the hottest show on Vamp TV."

Kat sucked in a breath. Maybe this hadn't been the best idea. But, hell's bells, she had to take charge of her life. Now.

"Sponsored by Swiss Storage. For memories of a lifetime. Trust Swiss Storage. And by Fang-zite. The all natural Male Fang Enhancer. Show her you've got a little something extra ... with Fang-zite."

"Go," the stage director ordered.

Kat smoothed her red silk top and, with more confidence than she felt, strutted out under the blaring game-show music and lights, her glam-girl earrings tickling her long pale neck. *I am immortal, hear me roar.*

The studio audience seemed to stretch for miles. Never mind the countless vamps watching at home. Her stomach tingled.

Her parents were going to kill her.

Stop it. There was nothing wrong with dating. Most vamps got to date. Only the royals were forced to marry people they barely knew. And because of their stupid rules, she'd endured centuries of a loveless marriage. She deserved a little fun.

Frankie brushed his lips against her cheek as the clapping from the audience died down. "Princess Katarina Volholme D'Transylvania," he said, rolling her name on his tongue like a fine wine. "You are the only daughter of the King of Romania. Newly single after 856 years and I must say you smell terrific."

Kat smiled inwardly. The perfume was her own creation.

"Are you ready to find the man of your dreams?"

"Bring 'em on," she purred.

Frankie urged Kat into a cute little perch on a barstool that had to have been designed for a giant. Add that to the fact that she didn't usually wear heels. The lights suddenly seemed too bright.

Relax. It was just like when Grandpa fought the Byzantines. *Move with purpose, move with power.*

Kate glided into the hot seat, and eased her glossy black hair from her shoulders. Frankie nodded in approval and she grinned despite herself. If she played it right, no one would even know she'd learned her modern English from watching *American Idol.*

A blood-red wall separated her from the male contestants. Frankie rested a smooth hand on her shoulder. "Are you ready to meet the bachelors?"

She nodded as the lights came up on the other side.

"Mozart," he called, "can we get a drum roll, please?"

The flame-haired bandleader spun his sticks and began pounding a wild, jungle beat.

"Let's say hello to our first contender," Frankie announced. "Bachelor number one hails from ancient Rome, where he wowed the ladies in the pits of the Coliseum. Today, he runs his own security firm and enjoys extreme sports. But will bachelor number one have the sword and the strength to win this lady's hand? We'll find out tonight."

The audience hooted and hollered. Kat fought the urge to peel at her Wildly Red nail polish. Bachelor number one sounded promising. Then again, her father hadn't liked the Romans since they'd invaded his lands in the second century. Stop it, she chastised herself. Nothing would please her dad except her marrying Vlad the Detailer. While he wasn't as obscenely old as her former husband, he was just as vanilla. Worse, he was chief of operations for his cousin, Vlad the Impaler. Kat had met them both at a dinner party a few hundred years ago and let's just say they were *bat crazy*, always trying to conquer something. Even if her dad thought Vlad would make a nice, ambitious husband for her, it just wasn't worth it.

"Our second bachelor hails all the way from England where he was a big hit as a royal executioner at the Tower of London. These days, he makes his living slicing and dicing news articles. Our bachelor is a journalism professor at the University of Missouri. But can mere words provoke the passion of a princess? We'll find out."

A group of women in the back started whistling. He must be good-looking. Most vamps were, but still, it took something special to get them going. Kat crossed her legs. She wouldn't mind being hot for the teacher.

"Bachelor number three hails from the Scottish Highlands. He's as comfortable in a tartan as he is at the table on the World Champion Poker tour. Want to finally know what's under that kilt? Bachelor number three is betting on true love."

She had always wondered about men in kilts. And she was more than ready for a little adventure after being cooped up for the last eight and a half centuries. Vamps mated for life and let's just say her husband hadn't exactly gotten out of the castle much.

To be fair, he was almost 2,000 years old when she'd married him. He'd been an old, old, *old* friend of the family's – her parents' choice, of course. He'd spent his nights dissecting the moths that flew into his study window. Or eating songbirds. He'd never had time for Kat. Marrying her had been a favour to her father and the crown, nothing more.

"And now," Frankie said like he was announcing the cure for sunlight, "it's time for our bachelorette's first question."

Kat sat up a little straighter and began reading the first pink question card. "As you may know, I haven't been out much in the last few centuries and I'm up for a fun time, maybe even a few *surprises*." She emphasized the last word as the card instructed. "Bachelor number one, where would you take me on our first date?"

"Well, Katarina . . . "

The Roman's voice sounded smooth, velvety. Kat succumbed to a very un-princess-like fidget.

"I'd take you to paradise, baby, because that's where you'd be after one kiss from me."

She forced herself not to gag. The Romans always did like their poetry, but sheesh – she'd expected more from a gladiator.

Kat glanced at the endless audience and immediately regretted it. After living quietly for so many years, it felt strange to be in front of so many people.

She cleared her throat. "Bachelor number two, where would you take me?"

Kat pasted on a smile – practised and perfected over the centuries – as he droned on and on about a picnic by a beautiful lake, one without food (for obvious reasons), without beverages (any and all consumables gave him gas) and not too close to the lake (he had a water phobia ever since his near drowning in 1754). Never mind that he was immortal. Well, she wasn't going to learn any more. Kat wasn't going anywhere with bachelor number two.

This simply had to get better.

"Bachelor number three? Where would you take me?"

"It's simple, Katarina." His voice was low, rumbling. If he'd had a Highland accent, he'd lost it years ago. "I'd ease you onto the back of my Harley, and rev up the engine. After that, it's anything goes."

She was suddenly aware of how tightly her black leather pants hugged her legs, her thighs. Kat tried to get her mind off it by focusing on him, but then all she could think about was what he *wasn't* wearing on *his* thighs – or anywhere else under that kilt. Did Highlanders really go commando? And was she ready to find out?

"Bachelor number three," she began.

"Number one," Frankie corrected her.

"No, we're skipping that." Kat waved him off. She needed to talk to the Scotsman again. She eyed the next question card: *If we were married . . .*

It would never happen. Kat flipped to the next card. She didn't need marriage again. She just needed a life, one where she called the shots for a change. Forget the cards. Kat shoved them underneath her. "Bachelor number three–" she folded her hands in her lap in anticipation "– what would you say is your best asset?"

"My attitude," he said simply. "I don't give up. I don't give in. And I know how to treat a woman." He lowered his voice. "When you leave here tonight, with me, I'll show you exactly what I mean."

Like he just assumed she'd go with him. Oh, who was she kidding? She'd made her choice. Kat was going to have her own version of a Highland fling with the utterly delectable Scotsman.

She stamped down a squeal of triumph. Finally! She'd been dreaming of going on a date since she caught her maid sneaking out with a handsome young blacksmith back in the seventeenth century.

Of course there was the issue of the rest of the show. *What's the strangest thing you've ever bitten? How many vamps can you fit in your coffin? Name the wildest place you've ever slept.*

She hardly listened to the answers. She wanted the Highlander.

Fionnlagh MacLaomainn had the little vampire exactly where he wanted her. Sure, he couldn't see the maverick brunette on the other side of the wall, but he felt her heat like the pounding of a battering ram. Her desire, too. She wanted him.

And why shouldn't she?

His kind specialized in giving the vamps exactly what they craved. Too bad he wasn't working for the eager Princess.

Finn cocked an arm over the back of his chair and shifted uncomfortably as the wooden stake he carried rubbed into his back. He never went anywhere without it. Vamps could be damned unpredictable.

Only the wealthiest undead could afford to keep an empath fairy like Finn on staff. Finn was undetectable to vamps when he wanted to be. Deadly too.

Still, he wouldn't have signed on for this job if it had meant hurting Princess Katarina. He didn't injure innocents. He would take her back to the King, however. She'd protest. He'd insist. After all, Vlad the Detailer had already arrived for the wedding. The vamp had a reputation for being sharp, focused and utterly obsessed with order. It would go much better for Katarina if Finn delivered her in good time.

Then he could get back to providing real security.

In his last mission, he'd staked a band of assassins. A king as old and powerful as Volholme had made his share of enemies. Still, Finn had a feeling someone new was gunning for the throne. There had been three attempts on the King's life in the past year. They needed Vlad's security forces, and perhaps even his cousin's, before another attack occured. It was a dangerous juncture – too dangerous.

It wasn't the time for the Princess to be running off.

Well, he'd tracked her, he'd found her, and now he'd bring her back. Finn ran a hand along his jaw as the host of the show asked the male contestants to stand.

In his three centuries with the royal guard, he was used to feeling the base emotions the more unstable vamps carried with them – fear, greed, hate.

Tonight, he was sensing something else entirely.

Finn stood, feet apart, as one by one, Princess Katarina met the poor saps she didn't choose. He shifted uncomfortably as the heat in his groin built.

Gods be to Glasgow. The vixen couldn't stop thinking about what he had going on downstairs and it was making him damned uncomfortable. Her father had claimed she was innocent, naive – untouched for at least the last several hundred years – locked in a fargalin' castle in Romania for God's sake. Seems it had given her plenty of time to work on her fantasies.

Think of the job.

He didn't need her approval. Didn't want her company. Even so, when he stepped around the wall to greet her, he couldn't help but swell with pride at the way she eyed him. A petite thing, as most women of her era were, with an upturned nose and pouty lips to die for. But there was something else that he hadn't seen in her file photo – a sparkle in her rich green eyes, an aliveness that he hadn't seen in a long time. He took her in slowly and wished he was the kind of creature who could give her what she clearly wanted.

The little royal was ready to let loose with about eight centuries' worth of sin and debauchery. Too bad for her she picked the wrong man to fool around with.

"Hello, Princess," he said, taking her small palm in his, giving in to the urge to rub his thumb against the soft skin on the top of her hand. "You can call me Finn."

Her eyes darted down to where he touched her then back up at him. "It's a pleasure," she said, her voice low and breathy.

She was more open than he'd ever seen a vamp. He couldn't read her thoughts, just her impressions. And what she was broadcasting right now made blood rush to parts that he'd rather forget about while on international undead television.

He couldn't help but grin. He liked a challenge. And this woman was more dangerous than a rabid vampire horde.

The announcer talked animatedly about their supposed dream date: a romantic getaway to Venice, Italy. There, they'd enjoy a cosy gondola ride for two before being whisked away to the terraced clock tower above St Mark's Square. As the moon rose above the city, they'd get a true taste of classic Venice by dining on a pair of donors descended from the great Renaissance painter Giovanni Bellini himself.

Finn tuned out the rest. It didn't matter anyway. They wouldn't be going to Venice. No, the Princess was coming with him.

Kat squeezed her toes against her slick, gold strappy sandals and knew she'd made the right choice. Fionnlagh MacLaomainn was even more delicious than she'd pictured him. Not to mention dangerous. He stood with his feet set apart, chest pulled back, and eyes that explored the entire quivering length of her, and then went back for seconds.

He wore a blue and green plaid kilt, a white linen shirt and had the roughened look of a man who wasn't afraid to get out there and live life. He had a squared-off jaw, an angular nose, and – her favourite part of all – auburn hair that whispered just short of his shoulders, with bits of gold and grey threaded throughout. Finn had the grace and bearing of a vamp who knew exactly what he wanted, which was perfectly fine with her.

The intimacy of being here, with him, caught her off guard. She felt claustrophobic all of a sudden and, at the same time, exposed.

Kat schooled her expression. He couldn't know how he'd gotten to her. Just because she'd never been alone with a man who wasn't a relative didn't mean she couldn't handle this. Times had changed. She had changed.

She willed herself to stop shaking as she marvelled at the warmth of his hand, the taste of the air around him. He felt and smelled alive and vibrant, not at all like her recently deceased husband, or even her father for that matter. Kat hadn't been this close to a vamp her age in, well, too long.

Finn slid a heavy leather coat over his shoulders. "Ready?"

"Oh yes," she said. She'd never been more ready for anything in her life.

He led her out of the studio and to the sleek black Harley parked outside. She hitched one leg over the monstrous machine and watched in sheer delight as he did the same. It was time to prove Princess Katarina Volholme D'Transylvania could take care of herself.

Finally.

She scooted forwards until her hips nestled against the bunched-up fabric of his kilt. "No helmets?"

"We're immortal," he said, leaning back into her, "what can happen?"

Kat curled her toes in delight as he took off for the open road.

The wind tore through her hair as the bike zipped through a row of posh stores on Kiev's premier Khreshchatyk Street. Wrought-iron street lamps cast a warm glow on outdoor cafes and the well-dressed pedestrians winding in and out of each other. Finn gunned the engine as he turned down the narrow Kiev Passage that led out of the city.

Free at last!

Her fingers played along his waist under his jacket. She ventured further, slipping under his fine linen shirt and feeling rock-solid abs. Oh my. Katarina stroked him lightly, revelling in the smattering of goosebumps she left in her wake. She'd ventured and he'd responded. How long had it been since someone, anyone, reacted to her with any kind of feeling other than respect? Or mere tolerance?

The one time she met Vlad, he'd looked straight through her, as if she didn't exist. She had no doubt he'd marry her without even seeing her, if it was at all possible.

Kat pressed her cheek against the back of Finn's buttery leather jacket. If the night ended right now, it would have been worth it.

Plus, she realized, a thrill rippling up her spine, they were going the wrong way. The airport, and Love Bites' private jet, was to the rapidly fading east. Finn was headed west.

She was *so* right to pick the Scotsman!

Kat wiggled against his firm backside and wondered if there might be a way to glamour him into kidnapping her to the coast. Royal blood had its advantages, or so she'd heard. Oh this was going to be fun, indeed.

On the way through the centuries-old town of Vinnystia, he took advantage of a stop light to twist around in his seat. He was rather dark for a Scotsman, and a vamp. The soft glow of the street lamps played off his features. The night was still young. Finn was supernaturally fast, even when he obeyed pesky things like traffic signals.

She licked her lips. "So what's the plan, Braveheart?"

He stiffened. "William Wallace was a patriot and a martyr. I'll not have you making glib comparisons."

She cocked her head to the side, studying the thunderclouds that rolled across his brow. "Did you know him?" Kat had certainly heard the stories. Her father had called the Scottish rebels a bunch of damned fools. Technically, she shouldn't have been in awe over a rebel to a king, but darned if she didn't find the whole thing a touch romantic.

Finn cranked the engine, almost as if he was buying time. Finally he said, "I knew him. I fought under Wallace, and King Robert the Bruce."

A vampire who fought human wars? Interesting. But not as interesting as what she wanted to do next. She ran her nails to his elbow and smiled inwardly as she felt him stiffen. "So where are you taking me?" she asked, her voice huskier than she'd intended.

Finn gave her a wicked smile. "I thought we'd go on our own adventure."

"Oh," she managed, almost surprised that her plan had actually worked. He wiped away that and every other thought when he lowered his mouth to hers.

His lips felt warm, firm and . . . *Oh goodness.* She'd dreamed of this for centuries and it was so much better than she imagined.

Finn was a man who knew how to take his time. Spirals of pleasure wound through her as he kissed her, slowly. Gently. There was an intimacy she'd never expected from all of the kisses she'd watched on daytime television. He took his time savouring her, tasting her. She loved every second of it.

Just for her.

He wasn't looking to her out of obligation, not because she was a princess or because this was something owed or something due. For once, it was about Kat as a person, as a woman. It was as if this kiss was the first thing she'd truly owned in her entire life.

She pressed herself against him, hands splayed on his chest. He was so warm, so vibrant. And the way he was making her feel. He took her mouth, her lower lip, her mouth again, with a raw sensuality that made her ache. When his tongue swept hers, she thought she might burn to a cinder on the spot. Just when she was thinking she could lose herself for ever, he pulled away, a mere breath from her.

Dazed, she watched him. The hunger in his eyes, the glaze of her kiss on his lower lip. She was glad to see how it affected him. Other, more modern vamps might do this all the time, but she certainly didn't.

The closeness, the feel of him. It was almost too much. Her confidence stuttered.

"I'm not easy," she told him. She didn't know why she'd said it, exactly – only that she'd needed him to know.

He levelled her with a conspiratorial grin, as if he understood how tough it was sometimes to reconcile this century with all the ones that had come before. "No worries, Princess. It was just a kiss." He leaned towards her again, ever so slowly, and, just when she thought she would erupt from the anticipation, he brushed his lips over her nose. "Green light."

She felt the sides of her mouth quirk as he turned forwards. The shock of the engine lurched her against him as they tore off into the night. It was almost like flying.

Closing her eyes, she relished the pleasure rippling through her veins. He couldn't have known he was only the second man she'd kissed. He made her whole body thrum with anticipation for – *Oh my*.

Whatever she was going to have to pay for this night, it was so going to be worth it.

She closed her eyes and savoured him for a long while, until the familiar scents of oak and hornbeam trees, roe deer and foxes ebbed into her consciousness.

Kat stiffened against him. Were they in Romania?

His muscles tightened, as if he could sense what she was thinking. "Trust me," he said.

Finn turned the bike onto a black asphalt road that led through a grove of immense beech trees, their bare trunks like hundreds of soldiers reaching up to the night sky.

Panic skittered down her spine. How could she trust him? She didn't know him. Not that she had to worry about defending herself. She was a royal vamp, and as strong as a Carpathian wild cat. Still, she wasn't about to be played for a fool.

Kat reached out with her senses. No, her father wasn't nearby. She sighed with relief. Still, why would the Scotsman take her to her homeland for a romantic getaway?

The blacktop ended at a painted monastery unlike any she'd seen before. North-eastern Romania was famous for them. They were usually large, ornate affairs, with striking medieval art decorating the outside and inner walls. This one almost looked as if it had been abandoned.

Smaller than the rest, and rounded, it hunkered in a tangle of wild flowers. Waist-high iron crosses ringed the outside of the structure, and garlands of large, fat cloves of garlic hung from the aged wooden roof.

It seemed that the villagers in these parts still had a healthy respect for vampires.

Good for them.

Finn held the garlic aside, so that it wouldn't bump her on the head as she entered. They didn't need assistance to see in the dark, but her date lit a series of tapers anyway. She savoured the way he moved through the large, round room.

Wooden benches backed against the brightly painted interior walls, almost as if this was some sort of old meeting place. Or storage area, she noted from the cluster of weather-beaten gargoyles and angels next to her. She watched Finn's military-precise movements as he touched a lighter to the last of the fat red candles.

She hooked a thumb through her brand-new gold belt. "Would you like to tell me what's going on here?" An amazing kiss was only going to get the studly vamp so far. It was crazy to come back to Romania. He wasn't looking at her and, even though she'd never been on a date in her life, this didn't seem like a happening place.

He turned slowly, as if he didn't quite want to face her. Candles cast deep shadows across his face. "I'm not a vampire."

"What?" Her mouth hung open. Thanks to years of ladylike training, she snapped it closed rather quickly.

He didn't bother to sugar-coat it. "I'm an empath fairy. I can pass as a vampire, or any other creature you can imagine. I can look like you, smell like you, feel like you –"

She bolted for the exit.

In a flash, he was around her, blocking the doorway. "I'm also faster than you."

Well, if he was like most men . . . she brought a knee up to his groin.

He blocked it just as swiftly. "The Princess likes to play dirty," he chuckled, avoiding a karate chop to his kidneys. "Look, I'm not going to hurt you." He looped a finger through her sassy gold belt and hung her out like a hooked sturgeon. "There's no escape, so don't even try. I was sent by your father."

It was worse than being kidnapped. More like being sent back to prison. "I won't do it. You can't make me go back there." Not without a fight. Kat mustered her strength and shot him with a full dose of royal glamour. "Your mission has changed."

He stared at her. "OK."

"Let me go."

He eased her to her feet, leaving her with the wedgie of the century.

She shook it off and locked the empath fairy into her thrall. If he could use her, she had no reservations about using him.

"You're going to be my transportation, my bodyguard." And, if she was lucky, something else. Of course she wouldn't glamour him into sex. That would be wrong. But perhaps she could glamour him into a peek at the best body she'd seen in eight centuries.

"Take off your shirt," she ordered, before she let herself think on it too much.

He hesitated.

Shoot. True, she hadn't used her glamour in, well, for ever, but this was supposed to come naturally. "Take off your shirt," she said again and was shocked when she found herself removing her red silk top instead. It slipped from her fingers and rustled into a silken pool on the stone tiles at her feet.

She couldn't have been more astonished than if she'd morphed into a bat.

Finn gave absolutely no reaction as she stood there in her black silk bra. And why should he? The man was under her thrall. Now if she could just get it to work right.

She tossed her hair off her shoulders and planted her hands on her hips. "Lose what you have going on upstairs, stud." She wanted to see that chest.

Instead, her hands found the clasp at the front of her bra. "Wait!" she said, slightly panicked as she popped the front clasp and tossed the scrap of silk over a bowing cherub.

Still, his face showed no expression. But her little striptease had done a number on him below the waist.

The truth crept over her. "You're not even under my thrall, are you?" The supernatural snake.

And now she couldn't even cover herself. She tried to cross her arms over her breasts. Embarrassment stung her. Fine time for reverse glamour.

"Do you mind?" she asked.

Candlelight flickered over his features and a roguish smile tickled his lips. "I was hoping you'd want to go another round. See if I might take off anything else."

"I don't think I could afford the humiliation," she said, even though she felt far from defeated. In fact, now that he wasn't bothering to hide his interest, she found his attention to her body quite stimulating.

Too bad he was on dear old Dad's side of things.

Planting one sexy gold shoe in front of the other, she sauntered up to him so close that the tips of her breasts almost – almost – touched his white linen shirt. That wiped the smile right off his face.

"Tell me," she said, her Transylvanian accent thickening with her mounting need. "How are you doing it?"

His Adam's apple bobbed as he swallowed. "I push your own glamour back on you."

"Indeed," she purred. "So what does my illustrious father have in mind?"

He gave her a stony look, but she almost detected a softening in him. He checked his watch. "In about two hours, King Volholme is going to meet us here. He wants to have a few words with you before we escort you back to the castle. Your wedding is tonight."

Dread settled in her stomach. She wouldn't do it. She couldn't. Kat did the first thing that came to mind. She elbowed Finn in the ribs.

She dashed past him, the night air cool on her breasts. Until Finn's hand clamped down hard on her arm. "I'm sorry," he said.

Tears welled up in her eyes. "Well, so am I." She whipped around to face him. "Do you know what it's like to have an eternal life where nothing you say or do matters? There's a reason the old ways die out. There's a reason things change."

"Princess, I – " He looked as helpless as she felt. He swore under his breath and shrugged off his thick leather jacket. "Here," he said, wrapping it around her shoulders.

It was super-heated from his body and held the dark, spicy scent of him. She wrapped it around herself, taking comfort in the sheer size and weight of it. How long had it been since someone actually cared about how hard this was for her?

"You have to understand," she said, "I can't be like this. I can't live like this."

She could see the muscles working in his jaw. "This marriage will offer the most security for you, and for your family. You don't have a choice," he said, losing steam with each word. "I don't have a choice, either."

The thing was, she *did* have a choice. And she was going to make it.

The Princess blinked away her tears and strode back into the old monastery, more resolute than she'd been all night. Finn braced himself. It was a bad sign.

She stood with her back to him in the circular room, which was fine with him. She'd broadcasted enough raw desire tonight to give him a hard-on for the next year. Burying her in his jacket made it worse. She might not feel exposed any more, but now it was almost like a part of him was covering those luscious breasts, the sweet curve of her back. Heaven help him.

Katarina tossed a wave of black hair over her shoulder and it was all he could do to keep himself from reaching out and touching it.

Which was insane.

He never should have let her take her shirt off. He could have just told her that her glamour wouldn't work on him. But no. He had to show off. He had to prove something to her. What did it matter anyway? She was leaving with Vlad, and Finn was going back to work for the King.

"Why?" she asked, the simple question stark against the quiet of the night. "You're not one of my father's subjects. Why do you have to follow his rules?"

"It's my job," he said, as if that answered it all. It did in Finn's mind. He'd been a soldier all his life and he was good at it. He had the power to fight war and aggression and he'd be damned irresponsible not to use it. "It's my life." He heard his voice go husky. "This is what I do." It was the only thing he did. If he didn't protect people, keep the peace, well, then he was nothing.

"You don't even play cards, do you?"

It was finally sinking in just how much he'd deceived her.

"No." He didn't have time for frivolity.

He reached a hand out to touch her and stopped just short of her shoulder. The memory of her soft, delectable skin was bad enough. He didn't need to feel it again – even through his leather coat. He curled his fingers into a fist at his side.

Princess Katarina didn't understand the sick creatures that were out there in the world, which was how he wanted it. It was his duty to safeguard her and other innocents. Sometimes duty came with a price tag attached. "Your marriage contract is final," he said, willing her to understand, to accept. "It's the way of your people. I'm not about to open up you or your kingdom to an altercation with Vlad and his family. Do you remember what his cousin did the last time a king double-crossed them?" The History Channel still did specials on that one.

"I can't give you your freedom. You'll have to convince your fiancé, or your father," he said, knowing at the same time that she couldn't. He closed his eyes. It was a bad situation all around. But it wasn't his fight.

She turned to face him, her arms in his bulky jacket folded over her chest. "So I go back and marry the crypt keeper and you spend the rest of your life saving the world."

He wanted to sigh in relief. Finally, she understood.

She considered him carefully. "So we're both trapped."

He blinked. "I'm not trapped."

She ran her hands along her sides, over her hips, down to where his jacket barely covered her backside. He wanted to close his eyes, but he couldn't. He knew the Princess wouldn't go down without one last fight.

It wasn't right. She shouldn't have to marry a cold, conniving vamp. But there was nothing either one of them could do about it. It was the way of her race. Feeling sorry for her wouldn't help.

Katarina lowered her hands and shifted so that his jacket hung open in the front. He swallowed hard, but kept his composure. Barely.

"You live for your duty—" a flicker of sadness crossed her face "– and it seems I will have to do mine." The candlelight threw shadows under her breasts, into the hollow of her belly. "But we should live first." She smiled at him like a goddess of old. Only a slight trembling at her collarbone gave her away.

He opened up his senses, readied himself for battle. Immediately, he felt her nervousness, but more than that, he almost staggered sideways at the brunt of her sheer, unadulterated hunger for him.

Oh hell.

"Be careful, Princess," he warned, his throat tight.

She lifted a slender shoulder. "You said it yourself. I can't escape you. I can't glamour you. In two hours, I'm going to be taken away, forced to live out what could be the rest of my life locked in another castle." She took one step towards him, then another. "You'll go back to your *job*." She toyed with the waistband of her downright addictive black leather pants. "Tell me, Fionnlagh MacLaomainn, what can we do with our last two hours of freedom?"

His mouth went dry.

She shot him through with a look that practically brought him to his knees. Her next words were mere whispers, but he heard her clear enough. "No one ever has to know."

Sweet heaven.

Maybe he couldn't change the way either of them lived, but they could have a night to remember. He specialized in keeping secrets. None of the vamps could read him. And she had no reason to provoke even more ire from her father. Besides, she and the King would have little or no contact once she was shut away in Dracula's Castle. By MacLeod's lock, was he actually considering this?

He gripped the hard leather belt at his waist. The mere thought of touching her had fire coursing through his veins. "This isn't going to change anything," he warned. He wasn't going to go soft. He wasn't going to let her go. He wasn't going to go off mission just because she let him touch her.

She tilted her chin up. "I know," she said, challenge blazing in her eyes. "At least give me a memory to last the next 800 years."

Her back smacked against the cool stone wall, as for her pants, well, she didn't really care what he'd done with her pants. Somehow the gold belt still rested on her hips, shimmering in the candlelight.

"Eager much?" she asked, wiggling her hips.

Finn stared at the flickering gold band snaking across her belly button. His gaze moved lower and he about choked. "Let's just say it's been a while for me too."

He growled most deliciously and swept her into a crushing kiss. She felt lavish, wanton, alive. And when Finn's hands trailed up her sides and cupped her breasts, she darn near bit him. She couldn't help it. This was all so new, so fresh, so utterly perfect.

She drove her fingers through his hair, revelled in the way her bare body scraped against his. He twined her legs with his, the wool of his kilt rubbing her in the most delightful place. Still, she wanted more.

Hadn't she said she was going to find out what Scotsmen wore under their kilts?

While his mouth did exquisite things to her upper chest, Kat drew her fingers down his back, pressing small circles along his spine. Down to where the tartan clung to that groove of muscle at his waist.

"Oh my," she said, as she observed how the evidence of his desire made the rough wool fabric stand on end.

He chuckled low in his throat. "You don't know the half of it," he said, spreading his legs for her.

Fingers shaking, she touched his knees, drew her hands up his legs, all the way to his "Bicycle shorts?"

He swallowed hard, as if the wait was killing him.

"It's ... " she began, wondering just how much bigger he'd be if he wasn't crushed into the shorts. It was an enticing, almost intimidating thought.

She lifted the tartan to get a closer look. Sure enough, his powerful thighs were encased in matching cloth bearing the Royal Arms of Scotland.

She lifted a brow.

"Trade secret," he hissed through his teeth. "It's the only way I can ride a Harley in a kilt."

"It's not a very good secret," she informed him. And with that, she liberated his kingdom once and for all.

Yow. The Scotsman did not disappoint. As she paused for a moment, trying to decide exactly what to do with her new find, Fionnlagh MacLaomainn took things into his own hands.

He kissed her cross-eyed before devouring her collarbone, her neck, that little spot behind her ear. He nibbled, he sucked, he trailed his hot mouth all the way down to her – *Oh my*.

Finn used his tongue on her breasts, his teeth, and she darned near slid down the wall, undone by the pleasure of it all. Only one thing kept her standing – she wanted more. She held the back of his head, raked her fingers through his hair and willed him to go on for ever.

She almost climbed the wall when his fingers found the very centre of her. She was soaking wet with need and she gasped with surprise. It was like nothing she'd ever felt before. He caressed her, parted her, rubbing her in ways so that she thought she might burst. All the while, he kissed her breasts, her belly button, her ... "What in the world are you doing?"

Kat never knew one person could do that to another and she certainly hadn't imagined how bone-crushingly delectable it would feel. He licked her, sucked her, tasted her everywhere until she exploded once, twice. "Finn!" The ankle grip she had around his neck would have flattened the average man, but Finn was certainly not an average anything. She gave up, threw her head back and released a very un-princesslike scream of pleasure.

"Is this another one of your supernatural powers?" she gasped, only half joking.

"We haven't even gotten to the good part," he said, standing.

She wrapped her fingers around his length. Her excitement rocketed as she sensed her power. If only she knew what to do next. "I've only ever done it in a bed. In the dark." Even that had been a few hundred years ago.

Finn kissed her like he was ready to devour her. He broke away, chest heaving. "We'll go slow."

Slow was bad, she wanted to say. This night was not about holding back. She wanted him hard and fast and now.

"No," she said, and nearly shrieked at the loss when he stopped. "Wait," she said. "I meant not slow. I didn't mean, oh hell – now, Finn. Now!"

He groaned and surged forwards. It stung, but she didn't care. She grabbed his perfect butt and forced him forwards. "More!"

"I don't want to hurt you," he heaved against her ear.

"Then don't stop." He couldn't stop now.

With a loud shout, he pushed himself inside her. She gasped at the bliss of being completely and utterly possessed. She'd never felt it. Would never feel it again.

Don't think. Just feel.

At some point, they ended up on the stone floor, the kilt under her, Finn above her. She was surrounded in the scent of him, the feel of him, as he drove into her, over and over. She revelled in it. Clutched his back, luxuriating in the muscle and power and strength she found. It was bliss. He was heaven. And if he was trying to make up for the last 839 years, he was doing a bang-up job.

When she came for the third time, he came with her, groaning against her ear as he spilled himself inside of her.

When she felt sufficiently able to speak, she tipped her head forwards against his. "Is it always like that?" she asked. Because really, if it was, then her life before this was even more pathetic than she'd imagined.

He chuckled against the crook of her neck, "Princess," he said, pressing wet kisses across her skin that made her all squiggly again, "it's never like that."

A chill crept down her spine, despite the warmth of the man currently rubbing his cheek against hers. She'd never have this again. Never have him. What good was it to experience so much when she'd be forced to live without it for the next millennium?

She pulled him closer. After centuries more of neglect, she might not even care any more.

"It's time," he said quietly, pulling away from her. She let him go, and felt the cool air creep in between them. He really was magnificent. Lean and strong, all bone and muscle and . . . yum. Well, she might as well look. She'd never see it again.

Finn's entire body stiffened as he checked his watch. "By Skara Brae, we've been at it for three hours."

Mmm . . . she sat up on her elbows. Her entire body felt sated, and a little wobbly. "It couldn't have been three hours."

"And then some." Finn frowned, studying the shredded bottom of his kilt.

His fault for putting his tongue in places she'd never dreamed a tongue could go.

She stood slowly and ran her fingers through her tangled hair as she watched him dress. At least her father was late. She considered it a gift. The King had a reputation for putting business over everything else. And that, Kat sighed, was exactly what she was – an item to be bartered and handed off to the royal with the most influence to peddle.

Finn handed her a conservative, medieval dress like the one she'd worn for the last 800 years. And like the ones she'd wear for the rest of her immortal life. She stuffed the shapeless, long-sleeved, high-necked bundle of brown velvet and trim over her head.

The lace itched at her neck in a way it hadn't before, now that she knew what it felt like to live without a noose of fine Romanian needlepoint. She pulled at the intricately woven fabric, almost wishing she hadn't known how her life could be.

Finn gathered what little they'd brought with them, the muscles in his back working as he double-checked his weapons.

He was so powerful, so alive. Not just because he lived and breathed, or because he could walk in the light. Finn lived his life. And for a while, when she'd been with him, he'd made her feel that she lived hers too.

Kat reached into the pocket of her gown and found a royal headpiece – a shapeless, formless cap of black thread and pearls. Her fingers moved of their own volition, weaving her long hair into a braid around her head and tying the velvet ribbons under her chin.

Having him – if only for an evening – had almost been worse than not having him at all. Because now she knew what she was missing. And it would kill her.

Finn frowned at his black satellite phone and strapped it back into his pack. "Your father's party isn't answering. He sat back on his heels as he checked his watch. "We're more than an hour past the pick-up time."

Kat licked her lips at the fact they could have been caught.

"Impossible," he said, "I would have sensed them coming."

"Would you at least pretend you can't read my thoughts?" she asked. It was bad enough that her life was an endless, open book. She didn't need him telling her what she was thinking.

He slung his pack over his shoulder as he strode towards her, a contrite hitch to the side of his mouth. "I can't read your thoughts, just your feelings." He touched his forehead to hers. "And I apologize."

Finn folded her into his arms. Safe.

Kat closed her eyes and let his warmth wash over her. Yes, she'd be sad later, and she'd mourn him, but right now, she had him.

Finn rubbed her back through the heavy velvet. "I don't know how to say this easy, so I'm just going to say it." He drew back and considered her carefully, his expression sombre. "There's no reason for your father to have missed our rendezvous. Worse, he's not answering his phone."

Apprehension seeped through her. "Do you think something's wrong?"

"I don't know," he said, all business. "But we're not going to waste anytime wondering. We're going to the castle."

So this was it. She swallowed hard and stared at the grey stone floor. He was taking her back to Varstnic Castle. She'd be married before sunrise.

Finn had told her to expect it. Still, a tiny part of her had held out hope.

"Come on." He wrapped her hand in his and led her towards the door. "We need to leave."

"Can I at least wear your jacket?" she asked, feeling silly but needing it all the same.

With great tenderness, he helped her into the coat. She savoured the warmth and feel of it, wrapped it around her so tightly that something poked her in the back.

"Ow."

He rubbed his thumb along her jaw. "It's just a spare stake. It won't hurt you."

"Right," she said, proving they couldn't go five minutes without one of them thinking of his job. Well, unless they were occupied as they had been earlier. Parts of her body immediately turned to liquid at the thought.

Finn looked flustered too. "Just—" he closed the jacket firmly around her "—just don't touch it. That, either," he said, as she pulled a heavy black gun out of the pocket.

"Bullets can't hurt me."

"No, but that gun shoots holy water. Hard and deadly accurate. Put it away."

Kat considered the gun, before stuffing it back into his coat pocket. Too bad. Where she was headed, it could come in handy.

Like a true Scot, he rode commando. Had to. The vixen had ripped the biker shorts right off him. Not that he'd minded. What started out as an act of mercy had turned into something else entirely.

Finn gunned the engine. If he could save her from this, he would.

He'd promised to return her to her fiancé. It was the way of her people, what her family wanted. He'd clear up what he hoped was a misunderstanding with the King about the drop-off scenario. Then he'd go back to the kind of hard-nosed jobs that kept her world safer.

Problem was, deep down he didn't think the King had made a mistake about the pick-up time. The King was rigid, precise. In the three centuries he'd known the man, he never knew the King to ditch his part of a mission – especially when his family was at stake.

The lack of a royal entourage tonight meant one thing – while Finn had been off diddling the Princess, King Petronius Brasov Volholme D'Transylvania, Lord of the Seven Clans and Romania was under attack.

Finn turned on to Highway 11 to Brasov, Transylvania. Whatever was going on, he had to keep Katarina out of it. She might be strong, and downright wicked when she wanted to be, but she wasn't a warrior. And he didn't know what he'd do if something happened to her. The mere thought of it made his gut clench.

Because she was the mission.

Yeah, right.

Finn steadied his breathing, the way he'd been taught. Slowly, he disentangled himself from the emotions of the little vamp behind him. Her quiet sorrow was a thousand times worse than her protests.

As they neared her father's castle, he opened himself up to the night. Along with the pine and dog roses in the air, he smelled danger too, the sticky sweet remains of deception and evil.

His fingers tightened on the Harley as he zoned in on the threat – three vamps and something else.

Varstnic Castle loomed like a spectre on the mountainside. Finn had travelled supernaturally fast, but they were running out of night. It didn't affect him in the slightest. Finn could walk in the sun. As for Katarina, he didn't even want to think what could happen to her if he didn't secure the castle by sunrise.

Just under an hour.

Finn powered the bike up the steep mountain passage. The Harley spit rocks as the tyres fought for traction. He took them all the way to the limestone gorge that snaked around the edge of the property, and parked in a patch of Russian thistle. "We walk from here."

Worry clouded her eyes. "My father is in trouble, isn't he?"

Finn didn't answer.

Instead, he helped her unwind her long dress from the bike and led her down as she dismounted. It reminded him of the way he'd assisted the ladies of old, and he quickly dismissed the thought. Kat wasn't a simpering maiden. He wasn't a knight and this was no fairy tale.

Katarina's ancestral home jutted from the rocks above them as they made their way to the stone bridge at the edge of the property. The night was eerily silent. He didn't like it one bit.

Finn kept her hand in his, and focused on what lay ahead.

Moss clung to tightly packed stones of the ancient castle. It was four feet thick in most places. Little had changed in the last several centuries, save for the secret entrance Finn had commissioned for the King.

You never could be too careful.

Kat clutched Finn's arm as he led them through a thick forest of spruce. She knew what was coming: home. Well, Finn was just doing his job.

She hesitated as he drew her into the clearing that housed her family's small cemetery.

"Not this way." Kat held back, shivering against him.

He hated bringing her here, but if they were going to get into the castle undetected, this was their only choice.

Life-sized brass effigies stood ramrod straight, in concentric circles. The earlier statues dressed in ancient robes, the latter in medieval garb, some in nothing at all, green tarnish staining the joints.

Kat spoke her words as if drawing each one from somewhere deep inside of her. "I haven't been here since . . . "

"Your wedding. I know," Finn said quickly.

Finn ran a thumb along the smothering velvet at the waist of her gown, and caught it against the loop of the gold belt she still wore underneath. If he could save her from this, he would.

Like peeling the layers of an onion, Finn took Kat's hand and began leading her through the generations. He felt her pause at the memorial to Baghatur the Decapitator, the infamous Byzantine Conqueror, but he pulled her onwards. His job didn't leave room for sentiment.

As they neared the centre of the graveyard, she stiffened and clutched her hand to the neck of her gown.

He gave her a quick once-over. "Are you OK?"

She wound her fingers through the stiff lace at her throat. "Do you have to ask?"

"For the record, this isn't my idea of a dream date, either." He diverted a portion of his empath senses her way and was hit immediately with her overwhelming desire to flee. He paused when they reached the centre of the inner ring, the final resting place of Illi the Father. The statue, as naked and muscular as Michelangelo's David, held aloft a bronze dagger. "I need you to stay here."

"Of course," she said, eyeing the path they'd just taken.

"If I'm not back before the sun rises, go to ground."

She nodded.

"Kat." He cupped the back of her neck and leaned in for the last best kiss of his life. He descended on her with mouth and tongue, pushing her, tasting her, scorching them both with the intensity of what they had found together.

Pleasure swamped his senses. He ground her closer, needing her like he'd never needed anything before in his life. He couldn't have her, didn't deserve her. But he would save her.

He smoothed her arms to her sides, his body aching for one final touch before he unleashed the full force of his empath abilities and froze her on the spot. She stood stock still, the epitome of desire.

Finn stepped back from her immobile form. "I'm sorry," he said, and meant it, even as the expression in her eyes went from confused to downright hostile. He couldn't let it affect him. Finn had work to do.

He knelt at the feet of Alulim the First. Brushing aside the leaves at the base of the statue, he quickly located the security punch pad and dialled in the code. "Don't worry," he said, refusing to let himself look at her, "I'm not leaving you defenceless."

Why did he have the sudden urge to show her? Touch her? It was ridiculous. Finn gripped the heavy metal trapdoor. It opened with the groan of joints that hadn't been worked in years.

A ladder led down into the dark. Finn launched his fairy sixth sense down the narrow opening and found it empty of life.

"You stay here," he said, glancing back at her and immediately regretting it.

He made one final check for the stake at his back and the knife at his belt before descending into the darkness. "Once I leave you, you'll be able to move again. But don't even think about following me. You can't." He'd designed the maze of passages under the castle long after she'd been married off the first time. No one, except for him and the King, knew how to get in or out. Smelling him, tracking him would be impossible.

She had to know he was doing this for her, and her family. But somehow, he doubted she'd gotten the message. And when Finn slammed the door behind him, a small part of him broke.

Think of the job.

He moved down the ladder soundlessly and with no need for light. Not that he could see in the dark like Katarina, but he could sense the objects and creatures around him.

The wet brick walls felt cool to the touch. Finn hadn't been down here in at least a century, yet he recognized the familiar odour of mildew and clay. Above, he heard Katarina's fury as she shook off his trap. She had to understand why he did it. From the way she cursed, Finn could almost believe that she was a mercenary, like him.

He did it for her own good. He had a feeling he was about to walk into a bad scene and he didn't need to be worrying about the princess.

And he sure as heck didn't need her to see what might happen to him – or her father. As he drew closer to the King, he could feel more of the old vampire's life force. It was weak, threatened.

Finn wound his way through the underground passageways. He slid through an opening in the panelling of the throne room with hardly a sound. The immense chamber lay dark and heavy from neglect. Years ago, this had been the centrepiece of the King's court, but Volholme had tired of parties long ago. Too bad. A few extra vamps could have come in handy tonight.

Finn moved soundlessly through the house, edging along the main corridor as the King's scent grew stronger and stronger. The unknowns were holed up in the King's study. Finn knew from experience that there was only one way in or out. He flexed his hands, ready.

He'd have to take out the empath fairy first.

Finn paused outside the door.

"This is your final warning," a cold voice stated.

Finn's heart pounded. Inside, the grey-haired King lay back in his leather chair, a war axe with a blade as long as a man's forearm threatened his carotid artery. One wrong move and his head would be off.

Katarina's fiancé, Vlad, held the axe.

The truth of it slammed into Finn. Vlad had been behind the attempts on the King's life – the promise of security forces, a mere trick to facilitate a hasty marriage with Katarina.

The ruthless vamp's chin shook and spittle clung to his yellowed fangs. "Sit up. Up! Do it or I execute your only heir."

Finn about choked when he saw Katarina's brother frozen to the spot, pink tears of rage in his eyes. Behind her brother stood an empath fairy. His yellow beard had grown longer and he had a new scar over his left eye, but Finn would have recognized Athol Grim anywhere. Shite. Athol had fought with Longshanks. And he was damned good at killing.

Adrenaline surged through Finn.

It was a power grab – plain and simple. Vlad couldn't assume the throne without direct ties to the Volholme bloodline. He needed to marry Kat and drink from her. If he couldn't do that, he needed the King dead. But not by his own hand or retribution would be swift. No, Vlad needed the King to kill himself.

Finn didn't have much time, but he did have a plan.

Silently as the night, Finn moved back through the corridor and into the music room. He pressed his back to the bronze-leaf wallpaper and, with every bit of will he had, he forced himself to take on the intoxicating scent and spirit of Katarina. He thought of her joy in finding him, her lust for life, that damned gold belt. He called up everything that was good about her.

And then he waited.

"I smell her," Athol said from the study.

"Well, go get her!" Vlad demanded.

Finn fought back a growl as he projected thoughts of Katarina, *his* Katarina, just inside the music room. He pictured her running her long fingers over the edge of a snow-white baby grand.

Finn could practically feel Athol salivating.

He'd kill the traitor. He'd kill them both. Finn only wished he could do it slowly.

Athol surged into the music room, a gleaming silver hook raised to snare Katarina. Finn stepped behind him and slit his throat.

He lowered the fairy to the floor and thanked the gods that the real Katarina wasn't here to see any of this.

Then Finn morphed into a spitting image of Athol. Well, at least the vamps would see it that way. Finn stuffed Athol's wooden stake into his belt and hoped he could get close enough to Vlad before the King did something they'd all regret.

What he needed was a distraction.

Finn strode back to the King's study, still trying to figure out the second part of his plan. His instincts had never let him down before. But as he came upon the portly King at the end of a blade, he wasn't so sure he was going to like what happened next.

"I can't find her," Finn said, imitating Athol's gruff voice.

The vampire's face reddened. "I can't kill him until I take her blood!" He pressed the blade into Volholme's skin, licking his fangs as a trickle of blood ran down the King's neck.

Almost to himself, Vlad said, "I can't kill the King—" a twisted smile formed on his lips "—but I can kill the boy." He turned to Katarina's brother.

Finn braced himself, ready to blow his cover, when Vlad stiffened and gasped. A volley of acid rained down, scorching the vamp's face. Finn ignored the poison and went for the blade, wrenching it away.

In a split second, Finn separated Vlad's astonished head from his neck.

Blood poured from the vampire's throat as his body thudded onto the thick green carpeting.

Finn wiped his face. Water. Holy water.

He hastened to the King's side. "Are you all right?"

Volholme nodded while Finn did a quick once-over to make sure the King was, indeed, free of holy water and in one piece. When he was satisfied he'd done his job, Finn glanced back at their rescuer.

Katarina stood in the doorway wearing nothing but his leather jacket and the black lace bra and panties that had driven him wild back at the monastery. She held his holy water gun in one hand and rested the other against the door jamb like a Playboy bunny. For a moment, nobody moved.

"Katarina!" the King boomed, the ruddiness returning to his cheeks. "For Varstnic's sake, cover yourself," he said, more affronted by her lack of clothing, it seemed, than with his brush with death.

"Yaaa!" Katarina's brother lunged at Finn, fangs out, until Finn froze the unfortunate vamp once again.

"It's me," he said quickly, morphing back into himself.

"Thank the ancestors," said the King, who looked quite relieved to see Finn instead of Athol in charge.

Katarina strode up to Finn.

"Nice jacket," he said.

"I was cold." She laughed and wrapped her slender arms around Finn's waist.

Finn looked down at her, never so glad to see anyone in his life. "How did you make it through the underground passages?" He racked his brain. "You can't smell me, sense me."

"Ah." She winked. "But I can smell me on you."

Finn warmed just thinking of it. It didn't help that she was beaming up at him. Finn found himself wearing a lopsided smile of his own. "You should wear that outfit more often."

She blushed. "I got the idea from a contestant on *American Idol*. She wanted to shock the judges."

Finn raised a brow. He wasn't one to argue with unusual tactics.

"What did you mean 'smell her'?" the King demanded, rubbing at his neck. "And unfreeze my son!"

Finn did and the Prince staggered forwards and caught himself on the edge of an antique suit of armour.

"What have you done to my daughter?" the King demanded.

Katarina straightened. "Nothing that I didn't want done," she said quietly. All eyes turned to her. She stood, arms folded, the prim and proper aristocrat in a leather jacket and a thong.

The King spared a glance at Vlad's wilted, headless body to the left of the red velvet drapes. His eyes hardened as he assumed the chair behind the desk like an executive.

Katarina balled her hands into fists. "Stop looking at me like that. None of this would have happened if you didn't try to force me to marry again." She wrinkled her nose at the body on the carpet. "All he ever wanted was my blood so he could kill us all. Great matchmaking, Dad."

The King remained silent, thoughtful.

He might have the luxury to ponder the old ways, but Kat did not. She might have run away before, but now she was ready to stand up and fight for a new life. Her life. She squared her shoulders and took one bold step towards her father, then another. "I'm not property that you can barter off. I'm a living, thinking being." She closed the gap between them. "I've lived with this for 800 years. Eight hundred years! Don't you think it's time I get to choose what I want to do with my life?" She looked at him earnestly, her emotions naked on her face. "It's my time now."

Her father rested his thick arms on either side of the chair. He suddenly looked very old. "OK."

"What?" Kat asked.

"You're right." Her father waved his hand. "You're right. Your mother's right." He bit at his thumb and took stock of her. "You know she ran off to Bulgaria when I told her you were to marry right away. Let's just hope *she's* not on a dating show."

Kat looked at him like he'd sprouted an extra set of fangs. "Are you all right?"

"Yes, yes." He nodded. "As long as no more of your future husbands try to kill me. Perhaps your mother is correct when she says you should stay single for a while." He dug something out of the pocket of his brown velvet waistcoat. "One moment." It was a BlackBerry. Kat almost fell over as her father started texting. "I've been bowing to the pressures of old traditions—" he gave her a knowing look "—but maybe it's time the King stops bowing."

She didn't even know her father owned a phone. Then again, her late husband had forbidden phones, so it wasn't as if her Dad could have called her anyway.

"There," the king said, hitting send. He eyed Kat. "Your mother will be thrilled. Everybody else will have to learn to deal with it."

She drew Finn's jacket around her and stood before her father. "As long as we're shaking things up," she said, ignoring the fluttering in her stomach, "I want to date."

The King's eyes widened and he tipped forwards in his chair as if she'd just said she wanted to streak naked through Kiev Square.

The Prince barked out a laugh. "Princesses don't date."

"Says the old, archaic law that you just changed," she said to her father.

Volholme frowned. "Who would you even date?"

Kat's hope surged as Finn stepped forwards.

Finn turned to Kat. The earnestness in his expression almost made her melt. "Katarina," he said, as he took her hands in his, "I'm sorry. I can't." He chose every word carefully. "I care about you too much."

"What?" Kat and her father both asked.

She couldn't believe it. Men. No matter how many centuries they lived on this Earth, they were still clueless.

"I have to protect you," Finn said, as if that explained it.

The King ground a beefy hand over his mouth, thinking. "You know, that's a good idea," he said. "I can't think of a better way to protect my only daughter than to stick her with an empath fairy. Besides," he said, sizing up Finn, "314 years without a vacation day is too long for anybody."

"Father!" Katarina rushed to him and clasped his hand to her cheek.

"But what if there's another assassination attempt?" Finn asked. "You know as well as I do that we're going to be hearing from Vlad the Impaler."

"You're not the only empath fairy on the planet," the King said. "Relax. Seize the day. *Carpe diem* and all that."

Finn couldn't have looked more shocked if the King had sprouted wings.

Volholme rolled his eyes. "What? You've never seen the *Dead Poets Society*?" The King shrugged. "Never mind. It's not about vampires anyway."

Finn broke out into a smile as it finally began to sink in.

Kat swelled with gratitude, hope and pure joy. She couldn't have hidden it even if she'd wanted to. She ran to him. And that's all it took for the immortal warrior to surrender.

With a whoop of joy, Finn lifted Katarina in his arms. She revelled in the feel of him as she slid down his body and back to her gold sandalled feet.

The King stiffened. "Just don't let her out of your sight," he warned.

Finn wrapped his arms against Kat, his grip warm and steady, his wide mouth set into a permanent grin. "Believe me, I won't."

Flotsam

Caitlín R. Kiernan

The moon is three nights past full, and I sit here alone at the edge of the low dunes while the tide goes out again. That moon, so high and cold and thoroughly disinterested, one great all-seeing, uncaring eye slowly beginning to close in the lazy, inevitable wink of lunar cycles. There's a warm late summer breeze rustling through the green tangle of dog roses and poison ivy, cordgrass and sea lavender, back towards the brackish expanse of Green Hill Pond. And Block Island Sound stretches out before me, restless and muttering beneath the moonlight, describing time and the night with the rhythmic language of troughs and cresting waves and breakers. I come here when she calls, which is more often than it used to be. I come here, and maybe there are others she awakens, on other nights, but, if so, I have never seen them for myself. I drive down from Charlestown, always stopping somewhere along the way for a few bottles of beer, a pack of cigarettes, following her voice and carefully minding the gauntlet of traffic signals and stop signs. I never play the radio. On these nights, there's room in me for no song but the one she sings, and it pulls me east and south towards the sea. By the time I cross the iron, concrete, and asphalt bridge where Green Hill and Ninigret ponds are connected through the narrowest of confluences, the song is the only momentum I need. All else has become distraction, annoyance, if I listen, and I freely admit there have been nights I've stopped there on the bridge. I've pulled over and stood gazing out across the soughing marshes, contemplating the life I lived before. She has left me my will intact – or so she swears – and I will say that it seems as though, in those rare moments of hesitation, my license to turn back, to simply *stop listening*, is right there before me. I only need the courage to turn away. I linger near my idling truck, hands shaking, smelling the stink of my own anxious sweat (which smells not so very different from the ponds and the sea), smelling the night, and I can *almost* comprehend the restraint and abnegation that would be required to turn around and drive home again. I have never yet done so, and I don't believe I ever shall. It is not my will. So, tonight I sit here at the edge of the dunes, beneath the indifferent moon as the tide slides steadily away down the berm, here and there exposing a few stranded jellyfish and an unlucky, gasping cod. Never yet has she asked me to come any nearer to the water than this. I think that's part of our peculiar symbiosis: she leads *me* down to the sea, but I am the magnet that pulls *her* up from the depths where she sleeps away the days, wrapped safe from the hungry sun, shrouded in veils of silt and darkness. Half a mile out, there's the wreckage of the *Caoimhe Colleen*, a trawler that went down during a gale, back in '75. She sleeps in the wheelhouse, most days, coiled up snug as any eel, tight as an oyster in its shell. I don't know where the sea hid her before the trawler sank; I've never thought to ask. It hardly seems to matter. I do, however, know that once, many years ago, she still slept on the land, keeping to one boneyard or another like any good cliché. I know she spent a decade haunting Stonington Cemetery, and the local teenagers still swap ghost stories that must have begun with her. And I know, too, that, farther back, she once rested among caskets locked safe inside a marble vault at Swan Point in Providence. It was there that she first thought of the water and so traded the mausoleum for the succour of the muddy Seekonk River. The only time I ever asked her why, why the water, why the sea, and even though I understood she does not breathe and has no need of air, she leaned close, laughing, and whispered, "You really have no notion how delightful it will be, when they take us up and throw us, with the lobsters, out to sea." Her laughter makes the night flinch, and sometimes I imagine it is harder than diamonds. She loves Lewis Carroll, and there have been evenings I've gone to her when every word from her lips is something remembered from "Jabberwocky" or "The Walrus and the Carpenter". When she bothers to speak at all, and there certainly are enough nights when we have no need of mere words for this necessary exchange. And now I realize that I have been woolgathering, partway drunk on convenience-store beer and drawing circles within circles in the sand. There was a noise, or, rather, there was the most minute alteration in the familiar sonic tapestry of the beach, the wind, the night, so I look up, and there she is, walking out of the waves towards me. She trails some dim bluish phosphorescence, something borrowed from dinoflagellates and tiny shrimp, only by accident or because she thinks it suits her. Beneath all the valleys and mountains and dry basaltic maria of the waning moon, she glistens. Not for me, but this is of no consequence whatsoever. I have never imagined myself at the center of anything, nor asked the paths of stars to bear some relevance to my own existence. She glistens, and it is sufficient that I am permitted to bear witness. For a while – I can never say how long – she stands over me, dripping and murmuring about the gravity of appetite and all the epochs that have come and are yet to come. Or this is only my straining imagination, and, instead, she mutters a bit of "The Lobster Quadrille", or there is not any shape or sense to her voice. Or there is not even her voice. For the song requires so much from her, and there is no need to keep singing when I am sitting at her feet. She kneels before me in the sand, though I must be clear that she is not kneeling *to* me. If she has ever deigned to play supplicant to any god or goddess, any demon or angel or pagan numen, it is a secret known to her and her alone. For my part, I like to think she has never prayed and never will. She kneels before me in the sand, naked save the limp strands of knotted wrack and ribbon weed woven into her black hair and hanging down about her shoulders and breasts, the sharp scatter of barnacles like freckles across her cheeks and belly, the anemone she has allowed to take hold in the cleft between her legs. One day, one evening, I know, she will become a garden, and no longer will she need to sing across the nights to insomniacs and mad men, suicides and lonely women. If she does not forsake the sea, it will, in distant centuries, make her well and truly its own. She will be nourished not with the warm blood of creatures that walk beneath blue skies, but by the photosynthesis of kelp and pink leaf, by sponges and colonies of encrusting bryozoans straining the murky sound for zooplankton and detritus. She will wear lady-crab garlands and sand-dollar brooches. These visions she has passed along to me, over the months and years, and I think they are a sort of comfort to her, the possibility of an end to untold ages of predation, an end which she accepts with the resignation of one who has been so long in agony and understands that death is, at least, release. She will not end, as my human consciousness will one day end, for that luxury was stolen from her long ago, but she might yet be permitted in this sea change to *fade*, diminishing as all unperverted Nature diminishes. She kneels in the sand before me (which is only to say in *front* of me), her eyes the still hearts of hurricanes, and then she smiles the smile I have driven through the South County night to see. She leans forwards, kissing me, and so I taste salt and estuary sediment and, beyond that muddy, saline veneer, the harsher flavours that I know are truly her own. Maybe she is speaking now, words hardly even breathed they fall so softly on my ears. Maybe she is thanking me for following the song again, or maybe she is merely reciting Lewis Carroll, or maybe she is describing some careless, wanton conclusion to our meetings, a crimson abandon that would leave my body torn apart and strewn among the dunes. But it's all the same, really, as I am hers to do with as she will, no strings attached, no farthest limits to my devotion; I made that promise the first night and have not yet regretted it. Her tongue, rough as any cat's, probes eagerly past my lips, and now she is pushing me down into the sand. She is the weight of all my joys and disappointments, the bitter weight of *living*, bearing down upon me. She rises from the ocean and delivers to me the merciless press of fifty or sixty pounds per square inch, and with a single inhalation she could collapse my fragile lungs. *Her sighs and cries would rend the skies for her lover that was drowned.* And when the kiss has finally ended (for, like a hall of mirrors, it only *seems* to go on for ever), I show her my throat, my paltry, insufficient offering. She trills enthusiastic approval, though, so never mind my own insecurities and misgivings in this moment. We cannot ever know the minds of the gods we serve, and we cannot second-guess their approval or disdain. *O Mother, even a dullard becomes a poet who meditates upon thee raimented with space*, and at best I am a dullard as the terrible, exquisite crucible of her mouth opens so wide and her long eye teeth flash the moonlight like pearls. *Creatrix of the three worlds, whose waist is beautiful with a girdle made of numbers of dead men's arms, and who on the breast of a corpse* . . . and I do not flinch or cry out or attempt to pull away as those fangs honed hundreds of years before my inconsequential birth divide skin and fascia and muscle to find the hot stream of my carotid artery. I do not turn away from the pain, but embrace it, as she is embracing me in her long white arms. The pain is one part of my penance, one part of my reward, a sliver of agony to last me until the next time, which I understand, as always, may never come. She clamps her jaws tight about me, and in this instant we may almost be as one, the embanked river spilling itself out into the boundless sea, and yes, yes, I am but a dullard, at *best*, and this is not poetry at all, Shri Kalika Devi, Morrigan – virgin Ana, mother Babd, great crone Macha, Queen of all the Phantoms – Circe, Nerthus, Al-'Uzzuā, al-Manāt, al-Lāt, Demeter: the devouring, loving, enveloping, consuming mother who draws witches to their sabat bonfires and men to sacred crematoria and priestesses to shrines in secret groves surrounding bottomless, serpent-haunted pools. The circle drawn about a stone to render it a mystery, and my mind reels and is all but lost in this ecstasy that I am well aware is not *my* ecstasy but hers and hers alone. I am, at most, vicarious. Dullard. Grateful, weeping dullard on a beach with the summer sea pulling back towards the fullest extent of low tide as she feeds. You do not satiate that hunger, but only placate it. She could devour the world and not be filled. Her thirst is as profound and abyssal as the "hole" proceeding a star's collapse, and I am damned and blessed to circle this event horizon for evermore, until she is done with me. Let me pray here for death, which is the same prayer I would utter for life, being and unbeing, and the blood that escapes her greedy, sucking lips trickles down my throat and chest and spatters like ink across the brown-sugar sand. I close my eyes, that shrinking moon, the single eye of all goddesses, glaring down at me. I will not, even now, forget those few lines memorized from the Sakti Sangama Tantra – ... *there is not, nor has been, nor will be any holy place like unto a woman* ... – but these are only a lunatic's ramblings, an idiot grasping at straws, and a dullard worshiping at the alabaster feet of the incomprehensible universe. I close my eyes, and the night falls away, and the sea is forgotten, and she is only my dream of purity and taint. She folds me open, and folds me shut and, when I awaken, shivering, in the morning to the giggle and screech of the gulls and the roar of the tide coming up again, I shall say my wicked, heathen prayers, and imagine her sleeping in the ruin of the *Caoimhe Colleen*, and already I will have begun waiting all over again.

The Murder King's Woman

Jamie Leigh Hansen

> "Ninety-nine veins of blood to tap,
> Ninety-nine veins of bloood . . .
> Pick the best flavour and drain it dry.
> There'll be ninety-eight veins of blood to try."

Sasha sashayed her curvy human body across the busy foyer of the San Francisco Vamp Palace, her booted steps in sync with the rousing chorus of vamps in the next room, her jaunty nurse's cap bobbing with the tune. Grasping hold of the song, she continued the refrain silently as she pushed the empty black wheelchair through the crowd of costumed, but deadly, vampires.

She wore a traditional white nurse's dress, with the neckline cut low to the thick, black belt on her waist. A bright-red Wonderbra pushed everything she had out and up in a bountiful display. The skirt stretched high on her thighs, leaving a few inches of skin bare to the tops of her thigh-high black boots. With her vivid, glossy make-up and her latex-gloved hands, her costume was perfect.

Sasha pushed the wheelchair to the elevator behind the grand staircase. A Bela Lugosi lookalike cast lascivious glances all down her body as a Queen Elizabeth smiled at her with condescending indulgence. Contrary to modern myth, vampires loved Halloween. It was the one night a year they could let their fangs hang out. Though, tonight, their fangs were a bit sharper than usual.

Smiling vacuously, her mind only shielded with the most basic of barriers expected from an average mortal like her, Sasha continued to sing silently. *Ninety-eight veins of blood to tap . . .*

Sasha entered the elevator, pushed the button for the fourth floor, and gripped the wheelchair handles tight. She smiled, wide and excited, for any who glanced her way. *Ninety-five veins of blood to tap . . .*

The elevator doors slid open to reveal a long, darkly panelled hallway with doors on either side. Some were open, some weren't. At one, a beautiful ice-blonde in a dress Cinderella would envy smiled teasingly at a dashing, kilted Scotsman. Her voice was a smooth purr. "You can look under mine if you let me look under yours."

He chuckled, his voice low as he leaned forwards and opened the door behind her. "Only look?"

Sasha's smile came easier as she passed them, the chair rolling quietly along the deep red carpet. *Eighty-nine veins of blood to tap, eighty-nine veins of bloood . . .*

At the end of the hall, between two closed doors where the wall only appeared to be a smooth mural, she deftly swiped a card through the nearly hidden slot. The hallway was silent for the moment, but the pounding of a human heart would carry easily through the walls and into the many bedrooms. She only had seconds before someone would come to see why hers pounded.

Adding even more joy to the refrain in her head, she slipped into the secret hallway, its walls thick enough to hide almost anything thought or spoken, and pushed the chair down the narrow tunnel. Halting outside the guard room, she parked the chair and stepped into the opening, leaning against the door frame in a seductive pose.

There was only one guard, sitting with his feet propped up and staring morosely at the monitors. He glanced back at her then did a swift double-take, nearly falling off his chair. Sasha grinned wickedly. "I heard you were hungry."

As he stood, the light hit his name tag. Stan. Stan took his time, gazing from the pulse in her neck, down her exposed cleavage and lower, to the inches of thigh exposed between her skirt and boots. In less than a blink, he stood before her, taller, faster, stronger.

Sasha shivered.

Stan wrapped his large hands around her sides and grinned with anticipation.

Pick the best flavour and drain it dry.

Stan groaned, "Oh, yeah."

There was a reason the little ditty was popular among vampires. Stan leaned forwards and licked a trail from the curve of one breast to her neck, meaning to tease her.

Instead, Sasha held him as he slid silently to the floor. Any of her personal taste he'd managed to pick up would be disguised by the knock-out gel she'd smeared all over her skin. It left a brutal aftertaste.

From one of the large front pockets of her dress, Sasha pulled a flash drive and plugged it into the computer tower. Three key strokes and Enter executed the desired file upload. The monitors and hard drive were busy recording an old episode of *Buffy* when she left the room.

Eighty-five veins of blood to tap . . .

Eighty-five veins of blood . . .

Only intense practice kept her focused as she pushed the wheelchair into the next room and saw the once healthy and robust vampire lying there. The bed holding him was more like an incubator, enclosed with glass and bright UV heat lamps shining directly on his skin. He wouldn't burst into flames from this false sun, but he was burned a deep red from head to toe. Tainted blood flowed through an IV into his right arm, while the blood he'd filtered through his ancient system flowed from an IV in his left thigh, to be used in other ways later.

A small, horrified moan passed her lips and she stiffened. If she broke her mental block now, she'd never have the calm concentration to get it back.

Eighty-three veins of blood to tap . . .

Her movements trained to smooth efficiency, deep breaths keeping her heartbeat slow and regular despite the strain, Sasha set the brakes on the wheelchair and opened the "legs" to give her room to seat him. Then she lifted the clear lid and removed the tainted IV from his emaciated arm and thigh.

From the backpack hanging on the back of the wheelchair, she pulled a bundle of clothes and a bag of fresh blood. She attached the blood bag to a new IV to begin feeding him immediately. Pulling him into a sitting position, she managed to snap a hospital gown on him and belt a large, fluffy bathrobe around him. He wasn't his regular weight, though still tall and bulky, or she couldn't have manoeuvred him so easily. By now his eyes were blinking and he was trying to steady himself so he wouldn't hamper her further. His small amount of balance helped when it was time to swing him into the chair.

Gently, Sasha placed the bag of blood in a discreet pocket she'd sewn to the inside of his robe. Slippers and a thin cashmere blanket covered his skin from the toes up. She tucked the blanket snug around his legs and inside the legs of the wheelchair so nothing trailed to catch in the wheels. The sleeves of the robe bunched over his clasped hands, where they rested in his lap.

Moving even more quickly now, Sasha powdered his face to transform his skin from the quickly healing UV burn to a sickly white-yellow. Then she turned his blue eyes brown with contacts and wrapped a scarf around his neck. Almost done. A yellow hospital mask, a dark brown curly wig to hide his straight black hair, plus a cap to hold the wig in place, and he was ready.

She didn't have much time and the urgency to leave warred inside her with the necessity of his disguise. To push the wheelchair, she'd be standing behind him, unable to shield him by drawing all gazes to her body. No, with him in front, he would need a costume no one would want to stare at. This was as close as they had time for.

Twenty-nine veins of blood to tap . . .

Sasha pulled two canisters from the bag. Five seconds after being set, the canisters would release a gassy burst of ammonia and bleach in the tightly sealed room, filling the air and erasing any traceable scent. She set the first one on the bed he'd been in, the metal of the can clicking against the frame. Rushing, she pushed the wheelchair to the guard's office and released the second canister. Holding tight to the handles of his chair, she ran down the tunnel to the hallway exit.

One deep breath to slow her heart, and they flowed out from behind the hidden wall, quick and brazen, as if they'd exited the room next to it. Behind her, the trick wall slid shut and a part of her eased. So far, none of the vampires moving in and out of the rooms in the hallway had paid them any attention, but her heart was beating too fast for a fun little song to explain. Seamlessly, Sasha switched her thoughts to a vampire movie she'd watched, in which a seemingly sick vampire chased his sexy nurse around the hospital room. Only, in her mind, *she* was the teasing nurse evading an easy capture. And her patient was no longer in a wheelchair.

The imagined chase made her heart beat faster, nearly bringing life to the heart of her vampire patient as he followed her around the bed and pushed her to the mattress. Her belt popped open, displaying her from her vulnerable throat, two tiny spots dripping blood, to her bright red I-Wonder-How-It-Holds-'Em-In bra. She landed with her thighs spread, exposing the matching red panties under her skirt.

At least two of the male vampires in the hallway glanced her way because of that image, their eyes burning red at the centres while their fangs pressed against their lips. Sasha bit her lip coyly and thrust out her chest and she played the fantasy further, focusing their attention on her.

At the elevator, Sasha pushed the chair into the corner, pressed the down button and planted herself in front of the wheelchair while they waited for the elevator to arrive on their floor. When the doors slid open, she froze, her mind going blank as she stared into the sharp eyes of the Master of San Francisco. David. He did not look happy. In fact, he looked a bit panicked.

Sasha looked his tall frame over, her mind still empty of thought. When his gaze swerved from her to the chair behind her, she licked her lips. Imagining flesh and sweat and blood, anything to recapture his attention. David's gaze snapped back to hers, his look considering, then all too interested. He arched forwards, exiting the elevator.

With wide eyes, Sasha glanced to the man at David's side. His second-in-command, Alexander. He was also tall and well formed, thick veins branching down his forearms and over his hands. He looked at David and in her mind she exaggerated his expression. A touch heavy on the possessiveness, more than a touch to see a spark of lust for David.

David jerked, his attention snapping to his second as he followed from the elevator. David set a startled, analytical gaze on Alexander as his second frowned in confusion.

Sasha stepped past them, pushing the wheelchair inside the elevator then turning and pushing the button for the lowest level. With nothing between her and the Master but her imagination, Sasha pictured both of the men bare, tanned and wrapped around each other. Posing for her.

Both David and Alexander stared at her with wide eyes, both aroused and nearly comically shocked at her vivid mind. In the second it took for the doors to slide closed, Sasha projected one final thought.

If Alexander were on top, would he take advantage of the power exchange?

David snarled at his second-in-command while Alexander tried to look innocent.

The doors clicked shut and Sasha turned the wheelchair, tugging down the mask to examine her vampire's healing skin. Familiar eyes, despite the brown contacts, twinkled up at her and his lip tugged up slightly at the corner. In the depths of her mind she heard his whisper.

Diabolical.

Sasha replaced the mask, her lips twitching at his praise. Circling behind the chair, she began a new fantasy for those who might listen, this one in the maze hedge at the back of the grounds. The leaves were dark and dense, turning the night from the darkest of blue to an inescapable pitch black. Perfect for the predator vs. prey game her fantasy master loved.

This is a side of you I've never known.

And he knew nearly all of her. Sasha grimaced. All except the grown woman struggling for freedom inside her. The woman with her own needs and desires. Sasha changed the course of her thoughts as her heartbeat slowed during the elevator ride, even her breathing sedate and regular by the time the doors slid open.

Twenty-eight veins of blood to tap ...

Sasha opened the door to the guest parking area. Rolling him to her SUV, Sasha aided him inside and loaded the wheelchair in the back, to be sterilized later. Taking her place behind the wheel, she pulled out and drove down the long, tree-shrouded driveway. Her watch beeped its notice. Five minutes. The rescue was on schedule. She needed to hurry a bit, but nothing obvious.

Flipping on the radio, she hummed the words, picturing the stories the songs told. Soon, she passed the guards at the end of the drive, giving them a jaunty wave goodbye as she did, and upped her speed just understandably past the limit. With one hand, she reached into the console between them and handed him another bag of blood.

He pulled off his hospital mask and pierced the plastic with his fangs, too starved to care that it was lukewarm. He took out the contacts, dropping them in the garbage sack she handed him. The empty bags and IV followed.

Singing louder, Sasha unpinned the nurse's hat and shook out her hair, then released the belt and unbuttoned the nurse's dress. Before it was fully off, she pulled on a loose, scoop-neck blouse. Changing was a trick while driving, but doable. It would be wonderful if she could give him her wrist and let him feed while she drove, but passing out at the wheel would be bad. Besides, she would give him fresh blood as soon as she could wash away all the knock-out gel coating her skin. It was the least she could do. This whole evening was the least she could do. She owed him her life.

He covered her hand with his and his voice was deep and raw. "Not any more."

"Always."

Ten minutes until dawn. It was a huge risk, but the only way this could have worked. Vamps weren't locked in sleep at dawn, but they would have to stay inside, well away from any light. She looked to the side. All of them have to take these precautions – including *her* vamp.

A few miles down the road, she pulled into a parking garage. Up and up, she drove to the top end, to a dark, lonely area that few people preferred. She backed into the parking spot so the passenger side of the SUV was near the passenger side of a blue Dodge half-ton.

Sasha parked and left the keys in the ignition. As she exited the SUV, she pulled out a long, flowing wrap-around and tied it at her waist. Taking the key from its hidden spot under the truck, she unlocked the doors and exposed the truth of the extended cab. The back seats had been removed, allowing a long, deep, light-proof box to fit snuggly behind the front seats. The box's camouflaged top made it appear to be a set of large speakers.

Sasha helped her vampire to the truck and disconnected the drained blood bag, replacing its tube with a tube that led through the bottom of the box to a closed garment bag hanging over the speakers. The garment bag held ten large bags of blood, all now hooked up to his IV. Sasha looked meaningfully into his healing face, knowing he read her thoughts easily.

He nodded, his blue eyes clear and warm. "You're an amazing woman."

With a grateful peck on her lips, he crawled into the box.

Lips tingling, Sasha sealed the box and closed the doors. Gathering together the used blood bags, she added them to the garbage bag. Then, like before, Sasha pulled an ammonia and bleach canister from the centre console, clicked it to activate the detonator, and left it on the seat of the SUV she was abandoning.

In the back of the truck was a cooler full of bleach. She tossed in the bag, her boots – as sad as that was, but they were too noticeable to keep – and pulled off her short skirt.

Seconds later, the truck roared to life and she headed for the Golden Gate Bridge. Within an hour, she was firmly on HWY 101 and heading north. The most beautiful and scenic drive in America had two other benefits – minimal traffic and a cool, comfortable climate to drive in. Small clusters of towns gave way to long, winding roads and gorgeous ocean vistas. And best of all, she was finally too distant for any vampire to read her mind.

Sasha?

Except that one. Mary grinned and relaxed into the driver's seat. "A nurse wears a name tag and I have a nasty habit of talking to myself. I had to make up a name for both. It seemed bad form to announce I was the Murder King's human, here to rescue him."

Yes, that wouldn't have worked nearly as well.

In a world of exotic vampire names, human names stood out. Hers, especially, considering she'd been raised by the Murder – a group of vampires charged with policing their own kind. Their title was linked with the phrase 'a murder of crows', though which came first – the murder of crows or the murder of vampires – was anyone's guess. The group consisted of the Murder King and his Crows, a mix of vampire and werewolf warriors.

If any vampire stepped out of line – or say, went on a killing spree, like the one who'd killed Mary's entire family – then the Murder came for him. In her case, the rogue had captured her family during a camping trip, forcing them deeper into the mountains and into a network of tunnels where they would be too lost to escape and he could have his fun and food without interruption. Three days of blood, screams and horror had followed in the darkness of that tunnel. It was a nightmare she'd never forget.

She'd thought she would die. Almost had. The next time she'd seen moonlight again, it had been splashed across Sebastian's face. She'd been the only one left alive. An orphan too traumatized by the gruesome deaths of her brother and parents to be mesmerized into forgetfulness, but too young to reliably vow silence and go her own way. Sebastian – the Murder King – had taken her home. A temporary fix that long ago became permanent.

Why the hell did they send you?

Mary buried the pang his question caused and, with a tight grip on the wheel, focused on the logic. She didn't heal as quickly. Wasn't as strong. Couldn't move as fast. Couldn't prevent the powerful vampires from reading her mind or mesmerizing her. God, the list was endless. She was the worst choice for rescuer.

"There were several plans to extract you. But David expected the vampires and was prepared for the wolves. In the end, we knew he wouldn't keep you forever. His Halloween party tonight was largely a show for gathering all of his people into one place for protection. Several attempts were made from different angles tonight. Some failed, some were back-up. All were distractions, because amid everything else, he'd never expect them to send me."

Not the protected human of the Murder King. Everyone knew she wasn't to be allowed around anything seriously dangerous. She pressed her lips and buried the issue. Not the most important thing to focus on at the moment.

She'd been safe tonight, unless she'd screwed up. She'd learned all the vamp tricks at Sebastian's knee as a child, not to mention those she'd created herself as a rebellious teenager, trying to circumvent her vampire and werewolf foster family.

Many had argued. Violently. She was too weak. Sebastian would go insane at just the suggestion. This was too important to leave in the hands of a human. In the end, she'd come up with the best, simplest plan. And if she failed, well, hopefully at least one of the other strategies wouldn't.

"And it worked." She smiled triumphantly into the rear-view mirror, thinking carefully over the last few days and all the plans she'd made, picturing them in detail so he could pluck them from her mind.

At great risk to yourself.

Mary sighed. She knew he wouldn't like that part. To Sebastian, anything that put her at risk was unacceptable. But did he realize the terror she'd felt when he'd been captured? She'd never forget the sight of him – his once vital, invincible body strapped helplessly to that table, tubes draining him of the powerful blood he needed to survive. His skin greying with a sick red tinge as they took him from her, drop by drop.

Mary checked her mirrors, blinking and rolling her eyes to air-dry them of tears as she breathed deep to fight the brutal images. It was only today that she'd seen the terrible things they'd done to him, but every moment since his disappearance she'd imagined images just as horrible. Some even worse.

He wasn't just her childhood saviour. Or the dominating law of her youth. He was so much more important to her than any one of the roles he'd played during her childhood phases. *I* . . . the sound in her mind was similar to a sigh. An acceptance. *I do thank you.*

"You would do no less for me."

It would be much less dangerous for me.

Again she pictured his thinning skin, his sunken chest. His veins blackened by the poison they'd forced into him. The pain he must have felt was unimaginable. She'd tried. She'd seen first-hand what vampires could do, and not just when she was a child. Those memories would never leave her. Pain was pain. Torture was torture. No one, vampire or human, was exempt from the risk of agony.

It had all come down to one salient point. Which could she live with best: risk of death, be it quick or slow, or life with the loss of him, and the knowledge she'd done nothing to prevent it?

How did you know I still lived?

She'd felt it. "Intel."

Silence.

"Why the elaborate set-up, the snail's pace torture? If he wanted you dead, why not a quick, clean kill before he lost his chance?"

They didn't tell you?

And break the code of secrecy they loved so well? She snorted. The subtext had flown around, but no one had wanted to explain. At first because they didn't want her involved, then because she'd have less to think about, therefore less chance to screw up the rescue. She had a long way to go to prove herself to them. Or, at least, to the handful of Crows *willing* to let her prove herself.

You have nothing to prove and no reason to try so hard.

A blank wall rose in her mind. It was mostly white with a grey crack that split in so many directions she could mentally trace it for hours. Which she had done before. She'd been using this trick for years since it seemed the most effective way to disguise her thoughts. By the time he broke through, the thought she hid would be long gone.

He sighed again. *David had a sister. She crossed the line.*

The Murder had been created long before the vampires had expanded past the Old World, before the ruling Monarchy had been replaced with more of a republic (with Senators representing the territories they ruled). The Murder existed outside of all rule, as the law itself. Everyone, both citizen and ruler, answered to the Murder. Whenever a rogue believed he answered to no one, killed indiscriminately and risked lawlessness and war, Senator or peon – the Murder was called.

David's sister Tatiana ruled an area in France a hundred years ago. She took a page from the bloody countess and bathed in the blood of virgins, not for the youthful beauty the countess had sought, but for pleasure and gluttony. Her antics, while legal because she'd made them legal in her territory, risked the safety of all vampires. The Murder was called and I dealt the death blow. Her people, David among them, were ordered to watch. To learn that type of barbarity was not acceptable.

"And instead, he learned to hate you."

My mentor and predecessor was killed during the battle. Her death marked my ascension to Murder King.

Ahh. For Sebastian to have profited from Tatiana's death. That would have been impossible for David to accept. "Why wait so long for revenge?"

He waited until victory was certain.

Meaning David had thought the Murder King was finally vulnerable. That there had been a hole in Sebastian's security.

She tightened her grip on the wheel. This was all her fault.

Her first two years of college had been full of online classes backed with evening classes. But this year, the courses she needed were only at certain times – day times – and her presence was mandatory. She'd moved into a dorm, living the college student's life, separate from the Murder for the first time since her rescue from that fatal family camping trip.

She'd thought she'd needed the independence, the chance to mature away from the watchful eyes of the Murder or they would forever see only the defenceless child she'd been. Or the protected pet she'd become. Unless she got away long enough to become the capable woman she felt was her destiny.

But, dear God, she'd left the Murder King vulnerable. His guards had been with her. This was her fault.

No. He bit the word out with a sharp snap. *This is David's fault. He was coming for me sooner or later.*

"But he had a chance because of me."

I left myself in the open.

She could hear the click as pieces fell into place. Over the last week, she'd heard a few facts about his disappearance. He'd been out of the compound at the time, but not on a case – something that hadn't happened in a hundred years. He had come to check on her at school.

No wonder Sebastian's werewolf bodyguard had glared at her, his hazel eyes so accusing. Lucas was never off duty. Strong, lethal, loyal. Pretty damned hot.

Sebastian growled in the back of her mind and she bit her cheek, concentrating on the pain until the urge to smile left.

Lucas had blamed her for Sebastian's vulnerability. Then each of the others had fallen in suit, not wanting to include her in his rescue, not trusting her. They didn't just think her weak, did they? Did they also think she'd helped his enemies? Of course, that would have to be a consideration. They'd all lived too long not to consider every possibility. "They were angry you exposed yourself to danger just to check on me personally."

Silence.

"I knew you had me watched. I haven't fought having guards because I understand why I need them." And the guards had kept it low key, granting her as much freedom and privacy as possible while keeping her safe. The Murder King had too many enemies and his human ward knew too many secrets.

Those aren't the only reasons why.

"Did David threaten to kill me?"

Yes.

"And you came to get me?"

Yes. Then there was a fight and I was captured.

She sighed and focused on her driving. Music played softly in the background and she let her attention drift with the words and the scenery. A half-hour later, she pulled into a double-wide storage unit and parked the truck. Using a slab on wheels and a winch system, she transferred his light-proof crate to the back of another SUV, cleaned anything that could identify them, set the scent-scrubber bombs and drove away in a vehicle with Oregon plates. A quick trip through a drive-thru netted her a burger and pop and she continued on.

Through it all, he was quiet. Considering the height of the sun in the sky, he probably slept like the dead. He didn't actually have to, but after being tortured for a week . . . well. She finished her burger and bagged the trash.

Something had to change.

She needed college. Not just for her to give her credentials in the real world, but for the distance, the space. For years now, she'd had one dream. Likely Sebastian knew, bits and pieces at the very least. She wasn't *that* good at hiding her thoughts.

The fact was Sebastian had never really been a father figure to her. She remembered her own dad too well for that. No, Sebastian wasn't her dad, but he was everything else. He was the strength that rescued her, not only the once, but every night in her dreams. He was the wisdom that guided her growth, as well as the growth of a coven of fifty vampires, and as many wolves. Policing rogues wasn't a cushy job.

But beyond all that, his humour made her smile. His anger alternated between making her cringe and sparking her blood. And his big, hard, healthy body made her wet . . . in places she dare not think of with him in the car with her – whether he was asleep or not.

She couldn't have him. Not yet. She would *not* be a liability to him. Despite the years of training that could've earned her a blacker than black belt, or the excellent marks she'd made with all her tutors, she still needed two things before she could fulfil her dream. Unfortunately, they were the two hardest things for him to grant: time and distance.

She needed these two things so that her thoughts could be private while she worked on herself. So her gradual changes could be noticeable when she returned home. Then Sebastian would see a different person. A grown, mature woman, worthy of respect. And love.

Her dream was to become his woman.

She needed to become a strong partner worthy of the Murder's leader. The kind of partner he needed. Any weakness in her would reflect on him. A human could only do so much in his world, physically, but mental weakness was worse.

She also needed to age. He'd been turned in his thirties. She had a good five to ten years before she could stand by him without looking like his kid sister, or worse – as she looked now – his daughter.

Five to ten years of living, a degree in business, minor in politics, and then she'd ask him to turn her. Assuming, please God, that he wanted her by then. That she'd proven herself worthy.

Mary breathed deeply, pulling back from her vision of the future. She had a vivid imagination. Too much focus on it and she might forget she wasn't there yet. She'd imagine skipping the years of hard work and just race straight to the next step, lying beside him in soft cotton sheets, their bare bodies close. Touching.

Images which were much too detailed to think about two hours from sundown. Mary leaned forwards and cranked the radio. A quick check of the maps on her cell phone re-confirmed the directions to the safe house, and she settled in to sing with the radio, emptying her mind of all else.

The sky was a mix of orange and yellow, the last burst of the sun before it fell below the horizon. Mary pulled into the garage and closed the doors, making careful mental note for Sebastian of the placement of items, doors and switches and, especially, the alarm code. He wouldn't exit the crate until the sun was fully down. There were too many ways the house might not be fully light-proof. When he felt safe, he'd come inside the house.

Is this place secure?

Mary thought over her plans and precautions, letting him see the details. "I paid cash and rented it under that emergency name you gave me."

Then only the two of us know.

"What about whoever made the ID?"

I made it myself.

Mary smiled and continued into the house. The bagged blood would have smoothed the edge of his starvation and sickness, but for true healing he would need fresh blood. She found the master bedroom and en suite, set a duffel bag on the counter and took a shower. She had to scrub away the face-altering make-up and every inch of her skin that was slathered in knock-out gel.

Forty-five minutes later, Mary exited the steamy bathroom in a tank top and matching sky-blue cotton shorts. Her hair hung in a straight, wet curtain to the middle of her back and thin wisps, drying to blonde, framed her face. Finally, she looked like what she was – a youthful, relatively innocent college student.

Light from the doorway behind her spilled into the darkened bedroom, illuminating the man sitting on the edge of her bed. The light struck his eyes, making shiny sparkles in the vibrant blue. Apparently distance didn't affect only the way people saw her, but also the way she saw them.

She'd always loved Sebastian, in all his many roles. But this one was new. Still thin and weakened from his ordeal, his skin had healed the small wounds and discolorations. Now his bare chest gleamed golden and his veins had returned to blue from their previously poisoned black. His hair gleamed wet from his own shower, taken in the main bathroom closer to the garage, and he'd chosen a pair of comfortable cotton sweats for the night. His bare feet curled into the carpet and his elbows rested on his slightly splayed knees, as he studied her just as thoughtfully as she did him.

"You have nothing to prove. You will not risk yourself in such a misguided endeavour again."

His voice was the same commanding baritone he'd always used. His mouth settled into the same thin line, demanding obedience – unhappy until it was willingly given. But something was different. He seemed more approachable, and not because of the amazing amount of muscled skin on display. Being bare might make other people seem more vulnerable, but not him now.

No, it wasn't the lack of clothing or his relative illness that made him seem approachable to her, but she couldn't decide what it was. Whatever was different, she didn't react with a knee-jerk urge to rebel against his words. Instead, she stepped forwards with a calm assurance in her mind, her body and her tone.

"I will risk whatever I deem necessary in order to aid those I care for. No matter the labels you give it later."

Sebastian straightened, still sitting on the bed, until his spine was a strong line and his shoulders a broad wall against the darkness behind him. "You would defy my command?"

Mary came to a stop directly in front of him, her eyes not much higher than his though he sat. She met his gaze without flinching. "You would have me be less than the woman you've helped raise me to be?"

His eyes narrowed. "No, but I would have you safe."

She raised her brows, then her chin, asking the question they needed to have out in the open between them. "Would you have me be a coward?"

He stared at her in silence, the point of no return a firm line between them. He'd ruled vampires and wolves long enough to know there came a moment when each individual was no longer a child. Her moment had come and he had to accept it.

She accepted that she was young and there was still much for her to learn. There were levels of maturity she had to earn. Mistakes she had to make. She didn't want to die. Didn't want to risk herself in ridiculous acts of recklessness, but like with tonight, she'd had a plan. She'd implemented it with only the help of those she trusted implicitly, and she had succeeded. He was alive and safe. And well worth the risk.

His hands clenched closed on his thighs, the only sign of any struggle inside of him. "I knew the woman you would be the moment I first gazed into your eyes. And while these last few years have taken for ever in your eyes, in mine, they've been the work of but a moment. I'm not ready to set you free."

Mary lowered to her knees, settling between his and gently covering his fists with her hands. "I haven't asked for freedom from you. Only freedom to be me."

His eyes flared, the blue an intense beam cutting straight to her marrow. "Are you really so positive you know what that means?"

"It means I am not an empty puppet or a brainless doll." Her hands clenched tight over his, her eyes wide and earnest. "I am me. That is what you hold. *I* am yours."

His face lowered over hers, his gaze devouring, his lips a breath away. "You vow this?"

That quick breath left her lungs. She could barely move with the intensity of the moment. With one hand, she drew her hair over her right shoulder, baring the left side of her neck. He needed to feed. She could sense his hunger. But also, she could sense that he hungered for her, specifically. And her promise would be sealed with her blood. It was the way of the vampire. Blood was life. Blood was sacred.

Wetting her lips, she spoke softly but firmly. Her words brushed his cheek. "I vow that I am yours. Your human."

Sebastian lowered his mouth to her throat, kissing her pulse. Inhaling her scent from her ear lobe to the fragile line of her collarbone, he whispered against her, "I don't want you to be just my human."

Mary swallowed, her heart beating so hard in her chest it rocked her to her foundations. "When the time comes, I vow that I will be your vampire."

Sebastian smiled, his lips brushing the top of her breast. His tongue was soft as he traced the cords of her neck up to her ear where he whispered, "Closer. But I still want more."

Mary inhaled deeply, her chest rising. Her breasts ached against his chest. She held in the moan, searching for the promise he wanted from her.

Arousal tightened the muscles of her stomach. Her hands wrapped over his biceps, holding her before him. His skin warmed to her touch, sparking her temperature even higher. Her desire for him was unmistakable. And he wasn't pushing her away or forcing her to keep a respectable distance. Instead, he opened his mouth and scraped his fangs delicately along the vulnerable line of her throat. Helpless to hold it back, she moaned.

"I like to hear you think as you reach a decision. Your thought patterns are not the ruthless, linear logic that works for me, but they are logical nonetheless. There are so many of your decisions I would never understand if I didn't have this advantage."

Mary trembled, bare and exposed. There was nothing she could hide from him. No feeling, no plan, no dream. Licking her lips, she gathered her courage and gave him what she hoped he sought. "I vow that I will be your woman."

Instantly, he crushed her against his chest, his arms steel bands around her and his face buried in her neck. His voice, when it came, was ragged. "Thank you."

Mary nodded, her mouth open to respond when his fangs broke her skin for the first time. Her eyes sprang wide and her back arched against him as twin spears of pain punctured her neck and her blood rushed into him. Her right hand grabbed at his shoulders, holding him tight as if his own grasp had lightened. With her left, she drove her fingers into his hair, pressing his head against her, as she finally understood what had previously been only hinted at in her thoughts.

She was needed in the most primal, elemental way. He needed what only she could provide and what she willingly gave, nurturing him with the comfort of her arms and the life from her body. It was a cycle of bonding she'd never imagined could be this intense. This necessary.

Then it was even more as Sebastian tightened his hold on her and lifted her, his lips never breaking their seal against her neck where he licked and suckled slowly and gently, savouring her taste like the most delicate of fine wines. Her knees met the mattress with her straddling him. Mary moaned. The cycle wasn't complete. Not yet.

Sebastian brought his hot hands to the top of each of her thighs and slid up, his fingers delving beneath the legs of her shorts and going up her hips. In one burst of strength he tore through the seams of both her shorts and underwear, peeling the shreds of cloth from her wet skin. When he had her finally bare, his fingers delved and stroked in the swollen flesh he'd revealed.

Mary cried out, a high, desperate sound. She'd waited so long for this moment and already it was beyond the capabilities of her imagination.

Sebastian lay back, Mary lying over him as he arched his hips enough to slide his sweats down to his thighs. He curled forwards, the hard core of his abs holding him as one arm circled her waist, lifting her with the strength of his biceps and forearm. Mary poised to give him the rest of her body. Another first.

Sebastian shuddered, moaning against her neck. "Yes."

Dragging out each second of an experience that could never be repeated, Mary took him inside her. A sharp pain gave way to tense muscles pulled taut. The cycle was complete.

Sebastian licked his marks closed, sealing her blood inside her veins. Mary took her time, staring into his eyes and revelling in the intensity of his focus.

Mary collapsed into his arms, her ear pressed to the now racing sound of his heart. When Sebastian slept, his heart was near silent. When he was hungry, it was barely a sluggish demand. But, for now, it beat for her.

Sebastian's fingers tangled in her hair, brushing the newly damp strands from her nape. "I may have taken too much blood, though I drank slow."

Mary smiled. "I'm not worried. I'm taking a medication that increases my production of red blood cells. I knew you would need to feed often this first week, and I didn't want to risk having you appear to anyone at less than full strength. I'll be fine."

"I won't endanger you."

She kissed his chest and nuzzled up to his neck. "With the medicine, it would be more dangerous to my heart if I didn't lose some blood. But don't worry. I studied the limits carefully. One week won't hurt me."

He chuckled and traced her cheek with one finger, his blue eyes clear and inviting. "You have a plan for everything, don't you? Even to become the Murder King's woman."

Mary bit her lip and shook her head. "I've only wanted to be Sebastian's woman. I have no designs on your title. It just comes with the total package."

He eased her up, then set her back against the pillows, coming to rest alongside her. "I know. That's why you have me. All of me. Heaven help you."

She laughed. "I think it's you who needs the help. Or, at least, you will. David isn't done with you."

And with that, her laughter faded.

Sebastian tucked a strand of her hair behind her ear. "Don't you worry about him. He's mine to take care of."

"While I do what? Go back to college and play a young twenty-something with no worries?" Mary grimaced and shook her head. "I can't do that."

Sebastian disagreed. "That's exactly what you do. You have a plan, remember?"

Mary shook her head. "One that's pointless if something happens to you."

He pulled her close for a kiss, dragging out the contact with her bottom lip for one for ever moment. "You saved me. Now I will do my job and you will do yours. Or, specifically, in a week when our time here is up."

One week. They would have one week, then maybe in a few years a future. Or maybe not. She bit her lip, staring into his eyes. Just as he had to accept her as the woman she was, she had to accept him as both the incredibly sexy Sebastian and as the indomitable Murder King. Always at risk. Always in danger. Except for this one brief week.

Mary pressed her bare body against his, her voice hoarse but determined. "Then we'd better make it count."

Butterfly Kiss

Carole Nelson Douglas

The name is Louie, Midnight Louie. I like my nightlife shaken, not stirred.

A veteran PI can never know his home turf's dark side well enough, and I have padded the neon-lit Strip of Las Vegas and its byways and back-ways for a long time.

Vegas has always been known as Sin City, but the "Sin" part has gotten a lot deadlier since the Millennium Revelation at the turn of the twenty-first century revealed some of the bloodsuckers in Vegas were actually supernatural – vampires, and werewolves and zombies, oh my.

I admit that I am not *au courante*, so to speak, with all the varieties of crime and punishment on the paranormal side of the street, so I have made it my business tonight to find that nomadic subterranean pit of the dark side of sin called the Sinkhole.

I am not impressed. Sure, the full moon is putting on a show topside, so I must dodge werewolves in the street, but I find they are mostly living La Vida Loco after their nightly blood-thirsty runs and now are only running up bills in gin joints and casinos.

Midnight Louie is light on his feet and used to keeping a low profile – a very low profile – abetted by the fact that I am short, dark and handsome. My thick black pelt blends into the night, except for my baby greens, which can emit a demonic glow when the few street lights hit them.

My kind has had a bad rep since witches were burned at the stake. I find that useful in my work. In fact, a tourist couple happens to notice me and runs the other way, shrieking that I must not cross their paths.

Fine with me, folks. Your footwear bears an odour of bunions. Or is that "onions" from a zombie burger joint?

All around me echo the same sounds of merriment and debauchery you get in mainstream Vegas, interspersed with occasional screams, growls and moans.

Then I catch an aroma that perks my wing flaps and tingles my tail section.

Something feline and feminine this way comes, and it is not the shape-shifted leopard devouring a Happy Meal at the MacDungeon's across the street.

The faintest brush against my shiny satin lapels reveals a pale feathery plume tickling the hair of my chinny-chin-chin.

Wow. This first-class dame is draped in luxuriant furs, cream with crimson tips, the breed colour called a flame-point. If the Sinkhole is the path to hell and this hot little number is on it, I am homeward bound!

"My name is Vesper," she breaths in my perked ear. "I have not seen you in these parts before, Big Boy."

Actually, I am. Big that is, and surely a boy. Perhaps some self-description is appropriate now that the action has turned romantic. First, I am twenty pounds of solid muscle. Check. Hairy chest, check. Concealed weapons? Check. Sixteen shivs ready to slash from my mitts and feet in a street rumble.

Best of all, I have – as they used to advertise sports cars – four on the floor and come fully equipped from the factory.

All this means I am ready, willing and able to take on any Sinkhole-dwelling humans or unhumans, and also, of course, any lone ladies requiring defensive and/or intimate manoeuvres.

While I am planning the evening's escapades, the lithesome Vesper has diverted down a dim alley, only her flame-tipped train beckoning from around the corner. I hasten to follow her.

Now, any simpleton knows this is probably a trap. So do I. Not that I am a simpleton, although I am a simple fellow at heart. No, I figure I will find out what the lady *really* wants, and if it is a patsy, we will have a discussion. Either way, I intend to get to know her a lot better.

So I edge into the alley, my laser-sharp night vision kicking into full power.

Yup. Another flash of tail deep in the darkness. Classic. I slink along the dumpsters, ignoring the octopus tentacles writhing over the edges. This is no time for sushi.

Even the noise of the main drag has faded. I am invading No Man's Land. Luckily, I am no man. I have almost caught up with the elusive Vesper when I stumble across the expected trap.

It forms an unseen barrier, less than two feet high and six feet long. I peer over it only to see Vesper's eyes gleaming red in the reflected light of the street.

Hmm, I think to myself. We commune over a dead body. Whose? How? Why? I have my work cut out for me, I see.

Vesper hisses, baring long front fangs (so misnamed as "canine") also gleaming red in the night light. True, neon is common in Vegas, and below it. However, this looks like the sheen of blood. Could *Vesper* have killed this man?

Gorgeous as she is, she is a domestic cat. I have almost killed humans in the pursuit of my cases, but I am remarkably strong and clever. I cannot believe this bit of fluff is homicidal.

Then I reconsider. Never underestimate the female of the species, any species.

I sniff along the victim's upper torso and encounter a scent of . . . nothing.

The man is not only dead, he is not . . . um . . . how shall I put it delicately? He is not rotting.

Now that is a truly revolting turn of events! I do scent the odd combination of earthy odours. Either this gent wore an unusual cologne or . . . *aha*! My luxuriant whiskers follow the shape of a large, curved *claw* impaled near his heart.

Dainty Vesper certainly could not have wielded this large a lance.

By now someone has stumbled out of a nearby dive, leaving the rear door ajar enough to cast pale light on our tableau of three.

The deceased is indeed a young man. His dark hair contrasts a dead-white skin. He would be handsome if he had green eyes like mine, but his eyelids are closed. Vesper is rubbing back and forth on his black attire, shedding white hairs in her distress.

I realize that she has led me here. This man must have been her . . . companion. I dislike the word "owner" used in relation to my kind. I have been street smart and fancy free since I was a kit. True, I have a human female room-mate, Miss Temple Barr, a public relations expert and sometime crime-solver – with my immense help, that is – but it is a voluntary arrangement on both our parts.

Vesper releases a sad *mew* and tries to make like an ascot around the poor guy's neck. I understand the bond between human and animal, but this is over the top.

"You must remove her," a low, rasping voice says.

Easier said than done, I think as I whip around to see what human has arrived on the scene.

I can communicate in various ways with various members of the animal kingdom, but I do not speak to humans. This is not because I *could* not if I so wished, but, really, some of my kin have suffered much at their disloyal hands. I am not about to honour even the best of them with my voice.

As for the voice I heard, we three are still alone. No one has discovered us.

I stare at Vesper while she whines and buries her face in the dead guy's neck and runs her dainty muzzle along his jawline. You would think she was a Silver Screen drama queen. I am not the sentimental sort, but realize that this distraught lady must not disturb the evidence on the body.

"Vesper, no!" the faint voice says. "I will not. Never. Anyway, it is not enough now, and this strapping fellow you have lured here is not sufficient, either."

Midnight Louie not sufficient? For anything? I beg your pardon. I am the primo PI in this town and have been since before God made millenniums and the devil made brimstone. Well, so to speak.

"Go, you," the voice commands me and follows up with a demeaning order, as if I were not Midnight Louie, PI. "Scat! And consider your hide well saved. Vesper means well but this is beyond the abilities of cats."

I drop my jaw. And speak. I am not violating my vow to address no human being. This man is unhuman.

"You are still alive," I tell my handsome corpse. "For a vampire."

He coughs slightly. "Good. You hear my thoughts. My dying thoughts. My poor Vesper is offering her slender artery for my survival, but it is not enough. You must drive her away."

"Someone has staked you so you cannot move," I diagnose, on the right trail at last, now that I know the nature of the victim. The claw must be polished wood.

It is not every day – or night, I should say – that an investigator can interview the corpse, who is also a corpse-to-be even more.

"A long distance blow," he answers. "I staggered here to escape more poison wooden darts just before the curse pinned me here like a bug."

Vesper lifts her lovely throat and howls. "You good-for-nothing," she accuses me. "You have neither blood nor brains to offer! *Do something.*"

"I am a professional," I tell her. "Your fit of pique is not called for. And I am not about to trick some innocent tourist down this alley – although I could – so he or she can be drained to death."

The vampire's form stirs. "No, no. Not to death. I am a daylight vampire, the new breed designed to mingle safely with humans. I feed on a . . . circle of willing volunteers, a mere cocktail with each, one at a time. Only now, I have been immobilized and starved. I need more than a serial filling day by day. I need a full body's blood. Keep anything human away. My will to survive could make me drain a person to death and make them a vampire . . . one without my scruples."

I frown. "How many daylight vampires are there?"

"Only a few dozen, but the programme is promising."

"Is it possible someone is trying to sabotage the movement by driving you to savagery or death?"

He gives a hollow, almost spectral laugh. "Even likely, but I do not have the time to explore that possibility, my feline friend. Can you . . . will you . . . look after Vesper when I am gone?"

Vesper emits an anguished screech and casts herself on the vampire's chest.

What can I do but promise? Still, I know I am in no position to shepherd a vampire pussycat. I need help with this case, probably human help.

First, I stiffen my spine and judiciously pat down the fallen vampire. He is nicely dressed in silk-blend black from foot to, ah, neck, and well built as humans go under his fancy clothes. I find a couple of interesting objects in his sports coat side pockets.

One is a slick multifunction device the size of a credit card. My street-calloused pads manage to punch enough buttons to call up his client list of blood donors. This causes my eyebrow whiskers to lift.

They are all female, all right, and one is a well-known performer on the Strip. I could make some tidy dough from the tabloids if I outed her erotic . . . tastes.

But that would be unethical. A plan is forming in my agile brain, but things are always complicated for a guy of my physical type.

"What is this?" I ask Vesper, rolling a ping-pong-ball-sized object I found in his pocket from one paw to the other over the pavement.

She leaps down to swat it away from me. "My toy."

"Just a minute there." I manage to pull it safely against my hairy masculine chest. "There seems to be something inside." I perk an ear at a muted but frantic buzzing.

"*My* toy," she repeats. "My master bought it for me."

A tug of toy ensues, during which, thanks to my superior strength, the ball breaks in half like a perfectly split eggshell.

Well.

The buzzing, now loud enough to decipher, resolves into an indignant high-pitched voice, as the winged inhabitant gives us both what-for.

"It is a Whirr-away," Vesper says. "My master hurls it for me to chase and find."

"Hmm." I trap a tiny wing under one curved claw. "I have eaten bigger mites than this by accident. This is no 'toy', Vesper, it is an earth-bound pixie. Very rare. Your master must treasure you indeed."

"You would stoop to petty thievery while my master lies dying?"

"I would stoop to using your 'toy' for a much more serious purpose. What is your name, little fellow?"

"I am female," the creature buzzes back at me.

"Is it true that pixies are allergic to silver?" A lot of supernaturals can be injured by silver.

I feel the tiny wing tremble against my pad. "Awful stuff. It burns my skin and if it ever enters my blood, I will die."

"Then I imagine you could spot the stuff instantly, from a long ways away?"

Another shudder. "It is far too popular as human jewellery. I smell six women wearing it on the street out there."

"What if the silver sprang from a lock of long white hair?"

The tiny human-like body leaps atop my mitt, pulling its wing free. "Changeling silver. That is different. Very rare and powerful. Almost non-existent in this realm."

"What is your name?"

"Wasp-Wing."

"I take it you can fly far and fast, Wasp-Wing."

"Like bolt lightning. I have been leashed so as not to over-challenge the vampire's feline companion."

"I usually work with a human female on my cases," I explain to all who listen, which is a fading vampire, a heart-broken vampire cat and my new pixie pal. "We need human help and I am thinking of a new partner this time who might just have the paranormal talent to do the trick. Fly topside, find the woman who wears changeling silver and bring her back, fast as you can."

"That will depend on the woman," Wasp-Wing rustles, vanishing like a dust mote against the neon-lit night.

"My toy will never come back," Vesper mourns. "I always had to trap and fetch it."

"Nothing wins over an ally more than letting it feel useful and challenged, Vesper."

"You expect this silver-bearing human female to save my master?"

"At the very least, she can move the body."

She strikes at me with fanned claws, but I easily dodge the blow. Those vampire claws may be toxic, for all I know.

"Calm down, Vesper. We all need help sometimes."

"If my master cannot drink he will die," she growls softly, curling up along his side.

I gingerly mount his chest, which of course does not lift up and down, and examine the weapon that pins him. It is not a toy either, but a curved claw two inches long. Small things can be potent, I know. Including pixies.

Perhaps ten minutes later, a shadow fills the alley opening, then a figure strides to our location and stands, hands on hips, feet astride, looking down. She is wearing low-rise blue jeans and a grey leotard top.

On her right elbow perches a tiny, glowing, winged figure.

"It is a good thing I brake for butterflies," she says. "My windshield almost pulverized the pixie before I discovered what it was. Am I to understand I have been summoned to perform a 'professional courtesy' for another PI?"

"Nicely put," I tell Wasp-Wing, although the woman cannot hear me.

Now that a human is on the scene, I am back to my usual handicap: my vow not to speak to the breed. Pixies, luckily, have no such principles and this one has been buzzing her head off since she landed on my colleague's windshield.

The woman kneels beside the vampire, taking him for a fallen private investigator.

"Man, you are nearly gone," she murmurs as Vesper jumps up to rub back and forth on her bent leg, white fangs gleaming.

I know what Vesper is thinking – she is hoping my hard-won assistant will trip over her onto her master and become instant fang bait.

He struggles, feeling the temptation, and manages to whisper, "Stay away."

"No can do," the woman says. "The pixie blabbed all. The name is Delilah Street. I am a paranormal investigator who has met a daylight vampire. I know your more-evolved type is mortally harmless to humans. We need to get you somewhere private."

He struggles as her hand reaches for the claw dart in his chest.

"Bespelled!" Wasp-Wing whines a warning, hovering over Delilah Street's fingers.

"No problem," she says, jerking out the claw as if it was a mere thorn. "What is your name?" she asks the vampire.

His body still twitches from the stake's removal. "Damien Abbott," he gasps. "You planning my gravestone? A daylight vampire will not rise again, never fear."

"You had better rise now or you *will* die, and these cats and the pixie seem unhappy about that, which is good enough for me. My blood is a bit off, human docs tell me, but I am the only oasis you have got going, pilgrim. Can you take just enough to walk a few feet?"

"I am stronger unstaked, but my control is shaky."

"I will have to trust it. I have never been vampire-bit. A minor withdrawal does not put me on the road to turning, Damien, but just a sip, pretty please."

"You are not my client."

"No, *you* are *mine* now." She extends a brave, bare wrist to his lips. "As the Wicked Stepmother said to Snow White, whom I happen to resemble, 'Come, bite.'"

She is right. In the faint light I see her skin is almost as pale as the vampire's and her hair as dark. I never thought I would live to see a smart dame inviting potential disaster, but I have heard Miss Delilah Street is the nervy type. I position myself to take a big chomp out of the guy's private parts if he should overimbibe, and I can see his eye-white glisten as his gaze shifts to the threat I pose.

Miss Delilah Street shudders a pixie shiver and then all is silent and still in the alley until Damien jerks his head aside.

"I did not feel a thing," Miss Delilah says.

"I secrete an initial drop of anaesthesia."

"In fact," she adds, purring a little like Vesper, who was now kneading her master's arm, "you remind me of my daylight vampire acquaintance, who is quite a sexy guy."

"I secrete an aphrodisiac as well."

"Oh." She jerks back, then moves behind him and bends to get an arm under his shoulder. "Upsy-daisy. Does my blood have any special effects?"

He lurches upright and actually cracks a smile. "It is a bit on the effervescent side. You enjoy your champagne, Delilah?"

"I am the Cocktail Queen of the Inferno Bar from time to time," she quips. "I invent 'em more than drink 'em. Come on, you had the smarts to get darted just feet from the back of Wrathbone's Bar. I called ahead for a private room."

"You are confident. What about –?"

"The cats are following."

"No, the, the –"

Miss Delilah Street looks down at me. Wasp-Wing had curled back into her ball, which I had rolled shut. Right now the lot was in my mouth, in my live prey carry, which would not dent a cotton ball.

"Who do you think told me your location? Handy little thing."

"Wasp-Wing is my cell phone, and Vesper's companion."

"Worry not. Your pocket-rocket pixie is safely stowed. Midnight Louie's custody is the safest place for it."

"You know this alley cat who has designs on Vesper?"

"Yup. He is a primo private eye, although I am surprised to see him walking on the wild side down here. He is not as young as he used to be."

I beg your pardon! I bare my fangs. But Miss Delilah Street is too busy planning her next move to pay any attention to mine.

"Get inside," she tells the temporarily revived vamp, "where I can nail the dart-thrower and save your undead life."

Miss Vesper pauses on the threshold, flaunting her fantail in my face to bring me to a sudden stop.

"So you are a notorious figure in the Overworld?" she says.

I sigh and let Wasp-Wing's carrier down to roll into the room beyond. "I do cut a wide swath," I say, striking a duellist's pose with my foreshivs extended.

"All you have done for my master is hang around *me*."

None are so unappreciated as the subtle. I step aside to permit the lady to enter first.

Wrathbone's is a rather rowdy venue, I have heard, with armed skeletons decorating the walls and a clientele that runs from adventure-seeking tourists to celebrity zombies to werewolf mobsters to vamps and narcs.

This room we have entered, however, is rather luxe, with an inner sanctum, i.e., bedroom.

"Perfect," Miss Delilah declares, ushering our wounded vamp onto the bed within. "You might as well husband your resources in your usual field of operations."

"I have only so many minutes before I will need more than your compromised blood to keep conscious, much less . . . viable," he warns.

"Relax," she tells him as Vesper rushes to claim what must be her usual spot on the bed. I well recognize the instinct. My Miss Temple has only one significant other (at a time; there are two vying for the prime spot), but that is another story in another place and time.

Poor Miss Vesper must share her master's accommodations with . . . several usurpers. I hasten to the anteroom and Miss Delilah's side. She has seated herself to scroll through our host's social register.

"Seven women," she mutters, "one for each day of the week, and all at staggered times. Six Thursday; nine am. Friday; noon Saturday; three Sunday; six Monday; nine pm. Tuesday. And midnight tomorrow: Wednesday."

She eyes my attentive presence. "Our vampire is a creature of habit, which makes him easy to target. I wonder if daylight vampires ever actually sleep."

I settle on my belly, forearms wrapped and abutting in my "wise mandarin" pose. Any minute now I would be calling Vesper "Grasshopper", were she not reclining in the bedroom.

"What is today's nine pm client, Corrine, besides late?" Miss Delilah asks herself, and me. "Is she at their usual rendezvous? Or does she know she need not bother? Why not text her to come here?"

"Now," she tells me, "that done, it is high time for an interview with the vampire."

I appreciate being kept abreast, so to speak, of the proceedings, and accompany her back into the adjoining bedroom. Vesper reclines beside her enervated master, although the crimson velvet bedspread is my main attraction. I would look terrific on it and my black coat would add a formal touch nestling next to Vesper's dazzling white one.

Damien probably looks tasty to human females, with his white silk shirt open to allow the wound to heal, and his black-suited form long and lean against the plush fabric.

I assume Miss Delilah Street must be thinking the same thing, because I hear her catch her breath.

"Shades of Sansouci," she murmurs mysteriously.

"I had no idea the Sinkhole had places like this," Damien says lazily.

"Vegas has always sold seduction," she answers.

"You realize I need to get back on my feeding schedule soon. Your blood is strangely soothing and exciting at the same time, but I took only what I needed to get to a safe place."

"I know all that. One of your ladies is en route."

"My nine pm? Corrine? Good. She has a calm nature. No hysterics from her."

I can see Miss Delilah register that at least one of his ladies is hot-headed.

Speaking of hot-headed ladies, Damien lifts a pallid hand to stroke Vesper's little pink ears, earning a slit-eyed purr. Pitty-pat goes my heart.

Miss Delilah sits on the foot of the bed. I see Damien's shoes have been slipped off and he is in stocking feet, like Vesper and myself.

"Tell me about your clients," Miss Dee says. "I know their names and appointment times from your BlackBerry."

He shuts his eyes to save strength to talk, and perhaps to picture the seven mistresses on whom his undead life depends daily.

"Corrine is a widow who deeply loved her husband and wants no other spouse. Midnight belongs to Violet, a goth girl who is dying to live the part. Dawn brings Petra, a career woman with no time for human love. Nine in the morning is Tess' time. She is an artist. Noon means I lunch on Suzanne, a retired nurse who enjoys ministering to the needy. At three, Nelda arrives for tea and sympathy. She has multiple sclerosis, but is doing well now. The ancients thought blood-letting beneficial for disease. Sunset falls when Vyrle comes. She is a chorus girl and finds our activity energizing."

Miss Delilah snaps Damien's BlackBerry shut and rises. "I will admit your nine pm appointment when she arrives."

"Corrine." He smiles, relieved. "What a lovely person."

It is hard to pull myself away from the vision that is a red-velvet reclining Vesper with her pink nose and ears and very sharp white teeth. I could certainly spare a little blood for a rendezvous with a hot tamale femme fatale . . .

Miss Delilah shuts the bedroom door and pulls a Mama-san chair with a huge round rattan back against the wall and sits. It provides an impressive background for her white skin, black hair and morning glory-vivid blue eyes. She would make one gorgeous blue-eyed black cat.

"The only thing to do, Louie," she addresses me as I arrange myself formally at her feet, "is to put each of Damien's ladies to the test. I urgently texted them all to come here. We must find out where hatred hides behind their vampire-loving exteriors, because that surely was the motive."

Hatred of Damien? I wonder. Or someone jealous of his attachment to his other lady friends? Human emotions get so messy when it comes to sex. My kind avoids that sort of trap thanks to a little inborn thing called "heat".

The door to Wrathbone's opens to admit a roar of laughter and the reek of booze, smoke and blood. In walks Miss Corrine. I see right away that Miss Delilah Street is dumbfounded. Me too.

Miss Corrine is at least sixty, which can mean well preserved these days, but still silver-haired and sedately respectable. One would not imagine her in abandoned intimacy with a vampire, but life is like that and it takes a lot more to surprise Midnight Louie.

"Who are you?" Corrine demands suspiciously. "I know it is nine-thirty. I was not on time for my nine o'clock, but he was not there . . . "

"I am Damien's . . . agent. I am afraid that he has been injured –"

Corinne ingests a gasp of horror.

"– and he needs a full measure of replacement blood at once. Perhaps a client would be willing to . . . give all to save him. As you know, a future eternal life as a daylight vampire would not be insurmountable."

"Oh, no! How terrible. Poor Damien. He is a dear, but I have several grandchildren. Surely my usual allotment would help?"

"Not enough fast enough."

Miss Corrine glances to the closed door and shudders. "I am so sorry. I live for my grandchildren. They need me. Several are in half-vampire, half-human families. I cannot give them up."

"I quite understand. Would you mind waiting at the reserved table outside the door? Damien's other clients are arriving. One may make the ultimate sacrifice and save him. Or . . . he may wish to bid you goodbye."

"I do not know . . ."

"Drinks, of course, are on the house."

"The others are coming? I know nothing about them. We have never met."

"Now is your opportunity."

It looks as if Miss Delilah Street knows females almost as well as Midnight Louie does. I have never seen a one who did not want to at least eyeball a romantic rival. Or maybe do her in. Or their common object of affection.

No sooner has Miss Corrine, the widowed grandmother, departed than another knock comes.

The entering woman wears an expensive navy power suit and high-heeled pumps. Her skirt and hair are short but sleek. She is a handsome forty-five but already consulting the Rolex on her wrist.

"Petra, I assume," Miss Delilah says.

"The message said Damien needed me. That is *some* role reversal. I have had an amazingly long day. Damien knows I start at seven am and go until whenever. He is the only thing that relaxes me, but once a week is all the time or blood I can spare. What is the 'emergency'?"

"He is dying."

"Oh. Is that possible? He is, you know, immortal. And unbelievably durable in bed, I might add. Are you another client?"

"His agent. He needs an entire blood replacement. I am sure the woman who volunteers would find the intensity ecstasy."

"Impossible. My schedule."

"Would you pause for a drink at the reserved table outside, then? He would wish to say goodbye if none of his other clients can accommodate him."

Petra eyes her glittering watch. "'Other' clients. He never would say a word about them."

She also falls for the cocktail table gambit and leaves.

I rub against Miss Delilah's leg to express my approval as we await the next woman.

The next knock announces a thirty-something woman sporting a long red braid down her back. Her tie-dyed leggings are turquoise and emerald under an oversized batwing tunic bearing the motto "Arty Party".

"Oh, gosh," Miss Tess Tampa says when told the situation. "Damien is the sweetest, sexiest thing and our sessions really free up my creativity. The whole point of our arrangement is no strings. A performance artist cannot be tied down to, like, rules. Vampires have lots of tiresome rules. Sorry."

"You did religiously keep the nine am meeting slot," Miss Delilah observes.

"Nothing else was religiously kept once I got there, though." Wink.

News of the drink table has her heading towards it with a "sorry" shrug I do not buy.

The following knock is tentative and the opening door admits a human version of Wasp-Wing, a petite woman with brown hair in a wispy cut.

"You must be –" Miss Delilah begins.

This one speaks too fast and too much to hide her nerves. "Nelda. I have never been to the Sinkhole before. It was . . . hard to find."

"That is the point. But you did it. You were brave."

"Well, for Damien. He has done so much for me."

"I hear your MS is in remission."

"Yes, my parents are so overjoyed. If they knew what I had been doing these past two years . . . I was so afraid. I mean, I never . . .

before. But Damien is so gentle and kind. I feel like a new person each time." She blushed. "How can I help him?"

She listens to Miss Delilah, sinking onto the chair near the door.

"How," Miss Nelda asks, "could he go without blood for so long? I know . . . there are others."

"That is a very good question, Miss . . . ?"

"Livingstone. Nelda Livingstone."

"You came . . . ah, your usual appointment is at three p. m.?"

"Yes. We have tea and talk and . . . lots of time. Such a wonderful break in my day."

"And what do you do during your day?"

"I am a computer tech at the Inferno Hotel. I will have to change to the night shift now, though."

"Are you saying you are willing to give Damien all the blood in your body?"

Her hands twist on her lap. "To save his life, yes."

"It is an undead life."

"Oh, he is far more alive than most people I have met in my so-called 'real' life. Is he in there?" She rises and heads for the bedroom door. "I should start now. I know what it is to feel weak and like your whole body and mind are deserting you. I am very strong now."

"Yes, you are." Delilah Street manages to step in front of the determined young woman. "This must be done carefully, not impulsively."

"But why delay? His existence –"

"We must give all the clients a chance to volunteer."

"All?"

Miss Nelda seems stunned, as if she had forgotten the others. My sincerity meter registers one hundred per cent. She thought only of Damien and their relationship, and had from the first.

Miss Delilah is not ready to end her serial interrogations, though.

"Nelda, you can finally meet the others at the reserved table beyond these rooms, share a glass of wine. The situation does not need to be addressed until, oh, midnight."

"But why wait? I could at least start him on the road to recovery."

I rise to stand before Miss Nelda, who is giving Miss Delilah a push-to-push resistance.

"Damien's wishes must be consulted," Miss Delilah says.

"Oh." The idea wilts the slender young woman's starchy resolve.

"You mean he might choose another to join him for eternity. I . . . I had not considered that. Of course. I will wait outside. Whatever he . . . Damien . . . wants. Needs."

She leaves in the same shocked condition as she had arrived.

"One," Miss Delilah says triumphantly. "She truly loves him. Whether it could turn the other way, I doubt. Yet strong love can breed stronger hate."

Me, I am not a huge believer in what humans call "love". Cupid is not my middle name. My usual stoic expression must appear dubious because Miss Delilah Street deigns to look down at me.

"I appreciate your adding your not inconsiderable weight to keeping Nelda's determined feet from heading right for Damien."

Another knock, followed quickly by a louder one. We peek out the open door to see two very different women arriving at once.

Va-va-voom! One is certainly my cup of sizzle on the hoof. The other is as different as she could be.

Ms Goth Girl struts in first, almost as tall as Miss Delilah, wearing high-heeled black patent leather boots laced down the back in scarlet. Her hair is a Bad Witch Glinda fall of artificial red, her stockings striped and her torso corseted.

"The name is Violet," she announces. "Where is my handsome vampy boy? I hear he needs some physical therapy and I am the gal to give it to him."

"I am his agent," Miss Delilah lies again. "And who is this?"

"I do not know," Violet huffs. "Some mundane broad."

"Young woman," the second lady answers for herself, "dressing over the top does not give you licence to talk over the top. I am Suzanne. I am a nurse. And I can certainly minister to the needy better than you."

"Violet," Miss Delilah says, "you are the midnight client and Suzanne has the noon slot."

"Whatever," Violet says with a shrug. "Damien loves me best. Show me to him and let the games begin."

Suzanne steps in front of the buxom goth girl. She has curly brown hair and must be fifty to Violet's twenty-two but her wiry frame is steel and so are her grey eyes.

"Look and listen, Missy. Damien is not a bone and a hank of hair to be fought over. He is a sick man and, as a nurse, I am best equipped to help him. I always was."

"Interesting," Miss Delilah notes. "Suzanne, you always considered Damien ill and your relationship like nurse and patient?"

"For heaven's sake, the man has a blood disorder."

Violet rolls her eyes. "He is a *vampire*, baby. Get real. That makes him a sex machine. That is what you craved, not some namby-pamby nursing fantasy."

Miss Delilah takes them both by the upper arms. "All his clients cherished a fantasy Damien fulfilled in many different ways. The question is, will you give him all your blood and your mortal life to keep him meeting with you, and the others?"

"Hey," Violet says, shaking loose. "I am in it for hot sex and the make-believe. Let *her* empty her veins; they look cold enough."

"Ah." Suzanne *hems* on the way to *haw*ing. "My *real* patients need me with such a nursing shortage, and the hospitals do not allow even daylight vampires on their staffs. Conflict of interest. Sorry."

Miss Delilah keeps their upper arms in custody and gives them the joint bum's rush while I silently cheer her on. Miss Midnight and Miss Noon equally disgust me. Not even a tremor of concern for Damien. Or his bereft Vesper. Or little Wasp-Wing. Maybe they do not know about his dependents, but tough. I bet he knows about theirs.

"One more," Miss Delilah said, peering out the door at the assembled women. "And here she comes, I think. Last but clearly not least."

I am curious enough to jump off the side chair and peer through my temporary partner's bejeaned legs.

Miss Delilah probably brushes six feet in her stilettos, but she is wearing low-heeled mules now and the oncoming female is likely six feet barefoot. She catwalks through the door in an off-the-shoulder red spandex top and Capri pants. She strides into the room on wooden platform sandals that tie around her ankles. Her hair is a blond ponytail that falls to where her tail would start were she feline, literally as well as figuratively.

"Vyrle, the six pm appointment, I presume," Miss Delilah says.

"Who are you?"

"The name is Delilah Street. I am helping Damien with his condition."

"Which is?"

"Terminal."

"A dying vampire? That is a new one." Vyrle hungrily eyes the closed bedroom door. "I can bring him to life again."

"So can anyone who will sacrifice all her, or his, blood to Damien and live as a vampire for ever."

"Not my ambition."

"What is your ambition?"

"To earn fifty thou a week at the Karnak Cleopatra spectacular show, and I am doing that. Damien was one of my daily pre-show energy-pumping techniques. And that alley cat is sniffing my shoes! *Scat!* Sultans have bid hundreds of thousands for a one-time onstage-used pair."

Eeuw. My nose retreats in haste. There are shoe fetishes, like women's high-heel collections, and then there are creepy shoe fetishes, which this lady's wealthy fans indulge.

Besides, I have learned all I needed to know. My first impression from her overbearing perfume has been confirmed by her stinky feet.

The nose knows. This Vyrle dame is the dart thrower, live and in person. All I need now is a way to tip off Miss Delilah.

But my partner seems to be following her own line of inquiry. "So you would not renounce all that fame and fortune to save Damien? If you were a vampire you would get to bleed your admirers physically as well as financially."

Vyrle snorts her disdain and tosses her ponytail so haughtily I am tempted to leap up, tangle my shivs in it and pull hard.

When Miss Delilah mentions the reserved table and the free drink while she checks Damien's condition, the Karnak high-kicker amazes me by accepting the offer.

"Excellent," Miss Delilah tells me, or the room, or just herself after Vyrle sashays out. "All our suspects are corralled for the denouement. Now to approach our would-be victim again."

Hot dog! As tragic as the situation could become, I will be able to feast on Vesper's beauty again.

Inside the bedroom, Damien lies, the usual pale and wan.

Miss Delilah arranges herself on the foot of his bed. "We have a candidate for your full revival."

"My clients came when you called?"

"To a woman. Every one. They are a varied bunch."

He smiles faintly.

"And some seem to owe more to you than you to them. Are you tamed predator or prey?"

"Neither, I hope. I am fond of all my clients, each in her own way."

"Well, one of them is not fond of you. Midnight Louie has tagged the dart thrower for me, and you."

I may swoon. I am actually being given full credit for my sleuthing powers. What a novel experience! I must work with this wonderful lady more often.

Damien frowns. "You know the motive?"

"Jealousy."

"How? I see them separately. They never meet."

"Now they have."

He winces.

"But none of that matters. I have found one who will happily give blood and be turned for you."

"That is amazing. I would never ask that of anyone."

"She volunteered."

"Was it Violet? I would think she would be thrilled by the opportunity."

"She was not, alas. The goth stuff is a pose, not a true vocation."

"Vocation?"

"The word surprises you?"

"It is just an . . . odd way to put it."

"I never mind being odd."

"Then," he says, "it must be Corrine. A sad, lonely woman with no hope of a human romance after losing her beloved husband. She would make a loving daylight vampire."

"So you consider your role therapy as much as a survival and sexual exercise?"

"There must be more than just sex for any relationship to endure, no?"

"I am asking what you think."

"I could not do what I do, give passion, if I had no compassion."

"Alas, not everyone is like that. Not every woman. But you will be pleased to know that your secret enemy is not an ordinary woman."

"If Violet and Corrine are not willing to become vampire, it must be Suzanne. She is the soul of tenderness."

Miss Delilah Street smiles. "Your expectations do you honour,

Damien, but then it is always about honour for you, is that not true?"

"What little honour one can find in these days," he mutters.

"Such an honourable man for a vampire. So methodical. One would almost say . . . canonical."

Can a vampire turn pale? At that moment Damien's bloodthirsty skin seems whiter than Vesper's fur, than the bedlinen, than bone and fang.

"I may not have . . . long," he says. "Yet I find even this half-life too precious to lose."

"Cheer up." Miss Delilah Street is displaying a shocking amount of insensitivity to the dying man, even if he is vampire. "You have a saviour, remember?"

"Must you put it that way?"

"Yes, indeed. I will end the suspense. She is Miss Nelda Livingstone – ironic last name, yes? – and she is wholly willing to give you every last drop of blood and die and live again as a vampire."

"Nelda! She has faced the most pain of them all! It cannot be Nelda. It will not be Nelda. I would rather perish."

"Then she will be condemned to a living death, for she loves you. I now see you clearly love her. There is no reason you should not be joined in eternal matrimony."

"God, no!"

"God, *yes!*" Miss Delilah Street says, leaning so close to Damien that Vesper leaps up and hisses. "What were you, and where were you, when you were bitten into a vampire?"

His waxen hands try to ward off her burning blue eyes and biting voice. I recognize a fellow truth seeker at her most ruthless.

"It was long ago. Centuries," he says.

"When, Damien?"

"The twelfth century."

"You must have been young," she notes.

"Thirty-four."

"Where?"

"England," he admits.

"Where in England, Damien? You know you cannot lie."

"At Gracethorn Abbey."

"You were bitten at an abbey?"

"Yes."

"Turned there?"

"Yes!"

"You were a monk there?"

No words issued from his whiter-than-death face.

"Damien?"

"I was . . . the abbot."

Of course, think I. Damien Abbot.

Miss Delilah Street jumps up. "Vesper. You out. Midnight Louie, see to it."

We felines obey as one, as if demons were on our tails.

Miss Delilah, in fact, strides out hot on our heels. She jerks open the door to Wrathbone's, admitting the noise of merriment and anger and passion and debauchery.

"Nelda, you are needed inside. Quick!"

Miss Delilah slams the outer door shut and locks it after Miss Nelda comes running in, white-faced herself, straight for the open bedroom door, which Miss Delilah shuts firmly after her.

Then she unlocks and opens the outer door and approaches the nearby table.

"It is all right," she tells the assembled clients of Damien Abbott. "Thank you all for coming and your time. You may go now. We will be in touch. Damien will be fine."

Amid the buzz and wondering and questions, Miss Delilah retreats and shuts herself in with Vesper and me.

Even a hardened street sleuth like me has to wonder – or not wonder at all – what is going to happen in that red-velvet-spread bed?

Miss Delilah Street folds her arms over her highly sufficient chest and keeps an eye on the outer door. I recognize top-alert guard duty from when my mama used to take us kits out to learn the ways of the world.

I would not want to try to pass Miss Delilah Street right now.

How she knows we will get an unwelcome visitor, I do not know. Me, my shivs are already primed.

The door breaks open and shatters to nothing, filled by a fury straight from hell. The noisy occupants of Wrathbone's are silent and frozen behind it, as if caught in a huge glass ball, like Wasp-

Wing. The hovering pixie shrills once and vanishes. Vesper growls like a tiger and stands shoulder to shoulder with me.

I eye our invader. It is Vyrle, only she is now seven feet tall and her hair is a floor-length cloak of fluttering, snapping, sparkling red and yellow and black flames that surrounds her figure and snarling elongated face – eyes, nostrils and lips slanted upwards in an expression of evil incarnate.

The only recognizable things about her are the telltale wooden platform shoes, currently sprouting sharp claws two inches long. I would not rub my muzzle there at the moment.

"I thought you got the message," Miss Delilah Street says. "You are not welcome here."

"He is mine!" the deep yet eerily feminine voice tolls like a bell. "Mine."

"Not at the moment."

"Mine for centuries, stolen from me, from my palaces under the hill, from my court, from my company."

"History does not support your claim."

The creature's bereft cry creates a crack in the invisible glass ball of frozen reality behind her. "He was almost mine, before a vampire gypsy turned him. I assumed a foul, stumbling, stinking form here and sought for two years to lure him to the Sinkhole, where my powers can flower. That human female is with him now and weak and soft and powerless."

"But I am not."

"You! You are nothing but a meddler."

Midnight Louie has been called such a thing before, by those who underestimated me. I hope that Miss Delilah Street is being underestimated too. I know better than to interfere. Sometimes it is wiser to be Zen than kung fu.

I notice something glitter at Miss Delilah Street's right wrist. The finest silver chain . . . changeling silver. It could harm Wasp-Wing if not undercover and under control. Are Vesper and I going to be treated to a manifestation of the infamous silver familiar born from the long lovelock of the Inferno Hotel's albino rock star owner, Christophe? Who knows what powers he commands? Not anyone in Vegas.

"When meddling is successful in my world," Miss Delilah Street purrs at this horrific entity, "they call it 'case closed'. Get out of here."

A roar and shattering echoes all around us, Vesper and I cling together, clawing our shivs into the floorboards to stay put, our coats rippling. Nice.

"I am queen," our invader declares.

I notice the fine silver chain is spinning and turning on Miss Delilah Street's wrist as if her bone and body were a loom. A glittering web is churning up her arm and shoulders and down her other arm, shining like the full moon.

Vesper's and my pupils become slits, as against the morning sun.

Vyrle's engorged furious figure spits thorn darts and daggers in a blinding blitz from the cold flames of her cloak of many colours.

Miss Delilah lifts her arms across her body and above her head unfolding lacy silver metal wings that look as delicate as cracked crystal. The queen's weapons stop, fall into nothing as her final wail peaks and fades and the glass behind her cracks from side to side and she vanishes into the bluster and rowdy noise and commotion that is Wrathbone's.

Nothing is left behind but her wooden platform spike shoes, which I had rubbed my face against to draw attention to the thorn nubs that pocked them. Miss Delilah Street's powers of observation and deduction are all that I could wish for in a temporary partner.

Miss Delilah fists her hands on her hips as a silver tinsel rain evaporates into the air around her. She is bare of all jewellery.

"Good riddance! What a witch!"

She bends to pick up a shoe, running her finger along the newly clawed platforms.

"We are seeing her true 'sole'. These have sprouted acacia thorns like the one that skewered Damien. I had my suspicions when I removed the clawed dart from Damien, but you detected the strong acacia scent of Vyrle's wooden platform shoes in their harmless guise," she tells me. "Many plants have both benign and malign applications. The thorn tree is used in perfumes, medicines and herbal preparations. It is also protected by the Fey, who can use its poison qualities, as you sensed. You and I and little vampire Vesper have just met the Dread Queen of the Fey, Louie. I guess a cat may look at a queen, after all, and rat on her too."

"*Ooh,*" Vesper purrs in my ear. "You are much better than you look."

That is more than somewhat promising.

*   *   *

By now the bedroom door has opened and the bedazzled lovers are creeping out.

"We heard a kind of mewing out here," Nelda says, brushing back her hair with a blush.

All that storm and fury. Were they dead to the world!

"Not to worry," says Miss D. "I was just shopping for a new pair of shoes." She waves one. "You will not be seeing the imposing and possessive Vyrle any more, Damien. You may be a vampire, but she was not of this world."

"She was the one who staked me with a claw?" he asks.

"Wooden, from the acacia tree."

"How did you know?" Nelda asks, shuddering. "Also about my deepest secret feelings?"

"The deduction process was simple. If someone hates Damien enough to kill him softly and slowly, someone must love him enough to make that would-be murderer jealous."

"Of me? Or of my . . . companions?" Damien asks.

"Of you all. Of us all, humans and unhumans. Vyrle is something else, something greedy and merciless. Fey. She almost had a handsome abbot in her power at Gracethorn Abbey centuries ago, but vampires are immune unless they venture into a former Fey touch-point, like the Sinkhole."

"Miss Street," he says, "grateful as I am for your detective *and* matchmaking talents, you assembled all my appointments. I could have sipped from the innocent five you dismissed tonight. We will have to continue as usual anyway, and find Nelda clients in addition."

"Call it a couple's practice." She shrugs. "Look, Damien, I go for long-term satisfaction on my cases. Even humans would rather drink deeply of life than sip it up in instalments."

Damien remains silent, but I do believe he blushes. Fresh blood will do wonders.

Miss Delilah adds, "To keep from killing your victims, you gave up centuries of celibacy to become a daylight vampire. If you can't be celibate, you can at least have a life partner, and Nelda will benefit from being a daylight vampire. Research shows vitamin D in sunlight is good for people with MS, which is not a blood-related malady. Come on; you and Nelda have too much love and compassion not to share it with others. You *can* live on love."

Nelda nods. "I lived on two hours a week. Now I have eternity."

She smiles seductively over her shoulder – nervous Nelda! – and returns to the bedroom.

Damien is torn, but lingers to question my partner more.

"I was pretty out of it, but what did you mean in the alley when you first arrived and said you 'brake for butterflies'?"

I give Vesper a lick and a promise to keep her attention and wait for the Divine Miss D to answer the vamp. I have been wondering about that myself.

Miss Delilah Street smiles. "To understand, you need to know about Dolly."

"A friend of yours?"

"Sort of. She is four thousand pounds of shiny black Old Detroit metal and wears chrome like Mae West draped herself in diamonds."

"A car?"

"Oh, please. She is a 1956 Cadillac Biarritz cream puff I got at an estate sale when I was on a scholarship in college. She can outrun a Porsche and outmuscle a Hummer."

"Kind of like you," he says with his own smile.

Nice fangs. Shiny and white. I always admire a guy with good grooming.

"Maybe. Anyway, when your messenger pixie, Wasp-Wing, came barrelling straight for me and my 'changeling silver', on the Strip, she got caught in Dolly's slipstream and almost crashed on the windshield, except that she looked like a butterfly, and I always avoid hitting them."

"You have my thanks, but I remain curious as to why."

Miss Delilah folds her arms and cocks her head. I smell a reminiscence coming on.

"Before I found Dolly and could drive myself," Miss Delilah Street says, "I was on a road trip with some college classmates heading for an out-of-town basketball game. A monarch butterfly hit the windshield. It got caught in the windshield wipers, its wings totally intact. They fluttered there at sixty miles an hour, looking alive.

"I asked the guy driving to pull over so we could at least free it. The monarch had to be dead, but those wings were so alive as they fluttered, so beautiful and miraculously whole.

"He would not even slow down. We would be 'late' for the precious 'game'. Sick at heart, I watched those wings flutter and kiss the windshield as if performing a dance just for me for forty damn miles."

"But the butterfly was dead," the vampire says. "Why would you care?"

"It was still beautiful, and so alive in its way."

"That story says something remarkable about you, Delilah Street."

"It says something remarkable about *you*."

He gets the point and nods. Humbly.

"I have secretly hated my lot in undead life all these centuries," the vampire confesses. "Even when I could convert in recent years to sipping human life rather than taking it. I divorced myself from feeling, as you had to while you watched, the sole attentive audience, while the butterfly wings did their fatal danse macabre. But you are right. The imitation of life is life in its way."

He turns to regard the doorway to Nelda. "I hated the idea of her losing and wasting her precious life on loving a dead thing, but you say love is immortal."

"I say to each his and her own," Miss Delilah Street answers. "Should I leave Midnight Louie with Vesper, or return him to his usual haunts along the Vegas Strip?"

"I say we should leave it up to them," he says with a smile while Wasp-Wing dances above everyone's heads in excitement like a butterfly, expecting many interesting future fetches.

I nuzzle Vesper's perfect pink nose. I say that Damien Abbott is one stand-up vampire.

Crimson Kisses

Diane Whiteside

Annapolis, Maryland, 31 December 1865

"May I have your blessing upon our marriage, sir?" Edmund Devereaux injected a coaxing tone into his request, rife with hope and a nervous suitor's eagerness.

Silence echoed on the other side of the room, bitterly suspicious. The room was like a banker's boardroom rather than a relaxed family parlour.

For the first time during Edward's long-rehearsed speech, terror pricked Sarah's spine and her smile thinned. Was Edmund's request more than her father was able to grant? Certainly not. Besides, he'd given his word to listen and Edmund, normally so cavalier towards the opinions of others, was trying very hard to be humble on this all-important occasion.

They stood in the library, the very heart of her father's power at the family plantation outside Maryland's capital. A single chandelier focused all attention on her father – the great estate's lord – where he sat enthroned behind the immense desk, its mahogany gleaming like old blood from decades of polishing. Inlays of ebony and swirls of brass accented more mahogany climbing the walls to meet the enormous collection of medieval daggers, their blades a veiled warning.

The gaslight from the library's chandelier lovingly burnished her lover's dark hair and lit flames in his blue eyes until he seemed an angel come to earth. Tonight he wore American-made evening dress, not his native London-made clothes, and he stood before her father's desk as politely – if not quite as meekly – as a political crony, come to buy a favour from Maryland's mightiest broker of votes.

Only an expert eye could have discerned the knife hidden up Edmund's sleeve and George Calvert, her father, had always hired that type of skill.

Sarah tilted her chin just a fraction higher, denying the demons of fear and doubt. She smiled at her lover even more warmly, to deliberately, silently, unite his request with hers. The crystalline music of a Chopin waltz whispered through the door, inviting them to better places.

"No," said the Calvert patriarch and folded his arms across his chest, arrogant with an assurance that came from generations of never losing a serious fight. "My daughter is far too young to settle down."

She gaped at him, unable to speak. He regularly lied in political circles but he'd never reversed a family pledge before, let alone one given as recently as a few months ago.

"You promised us last spring, sir, that if we waited until after Christmas," Edmund began, diplomacy shading into anger in his deep voice.

"I said I would consider your suit." Her father's thick beard folded over his crisp shirtfront like a pagan sanctuary's veil, concealing wisdom only its initiates cared about. "She has seen too little of the world to know her own mind."

"I am nineteen, sir." Sarah forced herself back from an angry retort. "By the laws of this state, that is more than old enough."

"You asked for my permission and I will not give it. More than that, I insist on protecting my daughter from a misalliance with an older man." His stare was knife-studded.

Dear heavens, Sarah thought, if he only knew how much older. . .

"She has lived outside a war-torn city for the past five years. How much more of the world does she need to see to become an adult?" Edmund demanded.

"She needs to spend at least six more years under her father's roof, as his hostess." The old autocrat bared yellowing teeth at them in a smile's mockery, certain of his advantage.

"In six years I'll inherit my trust fund from Mother and you won't have the interest to live on any more!" Her future would be acid-etched without her lover.

"You scurrilous, money-loving whoreson," Edmund finally, neatly summed up her father.

Sarah stomped her foot in agreement – and destroyed any chance of obtaining George Calvert's consent to her marriage.

South of Annapolis, Maryland, summer 1866

Hoof beats threaded the night like a spiked chain. Metal rattled and clanked in accompaniment, singing of their riders' guns and sabres. Salt gritted the heavy mist of the marsh, clambering among the thick groves of trees. It probed the two faces of the riders beneath the deep hoods of their cloaks, just as the few glimmers of silvery moonlight did.

A hound howled and was answered by another, then a third, and finally the entire pack.

Ice sliced through Sarah's veins more strongly than the late summer's night heat would account for. Mother of God, her father had brought the entire kennel out to hunt her. He was angry enough to want more than the troops his political connections at Washington City had sent him.

The familiar sound of the hoof beats made her mare falter and try to turn back to join the horses pursuing them. Sarah checked her mount instinctively, ruthlessly, her heart beating somewhere in her throat.

Edmund's hand shot out to grab her horse's reins but she'd already brought Daisy back on course. They galloped on, side by side. They had to reach Baltimore before dawn to catch the tide and the next boat to Europe.

But how could they escape the dogs she'd helped whelp and train, and who knew her scent better than their own?

Cassius and the other hounds bayed again, the high piercing notes which meant they'd found her trail. The hoof beats behind them sped up and her pulse stumbled. She'd never thought her father could string together a farrago of lies sufficient to draw troops out of Washington, no matter how nervous they were after Lincoln's assassination last year. God willing, they wouldn't be so hot on the chase that they'd shoot her and Edmund, no matter what their orders might be.

She glanced sideways, desperate for the reassurance which had never failed her.

Edmund rode beside her, his big body as perfectly poised as any cat, his long-fingered hands relaxed on Firedrake's reins. His crooked smile flashed for a moment below his broad-brimmed hat and he waggled a single finger at her.

Warmth glided over her skin, sweet and golden as the single drop of his blood he sometimes let her taste. She turned towards him, forgetting the rutted track and the tree branches grabbing for her cloak, the gibbering moonlight and her unhappy mare, or the Chesapeake Bay only a few feet away. She might be too young to settle down, according to her dictatorial father, but she knew where her future lay.

The road swerved diagonally in front of their pursuers. The mist melted towards the ground, trapped in a dying bramble bush.

BANG! A giant fireball slammed into her right shoulder and she tumbled forwards, over Daisy's neck and almost out of the saddle. An agonizing, ferocious, bestial pain overwhelmed her senses.

"Ahhh. . ." Sarah bit her lip before she could scream. Daisy stumbled, unbalanced by her rider's strange antics.

Edmund snatched Sarah out of the saddle and swung her up in front of him onto his horse, sending another jolt of fire-bright agony lashing into her.

She would not scream, she would not.

His arm was iron-hard around her, promising safety, and she turned her face into his chest, instinctively making herself into the smallest, easiest to carry bundle possible. She would stay with him for ever, no matter what happened.

Edmund gave Daisy a single, ferocious slap on her flank and the poor mare, who'd never been treated with anything but kindness before, galloped desperately away. Sarah closed her lips on a protest.

Cursing under his breath, Edmund wheeled Firedrake and sent him through a tiny gap between the trees and across a small creek. Soon the big stallion stood in a clearing at the centre of a thicket perhaps a hundred feet from the road, his master's unyielding hand on the reins forcing him to remain still. The moonlight was clearer here but scattered by clouds scudding across it and tree branches clawing at its edges.

Sarah closed her eyes and wondered how Edmund was keeping Firedrake silent. It was better to think about that than about the thousands of demons still digging the bullet into her shoulder, or about how much blood she had lost to make her cloak, dress, corset cover, corset and chemise cling to her skin within so few minutes.

She reached to pull the sodden clothing away from her aching skin with her wounded arm but it wouldn't move. A moment's ferocious concentration only encouraged the demons to pound harder and she managed to make her fingers brush across Edmund's arm. Nothing more. She was helpless.

Oh no, no, no.

Hoof beats pounded down the road towards them and went past, following Daisy. The dogs hesitated but her father angrily called them to heel.

Terror washed over Sarah, its crystalline bite cutting through her shoulder's agony. She stiffened and tried to pull away from Edmund so she could hear more easily, but he held her closer, his body curving to place himself between her and the road. His heartbeat, which had been steady even while guiding fugitive slaves out of Virginia, thudded fast and hard under her cheek.

She kissed his chest, nuzzling his brocade vest. No matter what happened now, she had to believe they would remain together.

Father roared a profanity and sent the far wiser dogs on with the horsemen. Then a single, isolated set of hoof beats told of his departure and Sarah allowed herself to breathe once again, just a little.

"Beloved." Edmund peeled her cloak back, sending another jolt of night-dark agony deeper into her gut. She bit down hard on her lip to stop the answering scream, not caring what she looked like.

"'Fore God, sweeting, how much blood did you lose?" As ever, when he was truly disturbed, Edmund's language escaped to his youth of three centuries ago.

"Too much," she answered honestly. Besides, she'd learned over the past seven years of working with him – first on the Underground Railway, then conveying spies into Virginia – that lies didn't work with somebody who could read her mind.

"I must take you to a chirurgeon. A doctor," he corrected himself.

Up ahead, the hoof beats had stopped and blended into a single massive drumbeat. Sarah stroked Edmund's cheek, high up on his cheekbones near his steel-blue eyes, but not too close to the serpentine scar carving his face. The sky's darkness was starting to claw at her vision, its edges tinted in crimson.

"Not without endangering them," she reminded her lover, gathering her words carefully to aid her ridiculously weak chest.

"Remember how the authorities slaughtered all those who helped John Wilkes Booth last year."

His features turned to stone under her fingertips before he caught her hand and pressed a kiss into her palm. "Will you trust me to heal you, my heart? With my blood?"

"Always." Her heart melted into the longing in his eyes and she gave him the simplest answer in the world.

He peeled back his glove and folded the empty leather, his breathing as ragged as her own. "Don't watch, sweetheart. This might offend you."

Her eyelids had been drooping, letting her drift into a warm darkness surrounded by his wonderful sandalwood scent. But such specious nonsense made her blink in astonishment.

"Are you worried I'll be offended by your *fangs*?" she demanded, almost too astonished to keep her voice down.

He shrugged and his chin jutted stubbornly.

"When you've drunk from me so many times before, however lightly? Do you think I haven't looked at least once?" She vehemently shook her head. "I love you, you dolt, no matter how long your teeth are or how bad your scars are – on your face, back, or elsewhere."

"Sarah, my angel." His harsh features softened and took on that glinting smile she loved – until he frowned again. "But are you certain?"

Her senses were swimming in a sea of grey mist. She truly shouldn't have restarted an old argument, not here, not now.

"But if it will help *you*, I won't watch," she conceded as graciously as possible. If nothing else, closing her eyes might allow her enough concentration to feel better. She laid her head back against his shoulder and tried that strategy.

"God's blood, Sarah, don't you dare die now!"

A sharp whoosh and the sweet, metallic scent of blood sprang into the salt air. He pressed his wrist to her lips – strong and vibrant with life, framed by woollen cloth and leather, and pouring blood like a rich, tangy fountain.

She stared involuntarily, ice spilling into her stomach. There was so much more blood than he'd ever given her before, even during the most decadent love play.

"Drink, my love," he crooned, his voice more alluring than the finest silk velvet. "I'm a *vampiro* mayor with three centuries under my belt. You need drink very little of my blood to live."

Her head spun for an instant between a coal-grey abyss and red-spangled clouds. Edmund would never hurt her. In fact, he'd saved her life more than once during the late War between the States. She could trust him. More importantly, no matter what happened, she'd rather drink deep and remain with him to face the future.

She kissed his wrist, shaping her mouth to his gaping wound. It was healing fast, the way his injuries always did, and was now barely an inch across.

A mouthful of the scarlet liquor spilled down her throat. It was hot and tangy, sweet and pungent, something to savour and something to gulp all at the same time. Its scent sang through her nose and warmed her bones. It seemed as if flowers somehow dwelt in it and the promise of sunshine.

"Edmund," she murmured. Her fingers tightened around him with all the strength that a lifetime around Maryland's finest horses had given her. The darkness fled and heat sprang into life deep within her core. "Edmund, darling."

She gulped greedily once again and he stroked her hair, his big hand shaking a little. "There now, my darling, there. All will be well. I'll tell you when to stop so you won't become a vampire, like me."

She muttered something, more concerned with the sound of his words than their meaning, and took another swallow. Giving him blood had been more pleasurable – ah yes, the joys of being his lover! – but drinking from him carried its own delights.

The hounds bayed their hunting cry to the moon, long and loud. An instant later, the hoof beats seemed to stretch out into a vicious spike and pinpoint their exact hiding place with terrifying precision.

Sarah broke free from Edmund's life-giving wrist. Her lungs powered her again and she could now balance herself against him, if she still couldn't lean her weight fully on her injured side. But her heart was beating so hard it could have rattled her ribs.

"Damn their stubborn hides to hell!" Edmund half-raised himself in his saddle, then sat back down, making Firedrake sidle. "They should have followed Daisy halfway to Baltimore by now."

"Cassius and the pack wouldn't want to leave me." That dog loved to find her, no matter how well she hid herself. It had always been a game before but the friendly hound couldn't know that this time she truly wanted to be left alone. He'd bring her father and troops from the capital with him. There'd be the devil to pay.

A snow bank lurked inside Sarah's bones, colder and heavier than after she was shot. But she could travel, albeit not far, thanks to drinking Edmund's blood. Even so, where would they go? A hundred options lay before them but each one seemed guarded by a massive sword.

"We'll circle around." Edmund gathered up the reins.

She embraced the option that brought him the most safety. "You have to leave me behind."

"Never." Below his carved cheekbones, his lips were a slashing line in the shimmering light.

"Firedrake will travel faster if he only carries one." She gave him the simplest excuse first, hoping he wouldn't press her.

"We will do well enough." His words were as hard-edged as his jaw.

"I cannot yet travel far," she whispered, giving him the last of the truth. Wonderful as his blood had been for her, it hadn't been enough. The musket ball was still lodged in her right shoulder and blood still seeped out.

"I cannot leave you here!" His words tore through the night and ripped at her heart. "I never hoped to find anyone like you to love and cherish. I will not permit you to depart my life."

The hounds howled again. The horses carrying the troopers were near enough to be counted and their accoutrements named. Sarah shuddered from more than the night air but kept her eyes fixed on Edmund, willing him to be reasonable for once.

"If you leave now, the hounds will stay with me. Father will only be concerned to guard me, not hunt you. You and I can be reunited later."

"How?" Edmund asked suspiciously, his eyes more shadowed than his hat brim could take credit for.

"Father has spoken of sending me to my aunt's, a thousand miles away. I will agree to go, then wait for you to come for me."

Edmund was silent, the skin on his face pulled taut.

The tack of the pursuing horses resolved itself into a cacophony of stirrups and bridles and bits. Father must be riding Lookout, the only horse with enough stamina to last the rest of the night. Firedrake's ears flicked forwards, seeking his competition.

Sarah's hand involuntarily tightened on Edmund's sleeve. He covered it quickly with his own.

"Very well. You need a doctor and rest, which I cannot provide." He kissed her fingers. "Tell me where to join you and I will be there."

"Texas."

"Texas?" His face suddenly seemed very white but surely that was impossible. His skin never changed colour, not even to darken or turn red under the sun.

"Austin, to be precise."

He made a strangled sound, deep in his throat.

Terror flashed through her, carving into the sullen, roaring pain in her shoulder like a butcher breaking apart an ox. What other option did they have?

She watched him, hanging on every indrawn breath, every averted gaze.

When he didn't voice anything more, she went on quickly, one ear tuned to the sounds coming from the road. "My aunt gives a grand ball every New Year's Eve for all her neighbours. If you come to that. . ."

"I will be sure to find you." He rubbed their linked fingers across his lips, his expression very grave. "I will come for you at midnight on New Year's Eve, Sarah."

Fear, as sharp as ice, lifted her skin from her bones.

"I will watch for you," she assured him fiercely. "I will wait for you for ever."

A very small smile touched his mouth then he kissed her, sweetly and all too gently, barely brushing his lips over hers. She whimpered deep in her throat, begging for more of him. Instead he lifted his head and nuzzled their intertwined fingers. "Dear, dear Sarah."

Words of love and passion, of a desperate, futile plan to escape with him to London or Paris jumbled together on her tongue. The hoof beats of the hunters filled the marsh air, guided by the eager barking of the hounds. They must have almost reached the place where Firedrake had turned off the narrow road.

Edmund flung up his head to listen, his hat brim's shadow snatching away his face from her eyes. But he dismounted with a courtier's grace and seated her on a fallen log, wrapping her up in his coat as if she were a queen.

Sarah fought to hold memories of his warmth, his scent, his

beautiful speed and grace. But she didn't dare reach for him. He needed to leave. Even *vampiros* could be shot and killed.

Back up on Firedrake, he paused the great stallion at the clearing's edge in a patch of moonlight. The dogs were very, very loud now, while the horses of their enemies were splashing through the inlet's heavy waters to reach them.

"I'll come for you at midnight," Edmund said very clearly, "even if the devil himself should stand in the way." He bowed, flourished his hat over his heart, and Firedrake reared, pawing at the moonlight as if marking the road back to her.

Sarah half rose, torn between whether to go with them despite the blood crawling still faster down her back or yell at him to ride on quickly. He vanished into the forest before her wounded lungs could catch air from the mist.

She sank back and buried her face in her hands, just as Cassius and her father erupted into the clearing.

Austin, Texas, 31 December 1866

"Governor Throckmorton." Sarah sank into a deep curtsey and tried not to glance at the clock. For a moment, the spinning dancers and the candle flames from the overhead chandeliers blurred into a single, throbbing, fiery haze. Her stomach knotted but she desperately fought it back, promising it salvation later. Escape would come with Edmund but not for another hour.

"My dear Miss Calvert, how lovely you look. My wife and I are very glad you're strong enough to join us." He bowed gallantly over her left hand, his narrow dark eyes assessing her face.

"Oh, I would never miss my aunt's grand ball," she assured him, turning aside the former doctor's unspoken enquiry. Arriving at her first Texas party with one arm in a sling made her conspicuous enough; publicly acknowledging weakness would make her even more noticeable. Above all else, she could not admit her true reasons for being here. It was best to blame her attendance on loyalty and a feminine longing to experience this truly remarkable gathering.

Considering that the site of the party was a new hotel in a muddy town more frequented by drunken soldiers than reliable bankers, the atmosphere was remarkably urbane. Crystal chandeliers sparkled above burgundy velvet drapes and golden walls, an excellent orchestra played for the many guests, while fine wines enhanced the consumption of delicious foods. She'd ensconced herself in a quiet corner between the band and one of the great windows overlooking the side street below, from which to watch the whirling dancers and her Aunt Mary's triumphal progress among the throng. She also hoped to escape her relative's more determined efforts to keep her close at hand, no matter where or what she was doing.

"May I introduce you to Don Rafael Perez, a long-time resident, and his lawyer Jean-Marie St Just?" The governor, who normally treated Texas' military commanders with more brusque efficiency than courtesy, all but grovelled to the larger of the two men behind them. "We're very lucky he – they – could join us tonight."

"Gentlemen." Sarah curtsied again. Both men were tall and wore superbly tailored eveningwear, probably from London. But any resemblance ended there. Mr St Just was slim and handsome, of the sort foolish maidens sighed over. Don Rafael was big enough to lift an enormous cannon, while his remote eyes beneath a brutal scar made him appear judge, jury and executioner all in one.

A thought brushed past her mind too quickly to be caught and vanished before she could examine it, but it was as if he'd heard her opinion of him.

"Señorita Calvert." Don Rafael raised a single dark eyebrow then bowed with an overly ornate flourish. "We are very pleased to make your acquaintance."

She flushed, convinced he was mocking her, and flashed her fan before her eyes for a moment's grace. How much would the governor – or her aunt, the social climber – care if she ruffled this rooster's plumage?

Thankfully, a ripple in the crowd provided a different distraction for her companions.

A man appeared at his elbow, clearly an Indian brave despite his formal white-man's clothing. He seemed caught between reliability and wildness, like a well-trained war horse waiting for the bugle to sound.

Mr St Just stiffened, alarm flickering through his eyes although his features never changed. Don Rafael's mouth tightened into a near snarl. For an instant, she thought she glimpsed pointed white teeth against his lips – like fangs. Impossible.

"And now, if you will excuse us, *señorita*? Governor? I fear we have urgent business elsewhere." Don Rafael inclined his head to them and departed, paying little heed to Throckmorton's veiled pleas for a rendezvous.

Heat pressed against her temples, heavy as a weighted cloth. A single bead of sweat gathered on the nape of her neck and sauntered down her spine.

Dizziness kicked Sarah again, vile as any jolt she'd experienced on the stagecoach trip from Maryland. Her wound had reopened along the way, leaving her ridiculously weak. She'd had to countermand her doctor's orders in order to come here tonight.

"Are you sure you're feeling well, Miss Calvert?" the governor enquired, his gaze passing quickly over her then sweeping the room beyond. She could almost hear him adding up how many important men he could speak to in his next few steps, now that he'd paid his duty to his hostess's niece.

"Entirely so, thank you, especially after I catch a breath of fresh air." She tilted her chin up, denying any longing to sit down. If Edmund were here, even that narrow chaise would be an ocean of comfort with him beside her.

"In that case, I'll give you a doctor's prescription and order you to step outside for a moment."

"In that case – I shall certainly obey, doctor." She smiled back at him and dropped a very small curtsey in mock humility. If she'd dipped any lower, she might have swayed and fallen.

She slipped between the curtains and onto the narrow balcony, a legacy of Texas' Spanish ancestry. Its ornate stone railing was draped in heavy blankets for colour, making it into a cosy nest from the waist down. The night was dark, with the waning crescent moon lurking behind scudding storm clouds. The narrow side street lay below her, full of heavy shadows except for a few stray beams of light creeping out of the hotel. Drunken revelry roared out of the saloons a few blocks away as men and their companions celebrated the coming year. The heavy curtains and thick walls confined the ball's cascading music to the interior of the building. Here and now, all was quiet.

One hour until midnight. Would Edmund come for her inside the party or outside? Would he be early or late?

Men burst out of the hotel and into the side street. Their scuffle was accented by the sound of fists slamming into flesh.

Could it be her lover? Sarah lunged for the railing of the balcony, her heart banging against her ribs.

A man cursed, only to be cut off by a gasp. Not Edmund, thank God. Sarah's pulse recovered enough that she could study the quartet facing her from the alleyway.

"Damn you, let me go, you greaser." A pig-faced man – his throat encircled by the Indian's forearm, and a big knife at his throat – glared at the immaculate Don Rafael. The brute tried to spit but failed miserably.

Mr St Just surveyed him coldly, then took up watch by the main street.

Sarah shrank back below the balcony railing, her heart in her throat, but she could still hear them.

"Not until you understand Texas law." Razors would have been gentler than Don Rafael's voice. "The only *vampiros* permitted in this town are mine."

Vampiros? He was a vampiro? *Like Edmund?* If she'd been feverish before, now she was colder than a glacier.

"Greedy bastard! There's plenty of food here for you and many other *vampiros* besides. Why won't you share it with visitors, like other *patrones*? Or are you afraid I'll kill you and take it all?"

Somebody growled down below but not Don Rafael.

Sarah glanced back at the window but stayed still, trusting in the merciful God which had kept her hidden so far.

"You should have asked my permission before you came here and started breaking the peace, Michaels." Don Rafael was unimpressed.

"I only did what all *vampiros* do – feed."

"You caused fear and death to create the emotion you needed to be able to drink that blood." Loathing cut through the night like a guillotine.

Death? But Edmund had only ever brought her great pleasure in exchange for a few drops of her blood. A horrified shudder shook Sarah to the bone.

"What of it?" The newcomer sounded genuinely startled.

"Not in my town."

Sarah nodded mute agreement for the first time.

"So let me leave."

"No. I rule Texas and I make the laws here. For this, you die."

Just like that? In the middle of the night, Don Rafael would announce sentence of death? What of a trial and witnesses, in case he was wrong?

Her skin was an icy shell somewhere miles away from her flesh. Sarah reached behind her for the french door's latch.

"But I did nothing I couldn't do anywhere else! Even if you don't approve of it, I swear I won't bother you again if you'll let me return to New Orleans." Terror rippled through the captive's voice.

Somebody spat into the street.

"Such behaviour may be common in that cesspool. Here, your life is already forfeit."

Dear Lord, Don Rafael truly did mean to execute the fellow. And she couldn't work the door latch while seated so that she could escape back into the ballroom. She rose stealthily to her feet and slithered along the wall to the exit. Slowly, carefully, she fumbled behind her skirts for the handle – and found herself looking back down into the alley again. She froze, afraid to move lest she be seen.

"Don Rafael—" Michaels began.

The big Spaniard caught the newcomer's head between his hands and twisted it sharply to one side. A sharp crack reverberated through the narrow street and the three Texans jumped back. The body of Michaels crumpled, dissolving into dust before it reached the muddy ground. His garments closed over the wisps like a shroud.

Sarah crumpled onto the balcony floor and knuckled her fist into her mouth lest she scream. Edmund would die like that someday. *Edmund, oh dear heavens, Edmund ...*

"God rest his soul," Don Rafael said finally. "I'll have a mass said for him tomorrow."

"Neatly done, sir, to break his neck like that," the Indian commented.

Sarah leaned her head back against the rough plaster wall and considered a thousand reasons why her stomach should hurl its contents through her throat. It certainly wanted to. It might even do so violently enough to have the results land on those arrogant brutes below.

"Do you think anyone noticed, sir?" St Just asked.

"No scent anywhere near except *prosaicos*," Don Rafael responded as casually as if they discussed a flower garden's spacing. "And we'd have seen or heard a mortal. Let us return home now so we can remove his scent."

"Excellent idea, sir," the others agreed.

Boot heels drumming along the boardwalk told of their departure but brought her little comfort.

Oh, sweet Mother of God, what would they have done if they'd found her? Killed her?

And what would the penalty be if they found Edmund here? Kill him for entering Texas without being one of the haughty Don Rafael's chosen few?

Darkness washed through her skull, more solid than the hotel behind her. By selecting this rendezvous, she'd summoned her beloved to his death. He'd known it, too – how could he not? – which was why he'd questioned her choice.

She couldn't risk his life; she couldn't. Perhaps if she wasn't at the ball when the clocks struck midnight, he'd leave, thinking she'd changed her mind. He'd be safe. She'd be alone – but he'd be alive.

It would have to be comfort enough through all the lonely years ahead.

She drew herself up and turned for the window, ignoring the slow tear trickling down her cheek.

Austin, 31 December 1867

The orchestra struck the quadrille's final chord and Sarah politely curtseyed to her partner, automatically removing herself far away from his clumsy feet. "Thank you for a most enjoyable dance, sir."

After all, Lieutenant Merrill had only stepped on her toes once and he hadn't ripped her flounce – this time.

"It was entirely my pleasure, Miss Calvert." The young officer drew himself up, his lean cheeks flushed with enthusiasm. "May I have the next dance, the midnight waltz?"

She accepted his arm, wishing he meant more to her than an occasional escort to church or charity work at the Blind Asylum. Texas was a frontier, where people made a fresh start. She should be able to respond to an honourable man's silent offer of devotion, instead of seeking ways to ignore the inexorable ticking of clocks.

She spent much of her time teaching at a freedmen's school, which horrified her aunt but kept her safely isolated from eligible young men. She only acknowledged its other benefit deep in the night when her pillow was utterly sodden with tears: it kept her from returning to Maryland with its flame-bright memories of Edmund.

Sarah patted her lieutenant's hand and gave him a variant on her usual answer. "No, thank you, I should return to my aunt. She needs my help for the midnight supper."

"Of course." His mouth twisted but he knew her too well to argue.

Her aunt's disgruntled glare tracked them from across the ballroom, even though she was standing between the new governor and Don Rafael. Aunt Mary sent weekly reports on Sarah's doings to the Calvert patriarch. Only Sarah's continuing aloofness towards Lieutenant Merrill had kept him from being chased off like every other young man who'd claimed more than two dances with her.

At least Aunt Mary was keeping Don Rafael away from her. Sarah had spent the past year dodging that top-drawer *vampiro*'s company and memories of last New Year's Eve. She loathed him – and prayed he'd never encounter Edmund.

A group of young officers and their partners accosted her and the lieutenant at the dance floor's edge, eager to discuss seating for the midnight supper where they'd plot tactics for the horse races tomorrow. Merrill joined in eagerly, soon gesturing with both hands to show exactly how a rival horse could be edged out of a turn. Sarah listened with half an ear, grateful for the enveloping throng, which kept her aunt from seeing her expression.

A single violin sent a long warbling note over the crowd, calling for dancers to celebrate ancient trees and water rippling under a moonlit sky.

A beloved whiff of sandalwood drifted past, long lost but never forgotten. Strong fingers clasped Sarah's elbow and drew her away.

"If you will excuse us?" a man murmured. It was not a request.

Edmund? Her heart gave an ecstatic thump and vaulted for the stars, only to fall back into Hell's lowest depths. If Don Rafael caught a glimpse of him . . .

Merrill's startled glance was countered by Edmund's scorching glare. When Sarah moved silently, subtly closer to the newcomer, Merrill fell back, yielding his claim. Bitter comprehension cut deep grooves beside his mouth before he returned to his friends.

Edmund swung her onto the dance floor, one hand firmly on her waist, the other grasping hers as if he feared she'd race away from him.

She gazed up at him, relearning every line of his beloved features under the brilliant gaslight. Every line was harsher, cut more clearly from the underlying bone. He seemed capable of carving through steel. Her fingers ached to tease his lips and teach him once again how to smile, despite the months and miles that had separated them.

The music swirled around them, sweet and charming like the delights they'd shared so long ago.

Why had she thought she could stay away from him?

"I have missed you so much," she whispered.

His jaw tightened still further. He swung her past another couple and through a tight turn, sending her blue velvet skirts flaring out like a carillon call for the truth. "Then why the devil didn't you wait for me last year?"

"Why didn't you tell me about Don Rafael's laws?" she countered. "I'd never have asked you to come if I'd known such an arrogant brute ruled here."

Terror flashed behind his eyes, dreadful as musket fire.

"God's death, Sarah, does he know you're aware of him?" His arm closed around her waist and he pulled her through the curtains and onto the balcony. A hard kick slammed the french door behind them and left them enclosed in an isolated world, separated by height from the few drunks wandering the main street. The night was brilliantly clear, illuminated by a full moon bright enough to almost touch.

"No, the man thinks of me only as the silent niece of a scheming hostess." She shrugged impatiently. What else was there to say after a year of minimal courtesy from the fellow? But she gave Edmund more details, to quiet the eyes raking hers and the hands rubbing restlessly up and down her arms. She needed him to believe her so she could convince her beloved to leave town.

"I spend my days with charities or the church, where occasionally we meet. Nothing more. But I saw him . . . kill another *vampiro*." An appalled shudder ran through her once again.

"'Fore God, such knowledge means certain death to *prosaicos*, Sarah! He's three centuries older than I am and a deadly killer." Edmund's hard fingers grasped her wrist the way he would grip an unruly dog. He turned back towards the ball. "I must take you away from here. Now."

Did he mean to haul her through the crowd? Sarah opened her

mouth to hurl a set of alternatives at his head. Thinking would be a good start.

Metal clicked softly and they both froze. Sarah's heart surged into her throat, too thick to let her draw air.

The latch turned and the french door opened.

With his hip, Edmund shoved her into the corner of the balcony and took up station before her. His big body blocked her view of almost everything beyond but, dear God, at what price to him?

"Good evening, Devereaux," Don Rafael purred like a tiger flexing his claws. St Just flanked him, cordial as an unsheathed sword. "What a delightful surprise to meet you here."

Sarah glanced desperately over the railing, hoping to see a carriage or a pair of horses waiting patiently. But the Indian's unreadable eyes met hers instead, matched by those of a dozen armed men nearby. For the first time in her life, she lusted for her father's command of profanity.

She hissed under her breath and glanced about for another exit.

Edmund's counter-attack came in a voice so sweet and reasonable, she might have thought it logical at any other time. "Release her, Perez. She's an innocent and has nothing to do with what lies between us."

"What?" Her instinctive objection died in her throat, strangled by the realization of an older, deadlier duel between them.

"Why should I? By all *vampiro* custom, *prosaico* mouths can only be stopped by death lest they wag too much." The Spaniard's dark gaze flicked over her like an executioner's axe considering the best place to strike. Her stomach surged into a knot but even that didn't seem small enough to escape him.

Edmund growled deep in his throat, almost too softly to be heard. He brought logic to bear on them again. "She knows nothing."

"Do not stretch the truth too far or it will strangle you." His enemy tutted. "You know she saw me destroy another of our kind. As for you, my fine-feathered English spy—"

"*Former* spy," Edmund's correction sliced through the other's taunt. His rage was all the brighter for how fiercely he kept it leashed. Both of them brandished their anger like weapons, turning the big Texan vampire into a heavy sabre and Edmund into a rapier – quick, lethal and razor sharp with deadly intent.

"As you wish. It matters little in the long run." Don Rafael waved the correction off like an emperor dismissing a scullion. "You know the price for coming here, especially when I swore sixty years ago to kill you the next time we met."

"I should have let all the Spaniards die when I had the chance, instead of trying to save them, no matter what I'd learned when I guested with the Inquisition," Edmund said furiously, his hands opening and closing at his sides as if hungering to close around the other's throat. "God's blood, Perez, will you never understand honour? Can you not recognize that you have to follow orders even when you don't believe in them and don't enjoy the consequences? Especially during a war?"

Don Rafael, his dark eyes boiling with murder, slammed the slighter man against the wall hard enough to shake plaster dust free. "Never question my honour, English dog!"

Edmund snarled in his face, fangs fully bared, and kicked him viciously in the knee. His old enemy snapped out a curse and they tumbled into a conflict like a pack of dogs, blood and growls flying faster than blows.

Sarah surged forwards to help but St Just's glare warned her off. Sick to the bone, more terrified than she could remember, she retreated to her corner.

How much of an advantage was three centuries to Don Rafael?

Something caught her heel and nearly tripped her. Edmund's knife glittered on the floor almost under her hem. It wasn't a butcher knife, which she knew how to wield, but perhaps she could accomplish *something* with it.

Pretending faintness, she stooped down and slipped the knife into her pocket, careful not to be seen by the preoccupied Frenchman.

The combatants were taking up more and more of the balcony until St Just was backed against the wall far away from her.

But Edmund was moving far too slowly. One leg dragged behind him and the wicked gash on his cheek had started bleeding again, badly enough to make his movements apprehensive. Don Rafael, damn him, fought as if he'd barely entered combat – coldly, quickly, unaffected by the blood spurting from his arm.

Surely her heartbeat could be heard in Maryland yet her thoughts were entirely clear. Sarah needed to help somehow, some way. For once, she could see the movements of the combatants very precisely, rather than as a whirlwind blur of saloon brawling.

How did one stop a very old *vampiro*?

When they rolled back next to her and Don Rafael was on top, Sarah leaped on him and stabbed him in the side. Somewhere, anywhere, who knew or cared where she struck? She only needed to distract him long enough to save her love.

She put her full weight – such as she had – behind the stroke. The blade went deep, slicing through wool and hard muscle and softer flesh. Damage, she was doing damage to a man's body. A fiery shock raced through her skin, more intimate than a handshake or a waltz, and she hesitated for a split second.

But this was Edmund's would-be killer, damn him.

She twisted the knife viciously, with every bit of strength and skill ever learned in a firelit kitchen.

Don Rafael's roar was loud enough to be heard across Austin. He broke away from Edmund and yanked the knife out, then stood staring at it. Anger repeatedly chased astonishment through his eyes.

Edmund staggered onto his feet and shoved her behind him. A few hard shakes of his head sent blood splattering across the balcony from his face.

St Just lunged for Sarah but his master snapped an arrogant finger under his nose. "Leave her be; the lady has won this bout."

Triumph's wings began to tentatively unfurl inside her heart. She must have greatly injured the far older *vampiro* to force him to back off so completely. But she and Edmund still needed to escape Texas.

The Frenchman retreated slowly, clearly unconvinced she could be trusted, while Don Rafael's men in the street below murmured angrily.

"My congratulations to both of you." Don Rafael eyed her, his saturnine features betraying little expression.

"Thank you. And thank you for the pleasure of serving beside you against Bonaparte." For the first time, Edmund too relaxed and Sarah allowed herself to rest her head against his shoulder. Perhaps they truly might escape both her father and this frontier.

The church bells began to ring in the New Year. One. Two . . .

She shook out her handkerchief and began to mop Edmund's face. He'd lost far too much blood and would need to feed very soon. Back in Maryland, she'd have seen that as an excuse for the delicious lovemaking necessary to infuse her blood with the most emotion possible. But here?

Don Rafael eyed her, coldly.

"Devereaux, at what time was your rendezvous with Señorita Calvert scheduled?" Don Rafael rubbed his bloody fingertips together, then pressed his hand back against his bleeding waist. St Just stepped forwards to offer an improvised bandage from his cravat but was impatiently waved off.

"Midnight, Perez. New Year's Eve at midnight." Edmund wrapped his arm around her waist, standing wonderfully close.

"I wondered who she was watching for last year." The big landowner stretched slightly and grimaced, hissing when the new movement put a new fresh strain on his wound.

Sarah pursed her lips and wondered if she'd ever gain any feelings of Christian charity for him. Then his words caught up with her. "What do you mean 'last year'?" she echoed. "You knew I was looking for somebody, yet you kept us apart?"

"Do you mean I spent an extra twelvemonth living in hell because you wanted to play God, you pestilential knave?" Edmund demanded furiously.

"Señor, Señorita Calvert was hardly well enough to travel last year, unlike now," Don Rafael snapped. "In fact, I suggest you depart immediately before her aunt comes looking – if you want a head start on the troops that female is certain to send after you, claiming you need a Maryland patriarch's permission even here in Texas."

Sarah sighed and grasped Edmund more firmly. At least this time, the army wouldn't have the advantage of Cassius as a guide.

Edmund kissed the top of her head, chuckling a little. Silly man, he always enjoyed a good challenge.

Don Rafael's eyes travelled over them, as encompassing as a scientist's spyglass.

"However, if you'd prefer. . ." He paused. "Since you have won this bout, perhaps you will permit me to assist you?"

"How?" Edmund asked bluntly.

"You could be married by my priest – I believe Señorita Calvert is a Catholic? – and spend your honeymoon at my ranch. I can vouch for my staff's discretion and their ability to keep your aunt at bay."

Under a *vampiro*'s roof?

Sarah glanced up at Edmund but he wasn't looking at her.

"If it's the fastest way to get married, we'll do it. Thank you." It might not have been Edmund's most gracious speech but it was certainly emphatic.

"It is nothing. After all, what are old comrades-in-arms for except to smooth the road?" Don Rafael bowed courteously, only to quickly bring himself upright. He'd need to feed soon so he could heal. But he undoubtedly had resources close at hand, since this was his territory.

"Do you wish to leave by ladder or through the ballroom, during the midnight supper, my friends?"

"Ladder," Sarah and Edmund announced in unison.

St Just snickered softly.

"Then if you will permit me a few minutes, I will have one brought round and you may depart. My friend here will remain inside so you may be assured of no interruptions."

"Thank you, sir," Sarah said, feeling much more cordial towards him. "You've been very kind."

"Perhaps." He raised a dark eyebrow. "Or a little foolish." He nodded to them both and was gone, still keeping his elbow tucked hard against himself. St Just shut the balcony door, ending a final glimpse of the fickle, grasping world inside, and left the lovers alone in the warm silence.

Edmund spun her around to face him, blood trickling slowly down his cheek. "Are you sure? We've been separated for more than a year."

Poor darling, he'd lived through such hell. What delight to spend a lifetime making it up to him.

"Dearest love." She caught his face between her hands and kissed him on the lips, giving him all the love, all the reassurance she could.

He caught her closer and his mouth devoured hers, tasting her breath, catching her joy, her trust in tomorrow, her tongue's willingness to make new words of love. Always him, only him.

"My darling Sarah."

His fangs pricked her lips and she moaned softly, moved closer, candlelight drifting behind her eyelids. Oh yes, giving him a small taste would be lovely now.

He nipped her and sucked, drawing on her like the breath of life itself. Her fingers tangled in his hair and his heart beat against her. Warmth surrounded her, swept over her shoulders, and down through her bones.

He rumbled her name and sipped her blood, while firelight warmed her veins. Tomorrow when they were married, there'd be a nova of stars to enjoy when they shared their first deep drink of each other's blood.

And centuries together to love one another.

Vampsploitation

Jaye Wells

Los Angeles, November 1979

The guy on camera wore a ratty ski mask, a black turtleneck stretched precariously over a beer gut and too-tight bell-bottoms. The wall behind him was covered in some sort of collage done in shades of black and white with accents of red. I tried to make out the details, but the poor video quality made the picture fuzzy.

I shook my head at the grainy image. If it had been anyone else showing me this, I'd think it was a joke. But the Dominae weren't exactly known for their senses of humour. I glanced over at Slade. He wasn't smiling. He rarely did from what I'd seen. Of course, I'd only known him for about ten minutes, and his lack of good humour was probably due to him not wanting to be saddled with a rookie.

"My name is Lord Viper," the guy on tape said dramatically. I barely managed not to roll my eyes at the fake name. "For too long we, the mighty Lilim, children of Lilith, have hidden in the shadows. The time has come to reveal ourselves to the sons of Adam. Unless—"

He paused dramatically. I knew what was coming and resisted the urge to fast-forward through his lame speech.

"—the Dominae gives me one billion dollars!"

I choked on a shocked laugh. Lord Viper wasn't the first vampire to try to extort money out of the Dominae. But he was the first to demand such a ridiculous sum.

"The money must be deposited by midnight Wednesday or I will give all the major media outlets in LA the story of the century."

He went on to rattle off the name of a local bank and an account number. Tanith cut the tape off as he started to rant again.

"Do you have the envelope the tape came in?" Slade asked, all business. His look screamed bad-ass assassin. Dressed in black from neck to toes, he wore a leather blazer, slacks and expensive Italian leather shoes. In fact, the only things keeping his look from being a Shaft rip-off were his pale skin and auburn hair.

Tanith shook her head. Of the three Dominae, she was in charge of the business side of running the race. Considering the sum of money this guy was demanding it wasn't a surprise she was taking part in this. "We had them dusted. No fingerprints."

Slade nodded. "Have you tracked the account he mentioned?"

"The account belongs to a Zeke Calebow." She slid a file across the table.

I scooted closer to Slade to get a look at the contents. He ignored me and focused on the papers. The picture clipped inside was a mugshot of a portly male vamp with shaggy copper hair and freckles. He looked stupid and mean – a bad combination. The guy in the video wore a ski mask, but my gut told me this Zeke and Lord Viper were one and the same.

"What do we know about Zeke?" I asked.

Tanith sighed. "Not much. Family is trash. Last known job was a strip club in the Valley."

Slade slammed the folder shut before I could read the name of the club from the dossier. "We'll check it out," he said in a clipped tone.

"You have forty-eight hours to neutralize this threat," Tanith said, looking from Slade to me and back again. "I don't think I have to remind you how sensitive this matter is. We want this guy dead yesterday."

"Consider it done," Slade said. Then he turned on his heel and marched towards the door. He didn't look back to make sure I followed. But I did anyway.

An hour later, Slade pulled up in front of the Tit Crypt. He hadn't said much to me on the way over. I tried to play it cool, but inside I was stoked. Even though I'd graduated with honours from assassin school five years earlier, most of my jobs thus far involved roughing up vampires who forgot to pay their tithes to the Dominae. This would be my first kill mission, which was why I'd been paired up with a more experienced assassin.

Among enforcers, Slade Corbin was a legend. The instructors at school spoke about his feats with reverence and had used some of his more daring missions as case studies. Rumour had it he was less than a century old, which was hard to believe. But looking at him, he obviously couldn't be that old. The light auburn colour gave him away. If he'd been older, the shade would be darker. For him to have accomplished so much at such a young age meant he was someone I'd be able to learn a few things from.

He turned the car off and leaned towards me. "OK, this is how it's going to work. You're going to shut up and stay out of my way. I ask the questions. I make the decisions. And when we find this asshole, we're going to split the payment ninety–ten."

My mouth fell open. "Excuse me?"

"Which word didn't you understand?"

I cocked my head to the side. Slade might be a legend, but no one spoke to me that way. "Listen, buddy, I don't know who the hell you think you are, but the Dominae asked us to team up on this. I'm not going to sit around and let you collect all the money." And the respect, I amended silently. I'd waited too long for a real chance to prove myself to the Dominae as an assassin for this guy to get in my way.

"No, you listen, sweetheart. You get in my way and I will end you. I've got a lot riding on this payday for some rookie to fuck it up for me. So, you'll march your ass in there and watch while I find our guy and get the job done. For your trouble, you'll walk away with ten per cent. And I'm being generous here. Ten large for doing nothing is a good deal."

I could tell this asshole wasn't going to listen to reason. Fine, I decided. Let him believe I was just some inexperienced hack. "OK, I'll tell you what. I'll let you do the talking in there if you agree to a seventy–thirty split."

He cursed under his breath, something about godsdamned stubborn females. "How about ninety–ten and I don't kick you off the case altogether?"

"You can't do that!"

"Watch me."

★　　★　　★

The bouncer at the door waved us in. Slade swaggered ahead of me, and I followed along, glaring daggers at his back.

I'd been in this place before. Being an enforcer for the Dominae meant I had to experience the seedier sides of the vampire underworld on a regular basis. Strip clubs especially seemed to attract tithe-avoiding repeat offenders, so I spent a lot of time staking them out. That allowed me to make contacts with the club owners and bouncers, who understood the benefits of cooperating with an enforcer. For me, the relationships meant I had access to the *who's who* in order to find out the *what's what*.

As far as clubs went, the Tit Crypt fell into the lower end of the spectrum. Instead of valet service and tight-assed chicks with glorious racks, it offered an all-you-can-eat buffet and hard-looking females who didn't even try to conceal the boredom on their overly made-up faces.

On the stage, a female with red hair twisted into Bo Derek braids swayed her hips in time to the disco tragedy of Donna Summer's "Bad Girls". I shook my head at the music. How a race that invented disco managed to outnumber my own escaped me.

In contrast to the disco-inspired fashions favoured by most of the strippers, I wore a "God Save the Queen" T-shirt covered in safety pins, torn jeans and biker boots. I topped the entire ensemble off with a beaten leather jacket I'd found at Goodwill. The confrontational look discouraged the roving hands and eyes of the club patrons.

I continued past the stage, and the interested stares of the men seated there. Fang, a male vamp with a moustache that would have made Burt Reynolds jealous, wiped the bar down with a dingy towel. His steady swiping slowed when Slade approached. I hung back, as instructed, biding my time.

Fang ignored Slade until he slammed a twenty on the bar. "I need some information."

The rag slowed its circling as Fang turned unfriendly eyes on him. "Ain't got none for sale."

Slade sighed and slapped another twenty down, harder this time. "I'm looking for one of your employees."

Fang leaned forwards. "Look, mister, you want to look at some titties, you've come to the right place. If you're asking me to squeal on my people, you'd best turn your ass around and go."

I choked on a laugh at the look on Slade's face. His jaw clenched, obviously a precursor to violence. I stood quickly, drawing Fang's attention to me.

His face transformed into a genuine smile then. "Amateur night is on Tuesdays."

I grinned and strutted over to the bar to run a finger down Fang's leather vest. "How about a private dance then, hot stuff?"

Fang leaned his elbows on the bar. "You sure your boyfriend here won't mind, Sabina? From the glare he's sending me, his mama never taught him how to share."

"Don't mind him," I said, waving away Slade's fierce frown. "Listen, Fang, I was hoping you could help me out with something."

Fang's moustache twitched. "Anything for you, good lookin'."

"We're looking for Zeke Calebow."

Fang frowned. "What you want with that lousy son of a bitch? I had to fire his ass."

"Why?"

"Bastard cut a peephole in the girls' dressing room. Caught him jacking off in the utility room with his eye glued to the wall." He shook his head. "Two of my best girls quit when they found out."

Slade spoke up. "Do you know where we can find him?"

Fang sent Slade a contemptuous look. "Last I heard he took a job at T&A Video over on Victory."

"Yeah, I know the place. Thanks, Fang," I said. "I appreciate it."

"I don't suppose you'd prefer to show your appreciation topless," he said with a twinkle in his eye.

I laughed and shook my head. "How about a rain check?" I slid a twenty across the bar. Fang pocketed the payment smoothly. "Will you call me if you see Zeke?"

Fang chuckled. "Yeah. I'll call you right after I beat his perverted ass."

I grinned. "Just as long as you leave the killing to the professionals."

Slade grabbed my arm and swung me around before I'd taken three steps out of the door.

"You want to explain to me what the fuck you were thinking in there? I thought we'd agreed you'd let me do the talking."

I jerked my arm free of his grasp. "First of all, 'you're welcome' for getting the information we needed. And second, Fang never would have talked to you if I hadn't been there."

"And why is that? You been doing some moonlighting?"

I gave him a look. "No, asshole. The vamps who don't pay their tithes usually spend them on one of three things: gambling, titty bars or prostitutes. I know every vamp bookie, club owner and pimp in the city." I stepped up on Slade, emboldened by the small victory of shocking him. "And if you'd taken two seconds to ask me, I would have told you that there was no way Fang would talk to you."

"Why not?"

"Because Fang's brother was killed by an enforcer for bootlegging blood-wine during Prohibition."

"Why does he talk to you then?"

"Because I flirt with him shamelessly." I smiled. "And because I saved one of his best girls from being raped by a patron several months ago. Fang loves his girls, and by helping one of them he considers himself in my debt."

"Oh," Slade said.

"Yeah," I said. "And if you drop the asshole routine, I'll tell you all about Larry, the vampire porn king who owns T&A Video."

A small bell dinged over the door as Slade held it open and motioned for me to go first. He'd been surprisingly quiet after our little chat. I took that as a good sign, since he seemed the type who liked to bark orders unnecessarily. So, as I brushed past him, I was feeling good. At least until I caught a whiff of the store – a charming perfume of stale cigarettes, body odour and dried semen.

T&A Video lay in the armpit of the San Fernando Valley. The introduction of VHS tapes a few years earlier had revolutionized the adult film industry, and T&A was just one of the many new establishments catering to the discerning wank-film connoisseur.

On the surface, it looked like your typical video store, except with sections dedicated to every fetish known to man – and sometimes beast. But in the back, it held one of the most extensive collections of vampire porn in Southern California.

As expected, Larry manned the counter. He had an unlit cigar clamped between his lips and wore a polyester shirt covered in a retina-burning psychedelic print. I thought the thick chain with the male symbol was a nice touch though. Over Larry's head, a TV bolted to the ceiling displayed a scene involving a pizza deliveryman and a woman whose undercarriage might be mistaken for a tribble from *Star Trek*.

Near the back of the store, a clean-cut businessman perused shelves labelled BARELY LEGAL. If he saw me come in, he was doing a pretty good job pretending he hadn't. He pulled a video from the shelf and added it to the three he was already holding.

A red curtain next to the checkout drew back and a young guy exited. His hand was busy zipping his fly when he noticed me. His cheeks went red and he scuttled by so fast he left a breeze in his wake.

Larry looked up from his racing forms as we approached. He ran a thick palm over his greasy hair and straightened his butterfly collar. His eyes groped my body in a way that left me wanting a shower.

"If it isn't Sabina Kane. How can I help you, sugar?" He completely ignored Slade.

"Is Zeke working tonight?"

Larry's eyes narrowed. "Sabina, you wound me. I was hoping you were coming to accept my offer to make a blood film."

I leaned back and tried to stifle my grimace. Fang films were fetish videos geared towards the vamp population. The last time I saw Larry he told me he could make me a star.

"Sorry, Larry, but I haven't changed my mind," I said. "I'm just looking for Zeke."

Larry's eyes narrowed. "You and everyone else."

"What do you mean?" Slade said, leaning in.

"Who the hell are you?" Larry demanded.

"This is my colleague Slade Corbin," I said.

Larry looked Slade over with what he probably thought was an intimidating stare. Slade simply stared back, cold as ice. I covered my smile with a hand. The thought of Larry intimidating anyone was laughable. The fact he was trying to intimidate a killing machine like Slade was downright hilarious.

Finally, under Slade's penetrating gaze, Larry cleared his throat. "Anyway, Zeke Calebow's dead to me. He was supposed to show up for work two days ago and I ain't heard one word."

"Any idea where we can find him?" I asked.

The male shrugged. "I think he hangs out at that strip club on Van Nuys."

"The Tit Crypt?"

He nodded. Shit, I thought. So far, all my clues were leading me around in circles.

"Do you have an address for him?" Slade asked.

Larry sighed. "Hold on, I got it here somewheres." His hefted his bulk from his stool and went to a file cabinet behind the counter. As he rifled through stacks of paper, he muttered to himself.

Slade and I exchanged a look. Chances were good Zeke wouldn't be at home waiting for us to put a bullet between his eyes. But if we had the address, we could search the place for any clues on where he was hiding out.

Finally, Larry came back over and slapped a coffee-stained job application on the counter. "The address is on that," Larry said. "You find that asshole, you tell him he owes me two hundred dollars for all the videos he checked out and never returned."

I nodded and handed the paper to Slade. "Thanks, Larry. I owe you one."

Larry shifted on his seat and leaned in again. "Let me know if you change your mind about making a movie. I'd love to get you on my casting couch, if you know what I mean."

Out of the corner of my eye, I saw Slade's mouth twitch. "No thanks."

"Aw, c'mon. It'll be fun." He wiggled his bushy eyebrows suggestively.

"I said no." Not just no, I thought. Hell no.

"Let me give you my card anyway." He pulled a greasy rectangle of paper from a stack at his elbow. "When you change your mind, call me. There's vamps out there'd pay good money to see a prime piece like you sink your fangs into a nice piece of meat."

Slade laughed out loud this time. I turned to him with an eyebrow raised. Slade paused and glanced warily at Larry. The porn king wiggled his eyebrows again, pointing a bony finger at Slade. "Don't laugh, good lookin'. I was talking to *you*."

One minute Slade stood next to me with his mouth agape and his cheeks red. The next, the bell over the door rang and I got a nice view of Slade's ass before it disappeared.

* * *

"I think we should hit Zeke's address tomorrow. I don't want to chance getting caught there if shit goes down." If the joke Larry had at Slade's expense was still bothering him, Slade didn't show it. But the clenched jaw hinted I should let it go. Instead, I glanced at the dashboard clock.

"Makes sense." Only about two hours until sunrise. Not a big deal for me. The only benefit of being mixed-blood I'd ever experienced was my ability to be in the sun. Granted, it weakened me, but I didn't have to dive for shelter like every other vamp on the planet. "You hungry?"

Slade smiled for the first time since I met him. "Liquid or solid?"

"Solid. I fed earlier."

He smiled and started the car. "I know just the place."

Slade insisted we go to the window to order, instead of using the drive-thru. Since I'd never been to In-N-Out Burger before, he insisted on ordering me something called a "Double-Double" with "large fries, well done". I wasn't sure exactly what any of that meant, but the heavenly aroma of grilled beef made my carnivore's heart go pitter-patter.

The chick in the orange apron handed over a box overflowing with burgers and cardboard boats filled with golden fries. Slade carried the feast to a small sitting area next to the parking lot.

He didn't wait for me to sit before digging into his burger. I smiled at the utterly satisfied sounds escaping between his bites. For someone who'd come across so cold all night, Slade seemed to have a passion for food. He finally slowed down enough to notice I hadn't tried mine. He pointed at the box with his own burger. "Dig in," he said over a mouthful.

I wouldn't quite call the experience orgasmic, but it was a near thing. "Godsdamn!" I said after I'd inhaled half the thing.

"Right?" Slade said, shoving two fries into his mouth.

We spent a few minutes munching companionably, watching cars pass by on Foothill Boulevard. Finally, I washed down my last bite with a gulp of cold soda. I was feeling good. Not just because of the burgers, either. What had started out as a disaster of a first mission – what with Slade being an ass and all – had turned into a pretty decent night.

"Slade?" I asked.

"Hmm?"

"Do you think we should review what we know so far?"

He grimaced, as if I'd just brought up a taboo subject. "Not much to review."

"But we have Zeke's personnel file. Maybe we should go through it for clues. You know, proof he's the one whose threatening the Dominae."

Slade raised an eyebrow. "Clues? Sabina, we're not detectives." He leaned in, whispering so the people at other tables wouldn't overhear. "We're assassins. It's not up to us to prove or deny Zeke's guilt. It's up to us to end him. Period."

"But the guy on the video was wearing a mask. How can we be sure it's this Zeke guy? After all, the perp could have opened the bank account under Zeke's name to throw us off his trail."

Slade cocked his head. "You've been watching too much *Magnum P.I.*"

My face went hot at his dismissive tone. Ignoring him, I opened the file. Zeke's job application was on top. I scanned the page, looking for something. What, I had no idea. I scanned past the work history since we already knew his last place of employment. Finally, my eyes landed on his chicken-scratch answers to a series of questions.

I snorted. "Listen to this. 'Why do you want to work at T&A Video?'" I looked up to make sure Slade was paying attention. He tilted his head, a facsimile of real interest. "Zeke said, ''Cause I like to watch people fucking.'"

Slade spewed a mouthful of soda across the table. "At least he's honest," he said once he'd stopped choking.

I smiled and continued, "'Please discuss your previous experience in the adult film industry.' Zeke put: 'Does whacking off to it three times a day count?'"

We both laughed so loud that the other customers started sending curious looks our way. Finally, I recovered enough to say, "The funniest part is that these answers got him the job."

Slade smiled and took another sip of his drink. A flash of fang peeked out when he pulled the straw away. "You surprised me tonight," he said, suddenly more serious.

"I know."

The corner of his mouth lifted. "I'm sorry if I was an asshole earlier. I just had a bad experience with the last rookie the Dominae saddled me with."

"Who was it?"

"Mischa Petrov."

I groaned and crumpled my burger wrapper, wishing it were Petrov's head.

"I take it you know her?"

"Unfortunately, yes." In addition to being my biggest competition in assassin school, Mischa Petrov was also my nemesis. She lorded my mixed blood over me whenever possible. And despite my higher grades, my grandmother, as leader of the Dominae, had chosen Mischa as the *Primora* of the class. The honour ensured Mischa was fast-tracked into getting the plum jobs, unlike the rest of us who had to serve time collecting tithes and tracking down petty criminals.

Slade laughed. "In addition to being completely incompetent, that female had the worst case of *fanged vagina* I've ever had the misfortune to experience."

I grimaced. "You fucked her?" My new-found respect for Slade took a nosedive.

He snorted and shook his head. "Are you kidding? I wouldn't let that she-devil anywhere near my unmentionables."

I smiled. "Good for you."

"Anyway," he said, "after that horrific experience, I didn't expect you would be a pleasant surprise. Especially since—" He cut himself off and looked away quickly.

I nodded. "Let me guess, the mixed-blood thing?" He nodded, looking sheepish. "Don't worry. I'm used to it."

He shifted uncomfortably on the small seat. "Anyway, I just wanted to apologize for earlier."

"Do you feel bad enough to split the take with me fifty–fifty?"

He threw back his head and laughed. "How about eighty–twenty?" His tone made it sound like he thought this offer was magnanimous.

I leaned forwards, looking him in the eyes. "Sixty–forty."

He pursed his lips and narrowed his eyes at me. Finally, he sighed. "Seventy–thirty. Final offer."

"Gods, you're stubborn," I said.

He shrugged. "Despite your luck tonight, I'm still the lead on this mission. When we go in tomorrow, you're going to have to let me call the shots."

I saluted him. "Yes, sir."

His lips twitched. "Smart ass."

Slade picked me up at my apartment the next night. I was waiting for him by the kerb when he pulled up in a black van.

When I got in, I asked, "What happened to the Karmann Ghia?"

He shrugged. "This has better storage." He jerked his head towards the back. I looked over my shoulder and my eyes widened at the treasure trove of weaponry. He'd installed racks filled with guns, knives, crossbows and various other implements of death. Along the opposite wall, a low bench featured manacles instead of seat belts. Red shag carpet completed the dungeon-on-wheels look.

"Nice carpet," I said.

"Hides blood well." He turned the key and the engine roared to life. "All set?"

An hour later, we pulled up in front of Zeke's house in Glendale. Calling it a dump would have been generous. It looked like someone dropped a cinder block and then stuck a door and a couple of windows on it. Although, the weeds, beer cans and cigarette butts added a certain charm to the landscaping.

"Looks like peddling porn doesn't pay as much as I thought," Slade said.

"Yeah, extortion is much more lucrative," I replied, scanning the dark windows for signs of life. "Doesn't look like anyone's home."

"Let me grab some party favours, just in case," Slade said. He ducked back into the cargo area. He opened his leather blazer and started filling interior pockets with assorted stabby things.

Let me just say, nothing is sexier than watching a male strap weapons to himself. Slade was no exception. For an ass, he had a certain alpha-male sexiness going for him. But I knew better than to entertain those thoughts for very long. I needed to keep my mind on the mission. So, I took my eyes off his physique and focused on his weapons. That's when I noticed he didn't bother grabbing any guns.

"No firearms?" I asked, checking the chamber of my own.

He paused. "Never use 'em." He pulled up the leg of his bell-bottoms and strapped a nylon sheath around his ankle. Into that went three wooden spikes.

"Why not?"

He paused, as if considering the matter for the first time. Finally, he shrugged. "Just don't like guns."

"Oh, I get it," I said. "You're *old*."

He laughed. "I'm only sixty, Sabina. Hardly *old* by vampire standards."

"You're joking. Sixty?"

He shook his head and grabbed a few throwing stars made from apple wood from the shelf. Judging by the smirk on his face, I'd managed to amuse him. As much as I didn't like being the source of anyone's amusement, I had to look at him with grudging respect. To have accomplished so much as an assassin at such a young age was mind-blowing.

"Ready?" he said, breaking into my thoughts. I nodded and cocked my gun. I might want to learn from Slade, but I drew the line at giving up my weapon.

We went in through the back door. In his haste to leave, Zeke must have forgotten to lock it. I shook my head at the oversight. For someone who'd managed to elude us this long, Zeke sure was an idiot.

The kitchen stunk like weeks-old trash and spoiled food. Even in the dark, I could see the dishes piled up in the sink and the pile of pizza boxes stacked next to the overflowing trashcan. Even in the dark, I could see food caked on the harvest yellow fridge and the avocado green counters.

Two doors led off the kitchen to other rooms in the house. Slade pointed to the right, indicating we should split up. I nodded and went through the breakfast area.

The only signs of life from my perspective were cockroaches crawling over forgotten cereal bowls and glasses coated with dried blood. Zeke, in addition to being a pain in my ass, also appeared to be the biggest slob I'd ever encountered.

I moved silently to the corner leading into the living room. When no sounds came from the room beyond, I slowly turned the corner with my gun ready to shoot anything that moved. Maybe I was being paranoid, but carelessness didn't pay the bills. More than one enforcer had gotten dead by being cocky.

This room was decorated in bachelor chic. Posters of a scantily clad Farrah Fawcett-Majors and the Dallas Cowboy cheerleaders lined the walls. The furnishings consisted of a battered orange Barcalounger parked in front of a TV the size of a compact car. I moved through the room quickly and headed towards the back hallway, which I assumed led to the bedrooms.

Through the doorway, I encountered a linen closet filled with *Hustler* magazines and ratty towels. A sound to my left had me swinging my gun around. Slade held up his hands and stopped. I blew out a breath and lowered the gun a fraction.

"Anything?" I whispered.

He shook his head. "All clear. You check that last room?"

A closed door waited on our right, which presumably led to a guest room or office. I shook my head and moved towards it. Slade had my back. Not that it made me feel any better. Despite his obvious experience in the field, his presence unsettled me. I was used to working alone, and adding a partner to the mix brought in all sorts of variables I couldn't control.

Still, I sucked in some air and turned the knob. When no one rushed me or shot me in the face, I let out my breath and walked in. Slade clicked on a flashlight behind me and shined it into the stuffy room. Dust particles glittered in the beam while my eyes adjusted. Once they focused again, I made out a utilitarian metal desk pushed up against the far wall. Confident we were alone in the house, I walked over and clicked on the desk lamp.

I busied myself opening desk drawers, rooting around for any clue of Zeke's whereabouts. All I got for my effort were a few back issues of *Hustler*, gummy rubber bands and a matchbook.

"Um, Sabina?"

I pocketed the matchbook, and looked over my shoulder to see what had Slade sounding spooked. He had his back to me, his gaze intent on the wall.

At first, I thought more beer posters plastered the wall. But when I turned around to get a better look, my mouth dropped open. The same collage used as a backdrop in the video covered the wall.

"Godsdamn, that's creepy," I said. Made from newspaper clippings, photographs, bits of string and what appeared to be bloody handprints, Zeke had crafted his very own serial killer-esque *objet d'art.*

I moved closer, careful not to touch anything. Zeke had been a busy boy. Upon closer inspection, I realized the pictures and clippings all served to prove the existence of vampires. From shots of vamps sucking on the necks of victims to headlines about unexplained murders, he had enough evidence to convince even those most doubtful mortals that the stuff of their nightmares not only existed, but walked down the same streets and ate at the same restaurants as the Sons of Adam.

"He wasn't bluffing," Slade said quietly. "He really intends to expose us to the mortals."

I backed away from the scent of dried blood and newsprint ink. "Do you have a camera in that van of yours?"

Slade opened his mouth to answer, but a crash made us both go still. The sound came from the other end of the house, probably the kitchen. I grabbed my gun and went to turn off the light. The room fell into darkness. Something about darkness always amplifies sounds. And this was no different. My breath sounded harsh to my ears as I listened to footsteps advancing through the house.

I glanced at Slade. He held a finger to his lips and went to stand with his back against the wall next to the door. I took point in the corner, diagonal to the doorway, ready to shoot first and ask questions later.

Floorboards creaked in the living room. Amateur, I thought. Or someone who wasn't expecting two vampires to be waiting for them. I crouched down in the shadows, giving myself the advantage of being able to see the intruder before they saw me.

The darkness in the hall shifted. I aimed the gun directly at the silhouette, tracking the figure. Finally, it crossed the threshold and stopped.

"Stop right there." Slade's calm voice sounded unnaturally loud in the dark.

The intruder jerked. Three panic shots exploded in quick succession. I covered my head with my hands as a shot zinged past my ear. "Godsdammit!"

"Stop!" Slade yelled. A scuffle sounded from the doorway. A female gasp followed by a male grunt.

I dived for the lamp on the desk. Light spilled through the room just in time for me to catch Mischa Petrov kneeing Slade between the legs. Gods love him, he held his ground, knocking the gun from her hand.

"Mischa, stop!" I yelled.

But she wasn't done fighting. The idiot was so pumped up on adrenaline she wasn't thinking.

"You scared the shit out of me!" she yelled at Slade, swiping at him and hissing like a feral cat. She was even dressed like Cat Woman in her one-piece black jumpsuit, which left little to the imagination.

I grabbed her arms and tore her away from Slade. She panted like an injured animal, ready to strike again. Blood covered Slade's lower lip, and two deep scratch marks bled freely next to his eye. Seeing the needless injuries, something snapped. I could understand why she shot without looking, but her disgraceful display of fear after the fact disgusted me.

"What the fuck were you thinking? You could have killed us!" I yelled.

She jerked away and rounded on me. "Me?" she spat. "You two were skulking in the shadows like a couple of thieves."

"I told you to stop." Slade said it in the same tone one might use to share the time. His complete lack of anger impressed me. Sure, he was probably pissed on the inside. But outside? Total control. That was the sign of a real professional. Unlike some bitches I could mention.

Mischa seemed to have collected some of her composure. She smoothed her palms over her ruby-red Crystal Gayle hair which, in my opinion, was completely ridiculous for an assassin. Now that she'd gotten control of herself, she transformed back into her typical dragon-lady persona. "Sorry, Slade. If I'd known it was you I never would have fired." She smiled at him in a way that reminded me of a lion eyeing a particularly plump gazelle.

"Shut up, Mischa. Flirting with me won't erase the fact you fucked up," Slade said. "Your lack of control makes you a danger to both yourself and anyone working with you."

Her eyes narrowed. "Fuck you, Slade."

"I'd rather gnaw off my own arm, thanks."

I didn't bother to cover my grin. "Looks like you've lost one of your admirers, Mischa."

She turned on me, practically spitting venom. "Shut up, mixed-blood. No one asked for your opinion."

I clenched my teeth and glared at her, refusing to let her get the best of my temper. I turned to Slade. "Can we go now?"

Slade shook his head. "Not until Mischa explains what she's doing here."

Mischa crossed her arms. "I'm looking for Zeke."

Slade's eyes narrowed. "This is my hit, Mischa. Back the fuck off."

"What are you talking about? The Dominae assigned me to this case."

"Bullshit."

She smiled, showing a flash of fang. "Guess they figured you'd be handicapped with the half-breed." She sent a venomous glance my way. "Face it, Slade. With her slowing you down, it'll be a miracle if you win this one."

I was still stewing when Slade dropped me off. After Mischa's insults, he had to physically remove me from Zeke's house. Lucky for her he had, because I'd been about two seconds from going Three Mile Island on her ass.

If Slade felt angry about the fact the Dominae brought Mischa in as insurance, he wasn't showing it.

"Stop sulking," Slade said. "If you let her get a rise out of you, she'll win every time." He pulled the van to a stop next to my car.

"I'm not sulking," I lied. "I was trying to come up with a strategy."

"Mmm-hmm," he said. "Do you always pout when you strategize?"

That was it. I'd been insulted enough for one night. I turned to Slade with a glare. "You know what? I don't think this partnership's going to work out for me after all."

He didn't seem impressed by my declaration. "Oh, I see." He nodded, as if he'd just had a revelation. "You're giving up."

"No, I'm not. I just prefer to work alone."

Slade sighed. "That's not an option and you know it. Until I give the Dominae the all clear on you, you're not allowed to pursue perps on your own."

I rammed my fist into the dashboard. He was right, but I didn't like it. I'd worked my ass off in assassin school and paid my dues for close to a decade to get this chance. Having to shadow an arrogant ass was insult added to injury.

"You're going to pay for that," Slade said calmly, looking at the dent I'd left in the dashboard.

"Fuck off." I slammed out of the van and stopped at my car. Anger and shame warred for supremacy in my gut. Anger because I was sick and tired of being underestimated. Shame because I was having a tantrum in front of an assassin of Slade's calibre.

Behind me, Slade rolled down the window. "Sabina?"

I whipped towards him. "What?"

"I'll pick you up tomorrow night."

I stopped cold. "What?"

"Which word didn't you understand?" he said, brow furrowing.

I blew out a breath, feeling like an ass for my display of temper. "No. What I meant was, are you sure you want to work with me?"

He frowned. "Why wouldn't I?"

I crossed my arms, hating him a little bit for making me spell it out. "Well, for one, not many vampires would choose a mixed-blood for a partner. And the Dominae obviously think I'm a fuck up, so I can't imagine why you'd bother."

He laughed at me. I narrowed my eyes, not understanding how anything I'd said was funny. "Grow up, little girl. This isn't about you and your pride. It's about the job." He paused and leaned out the window. "You want to be a good assassin?"

I assumed the question was rhetorical so I didn't answer at first. But he remained silent for so long it became apparent he expected an answer. I lifted my chin. "I don't want to be good. I want to be the best."

He bobbed his head, obviously approving of the answer. "You'll never be the best if you allow your feelings to get in the way of the job. So suck it up, sweetheart. Kill Zeke, collect the reward and move on. Self-pity has no place in our line of work."

On the outside, I probably looked as stubborn as ever. My arms stayed crossed, my chin stayed raised, and my eyes stayed narrowed. But on the inside, his words washed through me like ice water. It wasn't easy to accept that my emotions had been getting the best of me. But he was right. The longer I let my grandmother's underestimation of my abilities hurt me, the longer it would take for me to earn her respect. Females like Lavinia Kane didn't respect whiners. They respected doers – like Slade.

"Besides," Slade continued, "do you really want to let Mischa win?"

At that moment, something shifted inside me. Fighting against the prejudices I faced was a waste of time. From now on, I'd focus on being the best assassin I could be. I'd start by working with Slade and learning everything I could from him. And lesson number one was most definitely learned.

Finally, I nodded. "I'll see you tomorrow."

The corner of Slade's mouth lifted, and he nodded approvingly. "Yes, ma'am."

When I got into the van the next night, I handed Slade the matchbook I'd grabbed from Zeke's desk.

"What's this?" He held the book up to the light. It was from someplace called Jack's Hideaway in Long Beach.

"Found that in Zeke's office last night," I said. "I pocketed it just before we were interrupted by the trampire."

"And?"

"I called. Looks like Mr Z. Calebow missed the 'use a pseudonym' lesson in extortion school."

"What an idiot," Slade said. "Let's go."

We hit the 710 about seven o'clock. Big mistake. Traffic didn't just crawl; it oozed. I settled into my seat, prepared for a long wait.

"Thanks for the pep talk last night," I said.

Slade looked at me out of the corner of his eye. "No problem. We all need a good kick in the ass every now and then."

"I find it hard to imagine you ever need one."

He laughed. "You'd be surprised. I won't lie to you; the life of an assassin isn't easy. Since you're just starting out it's best to learn that early."

My life hadn't ever been what anyone would consider easy, I thought. "How long have you been doing this?"

He shrugged. "About thirty years now."

"Do you ever regret it? Becoming an assassin, I mean."

He paused, as if weighing his response. "Sometimes. It's a lonely life. And I have to admit I don't always see eye to eye with the Dominae." His words came out in a measured tone, each carefully chosen.

"I can see that, I guess. Have you ever killed someone and regretted it?"

He shifted in the seat. "Traffic's heavy tonight."

And with that, the door slammed shut on our conversation. The shades were drawn. And the "do not disturb" sign flashed like neon in the dark car.

Jack's Hideaway squatted on the side of the freeway like a beggar. The sign featured flashing neon palm trees and advertised rooms by the hour.

"Charming place," I observed as Slade pulled into the parking lot. The peeling turquoise doors opened directly onto the parking lot. The cars of choice for the discerning Hideaway patron seemed to be semi trailers and jalopies.

After making a circle of the building to make sure Zeke couldn't slip through a rear exit, Slade pulled into a parking space at the far end of the lot.

"OK, his room's on the second floor." Slade pointed to the door next to the metal stairwell.

"You think he's in there?"

Slade nodded. "My gut tells me yes. But he may not be alone. Be prepared for anything." He went into the back of the van and started filling his pockets with weapons. "I'll take point. You hang back. If he gets past me, put a bullet between his eyes. Got it?"

I nodded. My heart kicked up a notch. It was finally happening. My first kill.

The parking lot was deserted. The traffic from the freeway muted our progress up the stairs. It wouldn't cover the sound of gunfire though, so I'd made sure to slip on a silencer.

Slade took point on the left side of the door and I took the right, ready to get his back. Staying to the side, Slade knocked on the door.

"What?" a surly male voice called from inside. Zeke.

"Maintenance."

"Fuck off." The voice was closer now. A shadow passed over the peephole. Slade didn't bother responding. He kicked the door in, slamming it into Zeke's face. The overweight vamp fell back with his hands over his nose, screaming blood murder.

Then, with surprising speed, he barrelled past Slade and knocked me over. I fell on my ass just as he launched over the railing and took off across the parking lot.

"Fuck!" Slade yelled and took off after him. I scrambled to my feet with a few choice curses of my own. I jumped over the railing and shot across the parking lot.

Somewhere behind me, I heard a door slam, followed by the sound of high heels on pavement. A familiar female voice cursed loudly. I didn't look back, but I'd have bet cash money Mischa followed us to the hotel, hoping to cut in on the action.

With my eyes on Slade's receding back, I pumped my legs faster. I didn't want to miss out on the kill when it went down. I was closing in on him when Zeke turned right down an alley. As we rounded the corner, I came even with Slade.

Up ahead, Zeke jumped on top of a dumpster. With wide eyes, he glanced back at us. Then he jumped up to grab the bottom of a fire escape. He pulled it down and scrambled up the ladder onto the escape. Then he pulled the ladder up behind him.

Slade paused. "Go around the front of the building in case he comes back down!"

I stopped, panting for breath. "Why me?"

"Really? You're going to argue now?" He looked over his shoulder at Mischa, who ran towards us in her five-inch heels.

"Fine, but if you reach him first wait until I catch up."

Slade nodded impatiently and jumped up on the dumpster. "Go!"

I backtracked, zooming past Mischa without a second glance. I heard her skitter to a halt. "Where are you going?" She turned to follow me.

I ignored her and ran around to the front of the apartment building. The lobby was deserted, thank the gods. My boots clomped across the linoleum towards the stairs. The door opened behind me and Mischa's heels joined my boots in echoing off the walls.

"Sabina," she whisper-yelled. "What's going on?"

I needed to ditch her before she got in the way. Skidding to a halt, I turned. "Mischa, thank the goddess you're here. Zeke's on his way out the front door," I lied. "You stay here and bag him when he comes your way."

She narrowed her eyes, trying to figure out if she could trust me. "I don't know –"

I heaved a big sigh. "Fine. You can explain to the Dominae why you let him go when he comes this way."

She lifted her chin. "All right, but if I bag him I'm not splitting the money with you."

"Whatever. Just stay there and make sure he doesn't get away."

Without waiting for a response, I turned and ran up the stairs towards the roof. Four flights later, I burst through the metal door. Male grunts echoed across the barren landscape. Adrenaline surged. I rounded the corner to see Slade and Zeke knocking the shit out of each other.

As I rushed towards them, I was surprised to see Slade having so much trouble sealing the deal. Sure, he'd promised to wait for me to get there for the kill, but I hadn't expected him to follow through on it. Every assassin knows when you get an opening to finish the job you take it. But Slade didn't even have a stake in his hand. Sure, Zeke was fighting, but he was also winded and scared. Slade should have had the advantage hands down.

I pulled my gun from my waistband and advanced. Slade pushed Zeke back against the low wall surrounding the roof. Slade must've heard me because next thing I knew, he yelled, "Shoot him!"

Normally, I wouldn't have hesitated, but my hands shook and sweaty palms made my grip slippery. I didn't want to risk missing and clipping Slade by mistake. "I can't!"

When Slade looked over his shoulder at me, Zeke clocked him on the side of the head and took off running again. Slade swept his feet under Zeke's legs, knocking the fat bastard to the ground. Then Slade jumped over and grabbed the gun from my hands. He spun and took a shot.

The bullet whizzed by a good foot from Zeke's head. He lurched off the ground and rammed his good shoulder into Slade. The assassin cursed and fell on his ass. Zeke loomed over him, but Slade still had the gun.

Now, I thought, now he'll get him.

Slade pulled the trigger. The bullet went wide again and lodged itself in an HVAC unit. My mouth dropped open; shocked he could miss such an easy shot.

Zeke, spurred on by adrenaline, ran towards the door – and me. Driven by pain and fear, he barrelled right towards me. I bent my knees and pulled my spare gun from my waistband.

For one second, Zeke's face was a mask of rage coming towards me. Then time slowed, and the gun in my slippery grip exploded.

Blood burst from Zeke's right eye socket. His body jerked back, his arms going wide in forced surrender. He ignited before his body hit the rooftop.

I stood still for a moment as the shock of what I'd done soaked in. "I did it," I whispered. "I finally did it."

Slade groaned on the ground nearby. I walked over and gave him a hand up. "You OK?" I asked.

He nodded. "Sorry 'bout that," Slade said, motioning vaguely. "It's been a while since I shot a gun."

"No problem," I said, somewhat shakily. "At least we got him."

"You did good," he said. He gently pulled the gun from my steely grip. "You did real good."

I wiped my sweaty palms on my jeans. "Guess we'll need to call the sweepers to clean up this mess."

"We need to go back to the hotel to gather the evidence. I'll call it in then."

Just then, the door to the roof slammed open. Mischa exploded through it at full speed. When she saw the pile of ash smouldering on the ground, she yelled, "No! This was *my* kill."

Slade shot me a grin. "Day late and a dollar short as usual, Mischa."

Mischa stamped her feet and punched the wall – a vampire temper tantrum. Pitiful.

Slade turned to me and slung his arm across my shoulder. "Come on, Sabina. Let's go celebrate your first kill."

I couldn't sit still on the way home. By the time he turned into my neighbourhood, Slade looked at me with a rueful smile. "I remember my first kill," he said wistfully.

Needing something to do to distract me from my restlessness, I turned to him. "Tell me about it."

He shrugged. "Not much to tell really. It was a female. She'd cooked some of the Dominae's books. Siphoned a couple hundred thousand before anyone detected it. Easy kill. But I'll never forget how I felt after."

"Excited?"

He smiled, turning into my driveway. "More than that. The closest word I can think of is *aroused*." He punctuated the word by slamming the van into park.

"Yes," I said, looking him in the eye. "Aroused. That's the perfect word."

He watched me in the dark, saying nothing.

"Do you still feel that way after a kill?" I asked, licking my lips.

He answered with his mouth, but not with words. One second he was on his side of the van, watching me with heat in his eyes. The next he was on me. I welcomed the contact, revelling in another type of adrenaline. His fang scraped my lip, and he sucked on the sting, heightening the pain . . . and the pleasure.

We barely made it inside before the clothes came off. A small voice in the back of my head wondered if this was a mistake. After all, sex and business never mix well. But, another voice said, You're off the clock. The mission was successful, and it's time to celebrate.

I chose to listen to the latter voice, and welcomed Slade's tongue in my mouth once again. His copper scent combined with the musk of exertion from the night's battle. He slammed me up against the wall and I felt the drywall give with the force of his thrusts. I wrapped my legs around his hips, meeting him thrust for thrust. He filled me thoroughly, but I wasn't content to let him have control.

He reached up and grabbed a handful of my hair. I jerked away and lowered my legs. I pushed him back roughly towards a dining room chair. Slade smiled and obeyed. He fell heavily onto it and pulled me down after him. My legs bracketed his hips. I dug my toes into the hardwood floor for a better grip. My nails dug into his shoulders, leaving small beads of blood, which I licked away. Slade groaned and urged me on with delightfully lewd whispers.

I'd had sex before, but those had been restrained, polite affairs with upper-class vampires who thought bagging a mixed-blood would be an adventure. But behind Slade's tightly controlled facade lurked an animalistic lover. One spurred on by the excitement of the kill. My own internal beast rose to meet his and I gave him back as good as I got. Scratching, clawing, fucking until we were both left sweaty and spent on the cold floor. And when my orgasm exploded, the primal scream came from the dark place inside where the beast lived.

The next evening, I woke to Slade's hand caressing my hair. My eyes fluttered open. He sat on the edge of the bed. His clothes were on and he had his keys in his hand.

"You're leaving?" I said.

"Got to go pick up our payment, but I'll be back."

"Cool," I said lamely. The muscles in my shoulders relaxed. It's not that I expected him to declare himself just because we'd screwed. But still. No one liked it when their partner dashed out the door after a night of hot, sweaty sex. "Fifty–fifty, right?" I joked.

He smiled. "You don't give up, do you?"

"You'll find I always get what I want," I said.

He leaned down and kissed me. Unlike the frenzied kisses last night, this one was long and slow. Tender. Almost like he was saying goodbye instead of "see ya soon". When he pulled away and smiled, I shook off the heavy feeling of foreboding. "Fifty–fifty it is," he said.

"Excellent. When you get back we'll celebrate."

For a split second, I thought I saw a shadow pass behind his hooded eyes. But then he patted my ass and rose. "It's a date. Be back soon."

I leaned back in the bed and listened to him leave. His footsteps on the hardwood floor. The click of the door closing. Then, a few moments later, the van's engine roaring to life.

I clenched my stomach muscles against the tickle of excitement. Everything was coming together for the first time in my life. I'd finally made my first kill. Now my grandmother would have to accept my competence.

And the fact I'd managed to finally outdo that bitch Mischa Petrov made the victory so much sweeter. The look on her face when she realized we'd beaten her was worth more to me than any monetary reward.

And what about Slade? Right then, Slade was a big question mark. A very sexy, intense question mark. I scooted down into the covers as a smile spread across my face.

Sure, the job didn't leave a lot of room for romance, but there was no reason we couldn't be friends with benefits. Using each other to work off the post-job glow, as it were. And, who knew? Maybe we could even be partners. I allowed myself to daydream about us teaming up on more missions. He'd teach me everything he knew about being an assassin, and I'd reward him with hot, steamy sex. Seemed like a fair deal.

I slammed my fist into the table. "Where is he?" I demanded. All rational thought had flown out the window in the last twenty-four hours, but it wasn't until this moment that rage filled up the hollow place logic had abandoned.

"Calm yourself," my grandmother, Lavinia Kane, snapped. "We don't know where he went."

When Slade failed to reappear the night before, I'd spent the first hour in denial. Traffic, I'd reasoned. By the third hour, I'd paced a trough in my floor. By sunrise, after several unanswered phone messages, I'd gone into panic mode. What if something happened to him? Every now and then, even good assassins lost their luck and fell under the gun of a pissed off friend or relative.

I'd called the Dominae headquarters just before sunrise, hoping they'd heard something. Tanith informed me that Slade had come by to collect the payment as expected. She hadn't heard from him since, she said – not to worry.

After a sleepless day, my phone rang at about 7 pm. I'd rushed to answer, convinced Slade was calling to explain. Instead, my grandmother commanded me to report to the compound ASAP. I'd driven over with dread pooling in my gut like tar.

When I arrived, my grandmother gave me her theory on what happened to Slade.

"After you called last night, Tanith sent someone to check Slade's house. The signs of a hasty departure were unmistakable."

"But we don't know for sure he ran. Maybe someone kidnapped him," I said.

Tanith shook her head. "He also left this." She slid a note across the desk. As I read the letter, my dread morphed into black rage.

The note was addressed to the Dominae. The content was short and to the point: "I can't do this any more."

"How could he just disappear like that? Surely someone knows where he went," I said.

Tanith shook her head. "Sabina, Slade is one of our best assassins. He knows how to disappear when he wants to. We don't even know how long he'd been planning this or if it was a spur of the moment thing."

I closed my eyes. I'd been so stupid. A foolish girl blinded by hero worship and eagerness to please. On that first night, Slade had said he had a lot riding on this mission. I saw now that he'd been planning to leave before I even entered the picture. He'd played me for three days, allowing me to think we were a team. Truth was, I'd been nothing but a pawn in his plan to cut and run.

Why had he run? Well, he'd mentioned not seeing eye to eye with the Dominae. And when I'd asked him if he regretted killing anyone, he'd clammed up.

"Oh shit," I said as the rest became clear.

"What?"

"Does Slade ever use guns?"

Tanith and Lavinia shared a confused glance. "Of course. He's an excellent marksman. Why?"

I closed my eyes and shook my head. "He told me he didn't like to use guns. He only carried stakes when we were together."

"That makes no sense," Tanith said.

"It makes perfect sense. Last night, he deliberately missed Zeke twice. He all but forced me to carry out the kill."

"Why would he do that?" Lavinia asked.

"Don't you see? Slade lost his edge. That's why he ran. He said he couldn't take it any more." I held up the note. "He used me to kill Zeke so he could collect the money and run."

"Wait – you made the kill?" Lavinia said. "Slade told me you froze and he had to finish the job."

Before this little revelation, I'd been hot with anger. Now, the blood in my veins became an ice floe. "Did he? And I'm sure you bought that, didn't you? Easier to believe I choked than to believe that Slade was playing you all for fools!"

"That's enough!" Lavinia yelled.

"You're right. It is enough. I will not be punished for Slade's choices. I carried out the mission as instructed. I want you to clear me for solitary kills." I thought about asking them to pay me, but that didn't matter any more. I wasn't going to let Slade's duplicity screw me out of my chance to be a real assassin.

My grandmother stared me down with black eyes. I didn't flinch – didn't give her a hint of weakness to use as an excuse to deny me. Finally, she lowered her chin. "Fine. But you must promise to speak to no one about Slade's desertion. Is that clear?"

I jerked a nod. "Crystal."

"I'd hoped working with Slade would teach you lessons about how to be a good assassin," Tanith said, shaking her head.

"Don't worry, Domina. The lesson Slade taught me was much more valuable than any he could have planned."

"And what might that be?" Lavinia said.

I shook my head and turned to go. They allowed me to leave without comment. But as I walked out of the room and saw the hostile faces of the Undercouncil, and those other vampires who saw me as nothing more than a mixed-blood, the lesson echoed through my head.

I'll always be better off alone.

On the heels of that sad realization, I also knew I hadn't seen the last of Slade Corbin. I wasn't sure when. I wasn't sure where. But one of these days, I'd make sure he understood no one screws Sabina Kane – metaphorically or literally – and just walks away.

Trust Me

Stacia Kane

Chapter One

Whitechapel, London
3 September 1888

"So she was a prostitute?" John leaned back in his chair. He didn't want to hire a prostitute again. There had been too many of them, too many women he'd trained and come to know a little, only to have them leave again – usually carrying a piece or two of his silver and a bottle of liquor – and head back out to the streets.

At the same time, given the news that was all over the district this morning . . . how could he turn the girl away?

"She says no, sir." Mrs Langley smoothed her black skirts with her hands. "But I'm not certain she's telling the truth."

John nodded. He could easily find out. "Send her in."

Mrs Langley bobbed a quick curtsey and left the room, returning a moment later with the girl in question.

At first glance John thought her nothing special. Wisps of dark hair peeked out from under a respectable brown bonnet; her pale face floated above the neckline of an equally dull dress ten years out of date. She was slim and looked clean, and that was all that mattered. It wasn't until he looked again that he saw how pleasing were the angles of her face, how delightfully plump her lips. She was quite attractive, no matter how or why she chose to hide it.

"Sit down, Mrs Richards." He indicated one of the deep leather chairs in front of his desk, hiding his awkwardness behind a smooth, calm manner. Mrs Langley did all of the hiring and firing of household staff for his home in Westminster, and John barely noticed the maids who washed his dirty linens or scrubbed his fireplace.

But this was different, just as the house here was different. His home and offices in Whitechapel served a different purpose from his Westminster home, and if he hired this woman in front of him, she would be spending time here with him in addition to whatever other duties Mrs Langley would give her. He needed a woman who knew the area, a woman who would teach him about it. Most of all, he needed a woman who could be discreet.

For this Mrs Richards certainly looked the part. He would know more when she spoke. The thought of having a screeching Whitechapel harpie bludgeoning the English tongue in close quarters with him on a daily basis made the hair at the back of his neck stand on end.

Mrs Richards sat, folding her hands neatly on her lap. There was something dignified about her that John liked. It boded well for her.

"Tell me about yourself," he said. "Have you worked in service before? How did you come to be here today?"

Mrs Richards paused a half-beat before she spoke. There was vulnerability in that pause, and it made John oddly protective of her. When she finally did speak, her voice was low and soothing, with no trace of the horrible East End accent he'd so feared.

"My husband died, sir. Almost a year ago. I've been in service ever since." She paused again before the words "in service".

"What kind of service?" John leaned forwards. "With whom?"

"I did laundry for Mrs Grant on Varden Street. I cooked a little for Mr Bright on Cannon Street Road." She looked right at him as she spoke, steady and unflinching. Where had this woman gained such dignity, working as a laundress and a cook? Or had she always had it, and the travails of such employment had not managed to erase it from her?

He was intrigued enough to want to find out. "Did you do any other types of work?"

Pause. "What other types of work?"

John signalled for Mrs Langley to leave them alone, waiting until the housekeeper had bustled out of the room before speaking again. "Did you work as a prostitute, Mrs Richards?" He stood and opened the heavy sideboard, removing a crystal decanter of sherry and pouring her a glass. "Go ahead, take it. You look parched."

She smiled her thanks, but did not look particularly grateful. This was surely the oddest interview he'd ever had in his life. She seemed to be sizing him up, not the other way around. He liked that, though. He realized he liked *her*.

"If I had," she said, "I don't see why it should matter."

"I suppose it shouldn't. But I would like to know, just the same."

She shrugged. "Does the timing of my arrival here seem like a coincidence?"

"You mean the murders?"

"Yes." Two of them now. Martha Tabram and, only two nights before, Polly Nichols. Both of them viciously slashed . . . mutilated.

John sat down on the edge of his desk, close enough to her to look into her eyes. He realized as he did so that he'd been curious all this time as to their colour, and the discovery that they were green was quite satisfying. They were also large and steady, and now that he was closer to her he found she smelled faintly of lavender and rosewater. Her skin truly was perfect, as pale as milk, from her face down the slender column of her throat. He could see her pulse beating faintly there, betraying her outward calm.

"I assume many ladies are trying to get off the streets," he said as non-committally as he could. "Perhaps even ladies who just arrived on them."

"Perhaps that life was not to their tastes after all, sir," Mrs Richards said.

"Perhaps they could earn more money doing the same job privately, and enjoy it more as well."

The minute it came out of his mouth he regretted it. Was he mad? This woman had come here to be a secretary to him. Now he was actually propositioning her, and he couldn't for the life of him understand why, except he wanted to know what made her tick. He wanted to know what sorts of emotions hid beneath that calm face . . . what sorts of passions beat in the heart beneath the gentle swell of her bosom.

She blinked, once. The first show of emotion he'd seen from her. "Perhaps they could." Another delicate pause. "If the terms were right, and the employer agreeable."

"Do you find me agreeable, Mrs Richards?" His voice sounded hoarse, echoing strangely in his head; his trousers were uncomfortably tight. This was certainly not the type of interview he'd planned to have, but he found, as the minutes stretched while he waited for her answer, that he desperately hoped she would say yes. The desire to break through that calm exterior and see what lay beneath was almost overwhelming.

She shrugged again, a tiny smile playing across her face. "You're a handsome gentleman, sir. What woman wouldn't find you agreeable?"

He couldn't wait any longer. His hands gripped her shoulders, lifting her from her seat to press against him as he lowered his mouth to hers.

That first taste of her . . . it was like nothing he'd ever experienced before. Sherry and honey, and the pure sweetness of her mouth. Whatever she'd been doing for the last year, she still tasted like a virgin.

But she didn't kiss like one. The tongue that met his was sensuous, soft, accepting. The arms that wound around his neck as he squeezed her tighter were passionate, willing. He groaned into her mouth and she echoed it, and he believed. She wasn't putting on a show. Something was happening, some spark had caught fire between them, and he for one wasn't going to question it. Especially not at that moment.

His hands travelled down, cupping the curve of her behind and pressing her against him. He dipped his head, kissing that delicate throat. Beneath his lips her blood raced like a hare's. He had to fight to control himself.

Damn those heavy skirts! He wanted to feel her, really feel her, but it was impossible with so many layers of petticoats in the way. "Turn around," he managed.

She paused. Her lips looked plump and bruised from their passion. "Turn around."

Her brow furrowed slightly – he could only imagine what she must be thinking, if she'd truly been on the streets – but she obeyed him. Both actions pleased him. She had her own mind, but acknowledged his dominance. He'd never met a woman who did both before, not like this, with her particular cool control.

He couldn't wait to watch her lose it.

Gently he pulled the tie of her bonnet and removed it. The pins holding her tidy bun in place slipped out easily, releasing a soft mass of hair that caught the light from the candles and sent it back in sparks of deep blue. Black as night, black as a sinner's soul, her hair. He longed to see it spread over her pale naked flesh.

Still standing behind her, he reached forwards and unfastened the long row of buttons down her front. More of her neck and shoulders were exposed with every one. So pale. So beautiful. He pressed his lips over the delicate ridge of a collarbone, over the smooth curve of her shoulder, and swept her heavy hair off to the other side.

He glanced up. Her expression was still composed, but her lips were parted. Above the confines of her corset her breasts rose and fell rapidly. She may be able to hide her feelings on her face, but her body did not lie. Neither did his. When had he last wanted a woman this badly, been this desperate to take one?

Not yet. Not until he managed to break that steely composure.

Gently he slid the gown off her shoulders and down, so the pale ivory of her corset was her only covering from the waist up, her drawers and petticoat from the waist down. The petticoat he untied and tugged out from under the corset, letting it pool at her feet, before finally taking down the scrupulously clean and almost invisibly mended drawers.

Her skin was cool under his palm as he caressed one round cheek, then the other. He leaned forwards, running his hands down her front and resting them on her thighs, his thumbs barely touching the curls covering her sex.

Her breath hitched, but he saw no other reaction.

Those curls parted under his questing fingers easily, smoothly. His nose tingled with the musky, erotic scent of her. She shuddered in his arms, but still did not speak. Did not turn to look at him, did not move her hips eagerly forwards. But her throat worked as he began teasing her, exploring her with his fingertips.

"Mrs Richards," he whispered, letting his lips tickle her ear. Her pale flesh was turning pink, the colour spreading over her breasts and throat like a winter sunrise. "Do you find that agreeable?"

Finally she moved. She reached back and ran one hand smoothly over the front of his trousers. "Do *you* find *that* agreeable, Mr March?"

He couldn't take it any more. With a growl that seemed to come from somewhere below his waist he swung her around to face him, then moved once again so he could prop her on the edge of his desk. Desire glowed in her heavy-lidded eyes.

And her body . . . her breasts spilled over the top of her corset, her hips swelled like a cherry beneath it. Her thighs were slim and pale, the place between them perfect.

His cock leaped in his trousers, reminding him he had other things to do, more important things than simply standing here and staring at her all day. She was so calm. Even now.

And not a prostitute's calm. Not boredom. She wanted him, he knew it. The evidence stared him in the face and still coated his fingers. But she was hiding something, a part of herself, and John couldn't help but admire her for that. He did the same.

But he was better at it. He would defeat her in this.

He thrust his fingers under the cups of her corset and scooped her breasts out of it, dipping his head first to one, then the other, and rolling her nipples in his mouth. She gasped. A tiny gasp, but a gasp just the same. Otherwise she stayed still, with one lock of silky black hair falling over her shoulder and into her cleavage.

What would it take? He kissed her, taking another long taste of her sweetness, and found he could not leave again. The kiss continued while he put his hand back to work between her legs. Another gasp.

If he didn't get a real response, a vocal one, from her soon he would explode. "Tell me you want me," he demanded, his own voice none too steady. "Tell me."

She didn't reply. He withdrew his hand, withdrew himself, and faced her as she perched on the edge of the desk with her small pert breasts free from her corset and her legs spread. She looked, flushed with heat, less like a plain but alluring woman and more like a demon sent to tempt him, to steal his soul. Her eyes shone with hidden secrets.

Furiously he removed his own clothing, letting her see his excitement. Baring himself the way he desperately wished she would bare her thoughts. Her eyes widened. She bit her lower lip as he stepped close to her once more, until her heat bathed him. Her hips moved, urging him to enter her. He had to force himself not to close his eyes.

"Tell me."

Again she pressed her hips forwards. Her body begged him, but her lips made no sound, and it was her words he needed.

"Tell me!"

"Please . . . " 'Her calves wrapped around his waist, her wool stockings slightly rough against his bottom. "Please."

It was something. Not what he'd demanded, but something. Maybe she deserved a reward.

A reward for her or for him? Slowly, oh so slowly, he thrust into her. Her eyes fluttered closed, her head fell back.

He pulled out, all the way. Her eyes flew open. Her calves jerked, trying to force him back, but he held fast. "Tell me you want me. Say it!"

"Oh God . . . I want you!" The cool, sweet voice he'd heard earlier was rough, desperate. "I want you, I want you, oh please . . . "

The litany of her capitulation was lost in the roaring in his ears as he drove into her, hard, and kept driving, slamming into her with a speed and ferocity he'd not felt in years. He dug his fingers into her hips, bent to nibble at her throat. Her body thrilled him almost as much as her submission.

She found his mouth, sucking his lips, biting them softly, as her arms stole around his neck and her legs urged him faster, deeper. "Mr March," she gasped, her fingers tightening, gripping his shoulders almost painfully. "Do I have the job?"

"Yes, God yes!"

Mrs Richards would have to stay.

Chapter Two

Whitechapel, London
5 September 1888

The pile of laundry sat on the floor in the hot, damp kitchen. Glancing around to make sure the cook and scullery maid were still outside, she started yanking clothes out of the pile. One white shirt after another, all limp and smelling of her employer.

Her employer . . . her lover. She hadn't expected that to happen so quickly.

She hadn't expected to enjoy it so much, either. From the moment he'd propositioned her during her interview, to the moment he took her on the desk in his office, they'd hardly kept their hands off each other. And when they weren't together, she thought about him. Remembered him.

It scared her. If her suspicions were correct ... she shook her head. What did it matter? If her suspicions were correct, it would be worth it. If they weren't, it was worth it even more. John March was a truly talented man.

The shirts were clean. No spots of blood marred the white linen.

She hadn't really expected there to be any, not really. Surely a man cunning enough to commit the murders – a man the press was now calling "Leather Apron" – wouldn't put his bloodstained clothing in with the rest of his week's washing, not when servants talked as much as they did. It had been worth a look, though.

She stood up, peering once more out the window. The heavy skirts of the two servants were still visible through the dusty glass. Good. Now if she could get into his bedroom without being seen, she could search there, too. John had spent the night at his other home in Westminster, and she had spent the night at her room on Leman Street. There hadn't been much reason for her to be at the house if he wasn't, and of course neither of them would dream of suggesting she accompany him to Westminster.

His bedroom was dark. She lit the candle that stood on the small shelf by the door, not wanting to open the curtains even though the sun was barely risen. Most fashionable homes were dark to keep the sun from fading the beautiful fabrics and expensive furnishings, but John went beyond the desire into something of a mania. Three sets of heavy red brocade curtains hung on all of the windows on the second floor, and woe betide any maid caught opening them while the sun still floated in the sky.

There was nothing in any of the drawers, either. No weapons, no small boxes filled with locks of hair or bits of cloth.

Sighing, she sunk to her knees by the bed and felt around on the dusty floor. She should really get the housemaid in here to clean. Shameful to let things get dirty like that.

Under the bed was even worse. She stuck her head and shoulders beneath it, wishing there was enough room for a candle.

"Euphemia?"

Oh, no. "John?" She was acutely aware of her skirted bottom poking up into the air, of how embarrassing a position this was to be caught in.

"My dear, what are you doing?"

Oh please let me think of a good lie. "I was lonely," she said. "So I decided to come wait for you in here . . . but one of my hairpins fell out. I think it went under the bed." She paused. Did he believe her? "You ought to speak to Mrs Langley. It's very dusty under here."

The amusement in his voice was at once a relief and a further humiliation. "We can't have you getting dusty while you clamber around under my bed, can we?" His footsteps were quiet, but Euphemia felt them vibrate the wood floor just the same. She scooted out from under the bed, her feet hitting his legs in her haste, and straightened up, still on her knees but no longer bent over.

"Did you find it?" In the wavering light of the candle she'd set by the bed his eyes glittered. His skin looked almost eerily perfect, his handsome features slightly distorted. He was at once handsome and a little scary as he knelt on the floor just behind her. She had to crane her neck to look at him, but could not tear her eyes away.

"I'll look later," she said. "You're here early today."

"I've been here for an hour or so, in the office," he said. "I didn't see you there."

"I was in the kitchen." Her heart beat a little faster. Did he know what she'd been doing? Had he heard her opening drawers? He may even have stood and watched her doing it. She'd noticed he was incredibly silent when he wanted to be. "I was hungry."

"Hmmm." His hands found her waist and moved lower, stroking her hips through her heavy skirts. "I'm a little hungry myself." He gently guided her back to her hands and knees before him.

Fear added an extra bit of spice to her excitement as his hands continued to roam, unbuttoning the long row of ivory buttons up the front of her gown, pulling the dress down off her shoulders to her waist. She waited for him to untie the strings on her plain brown corset and remove it, too, but he did not, instead he pushed the dress over her hips and tugged her drawers down. She felt the waistband slip out from under the bottom of her corset and the cool air that now caressed her exposed bottom.

Surely it was wrong to enjoy this so much. To know that her employer may well be evil, but to still crave the feel of his fingers on her skin, slipping between her legs to caress her soft wet flesh. To crave the moment when his fingers disappeared and were replaced by something even more satisfying.

It was shameful, and Euphemia Richards knew it. But that did not stop her from crying out her satisfaction when John started thrusting into her, sending shivers of pure delight through her body with every stroke. His fingers dug into her hips, urging her to push back against him, to match his rhythm.

Her head swam. He moved so slowly, so steadily, as if they had all the time in the world. She tried to push against him faster, to intensify the sensations that already made her body shake, but he would not comply.

"Only one of us is in charge here, my dear Euphemia," he murmured. The words were almost enough to send her over the edge. Whatever this meant about her as a woman she did not want to analyse. All she needed to know was that he could control her with as much ease as he sipped his tea. A part of her she had never known was there responded to him like she had never responded to anyone else.

One hand left her hip, sliding down to touch her belly, to slip through the hair that covered her modesty and tease her most sensitive spot. She gasped and struggled to open her legs wider, but she could not.

The hard smack on her bottom caught her off guard, made her yelp in surprise.

"Only one of us is in charge," he said again, more forcefully. At once he froze in place. "Perhaps you need to remind yourself who that is."

She wiggled her hips, knowing what his reaction would be and shamefully craving it, too.

He smacked her again, harder this time. The imprint of his hand on her skin burned through her entire body.

"Who is in charge?"

She wanted to wait. For years her ability to stay calm, to stay controlled, had been her greatest charm. No silly giggling or ribald jokes for Euphemia Richards, née Euphemia Harte. She'd been born dignified, her mother once told her, and, as she grew up and realized she was too plain for such things anyway, she'd learned her composure attracted men as much as girlish simpering.

But something about John destroyed that placidity, as easily as a glass dropped onto a marble floor.

"You are," she whimpered. "You're in control." Just saying the words had a physical effect.

"Good girl."

His fingers found her again and he resumed his movements, thrusting into her hard and fast, his free hand bracing her hips in place.

It was enough. It was too much. Without warning or preparation her body clenched around him and burst apart, an explosion of pleasure so intense she was light-headed. She cried his name, her voice ragged and unfamiliar to her ears, and heard John join in her ecstasy, felt him jerk out of her to spill his seed on the candlewick bedspread beside him.

No man had ever made her feel like this, not her husband, certainly not any of the men she'd been with since becoming a widow and a sometime-prostitute in quick succession.

He lifted her gently, helped her onto the bed, and she lay there weak and shaking, wondering if it were possible to experience such pleasure and not actually die from it. And even worse, if it was possible to experience such pleasure at the hands of a monster, if one could fall in love with a man one could not trust.

Suddenly John spoke.

"Here it is." He leaned over to pluck something from the floor by the bed, kissing her knee as he did so.

It was a hairpin. "It wasn't under the bed at all."

Euphemia smiled and took the little pin. "Thank you," she said, but something cold and watchful had awakened in her breast. The hairpin, a cheap wire pin of the sort worn by local prostitutes, did not belong to her.

Chapter Three

Little Ilford Cemetery
6 September 1888

The setting sun cast long shadows as the women walked back to the road, leaving the grave of Polly Nichols behind them. On the dirt path the horses pulling the two mourning coaches made dull thumps, echoing the slow beat of Euphemia's aching heart. She had not particularly liked Polly. Polly had not been her friend. But Polly had not deserved to die. Neither had any of the others.

"Any news, Euphemia?"

They'd been waiting to ask her this, Mary and Peggy and Caroline.

All through the short service she'd felt their eyes on her. Now the other funeral attendees were barely out of earshot. Euphemia glanced around, hoping someone would be near so she did not have to speak. But she was unlucky. No one was there to overhear.

"I found something," she said reluctantly, pulling the cheap hairpin from her pocket and handing it to Caroline. "But it was in the bedroom—"

"So he had a prostitute in his bedroom." Mary snatched the pin away from Caroline and held it up to the sun, one eye closed. "You know, they think he might be killing some of them privately. In his home, I mean. And then bringing the bodies out. They say that might be why nobody's seen him." Her high-pitched voice never failed to get on Euphemia's nerves, more so today. It was unholy, somehow, that bright, tinny chatter in the silence of the homes of the dead.

"Just because he might have had a prostitute in his room means nothing," Euphemia said.

"It means he sees prostitutes," Peggy replied. Her bushy eyebrows lifted, making her hooded, beady eyes appear a little bigger. She took the pin from Mary and repeated the latter's actions, even sniffing it.

"Every man sees prostitutes, Peggy." Why the casual judgment of her friends was so upsetting to Euphemia, she had no idea. Hadn't she been just as certain that John was the killer? Hadn't a cold rush of pure dread run through her body when she'd found the hairpin?

Since then she'd managed to find a thousand explanations for it. None of them convinced her. She had to admit there was still every possibility that John was the killer she sought, that the man whose hands made her tingle and shake, whose smile made her weaken, could be the same man who slit throats and eviscerated women she cared about.

"Every man may see prostitutes," Peggy said. "But not every man has them in his home. Your John did. No lady of quality wears such things in her hair." She said it as if she had intimate friends among the gentry. "So if he's the kind of man who needs a woman for an entire night . . . well, he must be doing something special with them, mustn't he? Something most men don't do?"

The words sent a shiver of violent memory through Euphemia's body. The things John did . . .

"If she doesn't think he's the killer, we should listen," Caroline said. The other two rolled their eyes.

"We said we would all decide," Peggy said. "That when someone was ruled out, it would be because we all agreed."

The women were at the entrance to the cemetery now, ready to go their separate ways. "Do you have enough proof to convince us he's not guilty?"

Euphemia shook her head.

"Have you been able to account for his whereabouts during any of the murders?"

Again, she shook her head. John had a habit of going out at night. She had no idea where he went. She didn't always spend the night either, so she didn't know what he did when she was not there. Loath as she was to admit it, both because of what it said about herself and what it said about him, she could not rule him out at all.

"In fact, this hairpin seems to prove he's up to no good, doesn't it?"

Sometimes she really hated Peggy. "I suppose so," she mumbled.

Peggy sniffed. "Then get back there and do what you promised to do. Find us a killer, or prove he isn't one."

The three of them swept away, leaving her standing at the gate of the cemetery alone.

The Royal Alhambra was hot and crowded, just as it was every opera night. John paid his shilling to walk the promenade, past families – the women tired and clean-scrubbed, the men resigned to a late start at the public houses and dreaming of their first pint. He could smell the desperation of the women, the attempts to inject some happiness and semblance of respectability into their lives by doing something as mundane as attending the ballet.

Beyond the families, and in some cases intermingled with them, were the whores. Less of them than usual, since the murders had started, but still more than enough. Some people wondered why they didn't just get off the streets. John knew why. They needed to eat. They needed their gin. There was no other way to escape the misery of their lives, their terrible huddled existences spent with their legs spread and their chests pressed against walls while men they did not know took them from behind.

It was a life he could not even imagine. The misery and pain, the struggle to survive. But John knew what it was like to hate yourself for what you must do to live. He'd long ago made peace with that part of his nature that required violence. He'd had to. It was that or kill himself, and somewhere in the darkness of the everlasting night, he'd realized there were too many good things in the world. Things he did not want to leave.

Through the crowd he spotted her. She could be his tonight. Her pale hair was gathered under a tattered bonnet, her blue dress clean enough under the gaslights.

She was not Euphemia. She was neither as lovely nor as dignified. But none of them were like Euphemia. One of these days he would tell her how special she was becoming to him. How important. Maybe then he could tell her what he was, what he did, and she would forgive him. Maybe she would join him.

He could only hope and think of her as he crossed the room to talk to the frail blonde, the music from the ballet making his pulse beat in time, a steady rhythm. Already the taste of her blood was in his mouth.

8 September 1888
Whitechapel, London

"Another murder."

"Another murder."

Everywhere Euphemia went the same words fell from everyone's lips. Annie Chapman. Murdered. Eviscerated. Discarded like a tattered stocking not five feet from the back steps of a rooming house. What devil could have done this – and done it undiscovered? How had he disappeared so quickly, fading into the shadows of the night while steam still rose from the body?

The brows of the shopkeepers furrowed as she walked past. Women she knew eyed her with suspicion, and she knew why. John. He'd come to Whitechapel only weeks before – just before the death of Martha Tabram. Euphemia and her friends were not the only ones who suspected him. He kept to himself. He never went out during the day.

She had not seen him the night before. Mrs Langley had not seen him either, swore he'd not been in his bed when she'd arisen at five. But when Euphemia arrived at seven he was there, asleep.

Annie had died half an hour past five. Lizzie Long had seen her, about to earn her bed money with a dark man wearing a deerstalker hat.

John had a deerstalker hat.

Was this possible?

No. It couldn't be. She *knew* John. It had only been a week since the day she'd walked into his house, but she knew him. The way he spoke to her, the things they talked about, the way he called responses from her body and soul she'd never thought herself capable of experiencing.

No. No man who encouraged her to speak her mind so freely, who held her so tenderly, could do such a thing to a woman, to any woman. The words ran through her mind, a pleading litany, as she entered the house and placed her purchase – three new pens – on John's desk. She snuck into his bedchamber. On the shiny dark floor lay a pile of white linen in a graceful heap. The shirt he'd stripped off when he climbed into bed.

She picked it up. Even in the dim light the blood was evident. Just a few drops, dotting the collar. A smudge on the right sleeve.

She couldn't breathe. *It can't be him, it can't be him, it can't be him* ... But how to explain this?

Calm down, Euphemia. Perhaps the barber cut him while shaving. Perhaps he pricked himself with a pin while affixing his collar. This isn't a lot of blood, hardly any at all. Surely Leather Apron would have been covered in blood, bathed in it, if the tales she'd heard about the state of Annie's remains were true.

"Euphemia? Are you well, dear?"

The shirt fell to the floor. "John!"

"Yes. At least, I am fairly certain it's me." He smiled. In the gloom she saw him look down at his bare chest, so beautifully cut with muscle and bone, a sculpture in white marble. "Is something the matter?"

"I – There's been another murder."

He didn't move. Not a flicker of an eyelash, not a muscle. "Where?"

"Hanbury Street."

"But that's ... " He shook his head. "Come here."

She did. It felt like treading through sewer slush. Was that terror making her blood pound, or something altogether more base? What was wrong with her? There could be blood on his hands, and yet she still wanted those hands on her body. He could be a cold-blooded murderer yet she still felt, as all silly women did when faced with such things, that it couldn't possibly be him. Not this man, the one she'd started to think of as hers, the one she was falling in love with so rapidly it made her dizzy.

He pulled her onto the bed and tucked the covers over her, ignoring her protests about her shoes.

"I can't imagine how this must hurt you," he murmured into her ear. "I'm so sorry." In the circle of his arms she could feel her heart pounding against her ribcage. Did he mean the murders, or her suspicions?

Surely he meant the murders. He couldn't know why she was really here. "But that's . . . what?"

"Hmm?" His lips tickled her throat.

"You started to say something. 'But that's . . . ' You didn't finish. What were you going to say?"

"That it's terrible. I was going to say, 'But that's terrible.'"

She wasn't sure she believed him. She wasn't sure she trusted herself to believe him. But when his hand slid forwards to cup her shoulder, to gently encourage her to slide further under the covers to where his excitement awaited her attentions, she forgot everything.

Because she wanted to.

Whitechapel, London
17 September 1888

John adjusted his collar and headed out onto the chilly streets, with Euphemia's hand tucked firmly into the crook of his arm. It would happen again soon, he knew it. He could feel it in the air. Time was running out.

He tried to ignore the looks on their faces as he passed. Members of the St Marylebone Female Protection Society, handing out their flyers, trying to use the crimes to get women off the streets. Members of the Mile End Vigilance Committee, trying to seem casual and looking at nothing but, watching them. Watching him. Suspecting him. They'd zeroed in on him faster than he'd expected; the residents may be poor and uneducated, but they were not stupid.

He hoped this little trip out might calm them, might let them see he was nothing more harmful than a gentleman of means, but it seemed to be backfiring. He appeared to be taunting them with his presence, flaunting his money as though it made him better than they. Unapproachable. Uncatchable.

Arrests had been made. The man everyone had suspected, whose nickname of "Leather Apron" had been given to the killer, had been caught and released. He had an alibi for the night of Annie Chapman's murder, and for Polly Nichols' as well. The killer was still out there, increasingly nicknamed "Jack" by a public desperate to put a name to evil. The similarity of that name to his own did not escape him.

The streets filled with edgy prostitutes and edgier men. Drinking both soothed and angered them, making them even more unstable than they already were.

In the middle of the night someone had thrown a brick through the front window of his home. John was starting to wonder if it wasn't time to pull out. Let someone else take over.

But then he felt the warmth of Euphemia's skin through his clothing, glanced to his side and saw her sweet profile. She felt it too, the glares of the crowd, but was as always unflappable. Breaking through her silent reserve thrilled him, and the thrill wasn't getting old. Almost three weeks now he'd had her in his life, in his bed. The three best weeks he could remember.

Her body, so small and light and alive in his arms. Her voice, ragged with thrilling, ever-rising need. It had started as a curiosity, a desire. It was becoming a compulsion.

And more than that. He ... *liked* her. He cared about her. The story of her life was all too common – shopkeeper's daughter from the South-west, married, moved to London, left a widow. Never enough money. Never enough food or warm clothing. But through it all she had the dignity of a duchess.

Then he would make her laugh and suddenly she was a mischievous child, and he would laugh too. She made him feel young again. Carefree. Good about himself.

He knew she had her suspicions. He knew he would have to explain soon, to tell her what he did and why, and hope she would see what really lay beneath his actions here in Whitechapel. That she would be able to forgive him for not telling her.

For now, though ...

"You look lost in thought," she murmured, squeezing his arm.

"I am."

"What about?"

He hesitated. "I was thinking about you."

"Me?" She smiled, but it only took a second for that flicker of doubt to enter her eyes.

"About how lovely you look this evening." He glanced around them. They were passing St Mary's Church, and the pedestrian crowds were smaller. He thought he saw a few women behind them who looked familiar. Hadn't he seen one of them every time he went out lately?

No matter. He leaned over and gently scraped Euphemia's ear lobe with his teeth. "But how much lovelier you look without your clothes on."

Even in the dim light cast by the moon he could see her blush. "John . . . "

He kissed her again, on the lips this time, not caring who saw them. What difference did it make? Who cared about his social standing in Westminster, when this beautiful woman stood before him and bit her luscious lower lip, her eyes darkening with desire?

He'd have to leave London soon anyway.

"Who's in charge, Euphemia?"

"You are." No hesitation. Her hand slid a little on his arm, rubbing against his chest.

"Step into that alley."

Her eyes flicked back towards the women – ah! – that explained it. But she obeyed. He could smell her desire already, warring with the faint touch of nervousness and fear in her eyes. She squared her small shoulders as she walked ahead of him.

Her entire body shook as he placed her back against the high stone wall of the building behind. "Are you cold?"

"No." The word was barely a whisper.

"Euphemia . . . are you frightened?"

She shook her head. He knew it was a lie.

"Look at me."

She did, her big eyes glittering with tears. His heart nearly broke. Not just because she doubted him, but because he hadn't told her everything. He was falling in love with her, but still lying. Hiding.

"You're in no danger, my dear." He leaned forwards to kiss her, tasting her passion and worry, and the faint sweetness of her mouth. It intoxicated him, made him reckless. He wanted her, now. He'd meant to talk to her. It could wait.

He bent down, kissing her chest through the stiff fabric of her gown, kissing down her stomach, until he could lift her skirts up to her waist.

"John!"

"Hush." He returned to standing and kissed her lips again, and again, catching her thighs in the crooks of his arms and lifting them. His lips travelled down her neck, over her pulse, over the delicate smoothness of her skin. Her fragrance filled his nose. He was lost. Lost in her body, in her hands fumbling at his trousers and opening them. Lost as he tore away her drawers. Lost as he drove himself into her.

A soft cry escaped her. He barely heard it over his own, just as he barely heard the gasps of passers-by as they saw the two of them, against the wall, with her legs wrapped around his waist and his hat fallen off onto the cold ground at his feet. He didn't care, because inside she was all soft wet heat, gripping him, encouraging him to go harder, faster.

He didn't. He slowed down. Her fingers dug into his back. Her hips pushed helplessly forwards, begging him for more.

He wanted to give her more. Wanted to give her everything, anything, as long as she promised they could do this again, do this for ever. Her curious mix of passion and restraint, her clever mind, the way she challenged him everywhere but in bed. She was everything he'd ever wanted.

She gripped the hair at his nape with her right hand, tugging gently. He sped his pace, harder and faster, until he couldn't think or breathe or do anything but feel her around him. Her muscles contracted, hard, not on the wave but getting ready, and he was ready too.

"Come for me." He pulled his head back to watch her, her mouth open, her eyes closed, but did not slow his movements inside her. "Come for me, Euphemia."

"I . . . I . . . oh John!"

Her hips moved forwards as her back arched so violently he thought for a moment they would fall over. And then he didn't care, because she was exploding, and so was he, and it was the closet thing to magic he'd ever felt in his life and it wasn't until he managed to set her down some minutes later that he realized two things.

One, they'd attracted quite a crowd; and two, he'd forgotten to pull out of her as he came. He'd never forgotten to do so with any other woman.

Chapter Four

Whitechapel, London
30 September 1888
3.30 am.

"Send him out!"

"Send him out!"

Euphemia sat up in bed and instinctively felt for John beside her. The empty expanse of cold sheets taunted her. He wasn't there.

They'd gone to sleep together early. When had he gotten up?

The pounding on the door finally galvanized her. She slid from the bed and grabbed the silk wrapper he'd given her, tying it hurriedly around her waist as she ran down the stairs.

The light coming in through the gaps in the drapes looked eerily bright. Lurid.

Not daylight, but fire.

She glanced at the clock, and cold fingers squeezed around her heart.

"Euphemia!" Peggy's imperious voice carried through the windows. "Is he in there? You send him out!"

With the firelight hurting her eyes, it was hard to see Peggy at first, but there she was, on the street, only a few feet from the front door. Behind her was . . . what Euphemia would have termed a "crowd", if the word "crowd" had not implied innocence. This was a mob, an angry one, carrying torches like a sixteenth-century woodcutting.

"Two of 'em!" shouted a man from the back. "Two women he's kilt tonight!"

Two! It couldn't be possible. It couldn't be John, it just couldn't. No man so tender and caring could also be so vicious and cruel, so monstrous.

She dropped the curtain and stepped back, wishing the room wasn't so chill. She thought she might never feel warm again. They'd had dinner. They'd made love twice, once here, then again in bed, his fingers so gentle on her body, his mouth so warm . . .

They'd fallen asleep. And now he was gone and two more women – two! – were dead.

Mrs Langley wasn't in the house. No one was. Just her, facing a horde of drunken, angry people with torches.

She had to get dressed, at least. She would not, could not, open the door, not until she knew what was really happening. She felt too vulnerable with only the thin silk to cover her nudity.

"Euphemia." Something about his voice sent tremors through her body. It was not cool, not smooth, not amused. Not even rough with passion, but with something else.

She turned, her eyes adjusting to the darkness, and saw him standing in the hall beyond the stairs. He hadn't been there a moment ago, she was sure of it.

Nor was he usually covered in blood, but he was tonight. Dark smears of it decorated his face and shirt. She thought she might faint. *Dear God it was him. It was him all along, you stupid, love-struck fool . . .*

"Send him out, Euphemia! You give him to us!"

Euphemia didn't move, not even when the first brick sailed through the window with a terrible, high crash.

"How could you?" she whispered.

"How – my God, Phemie, you don't – Oh, no." He took a step towards her. She took one back. "Please, listen to me! I tried to stop him, I tried to catch him, I was too late—"

"Don't lie!" The scream ripped itself from her throat before she could think about it. "Don't lie to me!"

She'd noticed before how smoothly and silently he could move – just like a killer – but she'd never realized he was so fast. He was in front of her in less than the blink of an eye. Blood soaked his shirtfront and his coat, and slicked the knees of his trousers. He put his hands on her shoulders. She shuddered as blood seeped through her robe. "Look at me, Phemie, look at me! I know what you suspect, but I swear to you it's not me."

Tears ran down her face. She should be more afraid than she was, she thought, but perhaps it was resignation that made her stand and cry instead of fighting. She could not fight any more. She loved him, and if through her love she'd allowed him to commit more murders, she deserved to die at his hand. "I can't believe you. Look at you. How can I trust you when you're covered in blood, when that hairpin wasn't mine, when—"

"Because I love you."

"I heard 'im! He's in there!" The crowd outside started roaring, cursing. Another brick shattered a windowpane and clattered on the wood floor.

"I love you, Euphemia. Please believe me. You don't have any reason to trust me. I've been lying to you, I admit it, and I'll tell you the truth when we have time but we have to get out of here. You have to come with me *now*."

She could barely speak. "I can't."

"You must. He'll kill you if you stay. He knows who you are."

This time it wasn't a brick. It was a bottle. A bottle with a flaming rag stuck in the top. Fire leaped over the carpet. Euphemia screamed and tried to pull away from John, but he was too strong for her. Outside the crowd roared.

"We have to get out of here!"

"I can't, I can't go with you. Not after what you've done . . . "

"God damn it. We must go. The house will burn down around our ears if we stay!"

The curtains had caught now. Orange light flickered eerily off John's face; the blood on his clothing was a hellish design.

"I can go," she said. "I can walk out that door, and let you burn."

He recoiled as if she'd slapped him. "You could." He paused. "If you don't love me."

"How can I love a fiend? I don't even know you. You're not the man that I – the man that I thought—"

She wanted to finish the sentence but couldn't, because his arms were around her and his lips on hers. Feverish, tempting as a pact with the devil and ten times more arousing, he took her mouth without mercy, and she kissed him back with every bit of passion she owned.

"I love you," he whispered fiercely. "By God, Euphemia, I love you. And I'm not a killer. I tried to catch him. I'm here to catch him. I almost had him but he got away. He's too powerful for me . . . " His lips moved to her throat. "Believe me, I didn't hurt those women."

"But the blood on your shirt . . . " She wanted to trust him. Hearing his words of love made her ruined heart sing. She loved him, she did, and it might have been enough for her if only she hadn't trained herself to be quite so practical, so collected.

He pulled away, and looked down. His chest still rose and fell with his rapid breaths.

It was almost as bright as day in the room. The fire was growing, consuming the draperies and furniture. Sweat beaded on Euphemia's forehead and trickled between her breasts.

He spoke, but the words made no sense.

"What?" She couldn't quite make out what he'd said.

"I'm a vampire."

"*What*?" Dear God, was there no end to it?

He opened his mouth wide, and her fist flew to her lips. His teeth . . . so long, so white. How was this possible?

"I'll explain later. We have to go. Please, my darling, my love. *Please* come with me."

Her gaze flew back to the front door. Outside it lay freedom, from the fire and from blood and from the sight of John's unnaturally long . . . *fangs*. There was no word for them but *fangs*.

But inside was John. The man she loved and the man who, despite everything, she believed. And if he led her to her death, surely God's mercy awaited her on the other side.

Her neck felt stiff as she nodded.

His eyes widened. "You'll come with me?"

"Yes."

She expected him to kiss her, to tell her again how he loved her, but he did not. Instead he touched her hand and said, "I'll be right back. Don't move."

She watched him run up the stairs, her chest heaving. Somehow she'd been so focused on him she hadn't noticed the room filling with smoke. It was hard to see, hard to breathe. She coughed once, twice, and then she couldn't stop coughing; couldn't catch her breath.

"John?" She tried to shout, but between the crowd shouting and cursing outside, cheering as the flames grew, and her lack of air she didn't think he would hear her. No one would hear her. She'd made a mistake, a terrible mistake, and she was about to pay for it with her life . . .

Her back had been to the door. If she turned and walked carefully – crawled, perhaps – surely she could find it . . .

But before her knees hit the floor John's strong arm was around her shoulders, scooping her up, carrying her back towards the hall. Through the smoke haze she saw him twist one of the banisters on the staircase, saw a door open at the end of the hall, and then he carried her through it and darkness enveloped them both.

"John?" Before she was fully awake the word escaped her mouth, but she was glad it had when his hand grasped hers.

"I'm here."

She opened her eyes. Like all rooms John occupied, only a single candle illuminated it, but she could still see. Pale walls rose to a high, gilded ceiling. Heavy furniture sat against the walls, light glinting from shiny carvings. And silk-covered softness cradled her naked body.

Her throat hurt. "Where are we?"

"Westminster. We're safe, Phemie. You're safe."

The room swayed as she sat up. "Westminster?"

"The tunnels lead here. My house. We'll be safe enough, for a day or so. Until we get everything packed."

"Packed?" Her head felt stuffed with wool. What was he – Oh. It all came back, the fire, the blood, his . . . fangs.

"We have to leave London. We can't stay, not when they'll be after me. I'm sure your friends back in Whitechapel have told them everything they know."

Euphemia listened carefully for a trace of bitterness in his voice, but didn't find one. "My friends . . . "

"Don't fear. You were doing the right thing. We were on the same side, my dear."

"How did you know?"

His free hand stroked her neck, pushing her hair back over her shoulder. "Vampires know things. We see things. I wanted to tell you so many times, but I couldn't. If everyone suspected me it would put *him* at ease. I needed him at ease, so I could catch him."

"Him?"

"The killer. Leather Apron, or Jack, or whatever they're calling him now. He's not a vampire, but he's almost one. He's a ghoul, a thing made of pure evil, which eats flesh and bathes in blood. I was sent to Whitechapel as soon as we had word he was in town. We hoped to catch him before he managed to harm anyone, but . . . " His eyes darkened. "I failed."

"I don't understand this. I don't understand any of this."

"You will, in time. If you still love me."

She didn't reply.

"If you like . . . " She heard him swallow. "If you like I can send you back. I'll get my driver to take you, or give you fare for a hansom. And something more, to help you. If this is all too much for you, I . . . I understand."

She didn't understand why those words changed everything for her. Perhaps she never would. But it was at that moment, when he gave her back to herself, that she knew, really knew, that he was telling the truth. She'd believed him before. She'd trusted him enough to take the chance despite her fears.

But this was more than trust or belief. This was knowledge, rock solid. He loved her. He would never hurt her, or anyone else.

And she loved him. Her body filled with light, so bright it made her grin. A very undignified, un-Euphemialike grin, but it seemed to please John well enough.

"You think I'd give up a man as wealthy as you?" she teased.

His reply was a kiss, so soft and slow she felt her insides turn into liquid. "I don't want you to ever give me up," he whispered. "Not ever."

"I won't."

Their kiss deepened, their tongues meeting, entwining. Heat pooled between her legs, spreading up to her stomach, as if she'd just sat in a hot bath. There would be many nights in bed together. Years and years.

"Euphemia." His dark eyes twinkled. "Who's in charge here?"

"You are."

"And I always will be."

She smiled, too full of joy and love and desire to speak. He understood, she knew he did; knew she would never have to hide her thoughts or the wanton need he inspired in her. Never have to pretend anything, ever again. Because she'd finally found a man she could trust, completely and fully. For ever.

Whitechapel, London
9 November 1888
6 am

John and his brothers waited in the shadows outside 13 Miller's Court. Too late. John cursed himself. If they'd been a little more clever, if they'd gotten here just a little sooner . . .

The sun would rise soon. They needed to get back into the tunnels before it did. But so did he.

Finally the door opened, then closed. Their prey, who'd made so many women his, stood in the passageway between the two buildings, his work done for the night. His very presence coloured the air with stifling evil.

They fell on him. No more murders. His reign of terror would end, and end now.

The killer must have been waiting for them, must have known they would catch him eventually. He was prepared. His bloodstained knife sliced the air, caught Edward's neck, Cyril's arm, John's shoulder. He fought silently and hard, as the rest of them did, managing with the skills of their kind to avoid disturbing any neighbours. But just before the sun peeked over the horizon, John drove the stake into "Jack"'s heart as Cyril swung his sword and took the killer's head off. They stood silently and watched as he crumbled into dust at their feet.

It was over.

Truly over. The reign of terror in Whitechapel had ended, and with it the loneliness of centuries. John never thought he would be grateful to a ghoul, to something that never should have existed. But he was. Because if not for him John never would have met Euphemia, and as much as it made him sick that lives had ended, he knew his own had just begun again. His new life. The one he would share with Euphemia for ever.

The Scotsman and the Vamp

Jennifer Ashley

Hollywood, 1925

The best thing about a wrap party was the dancing.

Claire Armand loved the beat of the new jazz, its rapid staccato, the thump of the bass, the heartbeat-like pound of the drums. Silas Goldberg, the producer, could afford the best band in Los Angeles for his "it's in the can" party at his Hollywood mansion. Claire would start on a new picture in the morning, but tonight, she planned to dance her heart out.

The charleston was her favourite. It let her dance alone instead of risking a man's wandering hands in a foxtrot. Better still, she could show off her legs and the adorable silver shoes she'd bought to go with her glittering short sheath dress.

Coming to Hollywood had been the best decision of her life. She'd thrown off the shackles of the straight-laced, tradition-bound vampire community of London, and fled the role expected of her – vampire bride to Scotsman Ross Maclaren.

Sounded like a Hollywood film: *The Vampire Bride of Ross Maclaren.* Maybe she should pitch it to Goldberg.

"Oh, Claire, I love your dress." The heroine of the film they'd just finished, *The Ingénue and the Prince,* danced up to her. Lauren Cole, indeed, looked like an ingénue with her cherubic face, soft golden hair and big blue eyes. She was shy, however, and madly in love with the film's hero, the dark-haired heart-throb, Gavin Sanders.

"Thank you," Claire yelled over the music. "I had it made specially for tonight."

She didn't return Lauren's compliment because, as usual, Lauren had no clothes sense. The dress Lauren had chosen was frilly and frumpy and completely wrong for her figure. Claire would have to take her in hand.

"Gavin is right over there." Claire indicated the man standing by the bar, staring wistfully at them. "Go ask him to dance."

Lauren's eyes widened. "No, I couldn't."

This from a woman who'd declared her undying love to Gavin just this afternoon. But, then, the cameras had been rolling.

"You'll never get him to look at you if you don't talk to him."

"He's not interested in me. He's in love with you."

"Don't be daft. He told me the other day he found you a delight."

Rapture. "Did he?" Rapture faded. "I bet he was just being polite. It's you the men buzz around, Claire. You're so beautiful."

Of course Claire was beautiful. She was eternal. She never had to sleep or eat if she didn't want to. She could work long hours and always look good; she never complained or got tired. Film directors loved her.

When Claire had arrived in Hollywood last year, she'd been instantly cast as the femme fatale, a villainness to lure the hero to his doom. She had lustrous black hair, a pale face with sensual red lips, and dark eyes that smouldered at her command. She'd done six pictures so far, and her seductive stare had already become famous across the United States.

Off the set, Claire had no use for Hollywood men. She disliked their lasciviousness, their unveiled offers of sex, their conviction that all actresses were eager to leap into bed. Not one man she'd met in Hollywood was a gentleman, except Silas Goldberg, but that was only because he didn't see his actresses as women. They were dollar signs to him, nothing more.

Claire didn't care. She preferred dancing to men. She loved beautiful clothes, champagne, wild Hollywood parties, sneaking into speakeasies, and dancing all night. At home she'd been expected to remain quietly indoors in an English country house with the women of her clan, while the males were allowed to mingle with humans in clubs and restaurants. The world was deemed too dangerous for vampire women, who lived together in gorgeously appointed houses muffled against the sunlight. Elegant, luxurious and so very, very dull.

The music changed. "Foxtrot!" Claire shouted.

She grabbed Lauren and dragged the young woman to where Gavin Sanders stood at the bar. "Gavin, do dance with Lauren. She certainly doesn't want to dance with me."

Claire thrust Lauren's hand into Gavin's, kissed the tips of her fingers to them both, and whirled away, her good deed done.

A man in full Arab costume strode to her out of the crowd. He wore the entire outfit from *The Sheik* and had included a dark mask under his headgear. Claire held out her arms.

"Rudy, how screaming to see you. Come and dance with me."

Claire liked Rudy Valentino, one of the few men who didn't try to grope her. Rudy had supplemented his early career by dancing with elderly rich ladies in hotels back east, and Claire always found him graceful and light on his feet.

Tonight Rudy seemed ill at ease. He danced with her a few steps then swept her into surprisingly strong arms. Before she could ask what on earth he was doing, he ducked with her through the crowd and ran for the door.

Claire waved at the throng behind her. "Goodbye, everybody! The Sheik is carrying me off."

They cheered, far gone in champagne. Just before her abductor swept her out of the ballroom, Claire caught a glimpse of a man who looked exactly like Rudolph Valentino in a back corner. He wore a plain suit, was conversing with Goldberg, and never looked up at Claire.

"Wait a minute, who the devil are you? Put me down at once."

Claire struggled. She was strong, but so was he. He carried her out of the house and deposited her behind the driver's seat of an open roadster. He swung into the passenger's side before she could get out, and reached over and pressed the starter. "Drive," he growled.

In fury, Claire put the car in gear and screeched past the vehicles in the circular drive. She shot through the gates and yanked the big car to the right, roaring down the road that snaked downhill to town.

As she drove, Claire pondered what to do. She could easily wreck the car with her abductor in it and walk away without a scratch. But the man might die, and maybe he was only a foolish movie fan who wanted to see how far he could get with Claire Armand. She couldn't justify killing him because she was peeved.

Claire had no reservations about scaring the wits out of him, though. There wasn't much traffic this late, and she loved to drive. She zigged around a hairpin turn on two wheels then stomped on the gas. Wind rushed through her hair, and she threw back her head and laughed.

The sheik clawed the cloths from his head and face. "For God's sake, Claire, be careful." His voice was deep, rich, Scottish, and haunted her dreams. "This car is hired."

Claire hit the brakes. The car skidded sideways across the road then slanted into a ditch. Claire turned to stare at the big, dark-haired Scotsman who glared back at her with sinfully tawny eyes.

"Ross!"

"Aye. I've come t' take ye home, Claire."

Claire's body went hot, then ice cold. The tables had just turned. Instead of Claire Armand teaching her kidnapper a lesson, Ross Maclaren was going to teach *her* one. A big, fat terrifying, never-ending lesson.

What have they done to my Claire?

Was this his promised bride – this vixen in a shimmering dress that bared her arms and revealed her long, sexy legs? His Claire who'd danced with abandon in that ballroom, laughing like she'd never been so happy in her life?

Ross burned with fury but at the same time felt a touch wistful. She'd never laughed like that around him.

Now his promised bride glared at him with dark eyes that held a glint of red. Those same eyes had burned him from a cinema screen in Edinburgh not three weeks before. She'd been wearing a pseudo-Egyptian sheath that bared her legs and a large quantity of bosom for all the world to see.

His Claire. The woman who was to turn him into a vampire so that he could love and protect her for ever.

In the movie, Claire had languidly stroked her hand across the resisting hero's chest, while her lush lips moved silently. The next card had assured Ross that she'd said, "My darling, I burn for you with undying passion."

Ross had stormed out of the theatre and bought a ticket on the next ocean liner to America. He knew that what he'd seen had been a play, make-believe filmed on celluloid. But his urge to rip the hero away from Claire and throttle him had been too strong.

"Ross," Claire demanded of him now. "What are you doing here?"

"What am *I* doing here? What are *you* doing here? You are supposed to be home sewing your trousseau, preparing to become m'wife."

She shook her head, black hair glistening in the moonlight. "That's all off. I have a career to think of."

"It's no' off, lass. It can never be off. You're promised t' me and that's final. 'Tis the way of our lives."

"You truly want to become vampire and bound to me for ever? Don't you want a *choice*?"

"I did, when I was younger, aye. But after meeting you . . ."

"You burned with undying passion?" Claire rolled the eyes that had driven the hero mad in *The Pharaoh's Tomb*. "This isn't a film, Ross. It's our lives. Or do you want me only because I can give you immortality?" Bitterness and anger edged her voice.

"Claire, how could ye think that?"

Claire clutched the wheel of the unmoving car. "I decided I didn't want to be married off, to spend my days embroidering in some draughty Scottish castle. For ever. The world has opened up for women, and I want to live in it. Women are a large part of the movie industry now, and I see no reason why I shouldn't be, too."

"Aye," Ross agreed. "Tarts are a large part of it, too. Showing everything but their knickers to the world for a tuppenny ticket."

"Are you calling me a tart, Ross Maclaren?" Claire's eyes flashed dangerous rage, and her fangs brushed her lower lip. He wished he didn't find that so erotic.

Ross' reply was cut short by the sound of someone clearing his throat.

"You having some trouble, lady?" A man in a police constable's uniform strolled up to the car, regarding Claire with cynical suspicion. "Had a few sips from the hip flask, did you, ma'am?"

Ross started to growl in anger, but Claire turned an instant, heart-melting smile on the constable. "Oh, I am zo zorry, officer," she said, her voice deep and liquid. "I thought I zaw a cat in the road, and I didn't want to hit ze poor zing, did I? I had no idea ze car, it could stop zo fast."

Ross rolled his eyes in the darkness. The accent, the manner – all ridiculous, but the policeman stared at her with his mouth open. "Wait a minute. Aren't you Claire Armand?"

Claire tossed her hair. "I am she, yez."

"Hey, no kidding?" The policeman broke into a wide, delighted grin. "I just took my girlfriend to *Daughter of the Regiment*. You were brilliant. My girlfriend, though, she, um, thought you deserved it when you got shot."

Ross' protective anger rose like an enraged lion, but Claire put a slender hand on his arm. "Your lady is right, officer. Ze countess, she should die. She could not reform herself, no. She was too set on self-destruction. So she decides not to dodge ze bullet when it comes for her."

"That's exactly what I told her, Miss Armand." The policeman tugged a pen and paper out of his pocket. "Can I have your autograph? It would make my girlfriend so happy."

"She will cover you with kisses, no?" Claire tittered as the young man blushed. "Ah, I see zat zis is so. Certainly, I will write ze autograph. Zo long as it is not on a ticket?" She gave a throaty laugh.

"No, ma'am. I know now that you were trying not to hit a cat. Not your fault, and no one got hurt."

Claire wrote her name with a flourish and handed the pen and paper back to him. The policeman tucked the autograph into his pocket then guided Claire as she backed the car out of the ditch. The policeman waved goodbye, and Claire drove them away.

Ross finally unclenched his hands. "Good God, Claire, what was that all about?"

"I didn't want a ticket. And the nice constable can thrill his girlfriend with tales of meeting a famous movie star. I wager she really will cover him in kisses."

"I meant th' accent, and the rubbish about 'ze countess' not dodging 'ze bullet'.'"

"Oh, it's just a bit of fun. The movies only have pictures, so how does he know what I sound like in real life?"

"I see I arrived just in time. We'll go back together tomorrow."

Claire's good humour evaporated. "Hardly. I have another picture starting tomorrow, and I'm scheduled to do two more after that. I am getting so much work. My movies sell many tickets."

Ross gazed at the lights of Los Angeles spreading out from the bottom of the hill. Claire drove well, her hands resting lightly on the wheel. The weather was balmy here, the moon bright over the hills.

He found it intriguing, this strange world of warmth, with mansions tucked into hills above farms and orange groves.

"Where are you taking us?" he asked her.

"To my house."

"I'm staying at a hotel."

"My house is more comfortable."

"We're not married yet," Ross said sternly.

"Pooh. No one here cares about such things. Besides, I don't play innocent heroines, I play femmes fatales, so no one expects my reputation to be spotless."

Ross scowled. "You mean it isn't?"

"Don't be such a stick. The men here don't interest me in the slightest, if you are worried. They are either vain creatures who want me to admire them ad nauseam, or they smarm up to me to get parts in pictures. Boring."

"What about that disgusting bastard pawing at you in *The Pharaoh's Tomb*? I saw that one."

Claire smiled in delight. "Oh, Ross, you went to a cinema? How very modern of you."

"A mate dragged me there. I looked up from my newspaper and there was my lass, larger than life, on the screen in front of me. In a skintight sheath with that cretin's hands all over her. I knew it was only a play, but the man was enjoying his part a little too much."

Claire burst out laughing. The car swerved back and forth on the empty street as she laughed. "Oh, Ross. Oh, my love. How priceless."

"Watch where you're going. You'll have us in the ditch again."

Claire straightened the car but didn't slacken her speed. "You'll be happy to know that the cretin in question has no interest in women. He's Jonathon O'Dell, and he has a boyfriend."

Ross blinked. "A boyfriend?"

"Yes. A very nice young man who came with Jon to the studio every day. They've set up house together in Santa Monica. It's sweet."

"Bloody hell."

What kind of a place was this? Women wore next to nothing, men lived with men . . .

Look at Claire. The last time Ross had seen her, she'd been attired in a tight bodice and a long black skirt that enticed him by swaying when she walked. She'd looked shyly through her lashes when he'd taken her hand and declared he was honoured to have been chosen for her.

One year in America, and Claire was in minute dresses, driving cars like a wild woman, laughing up at the sky. Her hair flowed over the seat in a silky wave – at least she hadn't chopped it off like so many women did nowadays. Ross could get lost in her beauty.

But she was *his*, didn't she understand that? Promised to him since his birth. They would marry on All Hallows' Eve, and in their wedding bed she'd make him vampire. Then he'd protect her for ever.

Not every man in the vast Maclaren clan married and protected a vampire bride. Every hundred years or so, certain male Maclarens were chosen by mystics to marry a vampire woman of the Armand family. Ross had hated that he'd been chosen, had fought against it all his life – until he'd met Claire. Then he'd realized why men of his clan had agreed to sacrifice themselves for their vampire brides.

Claire was not only beautiful of face, she had a lush, curved body and a grace that made him want to watch her every move. Her smile was sweet, but she'd had a gleam in her eye that sent his fantasies dancing. He'd wanted to know her, talk to her, kiss her, hold her in the night. Was it the magic that made him feel this way? Or Claire herself?

Ross had been willing to find out. But now it seemed that Claire was not.

Claire pulled the big car up a hill, through a gate, and along a circular drive. She stopped in front of a Georgian house that looked a couple of hundred years old, but of course it couldn't be.

"This is *your* house?" Ross asked.

Claire threw him an exasperated look as she got out of the car. "Of course it is. I bought it after I finished *The Curse of the Mummy*."

"Did ye now?"

"I did, now."

Claire unlocked the front door and ushered him into a vast hall. A staircase curved upward to the left, and Ross glimpsed a comfortable modern bathroom through a door to his right. The décor was pale yellow with black accents, no gaudy marble or pseudo Egyptian gilt like at the hotel where Ross was staying. Claire at least had some taste.

She dropped her keys on the hall table and skimmed up the stairs. Ross admitted he liked the silvery dress, which cupped her bottom and let him watch her lovely thighs in motion.

He pulled off the rest of the Arab robes as he climbed after her and left them on the banister. Beneath he wore a suit coat and Maclaren plaid kilt. Americans on the trains had slanted puzzled looks at him all the way across the country, but since he'd arrived in Los Angeles, no one had batted an eye. They probably thought he was in a movie – *The Scotsman's Bonny Lassie* or some such nonsense.

His own bonny lassie flipped on the electric lights in a living room at the top of the stairs. Filled bookcases lined one wall, tall windows lined the opposite. Claire paused on her way to a drinks cabinet to turn on a phonograph and drop its needle onto a record.

"Cocktail?" she asked, taking up a silver shaker as the scratchy music began. "I've learned to make the most screaming drink called a Gin Fizz. They have Prohibition here, so it's terribly illegal, but the police never bother me."

Of course they didn't. Money and fame made the law look the other way in many countries. "I'd prefer malt whisky if ye have it."

"Good heavens, Ross, it won't hurt you to try something new. Expand your horizons."

"I did. I went to the pictures. Ye see where it led me?"

Claire opened bottles and poured things into the shaker. She put the top on and shook the container in time with the music, which made her jiggle agreeably. She poured the drinks into wide-mouthed glasses, twisting her wrist with a flourish.

Ross took the glass she handed him. "Where's th' cock's tail?"

"Silly. That's what drinks are called. Mixed drinks, anyway. Chin-chin." She clinked her glass to his and took a large gulp.

Ross let a swig roll past his lips, then he coughed. "That's bloody awful."

Claire looked at her glass. "It is rather. I prefer champagne myself. But cocktails are the rage."

Ross set his drink on a table and took the glass from her hand. "Never mind what's th' rage." He slid his arms around her and pulled her close. "I've not seen ye in almost a year, and I came a long way to find ye."

"Ross . . ."

"Don't argue with me, Claire. Just dance with me. Can ye do that?"

She ran her hands along his shoulders, her scent filling him. "I suppose."

"Good." The tune was rapid, but Ross knew how to dance, and he pulled her into the moves before she could protest any more.

Not fair. Ross looked at her with eyes the colour of the malt whisky he liked, pressed warm hands to her back, and Claire wanted to do anything he commanded.

His eyes now held fatigue from his long journey, his dark brown hair rumpled, his face hard and dusted with unshaved whiskers. She compared him to the carefully dressed, self-conscious male film stars, and decided she preferred Ross with his unruly hair and worn kilt.

The dance brought them close, her thin dress letting her feel the firmness of his tall, honed body. He glided with her around the room, skilfully avoiding the furniture, his gaze locked on hers.

"Come back with me, Claire," Ross said, voice soft.

Claire couldn't help but lace her arms around his neck. "You expect me to give this all up?"

"We were chosen to be together."

His words stirred heat deep down inside her, but she kept her tone light. "That was a line in *The Curse of the Mummy*. I, the evil countess, was to lure the hero to his doom so the mummy could kidnap the heroine. Mitchell, who played the mummy, had a devil of a time walking in that costume. He'd trip on the bandages and say the filthiest words I've ever heard."

Ross put his fingers on her mouth. "Hush now. Ye can tell me all about the debauchery later."

Claire wanted to keep babbling. "But there's a funny story about Mitch in his costume at a speakeasy . . ."

"Sh." Ross lifted his fingers from her lips and bent to her, his nearness blotting out all other thought, sight, feeling.

In the background, muted trumpets played a bouncing rhythm. Ross' warm lips covered hers, his hands moving in her hair. He smelled like the night wind and warm wool and soap. This was why Claire had fled England, travelling at night, hiding during the day. Pursuing her acting career had only been an excuse. She was in danger of losing herself to this man, this beautiful man who wanted to possess her.

"Ross," she whispered.

He licked the curve of her lip. "Tonight. Let us do it tonight and seal the bargain."

Fear wove through Claire's longing. She touched his neck, feeling the pulse pounding under her fingertips. The heat of his blood swamped her with need. The vampire in her wanted him – *yes, now, hungry*. She nuzzled his throat, licking the path of his artery.

"Yes, Claire. Do it."

Claire's teeth elongated before she could stop them, and she scratched his skin with one fang. *Mmm, salty, warm, good.* She licked away the crimson drop that welled from the cut.

Longing exploded inside her. Her need for him arose white hot. She wanted to rub herself against his body, feel his hardness between her legs, suckle his lips until they were raw. She wanted him in her bed, inside her, moaning as he came. She wanted her fangs in his neck, to taste his blood in her mouth as he drove into her.

"I want it, too," Ross whispered.

Claire gasped and pushed him away with all her strength. She folded her arms around her stomach, holding herself tight, tight, willing her fangs to recede.

Her incredible need for him wouldn't fade. The kiss had ripped something open inside her, something that terrified her.

"Go away."

"No." Ross smiled. Damn, but his smile could melt her like ice cream on a Los Angeles sidewalk. "You're mine, Claire. We are for each other. I'm not leaving this city without you."

"Well, you can't sleep with me." Claire's voice cracked as he came for her. What had happened to her liquid vowels, the languid confidence with which she'd outsmarted the constable this evening? "I'm starting another picture tomorrow and have an early call. I need my beauty sleep."

"Liar." Ross touched her face, his fingertips flaring her shrieking need. She was going to die if he didn't stop touching her.

Ross stepped back, and then she almost cried. Her body was flame hot, and the absence of his touch was like being doused with ice-water.

"But all right," he was saying. "I know ye don't need sleep, and you're as beautiful as you ever were, but I'll leave ye be. For now. Do you have guest rooms in this enormous mansion?"

"Next floor up," she said faintly. "Any of those rooms. They're all made up."

"Expecting company, are you?" Ross' whisky-coloured eyes flashed with anger.

"No, but my housekeeper likes to be prepared. Party guests might be too tight to drive home."

"All right then." Ross came to her again. Claire flinched, fearing what his touch would unleash, but he gripped her shoulders and planted a kiss on the top of her head. "Sleep well, my love."

He strode out of the room. Claire gazed after him, admiring how his Maclaren plaid moved across his firm backside. She grabbed her discarded cocktail glass and gulped down the contents, grimacing at the bitter taste, but the odd mixture cut through her bloodlust.

Claire wiped her mouth and moved to a window to look out at the moonlit night. How would she survive tonight, knowing he was one floor above her, sleeping, his bed warm and filled with his scent? She gripped the stem of her cocktail glass until it broke, tearing her skin and letting her thick, almost purple, vampire blood seep out.

She leaned her forehead on the windowpane to cool it, while behind her, the spirited song wailed to an end.

Has anybody seen my gaaaaaal?

Claire's driver picked her up while it was still dark and had her and Ross to the studio before dawn. Claire had found acting to be the perfect profession for a vampire. Unlike vampires in fiction, she didn't sleep like the dead during the day, although too much exposure to the sun could kill her. But a job that had her at make-up calls at four in the morning and kept her inside the studio until long after dark, suited her well.

"What do ye do when they want to film outside?" Ross asked her as they walked into the enormous, echoing building. Cameras zoomed past them on tracks, and actors, extras, costume ladies, make-up girls, set-builders and gaffers milled everywhere.

"Easy. When we do location shots I stay bundled up and under the tent shelter they fix for us. All the ladies do. They'd ruin their pristine complexions if they didn't. Plus the make-up keeps the sun from burning me. I can stay outside for a little while before I start to hurt. Then I feign fatigue, and they rush me back indoors."

Ross gave her a frown. "Too risky."

"We don't go out often. Most of the work happens right here in the studio, unless they need a grand outdoor scene. If they do distance shots they can use anybody dressed in the right clothes and not have to pay them as much as the actors. The only outdoor scene I've done is when Mitchell the mummy chased me across the desert until I died of thirst. We did most of those shots at night anyway."

Ross didn't look impressed. He'd insisted on coming with her today, but Claire decided it would give her the opportunity to show him exactly what she did and why she wanted to stay in Los Angeles.

Female heads turned as Claire led Ross through the throng towards the partitioned off dressing area. Claire was pleased that others envied her having such a handsome beau, but not pleased at all when a petite extra smiled and did a little undulation of her shoulders for him. The girl was lucky Claire didn't have to feed often. She could make do with a sip here and a sip there, always erasing her victim's memory before she let them go. They'd wake up happy, thinking they'd dreamed about being intimate with Claire Armand. With this woman eyeing her man, though, Claire might not be so nice.

Ross didn't seem to notice the attention. He focused on Claire and Claire alone, which made her feel both nervous and protected.

"Claire." Lauren smiled tiredly when they reached the dressing rooms. "How do you do it? You look fresh as a daisy, and I didn't dance half as much last night as you did."

"Clean living, darling. Did Gavin propose?"

Lauren's face fell. "He danced with me, then someone told him he had a telephone call, and he had to leave. I haven't seen him this morning."

"Oh dear. I'm becoming disappointed in Gavin."

Lauren gazed shyly at Ross. Ross wore his kilt, and he was watching the cranes and pulleys and other paraphernalia move about the studio floor.

"Who is he?" Lauren hissed.

"Ross Maclaren. My . . ."

"Fiancé," Ross said. He turned and bowed over Lauren's hand with old-fashioned gallantry.

"Oh." Lauren blushed and glanced at Claire. "Was he the sheik from last night?"

"Aye. That I was."

"He wanted to surprise me," Claire said, her voice weak.

Lauren actually laughed. "Well, you look surprised, honey." She led Claire through the curtains to the dressing room, lowering her voice to a whisper. "You gotta tell me *everything*."

Ross became interested in the filming in spite of himself. There seemed to be much chaos, but everyone knew exactly where to go and what to do. Claire emerged from the dressing rooms after about an hour, covered in yellowish paint, her lips a startling red. But even covered in greeny-yellow, she looked beautiful to him.

They filmed in a curtained-off portion of the studio. Behind those curtains was another stage in which another movie was being shot. Ross couldn't understand how anyone concentrated in the resulting cacophony, but film people seemed to be amazingly single-minded.

Ross did not know the title of the movie yet, but it was similar to the one he'd seen in Scotland. The scene they shot first involved Claire as the dark-haired villainess luring the heroine – small, blonde Lauren – into her lair. From what Ross gathered about the film, Claire played a rich femme fatale from Hungary who seduced men, took their money, and discarded them like soiled hankies.

She was to bring Lauren to her lavish New York townhouse, drug her, and ruin her reputation by arranging for Lauren to be caught on a bed with the villain. The hero, played by Gavin Sanders, would in theory be disgusted and marry Claire instead, giving Claire access to his riches. Or so Claire declared, rubbing her slender hands while her eyes smouldered.

Action! Claire, smiling evilly, succeeded in getting childlike Lauren to drink the drug-laced cocktail. When Lauren began to feel the effects, she begged Claire for mercy. Her words wouldn't be heard on the film, but her mouth would move in the dialogue.

"Please, please," Lauren said in a monotone as she sank stiffly to her knees and jerked one hand towards Claire. "Do not let me suffer a fate worse than death."

The director sighed heavily. "Cut!"

Claire relaxed. She smiled at Ross, then turned so a make-up lady could retouch her lipstick.

The director was shouting. "Miss Cole, she is about to destroy your chance of happiness with the man you love! For ever. You look like you're explaining that you don't want the chicken soup for lunch."

Lauren's eyes filled with tears. "But I don't know how else to do it."

"Like this, darling." Claire touched the heel of her hand to her forehead and managed to look both terrified and miserable. "*Please. Let me go. I beg of you, do not destroy me.*"

Lauren applauded, and the director said, "Yes. Exactly like that. Can you do that for me, Miss Cole? Thank you. May we press on?"

The scene continued. Ross sat back in the chair Claire had made someone get for him, and watched her performance. Most of the actors were jerky and unconvincing, including the villain whose oily smile set Ross' teeth on edge. But Claire had natural talent. She delivered her lines in a clear voice, her face telling the entire story. People in the studio stopped to watch her, enraptured, and applauded when she finished.

"She's amazing," the director, a thin man with pasty white skin, said to Ross. "A few more pictures, and she'll be a star."

"A star?"

"A top-billed actress. Box-office magic. She'll be so popular she'll wade through crowds of fans wherever she goes. She'll be able to ask for whatever picture she wants and command top money."

In other words, Claire would have wealth, respect, independence. Everything she wanted.

Where did Ross fit in to this new life of hers? He was still the man chosen as her protector, to keep his vulnerable vampire bride safe forever. The mystics said the signs had named *him* – Ross Maclaren – although Ross was beginning to suspect the whole vulnerability idea was bunk. The Armand vampires sequestered their females, claimed they could never survive in the world without a protector. That was the way things had been done for a thousand years.

But what about now? Claire was right, the world had changed. In this new age of motorcars and mansions, of film studios and cocktails, where actresses made fortunes like men, why would Claire need Ross? He loved her, but would that be enough?

Above him, a light burned out in a flare of sparks. Ross briefly wondered if it were symbolic of his relationship with Claire.

Then the sparks slid down the wire and lit a pile of papers on the floor.

"Cut!" the director roared. "Someone come and put out this fire."

Ross saw Claire instinctively recoil. She was vampire; the tiniest flame could destroy her.

Ross rose as someone ran over with a bucket of sand. The papers burned merrily, and a tongue of flame ran up a table leg and caught the costumes heaped on top. Lauren gasped, and Claire moved swiftly to the other side of the set.

"Damnation." The director grabbed at the costumes, cursing when he burned himself. The assistant dumped the bucket of sand on the papers, but the table continued to burn. The curtains between the stages caught. The director cursed again and tried to pull them down, but his jacket caught fire, and he flung it off him, eyes wide with fear.

"Everyone needs to get out," Ross said in a loud voice. He took up the megaphone the director had dropped and spoke into it. "Take the hand of the person next to you and walk out with them. Don't run. Let everyone leave while we get the fire contained. You too, Claire."

Lauren clutched Claire in terror. "Gavin! He's still in the dressing rooms!"

"I'll get him." Ross' heart hammered as the flames came too near Claire. "Go!"

Claire seized Lauren by the hand and started out with her. Just before they reached the double doors that had been rolled open to let everyone out, Claire stopped and looked back. She saw Ross reach the dressing area and, as he ducked inside, the curtains all around him went up in flames.

"Ross!" she shrieked.

The fire caught the beams that ran up to the roof, engulfing the back half of the building. Fire swirled in front of Claire, and the dressing area was lost to sight.

Claire shoved Lauren towards bright daylight. "Go."

"No, Claire, come with me."

The sunlight would be just as deadly for Claire as the fire. Claire's make-up would protect her somewhat, but it was a bright, cloudless Los Angeles day, with the sun directly overhead. Unless she got to shade quickly, she'd fry.

And while she tried to find shelter, Ross might die. He was mortal, and the smoke could debilitate him quickly. If she was fast, she could run in and carry both him and Gavin out. She had supernatural strength; they didn't.

Lauren cried out in despair as Claire dashed back into the studio. Fire was everywhere now, and smoke lay thick. She saw Ross' bulk as he tore the burning curtains from the dressing room partitions. Gavin was slumped over one of the tables beyond, half dressed and unconscious. Ross grabbed Gavin under the armpits and started to drag him off the chair. Then a burning beam fell across both men.

Claire swallowed a scream as she sprinted towards them. She felt her vampire body burning, felt the beautiful hair she was so proud of shrivel and crackle away.

She lifted the beam with her unnatural strength and threw it aside. Ross was still conscious. He looked up at Claire in horror, but when he opened his mouth to shout at her, he coughed on the smoke.

Claire flung Gavin over her shoulder and reached for Ross. He hauled himself to his feet, put his arm around her, and ran through the studio with her. A sound like a thousand nails raining on wood came from overhead, and then the roof collapsed.

With the last of her strength, Claire tossed Gavin to the pavement outside, wet now from fire hoses. Ross turned to her, and she pushed him, hard. He stumbled out into the sunshine and the pouring water and looked back just as the building collapsed onto Claire's burning body.

Tears rained down Ross' face as he drove through the streets of Los Angeles, heading for Claire's house. Claire was still alive, wrapped in blankets in the seat behind him, her little moans of pain breaking his heart. Her skin was black, her hair gone, and she could not speak or open her eyes.

What an idiot he'd been to think her invulnerable. Ross was supposed to be her protector, and he hadn't protected her. She'd risked her life to rescue him, and all he had to show for the adventure was a burn on his arm he barely felt.

Ross had defied the firemen streaming onto the scene and pushed aside the fallen beams to drag Claire out. He'd wrapped her body in blankets and run with her to the first car he saw, a roadster with a tiny canvas top raised against the sun. He didn't know whose car this was, but no one stopped him driving it off the lot as the studio burned under the bright California sky.

A hospital would be useless for Claire. Ross drove like a madman, dodging traffic, finally squealing the car up her long, curved drive. He lifted her from the back seat and rushed into the house and up the stairs with her, ignoring the startled questions of the Mexican housekeeper.

Ross slammed the door of Claire's bedroom closed then put her down on the bed and stripped away the blankets. Her dress and stockings had burned to tatters, and she lay bare on top of the bedcovers. Her lips moved, and a strangled sound came from her throat.

"Don't talk. I've got you home." Ross shed his clothes and lay down with her on the bed, carefully sliding his body next to hers. "There's only one thing to do, love."

Claire groaned again, trying to protest.

"No, sweetheart. It's the only way." Ross took the silver knife he'd kept in his sporran for this purpose, drew a breath, and made a shallow slice across his throat.

Bright pain quickly changed to numbness. Blood dropped to Claire's white coverlet and rained onto her burned body.

Claire moved. She wanted it, and yet he sensed her hold back. She could save herself, but even now, she was trying not to hurt Ross.

He loved her so much.

"Drink me," Ross whispered. He guided her mouth to the wound, his hand firm on the back of her neck.

Claire hesitated one more moment. Then her fangs elongated, and he felt the sharp pain of them on his throat. He fell back to the bed, holding her. Her bite grew stronger, then she gave in to her ravenous hunger and fed.

Claire's strength returned, swallow by swallow. Ross' blood was hot, heady like wine, thick and sweet. She filled her mouth with it then let it run down her throat, the sensation erotic.

She felt her skin grow smooth and whole. The remains of her burned hair fell away, and warm, new hair took its place. Her bite became stronger, more certain.

She felt Ross' heartbeat beneath hers. It slowed with each breath, fainter, fainter, dying away into a flutter.

Ross.

Claire's senses returned with a snap. She yanked her fangs from Ross' neck and sat up. Ross lay naked beneath her, his skin wan, his eyes closed. He still held her, his hands solid on her back.

"Ross!"

His whisky-coloured eyes opened to slits. "There, ye see? Ye do need me." His breath rattled in his chest, and then he went still.

"No." Claire gathered him against her, rocking him. "You aren't supposed to die. You're supposed to live so I can love you."

This wasn't how the turning worked. It should be mutual, a sharing of blood, Ross turning while he was still alive. He wasn't supposed to give up his life for her.

Claire snatched up the blade he'd dropped, dimly noting that it was the ritual silver blade for their wedding night. Ignoring the sear of the silver, she nicked her own neck. She caught the stream of blood on her fingers and dipped them inside Ross' mouth.

"Drink," she begged. "Ross, please."

Nothing happened. Claire smeared more blood on her fingers and again wiped them inside Ross' lips. She was healed now, his blood hot within her, making her stronger than she ever had been.

"Please." Her tears trickled to his skin to mix with her blood. "Stay with me, Ross. I love you."

Ross' eyelids fluttered. Claire bit her lip, not daring to hope. Then Ross closed his lips around her fingers and suckled, hard.

"Yes, love, that's it. Drink."

Ross raised his head, hunger in his gaze. Claire guided him to her neck and cried out when his teeth sank into her. He drank her as she'd drunk him, needy, ravening. She felt his body flush with strength, felt his arousal swell between his legs.

Claire's own need flooded her, mixing with relief and love. She slid her thighs open and guided him into her. Then for the first time in her life, she felt a man inside her.

Ross jerked his head up. A different hunger flared in his eyes, and he thrust. Claire felt pain, instant and hot, then it fled. A pleasure she'd never known before took its place. She loved it. Ross pressed her down into the mattress and rode her, harder, faster.

Abruptly Ross stopped, his eyes clearing as though he were awakening. He stared down at Claire in shock.

"You're all right," he whispered. Then tears poured from his eyes and he kissed her lips, her face, her throat. "Thank God, you're all right."

Claire wrapped her arms around him. "You saved my life. My lover, my protector. *Mine*."

Ross stroked her hair, still inside her. He filled her and stretched her and felt so damn *good*.

"Am I . . . vampire?"

"Yes." Claire bit her lip. "I'm sorry. I know it wasn't the proper time. But I had to save you."

His gaze softened. He could be so tender, could Ross Maclaren. "'Tis no matter, love. We'll marry, as the signs said we would."

"Yes." Happiness tingled inside her. "That's perfect."

"That is, if you'll still have me."

Ross looked worried. Worried? How could he worry that she ever wanted to live without him? "I'll have you, Ross. I love you, my mad Scotsman. I never want to lose you again."

Ross' smile turned wicked. "I love you, my bonny sweet vampire." He sobered. "Oh, God, Claire, when I thought ye were dead, when I thought ye'd never smile at me again . . ."

Tears filled her eyes, but she wiped them away impatiently. "No, no sorrow. You saved me, protected me, like I've always dreamed you would." She touched his face, loving him. "And anyway you're making love to me right now and I don't want you to stop. I *never* want you to stop."

"That can be arranged," Ross growled.

He pressed her down into the covers again until they were both shouting and laughing with the incredible joy of it.

"Look," Lauren said excitedly the next afternoon in Claire's favourite restaurant. "Can you believe it?" She waved a hand under Claire's nose, a large solitaire diamond sparkling on her third finger.

"Darling, that's wonderful." Claire hugged her. At a table across the room, Gavin waved, a little embarrassed.

Ross and Claire had gone to the studio an hour before in Claire's chauffeur-driven closed car to find that the entire building they'd filmed in, and the one next to it, had burned to ruins. The picture would go on though, the producer told her. They were moving onto another lot. A film there was scheduled to end the next day, and they'd resume production the day after that.

So the actors found themselves with an unexpected day off. Ross took Claire to the nearest jeweller's and bought her a fancy ring to seal their engagement.

Lauren now slid into the chair next to Claire's. "I held Gavin's hand until he came to after the fire. He smiled at me, and then he proposed. I'm sorry Claire, but I, um, kind of told him that I rescued him."

Claire clapped her hands. "Brilliant! You'll make an accomplished actress yet."

Ross grinned and raised his glass of whisky. "To Gavin and Lauren. May ye bear many bairns."

Lauren's dimples showed. "My real name's Myrtle, actually. Myrtle Bloomfield. But Mr Goldberg thought it wouldn't look good on a marquee."

"Gavin and Myrtle, then," Ross said generously.

Claire slid her own beringed hand along the table. "And Ross and Claire."

Lauren gasped. She seized Claire's fingers and studied the diamond with the intensity of an expert jeweller. "Oh, my, how *gorgeous*."

"Which means I won't be making any more films," Claire said. She felt a pang of regret. She truly loved everything about the movies – the cameras, the lights, the acting, even the early cast calls.

Ross closed his warm hand over hers. "Of course you will, lass. You'll be making plenty more. As many as you like."

"But I thought I was supposed to go to Scotland with you," Claire said in surprise. "What about your draughty castle?"

Ross shrugged, broad shoulders rippling. "I like it here. This movie-making looks interesting. I have one or two ideas that mebbe I can write into films."

Claire laughed excitedly. "I knew the bug would bite you. I just knew it."

"What bug?"

"Never mind. Let's go pitch your ideas to Mr Goldberg."

Lauren stood up as Gavin joined them. The four exchanged mutual congratulations, then Ross took Claire's hand and led her out of the restaurant. They dived quickly through the patch of sunshine into the back of Claire's car, which her chauffeur had pulled to the door.

"Did you really mean that, Ross?" Claire asked as she snuggled down against her new protector's shoulder. "You want to stay in Los Angeles with me? And I can keep making movies?"

"I wouldn't take that from ye, Claire. You love it so much."

"I can't do it for ever, you know. We won't age, and people will get suspicious. I can retire from acting and produce what you write. And your Scottish castle will make a lovely summer home."

"I'm home wherever you are, love," Ross said in a dark voice.

Claire shivered in delight. "I think it's *screaming* that you want to do movies too. You and I will be the cat's pyjamas for a while and then twenty-three skidoo."

Ross frowned. "What the devil does that mean?"

"You know, *scram*."

Ross growled and pulled her close. "What am I going t' do with you, lass?"

"I have one or two ideas. Then we'll go out tonight and celebrate. Champagne, jazz music and the charleston."

"Or we'll stay inside and celebrate." Ross leaned down and kissed her, lips bruising, possessive, then he grazed her neck with his teeth.

"Yes," she whispered, heat gathering inside her. "That sounds just fine, too."

I Need More You

Justine Musk

I look like an angel, but I am no angel.

"I know what you are," the boy said.

He had been following me for God knows how long, skinny white-faced blur swimming through the sand-tossed air. Under normal circumstances I would have noticed him much earlier, but there was nothing normal about tonight: not this temporary makeshift city deep in a desert nowhere, camps set along concentric rings that framed the area known as the playa: and not my purpose for being here, my mind enfolding the image of my lover like it were some dark, priceless egg on the edge of breaking.

He had summoned me here. He was so close, now – out there on the playa – I could almost taste how I'd be tasting him later.

He did not look like an angel any more than the fake ones I saw in the crowds, raggedy wings sprouting from naked or near-naked backs, bobbing along with each step. Different strains of music – house, reggae, acid jazz, dubstep – poured from the elaborately fashioned art-camps that rimmed the inside of the playa, thumped from the speakers of the outdoor clubs. White and neon lights picked out the art-cars moving along the playa, described the domes and twisting organic shapes of the theme camps. And the Man watched over it all: a giant, primitive figure lit up a ghostly blue, striding atop a wooden dome. On the last night of the festival, they would burn him and watch him fall.

"I know what you are," the kid said again. His voice came at me like a worm twisting through the sandy dark. "Sweet girl. Sweet, beautiful girl. I know."

"Get lost. I have nothing for you."

"I know what you have. I want it. Need it. Please."

He darted round to face me. The wind blew sand in our faces. I did not slow for him, forcing him into an awkward back-pedal as his eyes tried to meet mine and dropped away. A string of beads draped his neck, he was fingering it like a rosary, his shirt flapping on a decidedly unappealing torso. I have a penchant for lean human forms, their carved-out beauty of muscle and sinew, but this was a vermin body, starved and dirty and desperate, with the high-sweet smell of something rotting inside. "Please," he said again. "You are so beautiful. So fucking beautiful." Couldn't he bother to arrange himself more appealingly? Fall to his knees, lift his arms with dramatic flourish, tilt his head to expose that soft stretch of throat? Perhaps even quote some poetry. I can be a sucker for poetry. But there was no poetry in this one.

"I can give you what you need," he said. "I can give you –"

I stopped. "You presume to know my need?"

Small muscles jumped in his face. "I . . . " he said, and then, wisely, thought better of saying anything. That high-sweet smell came at me again: cancer. He was in the beginning stages of it.

I made a darting motion. Heat pulsed behind my eyes. I showed him my fangs, cold daggers in my mouth. Dropping my voice a full octave – a parlour trick, really, but it was a chance to amuse myself – I hissed, "You want my brand of cruelty? Because I can give you cruelty. I can give you pain."

His eyes widened. Behind him – and the forming puddle at his feet – drifted a double-decker bus reinvented as a pirate ship, electro-pop blasting from its deck. Bodies hung out the windows, yelled through September dark: "Come aboard! Come, my pretties! We love you! WE LOVE ALL OF YOU!" Some onlookers cheered. Two young men ran up alongside it and launched themselves through the door. By the time it had passed – only art-cars were allowed on the playa, and no faster than five miles an hour – my little vermin-stalker was gone.

The wind died.

The sand settled.

The vermin had thrown me off. I'd been in some kind of trance, lulled by my lover's scent in my nostrils, his taste in my mind, the memory and the anticipation. Now that was gone, throwing me back on nothing and no one but myself. I was alone on this dead Nevada land scattered with odd gigantic sculptures, over there some kind of laser show, and over there towering figures kneeling in worship of an oil derrick that, like the Man and the Chapel of Lost Souls, would be set afire at festival end. In front of me someone had set up a stand painted white with an antique telephone chained to a table and a sign reading TALK TO GOD. FIVE CENTS.

You bring me here, I said, streaming the thought-words out across the playa. Oh this desire, like a fierce blade twisting in my chest, his name engraved so deep there could be no substitute or replacement. It never truly went away. It hummed its dark addictive song beneath my days and nights – months and years and decades – while I travelled and hunted and loved (tried to love) and all the while pretending that I wasn't just marking time until he came again to my dreams, and told me where to go. Where to find him.

You bring me here, I said again, *to this bizarre place, this carnival on the moon, you summon me and I come, like the dog that you have made me. And I do it. I cross the country for you. I cross the world for you. I would cross time itself if I had to . . . because I want, I need, more you . . .*

But after tonight I am done with you.

I won't be caught on this chain any more.

I waited, probing the air for some kind of response. There was nothing. But then that seemed so much of what he was: creature of silence and void. He seemed most at ease in the in-between spaces, as if to look on him directly would do to him what full daylight would do to me.

"They're all over, this year."

So lost was I inside my own head, and so still and striking the woman who had spoken, that for a moment I thought she was another sculpture: desert Venus rising from the sand.

"The joops," she said. "Like the one that was bothering you. I thought you handled him well, by the way." She sighed. "That's what happens when we drink without killing. Word gets around. What a pain."

I tuned into her with interest: the smell of her evoked berries and cream, richly coloured silks, Belgian chocolate.

"I don't know you," she said, tilting her head. Reddish-brown hair spread along her shoulders. She wore a long suede dress that criss-crossed her torso in an elaborate assortment of straps. "I thought I knew all the nightsingers out here."

"Is that what we're supposed to call ourselves now?" My voice was arch. "Is that the politically correct term?"

Of course I knew the word, which had come into vogue at the turn of the new century – "nightsinger", meant to designate a certain class of vampire. Vampires come in all shapes and sizes, with varying degrees of appeal for our prey; the nightsingers, though, are the ones they write books about, and that the vermin – the so-called joops, a play on the words "junkie" and "groupie" – tracked and followed, begged to be bitten by, as if that same nightsinger beauty could enter them and make them something other than themselves.

Her eyes were pale gold, like a tiger's, and they took me in and read me. "So you're one of the rogues," she murmured. "Lonely path, that. No wonder your scent trail was so strange. How long have you been off the grid?"

"I have my own life to conduct," I said. "I don't need to be wired into some global psychic network."

"You don't worry about being left behind?"

"How can I be left behind?"

"Even our kind –" and she held out her hands, palms up, as if weighing some invisible substance "– evolves."

"Into what? We are what we are."

She tipped her head, but it wasn't a gesture of acknowledgment, more like sympathy for one in my position. I felt that – her sympathy – and the back of my mouth flooded with bitterness. I didn't have time for this.

"Come back to our camp," she said, "and have a drink – we have loveblood – and we can continue to argue the point."

I laughed. "Goodnight," I said, brushing past her, "nightsinger."

I passed a fire pit, humans huddling round it – had it gotten colder? Like others of my kind, I don't always register a change in temperature – and walked round a giant plastic cube in which a woman in pyjamas slept atop a shag rug. People were passing messages to her, slipping folded bits of paper through slots in the walls. They knocked on the plastic, trying to wake her up, but her chest rose and fell in the rhythm of oblivion. I looked at the woman in the cube. Then I couldn't help myself: I turned and looked back.

The nightsinger had not moved. People wandered the space between us, yanking up scarves or nursing masks as the wind began to move again. Green laser light streamed the air from a nearby installation. I could feel her gaze on me: fixed, unyielding. As if there was something she wanted to tell me, and that I desperately needed to know.

Your call: how I wait for it: how it thunders through my dreams, a tsunami of light sweeping me to you.

I come to you in Paris, a smoky cafe somewhere on the Left Bank, you wait in a corner booth with your notebook and glass of absinthe. I come to you in London, behind the rubble of a bombed apartment building, clouds mounting overhead, their promise of rain like a promise withheld. I come to you in the country town of Wagga Wagga and we lie down in yellow grass, kangaroos racing their shadows across the distant hillsides. I come to you in Kyoto, dripping silence beneath a stone bridge, cherry blossoms swirling in the water. I come to you in Starke, Florida, the night they executed a serial killer, people standing vigil with their signs that said BURN BUNDY BURN *and you took my hand and led me to the back of a van filled with flowers and candlelight. I come to you in Thailand, music pulsing down a beach crowded with dancing young backpackers, their pupils like full moons inside ecstatic faces. I come to you in Manhattan, on a windswept hotel roof, the spotlights of Ground Zero like ladders of light that souls were still climbing.*

I come to you.

I come to you, and you are waiting.

That is what I know. It is the fixed unchanging thing.

I come to you now, in Black Rock, Nevada, this ragtag city of tens of thousands that didn't exist a week ago and won't a week from now. I hitched my way here – getting cars to stop for me is never a problem – and walked the access roads marked with traffic cones to the Black Rock border, where dust-blown twenty-somethings dressed like refugees from a Mad Max movie checked tickets, searched incoming vehicles for stowaways, told people to make sure you take out everything you bring in, spoke about proper hydration and the increased police presence this year on the playa so if you have any drugs, keep them in your hidey-hole and no loose glitter or feather boas please, they drop and shed and litter. I walk the long, curving dirt road until it empties into the grid of "streets" – named and ordered on a map – and I walk past the RVs and the cars and the tents, the humble campsites and the more complicated affairs with their awnings and canopies and furniture, their whimsical signs and sculptures, their smells of barbecue. People in sarongs, shorts, bikinis, people in all kinds of costumes, people in degrees of nudity are milling around me, swigging water; they are lining up at the rows of porta-potties, they are riding bicycles, they are hanging out in deck chairs, on overstuffed sofas and love seats, on blankets, they are dancing on the roofs of RVs, silhouettes writhing in the harmless glow of dusk.

The last of the day bleeds out.

The wind livens, and I am out on the playa.

I find you beyond the Chapel of Lost Souls. Every year, I have learned, the Festival features such a chapel. Intricately constructed from small pieces of wood, this year's model is an ornate and rambling two-storey structure with a peaked roof and surround balcony. A playhouse for adults. People roam the tiny rooms, post drawings and pictures of loved ones, create their own shrines and leave eccentric little items of devotion. They use the proffered pens and markers to write messages on the walls.

I can't help myself. I grab a pen and scrawl furiously along the side of a column: "Jonas Alexander Stevens, 10 weeks". He was a good baby. The knife in my chest digs deeper, twists more. When I leave through the other side of the chapel I step out into a sandstorm. The wind cuts against my clothes so that even I can feel the edge. I blink the sand from my eyes. I see nothing ahead except blurred gritty dark. But that doesn't matter. Because deep inside the darkness of me a third eye opens and I see you striding towards me. I can smell you; I can breathe you in. You are night-blooming jasmine riding ocean air.

I feel your hand on my shoulder. I want to cry, and I am not the crying type, not even when I was just as human as those still back in the chapel. You fall beside me, your hand in the small of my back as you guide me through the sandstorm. The lights of the art-cars and sculptures and theme-camps thin out. We are at the far edge of the playa, as far out as we can go. Jagged rocks rise like teeth, cutting darker shapes against the dark sky.

We stand in the space you have created. Walls of sand swirl round us, a crazed and frantic periphery, but we are in a centre of perfect calm. The ground is layered with Turkish and Nepalese rugs; standing lanterns with textured bronze surfaces call a dance of gaslight and shadow.

I turn to you.

"I wish you would speak," I say, like I've said so many times before, hoping for a different response. "Say something. Anything."

You smile.

You are dressed in jeans and T-shirt, a tan leather jacket. You do not look like an angel. Then again, how is a creature like me to know? You look like an ordinary human male, if more attractive than most, just a touch of the uncanny in your sad, grey-green eyes. I stroke your face. Love your cheekbones, your wide, thin-lipped mouth, your olive skin. Love the way you pull me against you, bury your face in my neck. My hands move through your dark hair, trace the hard, sweet lines of your back and arms and shoulders. I can no longer catch my breath, or feel I need to. I take my sustenance, my life, from you. I am made full, turned whole, through you.

We sink into the rugs, and it is like all the times before. I freefall through a sweet and blasted oblivion. And in this oasis of space and time, you tumble with me.

But I hit the ground alone.

And shatter all over again.

Your seed in my body, your blood in my mouth.

He was gone.

The lanterns cast spheres of light into the calmed air. I tried to hold on to the bliss as hard as I could, talk myself away from the despair I knew was waiting: *If it bothers you this much – if he leaves you with nothing, worse than nothing – then put an end to it! Where is your will? Get over it. Get over it. Get over it . . .*

But then his absence rose up under me, made pure and perfect and new. It knifed my heart, my very bones. I started to shake. Who knew when I could have him again, or ever? I drew my knees against my chest and cried out once, twice. I tried not to scream. The sky unreeled above me and his absence seemed more solid than I was, my existence as tenuous as trembling ash. Scattered, lonely figures drifted the playa, heading home after a long night's revelry. An art-car with a pink shag canopy trundled past and took no notice of me. Morning crouched just beneath the horizon and I was exposed and alone. So be it. Anything was better than this loss that rang me hollow, this attack of the sweats, droplets of blood trickling on shivering skin. My body seemed to belong to somebody else. Let the morning have it then, and send flaming into the void what scraps of soul I had left.

The day's first sun lashed my skin.

And all thought dissolved into a soundless screaming.

*   *   *

I opened my eyes.

Pain streaked my torso ... or maybe just the memory of pain, because as my senses woke up one by one I realized I felt ... not bad, considering I'd expected to be a blackened crisp.

I was in a queen-sized bed, piled with pillows, the sheets stained my own sweat-pink. I knew by the black tape covering the windows and the bloodstained wine glass rolling on the floor that this was a vampire RV. It was also the most spacious RV I'd ever seen, not that I was an expert in such things.

I stood. I expected a sweep of dizziness but instead I felt ... not bad. Naked. I looked down at the whiteness of my body, the ridge of sunburn that ran from waist to shoulder. Someone had lathered me in ointment: I swiped off some of the glistening substance, brought it to my nostrils, but couldn't identify it. Whatever it was, it had taken the edge off the pain and faded the scar.

A robe hung in the door frame: ivory silk and tattered lace, lovely enough not to part with and ruined enough to bring here. Slipping it on, I moved gingerly into the hall, found the screen door and stepped outside. After the coppery, strange-vampire smell that filled the RV, night came as a relief.

The vampire I'd met out on the playa was sitting beside a fire pit, dressed in jeans and a blue plaid shirt, her hair pulled back in a braid. She was roasting a marshmallow on a spiked wooden stick. As the screen door whapped shut behind me, she turned her head a little. Then she said, "I don't actually eat them." There were vampires who developed an eating fetish, despite the damage it did to their systems. They were generally held in contempt. "I just like to roast them. I like the way they smell. How do you feel?"

"I'm alive," I said.

"And how do you feel about that?"

"Glad."

"My name is Anna."

Another RV, smaller and painted bright blue, was parked across the way. The space between had been turned into a lounging area, complete with oversized beanbag chairs, a Lucite coffee table, fringed yellow pillows. "You missed the others," she said. "They've gone to watch them burn the Man."

"You stayed behind?"

"I've been watching over you all this time, why stop now?"

"How long have I been out?"

"Three days." She looked at me with those pale golden eyes. "I still don't know your name."

"Vincent."

"You don't look like a Vincent."

"My father wanted a boy."

"You are most definitely not that."

"I renamed myself after my Changing." It seemed absurd to stay with my original name, given by people clueless to who and what I'd become. "After Edna St Vincent Millay. Her friends and family called her Vincent." I added, "She was a poet."

"I know who she was." Anna tipped her head back, said, "'My candle burns at both ends/It will not last the night/ But ah, my foes, and oh, my friends/It gives a lovely light.'" She slipped the marshmallow off the stick, lifted it to her nostrils. She grinned. "But that's not true for us, is it? Our candle burns for a very long time."

Popping sounds in the distance. Towards the far end of the playa, where a shadowed crowd of thousands gathered round the Man, bright lines streaked the sky: purple, blue and yellow, blossoming into fire flowers and breaking apart, falling. "I guess it's started," Anna said. She yawned. "Fireworks. I've seen so many of them." She looked at me sidelong. "You know, I thought they were just myth."

"What?"

"The fallen ones. He wasn't as stunning, or as otherworldly, as I would have expected. I would have thought he'd look . . . more like you, actually."

I shrugged. My beauty was no longer a subject that held much interest for me; and aside from singling me out to the vampire who had taken me for his own, before abandoning me for another pretty thing some sixty years later, it hadn't done so much for me. But then the implication of her words penetrated even my vanity, and I said, "You saw him?"

"He came out of the sandstorm, told me where you were."

"He spoke to you?"

If envy marked my voice, she showed no notice. "No. He put an image inside my head. I had to – I couldn't figure out, right at first, how to align the picture in my head with the playa in front of me, otherwise I would have gotten to you sooner." She stared at me for another long moment. "You thought he'd left you to die?"

"I'm nothing to him," I said. "A toy. A dog on a chain."

"Oh, I don't think so. But if you believe that, why go to him?"

I couldn't bring myself to say the response that came to mind – *Why do people put heroin in their veins?* – so I said nothing.

Anna grinned. "So what is it like, to bed such a creature? To drink from him? I can't even begin to imagine."

"It is like ... " I closed my eyes. Remembering. The moment he entered me, the raw wound of desire suddenly healed. The way everything else in my overlong life folded away and ceased to matter. The look in his eyes as he recognized my slow, shuddering rise to climax, and how he knew the moment to lower his throat to my mouth. I wanted to share this with her, but I did not want to put that feeling into words: such a feeling went beyond words, could only be compromised by them. I opened my eyes and said abruptly, "Why call yourself a nightsinger? I never understood."

"You don't like the term?"

"It's pretentious."

She lifted her eyebrows in what might have been amusement. "Eros and Thanatos," she said. "Love, which is the force of life itself, and destruction –"

"Thank you. I did not know this."

She ignored the sarcasm. "Everything you do, every choice you make, pulls you in one direction or the other. The nightsong," she said, "is about life. Why not align ourselves with that? It's as much of our nature as the rest."

"But you kill, right?"

"Not always. The joops are testament to that. They don't want to die, they only want the high that our bite can give them."

"But from time to time. You kill."

"Of course. " She drew back a bit, looked innocent. "But it doesn't have to be so ... crude. We give appreciation. We respect and celebrate our connection to what we eat, we make the conditions as humane as possible. The nightsong has a place for all of us, the predator as well as the prey. We're woven into its design like every other living thing."

"We cannot make that claim to life. We are the eternal outsiders."

"You are an outsider. You seem to like it that way."

"I don't like anything about it."

"Need, then. You seem to need it that way."

"I need *him*," I said. My voice broke out of me. "I crave him every second I don't have him. Do you know what it's like, to be linked to someone in this way? There's no room for anything, anyone else. It's the loneliest thing I can imagine." I hadn't expected to say any of that. Tears were at my eyes, and I blinked them back with fury.

"That's a fault of imagination," Anna said, with such easy certainty that I wanted to strike her. "Your world is a bigger place than you think. You're just too busy staring into this one little corner."

"I can't do this any more. I want . . . I want . . . "

"What do you want, Vincent?"

"More," I said, and couldn't help myself: "more *life*. All he does is lift me on empty promises and take me apart. I have to finish it before it finishes me."

"And you think he would just let you go?"

"Why wouldn't he? It's not like he sticks around."

"Did it ever occur to you," Anna said slowly, "that he's as trapped by the limitations of his own nature as you are by yours? Whatever chain existing between you is locked around his throat, my dear. He's your slave as much as your master."

"How could you know this?"

"The myths. They get passed along – to some of us, at least." She looked at me pointedly. "They're like vampire fairy tales, or at least that's how I always saw them . . . The allure that we have for them, the ones as fallen, in their own way, as we are in ours. We crave to bite, they crave to be bitten, and in the act of it both find a transcendence."

"It's an illusion."

"Who's to say?"

"Because I wouldn't feel like this," I said, "if that 'transcendence' were real. I would not suffer such an aftermath."

"There's always a price to pay," Anna said mildly. "You're just not used to being the one who has to pay it. Come with me. We'll head out to the playa, meet up with the others. If you like them – and I think you will – you're welcome to travel with us. We're a fun little dysfunctional family, and it's a lovely feeling," she said, "to make yourself a part of something. You should maybe give it a try."

I only looked at her. I wanted to say something, but didn't know what I might possibly express. "Come," Anna said, rising. "Come on," she said again, and there was laughter in her voice. I did not take offence.

She took my hand. It was a foreign feeling, this hand holding, and seemed a little awkward, and yet I did not mind it. We threaded through the camps to the nearest road and walked to the beginning of the playa. We passed a small group of people chanting, "Save the Man! Don't burn the Man! Save the Man!" and Anna tossed her head and laughed.

By the time we reached the dense walls of crowd, the Man was on fire. I could hear the flames, see the light cast into the sky, but my vision was blocked by the people in front of me. The art-cars and pirate ships – there was more than one, apparently – were parked along the crowd's perimeter and people filled the decks and roofs, or sat on each other's shoulders to get a better view. As Anna wove her way through the throng and I trailed behind, I caught the sense of restlessness beginning to sweep the crowd. "The damn thing won't fall," someone muttered, and someone else said, "They made it too strong, this is taking way too long."

I turned my head.

It was the kind of gesture you do for no reason, on impulse or instinct, only to lock eyes with someone who's been looking right at you.

He was standing about fifteen feet away from me, light from the nearby pirate bus falling over him.

His eyes were hooded, his face slack, as if he was held in a trance, and I felt my body and face mirroring his until I floated in a trance of my own. We moved forwards at the same time, and although I was not aware of crossing the space between us, suddenly I was bumping into his chest. My eyes fixed on the ground. I couldn't look up at him, didn't dare. I didn't know if it was shyness or submission or even naked fear. But then his hands were on my shoulders, and he dropped his head towards mine. I could see the wound on his throat; I had marked him, put my name on him.

His breath at my ear, and then he spoke.

"Love," he said, and his voice was hoarse and ancient and thick, and I knew he wasn't suited to language, had to fight to trespass this limitation. "Love," he said again, and very gently kissed my forehead.

His hands slipped off my shoulders and he backed away from me. I could no longer locate my knees; they slipped away; I was down on the ground. People, laughing and shrieking, two of them wearing angel wings, fell into the space around me. I was trembling. I cast about for Anna, but couldn't find her.

I found, instead, the vermin who had pursued me on the playa. He was huddled against a rock, clutching a blanket around his thin shoulders. I noticed how people were keeping a certain distance.

Something inside me shifted, broke open. I can't explain it any better than that. It broke open and spilled all through me: an ache and a tenderness and a kind of breathless awe. It filled me up. I looked at the joop and I realized that I was in him and he was in me. I let my gaze wander through the dense gathering of onlookers and understood that I was in all of them and they were in all of me. I had worlds within me.

The joop glanced up as I approached. His eyes widened as I lowered myself beside him and he started to speak, but I pressed my finger to his lips. I flinched at the contact, at his sick-sweet cancer smell. But I knew what it was within my power to give. I took hold of his wrist and brought it to my mouth. He drew breath. "Only a little," I warned him, "I will only take a little," and, closing my senses to the foulness of it, I sank my teeth into his underwrist. A cheer rose from the crowd, followed by yelling and whistling, the blowing of horns. The Man had started to fall. I listened for a moment, then began to drink.

Point of No Return

Jennifer St Giles

Chapter One

England, 1808

A stormy wind spewed from the North Sea, whipping up the craggy cliffs and punishing the dark walls of Castle Rue Morte before raking across the Yorkshire moor. Its chill stole what little warmth Christine Webber had gleaned from the late summer sun and she shivered. Since a child of ten, she'd often thought of exploring the abandoned castle and disproving rumours of its ghastly hauntings, but that day never seemed to dawn. The necessities of others always took precedence over her desires.

She pulled her worn cloak tighter and hastened her step as she gave a wistful glance at the castle and the rich, lavender blooms of heather stretching across the moor to its iron gates. Today being her afternoon off, she'd planned to explore a little and fill her basket with the sweetly pungent flowers, but her employer's regularly orchestrated crises always whittled away her personal time. Today was no different. This morning's errand for Lady Stafford to the neighbouring village of Scarborough had taken the entire day. And perhaps it had been necessary considering the enormous luncheon she was holding tomorrow to celebrate Lord Stafford's birthday. Since he was often too far into his cups at night, Lady Stafford didn't dare host a party after dark.

The waste of Christine's day didn't matter as much now as it did this morning when the sun was bright. With the coming squall, she wouldn't have had much time anyway and might have even been trapped at the castle until the storm abated – a thought that foolishly intrigued rather than frightened her.

Leaving the moor behind for the encroaching forest, she made her way along the gravelled path with a flutter of anticipation in her breast for what lay just ahead. She could already see him in her mind. She likened his magnificent form to that of a Viking or Roman warrior from ages past. Even Zeus maybe, for he had stolen his way into her heart like a powerful god and captured her imagination and desires.

Thickening trees eased the sting of the biting wind and deepened the evening shadows surrounding her as she made her way. The moment she rounded the bend into the graveyard and passed the eight-foot cross marking the entrance, she saw him. Tall and broad-shouldered, he looked as if he could slay dragons with a single blow from the sword he held. She slid back the hood of her cloak, feeling the chill of the restless breeze upon her face as she breathed in the scent of the approaching rain. Glancing quickly about to assure no one else was around, she sauntered forwards with a saucy swing to her step.

When she reached the bronzed statue, she angled her head back and slid her palm against its chiselled cheek. He stood, a lone warrior guarding over the dead as if he alone could keep the devil at bay. Such courage, noble bearing and – heaven help her – forbidden sensual appeal filled every contour of his likeness. How much more so had the man been in real life?

"Would that I had lived during your time. I would have loved you even if only from afar, as I am a servant and you must surely have been a lord."

She couldn't stop herself from sliding her hand down to press against the smooth curve of his breast, where she imagined his heart would have beaten passionate and true. Deep within the secrets of her heart dwelt the dream that one day he'd become real and steal her away from the loneliness and drudgery of her life. The warrior stood naked, save for his loin cloth and weapons, and she knew him well. Her hands had touched every part of him many times in her quest to draw him perfectly upon the page.

No one knew who the model was, but he'd certainly inspired the sculptor who fashioned him so perfectly in bronze, and drove Christine's hand to recreate him in the pages of her sketch pad.

One day she hoped to learn to paint and bring one of her many renderings of him to colourful life upon canvas. He was unlike any man she'd ever seen, and especially unlike the odiously obese Lord Stafford, whose ogling gaze grew bolder every day.

Christine seriously wondered if she would have to leave Castleborough and her beloved moors for the stench and grime of London's streets – the one place she could assuredly disappear from Lord Stafford. In any place smaller, she would be noticed for the vibrant red of her hair which marked her like a scarlet letter.

Inwardly sighing, Christine dearly wished that her mother's beliefs in otherworldly magic were true and that a cache of heather would be enough to protect her from men like Lord Stafford. If it was true, she'd go pick several baskets despite the storm in order to weave a suit of armour to wear.

Thunder ripped through the air and an icy gust blew up her skirt, giving her a sharp reminder that she had to hurry. She didn't want to draw any more attention from Lord and Lady Stafford by being much later.

"A kiss to hold you until I return again, my warrior." She lifted her lips to the strong breeze and waited a moment, imagining what she would feel if he kissed her. Then she patted his thick thigh and stepped back with a wink, before turning to leave. The path would take her past the church, the village, and on to the Staffords' estates. At one time there had been a church adjoining the graveyard, but it had burned down and those trapped inside had died. Instead of rebuilding on the same spot, the villagers had built the large memorial to honour the dead and moved the church closer to the town.

Aerick the Eternal waited in the shadows, watching the red-haired beauty as he had too many times to count. Frustration and longing pulsed with every beat of his heart. He knew her well. The scent of her blood, the fragrance of her skin, the softly sensual lilt of her voice. From the darkness of the memorial-crypt in which he stood, he'd often watched her with his bronze likeness across the graveyard. The way she spoke . . . the way she touched. And like a love-starved fool, he'd often stolen into her room during the dark of the night just to see her sleep, breathe of her essence, and imagine her touching him.

She was an innocent angel of fiery light whom he could only love from afar even though she bore the tiny birthmark of a vampire's mate – an hourglass – upon her neck. But with each passing season his resolve grew weaker, for his body throbbed to know hers from the tip of his fangs to the depths of his immortal soul. He would never claim her for his own with a blood oath, though. To condemn her to a life spent only within the darkness of the night would be a sacrilege. No sunrises, no sunsets, no heated kisses of nature's light – only a pale moon and the distant stars to illuminate, night after cold night. But even more importantly, his race was under siege. The slayers he battled grew in number every year and the prime vampires roving free upon the earth were few. Most now lived in asylums deep within the earth, giving up freedom for safety, and only having one child, if any. Aerick feared the vampire race would soon face extinction, despite the war in which he led the Blood Defenders.

The scrolled iron doors of the crypt and the confines of his hooded cloak kept him from seeing as much of her as he wanted, but he was close enough to breathe in her soft scent and sweet blood. It was a torture he couldn't resist. Fisting his hands, he sank his fangs into the flesh of his mouth as desire rushed through him in a hot, muscle-hardening wave of desperation. From the moment he'd seen her several years ago, he'd been unable to assuage his need with another, mortal or immortal. He often paced the halls of his castle with her on his mind, eating at his sanity. The place truly was haunted now.

He should be known as Aerick the Foolish for hanging himself within this tormenting limbo. Were she a widow, he could at least share the pleasures of the flesh with her. But he couldn't conscience taking her virginity without the honourable intent of marriage. He should leave Rue Morte and cut himself off from her forev–

A bloodthirsty howl roared over the echoes of thunder ringing in the air. A slayer! Aerick had centuries of practice in discerning their cry from that of a true Lycan. Vampire and Lycan had lived in nocturnal harmony until the form-stealing slayers crawled their way from the depths of hell by making a deal with Satan. Since the vampires and the Lycan refused to annihilate mortals for Satan, he sent slayers, beings that shifted into any form they chose. The slayers had brought about the War Of Distrust between the vampires and the Lycans, and preyed upon mortals in both the vampire and Lycan forms. Now, although they'd only ever protected them, humans thought of all vampires and Lycans as monstrous beasts of evil.

Aerick grabbed the metal bars of the crypt with gloved hands as he watched his red-haired angel stop on the path and glance about for danger. Though the storm had darkened the sky into a roiling brew of thunderclouds, there was still enough sunlight clinging to the day to painfully sear his skin. Aerick didn't know if the slayer was on the hunt for him, just prowling the area, or after the woman, but he knew without a doubt that the evil shifter would ravage and kill her if he could.

As he stepped from the crypt into the rapidly fading light of the day, his skin stung despite the heavy leather of his hooded cloak, boots and gloves. Ignoring the discomfort, he rushed forwards, unsheathing his sword – a Blood Defender was always armed to the fangs for battle. But his usual confident calm escaped him. Knowing he was seconds away from meeting his angel for the first time left him as vulnerable as a babe.

The slayer let out another blood-chilling cry, closer this time, coming through the forest. The bastard was hunting her and she knew it, even though the slayer wasn't in sight yet.

"Oh God!" she cried out and ran down the path to the church, leaving the darker shadows of the graveyard for the brighter light of the path. Huge droplets of rain splattered down and grew in force by the second.

Aerick cursed under his breath and raced after her, his skin burning despite the cooling rain and the protective clothes he wore. He reached her just as the beast broke from the trees in the form of a giant werewolf, saliva running down its fangs. It was hungry to kill.

Her scream rent the air and she fell back in horror. Coming up from behind, Aerick caught her and had a moment's rush of touching her for the first time before he thrust her behind him. He raised his sword, ready for the slayer's attack.

The towering beast sniffed the air and then laughed. "A bit early for a prime to be roaming about, isn't it? Your cloak won't hold in a fight, fool. I'll rip it and you'll burn to death watching me slake my appetites upon her."

Another cry came from his angel. The air trembled with the depth of her fear.

In all of Aerick's battling, he'd never hated a slayer more. He wanted to push back his hood just so the beast could read its death in his eyes. "Pray for mercy, slayer. For today you'll die." Aerick lunged, going for the werewolf's throat.

The beast twisted, lashing out with a long claw to rip off Aerick's hood. Aerick ducked low and the slayer's nails tore the back of his cloak. Fiery pain coursed through him as the rays of the fading sun penetrated and burned him. Aerick sliced into the slayer's furry arm, drawing a gush of black blood, before spinning around to place himself between his love and the beast. He braced himself against the pain searing his back.

The beast was larger than most of the slayers by several feet. Aerick decided to take it down from the feet up rather than risk getting close enough for another strike at its jugular. To make things a little more difficult, it started to hail.

"Is the human worth your life, prime?" the beast taunted. "Save yourself and return to the dark."

"Never, beast. Slayers are cowards. I'll engrave that on your tombstone. "

"Yours will read, 'A fool slain by Ghenghis'," the monster boasted with a sneer.

Aerick feigned another thrust to the slayer's throat, but at the last moment slashed downwards to its swollen groin. The beast's quick turn saved it from castration but Aerick's sword sank into the werewolf's thigh, hitting bone.

The beast roared in anger and pain then shifted into a fanged serpent to lunge between Aerick's legs. Aerick's slashing sword landed in the dirt as he slipped on the hail, missing the serpent by a hair's breadth. The girl's scream filled him with dread.

He swung around, already imagining the serpent's fangs sinking into her throat, but she wasn't huddled into a frightened ball behind him as he'd expected. Instead, she'd armed herself with a thick tree branch and swung at the serpent, hitting its head and knocking it into the air. The serpent shifted into a vulture and flew at her face.

Too close to safely use his sword, Aerick flung himself at his angel, his arms wide. He managed to knock her to the ground just before the vulture struck. Its claws dug into Aerick's back, tearing more from his cloak.

With sword still in hand, Aerick rolled to the side and slashed upwards, cutting off a claw.

"I'll see you both in hell!" The vulture, dripping black blood, added a shattering screech to his threat and flew off into the hailstorm.

In pain, Aerick smelled his flesh burning. He had to get out of the light.

"God in heaven! What was that beast?" The girl struggled upwards, face pale, blue eyes wide as she tried to block the bruising rain and hail. Leaves had tangled in her vibrant hair and a bleeding scratch marred her left cheek. The sweet smell of her blood set his churning hunger for her on fire. His fangs ached so badly that he bit the inside of his mouth, sucked at his own blood and fought hard to rein in his desire. He'd not lose his honour even if it killed him.

Taking a bracing breath, he clasped her gloved hand in his and helped her to her feet. Her body trembled badly from what had to be shock and fear, but her bravery didn't waver. It made him smile through his pain. "Come with me quickly," he said. "There is a chance the beast could return."

She shuddered harder and he slipped his arm around her and pulled her close to his side to protect her from the hail and guide her through the storm. The church was their closest shelter and he sighed with relief once the heavy, wood doors shut behind them. He only deliberated a moment before he decided to take her beneath the sanctuary.

She was soaked to the bone and the ferocity of the storm would keep her here for some time yet. He needed his skin salve and she needed warmth. Before she could catch her breath he led her to the secret panel and down the stairs.

The village of Castleborough was built with the secret help of varlets, human-like servants to immortals. Practically every building was connected by underground tunnels and had hidden rooms, stocked with furniture and supplies for a vampire's basic needs. When the light of day could kill, darkharbours were essential. Though it had been some time since he last visited the church, Aerick found the darkharbour in perfect order.

"Wait here," he told her as he closed the secret stone panel to the room and locked it. Ghenghis the Slayer couldn't get to them here even if he were whole enough to follow them. Aerick moved to the fireplace and took off his gloves and weapons. With the stored sulphur and phosphorus, he had a fire going in minutes. Then he lit an oil lamp and faced the girl, his heart pounding in wonder and his back searing in pain. Though she shivered, she didn't move towards the heat, but faced him, gloves in hand and brow knotted fiercely.

"Who are you? What room is this within the church?"

Aerick considered lying and telling her that he was just a man who happened to be near, but couldn't bring himself to cheat them both of the truth. With a groan, he unclasped his wet cloak and slipped off the hood. "Except for our names, we are already known to each other, angel. I am Aerick the Eternal. My bronze likeness guards the graveyard."

Christine's heart thundered even as her blood drained in a dizzying rush. In the flickering light, she studied the strong features of the man before her. She took in the breadth of his shoulders, the sculpted sinew of his muscles and the bearing of his stance, complete with sword, then stood in stunned silence. It was true. The man was the statue come to life, now wearing a loose white shirt, black pants and black boots.

Her gloves fell from her grasp and she leaned against the wall, needing support as her knees went weak.

He hurried to her, grasping her shoulders. "I'm sorry. I didn't mean to shock you. You've spoken to the statue so often that in my mind I thought I was already real to you. Forgive me, angel."

"You heard me?" she gasped, remembering her often improper musings.

"And watched. From nearby," he said. "You were too beautiful to ignore."

This couldn't be happening. This couldn't be real. Christine couldn't believe it, yet couldn't stop herself from touching him, from reaching up and brushing her fingers over his rough cheeks and chin. His skin was warm and vibrant and supple, but left no doubt of the iron beneath. His black hair fell to his shoulders in a wild mane and his green eyes were as sharp and fierce as the sword he'd wielded against the evil beast. The scent of sandalwood mixed with something arousing and exotic filled her senses. Yes, he was the man from the statue, but much bigger and more lethal and so much more ... everything. More valiant. More male. More predatory ... more sensual. Her thumb touched the full bottom lip that she'd drawn so many times and he gasped with pleasure, revealing a set of white teeth with ... oh God ... fangs. Her gaze met Aerick the

Eternal's and the dark hunger in them stole the breath from her lungs.

It was more than she could absorb and a suffocating veil closed over her, dimming the world to almost black.

Chapter Two

Christine wavered on her feet, her mind and body recoiling from the surreal sight of Aerick's fangs. Everything within her wanted to believe that the shape-shifting beast's attack, and all the rest of this, was some strange dream, but she feared it to be true. Which meant her mother's wild stories of supernatural beings and magic were true and . . . her warrior was real . . . and fanged . . . and a vampire.

Oh God. She couldn't breathe.

"Damn! Forgive me yet again, my angel," Aerick said softly, his expression pained as he hid evidence of his fangs. "It would seem you have stolen my wits with your beauty and your touch. You must understand, no matter how strange all of this is, you've nothing to fear from me." He scooped her off her feet, cradling her in his arms like something precious as he walked towards the hearth. She didn't know which was hotter, the fire or the heat of his body. Both seeped through her wet clothes to warm her skin.

"I swear upon my honour, no harm will come to you. Do you believe me?" He stood before the firelight, his gaze intent and earnest.

Caution warred with her dreams of the ideal man she'd imagined him to be. He'd already proven his noble courage to be true. He'd saved her life. Yet she had so many questions. And if he was a vampire, didn't she need to fear that as much as the slavering beast who had hunted her down?

"Yes," she whispered, then gasped for air, remembering to breathe. Call her a fool but she couldn't bring herself to truly fear him. She believed him and she believed *in* him.

"Thank God," he said, closing his eyes a moment.

She planted a finger in the middle of his white shirt. "But that doesn't mean you don't have a great deal to answer for, Aerick the Eternal. Now put me down and start explaining everything from the beginning."

His eyes popped open and an amused grin tugged at the corners of his sensual mouth. "Everything? I fear we'll be here quite a while then. I've been alive for a very long time."

As he set her on her feet, Christine had to remind herself that his beautiful mouth held deadly fangs. Rather than admit to being still too dizzy to stand, she moved two steps to the hearthstone and sat down, hoping that her heart would soon stop thundering in her ears.

He picked up a soft-looking pelt of white fur from the end of the bed and spread it before the hearth at her feet.

She watched him carefully, waiting for him to say more. When he didn't, she narrowed her gaze at him and cleared her throat, demanding his attention. "I should think you can start with the answers to these questions first. Who are you? What are you? How have you seen me in the graveyard? What sort of beast can change form like that?"

Aerick shook his head, seemingly bemused. Kneeling down on the rug before her, he caught a lock of her hair between his fingers. "Your hair gives testament to your fiery spirit. I will have your name first, angel. Then we will get you dry and warm before I talk."

"Christine." She swallowed, watching him run his thumb over the strands of her hair. Her body tingled warmly despite her chill.

"Christine,' he said softly, his voice a deep caress. "A perfect name for an angel. Now off with your wet cloak, so we can set it to dry as we wait for the storm to pass."

Her fingers fumbled with the clasp at her throat, but it wasn't the cold that hindered her. It was that he was so close and desire was burning unsettlingly in his eyes.

"Let me," he said. Brushing her fingers aside, he simply undid her cloak and leaned forwards to slip it from her shoulders. But inside her, she felt he did so much more to her than that. He stripped her defences bare. He made her wonder how his sensual mouth – so close now – would feel against hers. Her entire being knotted with expectation as she looked directly into his eyes. She had imagined his kiss so many times before.

He suddenly froze and stared back at her, then drew a sharp breath – pupils dilating and nostrils flaring.

A hot, branding fire swept down Christine's spine to her loins.

Aerick dropped her cloak, letting it fall down her back, and grabbed her shoulders, his mouth parting with expectation. She couldn't stop her gaze from dropping to the fangs he revealed. She knew she should fear them, fear that part of him, but she didn't. It fascinated her.

Releasing her, he cursed and stood to face the fire, his hands fisted. "Dear God, don't fear me. I can stand many things but not that. I'll never bite you, Christine. I'll never condemn you to a life of eternal darkness with a blood oath."

"I ... didn't ... fear you just now. I –" Her cheeks burned. Reaching up, she touched his arm. "I ... wondered of your kiss. If you've watched me at the statue then you know I often have." She ran her gaze down his form, knowing just how often she'd touched every curve of his bronze likeness. It was then that she saw his torn and bloody shirt.

"Good heavens! How could I have forgotten? You're hurt." She stood, urging him to turn his back towards her. "The creature clawed you."

He was silent until she brought her gaze to his as he looked over his shoulder. "Just a few scrapes. The sunlight burned my exposed skin, but there's a salve here that will help me heal quickly. It is the curse of my race to be free only within the darkness of the night."

"Where?" Christine muttered, ashamed of herself as she assessed Aerick's shredded shirt. He had more than a few "scratches".

He shifted his broad shoulder towards her and arched a brow that somehow made her heart flip. "Where what?"

"Where is the salve? We should have taken care of you immediately. We also need water and bandages."

"You would care for me?" He sounded incredulous.

Christine blinked at Aerick. "Of course. Why ever would I not?"

He shrugged then grimaced with pain. "I am a warrior breed of my kind. Besides the varlets who serve immortals, it would be rare to find another to care for me. Though warriors are essential to the survival of our race, they're seen as barbaric – a necessary evil to most, reviling and unclean to some. And for a human to care for one of my kind would be even more unusual, considering the reputation the slayers have built for us."

"What do you mean?"

"Slayers shift into any image they choose and often take the form of a vampire or werewolf when hunting mortals. That was a slayer that attacked us outside."

"So the ghastly stories are true, but we're blaming the wrong culprit?"

"Yes. A long time ago we tried everything we could to prove our innocence, but no mortal would believe us, even after seeing what the slayers could do."

"Forgive me for saying so, but most of your race and mine are ignorant fools then. How can they possibly revile the men who keep them safe? How could a mortal believe a slayer over a man like you? Thankfully, I am not ignorant. Now where is the salve?"

Aerick laughed. "You'll find the salve, bandages and towels in the cabinet by the table, but no water. This brandy on the mantel will have to suffice. The underground well for this darkharbour went dry a number of years ago."

"Darkharbour?" she asked as she gathered up the supplies.

"Hidden shelters to escape the sun when there's no time to return home."

"These places are everywhere?" She set everything on the table that stood to the left of the hearth.

"Most everywhere. There's even a place in the graveyard. It's the large crypt near the statue. That's where I first saw you several years ago," he said as he brought the brandy from the mantel and scooted a chair closer to the hearth. He opened the decanter and drank two long swallows from the bottle.

"Years?" she asked softly. Had she known it somewhere in her consciousness? Was that why she'd become so enamoured with the statue? Had she sensed he was there and fallen in love with his presence? Was that why she felt as if she already knew him?

"Years." He took another drink and then handed her the bottle. "You'd better have a bit yourself. It will warm you, and brace you for tending to my burns. Are you sure you want to do this?"

"Yes, I do," she said softly, eyeing the brandy. To Christine, the invitation to drink seemed like an open door to a world she'd only seen from afar. Gentlemen drank brandy, servants drank ale and she'd only ever had tea. Her hand trembled as she took the decanter, more from the brush of Aerick's fingers against hers than from the decision to take her first sip of brandy. She'd never be the same after today, so why not change everything about herself she could? Before she could think of any reason why she shouldn't take a drink, she lifted the bottle to her lips and proceeded to gulp a mouthful of . . . pure fire.

"Oh my!" she gasped. Her eyes watered and she shuddered as the brandy burned all the way to her stomach.

"Careful," he said, catching the decanter before it fell from her shaking grasp.

"People choose to drink that?" Her voice wheezed.

He laughed, a rich deep sound. She was sure she'd appreciate it later when she could function again. "Yes, just not all at once unless they're used to it."

"I think I'll stick with my tea for the time being," she said when she could finally breathe again. She shook her head as another shudder worked up her spine. "You're sure you want brandy put on your back?"

"The alcohol will cleanse the wounds and aid healing." He took off his shirt. If Aerick hadn't picked up the brandy for another sip then Christine would have done so herself. At least then she'd have an excuse for her sudden inability to think or speak. The bronze statue didn't match up to the man because the man surpassed the mere statue. He was a living work of art. His shoulders seemed to be three times the size of hers. Every hard-muscled curve of his chest and stomach flowed with perfection and oozed power. Her mouth watered and her fingers tingled. A warm glow centred in her belly and a hot rush of blood sang through her veins.

She closed her eyes a moment to gain control of her senses. Never before had the sight of a man's chest been notable to her, and her reaction shocked her, for she wanted to see more of him, all of him. She seriously doubted that any sculptor or painter could capture Aerick's perfection.

She opened her eyes for another look then gasped. Aerick had turned and straddled the chair before the fire, leaving his back to her. There were a handful of bloody cuts, but as he'd warned her, the burns were the worse. They were each about the size of his splayed hand, blistered and raw, as if the sun's rays had completely destroyed his skin.

Guiltily shoving away her wayward thoughts, she quietly set to work, cleaning the cuts first with the brandy he handed her. Next to him, she felt like a mouse before a lion that was growing tenser by the moment. But she refused to hurry. In fact, her every touch upon his tightening muscles seemed to linger longer than necessary as she ministered to him, for the emotion building inside her wouldn't let her do less than her best. She couldn't stay removed from his sacrifice and how much he had risked in coming to her rescue. She finished by putting a thick layer of salve over his burns, wrapping a wide bandage around his chest and securing it with a knot.

Looking down into his eyes, she brushed a silken length of hair back from his face and slid her palm to his rough cheek. "If that creature had succeeded in tearing more of your cloak, then you would have died as horribly as he said. You would have burned to death?"

He pressed his cheek tighter to her palm, slowly, almost reverently. His mouth was grim, and the intensity of his gaze burned like fire. "If it had been full day instead of evening, and if the exposure had lasted longer than the few minutes, then yes, it could happen. But the likelihood of the slayer gaining that much advantage over me in a fight is slim. Slayers like to instil fear, make their opponents doubt themselves."

"Then he was a fool as well. Even a blind man can see you've no need to question yourself." She pulled her hand back, but he caught her fingers in his and settled his gaze intently on hers.

"But I do doubt, Christine. Every time I have thought of you, every time I have seen you, I've doubted myself. And now that I have met you, I doubt myself even more. My honour tells me to stay away from you while everything else within me demands . . . other things." He brought her hand to his lips and kissed her fingers.

Lightning. That was the only way to describe the fire that flashed through her blood. Her mouth went dry and her pulse thundered.

"Other things," she whispered, her gaze dropping to watch his lips close over her fingertips. Her inner fire burned hotter. "Like a kiss?"

"To begin with. Yes." He urged her closer to him. As big as he was, sitting in the chair put him just a little more than a head shorter than her. "Do you want to kiss me, Christine?"

"Yes."

"Then kiss me, angel."

She knew another door was opening in her world. A change for ever. She was sure her heart would beat its way through her chest as she leaned down to set her lips on his. Warm and full and soft, his mouth was all that she ever imagined and more. His lips opened and pressed firmly to hers. It was magical. He was wondrous. The sweet brandy on his breath and the sandalwood of his scent washed over her senses, making her sigh. She could have stayed just like that forever, but reluctantly pulled back after a few moments.

"Perfect," he rasped. "An angel's kiss. So pure."

"There are different kinds of kisses?"

His gaze slid from her face down her body and back up, leaving a path as heated as the hearth fire. "Many kinds of kisses, many places to kiss."

Her fingertips still burned where he had kissed them. "Show me. Show me a warrior's kiss, Aerick."

He studied her for a long moment, as if drinking in every nuance of her. "I don't know that I dare. Every moment we spend together drives us closer to a point of no return – that irrevocable moment in time when everything changes for ever. But in truth, if I was going to leave before that point, I would have done so already. I am weak." He stood. "So, you would know a warrior's kiss then?"

"Yes," she said, looking up at him and meeting the dark hunger in his gaze head on. "I would know your kisses. All of them."

"God help me," Aerick whispered as he cupped her face in his hands and lowered his mouth to hers. His kiss began as hers, the firm press of warm lips. But the power of his kiss was intensified by the heat of his body and the feel of his hands upon her neck. The fire inside her flamed hotter and grew with each pounding beat of her heart.

His tongue brushed over her bottom lip once, then again and again, delving deeper into her mouth with each stroke, as if after having a small taste, he needed more and more.

She pressed closer to him, bringing her breasts to his chest and sliding her fingers into the dark silk of his hair. Suddenly everything changed in a heartbeat, as if her reaction to him loosened his invisible restraints. He growled deep in his throat and his tongue delved into her mouth, finding her tongue as she met him in a battling play of thrusts and parries. His hands left her throat and slid downwards. One hand covered her breast as the other went to her back, holding her firmly to him.

His hard-muscled thigh slid between her legs as he leaned her back over his arm. Unbelievable pleasure filled her. The pressure and heat of him against her intimate flesh, the rubbing caress of his palm over her nipple, the path of his kiss and questing tongue as he moved from her lips down her neck, and then back to her mouth to start the kiss all over again. He kept kissing her until she grew fevered, desperate. Her breaths became ragged and her body cried for more. She clutched his shoulders, arching to him. "Help! I am drowning in pleasure but can't seem to get enough," she whispered between gasps.

"Nor I, angel, nor I," Aerick said, his body trembling against hers, his breaths rasping harshly. He pressed his forehead to hers and his hair softly caressed her cheeks and chest. "That is why we must stop and I must leave here. I fear the hunger I have for you has no end. I could strip you bare and kiss you everywhere for ever and not quench my need." He eased back from her and she tightened her grip upon his shoulders. "Perhaps the storm has eased and I can see you home before it's too late."

Christine felt as if Aerick was suddenly closing a door he'd opened and she was about to lose something essential to her heart and her life. Did he mean to leave here? Did he mean this room, or did he mean Castleborough? Did she really want him to go and leave her untouched now that she'd finally found him? Did she want to leave this moment without knowing more of this incredible pleasure?

No.

He set her back on her feet and stepped away from her.

She bit her lip and he groaned, turning to face the fire with his fists clenched. After he drew a deep breath, he went right to the brandy and drank deep, his bandaged back to her.

Right or wrong, Christine didn't want this to end. Not yet. *I could strip you bare and kiss you everywhere for ever and not quench my need.*

She reached for the buttons on her blue muslin dress and undid them quickly, discarding all notions of propriety beneath the surging tide of desire. She'd never believed she'd actually be able to love this man and she wasn't sure she'd ever have this chance again. Her dress fell to a puddle at her feet and she slipped off her shoes then loosened the drawstring of her chemise. Aerick turned and froze, the decanter halfway to his mouth.

She didn't say anything yet, but slid her chemise up on her left hip, then her right, to untie her pantalettes and let them slide down her legs. She'd not worn a corset, and now stood before him in her chemise and stockings, feeling as if she'd just bared her very soul to him. "If I had lived during your time, Aerick, I would have loved you, even if only from afar. Now that you are near, how can I not share with you all there is to know of love?"

Chapter Three

In all of his years of battle, in all of his experiences during a life long-lived, Aerick had never come apart at the very seams of his soul before. Not until he looked up and saw her undressing for him, her fingers trembling and her gaze unsure, despite her valiant spirit. But it was her words and her question that went to the very centre of his heart. He still could not bring her into the dark bleakness of his life for ever, but could he love her as much as possible at this moment? She'd reached beyond all barriers of her life for him. How could he not?

He set the brandy down with a thud on the table and crossed the room to sweep her into his arms. He laid her on the warm fur facing the fire. Claiming her lips, he kissed her thoroughly again, drinking in the sweetness of her mouth before kissing his way down her throat. He could feel the racing beat of her heart and smell the heady scent of her blood pounding beneath his lips. His mouth watered and his fangs ached to make her his for ever.

The blood rushing through his veins sang her name to every part of him, making him throb with a consuming hunger so great that he trembled from holding himself in check. Any discomfort from the burns was negligible compared to the fire in his loins. He seemed like a beast out of control, for nothing would do but to keep a rocking pressure against anything Christine.

Pulling her chemise down to expose her breasts to his questing tongue, he cupped them in his hands and lavished each rosy nipple to a hard peak. He tasted and sucked and moulded and tweaked until she thrashed, her skin glowing from the heat of her desire. But it wasn't enough. He wanted her bare to his every lick, his every kiss. Kneeling at her side, he pulled her chemise down over her hips and tossed it. Then he untied her garters and slipped her stockings off her long, shapely legs until she lay nude before him, a picture of well-loved feminine perfection – red hair splayed wildly about her on the white fur, the firelight gleaming off her ivory skin, her blue eyes smoky, her mouth swollen and needy for his, her body flushed and ripe with the first bloom of passion. He would never forget this moment. He drew in a deep breath, savouring the scent of her arousal, a perfume of desire made just for him.

"Aerick?"

"Just admiring perfection. Seeing you like this is like looking at the glory of a fiery sun." Leaning down, he brought her foot to his lips and kissed her instep before moving to her ankle and lifting her leg higher.

"What are you doing?" she gasped and rose to her elbows.

"Exactly what I said, kissing you everywhere," he murmured, watching the tantalizing sway of her breasts. He licked his way up to her knee and then treated her other leg to the same kisses. Still angled up on her elbows, she watched him with her eyes wide with wonder. "You're beautiful, my love. More than I could dream possible."

"Aerick!" She tensed as if momentarily frightened when he touched her there with his mouth, then cried out in pleasure. He watched his angel come apart, a total slave to the pleasure overtaking her body. She fell back upon the fur, her back arched, and her breasts shook with every shuddering breath and every moaning cry. She screamed his name and convulsed against him.

He thought he would stop then, he thought he could stop then, but he couldn't. Being with her broke him, tore apart every notion of discipline he'd ever had as a warrior. His body shuddered so hard with his need to be inside her that he could no longer hold up his own weight. He freed himself from his trousers.

He expected her to tighten and fear the frenzy of his passion, but she didn't. She wrapped her arms around him and kissed him, rocking her body to meet his need. After years of celibacy, his orgasm slammed into him with such force and such pleasure that his vision faded to black for a moment. He hadn't even needed the taste of blood upon his tongue to reach his pleasure. Rolling to his side, he pulled her with him and collapsed in sheer wonder at the woman in his arms and what had just happened to him.

Christine looked into Aerick's dazed eyes, and brushed her fingers over his lips, touching the tip of his fangs lightly. He was breathing heavily, his body still shuddering from what she now knew had to be heaven upon earth. Pleasure still sang inside of her, brought to an even greater height because she knew that Aerick had experienced the same. What would happen next? She didn't know. It didn't necessarily matter because she belonged to him heart, body and soul. This love had been growing inside her for years, just waiting for him. She would follow him wherever he would go. "Why didn't you take me as a man would a woman?"

He pulled her close and kissed her softly then sighed. "Your virginity and my honour are still intact. As much as I would like to keep you with me for ever, I can't. Once the storm passes, I will see you back home. Then once I know the slayer Ghenghis is dead and you're safe, I will leave Castleborough."

Christine reared back in a mixture of shock and confusion. In the span of a breath, heaven shattered at her feet. Her insides trembled at the resolve in his green eyes. "What do you mean?"

"The slayer vowed to see you in hell. I'll die before that happens. You'll be safe. I'll gather the Blood Defenders and we'll hunt Ghenghis down."

Feeling too bare and vulnerable, she pulled from Aerick's embrace and pulled her chemise over her head. "At the moment the slayer doesn't concern me at all. What concerns me is what else you said." She blinked back the tears that threatened. "Why can't I be 'with' you? And how could you possibly even consider that you'll 'see me back home' and 'leave Castleborough', and that would be the end of everything we just shared?"

"Damn." Sitting up, he raked his hands through his hair and scrubbed his eyes, before facing her with a bleak expression. "What other outcome did you expect, angel? To stop now will save us both from greater pain in the future. The point of no return will only become sharper and more deadly the closer we become. I'll never condemn you to the darkness of my life, especially with my race in jeopardy of extinction. What honourable man or vampire would? And how long do you think we can share a passion as great as ours without me taking your virginity or your blood? You ask too much of me. My weakness for you is too great. Just look at what happened tonight within the mere two hours."

"Am I a woman of sound mind, Aerick?"

"Of course," he said, brow knotting with confusion.

"I am intelligent and capable."

"Extremely."

"Then I don't need you to make my decisions for me. I should be the one to decide for myself whether or not I want to share a future with you in your world or remain alone in mine."

"Unfortunately, I can't allow that," he said. Clearly agitated, he rose, pulled on his pants and marched over to the brandy decanter, then drank several gulps. "I've lived a great deal longer than you have, and I am much more aware of the sacrifices and dangers than you are. With knowledge comes responsibility. I can't conscience it. None of the Blood Defenders have women with them because almost all vampires with mates have gone to live within the protection of darkasylums, safe from slayers."

Christine didn't say a word, but rose and dressed herself. She wasn't going to beg to be loved, for if he loved her as she loved him, then all of his reasonings wouldn't matter in the end. Her fingers shook and her heart thudded with as much pain as it had raced with joy and excitement. She knew he watched her, expected her to agree with him. She refused to look at him. "I am ready," she said, slipping her cloak on. "It would be best for me to return home alone." She kept her gaze away from his eyes.

He'd put on his heavy cloak and his sword. "I will see you home, but none will see me."

She lifted her gaze then, meeting his for a brief moment before turning towards the door. "There's no need, Aerick. It would be better for me to cut things off here than to do so moments before having to walk back into the prison of my life."

"Damn it, Christine," he said. He crossed the room, caught her shoulders and turned her to face him. "Don't you understand that is exactly what I am trying to keep you from? A dark prison. Only this one goes on through eternity."

She shook her head. "You're making decisions for me. You don't know anything about my life at all, what it's like for me here . . . what I must face alone every day." A flash of Lord Stafford's lecherous gaze entered her mind and she shoved it aside. "But none of that is what really matters. It wouldn't be any different for me if I were the queen of England. A life without love and passion to fill it is a dark prison, Aerick, and that's most likely why you have no hope of a future. If all of the Blood Defenders see life as you do then it is no wonder you feel your race is doomed."

She hoped for a spark of understanding to light the grim darkness in his eyes, but none came.

"You don't understand. In my world it isn't that simple."

"No, it is you who doesn't understand. Love is that simple."

"Dear God, were it so," Aerick said. His mouth fell passionately upon hers and he backed her up to the door kissing her so deeply that she felt him all the way to her soul again. By the time he ended the kiss Christine was back to the desperation of desire, needing to be satisfied at that moment or her heart would cease to beat. Aerick himself was breathing heavily.

He pulled away from her with a cry of anguish. "Let's go."

She followed him up the stairs and into the church vestibule, where she was surprised to hear the sound of men's voices.

"If the chit don't 'pear by morn, we'll have to tell Lord Stafford the bloody wolf got her. For the life of me I've never heard such a bloodthirsty howl in me whole life."

"I'd bet a new shilling that if she met up with the beast, she'd walk away without a scratch. That red hair is the devil's own I tell you."

Christine whispered in Aerick's ear. "It's Billy and Will Jenkins. They're Lord Stafford's stable hands and must be searching for me."

"I can see they're working hard." The look in Aerick's eyes could kill.

Christine laid a staying hand on his arm. "It's all right. They'll see me home. They're just another part of my world."

"They'll wonder why you didn't reveal yourself when they first arrived."

"I'll tell them I fell asleep." She quickly searched the vestibule and pointed to a seat in a shadowed alcove across the room.

"I'll be watching," Aerick said and then fell back into the shadows.

Christine called out for the stable hands and all too soon she found herself riding back through the rain and chill wind and settled into her room at the Stafford Estates. Lady Stafford was quite put out that Christine had not made it back home before the storm and had thus ruined the quiet evening. Lord Stafford kept looking at her to the point that Christine pulled her sodden hood back up and pretended to be so cold that she shook droplets of water everywhere until Lady Stafford dismissed her for the evening.

After cleaning herself at the washstand and warming up with as much towel rubbing as her skin could stand, she climbed into her cot exhausted, but was unable to fall asleep. As she drifted in and out of consciousness, she relived every moment spent with Aerick. Sometimes she felt as if she could even smell him, as if he were lying next to her in the night. She felt him so strongly that she called out his name and reached out, only to wake alone and cold. She realized that it would always be so. All she would ever have of love were the stolen moments she'd shared with him. She didn't know how it would ever be enough. Tears fell then as it seemed her heart broke open and grieved, aching for the man she'd loved for so long, yet only known for a moment in time.

Aerick fell to his knees at the scent of Christine's tears. He'd watched her tossing and turning and knew that he was responsible for stealing the peace from her sleep and the light from her innocent eyes. She was wrong. To bring her into his world would only take more from her. Yet as he heard her muffled cries, his heart, his resolve, his whole being, broke beneath the pain. Without meaning to they'd both reached that dagger point of no return and it had plunged itself right through her heart and his.

He left Christine as the greying shadows of dawn appeared on the horizon. Before returning to Castle Rue Morte, he returned to the darkharbour he'd shared with Christine, extinguished the fire, drank the last of the brandy and, from the bed, took the fur on which she'd lain with him. Once within the stone walls of his own home, he didn't go to the kitchen for a meal as was his custom, but went to his study with a full decanter of brandy. His valet, Alfred, found him there a while later.

"There you are, sir. You quite had me worried when you didn't come home. I was about to search the darkharbours." Alfred blinked hard and leaned over Aerick's desk. "Looks as if you hit a spot of trouble, sir. What happened?"

"A slayer and a bit of sunlight. I'll live."

"If you don't mind me saying so, sir, you don't look like you will."

Aerick eyed the empty decanter. "You might be right, Alfred."

"Well, let's get you settled in to rest until the moonrise, and maybe you won't need a hair of the dog."

Aerick stood, but shook his head. "There's no cure, Alfred." He grabbed up the white fur and carried it to his chamber. He made it to the bed and fell face down, clutching the fur. Alfred fussed about and managed to pull off Aerick's boots and heavy cloak before he left, muttering about the idiocy of youth. Aerick lay in the dark. For a warrior who'd won many battles, he felt as if he'd just lost the most important one of his life. Everything within him ached for Christine.

Was it possible that she had learned more in her short life than he? Was it possible that she was right and he was wrong?

Chapter Four

Christine woke to discover the sun already on the rise. She'd overslept. She was in a miserable state. Her throat hurt and her body felt flushed with a fever. Aching everywhere possible, she rolled from her cot and dressed for the day, then hurried down to attend her duties.

The house was in a flurry of activity getting ready for Lord Stafford's birthday party.

"There you are," the mistress said sternly. "I want both the library and Lord Stafford's study in tip-top shape. The gentlemen are likely to retire for a port and a smoke after eating. So make sure everything is well stocked and not a bit of dust anywhere."

"Ye..s, mi . . . .tr . . . " To Christine's acute embarrassment her voice cracked hoarsely, barely audible.

The mistress narrowed her eyes. "Don't you dare become ill. Rumour has it that you were caught in the storm last night because you were cavorting like a trollop in Scarborough."

Christine stepped back in shock. Her appalled "no" came out no louder than a squeak, making her throat hurt even more. She shook her head adamantly.

Her mistress just gave her a disbelieving glare. Christine shivered. Once rumours spring up they're like weeds that keep growing no matter how hard you try to cut them down.

"Get to work – *after* you cover that devil's hair of yours with a mob cap."

Hurrying to gather the cleaning supplies she needed, Christine dug her cap out of her pocket and pulled it on. That she had forgotten to cover her hair before coming downstairs told her just how poorly she must be feeling this morning. Since Lord Stafford was often known to hide in his study when his wife was having a crisis – something she had before every big party – Christine decided to clean the library first. When she was finished, she walked tentatively to Lord Stafford's study and knocked. After several more tries with still no answer, she opened the door and breathed a sigh of relief at the empty, although odorous, room. Between the cigar smoke and the stench of alcohol (Aerick's brandy smelled so much sweeter), the room was in desperate need of airing out. She immediately opened the french windows that adjoined the terrace and looked out upon the day. Leaning against the cool glass and wood, she paused a moment needing to rest. She still had too much to do. It wouldn't be long before the guests arrived, then after that the night would come.

Would she ever see Aerick again? Did she dare go back to the graveyard after dark to find him?

It was the first time she'd allowed herself to think about him since rising, to delve past the "it doesn't matter" mantra running through her head.

The sun had broken through the grey clouds and it glistened off the green lawn and bright blooms. The breeze was light and fresh and felt good on her flushed skin. A rainbow arched near the forest, making her think a pot of gold lay just beyond the trees. This is what he didn't want her to give up. She seriously considered what life without sunlight would be.

Would she miss it? With her whole heart and every part of her being she would. She couldn't deny that. But was the warmth of the sun worth the loss of love? She could go blind tomorrow and never be able to see sunlight again. And as tragic as that would be, it wouldn't matter as much if she were in Aerick's arms. It wasn't as if she were giving up every aspect of life to be with him. The moonlight held its own beauty, and if she missed a rainbow, couldn't she paint herself one to see? As beautiful as the day was, it couldn't match the magical heaven of being with Aerick.

Sighing, she turned from the light and set to work. Lord Stafford was a swine. Cigar ash was everywhere, and tables were sticky from spilled drink. Everything might have had its place but that didn't necessarily mean anything. Christine set to work, forcing her body to function despite the increasing bouts of dizziness.

"Here she is, Claymore, the wench I was telling you about."

Christine whipped around to find that Lord Stafford and another gentleman had entered through the open french windows and had closed the door. Though she immediately felt uncomfortable, she gave a proper curtsey. "Lord Stafford. Forgive me. I am finished here and will leave you to your guest." Her voice was but a bare whisper, hardly audible.

She quickly crossed to the door, but before she could open it completely, Lord Stafford pressed his obese self against it, forcing it shut.

"Not so fast, wench." He reached out and jerked off her mob cap. Her hair tumbled down.

Christine reared back from him, clutching her arms to her chest.

"You weren't lying, Stafford. I've never seen hair like fire before," the other man said.

"And I wasn't lying about the other either. You should have seen her last night. Came back with her lips all swollen like a strumpet who'd been whoring all night long. Look at her now, her cheeks are still glowing."

Shaking her head, Christine backed away from Lord Stafford, smelling the strong odour of drink on him. He was very well into his cups already, but that didn't excuse his behaviour. She had to get out of the room. Going towards the desk would box her in more, but if she moved towards the fireplace, she might be able to get past the other gentleman and escape through the french windows.

"She does appear to be flushed, Stafford. And definitely a beauty – for a wench."

"Since she's now free with her favours, Claymore, I think we should avail ourselves of them. Sort of a birthday present to me. Just imagine piercing that hot fire."

The blood rushed from Christine's head and she wavered slightly as she made a dash towards the fireplace. "Stay away from me," she cried, but her voice was no louder than a peep.

"Now listen here, whore. You can make this easy on yourself and end up with a nice little trinket every now and then, or you can make this difficult. Either way, Lord Claymore and I are going to have a little fun with you now."

Claymore wasn't exactly encouraging Lord Stafford, but he wasn't calling a halt to the assault either. He was looking at her as if he wouldn't mind partaking in the birthday present Lord Stafford wanted. Christine didn't waste another moment. She grabbed the fireplace poker and brandished it before her. "Let me out of here now, or you both will pay severely for your crime."

Lord Stafford laughed. "Crime? The only crime is that I didn't get to have you first, whore. I've been watching you and that witch's red hair of yours for years. You were mine and now I'll finally have you."

He came at her and Christine held her ground until he was almost on her. Then she stepped to the side and brought the poker down hard on Lord Stafford's back, knocking him to the ground. Stafford screamed.

Before she could turn around, Claymore grabbed her from behind, one arm around her throat, the other around her breast.

"Drop the poker," he demanded.

She twisted, trying to hit him with it. Lord Stafford was still screaming, but now his body was shaking wildly on the floor.

Claymore tightened his arm around her throat, cutting off her air. He grabbed hold of her breast, squeezing until an agony of pain filled her. Still, she wouldn't let go of her weapon. It was her only hope. She struggled against him, her vision dimming by the second as her lungs burned for air.

Suddenly people burst into the room – men, women, servants, all screaming, demanding to know what was wrong.

"This witch," Claymore said. "She cast a spell on Lord Stafford so that he couldn't move and then began to hit him with the poker."

"I swear her mother was a devil's witch who up and disappeared in the middle of the night. Likely whoring for Satan, she is."

"Somebody get the magistrate!"

"Lord Stafford will be dead by then. Get her to break her spell first," someone else shouted.

Christine screamed. She tried over and over to explain that the men had attacked her, but her voice was no more than a scratchy screech. Her throat was on fire and her body turned to rubber as she fought Lord Claymore's hold. He choked off her air completely and the world went black . . .

. . . she was drowning. She couldn't breathe.

Christine gasped for air and choked as another glass of water was flung in her face.

"I tell you that unless you can get her to undo her spell, Lord Stafford will die," a man said.

She could hear Lady Stafford screaming hysterically in the background. Christine opened her eyes to find herself bound to a chair. "I'm not a witch," she cried. "I'm not a witch."

"Stop her from talking. She's making Lord Stafford worse. He's having another convulsion."

A handkerchief was stuffed in her mouth and pulled tight. She blinked at the people around her. Some of the faces she'd known for years, yet they were looking at her as if she were a creature worse than the beast she'd seen last night.

Dear God, Aerick! Her heart cried out. How could she have ever known that their stolen moments would bring such an end?

"There's only one thing to do," Claymore said to the crowd. "If you kill the witch, her spell will be broken."

"How?"

"Burn her! The fire will purify her sins and save Lord Stafford."

"Where? Where should the witch face God's judgment?"

"Before the graveyard's cross!" someone shouted and met with resounding agreement.

Men came forwards and grabbed up her chair, their hands groping indecently at her body as they carried her out of the house into the bright beauty of the day. She struggled wildly, screaming from her hoarse throat. She couldn't believe this was happening to her now, in this day and age. Something like this was only possible hundreds of years ago when ignorance and superstition ran rampant within the minds of people. But now?

Someone, somewhere, had to bring sanity to the mob. She tried screaming for help but the gag only became more and more nauseating the harder she tried.

Suddenly her grandmother's last words to her so many years ago hit home. *Take care, Christine. With hair like yours, you've been cursed with the beauty of the MacWebbers. Your mother left before harm could befall her. You make sure you stay sensible and pure and hopefully no harm will come your way.*

The nightmarish trip seemed without end as the crowd of people carried her through the village, holding her up like a severed head on a pike. As they reached the graveyard, she saw Aerick's statue and her heart broke in half. She'd had him in her arms and she'd let him go, though she knew with her whole being that all she would ever want in life was to be with him. Now it was too late, even though her whole soul desperately cried out for him.

It was too late to know his kiss again. To feel the race of his pulse as his body pressed intimately against hers. To know one more time the pleasure with which he'd taken her to heaven.

Aerick! Her heart wept.

They scraped her skin harshly with the ropes as they unbound her from the chair. There were so many hands grabbing at her as they forced her to the cold iron cross and tied her to it, hands bound over her head, waist lashed so tight she could barely breathe, her feet numb. They began throwing wood and branches at her that they'd gathered from the surrounding forest. The sticks bruised and cut as they hit her face and chest. She could do nothing to protect herself. She could do nothing to stop the insanity. All she could do was set her gaze upon the statue of Aerick and give her mind over to their few stolen moments of bliss.

Aerick came awake with a sense of terror grabbing him by the throat. He shook off the brandy-induced haze and rolled to his feet, battle ready. He gazed around his bedchamber. Gauging from the heat bombarding him through the sun-blocking panels covering the windows, his super senses told him it was still full daylight outside. He found no immediate threat near but the fear inside him doubled with every pounding beat of his heart. Something was very, very wrong.

He felt Christine's soul crying out for him, more strongly than ever before. He had to get to her!

"Alfred!" he shouted.

The valet came running. "Lord Aerick! What are you doing?"

Aerick looked up. He was donning as many layers of protective leather clothing as he could. "I'm going out. Something is very wrong."

"Dear God! Aerick! You can't. You know that no matter how many layers you put on, your skin will still burn. I'll go. Just tell me what the problem is."

"I don't know! I feel her terror. I have to go to her." He donned several heavy leather masks to protect his face.

"Whose terror?"

"The woman from the village. I've spoken to you of her before. I met her last night." Aerick explained the slayer's attack and how they sought shelter from the storm in the church's darkharbour.

"Then let me go to her," Alfred replied. "Or at least let us heat pitch to spread over your clothing."

Aerick shook his head. "There is no time. You can come with me if you choose, but as dire as I sense things are, I cannot wait. I'll take the tunnels as far as I can and then pray my exposure to the sun will be . . . survivable."

Armed with as many weapons as they could carry, Aerick led Alfred down to Rue Morte's dungeon and opened the portal to the underground caverns. With the lantern lighting their way, they travelled by boat beneath the moors until they reached the tunnels beneath Castleborough. Every pole stroke seemed an eternity to Aerick, for the closer he drew to the village, the stronger Christine's terror became.

Alfred tied off the boat as Aerick ran ahead through the tunnel. His mind told him that Christine's logical location would be at the Staffords' estates, but her spirit kept calling to him from the graveyard. There was a calmness about her now, as if whatever danger she had faced had passed and she now rested within a peaceful spirit realm. Dead?

"Nooo! Dear God! Nooo!" His fangs lashed his lip with the ferocity of a cry that continued to echo through the tunnels as he ran. He couldn't be too late.

He paused at the crossroads, torn over which way to go. Breathing deeply, he bit down on the panic inside him and focused his being on her spirit. He had to follow his heart. Alfred ran behind him as Aerick rushed through the dank tunnels to the stairs that led up to the surface. He looked out through the memorial's iron doors and his heart stopped beating. On the hillside, tied to a cross and surrounded by flames was Christine.

She wasn't struggling against her bindings. She wasn't screaming at the crowd who shouted, "Burn, witch, burn." She looked towards his bronze statue with an expression of total rapture upon her face.

Seething with rage, Aerick pulled on his hoods and burst from the crypt. He fought his way through the crowd with Alfred at his back. The mob parted like a sea but Aerick wished they would have fought him. He wanted to lash out, to maim and kill the ignorance that had thought to burn an angel to death. He felt his skin frying, despite the layers of clothing, yet kept running into the full light of the sun, knowing that every second brought Christine to the same horrific fate. He dashed through the scorching flames to reach her and cut her free, his heart and hope seizing as she fell boneless into his arms. Her skirts smoked but hadn't ignited into flames yet. Her skin was red and her hair appeared singed at the edges. So she shouldn't be dead. Unless the terror and the heat had been too much for her. He couldn't feel her heart beat. He couldn't feel her breathing. Her spirit still hung in angelic peace around him.

Screaming with rage and vowing to murder every person there, Aerick raced for the crypt with Alfred slashing a sword before them. The sun ate mercilessly at him, but nothing compared to the pain of holding Christine's lifeless body in his arms. Once in the darkness, Alfred barred the iron doors and they quickly descended to the secret door that led to the underground tunnels. Aerick made it to the safety of the tunnels before he collapsed to the ground. All he wanted to do was clutch Christine to his heart and send his spirit into death after hers. Instead, he flung off his masks, ignoring the raw burning of his skin, and laid her down. Then he began breathing his breath into her, compressing her heart to the rhythm of his, and delving his spirit after hers, calling her back to him.

One breath. All he needed was one breath. If he could get her to take just one breath, he could either sink his fangs into her and claim her for ever as his – giving her no choice in her future, and a life filled with eternal darkness; or feed her on his immortal blood which would strengthen her and leave the future up to her.

"Breathe for me, angel. Dear God, breathe for me."

At the faintest gasp from her, he had to decide. Instantly. Forcing his own wants and needs aside, he sank his fangs into his wrist and trickled his blood into her mouth, massaging her throat until she swallowed the immortal fluid. She jolted, her blue eyes popping open as she coughed and then sucked in large gulps of air.

"Aerick," she whispered, reaching out for him. "Are you real?"

"Painfully so." He smiled and pulled her into his arms. His burns would have to wait until his heart had drunk its fill of her.

Her blue eyes were dark with emotion, and welling with tears. "Oh, God. We have a second chance, a real second chance. I love you," she said. "More than sunshine, more than life itself, and I am never letting you go."

"Don't," he said with a half-laugh to cover the cry of relief flooding his soul. Then he said the one thing he'd never said before, "I love you, angel. Heart and soul through eternity, I pledge myself to you. You will be safe with me for ever no matter what the price."

Later, when they were stronger, when they were both healed, he'd ask her to share his life as an immortal, as a vampire. He'd ask her to take the blood oath with him. Then he'd leave the Blood Defenders and take her to live within the safety of a darkasylum, because he could never chance losing her again.

"How did you know to save me?"

"Our spirits are entwined. Your terror is mine."

Christine looked into the pain and desire of Aerick's gaze and realized what he'd sacrificed to save her. His whole body had to be as blistered as his face. Careful not to hurt him, she brought her lips to his, wondering why his pledge filled her with both joy and worry. But as he claimed her lips with his and she felt his love all the way to the centre of her heart, she thought of nothing except meeting and matching his passion, body and soul, for ever.

With Friends Like These

Dawn Cook

Greg peered into the fridge, not seeing the smeared takeout boxes and stale bagels any more. Bending to the lowest shelf, he grabbed two of his room-mate's juice bottles. The smoked glass clinked as he stood and shut the fridge, having to give it that backward kick so it wouldn't drift open again. Joe's music was cranked, the classical music vibrating the silverware in the rusted sink. He'd tell him to turn it down, but the only time his room-mate played the *1812 Overture* was when he was trying to impress his latest girlfriend.

Smiling faintly, Greg ran a hand over his late-night stubble and turned to the living room. Night had made the two large windows with their broken blinds into black mirrors. Shuffling to the couch, Greg twisted the cap off the first bottle and took a swig of the tomato juice/body-building protein drink before falling back into the worn leather. The smell of the puke of Joe's girlfriend from last week puffed up, and he shifted down without a pause. Setting the second bottle on the scratched glass table, he stared at the big, blank flat-screen TV, wondering if it was worth the effort to get up and find the game controller. Though the rest of the apartment sucked, Joe had the latest and best when it came to gaming. No one could say Joe didn't have his priorities in order.

The music from Joe's room started to build, right along with the feminine gasping moan, and Greg reached for the remote, turned on the TV and hit the volume to try to drown it out. Damn, he didn't know how the guy got the girls like that. It had to be his rep because he wasn't much to look at, thin from his running despite the high-energy protein he slammed down. Greg stood almost a foot taller than him, muscles defined from the running track in the corner, and still, when they went to the bar it was Joe who got the hot girl and he was left with her ugly room-mate.

TV blaring, Greg wedged his steel-toed boots off and kicked them to the side where they lay, the heavy dark mud from the September rains caking off to add to yesterday's dried clay. His gaze wandered over the pizza boxes from two weeks ago, the mismatched furniture and the bare, cold walls devoid of anything soft or clean.

The upstairs, two-room apartment had seen too many college parties and slipshod landlords to be considered anything but a place to crash for four years and forget about. A mishmash of styles from previous tenants had left their mark. A dusty beaded lampshade from the sixties dangled over the linoleum table. Beside the corded wall phone, a fuzzy print of Elvis was scrawled with the phone numbers of girls long since having gained their diploma, fifteen pounds, a mortgage and two-point-five kids. The matted shag carpet with an ocean of sand underneath was wall-to-wall ugliness, worn to nothing by the door. This wasn't where he was going to be for ever. It was temporary.

Yeah, temporary, he thought, sitting up in the flabby leather cushions when the buzz from the drink began to hit him. He'd moved in with Joe almost a year ago, a fight between him and his girlfriend over "World of Warcraft" forcing the move. He had offered to make her an avatar so they could kill pigs together in the woods, but she kicked him out after one too many gaming parties with the guys. He hadn't seen any of his old friends for months. Between classes and work, it was all Greg could do to remember to eat. Thank God for energy drinks, he thought, lifting the bottle in a silent salute.

The moaning from Joe's room was reaching a desperate crescendo, climaxing in time with the music – cannons, drums, horns and one frantic woman going off all at once. Greg couldn't help his smirk. The guy had talent.

Greg was mindlessly channel surfing when the door to Joe's room was flung open, hitting the wall to make the dent just a little deeper. "Hey," the lanky guy said as he crossed the living room to get to the kitchen, his quick strides making him almost a blur in his black boxer shorts.

Greg grunted something back, turning down the volume before the neighbours began pounding on the walls. Flicking through commercials, Greg paused to watch the one with the caveman. *Ooooh, poned again.*

Joe was on his fifth year of a four-year running scholarship, abusing the system that paid for everything as long as he kept coming in first. From his room came quiet panting and the soft strains of violins. It was a weird mix – Joe's classical tastes and low-income clutter. Greg figured Joe had money somewhere. Maybe one of those hard-ass families that wouldn't let you dip into the family fortune until you turned thirty or something. Joe had the attitude of killing time while he waited for something. The TV and electronic equipment *had* come with a service plan, not scrape marks from the back of someone's truck.

Greg's eyes flicked into the kitchen at the snap of Joe opening his own bottle. Joe downed half of it as he came into the living room. He was clean shaven despite it being night, smelling faintly like the girl's perfume and the shower he'd probably taken before she came over. His boxers hung loose on him, and sweat still shone on his shoulders between the new red marks from the girl's fingers. Eyes bright from the sex and exuding energy, he stretched out in the chair kitty-corner to the couch. A heavy sigh came from him, and his foot jittered. Up and down, that was Joe. If he didn't know better, Greg would say his room-mate was an addict, but he'd never found a pill or a syringe. Maybe he was just careful.

"Rough night?" Greg asked sarcastically.

"Rock and roll, baby." Eyes on the TV, Joe stared, lost, but his hand came out and they bumped knuckles. "Can't live with them . . ."

Greg sipped his drink, feeling it wake him up. "And you can't shoot 'em."

Joe laughed, still high on the woman in the next room. Greg clicked it to MTV, dropping the remote and stifling his envy. He'd been living like a monk the last eight months, not daring to bring a girl here. Not only would he have to clean, but Joe would give her that little grin of his, toss his hair, and she'd be singing soprano to the *1812 Overture* in three days.

"I wanna go for a run," Joe said, slamming the rest of his drink and standing. "Get up."

"Now?" Greg looked at the black window. Yeah, it was Friday, but he was too tired from his shift to hit the bar, much less the streets. "It's almost midnight."

"Chicken?" Joe started to do warm-ups. "Get up. Don't make me run down there alone. All kinds of weird crap out there."

"Which is why I don't want to go running in the middle of the night." Greg settled back into the cushions, eyes going to the mud he'd tracked in. Maybe he should vacuum tomorrow. Buy a mud mat with his next pay cheque instead of beer. *Did they even have a vacuum?* "Grow up, will you?"

A soft, slow laugh came out of Joe, and Greg looked askance at him, thinking his eyes were unusually bright. "The boogie man?" Joe intoned, wiggling his fingers at him. "Vampires going to get you? Ooooh. You'd better watch out. You'd better not cry."

"Piss on it." Greg began to click the remote. Pow – blow away the preacher man. Pow – waste the western. Pow – Billy Mayes hawking super knives, cut down mid-shout.

Joe laughed, and Greg's eyes squinted in anger even as he warmed. "Then you tell me how a freaky white kid can run up the side of a building," Greg said, eyes flicking to the open bedroom door as the sound of the shower filtered out. Yeah, it was embarrassing, and yeah, he might have been drunk at the time. But he had seen it, and his heart pounded just remembering it. It had given him the creeps, watching the small, dark-haired figure run straight up the wall like he was some kind of superhero.

"Dude, I told you to lay off the drugs."

"I don't do drugs, and you know it," Greg said sourly as he went back to clicking. The bottle was cold against his knee, and he downed it.

Joe had his leg up against the wall by the TV, almost doing the splits as he stretched. "I'm talking your food, man. The stuff they put in it. Look at my juice. One hundred per cent organic. None of that MSG, pesticide crap. It's going to kill you. Harden your cells till they can't move, stick in your brain and make you dumb. Look at me." Joe leaned in to his stretch to become about a foot thick. "No pesticides in this body. I'm keeping it clean. Only put top-grade into it."

Greg put his empty aside and cracked open the second. It burned going down, the heavy tomato flavour spiced with basil and some kind of pepper. The buzz was kicking in good now to make him feel alive. Joe got it where he worked, when he felt like it, at an organic food store. Greg wouldn't touch half the crap in the fridge that Joe brought home, but the juice was OK.

"Come on, run with me," Joe coaxed as he brought his foot off the wall and did a smooth, effortless back arch into a stretch against the floor. *OK, maybe that's how he got the girls.* "We can take the river route. Look at the hookers," he added, grinning.

Greg threw a T-shirt at him, which had been wedged between the cushions, and Joe put it on, hiding his thin chest and the new passion marks. "We'll look like a couple of gays down there," he said, remembering the feeling of watching eyes on them the one time they'd taken the river path after dark.

Joe leaned the other way, hamstring stretching. "Not if we're looking at hookers."

Staring at the TV, Greg tried to find a way to say no without looking like he was scared. The river route was a dark stretch of winding pavement between the bar district and the carnival about two miles away. During the day, the long riverside park was the realm of mummy daycares and lunchtime athletes, but at night, it became the property of gangs, dealers and stupid-asses that were too stupid to stay out of the stupid park after sundown.

"Come on, it's only a mile, then we'll loop back through the city," Joe coaxed. "Seriously. If I don't get out and move, I'm going to explode. Unless you think your vampire is going to come back? Bring your dog sticker if you're afraid."

Dog sticker. It was a shiny length of collapsible steel that Greg used to beat off pony-size poodles and yappy terriers who thought a running man was fair game, but the shiny point on the one end when it was extended would beat off muggers, too. Not that he'd ever had to use it.

Groaning, Greg clicked off the TV, got up and stretched for the ceiling to feel his back pop and crack. It would be nothing but crack heads, shooters and human trash down at the river once they got past the bars, but like Joe said, it was only a mile before they got to the better lit path beyond it. And he liked to run with Joe, especially at night when the air was cool and it felt like the world was sleeping. He had never been a slouch, but Joe pushed him. One more block, one more mile. He was in the best shape of his life for all the pizza and beer. "I don't know how you talk me into stuff like this," he grumbled.

Joe got to his feet, clearly eager. "Give me a sec to get rid of my bed warmer," he said, and Greg finished his second bottle in a rush, draining the last thin stream with his head tilted back.

"Dude. You gotta start treating your ladies with more respect."

But Joe was already walking away, cocky as all hell. "Yeah. Being Mr Personality has them lined out our door for you," he said, vanishing into the black pit his bedroom was. "Hey, bitch!" came his faint voice, joined by a high-pitched protest when the sound of the water quit. "You gotta go. Me and my man are going running!"

The woman's confusion grew louder, and Greg turned from balancing his empty bottles on the tower they were building in the corner as she made her stumbling entrance, hair dripping and clothes sticking to her wet skin as Joe propelled her, one hand on her shoulder, one hand on her ass, towards the door.

"Baby, what I do?" she asked, bewildered, bare feet on their nasty carpet. Maybe Greg's words had done some good, because Joe was more gentle than usual, giving her a kiss and devilish smile at the door before looping her purse over her shoulder and handing her a fuzzy, white, fake-fur coat.

"You're cool, sugar heart," he said, shoving a fifty in her pocket. "I gotta go do something. Get a cab, OK? Go eat some pie. Forget about me. I'm bad news. Make your heart break and your momma cry."

"Yeah, but baby!" she protested as he dropped her shoes on top of her coat and pushed her out. Joe shut the door and turned, the woman forgotten already as he went to the fridge. An exasperated half-scream echoed in the hall, and the sound of a pair of shoes hitting the door made Greg jump, but Joe only grinned.

Frowning and shaking his head, Greg went to his own room to change. Midnight at the river. Shit, those hookers better be hot.

The smell of dew-wet concrete was strong in the light fog, just enough of a presence to give a glow to the lights strung like pebbles on a string as they curved and twisted, following the path of the river. The stress and fatigue of the day was gone, his blood pumping and muscles moving to a rhythm that Greg could imagine went back to the beginnings of time when man fought to eat and ran to live.

Joe was beside him, their footfalls in perfect unison adding to the surreal feel, like they were floating in the muffled night, trees and empty benches passing as if they were momentary fragments of existence. It made Greg wonder if there wasn't a little magic mushroom in that "organic" drink Joe kept bringing home. He felt too damn good for it to just be himself.

They'd left the noisy, migrating, bar-hopping, street-wide party behind only a few minutes ago, but it seemed like miles now that they'd found a pattern of strides beside each other and the asphalt seemed to flow under them. The district had been busy for Friday, the unseasonably warm September evening bringing everyone out. He'd felt like malevolent eyes had been on him as he ran beside Joe in the district, straight down the middle of the blocked-off street, but every time he looked, it had only been laughing pedestrians saluting him with their open bottles, probably thinking they were asses for running in the night instead of partying. It had been a relief to leave the glow and alcohol-induced noise behind and let the cooler, muffled darkness enfold them, reminding him of why he'd said yes.

Before them, past the twists and turns yet to run, he could see the bright lights of the carnival, the Ferris wheel rising high above the trees still holding a few dry, brittle leaves. Behind them lay the bars, the sound of the music thumping like the heart of the night. Between was the river, the flat smoothness of the water contrasting with the darkness and the lumps of shadows looming and falling behind them as they ran.

Moving easy, Greg glanced at one of the city bridges that spanned the slow flow, empty of traffic at this hour. A glint of metal, a motion where none should be – something had caught his attention, and he stared, trying to figure out what he was looking at. Shit, he thought, his pace bobbling. There was a man, under the bridge, not standing under it at the edge of the water, but standing under it at the apex of the arch, hanging upside down.

Heart pounding, he came to a grit-sliding halt. "Holy shit!" he exclaimed, pointing. "Joe. Look!" The cool night air turned oppressive as the breeze from his passage stopped, and Greg felt a sweat born of fear break out on him.

Joe pulled up three steps ahead of him, turning to look where Greg was pointing.

"There!" Greg said, voice loud, but no one was there now. "There was a guy. Right there. On the bridge!"

"God, you're worse than a little girl," Joe said derisively.

He started to move, and Greg reached out, grabbing his arm. Warmth flooded his face at the mocking slant to Joe's brow, and he hesitated. He couldn't say that the man had been standing on the underside of the arch. Not now.

"Come on. Let's go," Joe said as he pulled away, a new eagerness to his eyes.

"No, wait." The man under the bridge forgotten, Greg panted, seeing his breath steam in the September chill. Something wasn't right, and he squinted at Joe ahead of him, breathing just as hard in the light of a street lamp. "How come your breath isn't steaming?" he asked.

Eyebrows high, Joe opened his mouth, but nothing came out.

A soft thump behind him spun Greg around. Autumn leaves drifted down around the spare man now standing there, his pointy-toed boots planted firmly on the asphalt. Shit, they were going to get mugged by a fashion-challenged gang member in a torn black leotard and funny hat.

"Because he's not warm-blooded, ass," the man said, confidence in his stance and words even though he stood almost a foot shorter than Greg.

"Hey, uh, hi, Michel," Joe said as he came forwards to stand beside Greg, looking both nervous and angry. "Long time no see."

Joe knows this guy? Panic ran cold through him, and his legs hurt now that he had stopped. What the hell was going on?

The man looked Joe up and down, not reaching for a gun or a knife, just standing there with a disgusted expression on his face. "Johann . . . Johann . . . Johann. I told you not to come down here. Ever."

Shit. It was a gang. An Asian or other foreign gang by the sound of the freaky accent the man had. He knew Joe was too up and down to not be on drugs. He could see the headlines now. TWO FOUND DEAD AT THE RIVER. LIFE GOES ON.

"And I told you I'd be back," said Joe.

Greg stiffened as he looked at his room-mate, his attention drawn by the never-before-heard hard tone to his voice. The casual, slipshod, sex-hungry guy was gone. He was mean looking, face showing new lines etched from a past anger, his stance aggressive as he stood with his fisted hands slightly from his sides and his head lowered.

"Is this your idea of a joke?" the guy said, jerking Greg's attention back to him.

"No, man," Joe said, his words casual, but his tone tight. "And he ain't a bribe. He's just with me. I wanna come home. You don't know what it's like being alone."

Greg tried to swallow. Shit, there was no one else out here, and the faint thumping of the music echoed louder. "You know him?" he said, then cleared his throat when his voice cracked. "Joe, you know this jack-off?"

"He's my brother."

The man facing them inclined his head, making a sort of half-bow, half-dance step back. It would have looked stupid on anyone else, but he made it look good, even as Greg could see the mockery in it. "I'm his older, smarter brother."

He began to circle with an eerie grace, and grit ground under Greg's heel as he turned to follow him, his skin prickling.

"You bring me a peace offering, and it doesn't have tits," Joe's brother said, eyeing Greg from under his shaggy bangs, looking at him like a dog wanting a bone.

"I thought you might be tired of them," Joe said, and Greg couldn't tell if he was kidding or not. "No, I told you, he's not a present."

"You taught him to run?"

It was mocking, and Joe was starting to lose his swagger, a hint of desperation beginning to show. "I wanted someone to run with, Michel. He runs good, even as big as he is. Leave him alone. I just wanna come home."

His chest had stopped hurting, but Greg's pulse still hammered. There was a shadowy figure on the bridge, standing at the railing as a car whizzed past. "Hey, look. You guys have a lot to talk about. Whatever. I gotta go," he said, starting to back up.

Greg sucked in his breath as suddenly Joe's brother was beside him, stinking of anger and domination. "I'm going to take your pretty boy," he said, smiling at Joe to show his teeth in threat. "And I'm not letting you come back. Bugger off."

A chill ran through Greg as the man turned his eyes to him, mocking and eager. "Run. I like it when you all get hot."

"Screw you, you asshole," Greg said, taking two steps backwards. There were two of them, and only one of him. But on the bridge in the thickening fog, were three figures now, standing apart but watching, silently watching. Gang members, or help?

Greg made a fist and dropped back to fight, but Joe was girling out, hunched and pleading. "Let me come home, Michel. I swear, you let me come home!" His jaw clenched, and a panicked determination coloured his voice. "Let me come home, or you're going to die tonight!"

"By your hand?" Joe's brother laughed, and Greg breathed easier when he turned his focus on Joe instead. "You can't kill me," he said, boots scuffing. "Momma would be pissed. Daddy would send his dogs after you. You'd be shredded before the sun came up." Lips parting, a slip of a moving tongue promised unwanted attention as he looked at Greg. "That's the rules. No fighting between brothers, or we'd all be dead in a hundred years. I can eat *you*, though."

"Michel, no!" Joe shouted, and his brother lunged.

"Hey!" Greg exclaimed, falling back when Michel grabbed his arm. Lashing out with a fist, he stumbled when he hit nothing. He found himself yanked upright and spun around until his arm was twisted to his back. Michel, though smaller by almost a head, had him.

His breath coming fast in his ear, Michel lifted ever so slightly on his arm, making Greg grit his teeth and grunt. "You're a strong little worm," the man behind him said eagerly.

"Mother f– Ow!" Greg yelped, going limp when Michel lifted his arm an inch more and pain flooded him.

"I bet you're a tasty little worm, too."

"What the hell is wrong with you?" Greg shouted, lunging backwards when he felt the grazing of teeth on his neck. *Shit, the freakazoide was trying to bite him!* His wildly darting eyes went past a wimping-out Joe to the bridge. There was a whole row of figures, all different in height from the size of a child on up – just watching.

Panic gave him strength, and he dropped, slipping out of Michel's grasp and lurching away, almost on his hands and knees. Regaining his feet, he stood beside Joe. His hands shook, and anger filled him. Why the hell wasn't Joe helping him? "Your brother is freaking insane!" he yelled, his voice going dead in the rising fog.

"Yeah, I know, man. It was a real drag growing up with him." Joe glanced at the watchers on the bridge. "Michel, I'm telling you. Don't touch him!" he said loudly, and, laughing, his brother came at Greg again, mouth open and arms grasping like it was a big joke.

Greg back-pedalled, his heart pounding and his only thought being to not let the freak get a hold on him again. This time, Joe stepped between them, the blur of his motion almost too fast to see.

"Out of my way!" Michel all but growled, and Greg watched in open-mouthed awe as he tossed Joe aside to land thirty feet away, stunned and unmoving on the grass. A shadowy figure seemed to melt from behind the nearby tree, kneeling on one knee to help Joe up.

"Son of a bitch," Greg breathed, hunched as he shook out his dog sticker. The click of the metal cylinders aligning themselves pinged through him, and he held it like it was a long knife.

"Michel, I'm telling you to stop!" Joe cried, but the man was coming at him, and Greg braced himself, jamming the point of the dog sticker right into him. A shudder went through Greg at the feel of the sudden give of flesh, and Joe's brother's eyes, inches from his own, widened.

"Stay away from me, you fucking ass," Greg said, even as his stomach turned. Shit, he'd just stabbed a man.

"Gaggh . . . oooh," the man leaning against him moaned, one hand on Greg's shoulder, the other holding the end of the stick jammed into him. But Greg's relief turned to fear when the pained sound coming from Michel turned into a chuckle, and then a laugh. Letting go, Greg backed up, horrified as Joe's brother plucked the metal stick out of him and tossed it to the sidewalk where it glinted wetly. His laughter grew, echoing in the fog where everything else seemed to be sucked up by it. And still the figures on the bridge didn't move.

"Michel, don't," Joe said from the shadows, his voice low and devoid of emotion. "I'm telling you now, as mother and father are my witnesses. Don't bite him."

Michel only laughed louder, the high-pitched edge making the hairs on the back of Greg's neck stand on end. "You lose!" Michel shouted, flinging a hand wildly as if grandstanding to the people on the bridge. "Everything that is yours is mine, little brother. It always has been, and it always will be. And that includes this. Your *friend*. God, it's pathetic!" He came closer, and Greg refused to back up, his heart pounding at the sight of Michel's eyes, glinting in the light when all else was dim and foggy. "Only vampire blood can kill another vampire," he said, a mocking smile quirking his lips. "But you're unusually strong. You might last long enough to be a diversion."

Vampire? Feeling his expression go slack, Greg remembered the figure standing upside down under the bridge, the feeling of being watched whenever he and Joe ran, the man he'd seen run up the side of the building only a week before his girl kicked him out and he met Joe on the bus.

In a jerk of motion, Michel reached for his shoulder, and yanked Greg forwards and into him. Pain seared his neck, and Greg screamed, howling as he realized the heavy weight on his throat was a head and that the man was taking a chunk out of him. His entire body jerked as a flash of heat burned. He was eating him. The mother was eating him!

And suddenly the weight and fire were gone and he was airborne. He hit the sidewalk and slid, his running pants tearing and the skin scraping from his thigh. "What the hell!" he shouted, orientating himself. He was thirty feet away, and that son of a bitch who had bitten him was kneeling in the golden haze of the street light, gagging as he vomited.

Ignoring the pain in his thigh, Greg got to his feet, awkward since his hand was clamped to his neck. "You're fucked!" he shouted as he strode back, shaking as he halted ten feet back. "You're all fucked! What fairy-tale-assed life do you think you're living in?"

They were two deep on the bridge. A handful more watched from the opposite side of the river, misty figures in the cloying fog. If they were gang members, why didn't they come beat the shit out of them?

Michel's head was on the asphalt. He tried to find his feet, failing as he choked on his own vomit. Face scraping, he turned to Greg's voice, and Greg's next wild outburst hesitated. The man's eyes were haemorrhaging, bleeding like tears. More blood leaked from his ears and nose in a slow flow. "You . . . " Michel gasped, and then he vomited a gout of blood, his body twisting with convulsions.

Greg stared, his neck throbbing as he shook. *What the hell is going on?*

Joe stepped into the light beside his brother. His narrow shoulders were stiff and the hardness was back in his stance. "What's the matter, big brother?" he said, nudging him in the ribs with his foot, and Michel vomited again, gagging into a wet moan. "My friend too spicy for you?"

Joe looked up at Greg, and Greg backed away, eyes flicking from the dying man to the one now jauntily coming his way. "What the hell is wrong with you?" Greg shouted, not knowing what else to do.

His voice was swallowed by the heavy fog, and the shadowy figures on the bridge began to become indistinct.

Running shoes scuffing, Joe halted beside him, then turned to look at his brother's last grasping motion, bloodied nails rasping on the asphalt. His expression held only a light disinterest and, turning to Greg, a sliver of his usual devil-may-care attitude started to show itself. "Let me see your neck," he said, and Greg smacked his reaching hand away.

"Oh, hey, relax, man," Joe said, dodging Greg's next swing and coming in close, too close for anything but a shove, but Greg's knees were shaking and he didn't move lest he push himself over. "I know you're freaking out," Joe said. "I'm still me. Still your friend. Let me see."

Breathing fast, Greg stood still as Joe prised his fingers from his neck.

"Look, you big pussy, it's stopped already," Joe said, smacking his shoulder to make him stumble. "You're going to be fine. Hell, you're going to be more than fine."

Greg caught his balance, looking first to the gathered figures on the bridge and then to Joe in mistrust. "Who are you?" he rasped, hand falling to hide his scraped thigh.

"I'm a vampire, dumb-ass. What did you think?"

Greg stared, trying to make sense of it. There was a man in a puddle of blood on the sidewalk. He'd bitten his neck. Joe said he was a vampire. He was losing it. That was the only thing that made any sense. Desperate for an answer, he looked to the bridge and the hazy outline of watchers. He was going to die. Game over. Hit the reset.

Giving him a sideways smirk, Joe strode to the unmoving pile of blood and nudged him with his foot. "You dead?" he said loudly, as if expecting an answer, and when the body was silent, he hauled back and savagely kicked him. Again and again, he slammed his foot into the limp body, sending it rolling in soggy spurts across the grass until it fell into the river.

"I told you not to eat him," Greg heard him say as Joe stood on the riverbank and watched the current drag Michel down and away.

Greg stumbled to stand beside him, running shoes going damp as he tried to figure this out. "Shit, man. What did you just do?"

Ignoring him, Joe took a deep breath. "I'm here now!" he shouted, his voice echoing on the flat river in the fog. "I'm here! It's me, now! *I'm back!*"

"Joe, you just killed him," Greg said, voice hissing as he looked at the people on the bridge, tall and short all inclining their heads in the mist. "You just killed your brother!"

Joe's eyes caught the light from a street lamp, making him look wild and unpredictable. "No, you did, my man. My man Greg."

"Me?" A cold feeling prickled through him. Joe's brother had bitten him, then fell down, vomited his stomach out, and died. It wasn't his fault. Frantic, he looked at the bridge and the witnesses, his face going cold. There was no one there. That fast, they were gone. *Had it even happened?*

Fists on his hips, Joe faced the river, breathing deep. "You feel that, man? That's a new wind blowing. Blowing my way, now."

Greg turned away, stumbling when the soft bank made his steps wobble. He thought he was going to be sick, but the memory of Joe's brother vomiting blood was too new, and he was scared to see what might come out of himself. "You're freaking me out, Joe." Head bowed, he dabbed at his neck to start a soft ache of feeling that quickly ebbed. It was hard to tell in the dim light, but it did seem like it wasn't bleeding any more. Maybe he hadn't been bitten as hard as he thought.

In a quick motion, Joe clapped Greg across the shoulder and pushed him back up the gentle incline as the fog began to turn into a soft mist. "I'll never forget this, Greg. I owe you everything. Hell, I'll give you everything." Once on the asphalt, he drew them to a stop, and Greg turned, pliant when Joe aimed him back at the river. "You all see him?" he shouted again, though there was no one left. "You get a good look. You fuck with him, you fuck with me!"

"Dude, what are you on?" Greg said, glancing over his shoulder at the red smear on the sidewalk and the funky hat, the only evidence left. "We gotta get out of here. This is a nightmare."

"The nightmare is over," Joe said. "It ended tonight. I can go home, and you're coming with me."

"Whoa, wait up, dude." Greg dropped back, hand raised.

"You don't want to go back to that peehole, do you?" Joe said, then grimaced, using a finger to tilt Greg's head so he could see his neck in the brighter light. Mist cooled Greg's face and neck, and he pushed Joe's hand off of him.

"Yeah, you're almost healed up," Joe said, leaning to scoop up the abandoned hat. "You've been drinking my stuff. You can't go back there. You're with me now."

"The protein drink?" Greg stammered, looking at the dark smear and pushing the hat away when Joe tried to give it to him. "Is that what killed him?"

"I told my mom you were a smart bastard." Joe looked at the hat, then wound up and whipped it into the river. "I can't kill my own brother. You heard me tell him to leave you alone. I tried to stop him. Everyone saw it. Not my fault."

The watchers. Vampires? "The juice?" he tried again, remembering how bad it had tasted at first, and then how it seemed to wake him up, make him alive. "It's vampire juice?"

Joe glanced sideways at him as he started them back in motion in a fast walk, headed for the bright lights of the carnie rides glowing in the mist. He looked totally slipshod, totally Joe, but totally someone new. It was like he'd taken off a homeless man's coat to show the three-piece suit of confidence underneath. "The juice is just juice. But I've been putting a little of my blood in there," Joe said, watching for his reaction and yanking him forwards when Greg threatened to stop.

"Oh my God!"

"God had nothing to do with it," Joe said, a hint of humour in him. "If God cared, he would have struck down my prick of a brother before he perverted the family. No, it took you to do that."

Only vampire blood could kill a vampire. That's what he had said. "Joe?" The sidewalk seemed to move under him on its own, and he kept moving by rote. "Joe, did you make me . . ." Shit, he couldn't say it.

"A vampire?" Joe laughed, and Greg exhaled loudly, scared. "No, man. You gotta be born one. You're better than me at surviving, warm-blooded and shit. You're my bodyguard now. No one can touch you. You're safe."

The wailing of sirens lifted faintly over the park's trees to them, and they both stopped. It was eerie, like they were linked somehow.

"Shit," Joe drawled. "Someone dialed 911. God, it was easier before cell phones." He looked at the bright lights a mile ahead of them. "Let's get out of here," he said, starting to run only to halt not three steps away.

Greg hadn't moved. He wasn't a vampire. But Joe was.

"You're not going to freak on me, are you?" Joe said as he came back. "You're under my protection. My dad would run his dogs for you, now. You'll be OK. No one will touch you. If they do, they die."

"You killed your brother." Greg pointed to the glistening asphalt, the blood slowly washing away. He half expected Joe to be gone when he turned back, but he was still there, thin body slumped to look like he always did with a half-smile on his face and the rain beading up on his smooth, always smooth, chin.

"No, *you* killed my brother," he said. "And stop worrying, lame-ass. I don't have any more brothers. I was the last. Seventh son of a seventh son. It starts with me, this generation. Shit, man, we're going to have fun."

Greg felt his face go pale. "I'm a seventh son, too."

Joe smacked him on the back to get him moving again. "Yeah. I know. Let's run. I want you to meet my family. They'll be waiting by the funnel cakes for me." Jogging backwards, Joe started putting space between them. "Come on, man. Let's go! We got chicks to pound."

Not knowing why but for that it felt good, Greg started to jog after him and, in a moment, he was beside Joe, feeling like he belonged there. His blood began moving, and the aches in his legs and knees disappeared. He was Joe's bodyguard?

They ran effortlessly from light to light, almost as if they were holding still and the earth was turning beneath them. "Joe?" he said, breathing fast, but not that bad.

"Yeah?"

He hesitated, not wanting to sound like an idiot. "Can you fly and shit?"

Joe started to laugh and, with that buoying him on, Greg ran in the rain, feeling pretty damn good.

Blood Gothic

Nancy Holder

She wanted to have a vampire lover. She wanted it so badly that she kept waiting for it to happen. One night, soon, she would awaken to wings flapping against the window and then take to wearing velvet ribbons and cameo lockets around her delicate, pale neck. She knew it.

She immersed herself in the world of her vampire lover: She devoured Gothic romances, consumed late-night horror movies. Visions of satin capes and eyes of fire shielded her from the harshness of the daylight, from mortality and the vain and meaningless struggles of the world of the sun. Days as a kindergarten teacher and evenings with some overly eager, casual acquaintance could not pull her from her secret existence: always a ticking portion of her brain planned, proceeded, waited.

She spent her meagre earnings on dark antiques and intricate clothes. Her wardrobe was crammed with white negligees and ruffled underthings. No crosses and no mirrors, particularly not in her bedroom. White tapered candles stood in pewter sconces, and she would read late into the night by their smoky flickerings, scented and ruffled, hair combed loosely about her shoulders. She glanced at the window often.

She resented lovers – though she took them, thrilling to the fullness of blood and life in them – who insisted upon staying all night, burning their breakfast toast and making bitter coffee. Her kitchen, of course, held nothing but fresh ingredients and copper and ironware; to her chagrin, she could not do without ovens or stoves or refrigerators. Alone, she carried candles and bathed in cool water.

She waited, prepared. And at long last, her vampire lover began to come to her in dreams. The two of them floated across the moors, glided through the fields of heather. He carried her to his crumbling castle, undressing her, pulling off her diaphanous gown, caressing her lovely body until, at the height of passion, he bit into her neck, drawing the life out of her and replacing it with eternal damnation and eternal love.

She awoke from these dreams drenched in sweat and feeling exhausted. The kindergarten children would find her unusually quiet and self-absorbed, and it frightened them when she rubbed her spotless neck and smiled wistfully. *Soon and soon and soon,* her veins chanted, in prayer and anticipation. *Soon.*

The children were her only regret. She would not miss her inquisitive relatives and friends, the ones who frowned and studied her as if she were a portrait of someone they knew they were supposed to recognize; the ones who urged her to drop by for an hour, to come with them to films, to accompany them to the seashore; the ones who were connected to her – or thought they were – by the mere gesturing of the long and milky hands of Fate. Who sought to distract her from her one true passion; who sought to discover the secret of that passion. For, true to the sacredness of her vigil for her vampire lover, she had never spoken of him to a single earthbound soul. It would be beyond them, she knew. They would not comprehend a bond of such intentioned sacrifice.

But she would regret the children. Never would a child of their love coo and murmur in the darkness; never would his proud and noble features soften at the sight of the mother and her child of his loins. It was her single sorrow.

Her vacation was coming. June hovered like the mist and the children squirmed in anticipation. Their own true lives would begin in June. She empathized with the shining eyes and smiling faces, knowing their wait was as agonizing as her own. Silently, as the days closed in, she bade each of them a tender farewell, holding them as they threw their little arms around her neck and pressed fervent summertime kisses on her cheeks.

She booked her passage to London on a ship. Then to Romania, Bulgaria, Transylvania. The hereditary seat of her beloved; the fierce, violent backdrop of her dreams. Her suitcases opened themselves to her long, full skirts and her brooches and lockets. She peered into her hand mirror as she packed it. "I am getting pale," she thought, and the idea both terrified and delighted her.

She became paler, thinner, more exhausted as her trip wore on. After recovering from the disappointment of the raucous, modern cruise ship, she raced across the Continent to find refuge in the creaky trains and taverns she had so yearned for. Her heart thrilled as she meandered past the black silhouettes of ruined fortresses and ancient manor houses. She sat for hours in the mists, praying for the howling wolf to find her, for the bat to come and join her.

She took to drinking wine in bed – deep, rich, blood-red burgundy that glowed in the candlelight. She melted into the landscape within days, and cringed as if from the crucifix itself when flickers of her past life, her false American existence, invaded her serenity. She did not keep a diary; she did not count the days as her summer slipped away from her. She only rejoiced that she grew weaker.

It was when she was counting out the coins for a Gypsy shawl that she realized she had no time left. Tomorrow she must make for Frankfurt and from there fly back to New York. The shopkeeper nudged her, inquiring if she were ill, and she left with her treasure, trembling.

She flung herself on her rented bed. "This will not do. This will not do," she pleaded with the darkness. "You must come for me tonight. I have done everything for you, my beloved, loved you above all else. You must save me." She sobbed until she ached.

She skipped her last meal of veal and paprika and sat quietly in her room. The innkeeper brought her yet another bottle of burgundy and after she assured him that she was quite all right, just a little tired, he wished his guest a pleasant trip home.

The night wore on; though her book was open before her, her eyes were riveted to the windows, her hands clenched around the wine glass as she sipped steadily, like a creature feeding. Oh, to feel him against her veins, emptying her and filling her!

Soon and soon and soon ...

Then, all at once, it happened. The windows rattled, flapped inward. A great shadow, a curtain of ebony, fell across the bed, and the room began to whirl, faster, faster still; and she was consumed with a bitter, deathly chill. She heard, rather than saw, the wine glass crash to the floor, and struggled to keep her eyes open as she was overwhelmed, engulfed, taken.

"Is it you?" she managed to whisper through teeth that rattled with delight and cold and terror. "Is it finally to be?"

Freezing hands touched her everywhere: her face, her breasts, the desperate offering of her arched neck. Frozen and strong and never-dying. Sinking, she smiled in a rictus of mortal dread and exultation. Eternal damnation, eternal love. Her vampire lover had come for her at last.

When her eyes opened again, she let out a howl and shrank against the searing brilliance of the sun. Hastily, they closed the curtains and quickly told her where she was: home again, where everything was warm and pleasant and she was safe from the disease that had nearly killed her.

She had been ill before she had left the States. By the time she had reached Transylvania, her anaemia had been acute. Had she never noticed her own pallor, her lassitude?

Anaemia. Her smile was a secret on her white lips. So they thought, but he *had* come for her, again and again. In her dreams. And on that night, he had meant to take her finally to his castle for ever, to crown her the best-beloved one, his love of the moors and the mists.

She had but to wait, and he would finish the deed.

Soon and soon and soon.

She let them fret over her, wrapping her in blankets in the last days of summer. She endured the forced cheer of her relatives, allowed them to feed her rich food and drink in hopes of restoring her.

But her stomach could no longer hold the nourishment of their kind; they wrung their hands and talked of stronger measures when it became clear that she was wasting away.

At the urging of the doctor, she took walks. Small ones at first, on painfully thin feet. Swathed in wool, cowering behind sunglasses, she took tiny steps like an old woman. As she moved through the summer hours, her neck burned with an ungovernable pain that would not cease until she rested in the shadows. Her stomach lurched at the sight of grocery-store windows. But at the butcher's, she paused, and licked her lips at the sight of the raw, bloody meat.

But she did not go in. She grew neither worse nor better.

"I am trapped," she whispered to the night as she stared into the flames of a candle by her bed. "I am disappearing between your world and mine, my beloved. Help me. Come for me." She rubbed her neck, which ached and throbbed but showed no outward signs of his devotion. Her throat was parched, bone-dry, but water did not quench her thirst.

At long last, she dreamed again. Her vampire lover came for her as before, joyous in their reunion. They soared above the crooked trees at the foothills, streamed like black banners above the mountain crags to his castle. He could not touch her enough, worship her enough, and they were wild in their abandon as he carried her in her diaphanous gown to the gates of his fortress.

But at the entrance, he shook his head with sorrow and could not let her pass into the black realm with him. His fiery tears seared her neck, and she thrilled to the touch of the mark even as she cried out for him as he left her, fading into the vapours with a look of entreaty in his dark, flashing eyes.

Something was missing; he required a boon of her before he could bind her against his heart. A thing that she must give to him . . .

She walked in the sunlight, enfeebled, cowering. She thirsted, hungered, yearned. Still she dreamed of him, and still he could not take the last of her unto himself.

Days and nights and days. Her steps took her finally to the schoolyard, where once, only months before, she had embraced and kissed the children, thinking never to see them again. They were all there, who had kissed her cheeks so eagerly. Their silvery laughter was like the tinkling of bells as dust motes from their games whirled around their feet. How free they seemed to her who was so troubled, how content and at peace.

The children.

She shambled forwards, eyes widening behind the shields of smoky glass.

He required something of her first.

Her one regret. Her only sorrow.

She thirsted. The burns on her neck pulsated with pain.

Tears of gratitude welled in her eyes for the revelation that had not come too late. Weeping, she pushed open the gate of the schoolyard and reached out a skeleton-limb to a child standing apart from the rest, engrossed in a solitary game of cat's cradle. Tawny-headed, ruddy-cheeked, filled with the blood and the life.

For him, as a token of their love.

"My little one, do you remember me?" she said softly.

The boy turned. And smiled back uncertainly in innocence and trust.

Then, as she came for him, swooped down on him like a great, winged thing, with eyes that burned through the glasses, teeth that flashed, once, twice . . .

Soon, soon, soon.

Eternity Embraced

Larissa Ione

Chapter 1

Andrea Cole had been hunting demons and vampires since she was eighteen, almost since the day she'd dropped out of college and returned home to witness both parents being torn apart by demons before her eyes. That was nine years, a hundred kills and two dozen broken bones ago. Killing evil creatures had never bothered her. Not once. But tonight was different.

Tonight she might have to kill the love of her life.

She gripped her stake so hard that she was surprised it didn't crack. Silently, she eased down the damp, narrow staircase that led to an underground chamber beneath the Oregon billionaire's mansion. The human scumbag was in league with demons who the Aegis, a society of human warriors protecting the world from evil, had been watching for two years. Andrea's division, a special vampire investigative unit, had concentrated all its efforts on bringing this guy down, starting with the vampires he harboured on his property. Beneath it, anyway.

Recently, an Aegis Guardian had disappeared into the bowels of the mansion. Under the pretence of delivering a kitchen order from a local bakery, Kaden had snooped around and got lucky when he spotted the butler opening a secret panel in the pantry. He'd followed the butler down a staircase, speaking softly into his hidden microphone as he described everything he saw. At the bottom, he'd found himself in a giant chamber filled with torture devices, several cells, dozens of tunnels and, unfortunately, more vampires than he could combat.

Andrea had listened in horror as Kaden was overwhelmed. When the sound had cut off, something inside her had died, and she'd done nothing but live and breathe revenge ever since. And now, revenge was within her grasp, because at this very moment there were twenty Guardians swarming the mansion grounds, armed to the teeth and working on three separate missions.

One: Capture the billionaire scumbag, Blake Alden. Two: Kill as many vampires as possible. Three: Find Kaden.

Find Kaden so Andrea could kill him.

The thought rolled through her on a wave of nausea. Maybe he was OK. Maybe the vampires hadn't turned him. And maybe she was freaking delusional, because she knew damned good and well they'd done it. Vamps got off on torturing Guardians – or worse, turning them. Nothing amused bloodsuckers more than dropping an enemy head first into their worst nightmare.

Cautiously, she stepped out of the stairwell and into a huge, cavernous basement. From the stone walls hung wicked-looking implements of torture. The floor was dirt. It wasn't exactly a basement, it was more of a cave, with cells carved into the walls. The doors were solid slabs of metal, with only a small, eye-level slotted window shot through with steel bars.

Ahead were tunnels she'd be willing to bet led to living spaces, and dozens of exits that would come out all over Portland. Behind her, six Guardians filed out of the stairwell.

"This is weird," Zach, a newer recruit, whispered. "There's no one here."

"They might have been tipped off and ran." Andrea moved towards the cells. "Or it's a trap and they're hiding. Be careful."

Zach and the others disappeared into the tunnels, leaving Andrea to clear the immediate area. The first cell was empty, the shackles on the walls hanging dejectedly from their chains. Some sort of spindly, man-sized demon occupied the second cell, cowering in a corner and trembling. A colleague would dispatch the pathetic creature later.

She moved on, slowing when the small hairs on the back of her neck stood up as she sidestepped a dark stain on the ground. Her gaze tracked automatically to the ceiling. Above her, meat hooks swayed, grotesque even in the dim light from the wall sconces. And there, in the corner, were Kaden's weapons, boots and shirt.

Andrea's heart dropped into the pit of her stomach. Where was he? Forgetting caution, she checked the third cell. The fourth cell.

The fifth cell . . . *Dear God, the fifth cell.*

Inside, sitting with his back to the wall in nothing but jeans and a metal collar around his neck, was Kaden. Andrea's breath lodged in her throat, her pulse went double-time, and though she knew better than to hope, she did exactly that.

"Kaden?"

His head swung around, his grey eyes bright and wide with surprise. His dark blond hair was alternately grooved and spiky, as though he'd been thrusting his fingers through it, and his tan skin was marred by fading bruises and cuts.

If the vampires had had him for the full two weeks he'd been missing, she was surprised he hadn't been hurt more. Then again, maybe they *had* put him through hell, but he'd healed already, thanks to a vampire's rapid regeneration abilities.

But so far, she saw no signs of him being turned. Maybe, just maybe, everything would be OK. *God, please let it be OK.*

"Kaden, don't move. I'm going to get you out of there."

"No!" He lurched forwards, only to be drawn short by the chain linking his collar to the wall. Panic put a chilling, grim light in his gaze. "You can't."

Dread draped over her like a shroud, suffocating her last breath of hope. She knew what he was going to say. She didn't want to ask, but the question fell from her lips before she could stop it. "Why not?"

"Because," he said, opening his mouth to reveal two extra-long canines, "I might kill you."

Kaden Quinn braced himself for Andrea's reaction. The sight of the stake in her hand put ice cubes in his blood – but whether his reaction was an instinctive one brought about by his new vampire status, or whether it was because he was a Guardian who knew exactly what that pointed shard of wood would do to him, he didn't know.

What he did know was that he'd been here for two weeks, tortured for the first five days and then turned into a vampire on the sixth.

Oh, and he was *starving.*

Andrea's gorgeous brown eyes glistened with tears. "No," she rasped, shaking her head so hard her ebony hair slapped her pale cheeks. "No. Those bastards!"

Her curses echoed through the chamber as she worked the slide-lock on the cell door. She was going to kill him. The knowledge should have comforted him. Upon becoming a Guardian, every Aegi swore that they would never allow themselves to be turned into any kind of monster – not vampire, were-beast, or demon. If you had to take your own life in order to uphold that vow, you did it.

Kaden hadn't been able to make good on his promise – he'd been knocked unconscious during the battle – and by the time he came to, it was too late. He'd awakened to find himself hanging from hooks outside this very cell. The physical torture hadn't been nearly as bad as the mental torture. The alpha vamp, an ugly bastard named Cedric, kept taunting that he was going to turn him. When Cedric finally latched onto Kaden's throat and began to drink, Kaden prayed for death. The alternative had been too horrible to imagine.

Then his nightmarish imaginings had warped into reality when Cedric opened a vein in his own wrist and, while another vamp held Kaden's mouth open, forced him to swallow his blood, activating the turn.

Kaden had drifted into blackness. When he'd come to the next night, his heart no longer beat.

He'd expected to feel different, as if getting dead and growing fangs would turn him into an insane, evil beast.

But nothing had changed. He still . . . felt. He still thought Andrea was the most beautiful woman he'd ever seen. He still hated vampires. Oh, sure, his senses were more acute and the sound of Andrea's blood rushing through her veins was making his mouth water, but he felt like he could handle being with her.

He'd warned her anyway. What if he was wrong? What if she got close and he jumped on her, ripped into her neck, and let that sweet lifeblood pour down his throat? Anticipation spiked, and lust stirred his sluggish body. While he drank, he'd take her and fist his hands in her thick black locks until she begged for mercy –

" . . . uh, Kaden?"

He blinked, realizing he'd been caught up in his crazy fantasy. Shit. He was freaking *starving*. The vampires hadn't fed him, and he'd had to watch when they brought unwilling humans to the basement to feed. He'd been horrified, yet overtaken by cravings and fascinated in a way that filled him with disgust.

Andrea was inside the cell now, crouching, the stake at her side. He eyed it warily. "Sorry. I was just . . . " *Thinking about sinking my shiny new set of fangs into you.* Cursing, he shoved his fingers through his hair. "Look, it's not safe for you here. Get your team out."

"The place is empty. I think they knew we were coming."

Adrenaline screamed through him in a stinging, hot rush that couldn't have jacked him up more if he'd shot it directly into his veins. "It's a trap." He leaped to his feet, startling Andrea to hers. "Get out."

"I can't just . . . leave you." Her voice broke, and his heart along with it. She'd faced an awful choice the day her parents died – stay, fight, and die . . . or flee, leaving them behind to perish. Her decision had been made when her father ordered her to save her sister, who had died anyway, leaving Andrea with a lifetime of regret.

She shouldn't have to make a similar choice now, but it was much too late for that.

His eyes latched onto the stake. He should tell her to kill him. He was a monster. An abomination.

But he didn't want to die.

"Andrea, you're a Guardian. You're tougher than this. You need to go."

She opened her mouth, but he didn't get to hear what she would have said, because suddenly the cell door slammed shut, trapping them both. On the other side was Cedric, grinning like a rabid coyote as he peered between the bars. He must have tripped a switch somewhere because the clamp around Kaden's neck snapped open with an ominous, metallic clang. He was free . . . in a manner of speaking.

Cedric's smile widened. "Now," he said, "let's party."

Chapter 2

Disbelief and anger clawed at Andrea. How the hell had she let herself be trapped like this? "You are so dead!" she snarled at the bastard who'd shut the door.

Through the barred slot, the ugly, scarred piece-of-shit vampire smiled at her idle threat, his pallid, fishy lips peeling back off yellowed teeth.

"We've slaughtered most of your colleagues," he said, his harsh words hitting her like a punch to the gut, "but I'm holding on to a

few. I'll have fun turning them, just like I did with your boy there."
He smiled again, then walked away, leaving her alone with Kaden . . .

. . . who was now loose in the cell with her.

Evil unchained.

Except she couldn't see her lover as anything but the man whose touch had lit her on fire, who had been a gentle or urgent lover, depending on his mood.

Then again, on the job he was a ruthless warrior, capable of cutting down entire nests of viper ghouls by himself. Oh, yes, she'd stood by and admired the way he used his hands with lethal skill, the way he could gut a demon twice his size and shrug it off like it was nothing. Afterwards, the jacked-up burn of the fight had sent him into her arms, a male on a mission to claim her as his prize.

She couldn't count the number of times they'd won a battle and then attacked each other, unable to wait for a bedroom. They hadn't needed anything but a wall or a tree to support her back and shield them from prying eyes. Their passion had heated up snowy nights, steamed up rainy days, and drawn lightning during storms.

And now he was looking at Andrea with that same battle-lust in his eyes, the adrenaline high that gripped all Guardians when the victory, the kill, was close.

Heartbreak and fear collided, making her clumsy as she settled into a defensive position, stake ready. "I don't want to have to destroy you."

And she wasn't sure she would be able to. They'd always been evenly matched in skill, but with his strength and size he'd had the advantage when they sparred. And now, as a vampire, he'd be even stronger, and faster as well.

"The idea doesn't thrill me, either." He closed his eyes and clenched his hands into fists, the way he did when he was angry and trying to keep his temper contained – something he rarely had to do. Kaden had always been cool, calm and level, to the point where Andrea sometimes needled him just to get a reaction. Now, it appeared that no needling would be necessary. "Andrea . . . I don't . . . I don't know if I can control myself."

"You want to kill me?"

His eyes flew open, the grey depths turning steely. "No. Never," he swore. "But I'm . . . hungry." His gaze dropped to her throat. His lush lips parted and he drew closer. For some reason, she couldn't move, was anchored to the spot, mesmerized by the fierce hunger in his expression. Everything around her, from the damp, musty odour of the dungeon, to the skittering sounds of scavenging rodents, faded into the background. Everything but him.

Swallowing nervously, she found her voice. "Kaden?"

He uttered a rough noise of anguish and threw himself to the far side of the cell, shuddering so hard his teeth chattered.

Something inside her broke, and she reached for him, only to jerk back when he hissed.

This was bad. Very, very bad. She had to find a way out of the cell before Kaden lost control and she was forced into the fight of her life.

Whirling, she attacked the door. She shoved at it, rattled it, trying to fight the panic that had wrapped around her chest like a clamp.

She'd always believed she could take down any vampire without mercy, but Kaden didn't seem like a vamp. He seemed like ... Kaden. With fangs. And maybe an extra scoop of menace. But other than that, he was the man she loved, and she couldn't stake him.

Thing was, she couldn't even be shocked by this knowledge. She'd failed at most everything she'd ever tried, from bowling, to cooking, to protecting her family. Never in her life had she stuck with anything when the going got rough or if she wasn't immediately good at it. Not until she'd joined the Aegis, anyway. She'd stayed, because she was damned good at killing.

At least, she *was*. Until now.

"Let me try." His voice was guttural, warped, as though every word was being funnelled through a shrinking pipe. She stepped aside as he hit the door with his entire body. His weight left a dent, but on his fourth try it became clear that the cells had been built to handle creatures much stronger than any man.

Or any vampire.

She shivered. God, the very idea that Kaden was undead ... it horrified her. And yet, as she watched him pound on the door with eye-blurring speed, the thick muscles in his chest and arms bunching and rippling, some secret, shameful part of her was fascinated – and maybe a little turned on by the raw power behind his every punch.

"Kaden?"

Slowly, he turned, braced his back against the door, and slid to his ass. Exhaustion put hollows in his cheeks, but his eyes were sharp as daggers. "Yeah?"

Maintaining a grip on the stake, she crouched and eased towards him. "What's it like?"

When he looked at the stake in her hand and growled, she set the stake on the floor and showed him her empty palms. She wasn't stupid though; she made sure the weapon was within reach. She also had an Aegis-modified squirt gun filled with holy water in her jacket pocket, as well as several blades stashed on her body. But he'd know that. His roving hands had long since learned the location of every one of her weapon hiding places. The memories made her body tingle and her mouth go dry.

"It's weird," he said gruffly. "I thought I'd feel like a beast. But I don't feel any different." He frowned. "No, that's not true. I feel stronger. And more . . . feral."

"Feral?"

He nodded. "It's like I'm a mass of instincts. Everything is magnified, from my senses to my desires. I don't know how to control them." He pegged her with a gaze so scorching she drew a harsh breath. "I've always tried to be gentle with you. But right now . . . " He threw his head back against the wall, and his throat worked on a hard swallow. "Damn. The things I want to do to you."

She didn't have to guess. His fangs had elongated into sharp, wicked daggers, and she could see his erection pressing against the fly of his jeans. Liquid heat flooded her body, a completely inappropriate response given what he was and where they were. But that dark part of her was enthralled with this new Kaden. Curious. Cautiously, she reached for him. The moment her fingers touched his knee, he went taut, his head snapped forwards, and once again she was in the cross hairs of his laser gaze.

Startled, she drew her hand away, but – lightning fast – he caught her wrist. For a breathless heartbeat, terror turned the air in her lungs to cement.

The stake was out of reach.

"I warned you," he growled. "I need . . . I *hunger* . . . " His fingers tightened, digging into her skin.

Common sense and self-preservation kicked in. He wasn't the only one with powerful instincts. Andrea threw a punch, nailing him in the jaw with her free hand. He didn't even flinch. She swung again, but this time he palmed her fist, stopping her throw as if she'd slammed her knuckles into a brick wall.

"Wow," she breathed. "You're really fast now."

"I wasn't exactly a slouch before." His voice was a husky purr that rumbled through every part of her body.

She snorted. "Becoming undead certainly hasn't done anything for your ego."

A slow, cocky smile turned up the corners of his mouth. Good Lord – were they really *bantering*? In this incredibly fucked-up situation? He seemed to realize the incongruity of it all and he sobered, releasing her as if she were a burning coal.

"Get away from me." He shoved at her, knocking her off balance and sending her sprawling. Instantly, he was on his knees beside her. "Oh, shit. Andy, I'm sorry."

She allowed him to help her sit up, but he didn't remove his hands from her shoulders. Neither of them moved a single muscle. Even the air went still with the uncertain tension hanging in the cell. Gradually, she became aware of the fact that Kaden's entire body was trembling, and, once more, his gaze was fixed on her throat.

Something touched her hand. The stake. He pressed it into her palm even as he lowered his head towards her neck. Her heart slammed into her ribcage and her stomach clenched, but she remained motionless. She focused all her energy on simply breathing, because that, at least, was still in her control.

"Don't let me do it," he rasped, but his lips were grazing her suddenly sensitive skin. He closed her fingers around the stake. His teeth scratched her throat – tiny, erotic pricks of pain.

His masculine need rolled off him in waves, and her traitorous body answered, going wet and molten hot. In the past, she'd always responded to him quickly, often after nothing more than his lustful look. But this was different. It was as though she was flame and he was fuel. There was nothing she could do but let it all burn out of control.

That's how they get you. Vampires are very sexual beings, they ooze sex appeal and are magnetic and irresistible to humans. They are spiders that capture careless flies.

The familiar words of Aegis leaders rang through her head, and though she knew she should fight, she couldn't.

"Please," he whispered brokenly. He lifted her hand, placing the point of the stake over his heart. "I can't hold on. Don't want to hurt you." His mouth was at her throat.

Andrea's entire body quivered, and a sob caught in her throat. What he was asking her to do . . . *oh, God.*

A shudder tore through Kaden's body. "Andrea . . . *fuck.*" Then his fangs pierced her skin. Her stake pierced his. They both gasped. Neither had gone deep, but there was no doubt that they both could kill.

They remained still, frozen in a twisted game of cat and mouse. He needed to feed, and she needed to kill him. But neither had the will power.

He squeezed her hand, putting pressure on the stake, driving it deeper into his flesh.

"No!" In one smooth move, she flung the stake away and grasped his head, pulling him firmly against her. His teeth penetrated her throat in a white-hot stab of pain that veered sharply to pleasure. His moan rattled through her, and she was lost to him.

Chapter 3

She should have killed him.

But now it was too late. Kaden didn't think he'd ever be the same. He'd crossed a line – vaulted over it – and there was no going back. Sensation stabbed at him, shooting like mini-orgasms through his fangs, all the way to his groin. He should tear himself away from Andrea. Do the right thing.

But he was so cold and she was so warm. She smelled like leather and cherries – a strange combination, but one that had always excited both the lover and the warrior in him. And best of all, *worst* of all, she tasted like sweet, sweet sin. Silky, warm blood filled his mouth and cascaded down his throat, filling that empty, hurt hole inside him.

No, not filling . . . because his chest cavity was truly empty now. His ribs caged a useless heart and his lungs still breathed even though they didn't need air. Some sort of cell memory kept his lungs filling, he supposed. He wondered when that would end, when his lungs would collapse and shrivel.

Andrea's pulse tapped against his teeth, and he moaned at the ecstasy of it. He'd been guided by instinct when he'd bitten her, and even though guilt knotted his stomach, he couldn't fight the drive to suck harder.

He also couldn't fight the desire to ease her onto her back and settle himself between her legs. Only the knowledge that there was a camera mounted in the corner of the ceiling kept him from tearing off their clothes and plunging into her body. But still, some instincts were too powerful to deny, and he rocked against her, drawing a low, heady groan from her.

Beneath him, she writhed, arching up to plaster their bodies more solidly against each other. An erotic surge crashed through him in a hot tide. Andrea tightened her legs around his hips so he rubbed against her. With each thrusting motion, she gasped, her panting breaths coming faster and faster.

Damn, he loved the sounds she made when she was making love. Granted, they weren't exactly making love, not while they were fully clothed, but the motions were the same, the feelings were the same and – oh yeah – the way she drove him wild with her fingers digging into his back was the same.

"Kaden," she whispered, "yes, *yes.*"

She was close, something he knew not from experience, but from his new senses. He could smell the delicious scent of her lust, could taste the zing of desire in her blood. It was like a drug he knew he couldn't kick. As a human, sex had been great. As a vampire, it felt out of this world, and he hadn't even gotten inside her.

Delicious agony.

He shuddered, sucked, rocked against her until the friction became nearly too hot to handle and a vibration sang through his veins. This was crazy, but his body had hijacked his thoughts, and nothing mattered but getting inside her. Impatient, he slid his palm down her body, but before he reached her zipper, she cried out, her orgasm hitting so hard and fast he could only hang on for the ride as she bucked beneath him.

She called out his name, over and over, her smoky, pleasure-soaked voice nearly sending him over the edge with her.

"I love you," she whispered. "God, I love you."

The words stopped him in his tracks like nothing else, not even his own will, had been able to do. She'd never said that to him, not in the entire year they'd been together. He'd suspected, but then, he'd suspected that he was in love with her, too. But it was something he'd never planned to admit, not when a Guardian's lifespan was as likely to be measured in months as in years.

Five years ago, he'd lost Gabrielle to this violent life just days after their engagement. She'd been bitten by a werewolf, had slaughtered several other Guardians, and Kaden had been forced to kill her.

He couldn't go through that again, and he'd guarded the words "I love you" with the ferocity of a lion protecting his pride. Andrea knew how he felt about love, and damn her for striking at him with a weapon every bit as dangerous and painful as a stake.

Roaring in agony and fury, he broke away from Andrea, surprising himself at the speed with which he came to his feet. Wide, glazed eyes blinked in confusion even as she slapped a palm over her throat. Blood seeped from between her fingers, and shit, he was a dumb-ass. A newbie vampire dumb-ass, who must look utterly ridiculous, standing half-naked in a cell with a raging hard-on.

Quickly, he seized her upper arms, yanked her to her feet, and swiped his tongue over the punctures he'd made, another instinctive move. Then he stepped away, but the cell was far too small to allow enough distance between them. An entire ocean of distance wouldn't be enough. Not when he still wanted her so badly it hurt, which was exactly what he'd been trying to avoid.

"Dammit, Andrea." He rammed his hands through his hair, needing to do something with them before he grabbed her again, and this time, refused to let go. "I told you—"

"Yeah, you told me." Her hands formed fists at her sides, and her face was flushed from her climax – and from anger. "Told me you never wanted to fall in love again, because it hurts too much when it ends. You told me when we first fell into my bed that our relationship could go nowhere except between the sheets. But it went a lot further than that, and you know it. It's time to stop skirting the issue and pretending that we only have *strong feelings* for each other."

Fuck. He flicked his tongue over one fang. It was a new habit he'd developed because he was now a vampire, a fact she seemed to have forgotten, even though two seconds ago he'd been at her throat and sucking her lifeblood out of her. How the hell could she be acting as though it hadn't happened? Acting as though she'd forgotten what he had become? For every second of every hour, until Gabrielle turned into a slavering beast, he'd been well aware of the fact that she had been bitten by a werewolf.

And yet, he'd been careless. Sloppy. Although it was Aegis policy to kill any human who had been bitten or scratched by a were-beast, he'd let his love for her cloud his judgment. He'd heard of humans who were immune to the infection, and on the off chance that Gabrielle was one of those rare people, he'd restrained her until night fell, bringing the curse of the full moon with it. Worse, he'd not wanted to hurt her, so he'd kept her restraints loose. When she turned, she got free and killed three of their colleagues before Kaden put a silver killing-bolt through her chest.

The pain, the guilt, had mired him in misery until Andrea showed up in Portland a year ago, a transfer from the Phoenix cell. She'd been like a whirlwind, sucking him into her life with her humour and fun-loving nature – exactly the opposite of the very serious Gabrielle. She was exactly what he needed after four years of loneliness and one-night stands.

"Well?" Andrea prompted, and he realized he'd been lost in his thoughts, which was not the place he wanted to be.

Not that their reality – locked in a dungeon – was much better.

Way to feel sorry for yourself. God, he was a moron. If growing up with two blind parents had taught him anything, it was that self-pity was a pathetic waste of time.

"Well, what?" he snapped, residual lust giving him the sharp edge he needed to do what he must. "You do realize that I'm a vampire, right? And you're a vampire slayer. Whatever *relationship* you think we had is over. The man you claim to love is gone, so you have two choices. You can stake me like a good little Guardian, or you can join forces with me to make an escape. But either way, there is no more *us*."

Crimson splotches mottled Andrea's cheeks, but he didn't need to see her fury to know she was bubbling over with it. His enhanced senses picked up her anger as a scent that was so bitter he could taste it on his tongue.

"You son of a bitch." Like a well-trained warrior, she didn't give away her next move, which was to snap up the stake. He could have stopped her; his reflexes were twice as fast as they had been. But in truth, he was curious to see what she'd do.

And when she came at him, he had his answer.

Damn him! Crazed with hurt and anger, Andrea launched herself at Kaden, her stake aimed right at his cold heart. Effortlessly, as though she were nothing but a minor annoyance, he blocked her with one upraised arm. Humiliation aside, she was glad he'd done it. Oh, she wanted to hurt him, but she'd planned to check herself at the last moment, not really wanting to kill him. And clearly, he didn't want to die. Or probably more accurately, he didn't want her to be the one to have to kill him. Not after the trauma he'd suffered when he'd had to put down his fiancée.

Yes, his words had put a fissure in her heart, but she wasn't stupid – he was trying to piss her off, to chase her away in order to save them both a lot of pain. She was sorry she'd told him she loved him, but she wasn't sorry for how she felt. She'd dated before meeting Kaden, but she'd never fallen in love. She hadn't known how good it could feel.

Or how bad.

Still smarting from his verbal smackdown, she struck out, slapping him across the face. His head snapped back and his eyes went wide, as though he couldn't believe she'd just done that. In an instant, he recovered, red sparks turning his eyes to molten metal as he grasped her wrists and yanked her into him.

Just as she'd wanted him to do.

Still, her heart thundered in her chest. Angering a vampire, even one you loved, one that had just given you a world-class orgasm, wasn't the brightest move in the world. "There's a camera in the corner," she said, angling her face away from said camera in case whoever was watching could read lips. "We need to fight, and you need to pretend to kill me. It's the only way to fool that psycho vamp into thinking you've truly gone over to their side."

She struggled, feigning fury, though she did put some power behind her knee to his thigh. He totally deserved that, and she smiled a little at his grunt.

"Good girl," he said through gritted teeth. "Didn't know you saw the camera." She didn't have time to bask in his praise, because suddenly, he spun her, put her back against the wall and his forearm across her throat. "So we fight." His teeth were bared and his eyes glinted, and if she didn't know any better she'd think he really was planning violence.

Then again, she *didn't* know any better. He'd changed. She shivered, but not with fear. No, once more, she was utterly turned on by the life or death game they were playing. And this was definitely life – heart-stopping, adrenaline-pumping life. Kaden had once said that you never felt more alive than when you were facing death, and if the way her skin tingled and heat blossomed between her thighs was any indication, he was *so* right.

"Fight me, damn you."

"Gladly," she snapped. Squaring her shoulders, she stomped on his foot and followed up with a swift kick to his shin and a hook of her boot to the back of his knee. His leg buckled, but before she could wrench free, he recovered.

"We've sparred for months," he said with an arrogant smile. "You think I don't know all your moves?"

She rocked her head forwards and caught him in the mouth. "You didn't know that one."

He grinned, flashing teeth smeared with blood. "Nice."

God, he was hot when he smiled like that and, again, the pseudo-battle stirred up something wicked in her. The puncture wounds on her throat began to throb in time with the pulsing between her legs, as if her body was preparing to take him inside her in any way he wanted. He was a very male animal, and her feminine instincts were answering without her brain's consent.

As though he sensed the change in her, his eyes darkened and his gaze dropped to her mouth.

"Kaden—"

He took her to the ground, twisting at the last second to absorb the brunt of the impact. In a smooth, easy motion, he rolled on top of her, pinning her with his superior strength and considerable weight.

Beneath him, she writhed, partly in a show of struggle for the camera, and partly because he felt so damned good pressed against her. She schooled her expression into one of rage – using her anger at her situation, at Kaden's transformation, at a past that robbed her of a normal life – to make the emotion believable, when all she wanted to do was roll around with him on a soft bed instead of hard ground.

Kaden fisted her hair in one hand and wrenched her head to the side, exposing her throat the way he had before. A raw, purring rumble dredged up from deep in his chest. Her breath quickened as he lowered his mouth to her neck and struck like a snake, with no warning. Like before, pain pierced her, a sweet, erotic agony that drained her of any resistance. No wonder humans succumbed to vampires so easily. Pleasure streaked from where his teeth penetrated her to every pulse point in her body.

Moaning, she arched her pelvis into his, and he shuddered even as he shifted his weight to press her flat again. Right. She wasn't supposed to be getting off on this. This was a show for the camera, and she was ruining it by wanting to ride him like a horse.

Again.

It struck her that she might be a little stupid in trusting him not to kill her, but what choice did she have? Besides, despite what the Aegis had taught her, she knew Kaden. She knew it would take more than an exchange of vampire blood to make him turn evil.

Too soon, he disengaged his teeth, but the motion was subtle, and he repositioned his mouth over the bite and stroked his tongue along the wounds to seal them. But he never lifted his head, and she barely heard him whisper, "This is killing me. Later, we'll do this right, but for now, I need to pretend to be drinking from you until you're dead. In sixty seconds, go limp and play possum. With any luck, he'll have fed recently."

God, she hoped so. Apparently, a vampire's ability to hear a heart beating grew more acute the hungrier they were. If their ruse had any shot of working, she had to appear very, very dead.

She waited as he mouthed her throat, his tongue swirling and flicking on her hypersensitive skin. How was she supposed to play dead when every lick brought her body to shivering, vibrant awareness?

And wait. He'd said "later". Did he mean it? Could there be a "later"?

She'd have to find out – *later* – because he pushed away from her. With a vicious (but oddly careful) shove, he nudged her aside with his foot like a dead animal he'd found on the road. She lay motionless, trying to not even breathe, as he paced.

She wondered if this was how he'd been while he'd waited for Gabrielle to turn into a werewolf. A restless energy kept him prowling back and forth, grumbling to himself. Had he prayed for her life, as Andrea had prayed for Dee's?

Poor, brave Dee. She'd been only two years younger than Andrea, and she'd wanted to stay and fight the demons that had attacked their parents. Instead, she'd only fought when Andrea had dragged her screaming from the house. Six months later, it had been Dee who had been approached by the Aegis to join their cause. Apparently, her bitter and rather public insistence that demons were real had grabbed the organization's attention. They were always looking for new recruits – especially those who wanted vengeance.

Andrea had joined too, desperate to uphold her promise to keep Dee safe. But Dee had never forgiven Andrea for deserting their parents. Within six months of joining the Aegis, Dee's reckless pursuit of revenge had gotten her killed, when she'd slipped away from Andrea to hunt down a demon in an alley.

She didn't know how long they went on like that, with her playing dead and Kaden wearing a rut in the ground like a big cat in a cage. Finally, she heard the ominous thump of footsteps.

"Kaden." The psycho vamp's voice sent a chill slithering up her spine. "You are now one of us."

Chapter 4

You are now one of us.

The words rang through Kaden in a deafening clang. Yeah, he was one of them. No, he hadn't killed anyone. But he'd fed. He'd sunk his fangs into a human – a human *Guardian* – and had filled up on her lifeblood.

And he'd enjoyed it. God help him, he'd enjoyed it.

He allowed Cedric to see his pleasure and his misery before averting his gaze in a show of shame. Which wasn't much of an act. But he needed the other vampire to believe he had gone over to the dark side ... reluctantly. Cedric wasn't stupid enough to think Kaden would convert without a fight. He'd have to play this smart if he wanted to get Andrea out of this alive.

"You've killed a slayer, *slayer*," Cedric said. "You are the worst kind of enemy to them. You know you can never go back. We can keep you alive."

"Go to hell."

Cedric didn't miss a beat. "The Aegis will hunt you to the ends of the earth. We can protect you. You know I'm right."

He was, but once he was free, Kaden would kill Cedric, which would draw the wrath of Cedric's entire clan. It was a trade-off Kaden was willing to live with. He'd survive as long as he could, inflicting damage and racking up vampire casualties until he could no longer fight. Until either Cedric's clan or the Aegis took him down.

Kaden swung his gaze around to Cedric, nailing him with every ounce of hatred he could muster. "The Aegis won't hunt me specifically. They'll assume I'm dead."

Cedric laughed. "We allowed one of the captured slayers to witness you killing the girl. Then we released him. I doubt it will be long before the Aegis issues an order of execution with your name on it."

Fuck. Kaden's death would be a priority by sunrise. "You son of a bitch."

Through the narrow window, Kaden saw the light of victory in Cedric's pale eyes. "So. Are you willing to work with us? I've tenderized a few slayers, and now they're just waiting to be eaten."

That shouldn't have made Kaden's mouth water, and the fact that it did pissed him off even more.

"Yes," Cedric purred. "I can sense your hunger." The crisp clang of the sliding lock vibrated the air in a concussion wave.

Kaden tensed up so hard he was nearly shaking with the desire to leap through the doorway and tear the other vampire apart. *Stay calm, stay calm . . .* He kept himself in check as the door creaked open. Wisely, Cedric stood back, well away from Kaden as he stalked through the doorway without so much as glancing at Andrea.

His shirt and boots lay in a pile, where they'd been left after the vamps had stripped him to prepare for his torture, and he went to them without asking permission.

Cedric watched, a creepy, satisfied smile on his gaunt face, as Kaden tugged on his long-sleeved, black turtleneck and combat boots. Kaden's weapons had been taken away at some point, but his captors had missed the razor-thin obsidian blade Guardians lovingly called the "demon-biter" which was hidden in his boot. The weapon was treated with holy water, which lost most of its effectiveness once dried, but the black stone reacted with the residue, leaving behind a caustic bite when activated by the blood of an evil entity.

Covertly palming the weapon, he swung around to Cedric. "Where are the humans?"

Cedric gestured to one of the tunnel entrances. "That way." Again, the guy wasn't stupid, and he waited until Kaden moved towards the tunnel before falling into step behind him.

They'd only gone twenty feet when Cedric ploughed into Kaden, struck from behind by Andrea. Kaden crunched into the wall, the impact bringing dust and stone down around him. Cedric wheeled around, Andrea's stake impaled in his shoulder. Roaring in fury, Cedric lunged at Andrea. Kaden's heart no longer beat, but it lurched with terror as Cedric's fingers closed around her throat.

No! Two weeks of torture and five years of self-loathing fuelled Kaden's strength, and he attacked, a whirlwind of unrestrained vengeance. A veil of red sliced down over his vision as he caught the other vampire with an arm looped around his neck.

In a smooth sweep, Kaden slashed Cedric's throat with the demon-biter, savouring the hiss of the holy water as it reacted with the vampire's blood. Andrea, in a coordinated move that reminded him what a great team they made, plucked the stake from Cedric's shoulder and plunged it into his chest.

A God-awful squeal rose from Cedric's body. The air around them heated and shimmered, and then the vampire flamed to ash. While the dust still swirled, Kaden swept Andrea into his arms.

"Thank God," she murmured against his chest.

"We're not done yet." He smoothed his hand down her spine, loving the way her muscles rippled under his palm. He wished they were anywhere but here so he could spend time touching her the way he wanted to. The way she deserved. "We've got to save the Guardians."

She nodded and pulled back, leaving him with an aching chest full of regret. Silently, they gathered what weapons they could from the dungeon and headed down the tunnel Cedric had indicated. It was dark, the walls seeping moisture from cracks in the rough stone, but his vampire vision allowed him to see as well as if it had been noon on a clear day.

Sounds drifted from the far end of the tunnel. Talking. Laughter. Some whimpers. The sound of flesh striking flesh.

Kaden crept into the shadows at the entrance to a large chamber. Inside, two vampires circled three Guardians who were bound and gagged, and sitting in the middle of the floor. Every once in a while, a vampire would kick or punch one of them and, while Kaden watched, the female vamp leaned over and licked the blood dripping down one of the Guardian's cheeks.

Kaden signalled to Andrea, and on the finger count of three, they went in. He took down the male vamp before the guy knew what had hit him. Even as his vampire flamed, Andrea's joined the fireworks show.

"That wasn't so bad," she said, as she holstered her stake with a sexy, confident shove home. Oh, yeah, he definitely appreciated a hot chick who knew how to handle wood. Pun intended.

But now wasn't the time to admire her warrior skills, or the way her full lips quirked in a satisfied smile, or the satin wisps of hair that curled around her flushed cheeks. Nope. Not the time.

"No, not bad," he acknowledged through clenched teeth. "But there are at least thirty vamps in Cedric's clan. They could show up at any moment." He knelt beside Zach, one of the newer Guardians in the North Portland Aegis cell, and sliced through his ropes as Andrea did the same for brothers Trey and Matthew.

The moment the three were released, they closed ranks, all glaring murder at Kaden. "Vampire," Trey spat. "You let yourself be turned."

Their weapons lay in a pile in the corner, and Matthew snagged a handful of stakes. Kaden didn't bother to stop him, but Andrea put herself between the Guardians and him.

"Stop it." She jammed her fists on her hips, looking all fierce and cute. "He just saved your lives."

Zach shot her an incredulous stare. "So? He's a vampire. He probably saved us from the others so he could eat us himself.'

Kaden couldn't blame them for their scepticism. He'd have been singing the same tune just a week ago. "I don't want to eat you." He stepped away from them and the exit, because what he'd said wasn't entirely true. "You need to go before the rest of the clan gets here." He grasped Andrea's arm and turned her into him. "You too."

"No. We stay and fight."

"That'll be suicide," Matthew broke in. "It was a trap. Probably set by Kaden."

Again, he couldn't blame Matthew for his line of thinking, but at this point, Andrea's safety was his prime concern. He wasn't going to let these guys put her in jeopardy because they were too blinded by training to see the truth.

Kaden swung around, baring his teeth and giving them an up-close and personal reminder of why they shouldn't fuck with him. "Get. Out," he said, with a calm he didn't feel. "I could kick your asses before, and you can't even begin to imagine what I can do to you now."

Matthew turned crimson with fury, Trey went wide-eyed with surprise, and Zach paled so fast Kaden thought he'd pass out.

Once again, Andrea put herself between Kaden and the three Guardians. It was a sweet gesture, but unnecessary. Kaden hadn't been kidding about being able to kick their asses.

"Go," she said firmly. "Wait outside the chamber. Give me two minutes." She must have delivered her command with a side order of glare that dared them to argue, because they didn't. They filed out of the doorway, but not without muttering obscenities under their breath at Kaden.

When they were gone, she turned to him, but he didn't give her a chance to speak. "You need to go too, Andrea."

Hurt filled her expression. "Not without you."

"I can't go back, and you know it."

"You're going to get killed if you stay and fight."

"And I'm going to get killed if I go back to the Aegis. I'd rather go down swinging." He couldn't bear the sadness in her eyes or the sudden, cavernous emptiness in his chest. Without thinking, he palmed the back of her neck and brought her in close. He dipped his head, and the moment their lips touched, he poured everything he felt for her into his kiss.

He just hoped she didn't feel his regrets, especially the big one, the one that had foolishly kept him from committing himself fully to her.

Then there was the other regret, the one in which he'd told her there would be a "later".

The kiss was goodbye.

Andrea knew it to her very soul, and she felt it in a shiver over her entire body. Eyes stinging, she jerked away from Kaden, but she clung to his hand desperately, even when he tried to extricate himself from her death grip.

"I can't lose you," she said. Pleaded, really.

The resolve in his steel-cut eyes sliced through her like an arctic wind. "We can't be together."

"I don't care what you are. I'm tired of losing people I love. I can't do it again."

He laughed bitterly. "Really, Andrea? You don't care what I am? How can you ever trust me? How can you think I won't turn into a ravenous beast and kill you?"

"Because you aren't Gabrielle." The words made his head snap back as if she'd slapped him, but she pressed the advantage, going right for his jugular, because they didn't have time for a leisurely chat. She had to get through to him *now*. "Gabrielle became a creature that couldn't recognize the person she loved, and she couldn't control her nature. But you *can* control yourself, Kaden. You were starving in that cell, and you could have killed me. You didn't. If anything, you wanted me. You've been turned, but you aren't evil. I don't care what the Aegis say. They aren't always right."

Strain put lines at the corners of his made-to-please mouth. "Even if what I've become isn't an issue for us, it'll be a damned big issue for the Aegis. They aren't going to welcome me with open arms."

"There has to be a way." Her mind worked furiously, searching the darkest, dustiest corners of her brain for anything useful. She could leave the Aegis, but that would be a last resort. Hunting demons was the one thing she was good at, and after an entire life spent quitting jobs, clubs and college, she didn't want to abandon this. Maybe she could transfer again. Someplace where having a vampire boyfriend wouldn't be a big deal. She almost laughed at that, because ... wait ... she sucked in a harsh breath at her sudden idea.

"I've got it." Andrea bounced on her toes, excited for the first time since all of this began. "We can move to New York. One of the cells there is rumoured to have a half-demon Regent. And remember how we heard that one of the Elders is married to a demon?" One of the twelve supreme Aegis leaders married to a demon? The story had spread like wildfire.

"Those are just rumours." Kaden's voice was tired, resigned.

Andrea's hope that they still had a shot at something began to wither. "I know, but—"

"Even if those things are true, life in the Aegis can't be easy for them. I won't subject you to that."

"I can handle it."

"I know you can," he rasped, "but I can't. I can't stand by and watch you be scorned."

"Then what are our options? Stay here and let yourself be killed? I don't freaking think so." She got right up in his face and poked him in the chest. "I've given up on everything in my life at some point. And I mean everything. If I attempt something new and I suck at it, I won't do it again. If I fail at something, I quit. The Aegis and you are the only things I've ever stuck with, and I will not go back to being a quitter. We will work this out."

Kaden stepped back, and the hardest thing she'd ever done was give him that foot of space. "And what am I supposed to do while you're out doing your job? Sit home and watch *Buffy* reruns?"

He had a point. Here she was thinking of her job, when he'd just lost his. He'd just lost everything, actually. Shaking his head, he looked up at the ceiling. "There's no way the Aegis is even going to let me live. Unless . . . "

Her breath hitched, just a tiny catch of hope reawakening. "Unless what?"

One of the guys just outside the chamber whispered for them to hurry up, but Kaden ignored him and scrubbed one hand over his face. "Remember how Tony brought up that radical idea once? When he was drunk and half out of his mind?"

She rolled her eyes. "You'll have to be more specific. We're talking about *Tony*, the guy who thinks fairies enchant his weapons while he sleeps."

He snorted. "Good point. You know, his nutty idea about getting a Guardian to turn vampire and infiltrate clans as a spy?"

"That was crazy," she said. "I mean –" She cut off with a gasp, as what he was saying slapped her upside the head. "That's what you want to do?"

"Why not?"

"Well . . . " She trailed off, because actually . . . why not? He was right about how the Aegis wouldn't accept him as a regular member any more. But if they went for this, he could still work, still do the job, but from the other side. "So instead of fighting Cedric's clan . . . "

"I'd join them."

The idea filled her with terror, but at least it offered a shot at keeping him off the Aegis' most-wanted list – and alive.

So to speak.

"What if they refuse?"

He slid a covert glance at the Guardians, who were still watching him with murder in their eyes. He wouldn't get any other kind of reception at headquarters. "They'll try. But look what happened when you attacked this den. Vampire ops are dangerous. If I can help, they've got to give it a shot."

Her chest constricted with doubt. "It won't be easy to convince them."

"Then we consider your idea about moving to New York. Or I work anyway, and feed you the intel. Either way, this is what I have to do, just as you need to keep working for the Aegis."

That all sounded great, but the most important part of this discussion was still an elephant in the room. "OK, but what about us?"

In a blur of motion, Kaden caught her shoulders and tugged her against him. Her heart went crazy in her chest, skipping around like a lovesick idiot. "I was a fool before. But dying kicked me in the ass and made me see things a little more clearly." Tenderly, he cupped her cheek in one palm. "Everything is intensified now. All my emotions. Including love."

"W-what?"

He crushed her to him, holding on so tight she had trouble breathing. Not that she would change anything. "I love you," he said. "I've loved you for a long time but was afraid to say it." He pressed a kiss to the top of her head and then drew back, but his intense gaze drilled into hers. "I still don't know how to handle my new status, and I've got a lot to learn, but my parents taught me that everyone stumbles, and it's OK to feel your way around. Took me until now to remember that. Still, I can't promise it'll be easy for either of us."

She pressed a finger to his lips. "One day at a time. All I ask is that we try. No quitting without a fight."

His smile stole her breath. "No quitting." His expression was serious once again. "You need to go."

"I still don't want to leave you here."

"You have to. Before Cedric's clan catches me with you. Right now they don't know I was involved with his death."

Outside the chamber, one of the guys cleared his throat impatiently, and she checked her watch. "It's nearly dawn."

"I'll be fine. At sunset, I'll meet you at your place. And remember what I said we'd do later?"

Her body heated up, because *oh, boy*, did she remember. "Uh-huh."

The sharp little points of his fangs gleamed, matching a wicked light in his eyes. "Good, because *later* I'm going to see just how much more intense *everything* can be."

She couldn't wait. They definitely had a rough road ahead, but it seemed that, for the first time in her life, the road wasn't a dead end. This was one journey she would not fail.

The Ghost of Leadville

Jeanne C. Stein

My name is Rose Sullivan. Although I've been on the earth for 200 years, I was turned on my twenty-fifty birthday. I am eternally frozen in the physical form of a twenty-five-year-old. Blonde hair, blue eyes, five feet two inches tall, one hundred pounds. I am small in stature which means men sometimes make the mistake of thinking a childish mind resides in this rather childish body. They only make the mistake once. I am preternaturally strong, as are all vampires, and have no tolerance towards those who try to intimidate me – or others. If I see an injustice, it is in my nature to correct it.

It isn't always easy being vampire. There are rules to be followed. Most humans are unaware of our existence. Just as they are unaware of other supernatural beings living amongst them. They have to be. The great secret must be preserved. Humanity has shown how it reacts to that which it does not understand. Destroy first. Ask questions later.

And so I have survived as a vampire for 200 years. Living in big cities, mostly. Able to last as long as forty years in one guise – the latest a museum curator in New York. My specialty was early Americana. Convenient since I was born to missionary parents in the American West in 1809.

But one can only do so much to disguise a face and body that do not age. It becomes apparent when all those around you take note of your "youthful" appearance that it is time to move on. A hasty resignation because of "family problems", a quick transfer of funds to whatever new identity I've adopted and a brief goodbye to the human hosts who have provided me sustenance during my stay. They, the few who are guardians of the secret, do not question. They are used to the plight of the vampire. They know to take the money and pleasure offered in return for blood and form no attachment. It has always been so.

And so I shed the skin of the old persona and adopt a new one in Leadville, Colorado in the year 2009.

I've decided this time around to eschew bright lights and settle into a quiet existence in a quiet little town. I've also decided to write a book. Why not? Look at a current best-seller list. The one hot topic on all the charts is vampire romance. Who is in a better position to write about vampire romance than a female vampire who has certainly experienced her share of romance? And besides, it's a chance to set the record straight, albeit under the ruse of *fiction*, about many things having to do with living a modern vampire life. It's not all bad. Not by a long shot.

There is another reason I chose to make this incarnation that of a writer. It's a solitary existence. I've had my fill of city life and being forced to live among people. The smells, the noises, the *desperation* of a population trying to cram all of life into a few decades burdens the spirit of a vampire. I'm ready for a change.

I bought a nicely restored Victorian on the edge of Leadville. I stumbled on the place last year while on a research trip, visiting early mining sites in preparation for a museum exhibit. Leadville nestles in a fold of the Rocky Mountains, hidden, protected. At the height of the gold rush, 50,000 called this place home. Now there are barely 2,000 people living here. The climate is harsh. The most often heard comment is that Leadville has two seasons – this winter and last winter. But temperature is irrelevant to a vampire. And Leadville's one lasting claim to fame is an opera house, built to entertain the miners during the long winter. It has been restored and opens its door to the public in the summer when a flock of faithful opera fans make the trek up from Denver to enjoy the old building's perfect acoustics. It is a gentle reminder of a gentler time. I fell in love with it at first sight.

And so I find myself comfortably ensconced on my living room couch, laptop computer open, finger poised over the keys to begin this novelist's journey. My eyes, however, keep drifting upwards, through the window at the other side of the room, drawn to the mountains rising like stark, grey monoliths against a cloudless November sky.

A familiar landscape.

Truth be told, this is not the first time I've lived in Leadville.

Memories flood back.

No, I lived here once before.

Leadville, 1884
Hyman's Saloon

"Rose. Come on over here, gal. I have someone for you to meet."

I look up. Sunny Tom's face is wreathed in a grin, his dozen gold teeth flashing in the bar light like fireflies on a summer night.

Are you sure? I ask him. I've been keeping an eye on the poker table. Miners flush with gold dollars and full to the brim with whiskey are normally good for business. But when the cards turn against them, the whiskey takes over. Bullets are never good for business and at this moment, both the whiskey and the cards are turning against one youngster new to both. I raise an eyebrow at Tom. *This could turn ugly.*

He shrugs. *He pay for his drinks?*

A nod.

Then fuck him. This is more important.

My gaze sweeps over the slight figure of a man standing beside him. Sunny Tom is six feet tall, two hundred pounds. The stranger with him is maybe five foot ten, one hundred forty pounds. He's dressed like a dandy – striped pants, white shirt, cravat with a diamond stickpin which winks at me as I approach. He has a hat in his hand and a big Colt revolver on his hip.

He watches me with a predator's eye. He's even-featured with a square chin, light brown hair, full moustache. Not bad looking. Must be a big spender if Tom is sending him to me.

I tilt my head, taste the air around him. He's sick. Consumption. It hovers about him in a bilious cloud.

I hold out my hand. "Rose."

He takes it, brings it to his lips. "John Holliday, ma'am. Pleased to meet you."

Sunny Tom probes my head, waiting for the connection to be made. I lift a shoulder in a half-shrug which prompts an exasperated, *John Holliday? You don't know the name? How about Doc Holliday? That ring any bells?*

Tom turns his smile back on Doc Holliday. "I will leave you in Rose's most capable hands. Have a very good evening."

He saunters away to take my place near the poker table, winking as he passes. *Have fun.*

With a consumptive? Tom is past before I can skewer him with a properly caustic reply.

He runs the saloon, I run the girls who work it. There are only two people who know the truth of our relationship. Sunny Tom and me. We are both vampires. Running a bar that specializes in whores and whiskey keeps us both in what we need. Human blood.

He's set me up tonight with a consumptive. It's not the illness I resent. Vampires are impervious to human disease. It's the *taste* of the blood.

My shoulders bunch a little at the prospect but I put on a sweet smile and take my place beside Doc at the bar. He half turns towards me and the diamond at his neck catches and reflects the light in a rainbow burst. I reach up and touch it with the tip of a finger. "Nice bauble, Mr Holliday."

His smile is tinged with bitterness and regret. "A gift from my mother before she died. Unfortunately not the only thing she left me." He is looking down the bar and with a flick of a finger, summons the barkeep.

Holliday orders whiskey for himself, turns to me. "What will you have?"

"Gin." I tap a finger on the bar. Sam has worked for us for twenty years and he interprets my order with a nod and a grin.

He turns his back on us and pours.

I touch Holliday's hand. "What brings such a famous person to Leadville?"

"I guess you could say my mother." This time there's no mistaking the irony heavy in his tone.

He reads the question in my eyes. He shakes his head, but the hard lines of his mouth soften. "The climate. I've been told it is better for one who suffers with consumption to live in a dry climate."

An honest answer. My eyebrows lift in surprise. It is only in the last few years that consumption has been found to be infectious. Yet he says it openly. Maybe because I am only a whore, bought and paid for, and the answer is of no consequence. The health of his wallet is all I should be interested in.

The bartender places our drinks in front of us. Holliday takes a long pull, draining the glass, orders another. I sip at my drink. It's only water. I learned long ago to keep a clear head when working. Alcohol goes directly into a vampire's system and we are as susceptible to its effects as humans. It took an unexpected and unprovoked attack from a drunken miner to teach me that lesson. Vampires are not easily killed, but we feel pain. I bore the marks of that attack for two days. The miner suffered the consequences for a much briefer period. He was dead in two minutes.

I watch Holliday surreptitiously, over the rim of my glass. Standing this close to him, his reputation as a cold-blooded killer seems exaggerated. His speech is soft, his inflection subtle. He is neither loud nor imposing.

Not an indication that he doesn't like his sex rough, I remind myself. The mildest mannered men are often the ones who find it satisfying to take their frustrations out on a female.

"So, Rose." Holliday dabs at his mouth with a finger. "What do you do for excitement in Leadville?"

"The gaming tables here, of course," I reply with a smile. "And Horace Tabor opened his opera house just last week. Emma Abbott is performing. Her voice is wonderful. If you're planning to stay for a while, you really should catch a performance."

He nods and signals for another drink. "Perhaps I will." He looks towards the tables. "Business appears to be good."

"It is. Silver was discovered two years ago and those lodes are as rich as the gold. There's money to be made for sure."

Holliday is watching me now, over the rim of *his* glass. "You don't talk like a whore. You don't look like one either. Your skin is milky white. Your hair shiny. Good teeth. Why hasn't some rich city boy plucked you up?"

I wave a hand and laugh. "You see any rich city boys around here? I'm doing what I want to do. I like men. They seem to like me. Men are allowed to indulge their passions. What's wrong with a woman doing the same thing?"

His eyebrows rise a bit. "Plain talk. I like that. I say let's you and me follow that passion right up to a room." He signals the bartender. "A bottle, if you please, and two glasses."

He tucks the bottle under an arm, scoops the glasses into one hand, places his other hand at the small of my back. "Time to properly make your acquaintance, Miss Rose," he says with a little bow. "Lead the way."

Tom's eyes follow us to the staircase at the back of the saloon. I feel his thoughts reaching out. *You need anything, you call.*

I smile at him over my shoulder. *You watch out for the other girls. Trixie should be back down in fifteen minutes. Annabelle just went up. Those two miners in the corner have monopolized Jane and Kate for too long. If they aren't ready to pony up for a fuck in ten minutes, kick 'em out.*

He grins and throws me a salute. *Yes, sir. How long should I give you and Doc?*

I put my arm through Holliday's. *As long as it takes.*

My room is at the back of the hallway, facing Main Street. It has big windows that are left open nearly all year around. The cold doesn't bother me and the bracing smell of air heavy with snow flushes out the human smell of sweat and semen that often permeates these walls.

Holliday crosses right over to the windows and pulls them shut. "Damn, woman. It's cold in here. Don't you feel it?"

No, the vampire answers. The human answers, "I forget sometimes to close the windows. Here. I'll stoke the fire. It will be as warm as a spring day in a minute."

He holds up the bottle. "Good thing I brought a little something to help heat us up."

He pours two glasses and hands one to me. I pretend to take a sip, then place the glass on the table next to the bed. "I know better ways to heat our blood." I slip the straps of my gown down over my shoulders.

His eyes follow my movements. He still has his own glass in his hand. By the time I've stripped down to my undergarments, that hand is trembling a little.

"You have a beautiful body," he says. "Tiny. You're no bigger than a minute."

"How about you, cowboy? You no bigger than a minute?"

He puts his glass down beside mine, crosses the room, eyes blazing with the challenge. He shrugs out of his jacket, lets it fall to the floor. He pulls the tie off, strips off his shirt. Only then does he take his gun belt off. He lets the holster fall to the floor. The gun he places on one of the pillows.

"You afraid you need protection from me?" I ask with a playful smile. I don't like guns, especially one within arm's reach of a man I'm fucking. Bullets can't kill me, but they sure as hell can hurt.

I reach out to move the gun. He's faster. He stops my hand, gives it a little shake. "Uh-huh. The gun stays where it is."

I twist free. "You paid for my time. This is my bedroom. I will fuck you any way you want, but not with a gun on my pillow. It either gets moved, or you both do. Out the door."

His face darkens with quick anger. Then it's over. The cloud clears from his eyes first. Then the corners of his mouth turn up in a grin. "Do you fuck as good as you give orders?"

My hand drifts down his stomach. "Take these off and we'll find out."

He fumbles a little with the buttons, impatience and desire making him clumsy. I push his hands away and free him myself. I throw him back on the bed, pull off his boots and slide his trousers down over his ankles. He reaches for me, but I've got the gun in my hand and have stepped out of reach to place it across the room on the bureau.

When I turn around, he's watching me with that predator's glare again, wary, suspicious, until I pull my chemise up over my head and stand in front of him as naked as he is.

Suspicion and doubt are swept from his mind. The only thing he feels now is a powerful lust, a hunger. My blood responds to the fire in his eyes. I let him pull me down on top of him, our bodies press together. My breasts are crushed against his chest. He grabs my shoulders and rolls me over. He thrusts himself deep inside me, pounding into me until he comes with a gasp and a moan.

It's over for him. The weight of his body on mine grows heavier as his breathing becomes deep and regular. I let him drift off, used to the ways of men. I am a whore whose value is limited to one thing – the vessel into which men pour their seed. But I am also vampire. I have needs of my own.

I have learned how best to fulfil those needs. When Holliday has slept for some minutes, I begin. I roll him gently off me and start first by calling up my own desire. My fingers probe my sex, finding the spot that brings the release denied me with our first coupling. Then, breathless, eager, I turn my attention to him. Holliday awakens, startled, to find this woman, this whore fondling him. But his body is already responding.

I straddle him, pinning him beneath me with my thighs. He tries once to grab my shoulders, thrust me back under him, but I am vampire. This is my game now.

He gives in, surrendering to my control. His hands grasp my buttocks. His eyes are closed and I bend forwards, kiss each eyelid, brush my lips against his. I trace a path with my tongue from the corner of his mouth to his jawline, find the pulse point just beneath the surface, wait until I feel the first spasms of his release, and bite.

Need consumes us both. He comes with a groan as his body pushes up against mine. I come with a shudder as I taste his blood, roll it around in my mouth, savour the life essence of this man. His blood is not as bitter as I expected. I drink, great breathless draughts of blood that warm and revive me. But I know when to stop. When to relegate the vampire back to the shadow. When to call the human back.

Holliday lies spent once more beneath me. I use my lips to close and heal the puncture marks. This is when I secrete the enzymes that make my host forget. The sex. The feeding.

But I don't want this one to forget. He won't remember my opening his neck. He won't remember my taking his blood. But he will remember the coupling, the pleasure we've given each other. I lie still and quiet beside him.

While I'm cradled against his shoulder, his right hand comes up and caresses the back of my neck. He doesn't fall asleep this time. He gathers me into his arms.

Imagine that.

Holding a whore after sex.

It makes me smile.

I'm sitting at the vanity, still naked, brushing my hair. Holliday watches, leaning against the headboard, a blanket thrown over his hips.

"You are no ordinary whore."

I shrug. "What kind of whore am I?"

He tilts his head, studying me. "I don't know."

He throws off the blanket, comes to stand behind me, takes the brush from my hand. He draws it gently through my hair. When he leans towards me, I feel his sex press into the small of my back.

"Are you ready to go again so soon?"

He lays the brush down, puts his hands on my shoulders, pulls me up. "If you do what you did before, I may never want to leave this room."

He is smiling and, for a moment, I see the younger, healthier man he must have been before illness and the fortunes of life claimed him.

A startling thought flashes into my head. He could be that man again. I could make it happen. I could make him forever young and healthy. I could make him vampire.

I feel him watching me. I've never done it before – made another like me. Would he want it?

His hands cup my face. "What are you thinking?"

A rap on the door brings me back to the present with a little jump. I stand back and away from Holliday and snatch up a robe. "Yes?"

"There's someone here says he's looking for Doc Holliday."

Sunny Tom's voice carries through the thick door. His thoughts project even better. *This could be trouble.*

Holliday reaches for his trousers. "Got a name?"

I've crossed to the door, pulled it open. Sunny Tom steps inside. "Says his name is Billy Allen. Says he's gunning for you. Name mean anything?"

A frown pulls at the corners of his mouth. "Yeah. The name means something." He shrugs into his shirt, tucks it into his trousers, straps on the holster. He grabs the gun from the top of the bureau, spins the chamber, slips it into the holster in a single, fluid motion.

"You don't have to go down there. There's a back entrance. Tom could show you and you could be out of town before Allen knows you're gone."

Holliday shakes his head. "No."

The answer sends a spark of irritation burning through me. "Why not? Why risk dying?"

His expression this time is one of amused indulgence. He chucks my chin. "I am dying, lady. Consumption, remember?"

"But what if you didn't have to die?"

What are you doing, Rose? Tom's voice is sharp-edged and heavy with disapproval.

Holliday is at my vanity, smoothing his hair back from his face, straightening the diamond tiepin at the neck of his shirt. "We all have to die, Rose. I'd prefer to do it with my boots on." He turns towards me and smiles. "How do I look?"

"Good. You look good."

He takes another step closer, close enough to lean down and brush his lips against mine. "Keep that bed warm. I reckon to be back."

And then he's gone, Tom on his heels.

Tom doesn't leave without a parting shot. He pauses at the door, grins back at me. *He must be one hell of a fuck.*

I push the door closed at his back and scramble for my clothes. There are too many of them with too many hooks and too many buttons. I give up, wrap the robe around me again and cinch it with the sash. Barefoot, I run into the hall.

The retort of the gunshot reaches me at the top of the stairs. I race down in time to see Holliday leaning over the end of the bar. In two seconds, I'm at his side.

Billy Allen is on the floor, his right arm bloody. He's yelling and clutching at the arm, his face twisted in pain and fear.

Holliday stands over him, pistol cocked, and takes aim.

"No." I put my hand on his arm, tug. "If you kill him like this, it's cold-blooded murder. If you stop now, it's self-defence. You'll have a fighting chance with a jury."

I recognize in Holliday's face a feeling I'm well acquainted with – the blood lust – when adrenaline is hot in your veins and the need for satisfaction swallows up your humanity. I'm not sure he heard or understood what I said. His heart is pounding with such force, I feel it deep in my own chest.

The crowd in the saloon has grown quiet. The only noise is the sound of sobbing from Billy Allen. Holliday remains poised over him. He glances down at me.

I shake my head. "Don't. Please."

He smiles.

Then he fires.

I jump, gasping.

There's a strangled cry from Billy Allen that continues to grow in volume until, as one, all of us take a step forwards to look.

The floor is splintered just above Allen's head. He's curled himself into a fetal position, rocking and crying. The air is foul with the smell of his body's waste. He's pissed and shit himself and all around laughter erupts.

Holliday holsters his gun. "Sorry for the mess," he says.

He looks around at the crowd. "I reckon someone should get Marshal Kelly. And call whoever you have in town who serves as a medical man to tend to Allen here. I'll be at the bar."

He holds out his arm and I take it. "You know you're going to pay for the damage to the floor."

Holliday grins. "You are no ordinary whore. That's a fact."

Sunny Tom is directing the music man back to his playing and the girls back to their hustling. He herds players towards the gaming tables to resume their interrupted poker game. I signal the bartender to give everyone a drink on the house. Soon Billy Allen is nothing more than a mewling distraction to be stepped around until the town's doctor arrives to cart him off.

Holliday and I sip whiskey at the bar.

"What's going to happen?" I ask. It's a stupid question. I know the answer.

Holliday's smile acknowledges that we both do. "I'll be arrested. If I'm lucky, they'll let me out on bail. If not, I'll be in jail until the trial."

"It's self-defence, though, pure and simple. Sunny Tom said Allen was gunning for you. You have a right to protect yourself."

Holliday laughs. "I'll be sure you're called as a defence witness."

"It will be my pleasure."

We lapse into silence. I can't quantify what it is about this man, this stranger, that has touched me. I only know that I want him to stay with me, if not for ever, than at least as long as human life allows.

"You better come right back here the minute you're released, y'hear?"

Another rumbling laugh. "You sure like to give orders."

"I do. And I'm used to those orders being followed. Don't make me come after you."

He puts his hand over mine on the bar and squeezes. "I'll do my best."

I lean towards him, rest my head on his shoulder, wondering again what he might say if I told him what I was and offered him eternal life. Would he believe me?

No. Worse, he might think me mad. Better to wait until he comes back. Until I have time to explain the gift I have to offer. What it means to me. What it can mean to him.

My heart is pounding so hard, I'm sure he must hear it. Maybe if I remind him of what we shared upstairs. Give him a hint of what could be. What *will* be when he returns.

I move closer, my lips at his ear.

He bends his head. "Yes, Rose?"

I don't get the chance. Marshal Kelly and two deputies appear at the door to the saloon and Holliday pushes himself away from the bar to meet him. He lets them take his gun and cuff his hands behind his back. He doesn't look my way. Not once. He carries himself straight and tall and with quiet dignity as they lead him away.

Sunny Tom comes to stand beside me at the bar. "Damn girl. Are you crying?"

I swipe at tears and snot with the back of my hand. "Of course not." I look around. "The excitement doesn't seem to have hurt business."

"Nope." He leans his elbows back on the bar and rests a foot on the copper rail. "Think we'll see Holliday again?"

"Of course. I told him he'd better come back the minute he's out of jail."

"And nobody disobeys one of your orders, do they?"

"Not if they're smart. I figure between all the legal wrangling and the trial, he should be walking through that door in six months at the outside."

Sunny Tom shakes his head. "Hope you're right. I'd hate to see you get your heart broke."

"What heart?"

One of the girls calls for Tom and he leaves me with a pat on the arm.

But I know.

Holliday will be acquitted and he'll come back.

He has to.

Turns out I am right and I am wrong.

Doc Holliday is acquitted. A jury agrees that Billy Allen spent the morning he was shot walking up and down Main Street telling everyone that he was out for Holliday's blood. They reasoned it would have been foolish on Holliday's part not to be prepared to counter force with force.

But I am wrong about something else. I am wrong about the most important part. I am wrong that Holliday will come back to me.

He never does.

For some weeks, I follow his story in the newspaper. How during the trial, Holliday's health deteriorated. How when it was over, he headed south for Glenwood Springs, to partake of medicinal waters found there that are said to relieve the suffering of consumptives. How somewhere along the way, he picked up a travelling companion.

At that point, I stop reading the stories. Stop waiting for him to appear. Stop making plans for when he does. It is finally clear that whatever we shared those brief hours six months before meant far more to me than it did to him.

Sunny Tom and I continue to run our saloon. We know it won't be long before we have to move on. The silver veins are petering out and prices are falling. In preparation we begin hoarding more and more of our take.

On 14 November 1887, I come downstairs to find Sunny Tom having breakfast at his usual table, the *Leadville Carbonate Chronicle* spread out in front of him. His hand stills and his eyes grow round as he reads.

I pour myself a cup of coffee and came round to join him. *What's wrong?*

He looks up at me, pity reflected in his expression. It's an emotion quite alien to his usually gruff nature. I raise an eyebrow in surprise.

He turns the paper around so that I see what sparked the reaction.

It is Doc Holliday's obituary.

I thrust it away. *I don't want to know.*

Sunny Tom takes the paper back. "You should at least hear this," he says aloud. He settles the paper on the table and begins to read: "There is scarcely one in the country who had acquired a greater notoriety than Doc Holliday, who enjoyed the reputation of being one of the most fearless men on the frontier, and whose devotion to his friends in the climax of the fiercest ordeal was inextinguishable. It was this, more than any other faculty, that secured for him the reverence of a large circle who were prepared on the shortest notice to rally to his relief."

He meets my gaze across the table. "He was a good man. It's all right to grieve."

No. I won't grieve any human. It's pointless. They die. We do not.

I push myself away from the table, turning to flee back upstairs when a man from the stage office appears at the saloon doors.

"Can I help you?" I ask.

He has a small package in his hand. "I'm looking for Rose Sullivan."

"I am she."

He holds the package out to me. "This came for you on the morning stage."

I fish a coin from my pocket and press it into his palm as I accept the package.

Sunny Tom asks from his table, "Sir, would you like a drink?"

I don't wait for the answer, but seat myself at a table in the far corner to examine the package. It's wrapped in plain brown paper, my name and Hyman's Saloon, Leadville, printed in block letters on the top. There is no indication of who it's from.

But something inside me knows. My hands tremble as I tear at the paper, fumble the top off the tiny box inside.

A diamond winks up at me.

Under it, a note. "For Rose. To remember me by. John Holliday."

Leadville
Present Day

A chiming tone from my computer brings me back with a start. I have an instant message coming in from my friends at the museum in New York. They tell me they miss me and ask how I'm doing and when I'm coming back.

"We know you won't last in Bumfuckville six months," one of them writes. "Rose Sullivan living in a ghost town? Never gonna work."

My fingers play with the small diamond pendant I've worn around my neck for over a hundred years. Holliday was the first and only man I ever considered offering immortality. If he'd come back after his trial, maybe he'd be seated beside me right now, adding his own words to mine.

My face is wet with tears. I am surprised how the memory of a man I knew only a few hours still has power to touch me. Or is it this place? Was coming back to Leadville a mistake?

Deep inside, I know it's not.

My fingers begin to move over the keyboard. Doc Holliday is here with me. I hear his voice, see his face and the words flow.

This will be more than a novel.

This will be our story.

The Vampire, the Witch and the Yenko

Tiffany Trent

Being a hired witch wasn't exactly the profession Dani had dreamed about as a little kid. A fireman or astronaut? Yes. Witch? No.

In fact, she hadn't even been aware that such a profession was possible until the Syndicate had quite forcibly made her aware. She'd always thought her ability to fix stuff was just a special talent, like reciting the alphabet backwards. But apparently not. Being able to fix anything, any broken thing from carburettors to crania, was not so much a talent as a *power*.

The Syndicate had snatched her up when she was a teen. Before things could get dangerous, they said. Before she could learn to break things. They told her she was fairly old to have her power come online.

At her look, the Questioner had said: "Ever wonder why there are so many missing children?"

That had stopped Dani cold.

She couldn't say she'd been entirely happy with disappearing into the Syndicate fold – never seeing friends or family again, always working undercover, never allowed to become too close to anyone. But the trade-offs were luxury, travel, protection and training. She'd seen first hand in her work what happened to the untrained. She was glad she'd been grabbed before any of that ugliness could happen to her.

She was also glad that she understood how the world worked a little better than most folks. Like the fact that every fairy-tale nightmare was true. Witches, ghosts, vampires, werewolves – all real.

Some people of course knew this far too well. Some people didn't understand the complexities and took out their fear and rage on any supernatural creature they could get their hands on.

And some people, like her present mark, were only after one thing – the Syndicate itself.

She stared down at Joey Martoni's craggy face. Mafia kingpin. Classic-car collector. Magic thief. No one knew exactly how he'd developed a means of stealing magic. He was like a vampire, only worse. He sucked witches dry, amassing all their magic for himself. He'd sworn to take the Syndicate down using its own power. And generally when Martoni swore to do something, it got done.

He'd infiltrated and destroyed an important cell around Washington DC that it might take years to rebuild. Some of the Syndicate's best witches had been lost. Some of them were the closest to friends and family Dani had these days. She didn't know if she'd ever stop missing them, or hating the man who had murdered them.

The Syndicate had heard that Martoni was appearing at the Island Cruise on North Carolina's Outer Banks, that he was even auctioning off a special car of his for charity. They decided to try a new tactic: use only one witch to catch him when he was isolated and exposed, away from his normal territory. If Dani could find a way, she might eliminate the Martoni threat and help the Syndicate rebuild. It was gratifying that so much trust had been placed in her and her alone to get the job done.

Trouble was, she thought, as she crumpled Martoni's photo into a ball of flame, all she really wanted now was to get out of the Syndicate for good.

Drake wiped his hands on the rag next to him and reached back into the guts of the '58 Corvette. She was a touchy beast, but such an old beauty that Drake couldn't resist the challenge. The biggest problem was finding someone willing to unload what he needed. He'd had Warren calling everybody he knew – and he knew a lot of people. The engine was fine but the carburettor was shot, and the owner was determined to have it back in time for the show next week.

The Island Cruise would be huge this year. A charity auction would feature one of the two known Yenko Camaros. When Joey Martoni had snatched it up about ten years ago, it had gone for $2.2

million. Hordes of collectors would be there, not just for the Yenkos, but for whatever else might catch their eye. The 'Vette had to be ready by then.

Someone was behind him. He knew it before the shadow fell across the plugs and hoses of the Corvette's innards. A chime sounded, a sweet, high sound that only he could hear.

A nasty tingle wormed up his spine as he turned.

The way her eyes scanned his naked torso, hugged his hips tighter than his jeans, and lingered on his crotch and thighs made him wish he wore a cloak from head to heel. He had back in the old days, and never thought he'd miss them when they went out of fashion. She glanced at the telltale shirt with his nametag on it draped over the bumper.

"I thought I felt you here when I moved in yesterday," she said, finally meeting his eyes. Hers were dark and wicked; he was even more certain that he wanted nothing to do with her. "I came by to make sure."

"Come again?" Drake said.

She purred, and Drake shook his head minutely. *They're all the same, damn them.*

"Do you need something?" He gestured towards the torn-up car. "I'm a little busy here."

"I just want to make sure you understand who calls the shots here," she said. She exuded a ripe sexuality that would have driven any human man insane with lust in ten seconds flat. But a human was not what she needed.

"Believe me, I'm perfectly aware," Drake said. He glared at her. She was young; this might be her first time. Some males would jump at that, but perhaps his nonchalance would give her a hint. "I've got business here, which as you can see I'm running behind on, so . . . "

He half turned, but she was there, her hand on his biceps pulling him back, with familiar force, to face her. More nasty shivers raced over his body, centred on where her fingers dug into his skin.

"I want you to understand fully what I mean," she said. Her fangs extended. Her other hand wandered down his ribs and into his jeans.

Drake looked down at her, at her hair snaking around her shoulders, down her back almost to her ass. The music in his mind compelled him to yield to her.

"Look . . . I'm not in that scene any more. I'm just doing my job here, doing what I love to do. I'm happy for you to do the same." He stepped back, pulling her cold hand out of his crotch.

She laughed, the long cords of her neck tightening. "Not in that scene? How precious! You know it doesn't work that way. Have you forgotten the duty you owe your species? You have three choices. Fuck, flee or die."

She pushed at his mind, trying to force him to cave in to her. Her song promised she would spread him across the hood of the car beneath her, riding him until he gave her what she wanted. She was in heat. And when vampires came into heat, their chosen sire had no choice. A vampire would travel continents seeking a sire for her offspring; they were worse than werewolves.

And if the sire wasn't strong enough or if he refused the mating, she'd kill him. That was the way it was, the way it had been since the *sanguinaria* virus had wormed into the blood of a Romanian village long ago. No one knew where the virus came from or why it worked the way it did, though there were theories. The comet debris theory was a personal favourite of Drake's.

But what he hated was all the shit about "siring" vampires off of hapless, tortured humans. Drake was grateful people didn't know how it really was, how twisted and humiliating vampire matings actually were.

"I'm waiting," she said.

He stuffed the compulsion of her lust deep inside his brain. He reached out and grabbed her by the throat, bending close so that his dark hair brushed her cheek. "You forgot the fourth choice, little vixen." He squeezed with a power that let her know he could rip her head off with his bare hands and freeze her bones if he chose. Her lips tightened and she dug her nails into the flesh of his arm until she broke skin. Black blood seeped out.

He threw her backwards and she tripped and fell, sitting down hard on the garage floor.

"Just keep that in mind," Drake said. "There's always another choice."

She stood, laughing as she dusted herself off, and tossed her long hair back over her shoulders. "And you've made your choice, *Drake*. I'm Ferrell. Remember that, because our next meeting won't be so pleasant, I promise you. You'll be screaming my name on your knees."

She stalked off and he heard the doors clatter closed behind her – all semblance of stealth gone.

The music went with her.

He narrowly avoided slamming his hands down on the Corvette. Instead, he turned and kicked a tyre so hard it sailed across the garage and sent a shelf of tools clattering to the floor.

He sighed and started cleaning them up, when a knock sounded at the door. Drake stiffened. He was pretty sure that Ferrell wouldn't bother to knock when she came calling again, nor would she return so soon after such a dramatic exit.

He walked over to the side door and opened it cautiously.

A man in black stood flanked by two well-dressed bodyguards who wore sunglasses even in the dark. The security lights made their faces bluish-white. Beyond them, a white limo sat next to a gleaming Yenko Camaro. It had the sport package – orange with white racing stripes, the Yenko logo emblazoned above the back fender.

Joey Martoni stepped uninvited into the garage. For just a moment, Drake thought one of the old princes had found him, so great was the power that rolled off him. But the great vampire princes were gone, lost in the Wars of the Matriarchs. Martoni must be something else entirely.

"You Drake Evans?" Martoni asked. The bodyguards stationed themselves on either side of the door. Drake caught a whiff of corruption under heavy cologne.

"Yes, sir." Drake decided to play the respectful card. For the moment. "What can I do for you?"

"I'm glad you asked that," Martoni said. "Glad you asked. Word is this is the best rod shop in town." His eyes travelled over the other cars as if they were garbage. "My ride needs an oil change and a little clean up before she goes to the auction block on Tuesday. Think you can manage that?"

Drake nodded. "I think I can handle that, Mr Martoni."

"Good," Martoni said. He walked out without another word.

One of the bodyguards handed Drake the keys and a business card. His cologne was overpowering. "Call us if there's a problem. Though there had better not be."

The limo pulled out, leaving Drake staring bemusedly at the heavy-bodied Camaro. Certainly not to his taste, but it was worth millions. He hoped Warren's insurance covered this.

He opened the garage door. Today, he had more important things to worry about than horny vampires.

Dani didn't have too much trouble sweet-talking Warren, the manager of Mal's Rod Shop, to hire her on for the night shift. People were already coming in for the Cruise and his best mechanic would soon be overwhelmed. Of course, it didn't hurt that Dani had more persuasive power than the best vampire prostitute. Witches had a rep that way, and that probably explained why Martoni hated them so much.

Her talents reminded her a bit too much of the old mind-trick scene in *Star Wars* for her comfort.

"Heard you could use a good mechanic to help out during the Cruise," she said.

Warren eyed her. He was a chesty man with a fat gold bracelet and tats up and down his hairy arms.

She smiled.

"Matter of fact," he said, "I probably could."

"When do I start – tonight?" she asked.

"Tonight! That would be great," Warren said, his eyes going glassy.

"What I thought."

They shook hands then. He gave her a key to the side door without being asked.

She tried to hide her huge grin as she left. If only Martoni could be this easy.

Between worrying over the Camaro and Ferrell, Drake barely felt rested when he rose at twilight. Very, very dangerous. If Ferrell were an older, more traditional sort, she'd call a quorum of the highest-ranking vampire females around. Usually, three crones assisted in capturing a recalcitrant male and forced him to stand at stud; three having some esoteric significance that Drake could care less about. If Ferrell wasn't a traditionalist – which he suspected – there was no telling what she would do. The younger vampires all acted like werewolves these days; it was all the rage. A pack mentality among normally solitary hunters was a terrifying thing indeed.

If he wanted to be ready, he'd need all his strength. When he'd started working for and with humans, he'd decided to eat only the ones who deserved it, and then only if he was desperately in need of nourishment. Tonight he feared he would have to feed, not only to prepare for Ferrell, but also because Danny, the new mechanic Warren had hired, was coming to help him on the night shift. If he was hungry or tired, things could get ugly.

He considered running again briefly. He'd certainly run before. But he couldn't run for ever.

And where would he go, anyway? He liked his work and the people he worked with. Warren was smart enough not to ask questions, and every night another car offered itself up to him like a beautiful patient that only he could cure. For the most part, he was left to his own devices. It was perfect.

These thoughts circled through his mind like vultures as he stepped out of his cottage and revved up his old Indian Chief motorcycle. He stopped to fill up with gas and got a newspaper, looking for the latest news on homicides, robberies, domestic or animal abuse. Police had found a body out on Dare Road. That was good enough.

Arriving at the site of the investigation was a disappointment, though. He sensed through the ground, through the memory of the place, that there had been no trauma here and thus no murderer to seek in retribution. The victim had been an old hitch-hiker who had died here of a heart attack. But . . . A heavy scent wafted on the breeze. There was a pig farm very close by. *Some* dinner was better than none, he reckoned.

Under the smell of the farm was an even sweeter scent, the chilling perfume of a vampire. It was as cloying as death; as alluring as absinthe. Soft, melancholy music drifted into his mind, threatening to take hold. He trembled a little, balling his hands into fists. Ferrell. This allure hadn't touched him in two centuries, not since Isobel. After her, he'd sworn off women, particularly of his own species.

"Damn it," he whispered through gritted teeth. He filled his mind with thoughts of cool metal, the 'Vette's red curves, until the music faded.

Had Ferrell followed him? The low murmur of voices came from up ahead. A human wouldn't have heard them, thinking his footsteps were only wind in the branches.

He hesitated. He wanted to be at the garage before the new mechanic but he still had to feed. If Ferrell caught him in his weakened state, it wouldn't go well with him. He recalled his words to her. *There is always another choice.*

Now that he knew where Ferrell and her gang nested, he knew he would have to come back and destroy them eventually.

But not yet. He sighed and headed towards the outermost building of the pig farm.

Dani didn't have much trouble locating Martoni's hotel. It was one of the few high-rises on the beach and swarming with security. She recognized one of Martoni's bodyguards from the de-briefing before she'd left her current cell. It was rumoured that Martoni didn't go anywhere without him, that his last wife had actually divorced him over it. Not surprisingly, the ex-wife had never been found, though of course no one could pin it on him or any of his people.

She was supposed to be at the garage soon for her first shift, but a little surveillance on the way wouldn't hurt. She parked her rusting Charade at a public beach access and hiked through the sand until she came up to the hotel from the back way. She missed her Lexus, but figured a beater was better cover. As she rounded the corner of the walk, she looked up to see four vampire females being ushered in by Martoni's security guards. No one else would have recognized this, of course, but Syndicate witches could always tell.

She chanted a spell of invisibility and hurried after them. Nothing but her shadow passed beyond the doors, down the carpeted hall, and into the elevator. She was gambling on the fact that Martoni wouldn't expect any witch in her right mind to attempt this.

The elevator doors slid back to reveal a warren of hallways and rooms. Bass boomed down the corridor. She followed the sour smell of the vampires to a room where several people – bodyguards and lackeys – attended the man himself near a fully stocked bar. The mirrors across from the door didn't register her as she passed into the room.

She got just close enough to hear what the vampires were saying, not enough to be detected by aural field or smell.

"And you will give him to us?" the youngest-looking vampire said. Older vampires always looked fragile, their skin brittle and cracked as old paper. The one who spoke looked fresh and the way she overused her voice belied her youth.

She handed Martoni something that Dani couldn't see.

"If this works, no problem. If it doesn't . . . " A tight smile quirked his lips.

The young vampire frowned. "Try it and see. We keep our word."

"But if there's nothing . . ."

One of the older vampires bent towards him. "Then your people are clean. Just try it," she hissed.

Dani backed towards the door. A flash from the thing in Martoni's hand and all her magic sloughed off like snakeskin.

Visible, clearly human, and standing in a room full of vampires, bodyguards and witch-haters, only one thing came out of Dani's mouth.

"Shit."

She ran.

Not for the elevator, but for the stairs. She hurtled down them with the bodyguards hot on her trail. They didn't stop to fire; they knew better than to waste precious time in a stairwell.

When she cleared the stairs, she headed for the boardwalk where she could mingle with the crowd. As she understood it, the nullifier Martoni had used would only work within a few feet of him so she slid into a glamour easily. Her mind worked at where the vampires could possibly have gotten such a thing. Only one had ever been known to exist, and the Syndicate claimed to have it deep in a vault. Unless someone had stolen it . . .

The guards hunted her everywhere, but realized soon enough they'd lost her in the crowd.

Her body shook. So much power fluctuation would make her ill.

She checked her wristwatch.

"Shit," she said again.

At the garage, Drake flipped through his usual supply chain websites, wondering where the new mechanic was. The Corvette's owner had evidently left a message with Warren asking about the car, saying that it "had better be ready in time for the show". And he wasn't the only one chomping at the bit. Ten classic cars and one truck were parked in the warehouse – all with issues to be solved by the beginning of next week. Drake didn't even have time to worry about Ferrell right now.

"Where is my damn grease monkey?" Drake growled. All he could find for the 'Vette was a Rochester fuel-injector, which was vintage '59. If the owner was a stickler, Drake doubted he'd go for it.

"Right here," a female voice said.

Though he heard no music, he swivelled with a tyre iron in his hand.

"Whoa." The girl held up her hands. "I come in peace."

Drake stared.

She was as gangly as a boy, and probably easily mistaken for one due to her rough hands and nearly non-existent breasts. But her dark eyes sparkled and her long, dark ponytail swung behind her baseball cap in a decidedly feminine way.

She came forwards, extending a hand. "I'm Dani," she said. Though she tried to smile, Drake saw that it was feigned. She was pale and tired.

Drake set down the tyre iron and shook her hand reluctantly. Her hand was pleasantly warm. "Drake," he said.

Her smile grew more genuine.

"What?"

"Not a name I would have picked for you," she said.

"Not the gender I would have picked for you," Drake said.

Dani's eyes narrowed. "A new place and already I get the usual treatment. You didn't get the memo I was a girl?"

"Warren didn't say anything about it," Drake said.

"I guess that could be good or bad, depending on how you look at it," Dani said.

"Guess so. Look, Miss Obvious, can you help me fix these cars or not? We've got a big show next week and I don't have time to chat up somebody who can't do her job."

She looked around and grinned. "Are you a betting man, Drake?"

"Why?"

"Because I bet you I can fix more cars than you can this week."

Drake laughed. "What's the prize?"

"If I win, I'll force you to eat your prissy little attitude by making you take me out to the Lone Cedar. If you win, I'll quit and you can hire someone who can do the job better."

"Deal," Drake said to Dani's retreating back. "You don't want to shake on it?" he asked.

She shook her head, looking back at him over her shoulder. "Nah. No time. Got to get to work if I'm gonna beat your ass."

Drake shrugged, suppressing a grin. Well then. He'd always liked a challenge.

*   *   *

Dani didn't recognize herself in the gilded mirror. Her hair curled in golden ringlets about her forehead and temples, and a tight chignon sat heavy on her nape. Her face was a different shape and porcelain pale, her eyes marble blue. Her corset was so tight every breath was a shallow hitch against the laces. Dark-grey watered silk embroidered with burgundy roses clung to her bodice and spread into glimmering skirts. Heavy steel hoops and layers of petticoats weighed down her narrow waist. She wore nothing underneath.

Her gloves rested on the foyer table beneath the mirror. She picked them up and slid them on without really knowing why she did so.

She barely heard the jingle of a sword before cold arms slipped around her and cold lips nuzzled her bare shoulder.

"Isobel, my darling," Drake murmured against her skin, "the carriage is waiting."

She turned. He was in spotless uniform – dress greys with yellow braid and the special red cord that denoted the vampire brigade. The CSA logo was emblazoned on the hat he carried under his arm. His dress sword curved at his side, the long tassels on the hilt trailing down. But he was still Drake – dark-eyed, broad-shouldered, exuding a lean sensuality that tightened her chest even more than the corset.

A mischievous smile curved her lips; her tongue clicked against pearly fangs. "Let it wait," she whispered. She ran a gloved hand over his coat, her fingers gliding over the braid and brass.

She saw her hunger answered in his eyes, but he took her hand, nearly crushing it in his own. "This is your cotillion, my dear. How would it be if your chaperone ruined your debut?"

She stepped closer to him, trapping his hand. She brought it to the curve of her silk-bound breast, where it rested like a longing bird. "Fine by me."

His mouth was on hers in an instant – hot, hungry, so shockingly mirroring her own need that she purred deep in her throat. He pushed her back until the table hit her steel hoops. He bit her tongue so hard he drew blood. Her music surrounded them like a symphony.

"Here?" he breathed in her ear.

"Here," she said. She didn't care if the servants or slaves saw. They'd seen stranger things in this household.

She worked at his trousers while he lifted her, skirts and all, onto the table. His eyes widened when he realized that nothing denied him access.

"Isobel," he breathed as he slid into her.

Dani sat straight up in bed. Everything in her body throbbed, down to her very toenails. She drew a shuddering breath.

"Jesus Christ," she exhaled. Though she'd given up smoking right around the time she'd sworn off men, she felt in dire need of a cigarette. Or a man. Or both.

She threw the covers off, realizing it was nearly twilight and she was already late for work.

"Damn." She fumbled for her cell phone as she crawled into her jeans and tank top.

"Hi, Drake," she said, hoping he didn't notice her breathlessness. "Listen, I'm running a little late . . . "

"It's your second day on the job and you're late already?" he said, his voice rising.

She grimaced and held the phone away from her ear. Better than a cold shower. "I'll be there as soon as I can. Guess you just might win that bet after all," she said.

"Sure looks like it," Drake snapped. He hung up.

She clicked her phone closed and grabbed her greasy coveralls off the chair. This was not going to be pretty.

The owner had agreed to the Rochester fuel-injection system with some grumbling. Drake had it express-shipped. "Two days," he muttered. He looked over the engine and sighed. Best thing would be to get to work on another car. All he could see of Dani was her denim-covered legs and work boots sticking out from under a black '70 Plymouth 'Cuda with a 426 Hemi. Its ghosted racing stripes glimmered in the shop lights.

She had pretty much avoided him since she came in – embarrassed, he guessed, at being so late the second day on the job. But he caught her once in a knowing look, as if she'd seen some intimate part of his past that she couldn't fathom. He'd scowled and she'd blushed. After that, she'd secluded herself under the 'Cuda.

He started in on a '72 Pierre Cardin-edition Javelin. He had been old when these cars came onto the showroom floor and he felt even older now as he remembered the original ads for these cars – a girl bounding up and down beside the Jav in a black and yellow leisure suit and matching scarf. He sighed, wiping grease off his fingers onto a rag. It looked like all this needed was a really good tune-up.

"That's boss," Dani said over his shoulder. She was as silent as a vampire.

Drake jumped. "How on earth do you do that?"

"Magic," Dani said, waggling her fingers at him. She grinned, but couldn't quite meet his eyes. Some sense memory lingered around her.

A name swam up out of her thoughts. *Isobel.*

He growled.

"Very nice Jav," Dani said, eyeing the Chinese red-, plum- and white-striped seats. Cardin had gone a little nuts with the interior design.

"I'm keener on her sort," Drake said, nodding towards the 'Vette.

"That girly old thing?" Dani said. She ran a hand over its curves. It was his turn to be embarrassed as he felt himself stiffen. Hers was a casual, almost condescending gesture, but something about the way her fingertips moved over the glossy, hard surface, the sense memory like a perfume lingering around her, stirred him.

He turned away to hide it.

"Nah," she continued, "I need more chunk to my ride." She returned to the 'Cuda. "Now this is an example of automotive perfection: 426 Hemi; Bassani X-pipes; Borla exhaust. That old girl couldn't hold a candle to it."

"Wanna bet?" Drake said. He bent back over the 'Vette. After Isobel, he'd sworn that nothing could make him feel again. And since 1867, when she'd finally discarded him, he'd managed that quite nicely. How had this slip of a girl gotten him so wound up?

He ground his fangs against his lower teeth when he felt her next to him, leaning to watch him tinkering uselessly with a hose.

"You are indeed a betting man," Dani said.

"When I get that Rochester in, we'll see what your 'Cuda can do," he said.

"And the stakes?" she asked.

He met her eyes. This close, he saw they weren't actually as dark as he'd thought. They were hazel, almost green now. Her lips were slightly parted, wet, a bit cracked. From the taut line of her neck, her stiff shoulders, the way her blood raced, he guessed that she'd not been this close to anyone in a very long time. He sensed that she was slightly embarrassed by her raw, gangly appearance, her tiny breasts, her thin legs. She had always been disappointed in her lovers; sex had been, for all its hype, ultimately less than what she'd hoped and yet such a basic need that she'd not fared well without it. And love? She didn't even want to go there.

All these things he caught like the soft, confessional notes of a viola played behind a closed door. And then an image. Of him in his officer's uniform, thrusting into Isobel, calling her name. The sound of the mirror shattering as Isobel's head smacked against it, the table rocking wildly beneath them.

His eyes widened.

Before he could speak, the garage door exploded.

Or, at least, that was how it sounded to Dani.

She ripped her gaze from Drake's. A piece of one of the garage doors had been torn apart and Martoni's bodyguards stepped through, followed by the vampire women.

Drake drew himself up beside Dani, his face as hard as iron.

A young vampire female sauntered up to him. She glanced aside at Dani and an amused half-smile played about her lips.

"You don't mean to tell me you'd rather consort with witches than your own kind, Drake? Were you not the only potential sire on the Eastern Seaboard, I might change my mind about this."

Drake didn't reply to Ferrell.

An image formed in Dani's mind. Sunset on a battlefield. Drake standing alone, looking out over the devastation, his uniform rusted with the blood of the fallen. Anger and resignation swept over his face. Just as they did now.

The bodyguards moved forwards to either side of Dani. She tensed. She saw the flash of the nullifier in the hand of the nearest one. She would have to do this the hard way.

"Wait." Ferrell held up her hand. "Let the witch stay."

"Mr Martoni—" one of the bodyguards began.

"—can wait for his prize while I enjoy mine," Ferrell said. "I want her to see what comes to those who think they can defy us. And," she said, walking up to Drake, "I shall enjoy your humiliation all the more."

Dani saw it before Ferrell did – the slight twist of the hip before Drake's palm came up and struck the vampire woman squarely in the breastbone. There was a crack as she fell backwards into the arms of the old vampire crones.

Dani dropped as one of the bodyguards reached for her. She swept her leg under the bodyguard as hard as she could, but it was like trying to sweep an iron telephone pole. The bodyguard wobbled a little and bent towards her. While she smacked away the hand that held the nullifier, she punched up at him from below.

The left lens of his sunglasses shattered. The nullifier slipped, sparkling, from his fingers and Dani dived for it.

Ice-white eyes ringed with blue stared at her as the bodyguard ripped off the mangled sunglasses and threw them to the floor, even as his human glamour faded.

Wendigo.

Now that she had the nullifier, she could smell him, too – the gut-wrenching odour of corruption, the desecration of flesh.

"We've got wendigo!" she shouted at Drake.

She tried to summon her power, but it was like trying to start a car with a dead alternator. The nullifier had drained her too much. She'd need some time to recharge. She had to get away from them to do anything worthwhile. They were much stronger than any creature she'd ever had to fight without magic.

The young vampire had recovered and advanced on Drake with a hard mouth.

"The Yenko," Drake shouted. He pitched the keys at her as the crones grabbed his wrists. Where they touched him, his skin turned white.

Dani caught the keys and dived just as one of the wendigo smacked her with unsheathed claws. Her face stung.

When she came up, she saw an ugly bruise blooming on Drake's mouth. With a flourish, the young vampire ripped his coveralls, T-shirt and jeans from him.

Naked and vulnerable, he knelt as the old vampires forced him down to the ground. Silver scars twined across his back, curling over his muscular thighs.

"Now, say my name," Ferrell said.

She didn't give him much time before she cuffed him on the side of the head again.

He spat.

She kicked him in the gut.

"Ferrell," he said.

Dani took a step towards him even as the wendigos closed in.

He half turned his head and saw her there. "Go, dammit!" he yelled at her.

Ferrell yanked his head back towards her.

Dani slid through the Camaro's open window and started it, slamming it into gear as the engine revved.

One of the wendigos tried to stop her, but she ran over him with a crunch and thud that made her want to vomit. His claws scraped down the hood, leaving thick furrows, and that made her want to vomit even more.

She hurtled through the gap in the garage door. The last image in her rear-view mirror was of Ferrell disrobing as the crones held Drake.

Tears sprang into her eyes, but she held them back as she roared down the highway. In her mind, she saw again the sweet, hot way he'd made love to Isobel. That hadn't been a dream. And now Ferrell was trying to force out of him what could never be forced. She was trying to take what could only be given. Just like Martoni – taking magic for himself when it should only ever come as a gift.

The hard edges of the nullifier cut into her palm. A slow smile burned away her tears. She knew what to do.

His head *hurt*. Cool hands cradled it. Cool lips slid on his. He'd been shot again, and Isobel . . . The last time it had been in the leg, and even though he'd been laid up, Isobel had come to him, giving him her blood to heal the wound. And then, well, they'd proved that even army cots could be put to good use.

He half smiled as her lips travelled down his neck, though the song, the music of Isobel, was all wrong.

"Have you had enough abuse then?" a voice said. "Are you ready to submit to me?"

Not Isobel. Ferrell.

It was dark but he could smell daylight. Late afternoon, approaching twilight. He couldn't sit up. She had him well chained to rock that dug into his bare back. A cave. Beneath the smell of light, the scent of decay – a mingling of pork and human flesh, the nest he'd smelled near the pig farm.

The crones sat silent nearby, but their cold music was all around him.

Ferrell moved down his body, her fingers like flies walking on his skin. He shivered in revulsion.

"End it," he said. "I won't give you what you want."

"Silly, stupid sire," she whispered. "I offer you such privilege! My mother is a Matriarch. Simply by doing your duty, you earn power and commendation beyond your wildest dreams."

"Which is why you are forcing me to impregnate you in a cave full of pig filth," Drake said.

Even though he expected the blow, it still hurt a great deal.

"This is your humiliation, not mine," Ferrell hissed. "It never had to be this way if you had properly served me from the beginning."

"Or if you'd left him alone in the first place," Dani said.

A flare of light and Drake could see her standing, her left hand wreathed in flame. Her tank top and jeans were filthy; her hair in dark disarray around her shoulders. Wendigo marks clawed shadows across her cheek.

She dragged someone behind her.

Martoni.

The crones hissed and shrank away from the hot fire growing in her palm.

"Let him go," Dani said.

Ferrell stood, her skin fish-belly pale, her eyes black with anger.

"He's mine, witch. Go steal someone else's stud."

The ball of fire grew, blazing white hot.

"You have two choices. I can lock you up tight with some man-food—" she shook the unconscious Martoni "—or I can fry you all to ash so that even your Matriarch won't be able to identify you."

"She escaped the wendigo. She does not boast," one of the crones said. "Ferrell . . ."

Ferrell unlocked his chains. Drake crawled past Dani and then stumbled to his feet. Before Ferrell or the crones could leap, Dani threw Martoni into them. Then she grabbed Drake and pulled him outside. She sent a hard blast of fire into the cave roof, melting and crumbling the rock into a hot tomb. Ferrell's music turned into a screeching cacophony before it disappeared completely from his head.

Dani helped him into the Yenko and he hissed as the leather caught at his bruised, naked skin. Dani hid her smile, tossed him some clothes and settled into the driver's seat.

"Hope I got the right size," she said.

He checked the tag blearily. He tried to nod but it hurt too much. "How'd you do that?" he asked.

"Magic," she said, looking over at him with a grin.

He winced when he tried to smile. The clothes rumpled across his lap.

"Do you need . . . ?" She leaned closer and exposed her throat. The freckles on her skin pulsed as her heart sped.

"I . . . " He sighed. He was tired and hungry and afraid that if he tasted her now, he would surely kill her.

"It's OK," she said in a small voice.

"There's a pig farm." He gestured.

She nodded, drove wordlessly down the road until he told her to stop. Out of the car, protesting against even putting on the clothes, he stumbled to one of the metal hog sheds.

When he came out later, she was leaning against the car, clutching his clothes to her chest. She looked a little green under the street lights.

He said nothing, but took the clothes from her, dressed, and returned to the car. She followed and gave him the keys.

"I'm going to Mexico," he said. "You should go somewhere, too. Wherever witches go that's safe."

Her hands fisted and he was certain she glared at him. "And that's your way of saying thank you?"

There's always another choice, he had told Ferrell. But he had never before realized how true that was.

He was silent for a long moment. Then he took her hand, banishing all sense memories, feeling only the magic-hardened angles of her palm. He drew her to him, putting his hands on either side of her face, trying to see her eyes.

"There are many other ways," he said. "I believe you may know some of them."

Her breath hitched as he bent close. He knew she was thinking of him again with Isobel, whether she willed it or not.

"I'll show you the others on the way down to Mexico," he whispered.

She shivered as their lips touched. A spark flickered between them and he drew back a little.

"Don't tell me," he said when she would have spoken. "Magic, right?"

She smiled and silenced him with her lips.

Circle Unbroken

Ann Aguirre

One

Red bled from the guttering neon sign, greasing dark puddles with an oily shine. Zane stepped over, his boots near silent on the wet pavement. All around him, dark, broken windows in tenement buildings hung like the razor-sharp teeth of some patient, predatory beast. The rain had stopped an hour ago, but everything was still glazed with a fine mist, as if the world sweated in anticipation of what was to come.

Or maybe that was just his mood.

One solitary window broke the surface of the wall beside that sign, and it bore black wrought-iron bars. Crumbling stairs took him right up to a solid metal door. From within, he could hear the soft strains of piano music. The player was a dilettante, pausing every now and then to add some unnecessary flourish. Oddly, the human vanity of the performance made him feel a little better.

He had nothing to worry about, he told himself. Nothing on his person would give away his intentions. It wasn't like he'd come bearing tricks of his trade. Even his cell phone was standard gear. This was strictly a recon mission, fact finding only.

Zane raised his hand and rapped in sequence with scheduled pauses and repetition. He'd gotten that much from one of the regulars before the man wound up in McLean, where they were studying his acutely paranoid behaviour. The skullduggery of it made him feel ridiculous, but it bore fruit when a metal plate slid back and a pair of dark eyes scrutinized him from head to toe.

"I'm here for a drink," he said.

No response. The peep slot closed and someone opened the door from the inside. His source claimed that was the pass phrase and, if given in conjunction with the knock, would get him inside. Unfortunately, he had no way of verifying whether the information was still good.

"Come in. Enjoy." From behind the heavy door, the voice sounded disembodied.

Zane shook off the chill and stepped through into the glowing warmth of the bar. He'd been investigating the place for months, but this was the first time he'd been able to get in the door. He took stock of his surroundings, and was oddly disappointed to find everything old-fashioned but tasteful. Mahogany panels lined the walls, softened with red embroidered tapestries. From the heavy, ornate bar to the chunky tables, there was something faintly Elizabethan about the place. In fact, he clashed with the décor in his worn army jacket and faded grey T-shirt.

He ran a hand through his hair, conscious of its uneven spikes in contrast with the suavity of the man closing the door behind him. The bouncer was enormous, biceps the size of someone's head, but his hair was meticulously styled, and he wore a superbly tailored suit. Even the piano player dressed better than Zane.

His source hadn't said anything about a dress code. But as he glanced around, he saw the other patrons didn't fit their surroundings either. A man sat at the bar in a badly rumpled dress shirt, sleeves rolled up and tie tugged sideways. He nursed something amber in a glass, staring at his own sullen reflection. By the scruff on his jaw, he might've been there for days.

Zane nodded to the bouncer and made for the bar, where the 'tender came over straightaway. "What can I get you?"

"Kamikaze," he said, pulling himself onto a stool.

When she began mixing his drink, he suffered a frisson of disappointment. He didn't know exactly what he'd anticipated, but this was sedate in comparison with his inchoate expectations. Maybe he'd expected a scene out of Anne Rice with human slaves twined around their vampiric masters, while they fed in veiled alcoves. This just looked like a private club, but it was stupid to imagine they'd work in the open. Before he got to see anything newsworthy, he'd need to earn their trust.

Such things took time.

Two

"Who is he?" Ysabel asked.

She never entered the public area without speaking to Marceau first. His family had been loyal for hundreds of years, and she could count on his candour as well as his keen judgment. The man beside her appeared older than she by more than twenty years, a father figure some might say. Her mouth curved into a wry smile at the idea.

Marceau folded well-manicured hands before him. He was a slim, dapper man in his mid-forties. His hair had gone silver prematurely, making an attractive foil for his dark almond eyes. As always, he was impeccably turned out in a Boss suit, his shoes polished until one presumed he could see his own reflection. Beside her, he stared out at the room, where the herd congregated.

To her surprise, Marceau shrugged. "I am not sure."

Ysabel's brows lifted. "You surprise me. No dossier to hand? Generally, you have them blood-typed before they enter our domain."

"He is nobody we've cultivated," he said repressively. "But he knew the knock and the pass phrase. Perhaps it is time we changed them both."

"To keep out the undesirables?" She mocked her retainer gently. "It would not do for our place of business to become sullied with those who wish to drink in anonymity."

"What of our anonymity?" he asked. "Purges have started with less moment."

Purges, crusades, hunters. Yes, she understood his caution.

Ysabel gave a short nod. "Make the change and inform Carvalo at the door."

She noted a number of regulars in her visual sweep, but the young man at the bar drew her gaze back. There was a fierce, savage quality about him from his shock of black, spiky hair to his lean, angular face. This wasn't a man who would bow to rules or regulations; she could tell that much from a single glance.

He shifted then, turning his face towards the wall through which she studied him. The man wore a diamond in his nose like a Barbary pirate. Ysabel had spent some time with a particularly roguish one in the islands; she recognized the type on sight. But where Jean Pierre had beaded trinkets into his hair, this one wore warpaint. Streaks of carmine and azure tipped the spiky points of his hair, like a peacock displaying plumage.

"It will be done." In another age, his ancestor would have swept a deep obeisance in speaking those words. Ysabel remembered another Marceau doing so. They never used their first names with her. In every generation, they sent the youngest son to replace the elder. One had stood at her side since before the French Revolution.

His demeanour said he would prefer to adhere to the old ways, but she had learned to her cost that clinging to the past could be fatal. The only solace came from living in the present, not reflecting on all that had been lost. That way lay madness and death, a ceaseless fall into melancholy.

"Thank you," she said, schooling her features.

She could not show weakness. Like a goddess carved from ivory and marble, nothing could touch her. Ysabel lifted her chin, watching the dishevelled man at the bar now. She could not feed from him again, no matter how he craved it. If she had any mercy, she would have barred him from the place, saving him from this desperate half-life, hoping against hope that she would call him to her private chambers again.

"Shall I have him escorted out?" Marceau asked.

At first she thought he was talking about the broken wreck of a man in the dingy white shirt. Then she realized he was looking at the fierce young pirate who had wandered into her lair. Ysabel smiled.

"Let him stay. I will speak with him myself."

"Is that wise, *m'selle*?"

"No." She laughed softly. "And that is precisely why I shall do it."

Marceau favoured her with a grave, measured look, as if to say he did not find her reckless manner amusing. But he said nothing; it was not his place to counsel her. In her way, she was akin to royalty, and there was no one who dared rebuke her.

She had outlived them all.

Three

She had hair like moonlight.

The woman wore a red dress that clung to her like a second skin, and Zane's next thought surprised him: blood and ice. Her smooth skin suggested that she was in her mid-twenties, around his age, but her eyes belied that initial impression. Those eyes were ageless, the deep grey of the sky just before a storm, and just as clouded with secrets.

Nothing in her demeanour hinted at violence, but he'd always possessed a strong sense of intuition. Though he had no proof, she was one of them. He'd stake his life on it.

To his surprise, she came straight towards him. She seated herself with liquid grace, putting an empty stool between them. Without taking her drink order, the bartender produced a glass of white wine. Zane watched her slim fingers curl around the glass, nails polished to match her dress. The crimson tips should have made her look hard and mercenary, but instead – well, he found himself unable to reconcile the conflicting signals.

"You're new here," she said without looking at him. Her voice carried the faintest lilt, not Irish, not Welsh, but as if ancient melodies danced on the tip of her tongue.

Something told him to be on his guard. "Yeah." The only line that sprang to mind was, *You come here often?* So he swallowed it along with a third of his now watery drink.

"Ysabel." The dishevelled man on the other side of Zane spoke for the first time.

So that's her name. Inexplicably, Zane thought of nightingales.

Despair in his face, the other man reached towards her like a supplicant. "Do you—"

"No." Though her tone was neither sharp, nor hard, it carried unmistakable finality. "You should go home, Steven. There is nothing for you here."

"It is to be exile for me then?" Though he didn't look poetic, Steven quoted verse nonetheless. "'And this is why I sojourn here, Alone and palely loitering . . .'" He shook his head bitterly. "It was you, wasn't it? 'La Belle Dame Sans Merci'. Keats wrote about you."

Zane didn't see her gesture in any fashion, but the bouncer from the door stood beside them, levering Steven to his feet. "I'll see that he gets home."

The woman inclined her head. Once the other two had gone, she said, "I am sorry you had to see that."

"Are you? Why?" His nerves tingled.

"I would not like to see you deterred from our company before you find what you're seeking."

He froze. "What makes you think I'm looking for anything?"

She faced him then, offering the full weight of her eyes, and he swore he felt the warmth of her touch. "We are *all* searching for something, are we not? Some gather wealth to stave off the long winter. Others yearn for power to leave their mark on the world. Yet others crave wisdom and knowledge. They are, perhaps, the most dangerous seekers of all."

"You think so?" He felt as if she employed an archaic form of mesmerism to slow his thoughts and leave him unable to focus on anything but her mouth.

Ysabel smiled. Her canines were delicately pointed. So subtle that if he hadn't known what he was looking for, he would've missed the slight variance.

"Who is more dangerous, the man who owns a bomb or the man who knows how to build one?"

He conceded the point with a nod. "One's capacity for harm is finite. The other—"

"Could destroy the world," she supplied quietly.

"I take your point." Belatedly, he offered his hand. "I'm Zane. I already know you're Ysabel, so it's only fair to offer a name for a name."

"Is it?" she asked, studying his palm like a fortune-teller. "How odd. I have seldom consorted with those who concern themselves with what is fair."

"Then you must've had a rough life, lady."

At length she took his hand and a sweet shock went all the way to his shoulder. It made him want to wrap his fingers around hers and draw her against him to see if the sensation would flood him from chest to knees. He restrained himself only through sheer will, pulling his flesh from hers quicker than was courteous.

She mused on that a moment, running her fingertips around the mouth of her glass, and a shudder went through him. He could feel her tracing circles on his skin. Desire rose, wholly unbidden, and he didn't like the loss of volition.

"I rather think that you are right." Sorrow wove through her storm-grey gaze like a colour. Cobalt, he thought, though equating emotions to the hues of her eyes shook him to the core. "They've changed the knock. And the password." When she demonstrated softly on the bar, he found himself memorizing the cadence. Then she leaned in to whisper the word in his ear, and pleasure spilled through him, so fierce it felt like fear.

He had to get out of there.

Zane stood and knocked back the last of his drink. "I'll see you around."

"Yes," she said. "You will."

Four

He stayed away almost five days. Ysabel knew he would return, but the time between visits told her something about the strength of his will. That made a pleasant change in an age where people made a life of self-indulgence.

In the end, though, Zane had no choice, for she'd laid her scent upon him, and it drove him back towards her with a quiet compulsion. But he'd struggled against the inevitability. She imagined him denying the pull, finding other things to do to prevent his feet from retracing the steps back to her. For the first time in a long while, the game promised more than basic satiation. Anticipation coiled through her.

This time, she kept him waiting a full hour before she came down to the public rooms. Her kinsmen – Galen and Cyrus – lounged in a corner booth, cultivating the acquaintance of two bar hags who would feed them before the moon waned in the sky. Ysabel shook her head when they started to slip away, indicating she did not require their attention.

The place was nearly full this evening. Their regulars liked the cachet of belonging to a private club, one that didn't choose its membership based on pedigree, lineage or bank accounts. No, Ysabel prided herself on operating the most eclectic – and the most deliciously varied – members-only club in the city. Whatever the pleasure, whatever the vice, one could find it here.

She was careful not to seek him out immediately, though she was aware of his every movement. Instead she flitted from group to group, making small talk with each party. It was her responsibility to make everyone feel welcome in her establishment. In some regards, things had not changed so much since she held intimate salons for the intellectual aristocracy several hundred years before.

By the time she made her way to the bar, he looked more than a little impatient. It was almost charming, the way he wore his emotions transparently. He'd never learned to school his face, and his gaze tracked her movements, as if he were a wolf with a rabbit in his sights.

The analogy amused her, when so clearly the opposite was true. Once more, he wore faded denims and the ancient army jacket. Beneath it, a black T-shirt clung to the lean muscles of his chest. Ysabel sat down beside him, and the bartender poured her usual, a glass of white wine. Red would make a stronger statement, but she didn't favour the taste.

"Thank you," she murmured to the server, then she shifted on her stool to face Zane. "I see you could not resist our charms."

"Apparently not." But he wasn't happy about it.

This time, instead of the diamond in his nose, she noticed the fierce, electric blue of his eyes. He looked angry and dangerous, not someone who would turn into a docile pet. But instead of deterring her, it only intrigued her further. To captivate someone like him would require a great deal of guile and effort. Her breath came a little faster, and she tasted his essence through parted lips: fierce, questing, savage. The modern age very seldom offered specimens like him.

"Are you ready to tell me what you want, Zane?" It was a direct challenge, and she would not have employed the tactic with anyone else.

By the way his head came up, he was torn on how best to answer. "I'm just hanging out," he finally muttered.

She was disappointed. Of all things, she would not have reckoned him a coward. Ysabel slid off her stool. "Then I shall leave you to it."

"Wait." The word sounded as if it came against his will.

She turned, one brow lofted in query. "Yes?"

Zane wore a hungry, frustrated look, as if he no longer understood what he wanted. "Can I talk to you? In private?"

Ysabel smiled. In answer, she curled her fingers around his wrist. The others knew what that meant: *This one is mine. Touch him at your peril.*

A little ripple went through the room as they speculated. What did she see in this one? How long would she keep him? Ysabel ignored the whispers.

She led him to her lair.

Five

Her touch felt unbelievably good.

Though she'd let go of him once they reached her room, the skin of his wrist still tingled. The heat seemed to be rising as well, spiralling out through his nerve endings to fire his entire body to a state of aching readiness. Zane wanted to strip naked, lie down on her luxurious white rug, and beg for her hands on him.

The strength of the desire left him suspicious. It couldn't be natural or right. He had to fight it. He had to remember what he wanted of her – a story, not sex. That was getting harder to recall since he'd spent the last four nights dreaming about her.

She was every bit as delicious as he thought, that first night. Tonight she wore black, a striking contrast to her pearly skin and the moonbeam glimmer of her hair. He'd never encountered anyone more sensual, more able to set him aflame with a simple touch.

Zane tried to make good mental notes. If she turned her back for a minute, he'd snap a few quick pictures with his phone, but she didn't seem inclined to wander away. Quite the opposite. She seemed downright intrigued by him, though he had no idea why.

They stood in an old-fashioned sitting room, decorated with gold and white striped damask chairs. There had to be several hundred books on the golden oak shelves that lined the walls. No mirrors, though. Was that more than an old wives' tale? How could she possibly look so gorgeous if she couldn't see her own reflection? A matching hutch offered basic wine and spirits. He'd give a lot to rummage around her room and learn her secrets.

This room had two doors, the one they'd entered through, and another on the opposite wall. He didn't know where that led, but he could guess.

"My bedroom," she said, smiling, as if she could read his mind. "Did you want to see it? I thought you wanted a *word* in private."

Zane felt his cheeks heat. What was it about her that made him feel fourteen and tongue-tied in the presence of the head cheerleader? God help him, he *did* want to see her bedroom – and not for the story. He reined himself in.

"I do," he muttered.

"Then why don't you have a seat?"

Heartbreakingly graceful, she eased into the chair opposite him and sat waiting. Zane had no idea what he was going to say. He couldn't start with, *Are you a dangerous, immortal bloodsucker?* Plus, even writing for *Weird Weekly News*, he still carried a certain burden of proof: blurry photos, bite marks, something.

Maybe that was how he could trap her. If he pretended to be into blood play, she might buy it. There were enough vamp fetishists who chased the lifestyle to make it plausible anyway. The only question was whether he could sell it.

He sat down, feeling more confident. At least he had an angle now. "Downstairs I couldn't help but notice your teeth."

Both her brows lofted. "And you want the name of my dentist?"

"I – no. I was just wondering what it meant."

"It's a cosmetic vanity," she said, smiling. "It lends the place a certain mystique, don't you agree? People like to feel they're in the presence of something miraculous."

"So they're caps?" Of course she wasn't going to admit she was the real deal, not until they'd built up some rapport – or maybe after she had him so enthralled he couldn't conceive of outing her. Zane thought about the man's face, Steven he thought his name had been. His eyes spoke of terrible addiction.

She gave a little nod. "I'm sorry to disappoint you."

"It's OK," he said. "I should've known it was nothing."

"So that's what you're seeking? Someone to bite you?"

Zane kept his face impassive. "Is that so surprising?"

"A little," she said. "I wouldn't have guessed that you want someone to command your will."

He didn't, of course. The very idea sent a thrill of horror through him. As a kid, he'd been subject to other people's whims, a victim of capricious fate, and he never intended to let it happen again.

"Maybe I just want to see what all the fuss is about."

"Do you truly think you can lie to me?" Her voice carried a queenly resonance, and he wanted to fall at her feet.

He didn't.

"Why not?" he asked. "You seem to think you can lie to *me*."

That surprised her. He saw it in the faint widening of her storm-cloud eyes. "You are a strange creature."

"Lady, you don't know the half of it."

"I know this – you pose a danger to me and mine. If I owned equal measures of caution and prudence, I would bar you from this establishment."

"But you won't," he said, smiling.

He saw her gaze linger on his mouth and he realized he was not without resources in this battle.

"I will not," she agreed. "The game is met, and I stand eager to learn who rises as the conqueror."

Zane touched her hand, his fingers light as the first snow in winter. "I am your undiscovered country, Ysabel. You have never met anyone like me."

Six

Within a week, Ysabel knew everything about Zane Monteith. He had lost his mother young, and his father drank. At fourteen, his father perished in a car accident, and his relatives passed him around – aunts, uncles and distant cousins – until he turned eighteen. Despite the odds, he landed an academic scholarship and went to Salem State College, where he majored in journalism. He'd found it challenging to get a job as a real journalist with no experience, so he wound up working for *Weird Weekly News*.

Now he wanted a scoop on vampires.

She smiled over that. Writing for such a rag, it was a little surprising he'd had the investigative skills to track them down. If he worked for a more reputable periodical, she might have needed to do something distasteful. But this . . . this could function in her favour.

Ysabel did not wait for him this week. One of the advantages of the modern age was that she didn't need to sit demurely in a tower, so she went to Marceau just before the club opened. By his tight expression, he didn't anticipate liking her plans.

"I won't be in tonight, Marceau. Leave Galen in charge. If he has any trouble, dispatch Carvalo to assist him."

"Noted, *m'selle*." Marceau hesitated, and she wagered with herself how long he'd take to voice his disapproval. No more than fifteen seconds; she counted. "Perhaps you should reconsider going out alone. Cyrus would be delighted to escort you."

Cyrus raised his ash-blond head, fixing jade eyes on the two of them. Once she'd thought him beautiful beyond belief, like an angel from a Renaissance painting.

"I would?" he asked, raising a brow at Marceau. "Pity. I had intended to cultivate the lovely Lily this evening."

"I do not think her garden requires any attention," she said dryly.

His green eyes sparkled. "You only say that because you know me."

Ysabel smiled despite herself. "True. But I will not interfere with your plans." She turned to Marceau. "I'm afraid Cyrus will not prove of any use to me in this endeavour."

"When have I ever proved of any use?"

"Fourth of January, 1857."

He thought for a moment, and then his smile slipped. "Yes. I suppose you're right. Be careful, Ysabel. It's been a long time since you went out alone."

She lifted her shoulders. "Things are different. The world has changed."

"But no less dangerous for a woman alone," Cyrus pointed out.

Her look chilled. "Then I misspoke. What I meant is that *I* have changed."

"True enough." Cyrus returned to his drink.

She left Marceau gazing after her, his brow furrowed in concern. If it were up to him, she would never leave the club without a full complement of bodyguards. But over the years, she had learned that sometimes all that did was give ruffians the notion that she possessed something worth guarding.

Ysabel did not go out the public entrance. Instead she passed through an inner door and stepped onto the street, rather than emerge in the alley. She had found that people enjoyed the hint of subterfuge as much as the exclusive feeling of the club.

Anticipation sizzled through her as she measured her steps along the damp pavement. If Zane had lived more than eight blocks away, she would've called for her driver, but he had a flat within walking distance, even on a night like tonight – perhaps *especially* on a night like tonight.

Rain drizzled on her lightly, leaving no marks on the white coat. She had bought it many years ago, after seeing Grace Kelly wear something similar in a film. She wore a pair of dark glasses to protect her eyes from the city lights. The world had become a place of neon and garish fluorescent beams when she could best tolerate candlelight or softly diffused bulbs specially purchased for their low wattage.

No one who passed her on the street would remember her tomorrow, though several men took a second look. She smiled as she paused at the crumbling brownstone. There was no security to speak of, not even an intercom system. Marceau would have a fit if he saw her entering such a place.

Smiling over that, she tugged the front door open. Inside, the air reeked of onions and peppers, underscored by a faint hint of mildew. The building reminded her a little of the tenements in New York at the turn of the century. They had left that city just after the last Great War. As she sought the stairs, she calculated. They had been in Boston for over six decades then, and she had not anticipated a diversion so soon in twice as many years.

Ysabel found the stairwell without mishap; Zane lived on the second floor. The second storey was divided in half. He had the flat at the end of the hall, 2A. She stepped lightly to the door and knocked.

When he answered, he wore nothing but a pair of old denims. They hung loose on his hip bones, showing the gently concave curve of his abdomen. His chest was lean and well muscled, fading bronze as if he had worked outdoors during the summer. Night-dark hair tipped in plumage stood in messy spikes; she could envision his restless hands working through it. He hadn't shaved in several days, so his jaw bristled. She should've been repulsed by the pure animal dishevelment of him.

She wasn't.

Seven

"You," he said stupidly.

Surprise didn't even come close. He felt like he'd been hit with a ball-peen hammer. Zane had thought Jablonski had come to ask him to fix something in her apartment again. Instead, he found an angel. It was madness that she would seek him out.

She looked like something out of an old movie: the debutante slumming with the gardener's son. Zane had never seen anyone so lovely. He'd wanted to believe it was the romance of the club that made him feel so helplessly captivated. But no, seeing her on the worn carpet in his own building left him reeling the same way. Raindrops lay on her moon-kissed hair like a fine web of diamonds.

It hurt him to breathe, his chest oddly tight. This reaction had kept him away from her out of a desperate sense of self-preservation. He'd feared the challenge she'd thrown down and, instead of pursuing the better story, he wrote a throwaway piece about how a butter stain on a pancake looked like the Virgin Mary. But even as he avoided her, he'd thought about her, about the way her skin felt beneath his fingertips. Such a trivial touch – he didn't trust wanting *anything* this much.

"Me. You've been thinking about me, have you not?"

Arrogant, he thought. But true. He nodded.

"I thought it time to give you what you want."

Did that mean she was going to bite him? A shudder of reaction racked him, horror commingled with desire. That was the last thing he wanted. He could not imagine anything so wrong as living off other people like a ghoul, a parasite.

At length Zane recovered his composure. "Then I suppose you'd better come in."

She brushed by him, smelling sweet and clean. He wondered what perfume she was wearing, for surely nobody smelled naturally of peaches, citrus, honeydew and water lily. He drew in a deep breath and fought the urge to touch her.

By the time Zane closed the door, he had himself more or less under control. He stood with his back to it while she strolled through his apartment, touching odds and ends as if she could know him through her fingertips. God knew, he wanted her to try, but not this way. Not through his things. His skin.

Distantly he knew she must be using vamp mojo on him. He'd never reacted to a woman like this in his life. Maybe he could use that in the story, make it a personal piece: I WAS A VAMPIRE'S LOVE SLAVE. His editor would love the confessional slant.

"Still working the angles?" she asked quietly.

"Always." He managed a grin. "Now then, what really brings you to my humble abode? I kind of doubt you're going to hand me a story on a silver platter." It was a calculated gamble. If she knew where he lived, she likely knew other things as well.

Maybe things he'd rather she didn't.

"I am, actually." She shrugged out of her white coat, revealing a sapphire dress that clung to her lithe body.

His apartment looked dingy and cluttered in comparison with her gentle elegance. She drew off the glasses last, her eyes full of storm clouds. Ysabel gave off an air of fragility, but some women made an art of concealing their strength.

"What do you want?" Cynicism spiked his tone. He couldn't help it. Nobody offered something for nothing.

Her gaze skimmed his bare chest. "You," she said softly.

Every instinct leaped at the word. She could take her sharp little teeth to his throat as she rode him. It took all his self-possession not to say yes and reach for her. To take her to his bed with its sagging mattress and rumpled sheets. But caution came hard won, and trust, for him, not at all.

"What you want . . . would it do me lasting harm?" No story was worth that.

"No," she said. "Not if we put a finite measure on our affair. You will recover your energies when I stop feeding from you."

There, she admitted it. A thrill surged through him. Zane wished he'd had a digital recorder handy.

"How long?"

"Sixty days," she answered. "I cannot take from you on a regular basis any longer than that without imperilling both your physical and mental health."

"So I'd end up like that guy at your club," he noted. "Steven."

Ysabel shook her head. "He has an addictive personality. If I'd known—"

"You wouldn't have used him."

"Chosen," she corrected.

Zane curled his lip. "So you're doing me great honour right now?"

Though he wasn't aware of her moving, she was suddenly much closer, close enough to touch. Her eyes caught his, and her scent swelled, going straight to his groin. "Does not it *feel* like one?"

God, yes. It did. He shook his head to clear it of sexual urges.

"The story. If I agree to this, you'll answer all my questions fully?"

"I will," she promised. "Thus, the bargain is struck. Shall we seal it with a kiss?"

Ysabel came up on her toes, and the taste of her went through him like white lightning. His head clouded. When he reached for her, he could no more have stopped that response than his own heartbeat. She felt unnaturally warm, as though she held fire enough to sear him to cinder and ash.

What was worse – he didn't care.

She became manna from heaven, the elixir of life itself, and he needed more. With a low growl, he swung her into his arms, dimly surprised at some level that she permitted it. But there was no mistaking the hunger in her hands.

His bedroom was dark, the sheets as rumpled as he'd recalled. Books and magazines lay scattered everywhere, a messy paper rug on the wood floor. For a moment, he felt ashamed to have her here, but she shook her head. "I will brook none of that between us, my chosen. There is no other I would have in your place this night, nor any palace that could offer more delight."

Chosen. The power of it rocked him. He'd never been chosen in his life. Everything he had, he'd earned or taken. Everything except Ysabel.

He set her lightly on her feet and she pulled her dress over her head. She wore nothing beneath it. The moon gilded her in argent and ivory, caresses that flickered over her skin in hypnotic patterns. In response, fire licked through him, tinged with a madness born of aching desire. If she was a dream, he did not want to wake. His hands trembled as he stripped out of his jeans, and then he came down to her.

Arms and legs tangled. They rolled, skin sweet and slick with yearning. Trembling, helpless, he thrust and found her hot, the loveliest thing he'd ever felt. He wanted her so that he couldn't hear for his own heartbeat in his ears. Her mouth seemed to be everywhere, her hair spilling over his skin like silver flax, and yet he could not hold her. Infinite, racking waves tore through him, boundless, unbearable. He felt her teeth on his throat, or thought he did, but he was beyond caring. She took him.

Eight

Ysabel lay beside him, glowing with his essence. He was frighteningly still, but she hadn't harmed him. It was rare for any chosen to surrender so completely the first time. Generally, such sharing only came after she laid the groundwork. She could not decide why he was so susceptible, though his claim she had never met anyone like him was valid.

She did not want to leave him, but she must return to the club before dawn, if not for the reasons he believed. His chest rose and fell in seductive rhythm, making her want to hold her cheek against his bare skin and bask in simple human warmth. As if in response to her thought, his arms came around her, drawing her against him. At first she thought it was no more than sleepy reflex, and then she saw his fierce blue eyes.

"Did you?" he whispered, fingers skimming his own throat. He winced when he found the sore spot.

"Yes."

"And that's it?"

She arched a brow, quietly amused. "Did you want there to be more?"

"I don't know." He shook his head. "I guess I just expected there would be."

"You thought it would be worse."

"Yeah. I've seen the movies," he added, defensive.

Then she did laugh. He took no offence from it. Instead he nuzzled her throat. To her surprise, he still had the energy to pull her on top of him. She didn't take from him again; instead it was pure pleasure that he gave. His slim, dexterous hands cradled her hips as she rode him. He lay beneath her, masterful in his submission, and she began to wonder in truth who would conquer whom.

The days and nights passed in a sort of divine madness, but Ysabel retained enough presence of mind to blur his perceptions when they tarried together. Despite what she'd said about answering his questions, she didn't intend to allow him any truth save that which she supplied. It amused her to see him struggle against her influence. No matter how many times they came together, he remained fuzzy on the details – and it must be that way.

If the others knew the truth about her latest plaything, it would not end well for him. Of them all, Galen retained an awkward amount of noblesse oblige, and he would see it as his duty to rescue her from her own folly. Marceau would simply shake his head with weary resignation if he realized what she'd done. Sadly, it was not the first time, just her first lapse in a long while.

But then, she'd always enjoyed playing with fire, and Zane burned with such a fierce light, she couldn't help but want a little warmth to kindle the endless ages after he fell to dust. She could see the fragile flicker of him, here now, and as quickly gone, no more than a shimmer in comparison to her kind.

Twenty-two of her self-allotted days with Zane had passed when Cyrus came knocking at her door. He'd fed recently, and that stolen energy sat on him like a nimbus, crowning his beauty with an incandescent glow. It was unusual for him to seek her out, but Ysabel made time for all the members of her camarilla, few that they were. Boston had not been kind to them, nor had the modern age. Without the glamour borrowed from writers of romantic fiction, they would have been hunted to extinction long since.

"You look well." She stepped back to let him enter her sitting room. "What brings you to me this night?"

In answer, he prowled the room, seeming unable to settle. Such distress was unlike him. She watched him for a moment, and then caught his arm as he paced by.

"Enough," she said gently. "Speak. There are no secrets between us."

His jade gaze fastened on her face. "Is that still true? It once was."

Cyrus alone knew how close they'd come to destruction, some 200 years ago. He alone had extricated her from the fearful truth. She'd thought the memory might have faded, blurred by years of pleasure, but she could see the spectre riding him tonight.

"It is still true," she told him with grave dignity.

"Then I must tell you – people whisper of your favour to this nobody, Ysabel. You seem besotted, as if *he* is the one who feeds from you. You shine when he comes to you. And I remember all too well the last time you displayed such marked affection."

Of course he would. The man had been his brother. Cyrus had killed him for her on 4 January, 1857. In return, she gave him what he craved most: immortality, a guarantee that his youth and beauty would never fade.

"And you think Zane is another Pierce, one who will gain my trust and betray me."

"I fear that," Cyrus admitted.

"Fret yourself not. Only forty-eight days remain in our agreement, and I shall not grant him anything that could harm us during that time."

"Do you swear it?"

Ysabel nodded and lifted her face. "Taste the truth of it for yourself."

Her kinsman took her lips in a sweet, lingering kiss. Though his mouth was lovely and warm, it left her quiet and still inside. Not even an ember stirred within her in response to his beauty, and that left her shaken, for it was wholly wrong.

"Dear God," Cyrus breathed. "You've mated to him."

Nine

Zane had no words to explain what was happening to him.

Over the past two months, he only lived when he was with her. Sure, he put in his time at *Weird Weekly News*, shopped for basic groceries and paid his bills, but it was work, all of it. Much as he didn't trust the sensation, he only felt alive with Ysabel.

That meant their affair couldn't be over too soon. He didn't know if he could hold out any longer than that against her allure, and he didn't want to end up like that guy, Steven. He didn't want to spend his remaining days pining for the sight of her, begging for scraps of her time. Zane couldn't imagine anything more pathetic.

No, when the agreed time period ended, they were done, and he was going to write a story that would make him famous. Probably not in any reputable way, but he'd long since given up on the dim dream of being the next Woodward. He'd settle for being the next Whitley Strieber.

Oddly, certain things didn't add up. Apart from the puncture wounds on his neck, there was never any blood on the sheets. Either she was the neatest neck nibbler ever born, or he didn't have the big picture yet. Still, maybe he was a victim of cinematic hyperbole. He'd give a lot to examine her teeth and see if they were hollow. Maybe she sunk them into his neck and took the blood straight through her fangs.

But she slept too lightly for him to check her dental work. The minute he stirred beside her, she opened her eyes. And once her gaze met his, he forgot all about his personal agenda. Cliché as it might be, the sex was earth-shattering.

Zane couldn't doubt she was drawing his strength away. He'd lost ten pounds, weight he couldn't afford to lose. In seven weeks with her, he'd gone from lean to thin. By the end, he would be gaunt and pale, visibly weakened.

The prize would be worth it.

He no longer needed a special knock or a pass code. Tonight he came via her private entrance. Night after night, he found her waiting when he finished his shift at the paper. It didn't seem to matter what time; she was content to take what he offered, and that seemed wrong. After all, Ysabel could rule the world with her smile.

Oh God, he had it bad.

A thrill tightened his belly when he came up the stairs and she opened her arms. Though he'd wanted to ask some questions tonight, he couldn't keep himself from her. He hardened as if in response to a silent command. For the first time, he could not wait for niceties; he could not wait for her to remove her clothes in languorous seduction. Zane had to have her or die.

He took her hard and fast against the sitting room wall. If she fed from him, he missed it in the blaze of wild rapture. Afterwards, he gasped into the curve of her throat, rubbing his mouth against her tender skin. "What's happening to me?" he breathed. "You *promised* me no harm, Ysabel. You swore it."

"You will take no lasting damage." But she sounded shaken. "Rarely such a bond forms, but time will wear it thin. In a year and a day, you will no longer recall my face."

Right now, Zane couldn't imagine anything closer to pure torment. "I don't want that," he protested, before he could recall the words that gave too much. "But . . . I don't want this, either." This helpless compulsion, falling upon her like an animal bereft of higher thought, terrified him. He didn't want to lose himself in her.

With some effort he straightened his clothing, but he couldn't make himself let go. All too easily, he could understand how Steven had turned into a pitiful shell of a man. Though he suspected he might be following in the other's footsteps, he couldn't open his arms and go. Instead he carried her to a chair, where she curled into him like a flower seeking the sun.

"Your thoughts are well-ordered tonight," she said, a note of surprise accenting the mysterious lilt of her voice.

She was right. There was no fuzzy euphoria clouding his mind, nothing to keep him from asking her anything he might wish. "Good thing," he muttered. "I was starting to think you weren't going to leave me a brain to interview you with."

Ysabel tucked her head against his shoulder. "Ask. I will answer."

"Do you mind if I record?" Taking her silence for acquiescence, he stifled his excitement at moving forwards. "I guess we should start with the basics. How old are you?"

"I have lived some five centuries."

That gave him pause. He was holding a woman who had been alive when Queen Elizabeth I was born, a woman who pre-dated Shakespeare. He'd touched her, kissed her. There was something awful – unnatural – about that.

Steeling himself, Zane went on. "Where were you born?"

"Looe." He didn't recognize the name, so he regarded her blankly until she added softly, "Cornwall. The world was different, then."

"How did you . . . " He hesitated, unsure how to ask.

"You wish to hear the story of my change."

Ten

Ysabel did not want to recall, much less share the callow young girl she had been. But she had said to him: *Ask, I will answer.* Such words had power when granted to a chosen. She could not deny him.

"Even in those days, Looe was old," she said then. "Once, William the Conqueror held Pendrym Manor. I came long after, born to a distaff branch of the Bodgrugan family. I was the youngest." She went silent, trying not to reckon how many years it had been since she'd even thought of them, so long gone. "My mother died in childbed, and I had seven older sisters. My father made a pet of me."

She felt him nod to show he was listening, so she continued in a bloodless monotone. "One by one, I saw them marry. Men and childbirth stole their youth, their joy, and for some of them, their very lives. I feared it as I feared nothing else."

"Marriage?" he asked, sounding surprised.

"You cannot imagine what it was like," Ysabel said sharply. "A woman expected no more than to live to see her third decade – and by then, she would be a crone."

"You were vain."

She did not deny it, for she had been. *Fertile ground for a chary tempter.*

"I begged my father to let me stay in his house. He would need me in his old age, I said. As I have already noted, he cosseted me; thus, he agreed. I avoided my sisters' fate, the constant swiving and breeding that would steal my youth and beauty. Then one night, a traveller stumbled to our door, blown by fierce winds and rain. There was naught natural in it. But he was passing fair and spoke with a minstrel's tongue. My father bade me, 'Unbar the door, daughter. Let us see what gift the foul weather has brought us.'"

A shiver rolled through her even now. In her mind's eye, she could still see the man who had changed her. "He was pale, pale as moonlight with eyes like silver fog. He had a smile like a knife, and a wit that kept my father laughing long into the night. He invited the bard to stay."

"And thus did you take the viper to your bosom."

Ysabel had to shake her head. "For weeks, he entertained my father with his stories. By night, after my sire had dozed into his cups, this stranger whispered to me of places he should show me, marvels I might never see unless I gave him leave to tear the veil from my eyes." She laughed softly, bitterly. "I thought myself wise in the ways of men. I thought it some double entendre. By then, the role of the ingénue had palled. I thought myself ready to play the seductress instead. I thought myself worldly. There was nothing he could do that would surprise me. I had seen the servants grunting in the back hallways."

"But he didn't want you for sex."

"Not entirely," she said, low. "There was that at first, and he was fearsome good. I loved him. Until he changed me, and left me with this hunger."

"Did it hurt?" he asked.

At first she didn't know whether he meant the loss of her virtue or the transformation. Either way, she answered the same. "Yes. And so I left my father's house."

"You went away with him."

She inclined her head. "Indeed. He had such wonders to show me, after all."

"Are you sorry?"

Ysabel considered for a moment. No one had ever asked her such a question before. "Yes and no. I have lived such a fearful span and, in that time, I have seen true miracles. But there is something wrong in it. I cannot survive without my chosen, and I miss the freedom of being beholden to no one."

"Last question for now," he said, as if she had given him a great deal to consider. "What happened to him?"

"He perished." Her stark tone gave nothing away regarding the old one's fate. She would never answer more.

His breathing deepened then, and she realized how tightly he'd leashed himself to focus on the questions instead of her body in his arms. Ysabel shifted on his lap, aware of his growing arousal.

"I lied," he breathed. "I must know one thing more."

"Ask."

"How does this work? How is it that I cannot be sated with you?"

Once, she would have called it magic. Now, science had supplied the answer. "I exude pheromones," she told him gently. "They stimulate the production of oxytocin, which increases pleasure, sexual stimulation, trust and reduces your fear."

"Which makes it easier for you to feed."

"Yes."

"Then do it. I want you again. I need—" Words failed him, but he raised his hips, rocking against her.

"You needn't feed me to have me," she murmured, warmth glowing through her.

One hunger was sated, but another blazed in her like an inferno. She lifted her skirt, and he unfastened his jeans. In one motion, he took her. Undulating her hips, she watched his face. She had never known anyone to respond as he did. Though he appeared tough and cynical, when she touched him, he gave everything.

"Yes," he whispered, lips parted. "Take everything."

That, she would not do. They shook together, and later she lay against his shoulder, spent and boneless. There had never been another soul that fitted her so.

"I shall miss you," she said softly.

"I don't want you to. Stay with me."

Ah, if only she could. She did not say this would be their last night together, unless – she hesitated, and then risked all.

"I cannot live in your world," she told him. "But you could make a place in mine. I have the power –"

"No." He stiffened.

"Not even for an eternity with me?" she asked lightly.

"No. I'm sorry."

He couldn't realize how deep his rejection cut. "Not everyone could turn down immortality so easily."

Zane shuddered. "I don't want that."

Her heart ached. *Nor do I.* Now she wanted everything she had spurned, so long ago. She wanted the freedom to be with him and share his life. But she would never say the words aloud. Across the centuries she had grown allergic to pathos, particularly her own.

"Then forget I spoke it." *Prithee, do it now, before Cyrus and Galen learn what I have done.* She brushed his temples and fogged his mind.

His hands sifted through her long hair, his fingers knotting. "I don't think I can bear this," he said unsteadily. "Our time is running out, and my heart aches with it. I want you as I've wanted nothing else in my life. Why can't you be a woman I could love?"

The question broke her heart. Pleasure she could offer, but love was forever denied her. She would always need a new chosen, always, no matter how tightly she bonded to the old. It would destroy him to see her with another, and so—

She rose, graceful and fluid. Her skin began to cool, lacking his warmth.

"Do you have further questions?" she asked.

"I'll ask next time, if I do." Zane stood, seeming to realize he had been dismissed.

There would be no next time. She let him go, knowing Cyrus would take care of the rest. The bond required special measures, but her kinsman would blot it from Zane's mind. For the first time in a hundred years, Ysabel the Untouched wept.

Eleven

Zane woke in a cold sweat. His head throbbed, but he couldn't put a finger on what was wrong. He tore his apartment up, searching in vain, but he couldn't for the life of him remember what he'd lost.

He went to work in a fog.

The building looked different to him somehow with its array of cubicles, worn brown carpeting and too bright lights. There was somewhere else he needed to be, but it wouldn't coalesce. Bobby, the photographer, stopped him in the hall, tapping his arm twice in agitation. "Are you high? Rogers wants to see you."

"Shit, why?" He tried to pull himself together. Having the editor-in-chief on your ass was never a good thing.

"I dunno, just go see him."

So he did.

He listened with growing incomprehension. Taking the story from his editor, he raised his brows at it. The piece was covered in red marks, but Rogers seemed excited. Zane couldn't remember writing the thing.

Which worried him.

"It's great," Rogers was saying. "Very hot. I'm using the headline you gave me." Skimming, he found it: I WAS A VAMPIRE'S LOVE SLAVE. "It would be better if you had pictures, but we can use stock footage. You said she was blonde, right?"

"Did I?"

"What's wrong with you?" Rogers shook his head in annoyance. "Anyway, I need you to get me these edits by the end of the day. Fix it up and send it to production, will you? I'm running it on the front page. Congrats, kid."

"Uhm. Thanks." Zane staggered from the office, peering at his own words as if he'd never seen them before. Had he been drinking? He'd heard of people bingeing into a blackout, but he couldn't remember much of the entire last week.

The story, however he'd come to write it, made his fortune.

At first it was just tabloid TV shows wanting to interview him. Then more serious journalists started talking to him about his experiences with the paranormal. He did a few radio interviews.

Tonight made his sixth, and he was starting to get comfortable with the process. But he couldn't shake the feeling that he'd lost his heart somewhere. Dusk till dawn, he never stopped aching, never stopped searching the crowd for a face whose lines wouldn't fully shape up in his mind's eye. Would he know her if he saw her? Who was she?

Breaking his reverie, the young woman who hosted *Boston Tonight* leaned towards him. "Zane, are you telling me that you slept with a vampire and lived to write about it?"

By this point, his answers were smooth and polished. The truth didn't matter. It didn't matter what he remembered – only what they wanted to hear.

"She wasn't a killer," he said. "And I'm no danger to her."

"So what was it like?" the woman asked. "Cold, I bet." She played a laugh track.

No, she hadn't been cold. She'd been quicksilver, love and lightning in his arms. Why the hell couldn't he remember her face? Zane started to wonder if he'd been doing hardcore drugs, and then he *considered* doing them, if it meant seeing her again.

Groupies started popping up at his apartment. Usually they were confused young things with barbwire tatts and dyed black hair. They bore the sad eyes of the eternal victim, and they seemed to think he could shift their sorrow. Without fail, he sent them away.

But pretty soon he had what publishers called a "platform". Most people seemed to think it was all a gimmick, which was fine with him. Wasn't that the point of the whole business? Entertainment?

Within six months, he quit working at *Weird Weekly News*. He had a bizarre compulsion to write a novel. Though he'd never wanted to do fiction – always, always it had been journalism for him – he couldn't get the heroine out of his head.

She haunted him.

Month after month, he banged out his magnum opus. The book was ridiculously long, epic in scope and spanning nearly five centuries. It began in 1513 with a girl in Cornwall. When it was done, it stretched to 150,000 words; the thing should've been unpublishable. Instead, he found an agent, who sold it at auction. To his surprise, Zane was credited with reinventing the vampire genre. He called the story *Ysabel,* and hoped that having written about her for more than half a year, she would leave him be.

Yet she still haunted him. Which was ridiculous because she wasn't real.

She wasn't real.

He tried to date, but the women never felt or tasted right. They didn't smell of citrus and peaches, honeydew and water lily. Night after night, he found himself holding the book he'd written, stroking the cover as if the cover model's skin ought to warm him.

He suspected he was going mad.

Twelve

"Still following him?" Cyrus asked with a touch of disapproval.

Ysabel knew he was right. It had been nearly two years, a wink of the eye to those such as they. Still, she should not clip articles from the paper about *New York Times* bestselling author, Zane Monteith. She should not watch programmes where he appeared as a guest. But she could not strike him from her mind.

Oh, he had served his purpose. He had gone away as she intended, swimming in false lore. She turned the jewelled pincers over in her hands then. They used these to mark the necks of their chosen, so they would not realize the true nature of the feeding: energy, not blood. That which flowed from sexual congress was the strongest, but they could feed off anger, grief, jealousy, terror – any of the fierce, dark emotions. In this way, they had hidden in plain sight for centuries. Not even John Polidori had gotten it right.

But Zane, Zane had been a particular coup. With one book, he had circulated more misinformation than she could have leaked in two human lifetimes. It was a pity she had made the mistake of falling in love with him; Cyrus had been correct in his judgment.

Once set, her kind could not undo the mate bond while the chosen yet lived. She had done her best to blot herself from his consciousness, but there was no such mercy for Ysabel. She must simply bear the loss. She'd offered him eternity, only to have him recoil in disgust. No, she had nothing he wanted. He was human, and proudly so.

Thus, she earned back her name, Ysabel the Untouched, and she fed on sorrow.

Belatedly she realized Cyrus was waiting for an answer. "Yes. I cannot help it."

"I hate to see you repine so," he said gently. "He is no one."

She offered a half-smile. "And so I was, once."

"What can I do?" He knelt beside her chair, sombre as he almost never was.

Ysabel ignored the question. "Do you know, Steven once quoted 'La Belle Dame Sans Merci' at me?"

"Steven," Cyrus repeated. "The suicide?"

At that, her burden became a bit heavier. "Yes. But I hear those lines and marvel that no one ever wonders what became of her, whether she ever mourned for the loss of her poet, or if she sent him from her in kindness."

He inhaled sharply. "I mislike your look, Ysabel. I do not like it when you speak this way."

She lifted her shoulders. "If I must bear it, so must you. Or . . . you can leave me, Cyrus. You are more than old enough to start your own demesne."

"I will not," her kinsman said quietly.

"Why?" she asked. "Why stay now? My house crumbles, and I cannot find the will to care." It was true. They were down to three now. Antoine had yielded the melancholy, and she should be looking for someone to replace him.

She could not. She no longer believed perpetuity was a gift.

He lowered his lovely face, unable to hold her gaze. "All this time, you never knew. I never spoke it. But anything I have done, anything over these long years, I have done for love of you."

Even to the murder of your own brother. I ought to have known. Alongside his twin, Cyrus had been her chosen, once.

"'Hell is empty,'" she breathed in self-loathing, "'And all the devils are here.'"

He shook his head with doleful tenderness. "'There's nothing ill can dwell in such a temple. If the ill spirit have so fair a house, Good things will strive to dwell with't.'"

"Mayhap so," she said, sighing. "Mayhap so. Yet I cannot help but weary of it all."

She remembered trying to persuade her sire otherwise. Tonight she heard his voice, whispering down the centuries. *This, this is the beginning of the decline. First, you gorge on sorrow, and then the melancholia fills your soul. From this, my love, there is no return. You have cheered me these many years, but I can stay no longer.*

Now, this too she would inflict upon Cyrus. He would bear the burden of her death.

But he knew her too well. "No. That is the one thing I will *not* do for you. Is this so dreadful? Would you be mortal again, truly? Would you give up eternity for him?"

Bowing her head, she acknowledged she had asked too much of him; her silence formed her answer. Ysabel went to don her white gown. To feed, she spent her nights at the hospital, ministering to those who were sick unto dying. There, she ate their misery like candy, and they lived three days in peace before passing on. They whispered in the wards of the White Lady, and some prayed for her to ease their pain.

Three years after she had sent Zane from her sight, Marceau came to her. She had not known Cyrus had confided in him, but she was not surprised by his knowledge, only his demeanour. She raised her brows expectantly.

"*M'selle*," he said, unwontedly diffident. "For the last year, I have been seeking an answer. I am your man in all things, and thus, I delved into the old books. Today, I come to say – there is a way. But there is risk. You . . . you might die of it."

"Marceau," she told him gently. "I am dying anyway. Will you try?"

They told her only that Cyrus must drain her energies completely, and then she must be laid out on hallowed ground, anointed in olive oil, holy water and myrrh. At the end of three days, she would be mortal or dead. She was willing to take the risk.

On the appointed night, she went to the cathedral and was surprised to find Cyrus waiting. Candles flickered all around, glazing the marble. He paused in his pacing when she entered. Gently, he took her hands.

"Are you certain this is what you want?"

"Yes," she said without hesitation.

He nodded grimly and drew her to him. Ysabel felt everything she was rushing towards him. Memories, brightness, love. She had to struggle not to fight. Cold now. Weak. Her body went limp.

As through some distant tunnel, she heard someone burst in, but she could not open her eyes. Galen's voice, angry. "What have you done?"

She could not explain. Marceau spoke then. "You must go, *monsieur*. Only Cyrus can stay with her now. Three days and three nights must he hold her, and when that time is done, he will bear her hunger as his own."

Oh, no. No. They did not tell me that. It is too much. But her eyes were weighted with lead, and all had gone dark.

"We are too few already. It's bloody fucking stupid," Galen raged.

Something crashed nearby.

"No," said Marceau. "It is love. And the key to all magic is sacrifice. Go now, Galen, and drink to her memory. She will not remember you if she survives."

She felt Marceau knotting a cord around her wrist. Symbolic. It joined her to Cyrus, and offered the umbilical of rebirth.

Epilogue

Their eyes met across a crowded coffee shop.

Zane felt as though he had been looking for her his whole life. She was lithe and fair, smiling as if she knew him. It could be that she recognized his picture from the back of a book jacket, but she didn't demand an autograph.

The thundercloud grey of her eyes took his breath away. Before he knew what he meant to do, he found himself beside her. He offered his hand and, when she took it, pleasure went straight up his arm, leaving him reeling. Breathless. He'd felt like this before.

Sometime. Somewhere.

"I'm Zane," he said.

"Ysabel."

And somehow, he knew, beyond remembering. Truth bore him up. It was she, the woman who had haunted him for years, who held his heart fast and would not let him go. She seemed equally transfixed, her fingers twined through his.

He kissed her, and it was right. He held her to him fiercely. She was heaven on earth, and the fear that she was no more than a figment of his imagination finally receded.

"I thought I dreamed you," he whispered.

"And I, you." She swallowed, seeming to have trouble finding her voice. "I do not remember everything I should, and yet I know this as truly as my own name. I have but one thing to offer you, and I am afraid you will not want it."

"What's that?" he asked, gently.

"My heart. Will you have it?"

"Lady," he said in an odd, courtly tone, "I will."

"Linden?" she breathed.

He remembered coming to her door on a rainy winter night, and how the rushes in her father's hall smelled of rosemary. He had recognized her then, too, and tried to keep her with him at any price. That cost him her love; he was glad she had not repeated his mistake. Over the centuries he'd known many names – and known *her* by many as well – but this time, they came together in the way that was right, destined to live and die together.

And then, and then, they would find each other again, a circle unbroken.

Skein of Sunlight

Devon Monk

Maddie's hands shook as she angled the visor mirror and applied her lipstick. Even with the make-up, she felt naked. Why had she let Jan talk her into going out tonight?

Jan sat in the driver's seat finishing off a cheeseburger. "You aren't nervous are you?" she asked around a mouthful.

"No," Maddie lied.

Jan stopped chewing to suck up the last of her diet cola and squinted at the quaint Victorian house just up the block from them. It was bathed in light from the street lamp, and practically glowed from the lantern beside the door.

"Might be the most dangerous looking yarn shop I've ever seen in all my days on the force," she said.

Maddie laughed. "Stop it. This is hard."

"No." Jan wiped her mouth with a wadded up napkin. "Chemo was hard. And you got through that. This is fun, remember? A real night out. A little adventure."

"I know, I know. It's just ... " Maddie touched her hair; long enough now, it was styled short and spiky in what Jan called a "vixen cut".

"Why you picked a yarn store is beyond me," Jan muttered. "There's a bar just a couple streets down. That's where you'll find adventure. Good beer, lots of hot young 'uns. We could go Cougar for the night. Lord knows it's been a long time since you had a man in a meaningful way."

Maddie cut her off before she could launch into the sex-fixes-everything speech. "Sounds great. You go check out the young 'uns. I'll prowl for yarn."

"You don't want me to go with you?" Jan tried, but failed, to sound disappointed.

"Like you'd last five minutes in a yarn store. Plus, I want to touch, stroke, savour."

"So do I," Jan said.

"Yeah, but I want to fondle *yarn*. See you in a couple of hours." She got out of the car and started up the street before Jan had any other bright ideas.

It didn't take long to reach the shop, but Maddie's heart rattled in her chest. She had a thing about yarn stores. She didn't know why, but she had always wanted to own one. Every town she visited, she made sure she tracked down the yarn shop. She'd never found the perfect store – the one she'd be willing to offer her life savings for – until she'd set her eyes on this beauty.

She didn't know who the owner was, but if she was there, and if the conversation turned that way, Maddie was going to ask if she'd be willing to sell.

Maddie pulled her shoulders back, opened the door, and stepped in.

The store was a lot bigger on the inside than it looked from the street, walls covered by wooden shelves that held skeins upon skeins of colour and fibre and texture. There was enough walking space to be comfortable, even with the two cosy love seats on either side of a small table that took up the centre of the room. At the far wall was a counter, a cash register, and no one behind either.

Maddie took a deep breath and smiled. She didn't know what it was going to take, or how she was going to do it, but this was it. She belonged here. This store was going to be hers.

"Hello," a soft baritone said from somewhere above her.

Maddie looked over to the left of the room where a staircase arched up. There, in the middle of the staircase, stood a man.

Tall, wide shoulders, lean. His black and grey hair was a little longer than was fashionable, his moustache and beard trimmed tight around his lips and shaved clean along his jaw. He smiled. Laugh lines curved at the edges of his eyes, hooked the corners of his lips, and set his age at somewhere around old-enough-to-have-tried-it-all and young-enough-to-do-it-again.

His wore a dark green sweater, rucked up at the elbows, his muscular forearms bare. No watch. No ring. Yes, she looked.

She also looked at the sweater. Handmade, cabled in a complicated Celtic knot up the arms where it wove like vines across his wide chest. Slacks for his long legs. But a pair of those deck shoes the skater kids liked to wear made her rethink his age again. Thirty? Fifty?

He waited, not moving, while Maddie took what she realized was a little too long to stare at him.

OK, a lot too long.

Forget the young 'uns. One look at this man had her wanting to stroke and savour a lot more than yarn.

"Come in," he said. "You are welcome. Most welcome. Are you here for the class?" He said it slowly. She walked towards him, paying absolutely zero attention to where she was going, each word drawing her in, closer and closer, until she bumped her knee into the arm of the love seat.

A rush of blood heated her cheeks. That got an even wider smile out of him. He showed his teeth, straight, white, strong, the incisors pressing into the soft flesh of his bottom lip.

Sexy.

What was wrong with her? She never acted like this.

He strolled down the stairs, paying particular attention to his shoes.

Released from his gaze, she found her voice again. And her brain. "Class?" she asked.

"Mmm," he agreed. "Knitting. No need to have brought supplies."

He crossed the room, moving like a cat. He paused beside the love seat and rested one hip against it, his arms crossed over his wide chest. He was so close, she could smell his cologne. Something with enough rum and spice to remind her of the Jamaican vacation she'd taken just out of college. The one time in her life she had really felt free and alive. Every day she had let the sun drink her down, and every night she had let the darkness, and the passion of a man feed her soul.

In all these years, she had never once thought of that man, that pleasure. She couldn't even remember his name. How could she have forgotten that? And how could the scent of this man's cologne bring those memories back to her?

He looked into her eyes, smiling, enjoying his effect on her. "We have everything you could possibly desire here."

He means knitting, she told herself. He means yarn. Still, the opportunity was too good to pass up. "Everything?" she asked. "I have an insatiable appetite for fine fibres."

A small frown narrowed his eyes, and he studied her face.

"Have we met?" he asked.

"No," she said. "I'm sure we haven't. I would remember you."

His response was cut off by the sound of the door opening behind her. A group of people, chatting, laughing, paused in the doorway.

The man in front of her gazed over her shoulder. He still smiled, but his demeanour shifted to the look of someone tolerating a pack of puppies wrestling over a toy.

"*Dobry vecher*, Saint Archer," a younger man's voice called out.

"Saint?" Maddie said.

"Good evening, Luka," the man in front of her said. "Come in, all of you. Welcome." To Maddie, "Please. Call me Archer. And your name?"

"Maddie," she said. "Madeline Summers."

Archer raised one eyebrow as if he hadn't heard her correctly, but Maddie had to move out of the way for the newcomers filing into the shop.

Luka, thin, young, beautiful, had that teen heart-throb smoulder going, marred only by his polo shirt uniform with the emblem of the local movie theatre over his heart and sleeve. He smiled at her, looked at Archer as if they were sharing a secret, then away.

Father and son?

No, Luka was an angel boy – light-haired, dark-eyed, while Archer was dark-haired, blue-eyed. Plus, Luka had delicate features, while Archer's wide shoulders and nose (which looked like it had been broken at least once) spoke of a different heritage.

Next to Luka was a girl who probably still went to high school. Her black hair shifted with stripes of pink and red like pulled taffy. Cute. Another, slightly heavier girl wore a gorgeous knitted beret and matching scarf. She held up a hand in wordless greeting as they tromped off across the room, heading towards the stairs.

"My apologies," Archer said. "For the children. They can be rambunctious."

"Are they yours?" she asked.

"Oh, no." He chuckled. "Students. They come here to knit."

"There's a class tonight? Now? I only came to look—"

"And why not stay?" he asked. "For the time we have. Tonight."

That was familiar. A voice she had heard in her dreams.

"I haven't put my hands on balls for years. Of yarn," she corrected, "on a ball of yarn for years. I just came to touch them, not to do, you know." She made a fake knitting motion with her fingers, which only came off looking obscene.

God, she hated it when she went into idiot mode.

He took a step forwards, and she was struck by how tall he was.

"What is there to lose?" he asked softly. "Some things, our bodies never forget."

This time, Maddie managed to look away from his smouldering gaze. "Like knitting?"

"That too."

She grinned and looked up at him. "So how long is the class?"

"An hour. Sometimes people linger. Will you?"

"Stay for the class?" she asked.

"Linger."

She couldn't think of any place she'd rather be. Certainly not hanging out in the bar while she watched Jan find boys half her age to buy her drinks. It was quiet here, except for the students upstairs laughing and arguing over a movie they'd just seen. It was comfortable here. And she liked the look in Archer's eyes as he pulled out all his manly charms to lure her into his knitting lair.

"I'll give it a try."

"Excellent." He looked happy, and something more – relieved. "Let me gather a few things. I'll follow you upstairs in a moment."

Maddie walked around the love seats and over to the stairs. Just as she reached the first step, the door opened again and two more women, women closer to her age, no, she realized with a wince, younger, maybe even still in their twenties, walked into the store. They greeted Archer warmly. Maddie bit her bottom lip, wondering if he was going to lay the charm on thick with them too, if maybe him flirting with her was just an act he used to lure in the female clientele.

Oh, he was a charmer all right. Kissing them both on the cheek and holding their hands just a little too long while complimenting them.

Great, Maddie thought. He'd been playing her – that was all. She'd been suckered in by a guy who flirted with every woman who walked through the door. And she'd actually believed him. She must have looked like an idiot. How could she have been so stupid?

Or maybe she was just that desperate not to be alone, even for only one night.

She almost turned around and left, but she had come here looking for the owner of the shop, and she wasn't going to leave without her name.

The room upstairs was filled with skeins of yarn and cosy couches. It also had a small kitchen nook where a pot of coffee and tea was set out. The teens were clumped together on a couch too small for the three of them. To her surprise, they were already knitting. Even the angel boy Luka had needles in his hands and was quickly working his way through a lace-patterned shawl in blood red fingering weight.

When Maddie was young, there wasn't a boy in a fifty-mile radius who would lay a finger on knitting needles, much less knit in front of his girlfriends. Although with the way the girls, especially the one with the multi-coloured hair, looked at him, Luka had a good thing going.

He caught Maddie looking at him and grinned, showing a row of straight teeth, his canines just a little too long, his eyes just a little too old in that young face. A chill ran up her spine. She rubbed her arms and walked away from the couches to a row of shelves with skeins of bamboo and silk yarn.

She got in a fondle or two, savouring textures and colours, feeding her senses through fingertips and eyes. Why had she stopped knitting? Probably the same reason she had stopped taking hikes, going to concerts, eating at fine restaurants. Somewhere in her battle to make her body her own again, she had lost touch with living in it.

No more of that. Her new life started tonight. With the owner's name.

The sound of footsteps on the stairs punctuated the teen chatter, and soon the two other women were in the room, taking their places in cushioned armchairs, and setting their knitting bags – more like stylish purses than grandmotherly baskets – by their feet.

She wondered which of them was the teacher.

Then Archer climbed the stairs. She could feel him, every step he took, like an extra heartbeat in her chest, a pulse in her veins. She could feel him drawing near even though she kept her back stubbornly towards the stairs and her fingers plunged deep in the silky softness of a pliant skein of cashmere. She held on to that skein of yarn like it was her only anchor to her own resolve.

And it was. Jan was right. It had been a long time since she had been with a man. Much, much too long.

Archer paused at the top of the stairs. She could feel him looking at her, watching her, a warm pressure against her skin that made every nerve in her body remind her she was alive.

Was it getting hot in here?

"I think this is everyone," he said. "Maddie, are you ready to join us?"

This was it, her chance to make a break.

She turned away from the shelf. No eye contact this time, that man had some kind of power in his gaze. She stared very solidly at the middle of his forehead.

"I can't. I . . . I have a date."

Even though she stubbornly stared at his forehead, she could see the rise of his cheeks as he smiled.

"Ah. I see. I'm sorry you won't be able to stay."

Maddie nodded, gaze on the forehead and forehead only. So far, so good.

Archer, apparently, had not gotten the memo that she was avoiding eye contact. He strolled over to her, his shoes quiet on the plush rugs scattered across the floor.

Without trying to, Maddie's eyes slipped, shifted, and her gaze met his. Her lips parted, and all she could think of was him kissing her, touching her.

"I hope you will reconsider my offer," he said.

Then the powerful gaze and the mind-numbing draw were gone. He looked like a man, a very handsome man, but just a man. A little concerned, maybe a little uncomfortable. Vulnerable.

He pressed the handle of a small paper bag into her hands. "A token. If you ever wish to stop in again."

"No, no. I don't think—"

He stepped back, quickly and smoothly out of her reach, so she'd have to follow him around the couches to give him back the bag.

That was when she noticed everyone in the room was silent, knitting. They were all smiling. Enjoying this. None of them looked at her, but she could tell they all thought this little exchange was funny. Fine. She'd come back tomorrow and get her answer. Let them have their laugh.

"Thank you," she said, pouring on the sugar, and not meaning a word of it. "It's been lovely meeting you all."

She walked down the stairs without stomping, and stormed across the floor. All she had wanted was some time to browse, and maybe a chance to buy the store. Was that too much to ask?

She yanked the door open, and nearly ran into the woman standing there.

"May I come in?" The woman was beautiful. Even when Maddie was young and in great shape, she had never been that pretty.

The woman's long, straight hair was so blonde it was silver in the lamplight. Her kitten-wide eyes were green and lined with thick lashes. Her lips were full and perfect, brushed with red lipstick. When she smiled, Maddie realized she could not look away.

"Please," the woman asked. "May I come in? There's a class tonight."

"Oh," Maddie said, catching her breath. "Right. Come on in. They're all upstairs."

A wicked light sparked in the woman's eyes, and was gone before Maddie could blink. "Thank you," the woman purred.

Maddie moved out of the way and the woman stepped over the threshold and into the yarn shop. She moved like a dancer, smooth and silent, her face tipped upwards towards the stairs as if following a string. She licked her lips and smiled.

She must really love knitting.

Maddie walked out. As she turned to shut the door, she noticed the woman's bag. Black, bulky, it looked more like an old-fashioned doctor's bag than a knitting bag. And as the woman climbed the stairs, she opened it and pulled out a pair of metal needles, each as thick as a tent stake, filed to a razor's edge.

One thing Maddie could say for Jan was that she was a cop, through and through. Even though she was off-duty and had probably had more than one beer, her smile faded as soon as Maddie stormed into the bar and plunked down on the stool next to her.

"Gin and tonic," she told the bartender. He nodded. But instead of getting on with the drink mixing, he leaned forwards and flirted with the little jailbait downing shots of tequila in front of him.

Men.

"Did you get a look at his driver's licence?" Jan asked.

"What?"

"The guy who pissed you off. It will make it easier for me when I pull his files and find out if there's anything worth throwing him in jail for."

Maddie put both elbows on the bar and rubbed at her temples. "That obvious?"

Jan shrugged. "You almost burned a hole in the back of the bartender's head. Want to tell me about it?"

"No. There was a man at the yarn store, he said there was a class and invited me to stay, and I thought, I thought . . . " She took a deep breath and crossed her arms on the bar, looking over at Jan. "I thought he was coming on to me. Flirting, you know? So I flirted back. But he was just playing me to fill out the ranks of the knitting class. Some other women came in, younger than me, prettier, and he tossed me to the side. I felt like such an idiot."

"Glad you decided not to tell me about it. Did you get this cad's name?"

"Stop making fun of me."

Jan grinned. "Stop making it so easy. I can't believe you're upset because someone flirted with you and you liked it."

The bartender finally sauntered over, placed her drink down without even looking at her, and walked away.

"Fine," Maddie said. "I liked the flirting. But did he have to crush my fantasy?" She smiled ruefully.

Jan raised her eyebrows in question.

"You know, that we'd fall in love at first sight. His favourite pastime would be doing dishes and going grocery shopping. I'd find out I was the long lost heiress to a fortune and we'd run away to someplace warm and sandy and make passionate love . . . " Maddie lifted her glass. "To reality. What a bitch."

"That's the spirit," Jan said, raising her own glass. "To Fantasy Crusher what's-his-name."

"Saint Archer," Maddie provided.

Jan's mood changed. She frowned. Took a drink of her beer.

"You know him, don't you?" Maddie asked.

"Yes."

"Is he a criminal?"

"No comment."

"Interesting. Witness protection programme?"

"OK, we're going to change subjects now," Jan informed her in her no-bullshit cop voice.

"Come on. You know something about him. Something bad, right?" Maddie took another drink, the warmth spreading out in her stomach and echoing back through her muscles. "It would cheer me up," she said. "Indecent exposure? Tax evasion? He runs a pornographic flower shop in his basement?"

"Not that I know of," Jan said. "Just the yarn store."

"What?" Maddie said. "I thought he worked there."

OK, the truth? One look at him and she had stopped thinking.

"So he owns the store?" Maddie asked.

"Yup."

"So . . . he's gay?"

Jan laughed so hard she snorted. "It's not on record, if that's what you're asking. Still. You know better than to assume things about people." She lifted her glass and muttered into it, "No one in this city is what they seem to be."

"But he has a record?"

Jan just gave her a look and took another drink of beer. She emptied half the glass, thunked it on the counter and refused to answer.

Maddie took another drink and thought it over. Maybe it didn't matter, but she had to ask anyway. "Do you think he's dangerous?"

"Would I let you go anywhere, alone, if I thought you were in danger?" Jan downed the last of her beer. "I'm going to the bathroom. Get me another beer, will you?" She was no longer smiling.

"Sure," Maddie said. And she didn't even point out that Jan had not answered her question.

Jan got her smile back when Tony Brown strolled into the bar. Tony worked for the city and he and Jan had the kind of history that led to him buying Jan another couple of beers, and them getting a table.

Maddie moped her way through another gin, then decided to call it a night. She handed her card to the bartender and her elbow brushed the little bag Archer had given her. She'd been so angry walking to the bar that she hadn't even looked in it.

She opened the bag and angled to see inside.

Two skeins of yarn caught light like summer fire, and a slick set of needles glinted dark beside them.

Maddie couldn't help herself. She gasped like she'd just found a kitten and pulled the yarn out of the bag. The fibre was exquisitely soft, with enough loft it promised warmth and shape and drape. Cashmere and silk. With a beautiful set of knitting needles.

Maybe it was the alcohol, maybe it was her sense of pride, or maybe it was watching Jan and Tony inch closer and closer together at the table.

Yeah, probably that last thing.

But whatever it was, Maddie knew she wanted to keep that skein of yarn near her forever, to hold it and fondle it and savour the possibilities of what it could become with a little time, a little hope and a lot of patience.

And she knew, just as quickly, that she had to return it.

This wasn't a token. This was a gift with strings attached. Well, just one long string, but still. That was attached. To a man whose name took her best friend's smile away.

Maddie settled her bill and told Jan she was headed home and was going to catch a cab.

Jan told her she shouldn't go home alone and even started to put on her coat, much to Tony's polite but obvious disappointment, until Maddie finally convinced her that she was plenty old enough to get home on her own. And then she made Tony promise to call a cab for both of them when the night wound down.

But instead of going home, Maddie marched back to the yarn shop.

The lantern outside the door was still on, and a light from one of the upper windows glowed brightly. The front window was dark, though. Maddie wasn't sure if the shop was open. Archer said people lingered, and it had only been maybe two hours since she left.

She walked up to the door and tried it. The door opened, so she stepped in.

The lamp at the back of the room near the counter was on. But other than the faint light tumbling down the staircase, it was dark.

Something felt wrong about the room. Maddie thought about dropping the bag on the counter for Archer to find in the morning, but the door was unlocked, which meant they weren't closed for the night. Someone still had to be here.

A shuffling sound, like something being dragged across the floor on the upper floor, made Maddie's heart pound. OK, maybe she should just go back outside, get a cab, and get the hell home.

Forget about leaving the yarn on the counter. Maddie hurried to the love seats and placed the bag on the table between them. That would have to be good enough.

The click of the door closing behind her made every nerve in Maddie's body scream.

She turned, hoping, and dreading it would be Archer.

"Hello, pet," a woman's voice cooed.

It was not Archer. It was the beautiful woman who Maddie had let into the shop. She held two very bloody knitting needles in her hand.

"I just came back to return the yarn," Maddie said, trying to think faster than her heart was beating.

"Aren't you sweet?" The woman tipped her head to one side, her ear nearly touching her shoulder. She inhaled. "Had a hard time of it the last few years, haven't you?" She straightened and clutched the knitting needles tighter. "Cancer. How sad. How alone."

She glided forwards. "Leyola can cure your pain," she sing-songed. "Leyola knows just what you crave."

Maddie was caught in her gaze. Even though it was dark in the room, it was as if a single light shone on the woman, illuminated her, made her incandescent, beautiful.

Something in the back of Maddie's mind was screaming – her reason, she thought – but she couldn't care less. She wanted to do anything the woman told her to do, wanted Leyola to take her pain away.

The woman was close now. Close enough that Maddie could see her more clearly. Her beautiful face had gone feral, eyes black without even a speck of white or colour, jaw elongated, fangs dripping with blood.

Holy shit. She was a vampire.

OK, maybe it was a little late in the game for her to put two and two together, but vampires weren't real. Sure, she'd heard of kids who liked to pretend they were vampires – it was popular in the high schools – but this chick wasn't a kid. And from the bloody knitting needles and fangs, she sure as hell wasn't playing around.

"You will give yourself to me." Leyola opened her mouth and bent towards Maddie's neck.

And even though every nerve in her body ached for this, for her touch, for her mouth, Maddie took a step backwards.

"No." It came out low, strong, born of years of anger against a disease that had nearly destroyed her. Maddie focused her mind, calmed her thoughts and put all her will behind it. "My body is my own," she said.

The woman jerked back as if she had been slapped. "That," she said, "will be your end."

She lunged.

Maddie got her hands up, banking on her coat to keep Leyola's teeth from tearing into her skin. But Leyola slammed into her, knocking her backwards. Maddie stumbled, trying to catch her balance and landed hard on the couch.

She needed a weapon. Now. Maddie scrambled back on the couch, her heels kicking into the soft cushions. The bag was just behind her, and in it were the needles.

Leyola strolled over to her, fingernails tapping against the needles in her hand. "You may deny death," she purred, "but you will not deny me."

Maddie yelled. She stretched to reach the bag.

A roar filled the room. Maddie rolled off the couch, caught up the bag and pulled the needles out.

She crouched, and thrust the needles upwards.

But Leyola was not there.

Maddie blinked, trying to make sense of the scene before her.

Someone was fighting with the woman. A man. Archer.

His shirt was off revealing the hard, defined muscles of his chest and stomach. The low light from the lamp painted him gold – a warrior from some ancient time. He and Leyola circled each other, speaking a language that made Maddie wish she'd taken Russian in college.

Maddie caught a glimpse of a tattoo spread across the back of Archer's shoulder – an angel in flight – and a trail of blood pouring over his ribs.

Leyola had circled so that her back was now towards Maddie. Archer said something to her, a warning. A command.

But Leyola only laughed and threw herself, needles and fangs, at Archer.

Everything suddenly seemed to happen very, very slowly.

Leyola, in mid-air, contorted like a gymnast, her feet hitting the ground as lightly as a cat, then pushed, not towards Archer, but towards Maddie.

Archer launched, a growl escaping his lips, his arms, hands, body, straining to reach Leyola.

Maddie still crouched, set herself, feet strong beneath her, shoulder forwards, knitting needles in her hand, ready for the impact.

Inhale.

Leyola bore down on her.

Archer plucked Leyola out of the air. Rolled her over his hip. Pinned her to the floor. He shoved his knee in her back and held both her wrists in his hands.

Exhale.

Time snapped back into real speed again.

"Maddie," Archer said, his voice a little husky. When she didn't respond, he glanced over his shoulder at her.

His hair hung wild around his face, and his eyes burned electric blue. Leyola beneath him squirmed and cursed. Archer's muscles flexed, but he kept her pinned.

Maddie found she was breathing hard, caught by his gaze and fully aware of how much she liked the primal hunger in his eyes, his anger, and his fear for her.

But it was his mouth that fascinated her most. His lips were parted, revealing fangs that grazed his bottom lip, pressing against the soft curve there, almost puncturing. Maddie wondered what it would feel like to kiss those lips, to feel the scrape of his mouth against hers. To open herself to his tastes, his textures.

"Maddie," he said again, his voice a soft growl that she could feel roll beneath her skin. "Are you hurt?"

Right. This was not the time to fantasize.

She did a quick inventory: no cuts, maybe a bruise on the back of her legs where she'd gone over the arm of the couch, but she was no stranger to bruises.

"I'm fine."

He smiled softly, a strange mix with the wild edge in his eyes. "Would you help me then?"

"You?" She glanced at the vampire pinned beneath him. What could she do that he hadn't done already? "Of course." She stepped out from between the couches. "What do you need?"

"Behind the counter, there is a drawer. A corner drawer."

Maddie crossed the room, let herself behind the counter, and opened the little triangular drawer. A strange assortment of things were gathered there: medallions, knives, bullets, paperclips and a small leather-bound book.

"Do you see the twine?" he asked.

Leyola spat obscenities.

Maddie picked up the ball of twine so small she could close her hand around it to hide it. "Yes," she said.

"Bring that to me, please."

Maddie walked over to him. Her adrenaline was starting to wear off and her knees felt a little like cooked noodles. Still, she held out the yarn.

"Unwind a length of it."

She did so. The twine was strange. It clung to itself and gave off the scent of green grass and something else she could not place. It was also cold, as if she'd just pulled it out of the freezer. She had no idea what it was made out of.

Once she began unrolling it, the entire thing seemed to release, flowing free from itself, and falling into a pile of string in her hand.

"What is it?" she asked.

"It is something very good at holding vampires until the police arrive." Archer shifted his grip, so both of Leyola's wrists were in one hand. He took the end of the string and tied her wrists together with the kind of unconscious ease that said he'd done this before.

Leyola moaned and squirmed harder, aiming a kick at Archer that did not connect.

"Enough," he said. "Your game tires me."

Archer leaned a little more weight on his knee in her back. He put his free hand on the back of her head and bent his face down, his eyes closed.

He looked like he was praying. Maybe he was. After a moment of silence, he cupped Leyola's head and thunked it into the floor.

She relaxed and was still.

Archer took a deep breath and rolled his shoulders. When he stood he didn't look at Maddie, but instead walked over to the wall and flipped on the lights.

Only one bank of the lights in the ceiling caught, but Maddie's eyes had gotten so used to the darkness she had to blink a couple of times to handle the glare. When she could really see again, she looked at Archer.

Still shirtless, it was no trick of shadow – he really did have the body of a god. A thick line of black liquid, blood, she could only assume, ran across his ribs, already dry.

In this light, his skin was pale, unfreckled, no chest hair, though there were several thin scars across his chest, one intriguingly low scar at his hip bone, and one scar near his collarbone that looked like a perfect pink circle the size of a coin.

The man had seen his share of violence.

And survived it.

Once her gaze lifted to his face again, she noted he was smiling at her.

And she was blushing.

"I feel there is some explaining in order," he began.

"I only came in to return the yarn," Maddie said. "I didn't know . . . I don't know . . . I shouldn't have even come here. Vampires? It's a joke, right? Knitting vampire dinner mystery theatre." She didn't believe that, not at all. But the reality was suddenly too much to handle.

Then Archer was in front of her, having somehow crossed the distance in an amazingly short amount of time.

"Maddie," he soothed, "I meant I should explain this to you. If you want me to."

He placed his hand gently on her arm. When she did not pull away, he wrapped his arms around her and held her close.

"I don't know if I want to know," she finally said.

"Then let's start with an easier decision. Would you like some tea?"

Maddie closed her eyes and inhaled the scent of him. One moment he looked like he could tear the building apart with his bare hands, and the next, he was holding her like she was made of fragile glass.

She nodded. "Tea would be nice."

He quietly led her away from the fanged, unconscious vampire chick tied up on the floor, into the adjoining room. Another couch and chair sat snug in the corner.

He left her there on the couch with the promise to bring her mint tea.

Maddie thought about leaving, about walking out of this mess, but she had some questions she needed answered. Questions about her half-remembered time in Jamaica, and the long nights he spent with her there.

The police showed up before Maddie's tea had time to steep.

No sirens, no flashing lights, just a knock at the door that made Maddie jump.

Archer, who had been sitting in the chair next to her, explaining that people in the city weren't always what they appeared to be, and how everyone needed a safe place in a storm – even vampires, maybe especially vampires, and how he had spent many years taking vampires in like Luka or taking them out like Leyola – stopped talking and gave her a reassuring look.

"I called the police," he said.

Archer had changed into a new sweater before bringing her tea, this one black, wool, and worked in a lattice-stitch pattern. She would have found the seaming fascinating on any other man, but Archer had a way of out-wowing even a sweater that beautiful.

"You called the cops?" she asked.

"I did."

"But you're a . . . isn't she a . . . "

"Vampire?" he said evenly. "Yes she is. As am I. Although, we do have our differences." He flashed a smile, showing just the edge of his teeth. "For one thing, I don't break into other people's places of business and try to kill them." He stood. Then added as an afterthought, "Well, not for many years."

He walked out of the side room and back into the main shop. Maddie got up and brushed her fingers through her hair, smoothing it, while she walked to the doorway so she could see what was going on.

Two police officers, one man, one woman, neither in uniform, walked through the front door, which Archer closed behind them. Archer motioned towards the still unconscious Leyola.

"She came in earlier this evening. I did not invite her. I was holding class upstairs."

"Who saw her?' the man asked.

"Luka and I. There were four women in class. Luka has taken all of them home, and made sure they have only pleasant memories of a class that was cancelled early. They were not harmed."

The woman cop nodded. "Do you know what she wanted?"

"Other than to kill me?" He said it like it happened every day. He shrugged, a roll of his wide shoulders that belied his injury. "I have not found anything missing. And I do not believe she was seeking my counsel. Nor asylum. She and I have . . . crossed paths before."

"So revenge?" the woman cop asked.

Archer crossed his arms over his chest and shrugged again. "When was she released?" he asked.

"About a month ago," the man answered. "We'll drag her back in. See if we can straighten her out. If not, will you press charges?"

"Yes."

The woman pulled something out of her coat pocket. Maddie couldn't see what it was, but she heard the telltale rip of duct tape being unrolled. The policewoman knelt, tipped Leyola's head to one side, made sure her hair was out of the way, then duct-taped her mouth shut.

"OK, we'll give you a call tomorrow night," the man said.

Archer walked to the door and opened it while the police officers got hold of the woman's upper arms and made a smooth, coordinated effort, carrying her out the door.

Archer left the door open and, within moments, another figure drifted at the edge of the doorway.

"Come in, Luka," Archer invited.

The teen heart-throb stepped in, glanced in Maddie's direction, his nostrils flared.

Archer put his hand on his shoulder. "She came back to return the yarn."

Luka licked his lips, swallowed. "Do you want me to take her home too?"

"No. I think I'll call her a cab." Archer raised his voice slightly. "Unless you have a friend you'd like me to call for you?"

Maddie sighed. He had known she was eavesdropping the whole time. "You could have told me you knew I was listening," she said as she walked out into the room with the two men. Correction: the two vampires.

"Hello, Luka," she said.

Luka gave her a half-bow. "I have other . . . commitments. If you'll both excuse me?"

Archer nodded and Luka turned and stepped silently back outside, into the night.

"So," Maddie said, "are you going to make sure I remember all this as a pleasant evening? Just like that summer in Jamaica?"

Archer smiled. "Ah, you catch on quickly." He strolled over to the love seats. "I could. If you asked me, I could leave your mind free of the memories of vampires. Give you back your easy world. Again."

He bent, retrieved the yarn that had spilled from the bag and found the needles Maddie had abandoned on the couch cushion. He sat on the couch.

Instead of looking at her, he gazed at the yarn in his hands, turning the luxurious hanks of sunlight between his wide fingers.

Maddie crossed the floor. "How many years have you been doing this?" she asked. "Taking in vampires, taking out vampires?"

He shook his head. "Many."

She sat on the couch next to him. When she could find her voice, she asked, "Why did you make me forget?"

He did not look up. Did not look away from the yarn that glowed like fire between his palms.

"Archer?" Maddie put her hand on his arm.

He lifted his head and met her gaze. "You asked me to. You were young. A full life awaited you. Sunlight awaited you." He lifted the yarn ever so slightly. "Not the night."

"Oh." She didn't know what to say. Too many emotions rolled through her. Loss. Regret. Hope.

"What if I don't want to forget any more?"

"Once a memory is taken, it cannot be returned," he said softly.

Maddie nodded. She knew that. "Is there ever a chance to make new memories?"

Archer stared at her, silent for so long, Maddie started blushing again.

"I know I'm older," she stammered. "I mean I'm not a college girl any more, not quite as thin as I was, as pretty as I was, but I love knitting, and yarn—"

And then Archer was bending over her, pulling her close, his lips hot, needful, his teeth scraping the edge of her mouth, inviting her to open for him, promising her pleasure, promising her more.

Maddie moaned. She touched him, stroked him, and savoured the textures and tastes of him, until her body and soul came alive, and she knew she would never forget this, never forget him again.

Author Biographies

Ann Aguirre
National bestselling author of urban fantasy, romantic science fiction and high-octane romances, she lives in Mexico with her family.
www.annaguirre.com

Jennifer Ashley
A RITA-award winning and *USA Today* bestselling author of more than thirty romances and mysteries, she also writes as Allyson James and Ashley Gardner.
http://www.jennifersromances.com

Camille Bacon-Smith
Author of the Daemon Eyes mystery series. She has a Ph.D. in folklore from the University of Pennsylvania and currently lives in Philadelphia.
http://camille-is-here.livejournal.com/
http://www.facebook.com/pages/Camille-Bacon-Smith/39649589596

Dawn Cook
Fantasy author of the Decoy Princess and Truth series, she also writes as *New York Times'* bestselling writer Kim Harrison.
www.dawncook.com

Deborah Cooke
Since selling her first romance novel in 1992, she has published forty novels and novellas. She has written medieval romances as Claire

Delacroix; time-travel romances, paranormal romances, chick-lit and contemporary romances as Claire Cross, and the Dragonfire series of urban-fantasy romances as Deborah Cooke. She lives in Canada with her husband and family, and knits far too much.

http://www.delacroix.net
http://www.clairecross.com
http://www.deborahcooke.com

Carole Nelson Douglas

New York Times' Notable Book of the Year winner and the author of fifty-some mystery, fantasy and romance novels, whose fiction often combines multi-genre elements, her early high fantasies were Top 25 chain bestsellers. The first two books of her current Delilah Street urban fantasy series, *Dancing with Werewolves* and *Brimstone Kiss*, received starred *Publishers' Weekly* reviews and made Nielsen Bookscan bestseller lists. She is the author of the popular 22-book Midnight Louie, feline PI, mystery series. *Vampire Sunrise*, the third Delilah Street novel, comes out in late 2009.

www.carolenelsondouglas.com
www.dancingwithwerewolves.com

Angie Fox

New York Times bestselling author of the Accidental Demon Slayer series, she claims that researching her books can be just as much fun as writing them. In the name of fact-finding, Angie has ridden with Harley biker gangs, explored the tunnels underneath the Hoover Dam and found an interesting recipe for Mamma Coalpot's Southern Skunk Surprise.

www.angiefox.com

Jamie Leigh Hansen

Paranormal romance author of *Betrayed* and *Cursed*, she loves to combine love and the eternal fight between good and evil in stories both supernatural and real.

www.jamieleighhansen.com
jlh@jamieleighhansen.com

Nancy Holder

USA Today bestselling author of the Gifted series, and co-author of the *New York Times* bestselling Wicked series, she has written many

novels tied into the *Buffy the Vampire Slayer/Angel* universes.
www.nancyholder.com

Larissa Ione
The *New York Times* and *USA Today* bestselling author of the paranormal Demonica series, she also writes contemporary romance for Red Sage and Samhain. In addition, she pens erotic sf action suspense for Random House under the name Sydney Croft, with partner Stephanie Tyler.
www.larissaione.com

Dina James
After writing three Destrati vampire stories featured exclusively in the *Mammoth* paranormal romance anthologies, her first fantasy story for young adults is published in *The Eternal Kiss: 13 Stories of Blood & Desire*.
www.dinajames.com

Stacia Kane
Author of the Megan Chase paranormal series, she is the mother of two little girls. She likes french fries and gin.
www.staciakane.com

Caitlín R. Kiernan
Author of the award-winning *Silk* (winner of the International Horror Guild Award for Best First Novel, and a finalist for the Bram Stoker Award for Best First Novel) and *Threshold*, among many others. She writes science fiction and dark fantasy works, comic books, short stories, novellas, and vignettes.
www.caitlinrkiernan.com

Caitlín Kittredge
Author of the bestselling Nocturne City series, as well as the Black London adventures (featuring mage Jack Winter), and the Iron Codex, a steampunk trilogy geared towards young adults, she lives in Seattle, is owned by two cats and loves pie.
www.caitlinkittredge.com

Rosemary Laurey
USA Today bestselling author is an expatriate Brit who now lives in Ohio and has a wonderful time writing stories of vampires and

shape-shifting pumas. Her new fantasy series, set in Brytewood, England during WWII, is published under the pen name Georgia Evans.
www.rosemarylaurey.com

Karen MacInerney
Author of the Gray Whale Inn mystery series (the first of which, *Murder on the Rocks*, was nominated for an Agatha award for Best First Novel) and the *Tales of an Urban Werewolf* trilogy, featuring the reluctant werewolf Sophie Garou.
www.karenmacinerney.com

Devon Monk
Nominated for a Best Urban Fantasy *Romantic Times* 2008 Reviewer's Choice Award, she is the author of the urban fantasy Magic series.
www.devonmonk.com

Justine Musk
Author of the dark-fantasy novels *Bloodangel* and *Lord of Bones*, about a race of men and women descended from fallen angels who go to war against demons (and sometimes each other), as well as the YA supernatural thriller *Uninvited*.
www.justinemusk.com

Patti O'Shea
Nationally bestselling author and winner of numerous awards for writing, her books have appeared on the Barnes & Noble, Waldenbooks and Borders best-seller lists. Currently, she's working on the Light Warrior series about a society of magic users that protects humans from demons and monsters.
www.pattioshea.com

Jennifer St Giles
This *USA Today* bestselling author is a former nurse and home-schooling mother of three. She has won a number of awards for writing excellence including two National Reader's Choice Awards, two Maggie Awards, a Daphne du Maurier Award, Romance Writers of America's Golden Heart Award, along with RT Book

Club's Reviewer's Choice Award for Best Historical Gothic/ Mystery.

jenniferstgiles.com
jenniferstgiles.blogspot.com

Jeanne C. Stein
Author of the Anna Strong Vampire Chronicles. The fifth in the series, *Retribution,* is released September 2009.
www.jeannestein.com

Jordan Summers
With sixteen published books to her credit, her latest series is the Dead World trilogy, featuring: *Red* and *Scarlet. Crimson,* the final book, will be published in November 2009.
www.jordansummers.com

Tiffany Trent
Author and creator of the acclaimed dark fantasy series, Hallowmere. She lives and writes in Manns Harbor, NC.
www.tiffany-trent.com

Jaye Wells
After several years as an editor and freelance writer, she finally decided to leave the facts behind and make up her own reality. Her overactive imagination and life-long fascination with the arcane and freakish blended nicely with this new career path. Her Sabina Kane urban fantasy series is a mix of dark themes, grave stakes and wicked humour. She lives in Texas with her saintly husband and devilish son.
www.jayewells.com

Diane Whiteside
By day, she builds and designs computer systems for the federal government. By night, she escapes into a world of alpha males and the unique women who turn their lives upside down.
www.dianewhiteside.com